No Victory Won

Book 3 of the
No Glory Sought Series

by

Phil Geusz

Published by
Melange Books, LLC
White Bear Lake, MN 55110
www.melange-books.com

No Victory Won ~ Phil Geusz ~Copyright 2011

ISBN: 978-1-61235-263-3

Credits

Editor: Nancy Schumacher
Cover Artist: Mae Powers

No Victory Won

by

Phil Geusz

How can any conceivable military victory be worth the death and suffering of billions?

That's the question Commander Thomas Longo must confront as against all odds the tide turns against his Dracan foes and final victory begins to beckon in the distance. Yes, there's still plenty of hard fighting to be done as the Emperor holds out hoping for a miracle. The end of the tunnel, however, is definitely in sight. Paradoxically this makes things more difficult still for young Thomas, who now must also battle against those who'd pervert his victory into wealth and power for themselves. Which enemy will Thomas find deadlier? The Dracan Emperor?

Or his own government?

* * * *

Dedicated to LT John L. Close, CHC, USN

Author contact

www.resistingarrest.net

Other books available by Phil Geusz from Melange

No Oath Sworn, Book 1 of the No Glory Sought Series
No Battle Fought, Book 2 of the No Glory Sought Series
'December Moth' in the Hearts of Tomorrow Anthology

Part I

Chapter One

"It was so good of you to come!" Rolf whispered for about the hundredth time.

"Not at all!" Admiral Vlasilov replied yet again, his voice full of false heartiness and camaraderie. Well, perhaps "false" was an unfair choice of words. The admiral wouldn't have taken so much time out of his overloaded personal schedule if he hadn't been sincerely grateful to Rolf and everyone else who'd sacrificed so much to produce the tiny handful of superfighters that was turning around the war. But, certainly, his tone was forced. Visiting a deathbed was an awkward thing at the best of times; it was far worse when you barely even knew the patient.

Rolf smiled and laid his skull-like head back onto the blood-spattered pillow. The linen had been snowy-fresh when the admiral and I arrived, but the Stormcrow-plant worker's skin had become so delicate and fragile due to long-term radiation poisoning that nothing around him remained unsullied for more than moments. Watery red fluid leaked from Rolf's ears, from the wrinkles in his skin, even sometimes from his tear ducts. He'd have died long ago if the navy hadn't, true to its word, provided the best treatments and most skilled specialists available. "I still can't believe it! The saviors of the United Systems—come to see me! Our biggest heroes! I've done nothing to deserve such an honor! Nothing!"

I met Vlasilov's eye; he nodded slightly, suggesting that it was my turn to speak. "I think that you have," I replied, doing my best to find words that could never, ever be enough for a man who'd freely risked dying so horribly. They called me a hero, and I'd sure enough taken chances. But laser-bolts generally killed clean, and even if they didn't I could always turn off my pain circuits. Poor Rolf weighed perhaps a third of what he once had, and putrid ooze dripped from every orifice. The entire room reeked of death and putrefaction, judging by how everyone else's face was all screwed up. Vlasilov had turned a deathly pale color. Soon, however, he'd be able to leave. How it was for poor Rolf, the source of all the nauseous emanations, I couldn't even begin to imagine. "I think that you *have* earned such consideration, and so does Father.

5

He sends his best, by the way, and plans to be here tomorrow."

Rolf's smile widened further; he might've been the happiest corpse in the universe. "I did my best," he whispered. "Always, I gave my best for your father." He turned to face Vlasilov on the other side of the bed. "Willy Longo is a noble man, sir. Noble and good-hearted! One of the greatest Esteppans who ever lived! It was my privilege to serve him. Together, we stood off the entire universe!"

"Da," the admiral agreed. His voice was sad. After all, he'd been one of the besiegers. "That you did, Rolf. That you did."

There was an awkward silence. Then Rolf inhaled, doubtless to thank us for coming again. But this time I decided to head him off at the pass. "Rolf Wunderling," I said formally. "We have come not only to visit, but to honor you."

"Ja?" the patient asked, looking a bit confused. His mind came and went, according to his wife. So far, we'd been lucky.

"Ja," I agreed firmly, meeting Vlasilov's eye. He nodded back, a pre-arranged signal, then looked over at the soon-to-be Widow Wunderling. Smiling, she stood up and took her husband's hand.

"Rolf Wunderling," Vlasilov said, carefully repeating the name, "I hereby invest you with the United Systems Medal of Merit, civilian-grade, for your role in supporting essential military production under the most dangerous circumstances imaginable." He paused, then pinned the pathetic little ribbon to the blood-spattered pillow. Its crimson silk made it look like just another stain. Then Vlasilov offered a parade-ground salute.

"I...I..." Rolf quavered. But I didn't let him speak yet.

"And I have two decorations to present," I continued smoothly, allowing Mrs. Wunderling time to remove them from her pocket. My fingers weren't nimble enough to make the physical presentation, so she'd agreed to do it for me. "First, there is the Esteppan Cross for Gallantry, civilian grade, awarded to you by the Esteppan government in recognition of your services during the last war." I let my smile fade slightly. It should've been awkward to present this particular honor while wearing a United Systems Navy uniform, but somehow for me at least it also felt very right. "When," I explained as Mrs. Wunderling performed her pinning duties, "you did indeed play a crucial role in one of the most stubborn and effective defensive stands in recorded history."

Rolf began weeping, watery-crimson tears running down his cheeks. But I wasn't done. "And," I continued, "Though Father himself will be here tomorrow to thank you in person, he's asked me to also award you the Longo Enterprises Certificate of Service, the highest commendation our business has to offer. It's presented in gratitude for service and loyalty so far above and beyond the ordinary that I cannot find words to express the Longo family's gratitude." Mrs. Wunderland did the pillow-pinning again, then showed her husband the big parchment Certificate in its heavy wooden frame. I then saluted as best I could, though the result was far less impressive than the admiral's showpiece effort due to my slow-moving electric motors.

"The Certificate!" Rolf blubbered, staining everything downstream of his eyes a brilliant, odoriferous red. "Mein gott! I mean…"

"It's the first one I've ever been privileged to award," I explained, hand still held rigidly to my brow. "And, I'm quite certain, I'll never give one that's more deserved."

"Mr. Longo!" Rolf's face screwed up, as if he were suddenly in agony. Perhaps he was. "Sir! I…."

"Hush, now!" Mrs. Wunderling urged her husband, though she was looking at me. Her eyes shone with gratitude. "You need to save your strength."

Presently the dying machinist's sobs turned into coughs, and more artery-bright blood erupted onto the pillow. Then a nurse came and wordlessly ushered us out into the corridor. "Go now," he urged us. "He'll be asleep in a couple of minutes."

"Right," Vlasilov replied, his voice unusually harsh and distant. "Of course." Then he turned to me. "You did well, Thomas. In a difficult situation."

I shrugged. "He deserved the best I could give. And more."

Vlasilov shook his head then smiled and placed his hand on my shoulder. "You're a credit to us all," he observed, apropos of nothing that I could see. "Come now, and let us spend some time in a happier place. Or a busier one, at least. We have many important plans to make together." He looked down at his normally-immaculate white dress-jacket; like mine, it was now flecked with thousands of tiny aerosol-borne specks of red. "Just as soon as we change our uniforms," he added. "Certainly, the war can wait long enough for *that*."

Chapter Two

Perhaps the war *could* spare Vlasilov and me for a few minutes every now and again. But you'd never know it from our daily routines. The admiral and I barely saw each other anymore; he was in command of the United Systems' only effective striking force, and I was in charge of the squadron of superfighters that *made* it effective. Both of our forces were battered and bloodied from recent combat; the task force was down to a single light carrier and crucially short on heavy escorts. Meanwhile, my wingman Jimmy Knight and I were the only surviving Skybolt pilots. Which meant that the admiral spent half his time trying to coax repairs and new tonnage from the wholly inadequate Esteppan shipyards, while Jimmy and I alternated twelve-hour shifts mounted in our shiny new 'bolts, ready to scramble. This left neither the admiral nor I with anything like enough time for our real jobs, even though I got what I could done via voicelink from my hardstand. Soon there would be more 'bolts and more pilots; a dozen surgeries had taken place while Jimmy and I were out raiding. And, even sooner, Hans and Werner would be back in action; their Stormcrows had been seriously damaged while unsuccessfully defending their carrier, but they'd managed to land safely on *The Glorious First of June*. My father's factory was fabricating parts, and in a few days they'd be able to take over for Jimmy and me and give us some down-time. But for now, we were on our own.

"You need more rest, Thomas," Father Murton scolded me as he fussed with my uniform jacket. "They're pushing you too hard."

"Maybe," I agreed. "But what choice do they have?"

"None," my tutor acknowledged with a sigh. "As usual." He finished buttoning my clean jacket, then looked up into my eyes. "Promise me that you'll nap tonight while you're on alert. You're still a teenager under that uniform, and teens need extra sleep."

I closed my eyes slowly. Sleeping on alert was supposed to be one of the worst sins imaginable for a navy pilot. But times had changed, it seemed. Jimmy and I both had tried and tried to stay awake through the long, dull hours, but we just couldn't. No one had yelled us when we'd finally passed out; in fact, our ground crews had muted their microphones so they wouldn't wake us up by accident. "All right," I answered, since I knew that I'd never make it all night anyway. "But…"

Father Murton raised his eyebrows. "But?"

I shook my head. "I don't know. It just feels wrong."

"It probably *is* wrong," the priest agreed, his knees crackling as he stood fully erect and adjusted my tie. "It's also necessary, however. Like half the other things you and I have been doing ever since this lousy war started. It's *all* insane. So why fight it when for once the craziness benefits you?"

"Heh!" I chuckled darkly. "You're right. I'll sleep tonight. In fact, I'll even cancel my planning session with Ted. I *need* to sleep."

Murton smiled. "Good boy." Then he patted me on both shoulders affectionately, and bowed. "You're presentable now, Thomas. My mother would be spinning in her grave if she knew that she'd worked all those double-shifts so that her son could become a manservant, mind you. But at least I'm finally getting the hang of it."

I smiled and shook my head. Neither Father Murton nor I had said much to each other during the long, circuitous trip back to Esteppe from Drakkus, where Jimmy and Delana and Viktor and I had slaughtered more human beings than anyone would ever count. But now our relationship was returning to something resembling normal. We just didn't speak of certain things, was all. Nor did we pray together anymore, which should've bothered me but somehow didn't. "Thank you for the help," I told him for perhaps the millionth time.

"You're most welcome," he answered with a little bow. "And, where are you off to now?"

"The daily war status meeting," I replied. As CO of the Top Bananas, it was my duty to remain in touch with the general military situation. My superiors cut me a lot of slack on status meetings because of all my other responsibilities. Ted, my co-commander, never missed one for this very reason. That way, at least *one* of us was up-to-date. Still, it was a good idea for me to attend when I could.

"Right," Murton agreed, his smile fading. "Well… Do what you have to do, Thomas. I've got a counselor's meeting myself, where I'm going to raise hell about your workload. Not that it'll do any good." He shook his head. "You're still a boy, Thomas. In a sane world, you'd just now be starting your senior year of high school. They're asking too much of you."

I shrugged. "Thank you for trying, Father. But you're not going to get anywhere. You're not talking to the right people."

He tilted his head to one side. "What do you mean, not the right people? All the high-rankers will be there, even a representative from Vlasilov's staff. Thank God, they're at least making an *effort* to be humane."

I smiled again, then pointed at the ceiling. "The ones you need to complain to are the Dracans. They're fighting altogether too hard. If they were to ease off a little, then so could we." My smile widened. "Why don't you invite the

Emperor to a counselor's meeting? I doubt he could make it personally, but maybe someone from his staff could stand in for him? Everyone could take a nice little rest, then!"

My tutor's face froze, then turned bright red. "Very funny, Thomas," he said as he opened the door to our shared living space and gestured me out ahead of him. "Very funny indeed. But, I fear, all too true."

Chapter Three

"Attention on deck!" the Marine guard bawled out as I stepped through the meeting-room door, and suddenly the previously-calm room was awash in motion. I *hated* it when everyone stood up and saluted me; my rank was a joke, a joke that nobody seemed to be in on except me. But the medals were even worse. By tradition, holders of the Parliamentary Medal of Merit were always saluted first, by officers of any rank. I'd been issued one of those for the Battle of the Orion Nexus, and then an oak leaf cluster to designate a second award for my recent mission to Drakkus. Most of the time these medals went to genuine heroes-- men and women who honestly deserved them-- instead of teen-aged boys who just happened to be at the wrong place at the wrong time. So, maybe it made sense that, for their rest of their lives in uniform, the people who actually had *earned* such an award should be saluted like an Admiral of the Fleet every time they entered a room. In my situation, however, it was more embarrassing than anything else, and the fact that I was always running late just made things worse.

"At ease," I mumbled, so quickly that the slower-moving meeting-attendees still hadn't finished standing up yet. I'd tried to have the formality suspended for the duration, but for once Vlasilov had overruled me. "It's good for them to show homage to a hero," he explained to me gently in his office, where he'd chosen to break the news to me personally. "And especially good for discipline. Even I need reminding of what the navy's all about from time to time. What we're actually here for, in other words, and what we're supposed to be doing for a living. So please forgive me, but the salutes continue. Even from me." He half-smiled. "You'll get used to it."

Maybe I *would* eventually get used to it, I decided. But at the rate I was going, it wouldn't be until I was at least eighty or ninety. Everyone stood and silently waited as I inched my way across the room on my slow electric motors and sat down in my assigned spot next to Ted. Then, as if on cue, everyone sat down again when I did. "Hello, Thomas!" my co-commander whispered as he pushed my chair in for me. That particular motion was very difficult for my mannequin body. Therefore, I knew that Ted was helping me because he knew that I actually needed help, not because I'd won a couple of fancy medals.

11

Somehow, that was different. "It's good to see you."

I nodded back. "And you," I answered, even though yet another endless meeting was the last place I wanted to be. How I was absolutely *dying* to get away from the navy for a few days! Not that there was the slightest hope of that, of course. Though being with Ted was the next-best thing. I liked him a lot. Not only was he fun to be around and not overawed by all the useless junk I was expected to wear on my chest all of the time, he was a hero in his own right and far more responsible for the Banana's recent run of successes than anyone else seemed to understand.

"Well..." Commander Bard said from the podium. Then she picked up her long pointing-stick. Michelle was one of the navy's top strategists, and I enjoyed the special classes she sometimes taught us pilots very much. "Let me continue from where I left off, then. The broad situation remains unchanged..."

I sighed and then, rather to my own surprise, yawned as Commander Bard outlined the same strategic picture she'd been outlining every day for the past two weeks, ever since our task force had returned to Esteppe. We'd hurt the Dracans badly, very badly even, in our raid on their homeworld.

"There's been no further use of nuclear weapons by the Dracans against ground targets since the raid," Michelle explained. "Or at least, none that we yet have word of. Now that our side has retaliated, they seem much less willing to play with fire."

There was a short murmur of conversation in the room. "Is there any recent word from New Nippon?" another commander asked. He was with the Fleet, not Aviation, so I didn't know his name.

"Our last news is ten days old," Michele replied, her face grim. "As of then, the Dracans were still present in force."

Ted frowned, and so did I. Our task force had chased merry hell over half the universe trying to maneuver the Dracans away from New Nippon, in order to break the blockade of Earth. Yes, we'd shot up lots of Dracan ships and supplies, and yes, we'd delivered our fusion weapons to the enemy's home world. Even the capitol. Because of this the media was calling our raid a great victory. But it wasn't, not really. Not unless the Dracans pulled out. That was the only test of success that really mattered. The United Systems could fight without Earth, for a time. It could even fight hard and well. We were cut off from the bulk of our wealth and resources, however, and Earth was in turn cut off from her vital imports. So long as Dracan forces held New Nippon, Earth's sole gateway to the rest of the universe, they were unquestionably winning the war.

Bard shook her head and sighed aloud. "Frankly, we don't know how they're doing it. Our traffic-studies show that Dracan molecular-battery deliveries must be down to a trickle. But..." She shrugged. "Intelligence estimates are notoriously unreliable. Eyewitness accounts from friendly neutrals are *not* unreliable, however, and they're who's telling us the Dracans are still blockading in force. Somehow or another, they're managing the impossible. And, Earth's not doing well. Details are classified at an even higher level than this meeting, but... Let me just say that they're howling for help back home. More desperately every day, they're howling for help."

There was a long, profound silence in the room. Then Michele moved on to the rest of her briefing, dealing with our own molecular battery situation—excellent, since we had so few ships—estimated repair dates when various major fleet units would be spaceworthy again, and a report on Skybolt production.

"We'll have a dozen 'bolts up and flying in ninety days," Michele reported, looking happy for the first time. "That includes a minimal acclimatization and training period for the pilots, though of course we'd always like to give them longer."

"Will a dozen be enough to crack on through to Earth?" demanded an Esteppan commodore I knew slightly from previous meetings; he was the officer in charge of the planet's dockyards.

"Maybe," Bard replied, choosing her words carefully. "And maybe not. The answer depends on many factors, most of which we can't possibly predict ahead of time. For example... How many Dracan superfighters will be present?"

"Ja," the commodore replied glumly. My report of encountering Dracan superfighters defending their capitol had made many officers glum, I couldn't help but notice.

"Exactly," Michele replied. Then she pressed her lips together and made a decision. "It doesn't take a particularly gifted strategist," she suggested at long last, "to see that before very much longer we're going to have to try to break the blockade regardless, using whatever forces we have at hand. I'm not revealing any state secrets when I say that the outcome of the war is at stake here. And Earth's already held out longer than anyone ever though she could." She looked down at her notes, then shut off the viewscreen switch with a loud, decisive snap. "We've had two weeks of relative quiet, ladies and gentlemen. It can't go on much longer. If I were in any kind of responsible position just now, I'd be planning accordingly."

Chapter Four

I thought long and hard about Michele's briefing as I walked ever-so-slowly down most of the length of *The Glorious First of June* to my cabin. It was located at the far end of the gunroom, the area of the ship where military discipline didn't apply to any of us under-age types. Which meant that every time I came and went, I had to walk first past Viktor's now-empty cabin, and then Delana's. It was harder than I'd ever dreamed, losing my fellow pilots. Even now, after the memorial services and the talks I'd had with Father Murton, it was all I could do to keep moving as if nothing were really bothering me at all. They'd been kids, was all. Just kids, who'd trusted me with their lives. Ted and I had done all that we could; we'd planned things out to a tee. But then my nose gear had failed and our mission's timing had been ruined. The enemy fighters, their attention undivided, had swarmed Delana and Viktor, first dozens and then hundreds, and then...

"Hello, Thomas!" a friendly voice greeted me.

I started abruptly; somehow, I'd frozen outside Delana's door without even realizing it. But it was just Petty Officer Brooks, Jimmy's counselor. It was almost time for our shift-change; probably Brooks was on his way to help dismount my friend from his 'hopper. "Hi," I answered, looking away. Everyone was watching me, I knew. It was no secret, how bad I felt over losing Delana and Viktor. Father Murton had tried to have me grounded; he'd told me so, right to my face. Deep down I knew that he was probably right. But I couldn't be spared, and that was that. Jimmy couldn't be on alert twenty-fours a day. No one could.

Brooks sighed and crossed his arms, but didn't speak for a long time. Then he shook his head. "Son," he finally said. "You've got to get past this."

Past what? I didn't ask. Brooks wasn't an officer, but I'd been in the navy long enough by now to recognize that officers held no monopoly on smarts. "Delana's dead," I answered. "She'll never get over *that*."

Jimmy's counselor winced.

"And, Viktor's gone too. We've got the telemetry."

"Viktor's gone as well," Brooks agreed, nodding sadly. "And we all mss him something fierce. Did you know that he asked for me to be his counselor, too?"

My eyebrows rose. "No."

"It's true," Brooks replied. "He never really liked Diane very much, though they both tried their best to make things work anyhow." He shrugged. "You can imagine how *she* feels."

I probably should've said something nice about the elderly Diane, who'd mostly been living on happy-pills ever since the bad news came in. But suddenly I was too angry. "Everyone's dying!" I complained. "Colonel Rotte, Gustav… Everyone! Do you know where I went today?

"No," Brooks answered. "Tell me."

"To an entire verdammt *hospital* full of dying people! To pin medals on a soon-to-be corpse's pillow. He smiled when we did that, Chief! Smiled! And he was dying ugly; I never, ever want to see uglier." I shook my head as violently as my motors would allow. "He was a Stormcrow worker. If he's not lying in his grave by this time next week, it'll be a miracle."

"Ah," Brooks answered. There was another long pause. "I'm sorry, Thomas."

"Sorry!" I exploded, waving my arms in rage. Anywhere else I'd have kept my feelings bottled up tight inside of me, the way I always did. But this was the gunroom, where it was supposed to be okay for us pilots to be kids. Even for the great hero Thomas Longo, it was supposed to be okay. "You're sorry! Chief, he was *oozing*! Leaking from everywhere!"

"It's always hard to watch others suffer," Brooks observed, arms still crossed. "When I was just a little younger than you, a friend of mine was burned up in a house fire. It took him a month to die."

I opened my mouth to yell some more, then shook my head again instead. "So he's dead too. Gone for who knows how long; since before I was born, for sure. Everyone's either dead or dying. And there's no point to any of it!"

"Maybe, maybe not." Brooks uncrossed his arms and tilted his head to one side. "Who the hell knows, anyway? Not me, for sure." Then he sighed. "My friend got burned up trying to get two kids out. Their mother was out front, screaming. She pointed towards their room, and we went in for them."

"We?" I asked.

He shrugged. "We. Otis was heavier than me, and the floor gave way under him. I got one of them out; the other was in his arms." The petty officer shuddered and his skin visibly paled. "They screamed, Thomas. God they screamed, for what seemed like hours. The fire department arrived as quickly as they could, but by then the little girl was dead." He shook his head. "She was the lucky one, Thomas. Trust me on that. Please. I don't want to have to explain."

"Everyone's dying," I repeated, not shouting this time. "All around me. Everyone. Either they're dying, or I'm killing them."

"I know," Brooks whispered, a most unexpected tear trickling down his cheek. Clearly, he could remember the fire like yesterday, would never forget it for as long as he lived. Just as I... As I...

Then, suddenly I was hugging Brooks, messing up his immaculate uniform something terrible. "Everyone's dying!" I repeated. "Father and Sven work in that plant, too! Without radiation suits, because the workers don't wear them! And Jimmy! My best friend Jimmy! He'd be dead too, if I hadn't... if I hadn't...."

"Shhh!" Brooks encouraged me as my false body was wracked with false sobs. I'd cried and cried and cried ever since coming back from my last mission; would I *ever* be all cried out? "It's all right, Thomas. God knows that what you've seen is worth a few tears now and again."

I was going to be late relieving Jimmy, just as surely as I was making a fool of myself in front of his counselor. But somehow, try as I might I simply couldn't stop bawling like a little boy. "It doesn't make any sense!" I protested.

"Life and death rarely does," Brooks agreed softly. "My friend Otis died, while I lived. The kids were hiding in a closet right next to each other. I grabbed one, he grabbed the other. One died, one lived." He shrugged. "It was the purest of chance, which was which. There was no sense to it at all."

"No sense," I agreed, feeling a little better though I didn't know why.

"But..." Brooks continued, pulling away slightly and looking me in the eye. "My friend was conscious most of the time, right up until the last few days. I visited him whenever I could; I was burned too, though of course not nearly so bad. So I was only a couple floors away." He looked away; clearly, the memory was extraordinarily painful. "Otis told me that it was worth it, Thomas. Even when he knew that he wasn't going to make it, he said that it was worth it. 'How could I live with myself,' Otis asked me, 'if I'd just let them die? If I'd ignored that poor mother, and just stood there while you went in alone? A man's gotta die someday, Greg. This way, at least I don't have to go out ashamed. That'd be the worst thing of all.'"

I thought about it for a long minute, but said nothing.

"Your dead pilots volunteered," Brooks continued, nodding towards Delana's door. "And, for that matter, so did the others who've died in training and in surgery, and so will all those others who are yet to die. Each and every one of them volunteered of their own free will. Fought for their chance, even. Sure, they're mighty young. But my friend Otis was only fourteen, and I'll not have you or anyone diminish his heroism by trying to claim that he was too young to make life-and-death decisions. Nor will I allow anyone-- including you, Thomas-- to demean Viktor and Delana's sacrifice." His eyes narrowed. "They chose as freely as you did. Just like the Stormcrow worker you visited today chose to risk his health. He's a hero, too. I've been over and over Jimmy's mission a thousand times; being who and what I am, it's my business to know everything he's done. And having been through your wingman's records, I can't help but know in intimate detail what you went through, as well." He frowned.

16

"Thomas… You really should've left Jimmy for dead. We both know it."

I gulped, but still couldn't speak.

"But you didn't. Just like Delana and Viktor didn't run away when every fighter on Drakkus seemed to be after them." He frowned. "You were lucky. And due to your greater experience, perhaps a somewhat better combat pilot as well. But you could've been killed every bit as easily as Viktor was. Right?"

Wordlessly, I nodded.

"And yet, despite having flown two of the hairiest missions in modern air-combat history, and therefore knowing fully what the odds against you really are, you're on your way right now to be mounted into a Skybolt yet again, on the off-chance that the Dracans might try raiding us here tonight." He shook his head. "Thomas… I don't know what more I can say. Delana and Viktor didn't die because of anything that you did, or anything that you failed to do. Nor did the Colonel." He paused. "When your nose gear failed, you had every opportunity to honorably abort the mission. No one would've said a word if you'd scrubbed. Would they?"

"No," I admitted. "I don't think so."

"Not after what you'd already done in the past," Brooks confirmed. "They wouldn't have dared. Yet, you demanded to be launched anyway, with nothing left on the mission clock. It was a suicide mission at that point; no one had thought about holding *Roman Nose* back to recover you yet." He paused. "Do you believe that Delana and Viktor would've done any less?"

"Well…" I spluttered. "I mean…"

"*Honor* them, Thomas," Brooks urged, taking me by the upper arm. "Don't mourn them; *honor* them. They died doing exactly what they wanted to do, of their own free choice. They chose their path because they cared about their fellows. And while I wasn't there, I suspect that like my friend Otis they died serene in the knowledge that they'd passed the most difficult test that anyone can ever face. Just as you've passed it yourself, even though by pure luck you didn't actually get killed in the process. Everyone dies, Thomas. Both you and I must die someday as well. I can only hope that when my time comes, it'll be while I'm doing the right thing. No mortal man can dare hope for anything more." He squeezed my arm gently. "You have to let them go, Thomas. For the sake of their dignity and honor, every bit as much as your own." He gently led me down the hall towards my own cabin. "Let them go. Soon there will be others who need you every bit as much as Delana and Viktor did. Be there for them, son. Then no matter what happens you can hold up your head as well."

Chapter Five

Honor them, Brooks's voice rang through my head that night as I stood parked on the gently rocking weather deck of *The Glorious First of June*. The navy generally operated fighter squadrons from land bases when their carriers were dirt side, so that the hanger-decks could be cleared and routine maintenance performed on the mother-ship. Besides, it made for a nice change of scenery for the pilots and crews. In this case, however, with only two operational 'hoppers left there was plenty of room for operations topside. Neither Jimmy nor I planned to take off in anything less than a major emergency, since we couldn't afford any more operational losses. So our 'bolts were set up side-by-side, and the off-duty pilot remained within a few minutes of his 'hopper at all times. The only exceptions were when I had to make especially important appearances, and even then the navy ferried me everywhere I went by high-speed courier in case I needed to rush back.

Honor them, I thought over and over again through the long dark hours, between little fits of half-sleep. *Honor them*. Jimmy's counselor was right, I supposed; what Delana and Viktor had done certainly deserved to be honored. But... In the end, all they'd accomplished was to incinerate, starve and poison almost as many people as Jimmy and I had. On Drakkus at this very minute dying men, women and children were probably crouching huddled in the dark, cursing all four of us with equal venom. Who was to say that Brooks was right and that the Dracan civilians were wrong? What *was* right and wrong in the middle of a war, after all? Could such distinctions even be drawn? For that matter, was there even really a right and wrong *outside* of war that everyone everywhere could agree on? What did it mean if we *couldn't* agree? And, did it really matter?

I thought about it for hour after hour, my dimmed-down readouts sometimes transforming themselves into squadrons of *Imperial Throne*-class battleships pumping broadside after broadside into a helpless, shattered *June*. Meanwhile, Father Murton begged forgiveness for our sins, the Dracan admiral screamed "Horrido!" at the top of his lungs, and I floated powerless and unable to do anything but watch, drifting further and further out into the cold black that went on forever and ever and ever. I never truly slept, I supposed. On the other hand, a lot of the time I wasn't exactly awake either. And once-- when I screamed out loud for Jimmy to break left-- my brand-new crew chief offered to get Father Murton for me. But it was just a nightmare, I explained. Something he should get used to, if he was going to be working with me for very long. "I'm sorry, sir," he mumbled. "So sorry that you should have to... I mean..." But somehow he never quite finished what he had to say.

By then it was after seven in the morning. Jimmy was supposed to relieve me at nine, and after that in theory at least I was scheduled for eight uninterrupted hours of rest. There were always reports to read, however. Reports on the new pilots, on proposed Skybolt modifications, on the estimated capabilities and numbers of the Dracan superfighters... It was more than I could possibly keep up on while standing heel-and-toe alerts with Jimmy, and yet as squadron commander I *had* to keep up. "These are going to be a very bad few weeks," Ted had warned me as we'd prepared for splashdown on Esteppe after our long, successful raid. "I'll do everything I can to help. But, in the end, you're going to be carrying far too large a load, and there's nothing anyone can do about it."

Well, I decided, there *was* one thing I could do. "Ben?" I asked.

"Yes, sir?" my crew chief replied.

"I'd like to read, if you don't mind."

"Of course I don't mind, sir," the young sailor replied. A new indicator lit up in my mind, and suddenly I was staring down at a plain, unadorned metal desktop. A hairy hand, presumably Ben's, hovered at one edge of my field-of-view. "What would you like me to set up for you first?"

I was still trying to make up my mind when another indicator lit up. It was my outside comm line. "Excuse me," I told Ben. "Someone's calling me." Then I answered my new phone. Both it and the reading-camera had been my brother Sven's idea, and I was very grateful. "Hello?"

"Thomas?" a feminine voice asked, and it was as if a cool breeze was suddenly blowing through my soul.

"Alicia?" I replied. "Is that really you?"

"Oh, yes!" the Deputy Prime Minister replied. Then she chuckled. "How many other people on this planet do you suppose can dial you direct while you're on duty?"

"Heh!" I answered, trying to grin. But of course I couldn't when I was a Skybolt.

"Seriously," Alicia replied. "I've got a hole in my schedule this morning, and a little bird told me that you were up and at 'em." She paused. "I'm not keeping you from sleeping, am I?"

Suddenly, two and two came together in my mind. "Father Murton asked you to call, didn't he? Because he's worried about me?"

"Well..." the rabbit-woman replied, clearly not wanting to give me a straight answer. "We're all worried about you, Thomas. You and Jimmy both, to be quite frank. You kids have been through a lot." There was a short pause. "I *do* care about you, you know."

I sighed to myself, not letting Alicia hear. She *did* care, I knew, and not just because it was her responsibility to ensure that her government's most important weapon systems were functioning at peak efficiency. "Yeah," I answered eventually. "I know." There was another long, awkward pause. "Have you heard anything from Spence?"

"Why, yes!" Alicia replied, her voice suddenly full of sparkle and cheer. She'd been married to her husband for well over a century, and being separated from him was terribly hard on her. All marriages were partnerships, but even as young and inexperienced as I was I'd come to understand that the Wistons were more dependent on each other than most. "I just got a note from him through the Gambian Embassy. He's fine, thank god! Or, at least he was nine days ago. He's found another safe place, he says, or at least another place that's as safe as anywhere can be for him. He says that the Resistance is stronger than ever, and that they think they killed over five hundred Dracan enlisted men last week by poisoning their rations with something-or-other; I forget exactly what. Nasty stuff, whatever it was."

I didn't wince, as Skybolts couldn't do that, either. While my efforts with fusion weapons might exceed those of Spence's resistance movement in total number of corpses generated, his organization's war certainly eclipsed mine in terms of sheer nastiness. Not that the Dracans hadn't earned such enmity; I'd been there and seen Dracan rule first-hand. What came around, went around. It was a law of nature, practically.

"He also wrote you a letter, Thomas," Alicia continued, "Instead of just asking me to send his regards as usual. I haven't opened it yet. Would you like for me to?"

"Really?" I blurted. "A letter? To me?" I'd spend several months living in a cave with Spence and Alicia back on Churilla; this was why it wasn't strange for me to receive a casual phone call from the Deputy Prime Minister. But still… Spence and his Freedom Fighters were rapidly becoming heroes everywhere that the United Systems flag still flew, so much so that people across the galaxy were greeting each other on the street with rabbit-ear finger-signs as a gesture of their common belief in ultimate victory. The sign originated on Churilla, but had spread everywhere. Not even Alicia was more famous and beloved than her husband these days.

There was a gentle tearing sound on the phone line, then Alicia began to read.

"Dear Thomas," she began; I could almost see Spence's spidery, archaic script. "I learned with pride today of your latest exploits against our common enemy. Well done, Thomas! Well done indeed, to you and to everyone who helped make your mission such a resounding success!" Alicia paused for a moment. "I said the same thing, you may recall. When I pinned your medal on you."

I didn't answer, and eventually Alicia read on. "You were already a hero when I last saw you, Thomas, and you're twice a hero now. By this time tomorrow, your name will be on the lips of every Churillian. And they will smile when they speak it. Your victory has brought them hope and joy. Because you spent so much time here, we've adopted you as one of our own. Like it or not you're a Churillan now, just as you were already an Earther and, dare I say it, a bit of an Esteppan. Which is something to be proud of, Thomas. Not ashamed. Just as you should be proud of your father and who and what he is. I still very much wish to meet him someday."

"Ha!" I interrupted. "Was it that obvious even back then? That being from Esteppe bothered me, I mean?"

"To both of us," Alicia replied. "But you're over it now, and that's all to the good." Then she went back to reading. "War is hard, Thomas. You know that better than most, probably now more than ever. It's the hardest thing that there has ever been or, most likely, ever will be. It brings out the best and the worst in us; every other human enterprise pales in comparison to it. You didn't love war when I knew you here, and I expect you love it even less now. Certainly I hate it more than ever. Though I've studied war all of my life and held few illusions as to its true nature, the reality has exceeded my worst expectations. When the fighting is done, if you and I are lucky enough to count ourselves among the survivors I expect that we'll loathe war more than anything else in the universe. Except tyranny and oppression, of course. And there's the rub that keeps the whole awful cycle going, over and over and over again.

"Alicia mentioned in one of her letters that you wanted this war to be different, for it to have meaning in that winning it would allow for a better, more enlightened form of government that would render future wars unnecessary or even unthinkable. The sentiment does you credit, Thomas. However, this is a problem that has defied solution since the very beginning of things. One underlying contributor is that violence *works*. Because it works, so long as there are great issues at stake people will continue to resort to it in order to get their way. As we've seen so clearly demonstrated, it only takes one side to make a war. The Emperor's apologists may claim otherwise, but I'm not having any of their poisonous garbage. This was a power and resource grab on the part of the Dracans, pure and simple. Whether or not they succeed will be decided on the battlefields, not at negotiating tables.

"Violence works even for *animals*, Thomas, and they often employ it as well in resolving their disputes. The Universe itself, in its most basic structures and laws, seems almost purposely designed to evoke violent conflict among we who populate it. Where resources are finite and potential wants and needs infinite, how can there *not* be conflict? So long as we are material beings with material wants and needs, living in a universe where such resources are limited and under conditions where violence is an effective and successful means of resolving disputes, it's no wonder there are wars. Indeed, the miracle is that there's ever any peace!

"That said, Thomas, I applaud you again for wanting things to be different this time around. Billions have died. Billions! More than have ever died in any war before. And the dead must weigh especially heavy upon you. In fact, for all the blood on my own hands I can't even begin to imagine what you must be going through. There also must've been losses among your own people, and probably you're feeling bad about them as well.

"So know this, Thomas. In my own studies of war, I've become convinced that, in those conflicts where significant cultural and philosophical issues are at stake, the more brutal and violent the war the sooner the fighting ends. Trying to fight a 'gentleman's' war only piles the corpses higher in the long run, and increases the suffering for all involved. Not only that, but the more overwhelmingly the enemy is crushed, the stronger the resulting peace. It's only when defeat is unquestionably complete that a people can accept the loss of their hopes and dreams and resign themselves to adopting the alien values and ideas they struggled so terribly hard against. This acceptance of the unacceptable is the essential component of defeat. It cannot be achieved without massive bloodshed most of the time, yet without it there can be no true peace-- merely a cease-fire. If the victory is incomplete, then, generally speaking, so is the peace.

"Thomas, you've fought hard and well in what I at least consider to be a noble cause. You've sacrificed more than you probably understand; a person's teenage years are meant to be a time of discovery and joy, not of military discipline and death. But there's still much fighting ahead of us both. To paraphrase a favorite historical figure of mine, your raid might not mark the beginning of the end, but I suspect that it marks the end of the beginning.

"I'd very much like to be able to tell you that this can be a war to end all wars, Thomas. The longer and harder we Churillians fight, the more I wish it could be made so. But no victory won has *ever* produced such a peace, else you and I wouldn't be fighting today. We're mortal men and women, we who run things behind the scenes, not fairy godmothers who can make wishes come true with the wave of a wand. We live in an imperfect universe, with only imperfect solutions available to us. All that we can realistically do is be certain in our hearts that what we're fighting for is true and just, and then do what we think will best ensure the most humane outcome possible consistent with the long-term good of humanity. Once the victory is won, we movers and shakers will sit down and craft the best peace we can, hopefully one better and more perfect than any ever crafted before. Even so, only the fools among us will imagine that our shiny new peace will last forever. Instead, it will surely prove to be as imperfect as the hearts and souls of we who will craft it.

"Even so, Thomas, there are always new things to be found under the sun.

22

We might not find an ultimate answer to the problem of war, we would-be peacemakers, but Alicia and I can guarantee that, if we survive and our side wins, there will be at least one innovation that, we hope, will make things incrementally better for us all. I cannot tell you what it is, Thomas, though I'd very much like to. But, when the time comes, I am quite certain that you will recognize Alicia's and my ploy for exactly what it is. And, I hope, will support or even join us in it.

"At any rate, I look forward very much to seeing you again, once the shooting is over and the dead are buried and our most capable men and women need no longer make killing each other their primary concern. Our home will always be your own, until the very end of things. I'd like to write a book with you someday about your travels and experiences; your memoirs, I suppose. But, until that happy time when we can meet again, may you remain safe and kill many, many more Dracans. Respectfully, your friend Spencer Wiston."

Chapter Six

I couldn't say precisely what it was that did the trick. Talking personally with Alicia helped, I was pretty sure, and certainly both Spence's letter and hearing Chief Brooks's story about the fire had an effect. Perhaps Father Murton's prayers were finally answered, or, most likely of all, it was just time. But that morning when I came off of alert I slept both deep and hard. It was the first good rest I'd gotten since fusion-bombing the City of Imperial Peace.

I didn't realize how good I felt at first, however. Normally, Father Murton woke me up, since he had to help me dress and such anyway. But this particular morning my cabin suddenly began heaving up and down, and bright sunlight flashed in my eyes. At first I panicked a little; *the Dracans are attacking!* Then I figured out that the motion was just *June* reacting to another ship splashing down in our little fjord. I clambered out of bed and staggered over to my porthole; it wasn't easy with my slow-reacting legs, but because *June* was designed with free-fall in mind there were handholds everywhere. I was lucky; the new ship was within my field of view. She was a merchantman, strangely enough, a bulk-cargo carrier riding low in the water and thus fully-laden. Generally the navy didn't like sharing anchorages with merchies; there were a thousand good reasons for this, ranging from security issues to overcrowding at the local bars. But, just as soon as the *Spokane Maru* settled in another big bulk-carrier settled in right behind her. This time I couldn't read her name; she was too far away. And then, in came a third!

"Good morning, Thomas!" Father Murton greeted me as he opened the door to my private sleeping-space. "How are you feeling today?"

It was an old ritual, dating back to long before I'd been brain-cored. "Fine," I answered, just like I always did. Then I looked at the clock and my eyes widened. "You let me sleep in!"

"Yep," he answered, stepping over to stand alongside me by the porthole. A fourth merchie was splashing down now, and *June* was rocking again. "I canceled your entire afternoon schedule, Thomas. Everything. You don't have a thing to do today except meet with Vlasilov, in his cabin. At your convenience, I might add. Not his."

I pressed my lips together. How could I possibly keep up with everything if my meetings were cancelled? "Look," I began. "I know that—"

But my tutor wasn't having any. "Talk to Vlasilov," he interrupted. "Not to me, though heaven knows I'm on his side." He smiled. "Or on *somebody's* side at least; I suspect that this originates from an even higher source than the admiral." He shook his head. "You're free to go see him any time you like. I take it that you'd prefer for it to be right away?"

It only took us twenty minutes or so to get me dressed. Since Father Murton had called ahead for me, I didn't have to wait at all. The admiral's office door was wide open as I strode up to it. "Thomas!" he greeted me, his eyes lighting up with genuine pleasure as he looked up from his paperwork. "I hear that you rested well last night. You're looking better already!"

I blinked in confusion as I stepped in and closed the door behind me. All that Vlasilov could see of me was a plastic-skinned, inexpressive mannekin body; I didn't get rings under my eyes or stress-lines in my skin. So, how could he tell if I felt better or not? "I—" I began.

"Sit down!" Vlasilov urged me, pointing to the chairs by the big stern-gallery windows. "I'll join you, and we can talk for a time."

My limbs moved slowly due to their electrical nature, while Vlasilov's body was stiff and a bit arthritic for another reason entirely. By the time he settled in next to me yet another merchantman, this one a huge tanker of some kind, was settling into the fjord. "Like a big fat goose landing," he observed, scowling in disapproval. "All ships are like that, you know. Sleek and graceful in space, yes. But hitting the water, they are like clumsy fat geese."

I nodded slowly as *June* bobbled up and down in the ripples. "Just as easy to shoot, too," I observed.

"Da," Vlaslov agreed, frowning slightly. Then his smile returned. "I have good news, Thomas."

My eyebrows rose. "Indeed?"

"This afternoon, both of our remaining Stormcrows will come back into service." He gestured out at the floating ships. "We'll have two more superfighters to help protect our fat geese."

I smiled too. "Great! I've been thinking this through, sir. If you put Jimmy and I on the night shift—"

"Heh!" Vlasilov interrupted, smiling. "How did I know that this would be your answer? You want to be put on the night shift so that you can keep up on your staff work during the daytime. Da?"

"Well…" I answered, looking down at the carpet. "I know that Heinz has staff work too, now that the Colonel's gone and Gustav with him. But—"

"But nothing!" Vlasilov interrupted; my heavens, but I was being interrupted a lot today! "Heinz will get the night shift, and that is settled. So that he can at least partly keep up on staff work, just as you said. And that is final."

My mouth opened, then closed. Sure, Heinz was an adult, and I was just a kid. But wasn't I entitled to some consideration too? "Well," I finally answered. "At least I'll be back on the same schedule with Jimmy. I miss him."

Vlasilov's eyes narrowed. "You wish to spend more time with your wingman?"

I felt my face harden slightly. "He's my friend," I said at last, after squirming in my chair for a bit. Didn't the admiral understand *anything*? "I don't have many friends."

"Ha!" Vlasilov replied, leaning his head back and looking up at the ceiling for a long, long time. When finally he turned to face me again, he was grinning from ear to ear. "I think we can arrange this," he said finally. "If Jimmy is willing, that is. It'll be his decision, as well."

Now I was totally confused. "I... I mean... Sir..."

"Ha!" Vlasilov repeated. Then, after gesturing for me to remain seated, he got up and retrieved the file-folder he'd been examining when I arrived. "I have a special assignment for you both," he explained. "One that has been deemed vital to the security of the United Systems, and which has been approved by Madame Deputy herself. You're being asked to volunteer."

I should've figured it out right then, the moment Alicia's name entered the picture. But I'd been working very hard, for a very long time. "Sir?" I nodded out at all the ships bobbing helplessly at anchor. "What could possibly be more important than covering the fleet?"

"We shall have air cover," he answered, though his voice seemed a little less certain than it had been. "Heinz and August will be taking over for you and Jimmy when he comes off duty tonight."

I pressed my lips together. "Sir," I objected. "Four 'hoppers are better than two. Even that really isn't enough."

Vlasilov's smile faded, and he sat down next to me again, folder still in his hand. "Thomas," he said eventually. "I won't lie to you. Four fighters are indeed better than two. But..." He turned and looked me in the eyes. "We could've had the Stormcrows operational again a week ago. You know that."

I snorted. "Half-operational, maybe! On backup systems, and maybe fifty-percent effective. It was a lot smarter to fix them right, in the long run."

"Exactly," Vlasilov agreed, still looking me directly in the eyes. "Thomas, how long have you been in combat?"

"About three hours total," I answered, finally beginning to suspect where this conversation was going.

"I don't agree, son," the admiral replied, shaking his head. "Three hours of Skybolt combat, yes. But then there was your time on Churilla, first with the army and then with the guerillas. Most people would count that as combat, Thomas. Some of it was *worse* than ordinary combat."

I shrugged, but didn't say anything.

"Then you spent most of your shipwreck leave working as a test pilot for your father and helping to form your squadron. The navy allowed and even encouraged this not because we didn't know better, but rather because we had little choice. God only knows how we'd have managed if you'd been less mature or capable." He sighed. "Then there was the breakout from Earth. Perhaps you don't count that as combat, but the navy disagrees. Your personnel record lists you as a participant in the Second Battle of New Nippon, even though all you did was sit and watch. Someday you'll get a medal for that, too. We all will." He shook his head. "That was plenty traumatic enough, for a boy your age. And then, well… We don't need to go over it all in detail, do we?"

"Maybe not," I agreed. "But—"

"No buts, Thomas!" Vlasilov interrupted. "Not this time! It's not just skyhoppers that require repair and maintenance. This is also true for the men and women who fly them." His expression softened as he handed me the folder. "You require maintenance, Thomas. So does Jimmy; he's been through less, but in this case 'less' is still 'plenty'. You've held on far longer than any of us would've willingly asked without a proper rest; it was only through sheer lack of options that I've asked you to remain on duty these past few weeks. And, believe me, each and every day I've kicked myself for having had to do so."

"Father Murton's been kicking you too," I observed.

"And Madame Deputy as well," Vlasilov agreed ruefully. "It's a bad idea, generally, for someone closely associated with a head-of-state to take on a critical military role. It affects discipline, and can make for poor decision-making." He smiled. "But in your case, as in so many other things, an exception simply must be made."

I couldn't help but grin. "Sorry."

The admiral grinned back. "You've been well worth the extra trouble." Then he handed me the folder. "It so happens that the people of Esteppe are for some unfathomable reason unusually fond of you and your wingman. Grateful to you, even. I can't imagine for the life of me why this might be so, but have come to accept that this is the case nonetheless." He rolled his eyes to show that he was kidding. "I've taken the liberty of having my staff put together a list of places and people who would welcome you, should you choose to pay them a visit. Looking at it, I don't believe that you'll lack for things to do during your shore leave."

"Shore leave?" I asked.

Vlasilov nodded. "Shore leave. Two weeks for both of you, and not a day less. I'd give you sixty days if I could, or even longer. Not only have you earned it, but that's what the experts suggested as well. However, I fear that in two weeks I'll need you back."

"Two whole weeks?" I asked, gripping the bulging folder nervously. "But… I mean…"

"Two weeks," he repeated as *June* bobbled again. Another ship must've splashed down, though apparently it'd landed someplace where we couldn't see it. "You will immediately remove that uniform, Commander Longo. And if I catch you in it again before fourteen full days have elapsed, so help me I'll make you regret the day you were born. Do you understand me?"

"Yes sir!" I answered, jumping to my feet as best as I was able. The effect wasn't very military, I was certain. But Vlasilov was willing to make allowances. As always.

He smiled and stood as well, then shook my hand. "Have *fun*, Thomas," he urged me. "Go laugh and play. Please?"

"I'll try," I answered, returning the handshake as best I was able. "If I can, I will."

Chapter Seven

My first day of leave wasn't spent ashore. Nor was it very much fun. Father Murton was waiting for me back in my cabin, with bright-colored athletic clothing already laid out for me. But somehow once I was out of my uniform I felt overwhelmingly tired again, even though I'd just woken up from a nice long sleep. It was strange, really; I hadn't felt all that worn down so long as I had important duties to perform. Once they were out of the picture, however, I wanted a nap more than anything in the world. I slept another few hours, got up and visited with Jimmy a little right before he went to bed, then slept yet again.

When I finally woke up the next day, everything felt different somehow. I wasn't nearly as edgy as I'd been, and when I walked down to Jimmy's cabin I smiled and waved at everyone I met along the way. I hadn't done that in a very long time, I realized with a little shock as I knocked at my wingman's door. Instead, I'd just kept my head down and ignored everyone around me.

"Hi, Tommy!" Jimmy greeted me brightly. He was wearing shorts and a cardinal-red sports jersey of some kind. His feet were bare, and the effect was so different from his uniform that at first I didn't recognize him. "I'm playing *Rocket Sledder*, Wanna come in?"

At one time, Jimmy and I had been top-notch Sledders. But we'd been on opposite shifts and drowning in overwork for a long time, and lack of practice took its toll. Two games later, Jimmy pushed his controller away in frustration and looked over at me. "This isn't any fun," he complained. "Not like this."

"It'll get better," I answered. "Once we're out on patrol. We'll have plenty of spare time then."

"I guess," my friend agreed with a sigh. Then he turned and looked at me. "We really ought to make some kind of plans, Tommy."

"Yeah," I agreed, even though I was plenty happy just playing video games and not having a big pile of urgent reports to read.

"Ted has four days of leave coming, too," Jimmy observed. "Starting tomorrow." He frowned. "He's my brother, Tommy. I ought to spend them with him."

I nodded; as much as Jimmy and I liked each other, some time apart would do us both good. Besides... "I ought to see my family too," I agreed. "If they can make time for me."

Jimmy smiled. "I bet they will."

I smiled back, though I had my doubts. It wasn't that Father and Sven wouldn't *want* to make time for me, of course. There wasn't the slightest doubt on that score. But, they were so important to the war effort that I'd be lucky if I got to so much as have dinner with them. "I've called the estate," I answered. "I'm welcome for a day or a year, anytime I show up." I half-smiled. "It's home, I suppose. Even though I've never been there."

We opened up Vlasilov's folder then, and pored over it together. "Wow!" I exclaimed at one point. "That's the best restaurant on Esteppe!"

"But we can't eat," Jimmy objected. "If you want scenery, you can always spend a night in your room at the Aerie. I could even be your guest."

My eyebrows rose. Jimmy wasn't in the Order of Blood, though I thought he should be. Probably would be, even, if he'd been Esteppan born. Was he jealous? "Of course, Jimmy! If you'd like."

"Naw," he answered, wrinkling up his nose. "Maybe if I could still ski, though."

I nodded in sympathy. Our biggest problem was that we *couldn't* do most of the things we really wanted to anymore, because of our mannequin-bodies. "The Youth Scouts are going to climb the Stahlberg next Sunday," I pointed out. 'It's supposed to be a really beautiful hike, and we'd be with kids our own age for a while."

Jimmy pressed his lips together. "They say you're not a real Esteppan until you've climbed the Stahlberg."

I nodded. "That's true. And, I never have. It's supposed to be an easy climb, one that we can make even as slow-moving as we are."

Jimmy nodded, and placed the brochure into a separate pile "I'll climb the Stahlberg, and be an honorary Esteppan. If..." He pulled out another brochure. "If, you'll come and visit the amusement park."

I gulped. I'd never been much for rides or the like, and Esteppe's one and only example of the breed was weak broth indeed in comparison to Earth's rich variety. "Jimmy, I..."

"Aw!" he complained. "Come on, Tommy! They're offering us *platinum tickets*! No lines, no waits, the best of everything. I know it's not Disneyland! But still! Do you have any *idea* how nice it'd be not to have to wait in line? Waiting takes forever!"

In truth, I *didn't* have any idea; I'd never been to an amusement park in my life. It wasn't that no one had been willing to take me; rather, I'd just preferred racing my skimmer on Lake Pontchartraine and riding horses and such. It'd always seemed to me that roller-coaster-type thrills were phony, somehow, compared to jumping wakes or taking a fence at a full gallop. But, if Jimmy wanted to go, that was fine by me. "All right," I agreed. Then I frowned. "Let's see. If we climb the mountain, that has to be on Sunday. And, the second Wednesday night I'm already committed to dinner with Alicia."

"I'm tied up that Wednesday too," my friend agreed absently. He stuck his tongue into his cheek in concentration, then re-arranged the brochures. "All right, then. Families first, for four days. Then the Stahlberg and the Youth Scouts. We split up again for three days, so that we can handle our Wednesday obligations and do other stuff alone. Then, we go crazy at Stormcrow Park. Deal?"

"Deal," I agreed solemnly, extending my hand for shaking. Jimmy accepted it, smiling, and our plans were made.

"You're gonna love Stormcrow Park!" Jimmy promised. "Trust me! You're gonna absolutely *love* it!"

Chapter Eight

I'd only been three when Father left Esteppe to try and expand family aerospace business to New Orleans. So, even though I'd actually lived on the ancestral estate for a time, I didn't remember anything about it. Lothar Longo had been one of the major financial backers of the original colonization ship, and so had been able to carve out a choice chunk of real estate indeed for himself and his heirs. Not only did we own, lock stock and barrel, one of the largest and most beautiful mountain ranges on the planet, but down underneath our feet mining robots labored day and night extracting tungsten and rare-earth elements from rich, seemingly inexhaustible veins. It was like owning a gold mine, save that some of the stuff we brought to market was worth a lot more than gold ever was. Our family didn't need Longo Industries to be rich; indeed, Father only started the company because the Autarch asked him to help develop ways to put Esteppe's unique brain-interface technology to work. And how Father had succeeded! His ex-professor had been pleased indeed.

My family home was surprisingly small; it'd been built during Esteppe's earliest days, when resources were limited and the colonists in a hurry to relocate off of their ship. There were only five bedrooms, though servants' quarters and a gasthaus had been added later. The Longos had never been noted for large families, and by the time Esteppe's economy had progressed to the point that a mansion might have been in order, tradition had set in and made the Old Home Place, as it was known, immutable. There were a few other members of the Longo clan on Esteppe, all of them distant cousins of mine. But Father was the heir of Lothar and so the mines and estates were his.

Though the mansion was small, I still rated a bedroom of my own. So did Father Murton, though just about anyone else would have been banished to the gasthaus. And, I had to admit, it was a pretty nice bedroom. I had a personal fireplace, just like everyone else did, though I never needed a fire since I didn't get cold. It was still pretty to look at, though. At the time the Old Home Place had been built, nothing had been more expensive or carried a higher status than Earth-imports. So, my fireplace was framed in New Hampshire black granite and trimmed with snowy-white Italian marble all done up in bas-releifs. The mantelpiece, like all the others in the house, was a rough-hewn plank cut from the trunk of a naturally-expired California sequoia, some of the most expensive wood in the known universe. And, best of all, almost an entire wall was taken up by a stuffed and mounted stormcrow, the biggest and perhaps most ferocious bird of prey yet discovered anywhere. They were extinct now, and the preserved specimen almost as priceless as my mantelpiece.

It was Longo family tradition, Sven had informed me upon my arrival, that I should carve my initials on the bottom of the mantel in whatever room I grew up in, using a knife made entirely of metal extracted from our own private mine. While I hadn't exactly grown up in this room I was already halfway wishing that I had; even as old as I was now, I could lie in bed and simply stare at the stuffed stormcrow for *hours*! So I didn't feel too terribly dishonest as I sat with my back to the unlit fire and scratched my initials into the soft, yielding sequoia wood right under those of my father. So *that* was the real reason why he'd named his first fighter design after Esteppe's most famous bird…

I was just finishing the crosspiece of the "A" when someone knocked at my door. "Come on in!" I answered, not stopping my work. The door swung open; it was Father Murton. "Hi!" I greeted him.

"Hi yourself," he answered, smiling as he looked around the bedroom. "Heavens, but I've missed this place," he said. "It's what I think of, whenever I remember Esteppe."

I nodded, then put my knife down. "It's about as Esteppe as Esteppe gets," I agreed. Then I nodded at the big preserved bird. "But that… Wow!"

The priest's lips curled in a half-smile. "It's something, isn't it? They were supposedly still common back when that one was shot. Pests, even." He sighed and shook his head. "We think we're such wise creatures, we humans. Despite all the evidence to the contrary."

I nodded, but didn't say anything. Then my tutor spoke again. "Your father's coming home, Thomas. He plans to spend all evening with you."

My eyebrows rose. "A whole evening?" Sven had managed only two hours; he'd just undergone brain-implant surgery to allow him to jack-in. I'd hardly recognized him; the shaven head was part of it, but there was more. His surgery was only two weeks old; the aftereffects had left him all headachy and, even less characteristically, a little grouchy. Or, perhaps that was due to all the sixteen-hour days everyone said he was working, trying to help Father pump out as many Skybolts as possible in the limited time available.

"I'm sorry, Thomas," he'd apologized over and over again, often for no reason at all. "You don't deserve to see me like this." His eyes had gone dull and gray where once they had twinkled so mischievously, and they peered out from over dark-smudged cheeks. Most likely it was just extreme fatigue, coupled with recovery from his recent surgery. If so, then I wasn't the only Longo overdue for a leave. But it might also be the first sign of radiation poisoning, from working at the plant with no protective gear. What could I do, though? What could *anyone* do, really? It had to be done, just as I had to fly combat. And that was that.

"A whole evening," Father Murton confirmed. "Though, he told me that he'll probably have to jack in for a couple hours early-on." The priest sighed and shook his head, but made no further comment.

"Right," I agreed, turning back to my carving. What would future Longos think, I wondered, when they looked upon my initials and realized who they belonged to? Would they be pleased to find themselves being raised in a room previously claimed by one so well-known? Or ashamed to share the sleeping-place of a mass-murderer? It was too early to tell, I decided. All I could do was make my mark, and let future generations judge for themselves. "What time is he arriving?"

"About six," my tutor replied. He smiled. "There's plenty of time for you to finish that up; it's terribly important, I know. It's a good thing we got you here when we did, otherwise, you'd have missed your one and only childhood opportunity to carve up your room without being spanked."

"Heh!" I agreed, not looking away from where my "L" was beginning to take shape. "How about if we get me dressed for dinner at five? That way you can have the rest of the night for yourself. You deserve some rest, too."

The priest smiled. "I'll get plenty of time off; Petty Officer Brooks is going to relieve me while you and Jimmy are together. But tonight I'll take you up on it anyway. I want to get a shot of the sun setting over the Lotharberg, if you don't mind. From the stables. I used to go back there to watch sometimes when you were little and taking your nap. But somehow I never took a picture, and, it's one of the most beautiful things I've ever seen. It makes me feel very close to God."

"Good," I agreed, turning to my tutor and smiling. "I hope you have a wonderful time."

Chapter Nine

Father arrived not long after my counselor finished dressing me for dinner; my family generally didn't go in much for formal clothing, but Father Murton had a suit and tie laid out for me and I knew better than to protest. Ordinarily I wouldn't have noticed his arrival; our 'hopper pad was well downslope of the Old Home Place. But the navy was maintaining a high-speed 'hopper there at all times, so that in case the Dracans attacked I could get into the fight as quickly as possible. This forced Father to land in the pasture; suddenly I winced, remembering that my counselor had been headed that way to take pictures, and to quietly commune with God and nature. I certainly hoped that his alone-time hadn't been ruined.

Father didn't come for me right away; I was a little hurt at first, until I remembered being told that he had to jack in for a couple of hours. That was reasonable enough; heaven knew that I'd lived on a killer schedule long enough to appreciate the need to remain caught up as much as possible at all times. Indeed, I reminded myself, I was lucky that he'd been able to work me in at all at such short notice. Most likely he was unaware that I even knew he'd arrived. So instead of bothering him I decided to go take a little walk of my own. The family estate would belong to Sven someday; while I would certainly be welcome as an honored visitor for the rest of my life, these few days, most likely, would be the only time I'd ever be privileged to actually *reside* at the Old Home Place. So, naturally enough I wanted to explore a little.

I didn't make it very far, however. While our home had five bedrooms, the rest of the living space was divided between a large formal dining room and an even larger common-living area. Apparently Father had decided to set up his at-home working facilities in the public area rather than in his own bedroom. I was halfway to the exit when I saw his now-bald dome sticking up over the back of his easy-chair, a heavy black cable drooping down from his golden skull-socket.

"Father?" I asked, practically whispering. I wasn't sure if I really wanted to disturb him or not; the fact was, I suddenly realized, that I didn't know much at all about jacking-in. Would it annoy Father if I interrupted him? Might it even harm him, somehow? But he didn't respond at all.

I pressed my lips together and thought things through. If being interrupted were even potentially harmful, Father wouldn't be working out in public. While the servants I'd met so far were quiet and discreet, they had work to do and were as human as anyone else. At any given moment a pan might drop, or a door slam shut unexpectedly. So instead of wandering outside and admiring the Lotharberg, I tiptoed across the room as quietly as my motors would allow and sat down in a heavily-padded leather chair directly across from Father.

My first surprise was his attire. He was wearing the traditional heavy black robe of the Esteppan Eliteman, adorned only with a sable collar and a gold fastener-chain at the neck. For the first time that I could remember he looked like he had in the old pictures, a war-criminal on trial for crimes against humanity. He'd *never* shaved his head or worn a black robe back on Earth; in fact, I'd never seen him in anything but brown or blue. *None* of us ever wore black, I suddenly realized. Not ever! I could understand why his head was shaved again; hair of any length, I'd read somewhere, could get down into the plug and foul the connections. Sven was doing it too, for the same reason I was sure.

But why the robe?

Father's hands were hidden, each being tucked, monk-like, up the robe's voluminous opposite sleeve. So all that I could see of Father himself was his head and face. He looked tranquil more than anything else, though his eyes were closed a little tighter than they would've been in sleep, and sometimes the lids twitched suddenly in long, complex bursts. Slowly a droplet of drool formed in the corner of his mouth, trickled down his chin, and then dripped down onto his otherwise immaculate garment. I shook my head in bafflement, then focused on the robe again. Gunther, back at the Stormcrow factory, had worn his Eliteman robe to greet Father. It had been intended as a challenge, I realized now. Maybe even an insult to a man he considered a traitor. Yet Father wasn't trying to insult me, or at least he wasn't that I knew of. So what other message might he be trying to send?

Another droplet of saliva began to form; I pulled out the normally-useless handkerchief my tutor always made me carry and gently dabbed it away. Father didn't notice, though his eyelids danced furiously. Was he even aware that I was present? I didn't think so.

Father had been a lot more than an ordinary Eliteman, I knew. He'd been the closest friend the Autarch had, the nearest thing Esteppe's once-leader had ever had to a son. They'd begun as professor and student, but the research they did together changed the universe forever. Father hadn't invented jacking-in, but the Autarch hadn't exactly come up with the technology on his own, either. Most of the patents, I'd learned in history class, bore both men's names. Father had never shared the Autarch's interest in politics, and hadn't taken an active role in the quiet revolution that left his mentor in control of an Esteppe that sincerely believed in his promises of a better, brighter tomorrow through direct brain augmentation. But he also hadn't exactly opposed his friend's takeover.

Nor had he hesitated for a moment when the Autarch summoned his old partner to help him defend the planet against an outraged universe. Indeed, his superfighters had almost succeeded in tipping the balance. Just as they were now keeping the Dracans at bay.

For a time, the ethics of the war had been at least arguable. Then the Autarch's mind broke and, absent any safeguards, Esteppe was plunged into the blackest dictatorship possible. Father turned traitor, and because of it the United Systems won a lot more quickly than they otherwise would've. Our family fled to Earth, Father let his hair grow long, and none of us had ever worn black again.

Until now.

I sighed and turned away; watching a person jack-in was interesting, yes. But only for the first few moments. After that it was like watching paint dry. So I decided to walk around outside for a little while, as I'd originally planned.

It was a glorious summer day on Esteppe, which meant that the air was merely chilly instead of bone-freezing cold. My homeworld was in the depths of an ice age, except that as far as the geologists could tell this one dated back all the way to when the planet had first cooled enough to permit the accumulation of frozen precipitation. While there was native life in abundance, it existed mostly in a narrow band around the equator, where the oceans were ice-free. If it hadn't been for the richness of the mineral surveys, the original colonists probably would've tried their luck somewhere warmer. But there *had* been the minerals and, so far, it looked like there always would be minerals. Esteppe was a geological treasure box, even more of one than Earth herself.

You couldn't tell by looking that the Lotharberg was made of such fabulous stuff. It rose almost a mile from our already lofty plateau, its near-vertical faces scrubbed sheer by eons of corrosive ice. No one had ever successfully climbed the peak without advanced gear, though many had tried. According to Father Murton's impromptu geology lecture, Esteppe was still quite a young planet and tectonically very active. The Lotharberg was a big piece of very hard rock that had formed deep underground, then been raised high into the sky by forces so slow-moving and yet so powerful that I had difficulty comprehending them. Along the way it'd been heated to incandescence not just once but again and again. This repeated heating and cooling, along with the effects of groundwater, had concentrated the exotic minerals to the point where commercial extraction was nearly as effortless as plucking gold nuggets from a stream bed. Yet the Lotharberg was more than a source of wealth to my family, I was beginning to understand. It stood tall, proud and defiant in the backgrounds of every Longo.

Except me.

"Hello," Father Murton said, interrupting my reverie. He stepped up beside me, looking even more dwarflike than usual in his bulky winter coat. "What a wonderful sight! I never tire of it."

I nodded but did not speak.

"Your father's here," he continued. "His 'hopper landed in the pasture." My tutor grinned. "He stepped in something nasty on the way to the house."

"Heh!" I chuckled. Father's feet hadn't been visible under his robe, so I wouldn't have noticed if he'd changed into his slippers. "I guess it happens to everyone. Even Elitemen."

Father Murton's smile faded. "You've seen him, then?"

I nodded. "He was all zonked out, wired up to his computer. Not a pretty sight."

"I imagine not," the priest agreed. There was another long silence while he admired the mountain some more. "And you noticed his robe."

I nodded again, not saying anything.

"Well…" My tutor wrapped an arm around my shoulder and gently urged me towards the house. "He certainly looks good in it."

I pressed my lips together. "Maybe he does," I admitted, forcing myself to be dispassionate. Then I stopped walking and turned to face my counselor. "But… Why, Father? Why is he doing it?"

The priest looked up at the mountain for inspiration. "He's been in the news quite a bit lately, Thomas," he answered eventually. "You've probably been too busy to notice."

"Really?" I asked. Father had been in the news before, of course. From the defendant's chair, mostly. So far as I knew, he harbored no desire to ever repeat the experience.

"Yes," my tutor agreed. "Of course. His return home would've been news under any circumstances. But with him restarting the Stormcrow plant, and the workers making the sacrifices that they are… Well, it's pretty stirring stuff, you have to admit. It was inevitable that the media would get hold of it. Heck, the government probably *encouraged* them to run the stories, because they stir others to sacrifice as well."

I nodded. It was wartime-- *everyone* had to sacrifice, or else we'd lose.

"Esteppe is being hailed as the salvation of the United Systems, and your father's being hailed, in the non-military sense, as the primary savior."

"That's reasonable enough," I replied. "Without the Skybolts, where would we be? He pushed for them when nobody but he and a few navy supporters were interested."

"He put up his own money and everything," Father Murton agreed. "People look at that, and they see a sincere man who had the good sense to foresee this war and do something about it at a time when their political leaders were refusing to build more battleships." Father Murton shook his head. "Plus, more and more people are coming to regard him as a hero for helping end the Esteppan war as well. Throw in the fact that the Longos have always been a respected family here, with deep roots in the society and, well… The fact is, Thomas, he could run for President of the planet tomorrow, and win easily. I suspect he may do exactly that, once Sven is able to take over Skybolt production."

My mouth dropped open. "Father? In *politics*? Don't... I mean..."

"Heh!" my tutor answered, grinning wide again. "I know exactly what you mean. And yet, think it though. Willie first gained notice as an Eliteman, one who'd proven himself worthy to be subjected to a brain-enhancing procedure so expensive that only a very limited number of procedures could be undertaken. Remember, the Autarch came into power on a wave of popularity, as the leader who was going to revolutionize society via enhanced brainpower and intelligence." He paused and looked me in the eyes. "People here *liked* that idea, Thomas. And, in the Autarch's defense, some of it came out quite well. Had the United Systems chosen to work with Esteppe rather than invade it, who knows? Perhaps the Autarch might not have gone mad. Perhaps we'd have millions of Elitemen by now. Perhaps our economy and technology might be so transformed that the Dracans would never have dared attempt making war on us. And, perhaps..." His face grew very serious. "Perhaps, billions who are now dead might still be alive."

Chapter Ten

All through dinner, I kept asking myself over and over again why in the world Father might want to get into politics. It was so unlike him! He stuttered and stumbled as he spoke, much of the time. Somehow, even though he dressed well, he always managed to look rumpled and a bit disarrayed when out in public.

Or at least he had back on Earth, I suddenly realized. Not any longer. Here, seated at the head of the table in his traditional family home and surrounded by staff and retainers, he wasn't at all the slightly-out-of-place but loving man who'd raised me. Instead he sat tall and regal in his fine black robe, his shaven, perfectly-shaped head emphasizing what must've been an aristocratic face all along. *Impressive*, I decided. If I had to sum up what my father had become in a single word, the word would have to be *impressive*.

"May I have another roll, Dodson?" Father asked his waiter. Dodson had been on the family payroll for almost half a century; I'd heard him mentioned many times during my growing-up years but never imagined that I'd ever actually meet him. He and his wife Marie were in charge of the estate whenever there was no Longo in residence. Which was most of the time, of course."

"Yes, sir!" Dodson replied, clicking his heels and doing everything short of saluting before marching back to the kitchen.

"So," Father continued, turning to me. "I'm glad that you and Jimmy are getting along so well. It's good that you have a friend, Thomas. It's something I've always wanted for you."

I nodded, then looked down at my empty plate. Father had changed in so many ways, yet there was still no doubting that he loved me. I should've been grown-up enough not to worry, but deep down I was still sufficiently a child that I felt deeply reassured. "I really like him," I explained. "We do stuff together."

He smiled. "Like climbing the Stahlberg, I hear. And going to Stormcrow Park."

I looked down at my plate again. "Yeah."

"Good!" he declared, nodding an acknowledgement to Dodson as his additional roll arrived. "Very good!" There was a long silence as Father buttered his bread. "Are they treating you well?"

I frowned. "The truth is, Father, they're working us to death. But, they *have* to."

He nodded. "Ja. I understand. But I don't have to like it."

I shrugged. "You're working pretty hard yourself."

"I'm not seventeen," he countered. Then he cocked his head to one side dismissively. "Things will get better for you soon, however. The plant is running well. In eight weeks, we'll have produced enough fighters to equip two full flights. In four months, there'll be enough to equip two full *squadrons*. And in six months, well…" He shrugged. "Dozens, certainly. Enough to win the war, unless the Dracans prove to be unexpectedly skilled at producing superfighters. Which I have reason to doubt."

"If anyone's an expert, you are," I acknowledged. Our best intelligence estimates were that the Dracan superfighters we'd encountered on Drakkus were probably early developmental models flown by test pilots. Close study had shown that they were all slightly different in size and shape; one of them had a fuselage a good six inches longer than the others. Plus, their tactics were very primitive. If they were indeed just beginning, we still had a huge lead.

"Assuming we can relieve Earth," I reminded him.

"Assuming we can relieve Earth," he agreed. "That's the most important thing in the universe just now. Relieve Earth, and we've won. The rest will be mere mopping-up. Painful and costly mopping-up, granted. The issue, however, will no longer be in doubt."

There was a long silence as Father picked at his steak. Eventually, however, he spoke again. "Have you given any thought to what you want to do after the war, Thomas?"

I raised my eyebrows. "Have you?"

He smiled. "A little, perhaps." Then the smile faded. "Sometimes I have business with Alicia Wiston. We speak of you often when this happens."

I nodded, not knowing what to say.

"She believes that you're a very bright young man, Thomas. You're brave and resourceful too, of course." His eyes narrowed. "She tells me that she thinks you're a young man of extraordinary moral courage as well."

"I doubt that," I replied. Then I frowned. "Though, Father, well…"

His eyebrows rose. "Yes, son?"

I fidgeted in my chair, not quite sure how to say what I was thinking. "Well… The older I get, and the more I learn about the world…" I sighed, then looked out at the mountain again. "What you did to end the war, when I was just little. *That* was an act of moral courage, Father. Colonel Rotte worshipped you like a god, if you didn't know it. Because he felt that you were braver than him."

Father blinked, caught at a loss for the first time since he'd starting wearing black again. "Well," he said eventually. "I'd never have guessed that."

"It's true," I assured him. "All the time I grew up, I never really knew you. I *still* don't know you, I'm beginning to understand. But the more I learn, the more I realize that the Colonel was right."

Father looked down at his plate, then raised his eyes to meet mine. "And you've been a son to be proud of as well," he said simply. "My most profound wish for you, Thomas, is that you will never, ever have to face the kinds of decisions I've had to make. Never!" He sighed. "And yet of course you already have."

I shrugged. The decisions had been difficult, yes. But *someone* had to make them.

Father turned and looked out at the Lotharberg, still silhouetted against the twilight sky. "The first winter here," he reminded me, "a third of the colonists starved to death. The robot-ships said the native life was edible, but it wasn't. Our ancestors brought too much mining gear and too few greenhouses; old Lothar had to fire into a starving mob."

I nodded; the story was well-known.

"It's not just war, Thomas," he continued. "It's the nature of life itself. Hard things have to be done over and over and over again, and hard actions imply difficult decisions. The truest measure of a man, I've long believed, is how he handles these decisions. We Longos have done well for the most part, or so I believe." He turned to face me. "When this war's over, there'll be more decisions to make than ever."

"Father Murton thinks you're going to run for office," I observed.

Father pursed his lips. "Does he like the idea?" he asked.

I squinted, trying to remember his exact words. "I think so," I answered eventually.

"Good," Father replied, crossing his legs under the table. "I'm glad. His opinion means more to me than he could ever guess."

"Really?" I asked.

"Really," he repeated. "I mean... Thomas! Do you honestly imagine for a moment that I'd entrust the raising of my son to a man I don't respect?"

My eyebrows rose; there *was* that, I supposed... "Anyway," I answered, after thinking it over for a time. "Are you?"

"Probably," he answered. "The greatest regret of my life is that I stood by and allowed my best friend to put himself in a situation that finally crushed him, and so many along with him. I feel an obligation, Thomas, not to hold back this time." He frowned, then fingered the socket in the back of his head. "This *works*. I can go places, see things... We *need* this, for the future of Mankind. I can't stand by and watch the Earthers throw away humanity's birthright. I *won't* stand by. Not again."

My eyes narrowed. "What's it like, Father? Really, now?"

He smiled. "Probably not nearly so spectacular as you imagine. The machine-elements simply reinforce the computing parts of the brain. When I jack in, there isn't a mathematical problem in the universe I can't solve, if it can be solved at all. Computation is effortless, in fact, so much so that with time and skill an Eliteman can sort of 'turn off' those parts of his brain that normally deal with such issues, and use them for more important functions like understanding and imagining and asking 'what if', the kind of things that no computer ever built can manage." His smile widened. "That's how I came to understand antigrav motors so well. My original area of expertise, the field of study I earned my doctorate in, was alloplasty. But through jacking in I was able to learn everything that was already known about antigravs, and then, through long hours of enhanced contemplation, see things that no one else could. Sven is the real aerospace engineer, both by training and inclination. Compared to him, I'm just an amateur. I expect *great* things from him, once he masters his link."

I pressed my lips together. "He didn't look good, Father. When I saw him yesterday, I mean."

"Right," Father agreed grimly. "I'm worried, too. He's scheduled for a full physical in two weeks; we're all getting them monthly, because of the radiation."

"Are *you* all right?" I asked.

"Healthy as a horse, they tell me," he replied. "Radiation can be like that, Thomas. It can kill right away, or it can kill years later, or it can have no effect at all. Some of it is natural resistance, some of it is luck, some of it the doctors are still scratching their heads over." His mouth formed a thin, grim line. "If we had more Elitemen, we could put someone to work on the problem. But the fools hung so many of us…"

I looked down at my plate. Sometimes, it wasn't so easy to keep track of exactly who "we" and "they" were. "Maybe once the war is over," I suggested hopefully.

"Maybe," Father replied. He cocked his head to one side. "You know," he said slowly. "Your brain is already wired for an interface, just like mine and your brother's. Currently the connection is fully employed transmitting physical sensations and motor-control and such. But, it's essentially the same thing. When we put you back into your body, it would actually be just as easy as not for you to have a plug, too."

"Maybe," I answered. "We'll have to see what the law is. And, I'd look silly with a shaved head."

"Heh!" Father chuckled. "Perhaps you'd look silly, and perhaps not. But…" He fingered his lapel. "As a member of the Order of Blood, it's traditional for you to wear a red facing on your robe." He looked me hard in the eyes. "If, of course, you were to choose to wear one."

I turned back to the window. The sun was down now, and the sky was star-sprinkled black. Yet the mountain was still there. Even invisible it was always there, part of every Longo's life. "I'm no Eliteman," I countered. "I can't even pass calculus."

"You *are* an Eliteman," Father replied. "The title was conferred on the basis of achievement, not ability. Some Elitemen never attended university at all; they were highly successful businessmen, mostly. Are you going to sit there, my son, and try to tell me that you haven't achieved at a similarly high level?"

"No," I replied eventually, though the single syllable sounded very hollow and alone. "I can't."

"Because you're not a liar." He sighed. "I asked you what you're doing after the war, Thomas. You've managed to out-maneuver me for a time. But now, you must answer."

I shrugged. "Go to school, I guess. College. Spencer wants to write a book with me, and I guess I'd enjoy that. I like him, a lot. He just sent me a letter, by the way. In it, he said that he'd like to meet you."

"And I him," Father agreed. "Indeed, if he survives I very much hope to work closely with him on several matters of mutual interest." His eyes narrowed. "Thomas, the opportunity to write a book with Spencer Wiston is a treasure beyond price. It's your decision, but I'd take him up on it. Even if it means delaying school."

I nodded. It was good to know that Father thought so well of Spence. He and Alicia had become very important to me, and I didn't know how I'd have handled it if Father hadn't approved.

"There's more to life than calculus," Father continued. "While it would please me if you did better in math, this is only because I know how much it bothers you." He smiled again. "You're *already* a success, Thomas, and you owe no one anything. If you choose to spend the rest of your life throwing wild parties and riding your skimmer, no one would deny that you've earned the right. Not even me. But..." He met my eyes again.

"But?" I answered.

"But," Father continued, pushing his plate slightly away from him as a signal to Dodson that he was finished eating. "Thomas, I've come to expect far more from you than that. Your mother was a politician; I learned much from her. While I can function as a leader at need, she was a natural." He smiled. "You must follow your own star, and I'll honor whatever choice you make. But you remind so much of my beloved Estelle sometimes that it hurts. Not only does your appearance favor her, but so does your whole demeanor. And I'll tell you a secret; she had to take calculus three times herself."

"Heh!" I laughed.

Father smiled. "It's your choice, as I said. But you're a leader, Thomas. If you remain in the navy, you'll rise as high there as you wish. Alicia, however, tells me that what you're *really* interested in is preventing future wars, doing your best to make sure that this tragedy never befalls humanity again." His smile faded. "That's a worthwhile goal, Thomas, for a man of your caliber."

44

He looked down at his plate for a moment, then met my eyes. "The navy helps keep the peace, yes. They're very important indeed, and their role in society is a most honorable one. The *real* mistakes that lead to war, however, aren't often made by soldiers or sailors. They're usually made by politicians, half of whom are self-serving liars and idiots at any given time-- individuals beneath even the lowest sort of contempt. More than half of them, even." He sighed. "I've allowed one incompetent leader to rise to power, Thomas, when I could've done something to prevent it. Instead I stood by and watched. I swear that I'll never do it again, even though it means taking on the job myself and getting my hands dirty in ways that I'd rather not. Politics is too important to be left to incompetent worms. I can be President of the second-most important planet in the United Systems, and I probably will be. Someday, I predict, it will become the *most* important. If I do my job well, that is."

His eyes met mine one last time. "Play your cards right, Thomas, and in a few years you can be Prime Minister. Will be, almost certainly. And, if you do *your* job well, there will be peace and harmony for everyone everywhere. There's never been anyone more perfectly placed. Or, I'll add, more perfectly suited for the job." A single tear ran down his cheek. "Though, of course, I'm prejudiced. Because I love you so very, very much."

Chapter Eleven

Peace and harmony for everyone everywhere. Father's words rang in my head over and over and over again that night as I laid and stared at the stormcrow mounted on my bedroom wall. *Peace and harmony for everyone everywhere. There's never been anyone more perfectly placed.* And the words were *still* echoing around my head not long before noon the next day, as Jimmy and I climbed the Stahlberg alongside what seemed like every Youth Scout on the planet.

"...still working on pilot training," Jimmy was explaining as we trudged along side by side Neither of us ever needed to rest or grew short of breath. Despite this large numbers of Youth Scouts continually passed us, their troop-standards fluttering gaily in the steady breeze. Almost all of them were wearing jackets despite this being one of the warmest days of the year, and at the peak they'd be sleeping in heated tents. Jimmy and I, however, were wearing nothing over the honorary Youth-vests we'd been presented with. It was embarrassing, really; where we should've been wearing merit badges, the Scouts had embroidered replicas of our military decorations. On Esteppe, I knew, medals were practically casual-wear. Still, everywhere Jimmy and I went we were surrounded by a thirty-foot or so bubble of empty space broken only by Petty Officer Brooks (who checked in with us from time to time to make sure there were no malfunctions) and a couple of the most senior Scout officials (who kept asking us if we needed anything).

"Training's going to be the pinch point," I agreed. Jimmy and I were under strict instructions not to spend too much time talking shop while on leave, but what else was there to do? I shook my head. "Jimmy, I'm so sorry I suggested this dumb hike. I'm bored too. And, I *like* hiking!"

Jimmy smiled; somehow, his plastic face captured the essence of his grin far better than anyone else's did. "It's all right," he replied. "I mean, the scenery is just as cool as you said it'd be. And, I actually liked the speeches. One or two of them, at least."

I shook my head again. Somewhere along the line, wires had become dreadfully crossed. What I'd envisioned for Jimmy and I was a hike with kids our own age, loosely supervised by a small number of adults and accompanied by the minimum level of fanfare possible. What we'd gotten instead was a highly formal social event, featuring us. The annual Scout hike to the top of the Stahlberg normally took a healthy boy or girl about ten hours, including scheduled breaks. Jimmy and I had felt we were imposing because, being unable to move as quickly as the others, our presence would stretch things out to eleven or twelve hours. Little had we realized that the Scout leadership would turn it into a sixteen-hour affair, complete with speechifying, ceremonial awards, and photo opportunities. I'd even been asked to make a brief speech about the war, though Petty Officer Brooks had whispered in my ear that I didn't really have to. But what was I going to do, after they'd made so much of Jimmy and I? It was just like selling bonds, though thankfully it didn't last as long.

And now all the other kids seemed to be afraid of us. Or more likely they'd been ordered to leave us strictly alone, respecting our privacy when what we really wanted was companionship and fun. What a mess!

"Look," Jimmy pointed out, his delight only slightly-forced. "Another generator!"

I smiled despite myself. The outmoded structures *were* kinda cool-looking. Esteppe's Stahlberg, or Steel Mountain, earned its name from the fact that it was festooned with steel towers and service facilities for what was still one of the biggest linear accelerators ever built. Prior to the development of antigravs and back when thrusters were still in their infancy, much of Esteppe's metal had been exported from here. The current hiking path once served as the complex's service road. "Yeah!" I agreed. Then I pointed up into the sky. "And look! There's a Steppesparrow!"

Jimmy smiled again. There *was* a lot of wildlife to be seen on the Stahlberg Trail, we'd agreed early on; the fact that it was only opened for use two weekends a year ensured that the flora grew undisturbed, and the fauna remained not in the least bit people-shy. Jimmy took eight or ten pictures before putting his camera away. Maybe he'd want to get it out again, I hoped, when we got to the top…

"Hey, boys!" Petty Officer Brooks interrupted my thoughts. "How are you doing?"

"Fine!" we chorused dutifully; Jimmy even kicked at a little rock on the trail, though his slow-moving foot didn't elicit much of a response.

"Good!" Jimmy's counselor replied, though his gaze seemed to linger on our faces for a just a fleeting second longer than necessary. "Isn't it a beautiful day for a walk?"

"Uh-huh," I agreed, and Brooks peered at me again. Then, for no reason at all that I could fathom, he smiled. "There's a rest stop up ahead," he pointed out. "The halfway point. You guys might be able to walk all day, buy I've got to visit the head. Do an old man a favor, and take a little break?"

"Sure," Jimmy agreed for us both; we'd do *anything* for our counselors, what with everything they did for us. "We'll sit on a bench. Take your time."

Sure enough, once we got close enough to the generator we could see that there was a major rest-facility built into the old power-house. It had heated benches and water fountains and everything; perhaps the old engineering plant was still producing a trickle of juice? All the places were filled as Jimmy and I came plodding up. But, as if by divine command, all the other kids got up and backed away, leaving us our choice of dozens of seats.

Alone, as usual.

It was nice to sit down, not due to fatigue or cold but because it was a change of pace. I was bored silly and it was probably twice as bad for Jimmy. We sat in silence for a time, then my wingman sighed. "I hope Stormcrow Park isn't like this," he finally said.

"Me too," I agreed. Minute after minute dragged on, and troop after troop of tired Scouts poured into the rest area until it was chock-full, all except for the invisible thirty-foot bubble around us pilots. The other kids didn't stare at us too much; they were at least *trying* to be polite. Soon the early-arriving Scouts were getting up and leaving, but there was still no sign of our counselor.

"I'm going to look for Brooks," I whispered to my friend. "Everyone and their brother is watching out for us, but what about him? This is a tough climb for an old guy-- maybe he had a heart attack or something."

"He can run your legs off," Jimmy assured me. "You ought to see his daily workout. But, yeah. I'll be right here."

No one seemed to know what to do when Jimmy and I split up. Almost half of the alleged Youth Scout Leaders suddenly began whispering to themselves as I moved away from my companion, and I realized that the security coverage was even thicker than I'd known. Brooks wasn't in the men's facilities at all, I saw almost immediately. Instead, he was standing face-to-face with a highly-decorated scout leader just outside the door, stabbing the man in the chest with his index finger over and over again. The scout leader's face was chalk-white, and his jaw was dangling as if by a thread. I couldn't help but smile; I'd seen this sort of thing before. A few weeks back a seaman second-class assigned to my wingman's ground crew had dropped Jimmy's brain-capsule during a drill. His face had looked just like the scoutmaster's when Brooks spoke with him after the incident. Most likely Brooks was employing the same well-proven motivational technique once again. It was probably a good thing that the wind was such that I couldn't quite make out individual words. Brooks spoke very fluent Navy; even Admiral Vlasilov had been impressed.

"He's fine," I reassured Jimmy when I got back to our bench. "Just taking care of business."

"Good," my friend replied, smiling again.

"We haven't really done much all that much climbing yet," I observed, raising my foot and placing it on the bench so that I could check the laces. I wouldn't blister if they worked loose, not in a million years. But I still didn't want my boot to fall off; it was embarrassing. "Soon it'll warm up. The animals and stuff'll come out. Maybe they'll even be some good pictures for you to take."

"Maybe," he allowed, not sounding very hopeful.

"Things are looking up," I reassured him, extending my hand to help him stand. "Trust me, and keep an open mind. I've got a feeling that the second half of this hike is going to be a lot more fun than the first part was."

Chapter Twelve

Sure enough, things *did* get better. Right after Brooks got back, two of the Scoutmasters came over, smiled nervously, and asked Jimmy and I if we'd be interested in being the special guests of a troop from New Copenhagen. We both smiled and nodded, and I did my best not to notice that the troop in question had been chosen simply because it was the one sitting closest to us. Jimmy still hadn't tumbled to who was really running things, and the last thing I wanted was to spoil it for him.

I ended up walking next to a scout about my age. His name was Evan, and he was very quiet at first. I almost asked him what his merit badges were for, since he had so many. But then he'd ask about my medals, and I didn't feel at all like explaining them. So, instead, I asked him if he'd ever climbed the Stahlberg before.

"Oh, yes, Your Excellency!" he answered. "Every year since I was fourteen." He turned to face me, thumbs tucked under the straps of his backpack. "Before that, I lived on Earth."

"Really?" I asked. "Wow! So did I!"

"I know," Evan answered, coloring slightly. "Everyone knows." He looked away.

"Yeah," I agreed. "It kinda sucks being famous. Believe me, it wasn't my idea."

"Heh!" my new friend laughed. "It looks pretty cool from this side of the trail." He glanced down at my embroidered medals, then courteously looked away. "Your Excellency."

I sighed again, then stopped dead in the middle of the pathway. "Please," I begged him. "Today, I'm not 'Your Excellency'. I don't mean any disrespect to the Order of Blood; if anything, the longer I'm a member the more I understand why people take it so seriously. But I'm on leave, Evan. Trying to rest and relax. Can we just be friends?"

Evan's brow wrinkled. "Sir…" he said slowly. "I mean…"

I turned and looked up the trail again to where Jimmy was happily chattering away with his personal guide, camera in hand. He wasn't being addressed as "Your Excellency", I was quite certain. "Please," I repeated.

"Evan, I'm Tommy Longo." I extended my right hand. "Just plain Tommy Longo, the very ordinary kid you've been assigned to keep an eye on all the way up to the top of the mountain. Can it be that way between us? Just for this one hike?"

Evan shrugged. "Sure, Tommy," he declared, his handshake a lot firmer than his tone. "If that's what you'd like."

"Thank you." I smiled and began walking again. "So, where did you live on Earth? And why were you there?"

"My mother's an exporter," he explained. "Earth doesn't buy many metals, but it's still the big trading center where agents meet to make deals." He frowned. "Or, at least it was until the Dracans came."

"Right," I agreed, not wanting to discuss Dracans. "Where did you stay? Were you a scout? And, did you do any hiking?"

"Not much," he answered. "Though I was a scout, yes." He pointed down to his merit badges. "About half of these are from Earth. But we lived in Manhattan so Mom could be near her work. We made it out to the Catskills a few times, and once we paddled down the Hudson. Mostly, though, we walked in circles around Central Park."

"I wasn't a scout," I answered. "Though now I sort of wish I had been. I feel like I missed something important. But I still spent a lot of time outside. Father made sure I learned how to ride and shoot and such." I smiled. "The only time I ever paddled a canoe was back in the bayous along the edge of our estate. I really liked it. So much that eventually I got into skimmer racing."

"You have a skimmer?" Evan asked eagerly.

"Yeah," I agreed, looking down at the ground. Skimmers were expensive toys indeed, even by the standards of someone who'd once lived in Manhattan. "I used to race on the lake, sometimes all day long when my schoolwork was caught up. We had a league and formal matches on Saturday, but we held our own races when no one was around. Those were even better."

"I guess you probably won most of the time?"

"Not really," I answered. "My share, I suppose. Skimmers take a long time to master, and I was only fifteen when…"

"Yeah," Evan agreed, not sure if he ought to ask more questions or not.

I shook my head. "It's not so bad, really," I explained. "I mean, I gave a lot of things up. But at first it was only going to be for a couple years or so, just civilian test-piloting. Then the Dracans attacked, and I got famous, and… Well, you probably know the rest."

"I do," Evan agreed. We walked along in silence for a time. "I'm going to join the army, I think," he said eventually. "At seventeen, if my parents will sign for me. They probably won't, though."

Wise parents, I thought but didn't say aloud. "You're not seventeen yet? You look it."

"Just a few days short," he replied, his face expressionless. "But if you can fight, so can I."

I didn't know what to say to that, really. While I hadn't exactly seen the best side of the army, well… The short time I'd spent with them had made thank my lucky stars that the navy was in charge of aerospace defense. Though I didn't think army people were stupid or slow or any of the silly things that navy people sometimes said about them, I still liked being with the fleet better. At least in the navy, everyone had a warm place to sleep all the time and good hot food. "There's plenty of fighting left to be done," I agreed eventually. Then I changed the subject again. "You say you've been up this trail before. What's the coolest thing you've ever seen?"

"A snow-lizard!" he answered, eyes lighting up. "Last year! A genuine, honest-to-goodness snow lizard!"

"Really?" I answered. "I thought those were endangered."

"Ja!" Evan confirmed. "Which made seeing one even cooler." He grinned again. "It was a female, full to bursting with eggs. And it was only about a mile up the trail from here. That's what I want to see on this hike, more than anything, is either her again or one of her young. Or at least that's what I wanted most until I heard *you* were going to be here!"

"Heh!" I laughed. "Believe me, a snow lizard is *much* cooler than I am. Ask Jimmy if you've any doubt." I frowned. "Aren't they dangerous?"

"A little," my new friend explained. "They're venomous, but the venom's evolved for native Esteppe life. So it works real slow on humans, No one ever dies from getting bit, though it hurts like the devil. But you do have to be careful. They're *really* fast. It's misleading, because they look like reptiles even though they're not. Cold doesn't slow them down."

"Right," I agreed, though I'd already known about the not-a-reptile part.

"They crawl right out of the snowbanks when it's warm," Evan explained. "And, it's extra-warm today. So I've got my hopes up."

My new friend and I hiked on in silence for a time after that, though a few other members of the troop came and snapped pictures of us from time to time. I couldn't blame them, I supposed. Besides, Evan would treasure them for the rest of his life. So I smiled and didn't complain, even when Chief Brooks walked next to me for a little while to make sure everything was all right.

The trail was ascending a series of switchbacks now; we were walking three or four feet back and forth for ever foot of altitude gained. Still, the trail had become very steep indeed, and Jimmy was nearly straight up over my head when I heard his amplified voice call out. "Tommy!" he cried out. "There's a snow lizard out! Just a little bit up ahead!"

"Really?" I asked, trying to sound surprised even though Evan was smiling knowingly. "Get me a picture, in case I don't make it in time!"

"Sure thing!" my wingman replied. Then his head disappeared over the guardrail and he was off with his camera.

"He seems like a really nice guy," Evan observed.

"You don't know the half," I answered. "His brother and father are something pretty special, as well."

"Yeah," Evan agreed, looking down at the path. Then he turned towards me. "I wish… I mean…"

Just then there was a thundering roar in the distance. It was an antigrav motor, giving all it had.

"Thomas!" Brooks cried out, sprinting up beside me. "We've got bogies, son! Incoming, fast and hard! The 'hopper's coming for us. Right now!"

I must've looked pretty silly, standing there with my mouth hanging open as Brooks sprinted on towards his other charge. Then the navy's high-speed 'hopper, the one they always kept standing by for us pilots, came surging around the side of the Stahlberg and hovered, its pilot trying to pick me out of the crowd. I turned towards Evan. "I… I mean…"

"It's all right!" he answered, backing away so the 'hopper could land for me. "I mean, like…" He grinned. "Way cool, man!"

I shook my head, but didn't have time to explain why what was happening was the uncoolest thing I could possibly imagine. Besides, even if I *had* time, I still probably couldn't have done the subject justice. War, I was beginning to understand, was something one had to live through in order to properly despise. Then the 'hopper landed, most assuredly destroying thousands of credits worth of the hikers personal electronic gear by its mere presence, and I was yanked unceremoniously aboard. There wasn't time for me to strap myself in before they repeated the process for Jimmy, tumbling his gyros in the process. Then the hatch closed and we sped away at many times the speed of sound…

…but not before I caught a split-second glimpse of a terrified juvenile snow-lizard, sprinting away from the terrible racket for all it was worth and then disappearing down its icy burrow.

Chapter Thirteen

Since Jimmy was out of action for the moment, I waited until our 'hopper stabilized and then moved over to an empty seat by the big conference table. Someone had installed a small pipper there, and one of Vlasilov's staff assistants monitored it at all times. It wasn't a very glamorous job, so it was performed by an ensign. Her name was Huan. "Hello, sir," she greeted me as I levered myself into the seat. It hadn't been modified for my strangely-proportioned body, and thus was a bit of a pain to get in and out of. "It looks like a major raid."

I nodded and watched as Dracan after Dracan poured through Esteppe's nearest Nikita point. First there was a whole flood of destroyers, then heavy cruisers. "Just as we've always projected," I agreed, leaning forward to examine the display. Even as I watched, *Crazy Horse* flared and died. She'd been the only blue pip on the screen, her duty to provide early warning honorably fulfilled.

"Exactly as projected," Huan agreed. "Every fast-mover in their fleet. Pretty daring of them, if you ask me. These are the same ships needed at New Nippon to guard the nexus there."

"Right," I agreed. The ability to generate a big vector was everything in a space battle, now that both sides were hitting nodes at previously unheard-of velocities. Therefore, fast ships were at an unexpected premium. Neither side had anything like enough of them. "If our projections are correct, then the heavies will be next."

I nailed it almost to the millisecond. Just after the last heavy cruiser transited the Nikita, an *Imperial Throne* class dreadnought came cruising through. *Imperial Wisdom*, her name read on the pipper. I pressed my lips together in concentration; Jimmy and I would be assigned to take her out, I was certain. We'd spent many hours working out attack techniques for capital units; now they were about to be put to the test.

But...

"Wait a minute!" I objected. "There's no way that's the *Imperial Wisdom*. She's still in the yards."

Ensign Huan's brow wrinkled. "That's right," she agreed. "Maybe the

Dracans completed her sooner than expected?"

Then another *Throne* popped through, the *Imperial Destiny*. "That one hasn't even been laid down yet!" I complained.

We hadn't been all that far from the big base at New Narvik; as we slowed I looked away from the developing battle and out the viewport. There were dozens of defenseless ships bobbing about in the water below, I realized sickly, maybe even hundreds. In fact, I doubted that anyone had ever concentrated so many ships together *anywhere*, unless maybe the Dracans did just before launching the war. The large majority were merchantmen; they were blunter and fatter-looking than the warships. Even as I watched, *Roman Nose* reared up out of the water and headed for space, followed by *Jimmy Doolittle* and a newcomer, the just-commissioned destroyer *Sitting Bull*. They were the 'ready' squadron. It would've been a beautiful sight, save that even in the passenger compartment I could hear the confused babble of voices as our pilot demanded and got absolute priority clearance from Esteppe Traffic Central. This was quite a feat, since half the ship-captains in the fleet were attempting to get the same priority clearance for the same airspace at the same time.

"It's a false alarm," I said aloud as *Graf Zeppelin* roared away after her consorts; she'd just been denied clearance but had launched anyway. Full-sized spacecraft simply did *not* up-ship without clearance; her captain would soon either be court-martialed or promoted. Very likely both, I decided. The navy had become a notably crazy place of late. "I'd bet anything that it's a false alarm."

"Probably," Jimmy agreed as, finally, he slid in beside me. "Geez. The admiral's gonna be *so*—"

Suddenly the pipper went blank, and Ted Knight's face appeared on our monitor. "Thomas?" he asked. "Jimmy?"

"Is it a false alarm?" my wingman demanded.

The non-scarred half of Ted's face colored. "Yeah," he agreed, looking down at his desk. "Word's just getting out. The staff people were trying to simulate what a Dracan raid might look like two or three years down the road, and…"

I let my head fall forward. *Zeppelin*'s high-risk takeoff, all the damage our 'hopper had done while flying over normally-restricted areas, all the Scouts who'd missed seeing the snow lizard… "So, it's just a computer glitch."

Ted nodded, then met my eyes. "The admiral's decided to try and make the best of it, though. We're turning it into a full-fledged surprise drill, though there won't be any more actual takeoffs." He grinned. "And what a surprise it was! Half the fleet got caught wrong-footed, and couldn't up-ship. That's partly because we're in an intensive maintenance cycle. Sure, you have to repair vital systems *sometime*. But still, half of our strength is way too many to have out of service at once. A whole lot of captains were doing work on the sly instead of when assigned, so as to make it look like things were getting done in impossibly short times. You ought to hear the admiral!"

I nodded. "Then Jimmy and I are going to go ahead and go on alert? As part of the drill?"

"No," Ted answered. "That's why I'm calling. Vlasilov stopped cursing long enough to ask me to specifically apologize to you two, and to let you know that you're back on leave." He smiled again. "I guess you'd like to get back to your hike?"

Just then, our 'hopper settled down on *June's* weather deck. I looked at Jimmy, but he shook his head. "No," I explained to Ted. "We'd rather not, if no one minds. It'd be almost over by the time we got back, and then we'd have to find the people we were with… Besides, it'd screw things up for everyone else. Not that we haven't done that already, maybe."

"We *are* very sorry," Ted repeated. "Everyone is." There was a long pause. "Welcome back aboard then. We'll try again soon. Stormcrow Park, isn't it?"

"Yeah!" Jimmy agreed, brightening up a little. "It'll be fun for sure! I sure wish you could come with us."

"Me too," Ted assured us, half-smiling again.

Chapter Fourteen

The one obligation that'd been pushed on me during my leave was dinner with Alicia on the second Wednesday. It wasn't that anyone had to press me to have dinner with my favorite rabbit-woman, not at all! But this was the only evening she had available, and her schedule was even less flexible than mine. So Wednesday it was and that was that. Since we'd gotten back a day early from the Stahlberg hike, Jimmy and I found ourselves aboard *The Glorious First of June* with little to do except play video games. While we were playing *Rocket Sledder*—and playing it far better than we had on out first day of leave-- Jimmy had an idea, something even better than anything in Vlasilov's folder. There was the whole fleet, better than half the entire United Systems Navy plus a bunch of merchies, all floating practically right next to us. What a shame it would be if no one took the opportunity to go exploring!

Our request went directly from Chief Brooks to Admiral Vlasilov, perhaps the shortest and strangest chain-of-command in history. Within two hours he'd not only approved, but also assigned us our own harbor-'hopper and pilot and issued an order explaining to all ships' captains that our visits were informal, there were to be no honors…

…and that we were to be allowed complete access to anything we wanted to see! How perfect could it get?

We spent our first day crawling up and down the length of the only dreadnought in the United Systems Fleet, the brand-new *Almirante Cochrane*. We ooh-ed and aah-ed at her huge guns, only marginally smaller than those of an *Imperial Throne*-class vessel, and Brooks got pictures of us sitting together astride one of the massive projector-barrels. *Cochrane's* main guns had been lifted from Seattle at the very last minute, her captain explained to us, and shipped as cargo aboard two cruisers to New Scotland where her incomplete hull awaited them. So instead of being designated with letters, as was normal navy practice, each of *Cochrane's* turrets memorialized a training fleet ship sacrificed during the breakout. The gun we sat on was from *Andrea Doria* turret, and the crew gathered around and listened as I told them about the two times I'd seen action alongside brave *Doria*. Somehow, I felt a lot better about her being gone when I was done. We toured *Cochrane* from keel to bridge, surrounded by smiling ratings who took the time to explain everything in terms we could understand. I liked Engineering best; the chief engineer took me all the way back to the extreme stern, where an experimental anti-grav had been fitted. "It's only strong enough for auxiliary use," she explained proudly. "But, it's still the most powerful antigrav ever built. And, Thomas, it's based on your father's feedback principle, the same as a Skybolt motor. You should be very proud. Someday it'll revolutionize space travel."

We also visited *Roman Nose*; the destroyer that'd recently saved Jimmy's and my life. Her captain had invited us to come and inspect the ship several weeks back, but we'd been forced by the press of duties to turn him down. Now there weren't any more excuses, so Jimmy and I went there next. Contrary to Vlasilov's request the entire crew was formed up and waiting for us on deck. Somehow, though, it was all right in this case because of the special relationship we had with this ship. "Hip-hip... Hooray!" a big petty officer bawled out as I led Jimmy down the ramp.

"Hooray!" the entire crew echoed. "Hooray for Thomas and Jimmy!" So, it wasn't quite an official greeting after all, though this time the captain did indeed make a big fuss about my using the entry port instead of crash-landing. Grinning crewman stood at two-foot intervals holding up handmade signs saying things like "This way, Thomas!" with a big arrow attached, and "Please, brake a little harder this time!" Then we were escorted directly to where a heavily-reinforced bulkhead was still creased and scorched from absorbing the impact of my previous visit. "It's not fixable, Thomas," *Nose's* captain explained. "That's why the forward armament hasn't been replaced; our basic structure can't support it anymore. As soon as she can be spared poor *Nose* will be relegated to training, and then I'll bet money she ends up as a floating war memorial somewhere. After the fights she's seen, she certainly deserves it." He handed me a permanent-ink marker. "Please?"

I laughed and signed the warped bulkhead, then Jimmy did the same. Meanwhile cameras clicked all around us as ordinary seamen jostled with their officers for a good angle. I *liked* the officers and men of *Roman Nose*, I realized suddenly, as much or more as I liked the men and women of *The Glorious First of June*. The other time I'd been aboard her I was fresh out of action, hurting in both body and soul. I'd met hardly anyone, since I'd largely been confined to sickbay. Even those I *had* met, I hadn't exactly been at my best for. Yet, this crew had arguably done and risked more for me than any other. So, since we seemed to be genuinely welcome, Jimmy and I spent the whole rest of the day gawking at the repaired places where heavy Dracan laser-bolts had struck home, and pausing respectfully before the memorial plaque dedicated to those who'd died crewing the plucky little vessel. It was no wonder she was Vlasilov's favorite destroyer, Jimmy and I agreed as we flew back home after it was all over. God help the Dracans, if all of our ships were as well-found and crewed as *Roman Nose*.

The next day, Jimmy and I decided on a change of pace. We planned to tour three different kinds of merchantmen; a general-cargo vessel, a tanker, and a liner that was being converted into a hospital ship. We did the liner/hospital ship first; *Red Crescent* wasn't much to see, really, though the medical staff in particular went out of their way to be nice to us. Most of the cabin walls were being knocked out to create long if somewhat cramped wards to treat the wounded, and her ballrooms were being divided up into treatment rooms and operating theaters. What was neatest about the ship, though, was that it was owned and crewed by the army. Even her captain was really a colonel, though his special uniform closely resembled that of a navy man. He'd been captain back when the ship had been the *Grand Vizier* of the Hassan Line, as well. "That's how the army does things," he explained to us with a smile. "When they need a specialist, they simply draft one." Most of the rest of the army ratings aboard were former merchies too, though they seemed to be taking well to military life. Their real test lay far in the future, however; another six months of work in the overcrowded Esteppan yards would be required before *Crescent* was fully prepared to space in her new role.

The *Nelson Rockefeller* was ready for space, however, and more than ready. "We've been floating here for days!" her captain complained as she drove us up and down the endless passages between the great vessel's cargo-tanks in a little cart. She was loaded to the gills with lubricants, solvents and bulk hydrocarbons that Earth's refineries could rapidly process into whatever might be most urgently needed. I'd never realized that a spacecraft could be so big; we must've traveled miles without ever seeing daylight. "Have you any idea what it costs to keep a ship like this just sitting here for no good reason like this?"

"I'm sure the navy knows," I answered as patiently as I was able. We'd sort of invited ourselves, after all. If our hosts were less than delighted to see us, well, maybe it was our own fault. "And, I'm equally certain they're paying a fair rate."

"Fair?" Captain Hazelwood protested. "What would be fair is if I were to up-ship and go see what the Dracans might offer." She crossed her arms defiantly. "*That* would be fair!"

I winced; *Nelson Rockefeller* was a Free Ship; meaning that she wasn't registered on any planet or bound to any government. My mouth opened, but Petty Officer Brooks beat me to the punch. "Clearly," he said slowly, "there's been a misunderstanding here. You've confused a good-will visit with a contract-negotiating session." His eyes narrowed dangerously.

"Contract?" Hazelwood protested, banging her fist on an oil-filmed bulkhead. "What contract? I'd die for a contract that'd let me space off of this goddamned iceberg of a planet!" She turned back towards me. "I bet you see Vlasilov all the time, right?"

Once again, Brooks beat me to the punch. This time, he literally stepped forward and placed himself between Hazelwood and I. "He does," Brooks agreed. "And so do I. Want me to lodge a formal complaint about your lack of hospitality? I've had lots of experience, I assure you. I know how to fill out the forms *real* good."

"Oh!" Hazelwood replied, rolling her eyes in mock-terror. "I'm just so freakin' terrified." She leaned around Brooks to address me directly again. The chief tried to interpose himself again…

…but by then, I'd had enough. Before Brooks could step sideways, I forced my way forward. "You're a Free Ship," I pointed out. "But, you're also part of a Free Company, aren't you?"

Hazelwood straightened her back in pride. "I am. Interstellar Cartage, the biggest there is."

"Right," I agreed. "I recognized the logo when we landed. I've seen it before, you see. Painted on the hull of the *Henri Deterding.*"

Hazelwood's face hardened. "What do you know of the *Deterding*?" she snapped.

"I killed her," I replied, smiling slightly. "Personally. About twelve weeks back. It's probably not declassified yet, which is why you haven't heard. It only took one torpedo; these big ships aren't nearly as sturdy as they look. She was sailing in a convoy. Under Dracan escort. Carrying Dracan goods."

Now it was Hazelwood's turn to stand open-mouthed but unable to speak. "I killed *Henri Deterding*," I repeated. "Just like I'll kill *Nelson Rockefeller* and you along with her if I ever even so much as hear rumors that you're *considering* carrying Dracan cargo. So help me god, I will! What kind of idiot are you, to make threats like that to *me*, surrounded by half the fleet? For that matter, what kind of dumbshit freebooter thinks they'll long remain in business under the Emperor? You think this war is some kind of a joke? A profit-center perhaps? Do you have any idea of how many good and decent men and women are dead? You'll sail where you're *told* to sail, and you'll do it when you're *told* to do it. If the navy weren't willing to let bygones be bygones, you'd already be locked up in an internment camp. You could *still* end up in one, you know." I looked around at the gaggle of slovenly crewmen who'd gathered at the sound of our argument. "I'll kill you all, by god! You just try me and see! Sail with the Dracans, and I swear to god that I'll kill you all!" I turned back to Brooks. "Bah!" I complained, jerking my chin at the Free Captain. "This woman has put a bad taste in my mouth." Then I turned to Jimmy. "Seen enough?"

"And more!" he replied. "If you miss, can *I* kill them?"

"Sure," I agreed, my smile widening. "Don't bet against me, though." Then I turned to Brooks, whom I expected to be furious with me for pushing him out of the way. But, somehow, he didn't look angry at all. Instead, he seemed to be trying not to grin. "Chief," I asked formally. "Can you lead the way off of this tub? Let's cancel the container ship and get back home."

"Yes, sir!" he snapped out, saluting every bit as smartly as I'd ever seen Vlasilov do it. "My pleasure, sir!"

Chapter Fifteen

Dinner with Alicia went the way it usually did; she wanted to know everything I'd been up to since we'd met last. Father always asked me the same kinds of questions that Alicia did, but somehow it was more relaxing to talk to my… stepmother, I realized rather suddenly as Madame Deputy paused to chew what appeared to be a particularly luscious leaf of something-or-other. The Deputy Prime Minister was my stepmother, and her husband the embattled Provisional President of the Government of Churilla in Exile had become my stepfather, all of this somehow taking place without in any way affecting my relationship with my real father or my tutor. What a mess my family life was! And yet, how wonderful it was as well! If we hadn't all been so famous and had so many responsibilities, it would have been better still.

"…really enjoyed visiting *Red Crescent*," I was explaining while Alicia chewed. "I mean, she's being rebuilt to help people instead of to hurt them. That's not to say that I think the fighting navy is bad or anything," I added hurriedly. When around Alicia I tended to babble on sometimes like a little kid. "But still, it's nice to see a ship with treatment rooms in it instead of magazines."

"Mmm," Alicia agreed through her mouthful of greens. Finally she closed her eyes in pleasure, and swallowed. "And I gather you had a nice visit aboard *Roman Nose* as well?"

"Uh-huh!" I agreed. "I think I might like to serve aboard a destroyer someday. There's a lot less spit-and-polish. Maybe because there's no senior officers around, most of the time."

Alicia smiled. "I need to make a special effort to tour her before she ups ship," she agreed. "After all, she helped save my life once too." Then, slowly, her smile faded. "What did you think of the *Nelson Rockefeller*?" she asked.

I pressed my lips together, then looked down at my plate. "I lost my temper," I admitted. "I guess you heard."

Alicia's eyes narrowed. "Yes," she agreed. "I did."

I wanted to apologize, for Alicia's sake. But the simple truth of the matter was that I didn't feel in the least bit sorry. So, instead I just sat and didn't say anything.

"You're in an impossible position," Alicia said at last. "You're a teenager, being asked to shoulder burdens that would break most grown men. Because of this, and for other reasons I prefer to keep to myself, I'd forgive you anything, Thomas. Literally anything. You know that, don't you?"

I nodded, still not saying anything.

"And yet," she continued, reaching down and pulling a bright red "Eyes Only" folder from her purse, "you've placed me in a very difficult position as well, regarding *Nelson Rockefeller* in particular and the Interstellar Cartage Company in general." The rabbit-woman opened the folder and pulled out a fat wad of paper. "They've filed a formal complaint over your behavior, Thomas." She handed a copy of the complaint to me. "Take your time."

It didn't take long to absorb the gist of it. The local office of Interstellar Cartage wished to protest the "high-handed" and "threatening" comments of one Commander Thomas Longo, while at the same time demanding to know if there was any truth to my "wild statements" regarding the disappearance of *Henri Deterding.*

I shrugged and pushed the paperwork back to Alicia. "It's all true. You know that already, I'm sure."

She waited again, as if for an apology. But I still couldn't make myself feel sorry. "Captain Hazelwood insulted the navy," I explained. "And those who've died, by inference. She said that she'd as soon sail for the Dracans." I shrugged. "That was when I lost my temper."

Alicia pursed her lips, then slowly nodded. "I see." Then she sighed and looked out the porthole. It was snowing a little, just enough to soften the silhouette of *Jimmy Doolittle*, anchored not far away. Then she picked up the paperwork and stuffed it back into the security-folder. "Thomas," she said. "I agree with the essence of everything you said and did. Don't doubt that for a second. Spence would've done pretty much the same thing in your shoes. Except that he doesn't wear them, of course."

I smiled a little, as I was sure Alicia had intended for me to.

Alicia grinned back, then her face went flat and serious again. "Thomas, it may appear to you that Spence and I have a completely harmonious marriage, and that we mesh perfectly when we work together. In fact, we both go well out of our way to present exactly that image to the world because doing so makes us both stronger. Besides, we really do love each other very much, so that we *want* people to think that way of us." She sighed. "But, it isn't quite how things really are."

I tilted my head to one side, not at all understanding what this had to with the *Henri Deterding.*

"Spence is more confrontational than I am," Alicia continued. "Much more direct in his methods and general approach to things." She sighed. "He'd have done almost exactly what you did, down there in *Rockefeller's* hold, when confronted by such an obnoxious, ungrateful wench. And, I'd have let him, because that very trait of complete directness is what makes Spence so effective as a leader and even as a scholar. It's a reflection of his fundamental honesty, the same honesty that's the root of all that makes him so good and so decent." She sighed. "And yet... You'll note that I said *almost*."

My eyebrows rose slightly.

Alicia sighed, then looked away. "You're a warrior, Thomas. Warriors break things and kill people. It's hard to be a warrior, I imagine, though thank god I'll never know." She shook her head. "War does things to people. Nasty, awful things, inside their heads and even their souls. In fact, according to my husband's books the absolute worst thing about war is the way it corrodes the souls of good and decent people and lowers them to the ethical level of savages." She shook her head. "Thomas, I don't know what kind of man I'm going to find waiting for me when I come back to my beloved Spence after the fighting's over. He's strong, yes. The strongest man I've ever known. But the terrible things he's had to bear responsibility for..." She sighed. "What will it do to him? Nothing good, I'm certain." Then her eyes returned to mine. "Thomas... It wasn't your voice I heard when I listened to Interstellar Cartage's tape of the incident. It wasn't Spence's, either. Even though I barely knew him, I recognized it in an instant. It was the voice of Colonel Emil Rotte."

I pressed my lips together, then folded my arms. "He was a great warrior," I pointed out.

"Oh, yes!" Alicia agreed. "I wouldn't imply otherwise for an instant! One of the greatest there's ever been, the very embodiment of a ruthless killing machine. I said so at his state funeral, and every man, woman, and child present stood and applauded. This wasn't only because they knew that it was so, but also because they understood that the colonel would've considered it the highest possible praise." Her eyes narrowed again. "Would *you* consider that to be high praise, Thomas?"

It was my turn to look out the porthole. "I... Uh..."

Alicia sighed. "The colonel was handicapped by his lack of a body, yes. But, he had over ten years between the Esteppan War and the Dracan War. What did he accomplish during that decade?"

"Not much," I admitted reluctantly. "Except for building a bunch of model ships."

"Not very much at all," Alicia agreed. "He could've achieved almost anything, Thomas, as famous as he was. Written books, run for office, become an educator, toured the galaxy, healed the wounds. Instead he just sat and waited for the next war. Because he'd become so hard and cold inside that he wasn't good for anything else anymore." Alicia waited a long time, letting her words sink in. "Thomas," she continued eventually. "Remember how I said that Spence would have done *almost* the same thing you did? He'd have threatened Hazelwood, yes. Threatened her so hard that the diplomats would've been abuzz for weeks. So would I, for that matter, though less bluntly. But..." Her brow furrowed.

"But?" I asked.

"He'd not have threatened directly to kill her," Alicia continued, her eyes now boring hard and cold into mine. "I know-- it's all a matter of niceties. Any threat that Spence or I might've made would also have implied her death, just as surely as your approach did. Still, it's a matter of degree. Or of coarseness, perhaps." She frowned. "You don't directly threaten to kill people, Thomas. Or, at least you don't when you're not on a battlefield. If you do you end up like Colonel Rotte, a lost soul no longer good for anything *except* combat." She frowned. "Thomas, I want better for you. I don't want to have to put you away after the war like a loyal but dangerous dog, to be held in honorable but distant storage until you're needed again to do the only job left for someone like you." Her eyes filled with tears. "I don't want that for you! Please, don't let yourself fall into the trap. Because if it can happen to you then it can also happen to Spence, and…"

Presently Alicia was weeping and I was hugging her from behind, trying to comfort the softly-trembling rabbit-woman with hard plastic limbs. "I promise," I said eventually. "I'll never do anything like that again. If you'll help me, that is. I think I'm going to need all the help I can get."

She squeezed my hand, then turned her chair around to face me. It was sort of funny, the way she was smiling so big while the tears continued to pour from her eyes. "I won't lose you," she swore. "Not that way. So help me god, no victory won could be worth *that* price. Yes, Thomas, you'll get all the help that can be provided, you and Jimmy and all the rest to come. But you above all because you've suffered so much. And, of course, because you're so beloved by so many."

Alicia took a few moments to clean herself up, and as if by magic the red "Eyes Only" folder disappeared. "I'll nationalize them," she explained when I asked. "It's what my staff wants to do, and now that I've had a little time to think things through I agree with them. For the duration; let the successor-government worry about compensation. And we'll intern the crew. Admittedly, there's a shortage of skilled spacehands. But we're not *that* short."

I nodded, eyes widening. I'd said a few silly, ill-chosen words, and it'd turned into an interstellar incident! My mind whirled.

Then Alicia took my hand again. "Now," she said, her smile returning. "It's time for more pleasant business. You don't think that everyone forgot what day today is, do you?"

I winced. There were so many more important things…

"Happy Birthday!" Alicia cried out, as the big double-doors at the far end of the messroom swung open. "Surprise!" A huge chocolate cake came rolling in, topped by what I knew must be eighteen candles and followed by Father and Sven and Jimmy and Ted and Admiral Vlasilov and Father Murton and, well, *everyone*!

"I…" I stuttered, trying to find words. "I…"

"Shut up and cut the cake, since you can't blow out the candles!" Jimmy interrupted me. "I want to see the look on your face when you open my present!"

"Yeah!" Ted agreed, handing me a knife. "Shut up and cut the cake. There's a good sailor-man!"

Then everyone sang while I clumsily guided the knife. It was a good thing that I didn't cry real tears anymore, I decided. Or else everyone's dessert would've been ruined for sure.

Chapter Sixteen

My birthday had been an emotional roller-coaster; perhaps it was fitting that the next day I should ride the real thing.

I'd never actually been to an amusement park, but one could hardly escape the advertisements and such. So I felt pretty certain that I knew what Stormcrow Park would be like. Some of it I got right; the cheap souvenirs, the big embarrassing hats that Jimmy insisted on buying, the whirling, colorful rides and gawking crowds. But I'd also gotten a lot of it wrong, as well. The hats were every bit as silly as I'd imagined them, but wearing them was *fun*. I even bought one for Petty Officer Brooks; it was shaped and colored like a huge banana. He grinned like a kid when he put it on. And the whirling, colorful rides were a lot more exciting than I'd reckoned on, too. Even after being a Skybolt, they were still fun! As for the souvenirs... Well, they remained cheap and tacky-looking no matter how hard I worked at appreciating them. But that was okay; two out of three was still a lot better than the Stahlberg had worked out.

Unlike the scouts, Stormcrow Park was no stranger to the art of playing host to celebrities. They not only issued us the promised platinum tickets for ourselves and Brooks, but detailed a park worker not much older than Jimmy and I to show us around and make helpful suggestions.

"...hurry if you want to see the Kabuki show," Brad was explaining. He was nineteen, and not in the least overawed by us navy types. "Stormcrow Park tries to offer an inclusive, multicultural experience. We can just make it."

Jimmy looked at me and shrugged; his hat was sculpted in the form of a bunch of ripe blueberries; I was wearing a cucumber. "I don't care," he said.

I pursed my lips and looked away. Jimmy *did* care, I knew. He wanted to ride rides. "How about we try the Gravity Hammer again?" I asked him. "It's been the best so far, I think."

"Me too!" my wingman agreed, his grin threatening to tear open his plastic skin. "Let's go!"

"Cool!" Brad agreed, smiling and leading the way back to the chauffeured private cart that went along with our platinum tickets. Jimmy and I climbed laboriously in, our motors humming in protest, and then we sped across the park for our third visit to Stormcrow Park's most famous ride. No less than three similar carts followed closely in our wake, filled with scowling navy and park-security types.

When we arrived at the special elevator behind the Hammer, Foehn Fox was waiting to greet us. The vulpine performed his first pratfall before we even came to a complete stop, tripping backwards over a knee-high rock wall and landing square on his soft, bushy tail. I'd always had a weak spot for a good clown, and whoever was inside the suit was one of the best I'd ever seen. As we climbed out of the cart he rose halfway back to his feet with the help of a snow-goose character whose name I didn't know, then tripped tumbled them both back to earth again. It was a silly joke, even a predictable one. Yet it was so well executed that I doubled over in laughter. "You really like that fox," Jimmy observed, looking at me strangely. "Is he from Esteppan folklore or something?"

"Beats the heck out of me," I admitted. "I'm mostly from New Orleans, you know. But yes, I like him a lot." Foehn, clearly overhearing my words, bowed elaborately and lodged his tail in an ornamental water-wheel in the process. As we walked away, the white goose was splashing through the shallows in a comical attempt to free him and I was giggling so hard I could barely walk.

The Hammer's elevator was very plain and ordinary, all the more so due to the way it contrasted with the rest of the gaudy park. This was, I assumed, because so few patrons would ever see it. Even gold-ticket holders, who paid a princely sum for the privilege of line-cutting, had to walk up the main ramps like everyone else. Only a handful of untreatable cripples and major celebrities would ever be permitted to take the elevator. Which were Jimmy and I, I wondered as we were whisked effortlessly upwards. Celebrities, cripples, or both?

The Hammer was fun, though not as much as Foehn, I admitted privately to myself. When the elevator slid open, as always, a little gasp passed through the crowd, and even the gold-ticket holders backed away. One of them, a girl of about eleven, curtsied. "Your Excellency!" she whispered, eyes huge.

I felt bad about cutting in front of everybody; it seemed unfair, somehow, at a very basic level. Certainly I knew that I'd *never* buy a gold ticket, even though I could easily afford one. But I also understood that the whole routine of the park was being disrupted for the sake of Jimmy and I, that the navy was spending heaven-only-knew how many credits on security for us, and that we had only this one day to visit where the other folks would mostly be able to come back time after time. So I tried not to feel like a pompous elitist as the ride operator called up an entire empty train for Jimmy, Brooks, and I, bowed respectfully before strapping me in, then sent us on our way with twenty-two of the twenty-five seats vacant despite the pressing crowd.

The Gravity Hammer was an anti-grav based ride, but with a twist. Instead of generating thrust, the way a Skybolt's antigrav did, or enabling someone to float in the air, as anti-grav boots did, the Hammer used the technology to *increase* gravity and create a false sense of acceleration, sometimes along many axis at once. The result was that, though our little train traversed what appeared to be a perfectly straight and level track, we riders felt like we were rising and falling and twisting and every other motion one could imagine, often all at once. No two rides were ever alike, the brochures had claimed, and so far as I could tell for once the promoters hadn't exaggerated. It was awesome! And best of all was the ending, where the train turned upside down and the safety bars raised themselves, so that only false gravity held us in our seats...

...until the field collapsed, dropping us like a rock for a clear hundred feet before catching us at the last minute and decelerating us enough to make a soft landing on a big air-cushion. It was *so* cool; even if you knew what was coming! Brooks especially seemed to like it. "Wow!" I said, accepting the ever-present Brad's help as I crawled laboriously to the edge of the landing-pad. "That was *great!* Jimmy had landed much closer to the center of the cushion than I had, and therefore he was taking longer in getting off. I shook my head; his and my presence must be ripping the carefully-planned ride-schedules to shreds.

When we got back out into the sunlight again, I realized it wasn't just the ride schedules we were upsetting. There, waiting for us by our cart, was Foehn and the goose. Our security escorts were quite deliberately moving us around the park from one quiet place to another, often via non-public paths and access-points. Foehn and his friend should have been out with the crowds making dozens laugh, not just our little group. But there he was, tail still soaking wet from the waterwheel, while the goose's paddle-feet squish-squished with every step. I laughed again at the very sight of them. "It's not fair!" I protested to Brad. "I mean... We shouldn't have these two all to ourselves. Think of all the little kids!"

For the first time since I'd met him, my assigned host addressed me formally. "Your Excellency," he countered, bowing slightly. "It's the least we can do, after all that you've sacrificed and done for us. We're deeply grateful. Everyone is." Then Foehn and the goose bowed again, this time sincerely. It should've been impossible to tell the difference, but somehow it wasn't.

"But..." I protested. "I mean..."

"Foehn and the bird are going to stay with us?" Jimmy asked as he stepped out into the sun behind me. "Cool! I kinda like them, too!" He waved, and they bowed a second time before waving back. Then he looked up at me and grinned. "You were *so* full of it, Tommy! You thought this amusement park wouldn't be any good, compared to the ones on Earth." He waved his arms and spun in a happy little circle. "This is the most fun I've ever had *anywhere!*"

Chapter Seventeen

We did end up watching a show, despite Jimmy's fondness for the rides. "Look!" Jimmy declared as we rolled past the Park's tridee theater. "Stop!" The driver slammed on the brakes, Foehn and his sidekick nearly joined us in the front seat, and one of the security carts rear-ended the other. But no one was hurt, the only real damage being a dent about the size of a hen's egg in one of the bumpers. "Look!" Jimmy repeated, pointing and practically dancing in his seat. "We've *got* to go see this on the big screen!"

I pressed my lips together and considered. "The Battle of the Orion Nexus", a big sign out front read. "See previously-unreleased footage in a twenty-thousand-cubic-foot display!"

"I don't know," I said slowly, turning to Brooks for guidance. But all he did was shrug.

"Oh, come on!" Jimmy urged. "Look. We're famous. We can't help that; it's too late. But just for once, let's try and see ourselves the way that everyone else does. Besides, it's only an hour long."

What the heck, I decided at last, climbing slowly out of my seat and down onto the pavement. Because Jimmy had stopped us so suddenly, we were alighting in a public area for once. Between Jimmy and the mascots and I, every tourist camera in the park must've been pointed at us, click-click-clicking away. A crowd formed seemingly out of nowhere, so thick that I wasn't sure I could force my way through it. I was just beginning to realize that I was a little frightened when a soft hand touched my shoulder. I spun my head around as quickly as my servo-neck allowed, but it was only Foehn. He smiled and bent down close to me, whispering so that only I could hear. "I'm not supposed to talk," he explained. "Don't ever tell anyone. But if you'll let me go first, I think I can get us through this."

I smiled back at the silly cartoon face and allowed Foehn to step around me. He looked around imperiously, then caught the eye of his snowgoose sidekick. Seemingly furious, the larger mascot pointed at the ground beside him. The smaller goose, looking dejectedly at the ground, sidled up beside him and shrugged its wings. Then, head held as high and regal as if he were leading a royal procession, Foehn led us off towards the theater entrance. As if by magic the crowd split before him, allowing us all to pass. It would've been majestic if Foehn hadn't somehow, from inside his costume, managed to drop his already droopy pants down around his feet without apparently noticing. His underwear had pink polka-dots.

The theater hadn't been a very busy place until Jimmy and I took an interest. Once we entered, however, the tridee show suddenly became the hottest attraction in the park. Security rushed ahead and saved us a block of seats near the front-center; Jimmy and I didn't have to be told to sit in the middle of this empty space. Then the guards crowded in around us to spoil any would-be assassin's aim. We'd been very lucky in our timing; the curtain was just rising as the security-types settled in around us. The credits rolled, and then…

…my jaw dropped as suddenly my picture flooded the tank. Under it, glowing letters formed. "Thomas Anthony Longo," they read. "One of many heroes."

At that, the place went absolutely nuts! "Hurray!" everyone was yelling, jumping up and down in their seats. "Hurray! Hurray!" Eventually my picture faded away, but the cheers simply would not. No one could hear the dialogue at all. The story moved on to footage of me testing the Skybolt against various navy squadrons; presumably the narrator was explaining how Father and the navy had been trying to persuade various government officials to buy 'bolts, though I couldn't be sure because I still couldn't hear a word despite the amplification. Finally they showed the old Top Banana squadron preparing to scramble, and I just *had* to do something because both Jimmy's father and brother had flown with the Bananas and might appear onscreen at any instant. It wouldn't be fair if Jimmy couldn't hear anything they might have to say, especially considering how badly Lofton had gotten shot-up. So, ignoring the unmistakably clear signals of my lead security man, I stood up and bowed, then raised my voice to the highest amplification I could. "Please!" I asked the crowd. "Please! Thank you for your support. But no one can hear. Let's all enjoy the film together!"

"Hooray!" they all cried out one last time. Something resembling quiet ensued, though a rumble-rumble-rumble of conversation never quite faded away. At least Jimmy got to hear his father's voice. "We need the Skybolt," he declared solemnly into a camera. Judging by the perspiration stains on his flight suit and the tired lines in his face, the interview must've taken place right after my simulated attack on the base he'd been assigned to defend. "Please, write your Parliamentarians and the representatives of your planetary governments and tell them that the Skybolt is the future of the navy."

"Hurray!" the crowd roared again, though this time the cheering faded almost immediately.

"Hey!" my wingman complained. "They didn't mention how Dad shot you down!"

I smiled despite myself. It felt like a lifetime ago!

Then the film turned dark and sinister. Hawaii was nuked, and so were the big military bases in Africa. Someone at the Army-Navy game apparently caught the Dracan surprise raid on film; from the way the camera lurched, I doubted that he'd survived. He'd been an army supporter, I could tell, because directly across the field were the navy bleachers, where I'd sat not too far from Jimmy. An expert photo-enhancer could probably have found our faces. Then the film moved on to the fleet launch…

…and my single Skybolt flying directly up through the center of the ascending heavy warships. "Hey diddle-diddle…" I heard my own staticy voice say.

"Right up the middle," Jimmy's dad replied, firm and confident and believing in me. It was odd, really. I'd reviewed the combat films a million times with Ted and others to see what we could learn from them. But somehow we'd never replayed that part. It wasn't significant. Or at least it'd never seemed so.

Until now.

It took the movie longer to tell the story of the battle than it took to actually fight it; by the time we got to the part where my 'bolt took its first hit and I turned away from the fight, my hands were balled up into rocklike fists and my jaw was clenched as tight as its motor could force it. Reviewing the tapes had that effect on me sometimes; when that happened, Father Murton always ended the session. But Brooks was made of sterner stuff; while he was clearly watching me instead of the movie, he didn't try and shut things down. Instead, he left the decision to me.

There weren't any high-resolution images available of the latter stages of the battle, or at least there weren't any available to us United Systems types. An arrow picked the insignificant fleck of my Skybolt out of what appeared to be a field of stars, and a little flare of light marked the firing of my last torpedo. Then the *Imperial Throne*, nameship of her class, exploded…

…and the film suddenly ended, because the last United Systems ship to get out had made good her escape.

Suddenly everyone was cheering again, and this time there was no stopping it. "Tho-mas! Tho-mas! Tho-mas!" the crowd cried over and over as the film moved first into an examination of the Dracan occupation of Churilla, then Spence's resistance movement, and finally footage of Jimmy's crippled father and wounded brother helping pin the Parliamentary Order of Merit onto my chest in the secret tunnel under the Gambian embassy. Eventually the projectionist gave up and brought up the lights during the navy recruitment promotion at the end of the film.

Then someone got on the PA system; I didn't know who, though he didn't sound Esteppan. "And don't forget that next month we'll be showing another war-film, *Raid on Drakkus*, starring Thomas and his wingman Jimmy Knight!"

The crowd roared out anew, this time an angry, aggressive sort of sound.

But the anger didn't last long; pretty soon the audience had switched to "Tho-mas! Jim-my! Tho-mas! Jim-my!"

"Wow!" Jimmy said, though he had to lean over close to my ear for me to be able to hear him. "Just... Wow!"

"Yeah," I agreed. I'd known we were famous; I'd have had to have been stupid not to. But, somehow, I hadn't quite understood *how* famous. Yes, I was finding more to enjoy in Stormcrow Park than I'd ever expected. It would've been better still, however, to visit as an ordinary, faceless tourist. Suddenly, down deep in my gut I understood that no matter how long I lived, I'd never, ever have that opportunity. Or, many other lost opportunities which I couldn't yet begin to enumerate. Though, I recognized sickly, I'd have plenty of time to regret every last one of them.

If I survived the war, that was. First things first.

Chapter Eighteen

The next morning, I was a Skybolt again. Jimmy and I were assigned the day shift. It was a pleasant change, for me at least. Now I could at least look out and admire the Fleet as it bobbed at anchor, waiting for I didn't know what. The fjord was full to bursting, and there was a sense of tension in the air that hadn't been present two weeks back, before we'd gone on leave. Or if it had been, Jimmy and I were oblivious to it because we were so tired. Certainly there was a lot more activity, even allowing for the fact that I'd previously been on the night shift. Our anchorage was practically crawling with small and not-so-small cargo lighters filled with supplies, molecular batteries, and last-minute cargo. The sky was nearly as crowded; in theory, Jimmy and I were supposed to remain fully up-to-date on traffic conditions at all times, so as to be ready for instant clearance and takeoff. But the traffic was nearly as bad as it'd been in London the night of the emergency session of Parliament. I couldn't *possibly* keep up with it all, and near as I could tell neither could the controllers. There'd been two mid-air collisions over the Fleet already, both while I was on leave, and in peacetime everyone would've been grounded until new procedures could be worked out. But it *wasn't* peacetime, so the 'hopper pilots, civilian and military alike, simply did their best to dodge their fellows while turning the ether blue with profanity. If Jimmy and I ever actually launched, we'd simply have to hope for the best and depend on everyone else's sense of self-preservation.

I'd suggested that we ought to relocate to a less-congested airstrip, but the admiral had vetoed me. "We don't want to take any chances on an operational loss," he explained, "No matter how slight. Besides, it won't be very long now."

While I didn't agree with Vlasilov's views on the risk of losing a 'bolt in a flying accident, anyone with eyes could look out over New Narvik Fjord and see that it was almost time to leave. There were so many merchantmen about, and all of them so heavily laden, that it was surprising there was any water left for the oysters lying in their thick bottom-beds.

Father Murton joined me on deck at about eight. He'd helped me settle in, then attended a counselor meeting. He looked a lot better for his spell of R and R. In fact, he seemed ten years younger.

"…tried to make them see reason," he was explaining to me. "But as usual they wouldn't listen. I'm still in command of the whole Corps of Counselors."

I blinked the light on my monitor-camera twice, shorthand for a nod. My tutor shook his head. "I don't have time to take proper care of you, Thomas, while burdened with so many other duties." He frowned. "The only way they'd allow you to have a full-time counselor of your own, they told me, was if I took the Corps job full-time. Then you'd get someone new, but all to yourself."

I false-gulped. Father Murton had done *so* much for me, and been so brave… "Do you…" I began. "I mean…"

"Of *course* not!" the priest countered, his mouth a thin, angry line. "I'd never dream of it." Then his face softened. "Though they have a point," he admitted. "No one else knows this job half as well as I do. There's hardly any experience to go around. And I have the rank. I *ought* to be in command."

"We'll muddle through," I answered, more relieved than I sounded. "If you get too busy, maybe you can ask Brooks for help?"

"You really like him, don't you?" he asked, looking sidelong at my long, red-painted nose. It had all kinds of kill-marks on it now, though I tried not to look too closely at them.

"Yeah," I admitted. "Not as much as you, of course. But, if you're extra-busy…"

"Gotcha," my counselor agreed, reaching up and patting my fuselage gently. "I think he's one heck of a good man, Thomas, and I'm glad to see that you think as much of him as I do. Expect to see more of him, then. And thank you for understanding." He frowned. "Though this trip shouldn't be too bad, with only the two of you aboard."

I blinked my light again. "Though I wish Heinz and Dieter were coming."

Father Murton frowned. The two Butcher Birds, last of their kind, were being left behind to defend Esteppe and the all-important industrial infrastructure from which Skybolts emerged. "I wish they were too," he admitted. "But I can't argue the logic. Besides, *someone's* going to have to train the new pilots." He shook his head. "I'd certainly hate to try and keep *their* schedules for the next few weeks."

I blinked my light again, but remained silent. Yes, the Birds were going to be on the schedule from hell. But Jimmy and I were shipping out to face the Dracan Fleet. Heinz and Dieter would gladly have come along, I knew. They'd fought beside us before, and their courage wasn't in question. Yet I couldn't help but feel a shameful stab of envy every time the subject of their staying behind came up.

A long silence dragged itself out, something that happened a lot while I was standing alert. Finally, my tutor spoke again. "So," he asked. "How was the rest of your leave? After you got rid of me, I mean."

I blinked my light rapidly many times, shorthand for a smile. "The hike didn't work out," I admitted. "Though I expected that to be the best part. And, we toured some ships; I guess you heard about that, too."

"I did," he admitted, gazing out to sea and revealing nothing by his expression.

"That didn't work out too well, either. Stormcrow Park was nice, though. The mascots, especially."

The priest nodded.

I sighed. "But, even the park was kind of a letdown." I changed to my wingtip camera and looked inwards at my tutor, but his face was unreadable. "I tried to have fun," I explained. "It was my *duty* to have fun, almost. And I'm really sorry that things didn't go better. I feel like I let everyone down." *Including Foehn and the little goose*, I added silently to myself. *Whose name I'd never even bothered to learn.*

Father Murton still wasn't saying anything, so I false-sighed and went on. "It was... I mean, you were with me at the Old Home Place. It's nice. But it'll never be *my* home. No matter whether my initials are carved there or not."

"I know, son," the priest whispered.

"Father thinks I could be Prime Minister someday. In fact, I kind of think he hopes I will be, even though he loves me enough that he won't push too hard."

"Do you think you could become Prime Minister, Thomas?" my tutor asked.

"Yes," I answered after thinking things over a moment. "I mean, I could try and tell you that I wouldn't have a prayer. But that wouldn't be true. Would it?"

"No," Father Murton replied gently. "It wouldn't. Which makes the reality all the worse, I'd imagine."

"So," I went on, hardly hearing the priest's words. "I was still all upset about that when I went to go climb the mountain." I sighed. "Father, I wanted to enjoy that hike more than anything in the world. But it wasn't a hike; it was a circus. I wanted to be with other people my age, was all, and see some wildlife and pretty landscapes. The scenery was all right, I guess. No matter how hard I tried, though, I couldn't be just another kid. Everyone else kept making me special and different. And finally, just when I was about to make a friend and see a snow lizard..."

"Brooks was livid," Father Murton said eventually, still facing out to sea. "You have no idea. He saw what you wanted, what you were trying to do... He even admired you for it, Thomas. For not *wanting* to be treated as a hero. It broke his heart when everything fell apart."

"Yeah," I replied, not really sure what to say about Brooks and his broken heart. "It wasn't anyone's fault, I guess. But it wasn't much fun, either."

"And the ship tours?" Murton asked.

I false-sighed again. "I'd rather not talk about them, if you don't mind. That time, the mistakes were all my own fault. My mouth ran away with me. I feel terrible about what happened, and Alicia has already lectured me on the subject. I know I was wrong."

"Okay," the priest agreed, blinking in apparent satisfaction.

"So," I continued. "After ruining an annual Esteppan tradition for thousands of kids and causing an interstellar incident aboard the *Rockefeller* here in the fjord, I suppose one could say that Stormcrow Park was a success, in the same sense that any landing one walks away from is considered a success." I blinked my light again, the long, steady light that indicated a frown. "I made thousands of people wait a little longer to ride their rides. Though, I suppose, in fairness, the fact that Jimmy and I were there gave them something unexpected and extra to remember about their holiday. So, we didn't totally ruin everything. But…"

"But?" my tutor asked.

"But," I repeated slowly, searching for the right words and somehow not quite finding them. "There's something I can't get out of my head," I continued. "It's silly. You're going to laugh. I just know it."

"No, I won't," the priest promised me. "I'm just glad you're talking to me again, Thomas. It's been far too long."

I didn't understand what he meant about it having been too long; we talked almost every day. But I could only converse on one subject at once, no matter how many speakers I was hooked up to. "Well…" I said slowly.

The priest waited, silent.

"They had these mascots," I explained. "A fox and a snow goose."

"Right," he agreed. "They're quite famous, even off-planet."

"Well…" I repeated, wanting to look down at my feet and not able to. "I'm not surprised, though I didn't know. They were funny, Father. I mean really, really funny."

"They get paid to be funny. And, they love their work. It's what they live for. Or at least that's the case with most performers of that sort; I don't know these personally."

"Oh, they loved it all right!" I repeated. "You could see it, every second. They clowned for Jimmy and me like we were the only audience in the universe. And, they were *good*! But…"

"But you couldn't laugh," the priest guessed.

"Right!" I answered. "Exactly! At first I could, sure. But then we saw a movie about the war, and everyone cheered us. It was like someone flipped a switch inside of me; after that, I couldn't enjoy Foehn no matter *how* hard I tried."

"I see," my tutor answered, thrusting his hands into his pockets. "Or, at least, I think I do."

"I want to laugh again," I explained to my counselor, the words coming now all at once, in a terrible rush. "I want to be able to go on hikes and make new friends. I want to be able to go tour ships and not be a VIP that causes interstellar incidents. I want to be able to go places and not have people make a big deal out of me." I sighed. "It's all gone. The important things, I mean. The stuff that really mattered to me in life. All of it's gone, turned upside down except for you and Father and Jimmy and a few others. And I want things back the way they were!"

Father Murton removed his right hand from his pocket and stroked his beard for a moment. "Thomas," he finally said. "I've always known that you were smart. Wise beyond your years, even. If you ever *do* seek to become Prime Minister, I'll support you to the hilt. My word of honor; we could do far worse." He paused again. "Not every man can claim to know the day and the hour that he ceased to be a boy. Yet I believe you've defined it almost to the second." He turned and looked into my wingtip camera. "You've grown up, Thomas. That's what happened to you at Stormcrow Park, and that's what hurts so badly inside. And, as you've already figured out, you can't go back. No adult can, though that's even truer in your case than most." He sighed and turned back out to sea. "Brooks told me about the movie and the cheering. And, that you liked the mascots at first, but that after the film they no longer worked for you. He thought that you were pushing too hard, going to see that movie. In fact, he almost warned you not to. But for all his life experience, he doesn't know Esteppans very well. Or at least not you Longos. Your kind doesn't go in for warnings, or at least not so you'd notice. You just plod recklessly ahead no matter what, daring everyone and everything in the universe to stop you. Which, somehow, it never quite does." The priest sighed, his shoulders rising and falling slowly. "And thank God for it! Where would we be today without you and your hard-headed natures?" He smiled again "Welcome to manhood, Thomas! I wish it'd come to you in a more normal way, in more amenable times. But like war adulthood comes when it comes and we have to deal with it as best we can with what we have on-hand." His smile faded a little. "Welcome. And know that I think you're going to do just fine."

Chapter Nineteen

It was just as well that I achieved adulthood while on leave; if I'd had to find time to do it while standing heel-and-toe watches I'd have still been a soprano at thirty. Once our first watch was finished, it was back to the same old endless grind of hurried meetings and boring situation-reports. I couldn't figure out why they even bothered holding the sit-rep meetings so often; things never changed much. Everything on our end was as ready as it could possibly be; obviously we were waiting for something to happen that was classified at a much higher level of security than most of us battle-fighting types were cleared for. At first it rankled that that we who were most likely to die weren't allowed to know certain things. Then I thought it through. We who were most likely to die were also the ones most likely to be captured. What we didn't know, we couldn't reveal under drugs or torture. So even if it wasn't very pleasant not to be in the know, I stopped asking questions.

One interesting thing *did* happen during our delay. *The Glorious First of June* had originally been designed to operate twenty-four Polecats, a half-squadron. Skybolts, however, were far more demanding birds than Polecats in terms of support staff and maintenance facilities; Father's special engine design, for example, required much more frequent teardowns. Even worse, doing this kind of work on a 'bolt required double the man-hours and three times as many tools and fixtures as the older fighter. Despite this, it was a terrible waste for *June* to hit space with so much empty hanger-space. I figured we'd probably transport urgently-required cargo to make up the difference, but on our third day back on duty a lighter came easing up to our hull. "Ahoy there, *June!*" her captain cried out through a megaphone. "This is the *Demetrius*, with aircraft and special cargo! Ahoy!"

I watched with interest from my usual position on the weather-deck; because so many of my on-watch shifts had been during the hours of darkness I'd never watched cargo being swayed aboard before. The lighter was equipped with a big crane; in minutes it was in action, lifting crates the sizes of busses and swinging them effortlessly across the yard or so of open water that lay between the two craft. The .operator was amazing to watch; she stood atop the lighter's superstructure with legs spread wide, swaying with the gentle dip and roll of the two big vessels and manipulating her little control box with what must've been decades of hard-earned experience. As the big containers swung outboard the lighter heeled further and further, but the operator anticipated every motion. Then once again everything shifted as the load was transferred to *June*, which in turn rolled imperceptibly as well. I got a headache, trying to picture all the angle-of-moment calculations that the woman was performing so effortlessly in her head. In fact, I was so fascinated that at first I didn't notice that all the boxes were painted up in Longo blue, and carried my father's logo.

"Wow!" I finally called out, interrupting Jimmy at whatever he was doing to kill time. My friend was on the other side of the deck, and therefore couldn't see a thing. "This is cool!"

"What's cool?" he asked. "Is another ship coming in for splashdown?"

"No!" I answered, making sure that our private channel was encoded, the way it was always supposed to be. You couldn't be too careful with security, even if the navy was operating in broad daylight. "We're taking on more aircraft!"

"No kidding?" my friend asked. "Polecats?"

"Skybolts!" I answered. "You can tell from the shipping crates." I switched to a wingtip camera, which had a telescope function, and zoomed. "Skybolt Mark II's, according to the labels." I switched to another container. "Or... Wait a minute. This one's a Skybolt Mark I*."

There was a long silence. "That's odd," Jimmy finally said. "We're just plain Mark I's. An asterisk after the 'I' is supposed to mean a minor modification-- I can see where your dad might've come up with an improvement by now, a little change they can make without slowing down production. But to go to a 'Mark II' designation means a major redesign. Why would they do that when there's such a terrible shortage?"

"I don't know," I responded. "And, even more, why didn't they tell me anything about this? If we're getting better 'bolts, don't you think they'd let me of all people know?"

"You and me both, I'd think," Jimmy replied after a time. "How many containers are there?"

"Ten," I replied. "We'll end up with a dozen birds and two pilots. Does that make any sense?"

"Not that I can see," Jimmy answered. "But then, as Dad always used to say, this *is* the navy we're talking about here. Keep watching, and let me know what else you find out."

I clicked my mike circuit twice and zoomed in further on the action. The loading was going more slowly now, as *June*'s deck grew crowded. Not only were the crates themselves taking up more and more space, but crewman were swarming around the new arrivals as well, removing the packaging materials. Things had almost come to a standstill by the time that the first sky-blue 'bolt emerged from its wrappings. Like my own fighter it had a red nose, which seemed almost to glow in the weak Esteppan sun. I virtual-frowned. Something was fishy here. Very, *very* fishy. Here we were, in broad daylight, out in front of god and everybody, openly advertising the location of a huge percentage of our most secret and effective weaponry. Why would we do that? Then a little light went on in my head. I swung my wingtip-camera outboard, to sweep the decks of all the nearest merchies. Sure enough, their rails were lined with bored idlers, half of them sporting binoculars.

Some of them were spies, I realized suddenly. And Vlasilov knew it. Just like I now knew that the Skybolts being swung aboard were no closer to being the real Mc Coy than was my social body. It was a beautiful thing! Simply beautiful!

"Ha!" I cried out aloud, over the private circuit to my best friend. No *wonder* the Longo markings painted on the crates had seemed larger than usual. It was because they *were* larger! So that no dimwitted amateur secret agent could possibly misidentify them!

"Ha what?" he asked. "Did someone trip and fall or something?"

"No," I answered, carefully choosing my words so as not to reveal anything even if our enemies could hear me. "Even better! But I can't tell you anything more until later. Face to face, I mean. Anything else might ruin the surprise."

Chapter Twenty

And what a pleasant surprise it turned out to be! Commander Knight was waiting for us down on the hanger deck when we came off duty, and by the time he was done explaining Jimmy and I were smiling so wide that our grins barely fit on just one face apiece. It was great, just great!

"…aren't quite as powerful as real 'bolts," Ted explained, leaning up against the nose of a so-called "Mark II". "But, they *are* four-fifths as powerful, so they ought to be able to keep up all the way through the approach." His smile widened. "They can be programmed to hold formation, as well."

"Wow!" Jimmy exclaimed, eyes wide.

I shook my head. "Jeez! They'll fall for it for sure."

"They won't have much of a choice," Ted agreed. "Intelligence work is always an imprecise thing even during peacetime, when spying is at its easiest. How can the Dracans be *sure* that we don't have a dozen operational 'bolts? They can't, of course. Which is the beauty of the whole thing." He reached up and patted the side of the Mark II's nose. "That and the big warhead, of course."

I hadn't thought it possible, but now I was grinning wider than ever. It wasn't every day that you ran into nuclear-armed decoys. Double-deceptions, I was beginning to understand, were even more fun than the more common forms of deceit. *Sven*, a little voice whispered in my ear. Sven had once been a missileer, and a highly-decorated one at that. This had been *his* idea; it had his footprints all over it!

"But there's more," Ted explained, walking slowly across the hanger deck so we could keep up. He nodded to the pair of Mark I*'s. "Those are real," he explained.

"Wow!" Jimmy repeated as he tottered up alongside what clearly was to be my new fighter; the Stormcrow workers had painted the nose red at the factory, as I'd seen from the weather deck earlier, and already my support crew was busily reproducing all of the kill-emblems as well. I wished they wouldn't do that, especially not the mushroom clouds. Just like I wished that the Stormcrow people wouldn't paint my nosecones up special, for that matter. But how could I ask them not to, when they took such obvious delight in it? So, instead of saying anything I smiled and waved at my staff, then walked over to examine

Jimmy's new 'hopper. It was identical to the old one, as near as I could tell. Or at least it seemed identical until I walked past the left side of the nose.

"Hey!" I pointed out. "They put the gun on the wrong side." I tilted my head first to one side, then the other. "And it's bigger, too!"

"Yeah!" Jimmy agreed, examining at the nose on my plane. "But… Wait a minute!"

"Yep," Ted agreed, eyes twinkling. "You've got twin cannon now, with a little more oomph behind each of them." He turned to me. "Your complaints have now officially been addressed."

I blinked, trying to remember complaining about anything.

"The head-on passes," Ted reminded me. "You complained about the fact that you were continually making head-on passes, which depend more on luck than anything else. Even an inferior fighter, you quite correctly pointed out, has a good chance of killing its enemy in a head-on pass, and because of the 'bolt's speed the most common way for the enemy to engage is from ahead."

"That's how I got shot down, all right!" Jimmy piped in. "Just exactly that way!"

"Yep," his older brother agreed. "And people took notice." He turned back to me. "There's only so much that can be done," he explained. "Most likely the head-on passes will continue; the Dracans can hardly do anything else. But we've more than doubled your firepower."

"What're the tradeoffs?" I demanded. There *had* to be tradeoffs; there always were, in weapons design.

"Increased mass," Ted admitted. "Though not as much as you might think; some genius back at your dad's plant came up with a system where the gun-barrels are now doubling as load-bearing structural members. We also had to cut back on your ammo supply some. But experience to date says the 'bolts were oversupplied to start with; even after the Drakkus raid you still had twenty-five percent left. To help make up for it, you can toggle either gun off or on if you don't think the target justifies firing both."

I nodded, though it was hard to imagine settling for anything less than the most firepower possible when in actual combat. "We'll have to try it out, I guess," I said, even though deep down I believed that the modification was probably a good one. "When we can fly again."

"Which'll be fairly soon," Ted answered, his face sobering. "The plan is to let you two wring these new birds out once we're spaceside, while on our way to New Nippon. If you give them the thumbs-up, you've got new rides. If not, we've still got the old birds." He shrugged. "Whichever you don't keep will form the seed stock for Earth's program."

I nodded again; Earth was the three-hundred-pound economic gorilla of the galaxy; we'd known all along that no matter how badly she was hurting, war-material production would still have to be a priority there. Especially Skybolt production. It might take as many as several hundred 'bolts to win the war, especially against Dracan superfighter opposition. If Esteppe had to produce them all, the war would drag on who knew how long?

"Great," I agreed, turning back to my own 'bolt. From this angle the only kill-marks that showed were those for Dracan warships; two *Imperial Throne*-class battleships, two troop-carriers and half a destroyer. Somehow they didn't bother me as much as the others, especially the battleships. Having seen in person what a *Throne*'s main guns could do, I loathed the things. They were an affront to decency in the same way as a fusion weapon or cluster bomb; all were abominations of engineering genius. "We'll wring them out when there's time." I raised my eyebrows. "Any word on that?"

"Not officially," Ted answered, his smile fading. "But a little bird tells me that a high-ranking VIP is scheduled to arrive aboard tomorrow evening, spend the night, then address the entire fleet early the next morning. And, Thomas, I've been told to reschedule the duty roster so that you'll be able to meet with said VIP before her speech. What does that tell you?"

"Alicia's addressing the fleet again," I sighed. I wasn't disappointed in the sense that I didn't want to see her; in fact, I was already looking forward to it. It was the combat that loomed beyond which bothered me.

"That's so cool, that she still comes to see you," Jimmy observed.

I nodded, then came to a decision. "Would you like to come too?" I asked my wingman. If my duty schedule could be juggled to please Alicia, I reasoned, then Jimmy's could be altered to please me. Or at least just this once, it could.

His eyebrows rose. "Could I?" he asked.

"I can't promise," I answered. "But I can try." I turned to Ted. "He's going to be in every bit as much danger as me," I pointed out. "It's not fair that he shouldn't get the same attention. And I'm sure that Alicia won't mind."

The elder Knight nodded slowly. "If you can pull it off, Thomas, and if Jimmy wants to go... Well, I'll certainly make no objection."

Jimmy looked down at his shoes. "Thanks, Thomas. Yes, it'd mean a lot to me. And it means even more that you're willing to try."

Chapter Twenty-One

It was just as well that Alicia met with Jimmy and me before her speech instead of after. In private she greeted us in her usual grandmotherly way, smiling kindly and commenting on how pleasant it was to be around such nice young men. When she addressed the Fleet, however, it was a different story entirely. She cursed the Dracan Emperor, naming him a villain and a fool, then shook her fist in the air until we were all shaking ours along with her. "Death to the Emperor! Death to the Emperor! Death to the Emperor!" It was chilling, especially the part where she explained how we'd know that we'd finally killed enough Dracans when the rest quit fighting. "*That's* when the slaughter can finally stop!" she declared, fist still raised high. "On the day that the Dracans lay down their arms and beg for mercy. Until then, however, we must strike and strike and strike again." It would've been a lot harder to take had the order of the two events been reversed; she hadn't been grandmotherly at all behind the podium.

"Wow!" Jimmy declared as we left the hanger deck to prepare for upping ship. *The Glorious First of June* was the task force's flagship again, and thus would be first of the armada to lift. "And I thought bunnies would be peaceful and gentle!"

"You ought to meet Spence," I answered as we made our slow, plodding way through the swirling crowds of rapidly-moving spacehands. "He's *twice* as bloody-minded as Alicia." I frowned suddenly. "Maybe it's *because* they're rabbits?"

Jimmy's eyebrows rose. "Huh?"

"Well…" I answered, my thoughts not fully formed yet. "Think about it. A rabbit's natural place in the order of things is near the bottom of the food chain, right? So, they're prey. Victims."

"I guess."

"There's two ways that one can deal with being a victim. One of them is to go all passive, like. Resign one's self to the inevitable; try to make peace with it."

"Uh-huh," Jimmy agreed. "That's what I'd expect a rabbit to do."

"But," I continued. "Just because someone's set up to be a natural victim doesn't mean they're going to like it, or even accept it. I mean…" I sighed. "Maybe Alicia and Spence are really, really angry about something inside of them. Like, having fur when no one else does, or not being able to have children of their own." I frowned again. "That's why they like me so much, I think. I wonder how many other kids they've adopted over the years?"

"Bunches, probably," Jimmy agreed.

"Yeah," I answered as the crowd finally carried us down the companionway to the gunroom. Negotiating the stairs was never easy for either Jimmy or I, so we made it our habit to suspend all conversations until we could give them our full attentions again. "I wonder how many?"

Jimmy shrugged. "It doesn't matter, that I can see. She really *does* care about you; anyone can see it. You're lucky!"

"Maybe," I answered. "But I have to wonder about something. Spence and Alicia are both super-intelligent as well as being bunnies. You know that, right?"

"Yeah," Jimmy agreed. "So?"

I pressed my lips together. "They're super-intelligent, and full of anger. They're *different* as well, in a society where their kind of difference is tolerated but not allowed to be perpetuated." My eyes narrowed. "They're a little mad, I think."

"Of course they're mad!" my wingman agreed. "Alicia was mad as hell!"

"No," I answered slowly. "Mad, as in insane. As in so angry that they're maybe even *glad* there's a war on and people to kill, somewhere deep down inside. I was with Spence when he wrecked a train on purpose. A lot of Dracans died, and it could easily have killed us. He loved every second of it." I stopped and turned to face Jimmy. "Is that sane behavior?"

Jimmy blinked, then looked away. "Not really, I guess."

I shook my head and sighed. "Don't get me wrong, Jimmy. I love and respect both Spence and Alicia as much as anyone I've ever met. It's a privilege and honor to know them so well. Even more…" I sighed. "They're winning this war for us, where I don't know that anyone else I've ever met could."

"Maybe you *have* to be a little crazy to win a tough war?" Jimmy asked, shrugging. "Maybe the side that's crazier has an advantage, even? I mean, look at us. We have to be nuts to fly combat. Sane people would take one look at what we do and run away screaming."

My eyebrows rose; I hadn't thought of that. Colonel Rotte had been more than a little insane, I now understood. His kind of crazy certainly won battles. Presumably it won wars as well. "True enough," I admitted.

"Maybe *everyone's* insane, when you look close enough," Jimmy continued. "Maybe that's why we have wars in the first place, is because everyone's crazy. If war itself is crazy, then maybe only crazy people can be really, really good at it? Who can know?" He looked into my eyes. "Now, here's what *I* want to know. Are you going to run for Parliament, like she wants you to?"

It was my turn to look away. That was the *real* reason that Alicia had wanted to see me; she'd asked me flat-out to go see the Prime Minister and volunteer once we'd broken through to Earth. I was eighteen now, which made me a voter. By law, anyone eligible to vote was automatically eligible for office. Parliament wouldn't be suspended forever, she'd explained to me, and she suspected that her coalition would need my help in order to hold onto a majority.

"I don't know," I answered. "I haven't had much time to think about it yet. The whole idea still sounds as crazy to me as the war itself." I sighed. "There's too much other stuff going on that I need to worry about first. Like testing our new 'bolts. And then surviving long enough to *get* to Earth. First things first."

"You'll win," Jimmy predicted. "If you run, you'll win hands down." He frowned. "I think you should. The navy needs more representation. We wouldn't be fighting this war, if Parliament hadn't voted for disarmament."

I shook my head. *I should run for public office in support of a woman I'm beginning to suspect is insane?* I didn't say out loud. My father had once made almost precisely that same mistake. And yet... And yet... Who *else* was there to support, anyway? Who else would fight the Dracans tooth and nail, and not worry more about getting naval ordnance contracts for their districts than about how many billions of good men and women were suffering and dying due to their poor decisions?

What good was a victory, I asked myself, if all it did was line pockets and guarantee the re-election of a bunch of amoral self-important pigs that more often than not didn't deserve the fancy offices they filled? Such a victory wouldn't be any victory at all, I understood suddenly. Not in any meaningful sense of the word. And yet... And yet...

"I don't know," I sighed as we arrived at the door to Jimmy's cabin. "I'm still 'way too young and immature for this kind of stuff."

"No you're not," my wingman countered, meeting my eyes again. "You're young, yes. But you're not *nearly* as immature as half of Parliament. Even a kid like me can see that. And..." He frowned. "You've seen stuff, Tommy. Bad stuff. We need people there who've seen what you've seen and done what you've done. To you, this war isn't just theory, something happening a long way off. It's *real.* And like she said. You could find someone in Opposition to pair your vote with and keep right on flying combat when you don't have anything important to say or do there."

"Maybe," I agreed, suddenly very tired. Perhaps I could work in a short nap after preparing my cabin for free-fall? Would I be allowed to plan even *that* far ahead, for once? "Or maybe not. Who knows?" I sighed again. "Do me a favor, Jimmy. Please?"

"Anything," he answered. "You know that."

I smiled; Jimmy was the best friend anyone could ever ask for. "Don't breathe a word of this to *anyone*. Not a soul. I need time to think, to work this through on my own."

"Sure thing," he agreed, eyes sparkling. "And I won't bring it up again either. Promise! Not unless you *want* to talk about it."

"Thanks," I answered, placing my hand on his shoulder.

"Don't sweat it," he agreed, placing his hand atop mine. "But…"

"But?" I asked.

"If you *do* run, I want to go out and campaign for you. Please?"

Chapter Twenty-Two

In a way it would've been nice if Admiral Vlasilov had chosen to fly his flag in *Almirante Cochrane* instead of *The Glorious First of June* again. *Cochrane* had been designed as a flagship from the keel up, whereas *June*, being merely a light carrier, had originally been intended to serve as little more than a fleet auxiliary. Aboard *Cochrane*, Vlasilov would've had an entire suite of offices for his staff, a larger cabin for himself, improved signaling facilities… The best of everything. But *June* was indeed the most important vessel in the Fleet, being the only one capable of operating superfighters, and apparently Vlasilov felt that keeping a close personal watch on Jimmy and I was more important than the comfort of either his staff or himself. It was good to be important, I supposed. But it would've been really cool to stay behind and watch the entire Fleet up-ship, too. It was the biggest collection of space-going ships ever assembled, and what a sight it must have been! But because *June* led the way, we missed it all.

At least I was able to watch the fleet forming up. This was a long, tedious process, complicated by the fact that the merchies weren't at all used to maneuvering in such tight confines. I spent most of an hour gazing out of my porthole once we cleared the atmosphere, but near as I could tell our formation was just as tangled a mess at the end of that period of time as at the beginning. What a shambles! Vlasilov actually had to cancel the daily situation-briefing because he needed every qualified navigator on the bridge averting last-second collisions. No one thought to tell us aviator-types that the meeting was off, however; Ted and I had been sitting alone in the briefing room for perhaps ten minutes when Commander Bard happened by. "Oh!" she said, raising her eyebrows. "Didn't you two get the word?"

By then, we'd both pretty much figured things out on our own. "No, ma'am," Ted answered; though he and Bard and I were all substantive equals in terms of rank, Michelle was much older than us two aviation-types. She was more a scholar than a naval officer, and everyone treated her more like a distinguished professor than anything else.

"I'm sorry," she answered, smiling gently. Then she pointed towards the bridge. "Everything's a mess up there. Someone screwed up when the sailing orders were issued; there's at least two different versions of them going around, and maybe three. They've just now figured that out."

"Wow," I answered, shaking my head. "What a dumb mistake!"

"We make dumb mistakes all the time," Bard pointed out. "All organizations do. The military seems to make more than their share, I know. But that's only because we're so often attempting such difficult things." She smiled. "There's not a corporation in the galaxy that could've assembled this convoy. Even the Dracans couldn't put together something like this, I'd be willing to bet. And if they did, I'll wager they'd make mistakes too."

"Maybe," I admitted, a little sourly. I didn't like it when the navy made mistakes; too often, people died.

"Every military organization in history has blundered," Bard assured us. "Even the most competent. The United States Navy, for example, made an error calculating the tides at Tarawa Atoll in 1943. People had been figuring tide tables for centuries by then. Yet somehow they miscalculated in a big, big way." She sighed. "Hundreds of marines, maybe even thousands, died over that one."

I snorted; this was hardly reassuring. But it was also interesting, as well. "What other big mistakes have navies made?"

Bard smiled. "Well… The US Navy also once sent out a large task force to bombard a Japanese garrison in the Aleutian Islands. The squadron was equipped with airplanes and state-of-the-art radar, but returned home about a week later with guns unfired because they *couldn't find the island*, even though it was United States territory and had been mapped many times."

Ted winced. "I'd hate to explain *that* one to a Board of Inquiry!"

"Heh!" Michelle agreed. "Then there was loss of a Royal Navy cruiser to a navigational hazard in 1940. She hit a rock, a charted one. The navigator, it was later determined, had drawn in the projected ship's track with a pencil. The pencil line obliterated the chart's notation of the rock so that no one knew it was there. It was most unfortunate that they happened to be *exactly* on course."

"Jeez," Ted sighed, looking out the porthole at the chaos all around us.

"The RN changed their navigational practices after that, so it couldn't happen again." She nodded out at the orbital traffic jam. "And we'll learn from this one, too. Next time, we'll do better."

"War is chaos," Ted agreed, "Or something very close to it."

"Indeed," Bard agreed. "Insane, murderous chaos. My doctorate is in military science, but I want to laugh every time I hear the words 'military' and 'science' used together like that. Sort of like 'war plans'. The terms are mutually contradictory."

My ears pricked up a little. Commander Bard was really good at explaining stuff, and I'd been thinking about Spence and Alicia a lot lately. "Are all great wartime leaders crazy?" I asked her. "Or, are most of them, even?"

The older woman blinked. "I don't know," she answered after a moment. Then she looked thoughtful. "A lot of them certainly were. I suppose it all depends on how you define 'insane'. Napoleon, for example, was a power-mad egoist. But insane? I'm not sure."

"A lot of them weren't," Ted commented. He nodded at the *Jimmy Doolittle*, closely formed up on our starboard side. "General Doolittle was a good example. He was a great warrior, yet sane as they come."

"True," Michelle agreed. "But also, not so true." She frowned, then turned to me. "General Doolittle, if you didn't know it, Thomas, was the commander of the United State's Eighth Air Force during the later years of the Second World War, when along with the RAF's Bomber Command it nearly leveled Germany. He did a good job as a General, but that's not what he's really famous for."

My eyebrows rose. "I thought that *Doolittle*-class cruisers were named for aviation pioneers," I objected. "Not generals."

"They are," Michelle reassured me. "Doolittle was also a famous air-racer and the first man to ever be awarded a degree in aeronautical engineering. He developed the world's first blind-landing system, too. But that's not what he's really famous for either."

"The Doolittle Raid?" Ted asked.

"Exactly!" Michele replied, smiling. Then she turned back to me. "Colonel Doolittle, before he became a general, once led a near-suicidal bombing raid on Japan, including the city of Tokyo, at a time when just about everyone in the world considered such a raid impossible." Her smile widened. "Like your raid on Drakkus, Thomas."

"Really?" I asked.

"Really," she assured me. "In those days, nuclear weapons hadn't been invented yet. Only a dozen or so planes participated, so there wasn't much real damage. Even worse, every single one of them was lost, at a time when there weren't planes to lose. The attack was a foolish, even stupid thing to attempt; the most effective remaining units of the US fleet were put at risk. It was only by the greatest of good luck that one or more carriers weren't lost. When the mission was over, Doolittle thought he'd be cashiered as an officer—that his career was over. And by any objective measure, he was right. It was a stupid waste of scarce resources. Instead of being cashiered, however, he received his nation's highest medal for valor."

Again like me, I didn't say aloud. "Why?" I asked.

"Because this irrational little pinprick of a raid ultimately did more to win the war for America than any other single military action," Michele explained. "The Japanese were deeply shamed, and reacted with equal irrationality to Doolittle's foolishness. They'd already achieved all of their primary war aims, but decided to push things one island further, to prevent any more such humiliating, albeit harmless, attacks. In doing so, they risked their entire fleet, just like the US had. But, the Japanese weren't so lucky."

"Midway," Ted interjected. "Their three finest carriers sunk, with all their best pilots."

"Four, actually," Bard corrected him gently. "And a heavy cruiser." Then she turned back to me. "So, Thomas, your question is actually a very complicated one."

I nodded. "Then, you're saying that it *does* help to be crazy."

"Maybe," she acknowledged. "I *can* say that war is a human activity, and that I believe that all humans are fundamentally irrational creatures. Indeed, war is probably the most irrational human activity of all." She frowned. "It wouldn't surprise me at all if a certain kind of madness were a vital military asset, now that I think about it." Her face brightened. "You know, I may actually write a paper on this!"

"Heh!" I laughed, smiling back at her. "What about peacetime, Commander?" I asked. "Do great wartime leaders make good peacetime leaders?"

"Almost never," she answered, her smile fading. "That question, at least, is one that's easy to answer. The history books are full of examples. Great wartime leaders, both military and civilian, tend to be seen as too abrasive and extremist in peacetime. They rise to high rank when the shooting starts, often with meteoric speed. Once the war is over, they're usually eased into quiet, honorable dead-end jobs where they don't have any real power anymore. The previous leadership moves back into place, and it's back to business as usual."

"Great trainers and great administrators usually don't make great leaders," Ted observed. "And vice-versa. At least, that's what Dad used to say." He smiled. "Dad's definitely a leader, not an administrator. And, it shows. Most of his classmates outrank him. Or they did the last I heard. That may have changed recently. Probably has, I bet."

"There's nothing rational about war," Bard added. "Or about leadership, or determination, or courage…" She frowned. "I think you're right, Thomas. The great ones *were* usually a bit mad. What a crazy universe we live in!"

Chapter Twenty-Three

The United Systems might be led by a madwoman, and certainly the Dracans weren't any better off. War might well be the maddest act of an incurably insane species, and surely I wasn't anything resembling a normal eighteen-year-old kid anymore, whatever normal was. But none of that had much of anything to do with anything, in terms of day-to-day life. Or at least it didn't that I could see. If we were all mad, if even the universe itself was mad, then the insanity was on such a huge scale that one didn't tend to notice. I had meetings to attend, plans to make, reports to study… It was enough to drive me crazy!

There were good things too, though. For example, Jimmy and I each had a brand-new Skybolt Mark I* to familiarize ourselves with and then evaluate for combat. We took a lot longer at the job than we really should've, I suppose, though it'd been so long since our last flight that we probably needed the stick-time anyway. The fleet's sailing orders were so badly screwed up that it took two entire days to sort everything out and get everyone flying in the same direction at the same time. Since we were still nice and close to Esteppe, where our antigravs had plenty of bite, I asked for and got permission to set up an area of clear space for Jimmy and I to really wring out the 'bolts in. Even better, Vlasilov detached *Cochrane* and *Graf Zeppelin* to work with us. We used them as targets, while in return they got tons of gunnery practice simulating firing back at us. It was fun! One thing we noticed right away was that *Cochrane*'s small close-defense guns couldn't traverse fast enough to follow us at very short range, though *Zeppelin*'s Esteppan-designed mounts, the ones the navy had originally rejected, could. *Cochrane* might as well have been throwing spitballs at us once we closed within a mile or so, for all the harm her guns could do us. This gave the navy's tactical geniuses a lot to think about, or so we heard later. From the perspective of we 'bolt pilots, however, it didn't really matter. We were planning on flying against Dracan-made mounts, and no one knew if getting in close against them would work or not. We'd never tried it. And finding out could be very, very expensive.

Another thing that Jimmy and I learned while making mock attacks on *Cochrane* and *Zeppelin* was that modern, up-to-date designs were a *lot* more deadly than the older ships we'd mostly taken on up until then. Even *Imperial Throne*'s weren't festooned with light mounts the way that the latest United Systems vessels were. *Cochrane* shot me down in simulation a good half-dozen times out of fifty or so attacks, and pegged Jimmy even more frequently. But *Zeppelin* was the real star of the exercises; while we 'bolts still had a better than even chance of destroying her before she got us, we'd *never* come up against such a difficult target. It was like trying to fly up a fire hose without getting wet, she put so many laser-bolts into the air! God help the Dracan who attacked either her or whatever she was escorting, I decided, especially if they weren't flying a superfighter. Some navy types had been eyeing the kill-tally on the side of my fighter's nose and saying that the capital ship was obsolete. *Zeppelin* was proof that for every new weapon there was a counter. Even *Cochrane* was a difficult target; re-equip her with *Zeppelin*-pattern guns and she'd make a terrible foe indeed.

As expected, the new 'bolts were indeed a shade less handy than our old mounts. The additional weight was small, but located far from the airframe's center of gravity. *Zeppelin* and *Cochrane* both claimed that we were slightly easier targets in our new rides. Yet, the Mark I*'s additional firepower was the best answer we had to all the repeated head-on fighter attacks we'd found ourselves facing while in actual combat. Jimmy and Ted and I talked long and hard about which to choose, then firmly decided not to make a decision after all. *June* was carrying a full complement of a dozen 'bolt support teams, though most of them were fresh out of training and lacked experience. There wasn't a reason in the world we could see why they shouldn't keep all four Skybolts airworthy instead of just two, so that we could hold our options open until the last possible minute. If it looked like there'd be enemy fighters present, we'd fly the Mark I*'s. If not, we'd go with the more agile Mark I's. If we *still* weren't sure… Well, I'd flip a coin or something. In the meantime, since we were still in orbit I was able to call up Father and let him know that overall I considered the Mark I* to be a success.

"The best solution," I suggested, "would be if one flight in each squadron was equipped with I*'s. They could fly cover for the rest."

"Ja," Father answered, sounding a bit smug. "I told the navy you'd say that once you'd flown one, but they didn't want to hear it. It's a good thing I set up the pre-production planning *my* way!"

I smiled, even though we were on a sound-only connection. The security was better on those. "How's Sven?" I asked. "Has he seen the docs yet?"

There was a short silence. "He's very tired," Father answered. "Designing the decoys took an awful lot out of him. He's resting now, and Gunther's helping carry his load. Good old Gunther! I'm so glad he's still with us!"

His cheerful tone didn't sound in the least bit genuine, at least not to my experienced ear. "Father," I said slowly. "You didn't answer my question."

"He asked me not to tell you anything," my father replied. "Sven doesn't want you to worry about him, with all the risks you're taking yourself. Most of the tests were inconclusive, and so far it appears that he's in no serious danger." There was a long pause. "Please, Thomas. Honor his request, and ask no more. He's a hero too, you know."

Suddenly there was a lump in my throat, artificial body or no. "Right," I agreed, switching back to "business" mode the way my family always did when feelings ran a little too high. "One flight per squadron, I think. Plus the staff flight, of course."

"Of course," Father agreed, his own "business" voice also up and running as if nothing at all was wrong. "I've recorded this call, and will play it for the procurement people first thing tomorrow morning. They'll accept your judgment, I think. I mean, who else are they going to ask?" There was a long pause. "Well," he said eventually. "I suppose this is goodbye, then."

"For now," I reassured him. "I'll be back."

"You will," he agreed, though it was more a prayer than a statement of fact. "And, Sven will be fine, as well. We Longos are practically indestructible. Don't you worry a minute about him!"

I nodded, even though the gesture was invisible. "Please, tell him how much I love and respect him." It was my turn to pause. "As much as I love and respect you."

There was a sharp intake of breath; it must be very hard, I realized suddenly, to be facing the likely loss of two children at once. "And we love you, Thomas. Both of us. Come back to us, son. And make our family whole."

Chapter Twenty-Four

Regular briefings didn't resume until our little traffic snarl was cleared up and we were well on our way out of Esteppan space. At the very first one, Admiral Vlasilov introduced our new flag captain, Rosalind Jones of New Harlem. No one made any mention of the old flag captain, an affable old man who loved to tell long-winded jokes. He'd been responsible for the botched sailing orders that'd delayed us for two precious days, we all knew, and that was that. The less said the better. Captain Jones stood, smiled, sat down again, and the incident was behind us. Nothing much had changed on the status board, except that our ships were now in transit instead of waiting afloat.

"Our force consists of this ship, one modern dreadnought, five heavy cruisers, three light cruisers of which two are of the superior new pattern, nine destroyers of which five are *Chief*-class, and one hundred and seventeen merchantmen." Vlasilov smiled. "For those who are wondering-- yes, this is indeed the biggest convoy ever assembled. Even the Dracan invasion convoys weren't so large." A little rumble of conversation passed over the room.

"These merchantmen," the admiral continued, speaking over the voices, "represent almost six typical months worth of trade for Earth. The ships contain food, raw materials, ores, medicines… Everything that the mother world has been screaming for." He scowled. "It's taken us weeks to assemble this much tonnage. Interstellar trade elsewhere in the United Systems has come to a standstill for lack of these bottoms." He gestured at the big pipper in the front of the room, which showed a live image of the great assemblage. "This is it. All. Everything we have. There are no reserves." His eyes turned to ice. "We will *not* lose these ships. No matter what. This is our prime mission, getting these ships through to Earth whole and undamaged. Everything else, including our own survival, is secondary. Is this understood?"

"Yes, sir!" someone from a few rows up called out, and Vlasilov nodded in satisfaction.

"Very good," he continued, eyes still cold. He walked over to the pipper and hit a switch. Instantly the view changed to an image of the New Nippon system.

I felt my upper lip curl in revulsion; the place was absolutely *swarming* with Dracans!

"This is smuggled imagery of our enemy's deployments," he continued, picking up a pointer-stick. "It's roughly two weeks old, but the pattern hasn't changed for over a month now." He pointed at a long line of capital ships . "Here's their main body. The entire Dracan battle-line of seven older dreadnoughts, minus the surviving *Imperial Throne* class vessel. She's been missing for some time, and we suspect that the Dracan High command is holding her back against more tip-and-run raids due to her high speed. Frankly, however, they don't *need* the *Throne* out here anymore. Not after destroying our own nearly all of our own battleships." He waved his pointer up and down the battle-line. "See how they've lined up, so as the cross the 'T' of any force entering via Nikita Two? Though this display doesn't show it, they're keeping their turrets bearing on the hyperspace point at all times, twenty-four seven." He lowered the pointer and tapped absently at the crisp seam in his trousers. "Ladies and gentlemen, Nikita Two is closed. We couldn't force it if we were twice as strong as we are, and even then we'd be fools to challenge that kind of firepower at such a positional disadvantage."

His frown deepened as he turned back to the pipper. "The situation at Number One isn't much better. The Dracans have concentrated their light forces there, the smaller ships heavy on torpedo armament. They've done this because Number One is close enough to Number Two for the battle-line to offer support." He swung the pointer reminding us how close together the Nikita's were at New Nippon.

"Jeez," Ted whispered in my ear. "That's worse than anything we've gamed out."

"Yeah," I whispered back.

"That leaves only Nikita Number Three," Vlaslov continued, "which stands further out from the primary than the other two." He frowned, then gestured with his pointer. "It's guarded only by a pair of destroyers. This is mostly to provide warning, one would assume, and to close the Point to unarmed merchant shipping. It'd be a relatively simple matter for us to enter the system by means of Number Three. It's even the most direct route; there's fewer Jumps between here and there by that route. But, of course, that's exactly what the Dracan Admiral *wants* us to do."

I nodded slowly; after so much time in the navy and a few classes, I was beginning to understand this kind of stuff. If we entered the New Nippon system via Number Three, the Dracans would have time to combine their forces and effect an intercept in overwhelming force. The outcome would be almost as one-sided as the slaughter of the Training Fleet.

"So," Vlasilov continued, his frown deepening, "We must choose between the line of battle at Number Two and the torpedo-equipped force at Number One." He lowered his pointer and looked at the floor. "Both, frankly, are more than a match for us. But, we feel that we're more likely to get at least some of the merchantmen through if we fight the light forces and then run for Number Four, towards Earth. That way the deadliest threats of all, the big guns, are kept at long range."

This time, there was no buzz of conversation. Finally, an officer in the front row raised his hand. "There'll be dozens of torpedoes, sir," he pointed out. "Maybe even hundreds."

"Da," Vlasilov agreed, nodding soberly. "That there will." He nodded to me. "Our fighter pilots will be instructed to destroy as many torpedo-carrying vessels as possible. They'll do all that they can, I'm certain. But it won't be enough." He grasped the pointer in both hands and held it backhanded across his chest. "There will be casualties. *Many* casualties. Still, the convoy *must* get through."

There was another long silence, then another hand went up.

"Sir," the female officer began when Vlasilov nodded at her. "We fought an entire campaign to deprive the Dracans of molecular batteries and the bottoms they need to ship them, in the hope of making the New Nippon system untenable for them. We even hit their homeworld, trying to force them to fall back." The woman shook her head. "And yet they're still there. Have our efforts had any effect at all?"

Vlasilov's eyebrows rose, then he turned to Commander Bard. "Would you care to field that one?" he asked.

Michelle's cheeks reddened slightly; the anti-battery campaign was her brainchild, and she still couldn't figure out why it hadn't worked. "Yes, sir," she said, standing up and walking down a long row of seats to the center aisle. Then she turned to face the entire room. "The fact is that we don't understand how the Dracans are maintaining such a strong presence so far from home. Logistics is supposed to be a fairly exact science; it takes so many bottoms to carry so many batteries across so much space. The Dracans simply don't have enough tonnage to support their fleet anymore, at least not where it's at. Something should've given, but nothing has." She shrugged. "The admiral noted that the *Throne*-class dreadnought is missing. *Throne*s are huge battery-hogs; I personally suspect that she was withdrawn for logistic, not strategic reasons. Plus, our intelligence shows that the Dracans are going to extremes to make their batteries last; there's been no live-fire drill, for example, and ships move only rarely." She pointed at the Dracan battle line. "In fact," she continued, "if you look closely, you'll see that their dreadnought formation is somewhat ragged and uneven; we presume that's because it takes power to keep things neat." She smiled slightly. "Imagine the kind of supply pressure it'd take to make a battleship admiral willingly accept a ragged formation, and you'll gain a deeper appreciation of how short on power the Dracans must be."

"Heh!" the female officer replied, smiling as well. Battleship admirals were notorious for being spit-and-polish sticklers, especially about formations. Even *I* knew how anal they could be! Then her face sobered again. "How will this impact the battle?"

"We can't know," Michelle replied. "We just don't have enough facts." She shrugged. "By our reckoning, the Dracans should've fallen back long ago. So you can see how reliable our projections are. While it's certain there'll be at least *some* impact, even if it's merely a slightly slower rate of fire due to the lack of drill, there's too much that we just don't know." She shrugged again. "Ma'am, your guess is as good as mine."

Chapter Twenty-Five

Michelle's guess was probably as good as Ted's and my own as well, even though we spent hours studying up on the Dracans. Not only did we read hundreds of pages of the most boring intelligence reports imaginable, but we stared at the smuggled pipper-image for so long that one morning, while Father Murton was scrubbing my face, I swear I saw the Dracan fleet's tactical disposition in the soap bubbles floating in the sink.

"There aren't any carriers," Ted observed for perhaps the ten-thousandth time. "But that doesn't mean there won't be fighters."

I nodded; the Dracans had invaded New Nippon and probably had taken over the bases there. "But... Why would they station fighters anywhere but Earth, where they're needed so badly?"

"Touché," Ted agreed his half-face long and mournful. Even ordinary Dracan fighters could operate near the New Nippon Nikitas, in part because of the proximity of the big gas giant. My co-commander sighed and pushed away his pile of papers. "Thomas, we can guess all day. But, we can't really know what to expect. There's just not enough data."

I nodded in agreement. "We can make contingency plans, sure. And we should. But unless we can figure out what's in the enemy's mind, we're going to have to be reactive. And, that's a bad thing." Being reactive, by definition, meant that the enemy would control the circumstances of the engagement. More often than not, that was a particularly effective way to lose. "So, let's look at our orders one more time," I continued, reaching for a particularly well-worn paper. "The primary mission," I read, "will be to safeguard the merchantmen and relieve Earth. All other considerations shall be secondary to this goal."

Ted frowned. "You'll have to take out as any destroyers as you can, just like the admiral said back at the briefing. Unless...."

I frowned as well. "Unless there's fighters around. They're even more dangerous than the destroyers, particularly superfghters."

There was another long silence. Finally, Ted broke it. "All right," he said, slapping the tabletop with his palm. "This isn't getting us anywhere. Put yourself in the Dracan's shoes. If you were their C-in-C, where would *your* superfighters be stationed?"

"They have to defeat Earth to win the war," I replied slowly. "Either starve her out or beat her into submission. That's what'll decide everything. Everyone thinks so, including Father."

Ted nodded, but said nothing.

"So," I continued, gazing out the porthole at where *Jimmy Doolittle* was holding her customarily tight formation, "I imagine I'd either station them at New Nippon or at Earth itself. Earth still has a Polecat force, a substantial one. It's no picnic to attack a planet that has lots of air cover, even old-style air cover." Ted nodded, understanding that I knew this from personal experience. "They *could* be at Earth," I reasoned. "It'd make perfect sense. But, look at it from their point of view. They *know* any superfighters we have will fight at New Nippon, right? I mean, we'd be crazy *not* to use them."

"That's true enough," Ted replied, his mismatched natural and artificial eyes meeting mine.

"Their fleet's at New Nippon," I continued, still not quite sure where I was going. "That's where they're going to make their stand, and rightly so. If they're already short on batteries, why strain their logistics one Jump further, when all Earth traffic has to go through the Nippon Nexus anyway?" I shook my head. "I predict that all we'll find at Earth are troop transports and carriers loaded with regular fighters. No more than *has* to be there, to alleviate the battery shortage."

"So far, I'm with you," Ted agreed. "That's certainly how I'd do things."

I shook my head and sighed. "So, there's going to be a decisive battle. Both sides know where, if not when." I looked down at the pipper-image and the seemingly-impenetrable line of Dracan dreadnoughts. "If you were the Dracan admiral, would *you* willingly do without your own equivalent of the enemy's most effective weapon?"

"No," Ted agreed after a long time. "Even more, in his shoes I wouldn't let you and Jimmy and heaven knows how many more like you zoom around and shoot up my fleet without opposition. Not if there was anything at all I could do about it."

I nodded. "Then the superfighters *will* be there. Agreed?"

Ted's head bobbed as well. "Yes. And if they're there, it only stands to reason that there'll be a substantial force of regular fighters to support them and back them up. In for a penny, in for a pound." He tapped the pipper-image with his finger. "All based right there. On New Nippon."

I nodded slowly. "It's too bad there's no Resistance there yet. Or else maybe we could blow them up on the ground."

Ted nodded. "They didn't have a Spencer Wiston to make things happen quickly. Men like that don't grow on trees. Maybe in a few more months."

"Maybe," I agreed. "But, it doesn't matter. We won't be waiting that long." I frowned and studied the enemy dispositions some more. "We have a lot of advantages on our side," I pointed out. "For one, even at superfighter speeds it'll take them a good ten minutes to scramble a 'hopper all the way out to

Number Two. And that's assuming they've got birds on alert status." I closed my eyes, remembering how tedious it'd been to be an 'alert' bird.

"There's no way they can maintain standing patrols," Ted agreed. "Not only would that eat batteries, but it'd also wear down pilots and hardware. And there's the maintenance issues, too, of course. Those are probably even worse for them, with first-generation tech."

I nodded. "They can't have more than two or three birds at most. Not after we shot down their prototypes and nuked so much of their homeworld."

"We might even have gotten the factory. In which case we're worried about nothing. But, that'd be *too* lucky."

I shook my head. We were *never* that lucky. "Two or three birds. Maybe more pilots, especially if any of the ones we shot down over Drakkus survived." My eyebrows rose. "Which is different from how things were for us on Esteppe. We had the same numbers of 'hoppers as pilots at first, and then right at the end more birds than pilots. Still more birds than pilots, really. So, we could maintain a continuous alert force." I smiled. "But…"

Ted's half-grin matched my own. "The Dracan's won't be able to, with so few birds. No 'hopper can fly with a half-installed pilot. It takes us almost an hour to do that. And that's with a 'bolt. It takes even longer in a Stormcrow, because your father has refined the design since then." His grin widened. "We have roughly two hours a day, then, during which they can't launch."

I nodded. "Do we have any intelligence on when the Dracans traditionally change watches?" I asked. "If so…"

Ted slapped his palm on the table. "If so, we can try to hit the Nikita right at the most likely time for their super-birds to be out of service!" He shook his head. "Wouldn't *that* be a pisser for them?"

"Yep," I agreed, trying to picture the look on Admiral Vlasilov's face should such a terrible misfortune overtake him. It wouldn't be pretty.

Suddenly Ted's hands became a blur of motion as he began developing a mission profile. "So… We'll give you two a full load-out, four torps apiece. You hit the light forces hard and fast, like the admiral wants, during the ten minutes we're sure you'll have before the Dracans can interfere. Then you whack the airfields."

"Right," I agreed. "We smoke as many warships as we can, then try to catch the superfighters on the ground, changing pilots. On the way in we'll avoid air battle as much as possible, just like we did on the Drakkus raid." I smiled. "We won't have time to re-arm with more torps anyway, most likely. And, I bet we'll tie up every single enemy fighter. Or, most of them at least. Every one that chases us, at any rate, is one fewer that attacks the merchantmen."

"Yep!" Ted agreed, scribbling madly. Then he raised his head and looked me in the eye again/ "You'll be flying the Mark I*'s, I presume?" he asked. "In anticipation of air battles?"

I thought about it for a moment. If we flew the Mark I's, we'd be slightly more likely to survive the anti-ship phase of the mission. But, overall… "Yeah," I agreed. "Why not?"

"We can schedule you more simulation time with them," Ted suggested, scribbling away again. "And put them in the hands of our best ground crews."

"Good," I agreed, feeling a little better now that at last some of the key decisions had been made. "Besides, it'll make Jimmy happy."

"How so?" my copilot's elder brother asked, not looking up from his paperwork.

"Two cannon," I explained. "Shooting a gun is always fun, but it's even better when the gun is literally part of you." I smiled again. "It feels, well… powerful. Very different from a simulated run. And, ever since he first laid eyes on those oversized twins, Jimmy's been dying to know what it's like to cut loose with both of them at once."

Chapter Twenty-Six

I'd felt very much an outsider when I'd first spaced aboard *The Glorious First of June*. Which was natural enough, I supposed, since I'd pretty much been exactly that. While I'd learned a little about the navy via my demonstration tours, I'd never planned to ever actively be involved in the Fleet. So, while I'd known a bit back then about recognizing rank designations and what a squadron commander did for a living, I wasn't *part* of things. Everything had been a sort of confusing swirl as the ratings performed mysterious functions and bells rang for no reason that I could discern. Not only had practically all the faces been strange, but the essentials of the culture itself had been beyond me. I'd been a stranger in a strange land, trying to keep out from underfoot when not called upon to make my own unique contribution.

Things were very different nowadays. Instead of getting lost all of the time, I wandered *June's* corridors with as much confidence as I'd once canoed the backwaters of Father's Louisiana estate. When ratings waved and smiled, as often as not I waved back and called them by name. Slowly, bit by bit, I'd become part of the living organism that was *The Glorious First of June*.

So it was that I was able to sense the ship's mood as we winged through space towards a rendezvous with the Dracans that none of us really wanted to keep. At first, everyone was taut and nervous and slightly out of sorts, as new shipmates were assimilated and the complex interlocking web of duties and responsibilities re-established itself. There was fear in the air during those early days; I could almost smell it as I wandered the ship in the course of my duties. Then things began to work themselves out. The new crewmen settled in, helped along by the not-so-subtle posturing and cursing of the petty officers. Roles and relationships were settled, reducing the stress level. The ship's chaplain spent a lot of time in the crew's mess talking to the sailors about this and that, but mostly about why the Dracans needed to be beaten and sacrifices had to be made. Slowly the various ship's departments solidified their plans, as Ted and I had already done. Nothing, I'd already learned, was better for morale than a battle-plan. Once you had a plan, you could drill and think ahead and work constructively towards increasing the odds of victory instead of just sitting around waiting for panic to set in. As one by one, the various departments began drilling, drilling, drilling, it was as if a great poisonous cloud was filtered from *June*'s atmosphere and vented into space. Where once there had been fear, soon there was confidence. Where once there had been chaos there could now be found calm resolve. Where once there had been doubt, well... Neither Admiral Vlasilov nor the chaplain tried to hide the fact that our casualties were going to be awful. It wasn't realistic for anyone to assume they were going to survive the battle; most of us were veterans and knew better. But what we *could* do was be fatalistic and then resolve to go down fighting.

Me? I made out a last will and testament for the first time ever, leaving everything except a few personal items to Father and Sven. Then I privately promised myself that if I had to die, I'd take enough Dracans with me to make Colonel Rotte jealous. Horrido! Kill them all!

"Well, Thomas," Father Murton said as he was undressing me on our last night of transit. "You seem calm enough."

I shrugged. "It's my third major mission," I answered. "I won't say I'm not scared, because I am. But, combat isn't something new to me anymore. I already *know* how awful it can be." I shrugged again. "I'm either a veteran or else I'm crazy. Take your pick. If there's a difference, that is."

"Heh!" Father Murton replied, eyes twinkling as he put away my shirt. "You're growing up fast, Thomas. It's a little frightening, really."

I smiled back. Father Murton had done so much for me, for so long. He'd been featured prominently in my will, of course. I'd left all kinds of sentimental stuff to him, things that I hoped would remind him of special times we'd had together. Like my primary-school diploma, for example, which he'd help me celebrate with a memorable day at the San Diego Zoo. But still... Suddenly it didn't seem like enough. "I... I love you, Father Murton," I heard myself blurt, probably apropos of nothing from his point of view. "And I'm grateful for all the wonderful things you've done for me. Thank you so very, very much."

The old man froze midway through opening my closet door. He looked hurt more than anything, though I knew that wasn't the case at all. "I love you too, Thomas," he answered, his voice betraying only the slightest of quavers. "You've been the greatest blessing I've ever known. There isn't any need to thank me for anything. The luckiest and best day of my life was when the court appointed me to be your guardian while your father was on trial and your brother was still a POW. The second-luckiest was when your father chose to keep me on when he could've chosen from any of dozens of old family retainers." He smiled, even though his eyes were filled with tears. "I loved you before you were a famous hero, Thomas. I loved you before you could walk, even. And all you've done since is fill me with pride at the man you've become and convince me that not a single effort was wasted."

I didn't know what to say. But it didn't matter, really, because before I could stutter and make a fool of myself my shirt was fluttering to the floor and

Father Murton was hugging me as tight as he could and weeping his eyes out. "Come back!" he wept. "Please, Thomas! Don't take any more chances than you have to. Come back, safe and sound! You're needed, son! *Needed!*"

I couldn't cry actual tears anymore, but my brain was still fully human. It was flooded with whatever the chemistry of sadness was, so that my not-eyes burned and my throat, which didn't even pass air anymore, seemed to close up tight. But it was okay that I couldn't weep, for Father Murton shed enough tears for the two of us. "We need you," he muttered over and over. "All of us, we need you. Our last, best hope."

Then, after a very long time, it was over. Rather embarrassed, my counselor hung up the dropped shirt and I retreated to my bedroom. "Are you ready, Thomas?" the priest eventually asked from our shared living space.

I nodded, knowing exactly what my tutor was referring to. He was honoring a special request I'd made a few days earlier for the evening before combat. "Forgive me, Father," I began, reciting the ancient formula as my counselor entered the room. "For I have sinned."

Chapter Twenty-Seven

The lead ship of our formation, the heavy cruiser *Orleans*, was scheduled to enter New Nippon space at precisely sixteen-hundred hours, the time we'd determined would probably be most awkward for the Dracan superfighters. *Orleans* was an older vessel, equipped with thick armor but otherwise not of much fighting value anymore. Her role was more to soak up lots of Dracan firepower than to do any damage in her own right; it'd take a little time for our enemies to kill her, we reckoned. During that time more fleet units would pop through behind her, out of the line of fire. Then the fight would begin in earnest.

Everything always seemed to happen in slow motion when I was a Skybolt and just sitting around waiting. It was bad enough when I was an alert bird, but knowing for sure that combat was in the offing just made things that much worse. I checked my four antiship missiles for perhaps the twentieth time; they were still green. Then I activated my tail-camera and looked down the line of five specially-designed decoys that would come off the rail behind me. I still loved the fact that they carried warheads; my eldest brother was going to get a very special thank-you when I saw him next. *The Glorious First of June* was scheduled to hit the Nikita about halfway through our train of warships, protected by *Graf Zeppelin*, *Jimmy Doolittle*, and *Almirante Cochrane*. Though there were other carriers building all around the United Systems, for the moment *June* was our only space-capable platform capable of operating superfighters. This made her the most valuable vessel in the fleet.

"It's a shame we can't hit the Nikita at high vector," Ted groused in my ear for about the tenth time. It took special equipment and training to nail a Nikita while moving fast, equipment and training that not only was lacking on all the merchies, but some of the older fleet units as well. Indeed, *no one* had been able to do a transition at high speed until just a couple of years ago. I clicked my mike twice in acknowledgement, then swung my wingtip camera over towards Jimmy's 'bolt. "You as nervous as I am?" I asked on our private channel.

"Twice as," he replied; it wasn't hard at all to picture the grin that should've come along with the words. "This waiting is the worst part."

"Yeah," I agreed. "I still don't like the idea of not having you covering my six, Jimmy. It makes me nervous, not having you back there." For the first part of our mission, each of us was going to lead a "flight" of decoys which hopefully would divide the enemy fire. Any survivors would then be used to attack the enemy, making use of the warheads. Until then the Dracans would think they were facing a dozen superfighters, not just two. How would they react? My friend and I would be among the very first to know.

"I'll find you when it's time," my wingman assured me. "Believe you me, I will! You always find the best targets, and I don't want to miss any good opportunities."

"Heh!" I replied, clicking my mike twice in appreciation of the compliment. I wasn't yet half as good as Colonel Rotte at being at the right place at the right time, but I was working on it. "Good luck, Jimmy!"

"And to you, Tommy! Kill them all!"

"Kill them all!" I agreed. Then I switched off. There was only a minute or two left, so I brought up the special camera-link that'd been provided to key personnel for this mission. It enabled me to see through the nose-camera on *Orleans*, or at least it would until she Jumped. All it currently showed, however, was a still very distant triangle of blue blinking lights.

"Good luck, Thomas!" Father Murton called out to me on his channel. He almost never used it, so I fumbled a bit trying to activate the right reply-mode.

"Thanks!" I answered, my mind mostly on the view from *Orleans*. Any second now... "See you later!"

Then there was a flash of space-warp induced light, something I'd never seen before because less-antiquated drive units didn't create the effect. It was beautiful, a sort of green cascading curtain that pulsed and throbbed in a million shapes that felt like they should make sense but somehow didn't. For just a fraction of a second I could make out the distinctive hump-backed shapes of Dracan fleet units through the green fog...

...and then everything went dark, as *Orleans* was suddenly I'd never bothered to find out how many light-years away and far out of communications range. Just for an instant, however, we'd received a priceless, precious image. I waited patiently as the image-techs first found the single frame, then displayed it again for me even as they were still enhancing it and cleaning things up.

Good Lord! *Orleans* had Jumped right down the throats of five Dracan light cruisers!

"Jeez!" Jimmy protested as the Nikita flared over and over again, this time from Dracan salvoes slamming home on the far side. "They are *so* dead!"

I didn't reply, there not being much to say. *Orleans* was manned by an all-volunteer crew, most of them with family on occupied worlds. Every effort would be made to rescue the brave vessel's survivors. If any. "Those five cruisers are yours," I decided. It was better to give Jimmy the sure target, the one easiest to locate. "I'll find something else. There shouldn't be any shortage of Dracans."

"Roger," Jimmy acknowledged.

Then it was the turn of an entire squadron of *Chief*-class destroyers to pound their way through, lean, mean and two abreast despite the tight confines of the Nikita. It was their mission to blast a hole for the rest of us by virtue of speed, torpedoes and sheer ferocity. The flashes grew a lot brighter after they passed through; one Dracan salvo, timed just right, passed through the Point intact and went flying off into the eternal black.

We were next. *Cochrane, Zeppelin, Doolittle* and *June* formed line ahead, and together we raced for the Nikita just as fast as our drives would carry us. We were the most modern units present aside from the *Chief*s; the heart of our force. While we would've preferred a less risky approach, it had soon become apparent during our planning sessions that unless *Cochrane*'s big guns and we Skybolts got into the fight and starting doing damage early on, our side didn't stand a chance.

The Nikita was flashing and flickering something fierce as we closed in on it, resonating from the colossal energy discharges taking place just on its other side. It flared up *huge* just before *Cochrane* disappeared; most likely, I guessed, a torpedo had struck home. Then the big dreadnought flickered and vanished, we traveled a few more critical yards…

…and, with the usual flash of nausea, we'd made our Jump!

"Launch! Launch! Launch!" cried the deck officer; it was his job to get us off the rails and into battle just as quickly as humanly possible and he was bound and determined not to be found wanting. I felt a tremendous tug on my nosegear, raced down the little shaft at twenty gees of acceleration, and then found myself in the middle of a confused space battle so quickly that my head would've spun, if I'd had one.

"Whoa!" I cried out on the common frequency as I broke left just as hard as I could; if I hadn't, I'd have rammed the hard-stricken *Cochise* just ahead of her engine room, probably destroying us both. It was *Cochise* who'd taken the torpedo that'd flared the Nikita, I could see from her still-glowing damage, and now she was out of control and reeling all over the sky right at the point of maximum traffic congestion. How had she been targeted so quickly, I wondered? It was supposed to be impossible to acquire and aim that fast. The Dracans must have simply fired a salvo at the Point, and hoped. Whatever they'd done, clearly it'd paid off for them.

Even though I'd been in the fight no more than a few seconds and had made my first violent maneuver, a few precocious Dracans were already firing at me and coming uncomfortably close to the bull's eye. I broke left again, then spared my rear cameras a glance. Sure enough, the decoys had found me and were forming up as if they were real Skybolts. Even I couldn't tell the difference at this angle. "Blue flight, blue flight," I heard Jimmy intone, to help make the illusion complete in case anyone was listening. "Form on me."

"Red flight," I echoed. "Prepare for attack!"

Sure enough, the sky was chock-full of targets. It was also filled with defensive guns, however, and searing laser-bolts freshly fired from said guns. My pipper wasn't registering yet, but I really didn't need it what with so much action taking place so close at hand. The Dracans were still formed up into a rough line, though there was an empty slot where one of their light cruisers was already missing. I swung a camera back along the vanished Dracan's vector to see if maybe there was a cripple that needed finishing off. But, no, I realized with a gulp. There was no cripple at all. Just two hulks welded together from the force of what must have been a truly colossal impact.

One of the hulks was *Orleans*; apparently her captain had elected to ram. There could've been no survivors on either side.

Not that there was time to look for survivors, not just then. I was looping and whirling and dodging laser-bolts coming from three sides, even as I negotiated a particularly difficult salvo one of the decoys behind me flared and died. The electronic pilots were very simpleminded-- they had to be in order to operate at all near an antigrav motor-- and therefore the fake Skybolts couldn't last long in combat. This would become especially true once the air-to-air fighting began. It was up to me, therefore, to take advantage of them while I could.

Just astern of the light cruisers lurked a full squadron of destroyers, still not engaged except for firing at me. They were just beginning to pile on vector for a torpedo run on *June* and company. I gritted my virtual teeth and swung my nose-heavy Mark I* towards the lead ship, positioning myself so that my decoys and I were running right down his throat. Destroyers were smaller than cruisers, yes, and therefore under normal conditions were less desirable targets. Typically, however, destroyers carried two or three times as many torps as a cruiser since the latter carried a set of heavy guns as their primary weapons. This would be a torpedo fight, primarily, and the more torps I could destroy before launching the better. So under the circumstances, destroyers were fine by me. What did I care if the pictures they'd eventually paint on my nose-cone were a little smaller, if I was helping win the war?

The Dracan destroyer-squadron leader might've been brave, but he wasn't suicidal. Instead of accepting my challenge, he swung hard to. If we'd begun the engagement at anything but point-blank range, his evasion might even have worked. As things were, however, we started out practically at knife-fighting quarters; I hardly aimed as I released a torp on the flagship and then another on the next Dracan in line, who was dutifully if foolishly following in his superior's track. There were two brilliant flashes in quick succession, and then I was by them, swinging around for another pass.

"Splash a cruiser!" I heard Jimmy call out excitedly. "Splash one!"

"And two destroyers!" I added. "Horrido!" It would've been nice to check the pipper, to see which cruiser Jimmy had sunk so that I could perhaps take advantage of the savaged formation. For that matter, it would have been *really* nice to know where the Dracan line-of-battle was and who it was engaging. But, the pipper *still* wasn't updated; had the battle so far really been so short?

This time I was running down the destroyers from behind. They were fast ships by starfaring-vessel standards, but nothing to a Skybolt with a nearby gas-giant to provide a mass-anchor. This time the two leftovers broke in opposite directions, one of them vectoring directly across the course of yet another destroyer squadron barreling in for the attack. I chose to let the badly-maneuvering Dracan live, as a sort of reverse-Darwin thing, and instead squeezed off a single torp towards the ship that had turned in the correct direction. Instantly the destroyer cut thrust and slewed sideways through space. It was a beautiful thing, as pretty as watching a dancer leap and twirl. But, pretty or not, it hurt to see my torp glide harmlessly past. "Damn!" I cursed; it was my first war-shot miss. And because of it, the Dracans would have another eight or ten torpedoes to fire into the helpless merchies!

I was down to one torp now, but there wasn't the slightest doubt in my mind as to where I wanted to place it. That Dracan destroyerman was *good*, and I didn't want to have to fight him again another day. Once was plenty enough, thankyouverymuch. Angrily I did an Immelman, followed by my surviving decoys. I'd lost another along the way, I realized, though I hadn't noticed the explosion among all the other fireworks filling the sky. Given the volume of fire, the decoys were probably the only reason that Jimmy and I were still alive. I was headed back towards the Nikita now, and there were the merchies, plodding through one by one into what must've seemed to them like Armageddon unleashed. There were torpedoes exploding, laser-bolts seemingly everywhere...

...and where are the big rounds from the Dracan dreadnoughts? I asked myself suddenly. They were surely within range. Why weren't *they* killing ships, too? These were good questions, I knew, pertinent ones that I very much needed to know the answer to. But since my pipper still wasn't updated, I had to do without the luxury of knowing. The only other way to find out would've been to search the sky by camera, and I hardly had time for *that*. Instead I focused on the job at hand, which was killing a certain Dracan destroyer and her too-brilliant commanding officer.

On the next pass I took her from dead ahead, like I had the first pair. This had the welcome effect of effectively cutting her defensive fire in half, as the stern guns couldn't bear, and also, I hoped, of scaring hell out of the crew. There was nothing—nothing!—so disconcerting to a spacer as a determined enemy on a ramming course. Carefully I aimed off a little to starboard and fired both of my new cannon. The laser-bolts narrowly missed the little ship's port side. Her helmsman flinched the other way...

...and sealed his shipmates' doom, as well as his own. It's impossible to instantaneously stop thousands of tons of mass once it begins swinging in a specific direction; one of the Butcher Birds had taught me the trick. My last torp sprang from the rail at much too short a range, aimed in the direction of the unstoppable swing. Now there was nothing at all her captain could do, brilliant or no. The unknown Dracan's war was over, as was his career and his life; my weapon impacted directly on the bridge. Fragments rattled off of my thick skin as I soared through the debris. But, they did no damage.

"Splash another destroyer!" I reported. Then I checked the mission clock. My heavens! I hadn't been aloft five minutes and already I'd killed who knew how many Dracans! "Are you ready yet, Jimmy?" I demanded. "Target Two awaits."

"Just a…" my wingman replied. There was a long pause, then a brighter-than-usual flash. "Aww!" he complained. "My torp was gonna hit her, but *Cochrane* got her first!"

"Robbed," I sympathized, though I didn't care who got credit for the kill so long as more Dracan guns were silenced and more torpedoes were destroyed unfired. "Form up. I'll hold position as best I can." I panned my camera around the sky; against all odds, as nearly as I could tell we were winning. There were several dead merchantmen about, yes. But not nearly as many as I'd have expected, considering that in essence we'd Jumped straight down the vent of an erupting volcano. Except for *Orleans* and *Cochise*, however, I couldn't locate a single friendly warship that'd suffered significant damage. Indeed, so far Dracan losses seemed far in excess of our own. *Something's wrong*, a little voice I'd learned to trust whispered in my ear. *Admiral Vlasilov predicted a slaughter, yes. But not a* Dracan *slaughter!*

Then the pipper finally beeped and I practically broke the virtual knob off of the thing accessing its imagery. Sure enough, things were pretty much as I'd pictured them in regard to the local battle. Four of the five Dracan light cruisers were dead. Their backup heavies were exchanging fire with our battle-line and, seemingly, getting the worst of it. Inexplicably, however, the main Dracan battle-line still wasn't engaged. Instead the dreadnoughts simply floated idle, remaining in their ragged, sloppy battery-saving line despite being easily within range of the fleet action. They still hadn't fired a shot! Why? Why in the universe would they just sit and watch while their light forces fought, and lost, the most crucial battle of the war so far?

Suddenly, I understood. "It's a bluff!" I crowed on the main 'hopper channel. "The whole blockade's been a bluff! Those battleships don't have any batteries in them! They *can't* fire their main guns! Michelle was right after all!"

"Yes!" Ted agreed. "We just came to the same conclusion here, on the bridge. If they could possibly intervene, they'd have by now. The whole blockade has been a farce since who knows when? They even conned us into hitting the part of their forces that was still fueled and ready for battle! What fools we are!"

I frowned. "Jimmy and I could hit them. We have the range, and there's still the warheads in the decoys."

"No," my co-commander replied. "Leave them be. Complete your mission as planned. Your original targets are more important. That's an order directly from the admiral.'

For just a second I considered protesting. Then I remembered. The merchies had to come first, and there were likely still fighters based on New Nippon. "Right," I acknowledged. Even as I spoke, *Cochrane* came about and turned herself broadside to the inert Dracan capital units, utterly ignoring the heavy-cruiser fire that was so ineffectively being concentrated on her. Her main turrets spoke…

…and a few seconds later, a hit flared bright on the last Dracan dreadnought in line. That was enough for the enemy admiral, apparently. And who could blame him? What use was it to expose such valuable fleet assets to enemy fire when they couldn't even respond? Small vector-arrows began to sprout behind the red dreadnought-emblems. They were bugging out, running for home with presumably the very last of their power!

Suddenly my mind was full of chatter. "Ha!" Jimmy cried out, for an instant overriding the rest. "We've won!" Ted declared, his voice full of emotion. Even Father Murton chimed in; "Thank god," he whispered. I pressed my virtual lips together; it was good news, sure enough. Better news than we'd ever dared hope for, in fact. But, the battle was *not* over. Almost certainly there were fighters based on the Dracan-occupied world below us. If so, they still posed a terrible threat to the unarmored ships we were sworn to protect.

"Jimmy!" I called out urgently, still weaving an indeterminate pattern through the Dracan fire but in general holding my position so that my wingman could find me. "Where are you?"

"Here!" he replied, suddenly sweeping up into his usual spot close in under my right wing. Two decoys trailed him; I still had three left. "Let's get this done, Thomas. I'm sorry I'm late. But it was worth it; I killed another cruiser!"

"Congratulations," I replied, swinging my nose towards New Nippon. Two cruisers was a good day's work, yes. An important, even vital tally, under the circumstances. One could hardly blame Jimmy for delaying a little in exchange for a second such kill; I might well have done the same in his shoes. But, could we still catch any of the enemy on the ground? I checked the clock; we were six minutes into the attack, a full ninety seconds behind schedule. "Let's leave the rest of the big guys for the ships' gunners, and go kill us some 'hoppers."

Chapter Twenty-Eight

It was too bad that we didn't have more battleships in our fleet; only *Cochrane's* big guns had the range to punish the Dracan dreadnoughts for the deception they'd gotten away with for so long. But, working alone, even the mighty *Cochrane* didn't have enough juju to actually kill any of the enemy main battle line before they exited through Nikita Number Two, in the sort of regal dignity that only dreadnoughts can hope to achieve. They even neatened up their formation along the way—it was probably more out of habit than anything else, though I'm sure their admiral was greatly relieved. *Cochrane* scored three more hits on the last ship in line, a vessel nearly as old as our own *Orleans* had been, but for some reason she just wouldn't give up the fight. When she finally vanished, the wounded Dracan still appeared functional and totally under control.

By then Jimmy and I were closing in on New Nippon and out of sightseeing time anyway. Eight full minutes had passed now since the shooting had started, and while our mission-timing might possibly have negated the super-fighter threat, no conventional 'hopper pilot worth his salt had any excuse for still being on the ground. But where were they? The pipper was still bereft of enemy aerospacecrat.

"I'm worried," I admitted to Jimmy. "I've had a bad feeling about this ever since we found out the Dracans really were out of molecular batteries after all. We always think we're smarter than them, and sometimes we actually are. But…"

"Gotcha," Jimmy agreed as we zoomed downwards towards the planetary surface. Or, satellite-surface, more correctly, since New Nippon was actually the satellite of a gas giant about twice the size of Jupiter. It was called Yamato. "I've been worried too. I mean, the Dracans *have* to win this battle, right? Just like we do. And, they *knew* that their battle fleet was helpless. So…"

But Jimmy never got to finish his sentence. Just then my pipper began beeping like a slot machine paying on a million-credit jackpot. Except that this time each beep indicated a new Dracan detected, squadrons and squadrons of conventional fighters appearing from behind New Nippon's eastern horizon. Then, as the pipper kept ringing away, a new swarm began rising from the location of New Nippon's largest commercial airfield, joining up in what was obviously a carefully-planned rendezvous with the huge mass of 'hoppers. Their target was clearly the merchantmen we'd sworn to protect.

"Oh," Jimmy said after a long, pregnant silence. "I see. Now."

"Our target is Saburo Sakai Field," I decided. "Then we turn around and kill as many Dracan fighters as we can."

"Roger," Jimmy acknowledged, following my lead as I turned slightly away from the cloud of 'hoppers. There were several reasons to prefer Sakai Field over any of the other available targets. First and perhaps most important, it was just over the *western* horizon and not the eastern one. If the Dracans wanted to mix it up with us, they'd have to chase us halfway around the planet to do it. Second, Sakai was the former United Systems naval airbase, located far away from any population centers. While the warheads in our decoys were only of tactical-size, and as clean as they could be made in deference to the fact that the New Nipponese people were on our side, it would be as well if we didn't take too many chances. And, third, since Sakai was a former navy base, it had the best support facilities in terms of hardstands and the like. While it was far from a sure thing, if there were superfighters to be found on New Nippon then they'd most likely be based at Saburo Sakai Field. And, with any luck, they were still on the ground.

It didn't take long at all to pound our way down through the atmosphere at just under the maximum safe speed; in deference to our decoys we couldn't quite run flat out. New Nippon was a terribly level place, there was virtually no terrain to exploit. So Jimmy and I ducked down as low as we dared, ran our pre-planned fake course towards another airfield, then swung hard for Sakai. In the absence of fighter opposition, Ted and I had figured that missiles would be the main threat. And, indeed, our missile-warnings beeped several times. But apparently the Dracans never got enough of a return off of us to fire. "We hit a sensor gap!" I crowed, just as the Sakai control tower reared up over the too-near horizon…

…and suddenly something hit my fighter, hard! Then, again!

"Break left!" Jimmy screamed, and instinctively I jerked my 'bolt around in the direction indicated, as we'd practiced so many times above the frozen wastes of Esteppe. "What—" I tried to ask.

"Gun!" Jimmy replied. "An old-fashioned triple-A gun! Firing metal projectiles! I got a good look as we passed."

Well, *that* was something new! How in the world had they obtained sufficient muzzle velocity to engage a 'bolt? I checked my damage-control center, and virtual-scowled. "Two hits," I reported as we zoomed off in the wrong direction. "Both in the engines. No further indications."

"Any power loss?" Jimmy demanded.

"Not at this setting," I replied. "But at higher ones, who knows?" Our engines were delicate assemblies indeed, and required perfect alignment and synchronization for proper function. "Not that it matters for now. Conform to me, and we'll try again."

I swung my nose slowly back to starboard, alert now not only for the deadly tones of a missile launch but also searching the featureless ground ahead for gun installations that might open up without warning. The visual search was especially difficult because I hadn't the faintest clue as to what an "old-fashioned triple-A gun" looked like. At one point I detected a patch of slightly-discolored ground dead ahead; instead of taking chances I employed both nose-cannon. It blew up with considerable vigor, whatever it was, and I could only hope that it had indeed been an air-defense weapon rather than, say, something to do with the civilian electrical grid.

Then the Sakai control tower poked up above the horizon again. "We'll expend them all in one pass," I ordered. "You take the tower as your aiming-point, and I'll find something else when we're a little closer. We don't have time to be fancy. I'm getting the willies, thinking about all those Dracans heading for the merchies."

"Click-click," my wingman replied wordlessly.

Then, quite suddenly, we were *over* Sakai Field, moving so fast that everything was a blur. I picked out a nice hanger, pointed my nose directly at it for a second, then flipped the switch that unslaved the decoys. They were in free-flight, now, and headed to where I hoped they might do some good. I swung my cameras about, both for my own benefit and to provide images for when the navy next came this way...

...and noticed a hardstand with a door open! "Break right!" I declared, swinging around towards it as aggressively as if I'd been Colonel Rotte. Sure enough, I could just make out the shape of the 'hopper's nose as it began to roll out. A superfighter, on its way to either intercept us or join up with the mass-attack on the merchies!

"Geez!" Jimmy added. "There's another at eight o-clock!"

I spun my camera that way; sure enough, there was a second Dracan super-'hopper even nearer to launching than the one I was aiming at. But it was too late. You could only aim at one 'hopper at a time. I lined up, made sure both cannon were activated...

...and blew the evil thing into a million pieces before it could get off the ground. It was dirty pool, sure. Unfair as all getout. But it *worked*, as the navy pilots who'd finally defeated the Stormcrows had so well understood. "Break left!" I cried out, trying to set up Jimmy for the second target; he'd have a far better angle than me. "Break..."

Just then the decoys began to slam home, one after another, each unleashing its fireball in rapid succession. While we 'bolts were well out of the lethal radius, it was still very unpleasant to be slammed about and disoriented so violently; probably, it was a lot like being trapped in a thunderstorm in an old-fashioned airplane. We also had to be doubly careful due to the fact that we were down so low. Both of us, in fact, were forced to pull our noses up and gain a little altitude, which made further strafing attacks out of the question.

"Did the bombs get him?" Jimmy demanded.

"How should I know?" I complained, searching the sky as best I was able. Which wasn't very, due to all the smoke and dust that was suddenly in the air. "My pipper's blanked, too. There might be more of them around than just that one anyway!"

"Yeah," my wingman agreed. We flew a complete circuit of Sakai Field; it was flattened and wouldn't be playing host to any more superfighters anytime soon. Even better, all but one or two of the hardstands, and presumably whatever might have been inside of them were flattened as well. They were built to withstand tactical nukes, yes. But only one at a time.

"We're not doing any more good here," I decided at last. "If there's still any superfighters alive, we'll never find them like this. Let's make our interception of the main strike while we still can."

"Roger," Jimmy agreed, conforming to my maneuvers as always. I raised my 'bolt's brilliant red nose skyward, then mentally shoved the throttles forward. At first I rose like a rocket. Then at just a little under full military power a red light appeared in my damage-control center.

"Damn!" I cursed, throttling back. "I've got damage after all! My motors are out of synch. This is all the power I've got!"

"Oh," Jimmy replied. Not that there was much else he could say.

It was time for a quick decision. "Jimmy, we're going to have to split up again; we can't afford a delay. Go without me and I'll catch up later."

There was a short pause; any single fighter alone was far more vulnerable than a trained pair, working together and flying the Thach Weave. I wasn't just being noble; Jimmy's life was at risk almost as much as mine. Then, like the good officer that he was, my wingman accepted his orders and obeyed them. "Aye-aye, sir!" he acknowledged. "I'll try to save a few of them for you!" Then, my friend piled on the power and became a rapidly-receding spot in the sky.

Chapter Twenty-Nine

Being a damaged 'bolt was a lot more akin to being sick than I cared to admit. It was hard, knowing there was something broken inside of myself that I couldn't reach or touch or fix. It might not've been so bad, except that the Mark 1* was equipped with an emergency manual engine recalibration system designed for exactly this situation. This *should* have allowed me to make rough adjustments, even in the middle of a dogfight. Predictably, however, one of the two rounds I'd absorbed had taken *it* out as well. Clearly, Father's genius was no match for sheer bad luck.

Despite the fact that I'd not received a single hopeful sign, I continued playing with the recalibrater as I raced away from New Nippon, following in Jimmy's tracks towards the main action to come. What a furball *that* one was going to be! My friend needed me, so I flew straight and level and true...

...right up until the second when dozens of laser-bolts came flashing by from the rear! "Whoa!" I cried out onto main channel, twisting away to the right just as quickly as I possibly could. Instantly the little flecks of fire receded, then swung back my way again. I barrel-rolled, reflexively trying to go to full-power again. But there wasn't any more power!

"Die, murderer!" a new voice rang out in my headphones. "You killed my mother, you bastard!"

I barrel-rolled again, this time to the left. It was an instinctive reaction, not something I had time to think about. If my enemy had a wingman...

And he did! More laser-bolts came flaring past, seeming to curve away from me as I spoiled my enemy's aim before the rounds were even fired. That was the very best time, Rotte had taught me. I leveled out, Immelmanned...

...and there they were, two Dracan superfighters in close formation. I wasn't in any position to fire. That was perfectly fine by me, however. Neither were they, which was a distinct improvement over how things had stood just a few seconds before.

"You killed my mother!" the voice rang out again, on the common frequency honored by all spacefaring peoples. "She was a doctor, in the City of Imperial Learning! You nuked her, Thomas Longo! You murdered them all! I've prayed for this day!"

I swung about in a long, undulating s-curve calculated to be difficult to predict. So, I'd killed this Dracan's mother, along with so many others. What could I say? He was right to be angry, I supposed. To the Dracans, I was probably the greatest war-criminal of all time.

"You can hear me!" the Dracan screamed. "I know you can! Say something, baby-killer!"

I pressed my virtual lips together. Rotte had warned me many times about exchanging banter with the enemy. "Only when it pays," Emil had drilled into me, over and over. "Only when it's another weapon in your arsenal. Otherwise, mere words are wasted breath. Distracting, too. Don't yell at them; *kill* them. Cannons settle arguments far more effectively than words."

The Colonel was a wise man, I thought as I rolled and dodged, denying my enemies any easy openings. Kill them, don't argue with them! Then I virtual-frowned to myself. I'd offered these two an easy shot, the easiest shot possible, in fact, by not watching my six closely enough. Yet they'd missed. Why?

"Murderer!" the Dracan screamed, firing his cannon at nothing. "And now you've dropped your filthy nukes on my friends, too! I'll kill you slow, you son of a bitch! I'll send your rich plutocrat father the gun footage, so he can see how you suffered. I'll kill you dead, dead, dead!"

Dead, dead, dead, the voice echoed in my head. But I wasn't really listening anymore. *Why did you miss?* I asked myself again. *Why, when offered the easiest shot in the world?*

Maybe because you're lousy pilots? I wondered. I barrel-rolled again, then Immelmaned halfway through the second spin. "Break right!" the Dracan voice cried out, still on the common frequency. He swung hard and fast...

...but did I detect a bit of hesitation on the part of his wingman?

The Skybolt program had been a nightmare of improvisation and sacrifice. *Everything* had been thrown to the winds in order to bring a handful of 'bolts into combat; training, traditions, ethics, lives... *Everything!* And yet, as insane as our own program had been, how much worse must it have been for our enemies? They were starting production up totally from scratch, without Father's practical knowledge and experienced staff. Even more to the point, how impossible must it have been to start up a combat organization without the benefit of *Rotte's* hard-won experience? Sure, the Dracans had good machines.

But, had they had the opportunity yet to work out how to really *use* them?

My 'bolt was no longer capable of full power, but it was still roughly as potent as a Stormcrow flown flat-out; instantly I cut the engines, spun about on my vertical axis, and began thrusting like mad on an intercept course. The Dracans could-- *should!*—have done the same and fought me head-on with the odds two-to-one in their favor. Or alternatively they could've sort of dipsy-doodled and threatened my own tail. But they didn't do either of these obvious things. "Break right!" their mouthy leader cried out instead, a purely defensive move.

Rotte had *hated* purely defensive moves. He'd hammered home the reason why over and over again in the empty skies over Esteppe. Purely defensive moves ceded the initiative, a deadly mistake against a skilled foe capable of dictating a fight on his own terms. Now it was my turn to pass the lesson on. Instead of backing off and circling as my enemies had done, I yanked my nose in even tighter and barged right in, letting fly a few shots just ahead of the enemy formation. My rounds weren't even close, but the Dracans panicked regardless. "Break right, Johnny!" the leader cried, his voice cracking with strain. Was this the first time he'd ever been under fire? Or, more likely, the first time he'd ever dueled with anyone other than a rank amateur like himself?

Of *course* it was his first time. Where would the Dracans find an experienced trainer?

Did they even *realize* how unready for war they were?

Suddenly I felt sick inside as I realized how this combat must end. I rolled right, and missed with a low-probability deflection shot on the wingman. Untrained as he was, he reacted in precisely the wrong way. "Break left!" I heard his voice call out.

"Wait!" cried the leader, who was still swinging right and couldn't possibly conform to the new maneuver. But it was already too late. The wingman had broken away on his own, all by himself.

"Paul!" he screamed, the true terror of combat finally sinking home. "Where are you?"

I was in just the right place at just the right time; Rotte would've been proud indeed. "Horrido!" he would have cried out as he fired both big guns and blew what I now understood to be merely a fifteen-or-so year-old kid out of the sky without a second's hesitation. But there *was* a difference between Rotte and I, I was beginning to understand. Just as I was learning that there was more than one kind of horror to be found in combat. "Splash one," I was supposed to say when I killed an enemy, so that the statistics-team aboard *June* could keep track of things. But this time I hadn't the heart. Instead, I maintained a cold, icy silence as I fired. So practiced and skilled an executioner had I become that it took me only five or ten rounds to kill the brave boy who might well have been Jimmy on *his* own first combat mission.

"*No!*" screamed the Dracan leader, giving voice to a horror that more nearly matched my own than he'd ever know. "You *bastard*! You're *dead*!"

I shook my virtual head. He was brave, this one. Given time, I could perhaps make a fighter pilot of him. But, as things were, well… The lessons currently on the syllabus were not exactly of the constructive sort.

"I'll kill you!" Paul the Dracan screamed again. "For my mother! For my widowed father, and my motherless baby sister! I'll kill you for John!" The scream turned into a wail of anguish. "Johnny!" he cried out again. "Are you out there?"

Johnny hadn't ejected. For a moment I was tempted to inform Paul of this, then decided it would be pointless cruelty.

Killing the wingman had drawn me well away from the other superfighter; indeed, the running combat had taken us both almost all the way back to the main fleet action. Because even a lame 'bolt was so fast compared to anything else in the sky, I wasn't too terribly far behind the large Dracan 'hopper formation on its way to attack the big ships. "Splash one!" Jimmy cried out; I'd been ignoring him for a little while due to the problems I was having on my own. "And another!" It was good to hear his voice after the terrible thing I'd just done.

"Great shooting, Jimmy!" I encouraged him, trying to keep my voice as calm and as normal as possible despite the deep pit of anguish gnawing at my guts. "I'll be there as soon as I can!"

"Right!" he answered in his usual cheery tones. "I've killed seven, Tommy!"

"Seven!" I replied. "Keep that up and soon you'll outscore me!"

Then Paul was back, with his dark, dire threats. They didn't scare me anymore, not with the way he was whimpering and weeping as he issued them. If he was a day over sixteen, I was a monkey's uncle. "...come back and b-b-blow you out of the sky!" he sniffled. "Out of the universe, even!"

Suddenly my pipper beeped, and I zoomed it to the max. There Paul the Dracan was, below me, slightly to the left, and flying as straight and level and stupidly as I'd been when the fight had started. Clearly, *his* pipper hadn't recovered yet.

I flew on for a precious second or two, not wanting to do what must come next. But then I thought of the lumbering line of merchies carrying food and medicine to a starving Earth, and decided to put the terrible deed behind me.

"...miserable c-c-coward!" Paul was muttering now. "Miserable c-c-coward, hiding in the dark! Gonna shoot me from behind, kill me without warning like all the rest?"

How else? I didn't answer as I swung in behind the Dracan. What moron had taught this guy about war, anyway? Was he expecting combat to be *fair*? A *Dracan*?

Paul was yawing slightly side-to-side now, though not enough to affect my intercept. Probably he was trying to sweep the skies where he expected me to be. I was less than a mile away when I triggered both cannon, practically on top of him. Paul's superfighter exploded in a blinding flash, and it was over.

"Splash two!" I reported a little belatedly on *June*'s frequency. "I say again, splash two superfighters! "

"Outstanding!" Ted's voice replied. "We've been following it from here. Excellent work!" My co-commander's voice was hearty enough, but his praise felt thin and false nonetheless. He was a fighter pilot too. Had he followed my enemies' radio chatter and felt the same emotions I had? Most likely. In which case, he was probably doing the best he could to sound genuine in praising a child-murderer.

I clicked my mike-circuit twice so that I wouldn't have to speak. Then I consulted my pipper; even at reduced power, I'd still be able to make one good pass against the big Dracan fighter force. "Hold the fort, Jimmy!" I said, switching to our private channel. "Here I come, ready or not!"

Chapter Thirty

There were almost as many Dracan fighters in the main attack force as there'd been back at Drakkus a few weeks earlier, when we'd made our big attack. This time, however, they weren't stripped clean and trying to intercept us. Instead they were loaded up with either two or four torps apiece, depending on how old they were. Conventional Dracan fighters had to attack en masse in order to present a credible threat to a Skybolt; while this swarm was certainly large enough to be dangerous, their loadout and mission orders rendered them relatively harmless for the moment. That would change in an instant, of course, once they'd fired off their heavy ordnance.

Jimmy was up to ten destroyed enemy fighters by the time I caught up with the formation; his voice was filled with glee as he reported in kill after kill. "Splash Nine! Splash Ten! Horrido!"

"Horrido!" I agreed, getting into the spirit of the thing once again as I fired from extreme range and flared an older-model Dracan that carried only two torps. Because I'd been held up by the superfighters I'd had to build up a very large vector in order to close the range, so that I was coming up fast. It was as well that Rotte had taught me so much about snap-shooting, for this was all I had time for as I zoomed up behind the enemy formation, braking just as hard as I could. "Splash One! Two! Three!"

Then, the Dracans did something unexpected. Instead of continuing their long, steady torp run, they braked as well, so that I went hurtling out in front of them. Now I was flying along straight and level in front of a dozen or more enemy guns at point-blank range, and the sky was full of fire. My heavens! Was I actually a higher-priority target than the merchies? If so, the Dracans had gone mad!

"Look out, Thomas!" Ted cried. "Brake, son! Brake!"

I *couldn't* brake any harder than I already was, or else I'd have been doing so to make my own gunnery easier. "I…" I replied as best I could, twisting and weaving. "I…" But it was too late. A fireball hit my port stub-wing, causing little damage, then a second slammed home into my already-hurting engine bay. There was a bright flash, then the starboard motor cut out entirely. I was down to one-ninth power, without the feedback effect of the two motors working together to help me. One-ninth power, in the middle of a dogfight!

I was dead! *Dead!*

"Brake!" Ted roared, suddenly understanding how terribly everything had gone wrong. "Brake with everything you've got! Get clear of those Dracans!"

"Tommy!" Jimmy's voice chimed in; I'd never noticed before how much he sounded like his older brother, especially when they were both really, really scared. "I'm coming!"

"Don't!" I countered, trying to dodge and weave with the feeble little remnants of energy my 'bolt was still capable of delivering. It wasn't working very well; I took another hit to the starboard motor, then a heavy blow to the fuselage that wiped out about half of my flight systems. "Kill Dracans! Think of the merchies!"

"No!" Jimmy cried out; he could read a pipper as well as I could and therefore knew exactly how dead I suddenly was. "I'm coming!"

"Punch out!" Ted ordered abruptly, changing tacks. "We'll pick you up!"

"They'll kill me in a minute if I do that," I protested, executing a neat little looping turn that, if I was lucky, might keep me alive a few seconds longer. Suddenly no longer in firing position, the two nearest Dracans broke off, leaving their quarry for the next pair. There'd be no evading them, I could see. It was over. "Horrido!" I screamed, swinging my big twin cannon onto the rearmost Dracan; they were about all that was left that still worked properly. He flared and died. "Horrido!" I screamed again. "I got another! Make sure it gets counted!"

"Thomas!" Jimmy wailed in despair.

Then a new voice broke into the channel. It was familiar, but I couldn't quite place it. "Thomas!" it shouted. "Stop braking! Run towards me, boy! Directly towards me! Just as hard as you can!"

"Who are you?" I demanded, beginning a sloppy, underpowered evasive roll. "Where do you want me to run?"

"It's Captain Jungmann!" the voice replied. "Of *Graf Zeppelin*! Try to ram me, son, if you can!"

I glanced at my pipper; *Zeppelin*, *Cochrane*, *Doolittle* and *The Glorious First of June* had formed a line, a last-ditch screen between the deluge of Dracan fighters and the soft-skinned merchies. I wasn't quite on an intercept course for *Zeppelin*, but it was close.

"Ram you?" I demanded. "There's too much vector! I'll die, you'll die… Are you nuts?"

"Ram me, Commander!" Jungmann repeated. "That's a verdammt order!"

I virtual-scowled to myself. I was responsible directly to Vlasilov, by special command arrangement. Not to every ship-captain in the Fleet. But still… It'd been Jungmann who'd up-shipped his cruiser without clearance during the big false alarm, back on Esteppe, when I'd been called back from the hike. The admiral had decorated him for it, calling him one of the finest, quickest-thinking, most daring officers in the navy…

…so I decided to trust him. Instead of braking more, I swung my nose back around and lined it up as best I could *Zeppelin's* bridge. Then I piled on what little power I had. "Aye-aye, sir!"

"Guten, Thomas!" he acknowledged, his Esteppan accent revealing showing itself under the stress of combat. "Is gut." There was a short pause as *Zeppelin* completed the task of centering herself in my sights; it was a strange sensation, having a target cooperate instead of evading. "Now, son. Do *nothing at all* no matter what happens. Do you hear me? Do *nothing*, even if you're being shot up. If you move an inch I'll kill you by accident. Acknowledge!"

"Right," I agreed, beginning to understand. *Zeppelin's* guns and gunners were the finest in the fleet, or at least I certainly thought so. "Not an inch."

Just then the Dracans began finding the range, and laser-bolts by the dozen flew by. I resisted the urge to maneuver, instead turning off my rearward-facing cameras. They wouldn't like where I was leading them, I reassured myself. Not at all! Then, finally, one of them found the mark. *Slam-slam-slam!* There were sparks and fire and pain…

…and then the enemy barrage was as rendered as nothing as compared to the combined efforts of *Graf Zeppelin*, *Jimmy Doolittle*, *Alimrante Cochrane*, and *June* herself blasting away at the fighters on my tail.

It was incredible, nothing at all like the wargames we'd played together. Where the simulation-images were semi-transparent so that we could see through them for safety's sake, the actual combined fire from the three great vessel's rapid-fire weapons formed a literal wall of fire. In all the fighting I'd ever done, I'd never experienced anything half as terrifying. I'd once described trying to attack even *Zeppelin* alone in simulation as being akin to trying to fly down a fire hose without getting wet. But the reality far exceeded anything I could've imagined. And now there were *four* modern rapid-fire ships blazing away in my immediate neighborhood, not just one or two! Even *June's* contribution, relatively small as it was, made the defensive fire of an entire Dracan destroyer squadron seem as nothing in comparison. It was *so* hard, not flinching away from the rivers and gouts of energy that surged by me, often mere inches away on all sides. Finally I shut off all my external cameras and flew dead-steady in total darkness. "Beepbeepbeepbeep!" went the pipper again, just like it had when the Dracans had first appeared around the curve of New Nippon's horizon. But this time each tone represented not the appearance of a new threat but the death of aknown one. Jimmy had picked away at the Dracans, yes, and I'd killed a few myself. But this was mechanized slaughter, death on a massive scale that I was quite certain no other fighter-force anywhere had ever known before. Nothing, no one could stand such losses. Not even the huge Dracan formation.

Then as if someone had hit a switch the light-show ceased. "Break left!" Captain Jungmann ordered. "Break left!"

124

Instantly I complied, reactivating my cameras with a thought and turning as hard as my mangled 'bolt would allow. I was practically on top of *Zeppelin*, I realized with a gulp. Too close! But the light cruiser was almost as responsive to her helm as the *Chief*-class destroyers she was descended from; as I swung in the requested direction *Zeppelin's* superstructure seemed to fall away as she spun about her longitudinal axis. I came closer and closer and closer, gained a short but vivid close-range impression of a triple-barreled turret still glowing white-hot from sustained firing…

…and then I was past, having shaved things so close that I was half-certain my 'bolt had left gouges in the cruiser's paint.

"He's made it!" Ted declared.

"Hurray!" Jimmy cried.

"Thank god!" Vlasilov's voice added.

Then suddenly the sky was alive again, this time with the flashes of Dracan torpedoes as they slammed home against our helpless charges. One, two, three, and then they were hitting faster than I could count. I wouldn't have been able to tell without my pipper, but one of the targets was the tanker *Rockefeller*, aboard which I'd made such a juvenile fool of myself what felt like so very long ago. She took at least three hits, and went up in a great flash along with, presumably, the new crewmen that the government had scraped up for her. *All of that oil*, I thought to myself, shaking my virtual head. *All of that expense, keeping her sitting idle in port for so long. All of the work involved in building her and fitting her out, all of the diplomatic problems she'd been the center off… It had all been for naught, all gone to waste. All eaten by the mindless war.*

Then the flashes stopped and I scanned the skies. There were still Dracan fighters about. But only a handful, out of range and retreating towards the relative safety of New Nippon. They'd lost eighty, maybe ninety percent of their 'hoppers. A catastrophe, in anyone's terms. And for what gain had our enemies suffered such a beating? I scanned the sky again. *Rockefeller* was gone, and another merchie, and another, and another… Twenty-eight, in all. A good sixty cargos would get through to Earth for sure now; there wasn't anything left to stop them. Sixty cargos, when Vlaslilov would've called forty a victory!

Then I re-examined my pipper; something had caught my eye the first time through, but, somehow, my mind hadn't accepted it. Now, however, reality was forcing its way in. I focused in on the last-ditch battle line, the formation that'd shot so many fighters off of my tail…

…and inwardly shuddered. *Cochrane* was fine, as was *Doolittle* and *Zeppelin*. But *The Glorious First of June* had been hit, and badly. She'd taken two torps, and as lightly armored and shielded as she was…

"*June*," I called out on the main frequency. "This is Red Flight Leader. Acknowledge."

There was a long, long silence.

"*June*," I repeated, "This is Red Flight Leader. Acknowledge."

Another long silence, as *June's* pipper image faded several steps towards dead-ship blue before stabilizing again.

"She's not answering me, either," Jimmy replied.

"Nor anyone else," Captain Jungmann interrupted. "Though we've made contact with the engineering decks via hand-blinker. It looks bad from here. Very, very bad," He sighed into the open microphone. "We're going to hold position on this side of the Nikita until we find out for certain how hard the flagship's been hit, kids. In the meantime conform to my vector, then take position port-and-starboard of me. I know that you're both damaged and that therefore it'll take you some time." He sighed again. "There's no rush. It looks like we may be here all day anyway."

Chapter Thirty-One

It *did* take almost all day before things began to straighten themselves out. Jimmy's 'bolt had taken a hit to one of the motors late in the engagement, so that he too was down to one-ninth power. Both of us had to fly huge, slow interception curves in order to take up our assigned stations; flying so sedately required little attention, which gave us all the time we needed to examine *June's* damage and worry.

"She took one to the bridge," Jimmy reported on our private circuit, which truly *was* private for once, more likely than not. It didn't seem probable that anyone from our mother ship could be listening in. "And another to the engineering decks. That's the really bad one; it looks from here like the bridge hit didn't detonate quite right or something."

"Part of the superstructure's missing," I pointed out, silently cursing the fact that all of my high-magnification cameras were out. Along with most of everything else; even my life-support systems were leaking, though if they didn't get worse I still had hours before I needed to even begin worrying.

"Yeah," Jimmy agreed. "There's that, I suppose." Neither of us wanted to mention the fact that virtually everyone we were close to, from Vlasilov to our counselors, had their battle-stations on or near the bridge. Ted was the sole exception; he shared office-space with the deck officer just abaft the port catapult. Otherwise, though…

"There's launches and ships' boats floating all over the place," Jimmy continued, knowing I couldn't make out such small details. "It looks like the other ships are sending people to help. That's a good sign, I think."

"Probably," I agreed, though I thought it more likely that the launches were rescuing survivors. On my pipper *June* was hovering just two shades above dead-ship blue. Somewhere, sometime, a ship might've been damaged that badly and recovered to fight again. But I'd never seen it. Idly, I switched over to the general frequency.

"..sheer off!" a gruff voice was complaining. With so many small craft in the sky, the frequency was badly overcrowded. "We have the right-of-way, *Cochrane*-launch! I've got a rescue team aboard!"

"Sheer yourself!" a woman replied. "I've got an enviro-igloo! Priority A-1, my officer says! Most important cargo of all!"

"The igloo it is," I heard another female voice add. It seemed familiar, but at first I didn't recognize it. Probably this was because it was so badly out of place. "This is Commander Bard, of *The Glorious First of June*. We're back on the air." There was a short pause. "I'm speaking for Captain Jones. She's too badly wounded to transmit."

"Michelle made it!" Jimmy cried out. "There were survivors on the bridge after all!'

But also casualties, I didn't add. "Thank god," I agreed. I liked Michelle.

"*June*," a new voice interjected. "It's good to hear from you! We've been worried. This is Captain Shepherd, of *Cochrane*. Is Admiral Vlasilov available?"

"No, sir!" Bard replied, after a momentary pause. "He's still missing; the upper decks took the brunt of the blast. Captain Jones is badly wounded, sir. She hereby transfers command of the rest of the task force to you as the next most senior captain, though she'll remain in charge here for as long as she can." There was another long pause. "There aren't many line-officers left, sir."

"Right," Shepherd agreed. "Send my best to Rosalind." There was another long silence, while he considered what to do. "Everyone's sent damage-control parties. Even the merchies want to help. Is there anything else we can do?"

"You've already sent more small-craft than we can handle," Michelle replied. "As you can tell from monitoring the traffic. The igloo will help a lot; we've lost pressurization except for most of three decks near the core of the hull. Engineering is toast; we're operating off of auxiliary power, and can't make any thrust whatsoever."

"Will you be abandoning ship, then?" Shepherd asked.

"No," Bard replied. "Captain Jones says definitely not. We're the only carrier in the squadron, and we've two serviceable superfighters aboard. We'll not be abandoning them without a struggle."

"Roger," *Cochrane*'s captain agreed. "We'll continue to support you in every way possible. If you need anything, you've but to ask."

"Captain Jones suggests you rig *Cochrane* to tow; she says that if memory serves your Jump coils are big enough."

"They are," Shepherd agreed. "And we shall. Godspeed. *Cochrane* out."

No Victory Won ~ Phil Geusz

Chapter Thirty-Two

Sometimes I didn't know which was worse, being a 'bolt or wearing an inflexible, clumsy mannequin-body. Being a 'bolt is cool, at least; you can sit and imagine that you're zooming across the sky, even when you're really just helping out with a deck-crew drill or doing a boring twelve hour shift on alert status. But in a mannequin body, you can fidget. Think that's not important? Try not being able to for a few hours sometime.

"This is awful!" Jimmy complained for about the thousandth time. "We don't even know who's dead and who's alive!"

I clicked my mike twice, not wanting to discuss the subject any further but also unwilling to discourage my wingman from talking about it if he needed to. Jimmy was a brave, loyal friend. I'd listen to literally *anything* from him, for as long as he cared to rattle on.

"I mean… The admiral's missing. And no one's said anything to us about Brooks or Father Murton." There was a long pause. "Don't you think they'd have told us, if the news was good?"

Probably, I didn't answer. Instead, I tried to be upbeat. "Vlasilov is *missing*," I pointed out. "Not known to be dead. He's a tough old spacehound; as likely as not he's floating somewhere in a survival balloon, waiting." It was possible enough, on the surface at least. The task force's small craft and even some of the better-equipped merchies were systematically homing in on the survival beacons and chasing them down, one after another. Most unexpectedly, they'd rescued three men from the crew of *Orleans*. One of them even looked likely to live through the night. I thought back to how *Orleans* and the Dracan cruiser had sort of melted themselves together, and virtual-shuddered. Rotte might've welcomed such a fierce, cataclysmic end, but it was something I hoped *I'd* never have to face.

"I'm scared," Jimmy admitted at last.

"Me too," I replied, being as comforting as I knew how to be. Which wasn't very, I knew, though I tried my best. In recent years I'd not spent a lot of time learning how to be a good nurturer. In fact, my career had taken me in rather another direction entirely…

It'd been six hours since *June* was hit, and despite my earlier pessimism her pipper-image had grown a single shade brighter. Captain Jones had died on the bridge, and despite the fact that she wasn't a line officer or even officially part of the ships' company Commander Bard was now in charge. This was only temporary; *Cochrane*'s first officer was en-route to take over, as everyone including Michelle was fully aware that she wasn't qualified. But the situation spoke volumes regarding the degree of carnage that must've taken place among my shipmates. Jimmy might need urgently to know who was dead and who wasn't, but I was in no hurry whatsoever. Ignorance was hope.

"Hello, Thomas and Jimmy!" Captain Jungmann cut in. He checked in on us every little bit, to make sure that we were still okay. It made sense, I supposed, considering that we were shot up almost as badly as *June* was. "How are my favorite fighter aces doing?"

"Fine," I let Jimmy answer for us both.

"I'm still leaking," I added. "But the rate's unchanged."

"Well," Jungmann replied. "That's not what I'd call *good* news, but it'll do for now." He paused for a second. "You won't have to wait much longer. Believe it or not, *June's* about to request that you land-on. Her recovery gear is undamaged, and casualties were light among your 'hopper wranglers. Your quarters are undamaged as well, I've been asked to inform you. Which I for one am glad of; you two have seen plenty of combat for one day. You're to proceed directly there and await further orders. Which, I suppose, may be quite some time coming."

"What about my brother?" Jimmy demanded. "Or Petty Officer Brooks?"

"Or Father Murton?" I heard myself ask, though I'd promised myself not to.

There was another long silence. "If I knew," Jungmann answered, "I'd tell you. My sacred word of honor as an Esteppan, given to a member of the Order of Blood."

I couldn't say much to that; if there was a more morally-binding oath that Jungmann could swear, it'd have to involve a deity. "Thank you," I replied.

"You're quite welcome, Your Excellency" Jungmann replied. "I admit that I'm worried about Admiral Vlasilov, too. He's a force of nature, that man. Not someone we can spare."

"No," I agreed. Without Vlasilov and his utterly ruthless drive, we'd have been defeated long since. "I'm worried as well."

But I didn't have time to worry very long. Suddenly a familiar voice was speaking. "Red flight," Ted's voice said in my head. "Attention Red Flight. Do you read?"

Even if I could've beaten Jimmy to the mike switch, I wouldn't have. "Ted!" he cried. "Oh, Ted!"

"I'm all right, kiddo," he answered. "Not a scratch, though I've been out of circulation for a while. The compartment I was in was surrounded by vacuum, and the power was out. But I'm fine now."

"Oh!" Jimmy cried, unable to find words to express his joy. "Oh! Oh!"

"It's all right, kiddo," Ted repeated. This time, I could make out a certain raspy harshness in his voice, a sound characteristically caused by momentary exposure to vacuum or something rather near to it. Apparently there was more to Ted's survival story than he was telling. "It's all right. Don't go all blubbery on me. We're on duty!"

"Aye-aye, sir!" Jimmy replied, attempting to suppress his sobs of relief but not quite succeeding.

"All right, then," Ted replied. "I'll see you just as soon as you're aboard. Until then…" His voice hardened. "Thomas?"

"Yes?" I answered, feeling a sudden chill. Was I about to receive the bad news I was so dreading?

"I understand that your life-support is damaged. You'll land first, on the starboard rail. The port is no longer in service; we've stripped the crew to help out in Engineering. So you'll make a standard approach and land on the starboard."

"Right," I acknowledged. So it had just been landing instructions, not something worse. This time. "Starboard rail. Acknowledged."

Chapter Thirty-Three

The landing was idiot-simple, even with my broken bird. I'd been formed up on *Zeppelin*, which in turn was hovering protectively near *The Glorious First of June*. So there was practically no navigating required; my destination wasn't moving in relation to my point of departure. In five minutes the thing was done, and the promised vacuum-suited ratings were disconnecting me from my 'bolt.

"Where's Father Murton?" I asked the first rating to connect herself up to my audio circuit.

"Now don't you worry about that, Thomas," the woman replied. I didn't know her; perhaps casualties had been worse among the aircraft-handlers than Jungmann had realized. Certainly the hanger walls were scorched, or at least those parts of them that I could make out from my limited viewpoint, and one of the big support beams was bent like a banana. "Let me get you out of there, and then you can head up to your cabin."

I wasn't in much of a position to argue, unless I wanted to fire my cannon or perform some other equally stupid and pointless act. But even though outwardly I probably seemed to be perfectly under control, inside of me something was beginning to slip. "Sure!" I agreed. Anything to get back into my mannequin body. Anything!

Dismounting me in vacuum was an even longer and slower process than doing so in a decent atmosphere; I'd never worn a pressure suit, but trying to work through such heavy, stiff gloves must've been a lot like trying to tie my shoes with mannequin-hands. Jimmy was aboard *June* as well and half out of his own 'bolt before I blinked my eyes and looked up…

…not at Father Murton, as was normally the case after combat, but at Ted Knight.

"Where is he?" I demanded, self-control broken at long last.

Where is who? Ted didn't reply, to his credit. "We don't know," he answered. "He's missing."

"Brooks?" I asked.

"Him too," Ted answered. "Part of the bridge is gone, several decks worth. That's where they were. Vlasilov and most of the command staff as well." His face hardened. "I won't lie to you, Thomas. The odds are about nil. The debris is being searched as we speak. But…" He shook his head in a very final gesture.

My jaw worked; I tried to speak, but couldn't. "Jimmy…" I finally manage to croak out.

"I'll take care of him," Ted promised. "And we're looking for someone to take care of you too, Thomas." He paused. "Is there anyone… I mean…"

Not in the whole universe, I suddenly realized. Not except Ted, and I couldn't take him away from Jimmy. "I'd rather be alone," I answered. "For a little while at least."

"If that's what you want," Ted agreed, showing that while he might have been one of the hottest Polecat pilots who'd ever lived and at least a near match for his father in terms of operational genius, he didn't know beans about the Counseling business. "I understand, Thomas."

It didn't normally take more than a couple of minutes to walk from the flight deck to the gunroom, not even in a dead-slow mannequin body. But now it was three times the distance it had been due to the need to remain in areas that still had life-support. It seemed to take forever; as long, even, as it'd taken me to climb out of the Kammhuber Pass while watching everyone die of radiation poisoning along the way. It wasn't just the extra distance, but nothing looked like it had just a few hours before. Everything was scorched and burned and twisted just a little bit out of true here and there. The crew was worse; there were men and women still on duty all over the place with untreated burns and deep cuts that'd only been field-dressed. Worst of all was their eyes; where even the day before they would've waved and smiled, today they stared dully at my clean, freshly-pressed uniform, probably the only one on board except Jimmy's. Then, wordlessly, they'd step out of my way.

It soon became evident that there were *many* routes I could follow back to my cabin, not just the most direct one. If I went the long way around, who would ever know? If I claimed I was lost, how could anyone tell that was I lying amidst all the confusion? Ever since Ted had told me that Father Murton was probably dead, something big and black and overwhelming had been growing inside of me. It wasn't right for an officer to disobey important instructions, even if they weren't quite orders. But, if I went back to my cabin, the big black thing would burst and overwhelm me. That was something to be avoided for as long as possible, the navy for once be damned.

I came to a branch in the corridor. My cabin was to the right. I swung left, not hesitating a second. Towards sickbay.

Almost immediately I realized I'd made a bad decision. The ship's medical facilities were totally overwhelmed. The first proof of this was an endless line of corpses, each neatly covered with a blanket, all pressed up against a bulkhead so as to allow room for a pedestrian to pass. I didn't try to count them, but there were dozens. Many leaked, so that after a time I was leaving little red gore-tracks wherever I went. That didn't particularly bother me; there were plenty of others like them.

Then I began to encounter the living, though in truth they weren't very different from the dead. These were clearly the soon-to-be-dead, generally missing large pieces of anatomy or suffering gross burns. They leaked too, even worse than the corpses, and sometimes despite what must have been the deepest drugging possible they moaned and shuddered.

"What are you doing here?" an orderly demanded as he rounded a corner, his gurney covered with a red, drippy sheet. "You're not authorized!"

I merely stared at him until he dropped his eyes and rolled his burden to join the other corpses. Apparently he was too busy to argue.

Closer to sick-bay proper, conditions grew both worse and better. Things were better in that while the wounded still lined the corridors, most of them were conscious and appeared likely to survive. But things were also worse because, unlike the clearly terminal cases, they couldn't be so heavily drugged. Many were in agony.

"Aaaah!" cried out a woman almost at my feet. She was writhing and twisting in pain, despite being tightly strapped down into her gurney. "Please, sir! Get me a medic! My arms! They burn! Oh, they *burn*!"

I bent over and smiled, though I had to force the expression onto my face. The woman's arms *couldn't* be burning; she no longer had any. Not even stumps. "Of course," I promised. "Right now."

"Thank you, Commander Longo!" she replied, falling back onto her gurney. "They *burn*!" Then she passed out, which was a blessing to us both. Now it was easy to see why there were so many untreated minor wounds among the rest of *June*'s crew; a man would have to have a heart of stone to demand anything but the most essential treatment when so many severely-wounded shipmates were lined up already.

Sickbay was located very near *June's* center, so as to be as protected from damage as possible. I decided that I'd seen enough, so instead of turning left at the main corridor I swung right, towards the officer's mess. There wouldn't be much traffic there, I reasoned, and so I wouldn't be in the way. But I figured wrong again. There was an auxiliary airlock across from the mess that I'd forgotten about, and it was working at maximum capacity. A grizzled old chief was in charge, which told me how terribly important the task at hand must be. I turned to leave…

…but just then the chief spoke. "Belay that!' he ordered a younger rating, who was reaching into the lock with a sort of boathook. "D'ye want to put the admiral's eye out?"

I blinked, then turned to watch. Someone had loaded the wounded into small cargo-canisters, which probably made sense as a quick-and-dirty way to move them in a hurry. Now, however, they had to be removed. "Get in there!" the chief roared. "It'll wash off!"

The rating pressed her lips together, then nodded and crawled through the hatch.

"Gangway!" a voice behind me sang out; instinctively I pressed myself up against the bulkhead as a gurney with an equipment-filled shelf mounted underneath it rattled by, followed by three men in bloody white coats. "Gangway!"

Then Vlasilov's head appeared; it was covered in blood, and a large flap of hairless scalp was dangling loose. His eyes were fixed open and glassy, while his mouth was gaping like that of a dead fish. It looked as if he couldn't breathe, though he was as much in good air as I was. "Now!" the lead medic screamed even before the admiral was halfway out the hatch. The three were clearly a trained team, and knew exactly what they were doing. One forced Vlasilov's jaws open and shoved a tube down his throat, while the other two plunged improbably-large needles deep into his chest. Then they stood back and stared at the instruments on their equipment. They were from *Doolittle*, according to their uniforms.

"Gangway!" I heard behind me; another cart was coming.

"Negative," one of the needle-shovers reported. "Try again?"

"Positive!" the other replied, as a green light appeared on the cart. "He's getting oxy!"

"Thank god!" the throat-tube man answered; clearly he was in charge. "If I lost Vlasilov to a simple case of vacuum-lung, I'd never hear the end of it. Someone might think it was personal."

"There may still be brain damage," the needle-man whose thrust had missed whatever his target had been reminded his superior. "He was high and dry a mighty long time."

"How could anyone tell?" the man in charge answered dryly; it was the first attempt at humor I'd heard in hours.

"Sir!" the chief in charge of the lock said. "I have more wounded coming in. Clear out, please!"

"Of course," the team-leader answered, suddenly all business. Moving quickly but carefully, so as not to dislodge the needle that had "taken", they loaded the admiral onto the life-support gurney and squeezed past first me, then the other, identical cart. There was a short pause while the vessel on the other side lined herself up again.

"Hurry up!" the chief growled to no one in particular. "Damn merchies are *slow!*"

Then the green light went on, the dog-wheels spun, and the now blood-soaked rating looked in. "Geez!" she whispered.

"Get in there!" the Chief railed, grapping her and physically thrusting her through the hatch; it was clear to me now why she'd been selected for the duty; the woman was a tiny little thing. First a male leg emerged, attached to nothing. "It's in my way!" the rating explained, though the Chief made no argument as he accepted the gruesome thing and tossed it aside. Then came a second. Unlike the first, it still had the lower part of a pants-leg on it. Then came two calf-stumps, tourniquet-ed very effectively with navy web-belts, as prescribed in the manual.

"He'll have lost a lot of blood," the cart-leader declared. She was from *Geronimo*. "Make your setting oh-fiver-three."

"Oh-fiver-three," one of her subordinates agreed.

Then the wounded man came the rest of the way out...

...and to my shock I realized it was a buck-naked Father Murton! He was covered with bruises and small cuts, and his eyes were glassy and listless just like Vlasilov's had been. Most likely, I decided, he'd been caught in the explosion, and then someone had bound his wounds and gotten him into either a survival balloon or some other air bubble.

He was *alive*!

Suddenly the cart surged forward, and the two big needles and tube came out. All three plunged home.

"Negative," the first needle-man reported.

"Negative as well!" the second said, his eyebrows rising inquiringly.

"Do it!" the woman in charge snapped, and both men yanked out their needles and sank them a second time into my tutor's chest. Blood gushed out of the other two wounds as if from a hose, but no one paid attention.

"Negative!" the first man repeated.

"Neg..." Then he paused and examined his instruments. "Wait one!" There was a long pause. "Positive!" he declared.

"Clear my damn lock, sirs!" the Chief ordered. The others might outrank him, but everyone knew who was really in charge.

"Right," the team leader declared, stuffing handfuls of gauze into the gaping holes in Father Murton's ribcage. "We're outta here!"

Somehow during all of this the little female rating had wormed her way back through the hatch. "Here's another!" she answered. A foot emerged, this time apparently still connected to something. "I need help! He's huge!"

"Thomas?" someone said at my elbow. I turned, and there were Ted and Jimmy. "We're not supposed to be here, but...'

"We looked and looked for you!" Jimmy complained. "But..."

"Ooof!" the Chief complained, tugging at the foot. "He *is* huge!"

"A chief," the rating's voice said from the darkness. "He's got more years-of-service stripes than I've ever seen. More than you, even!"

A shadow crossed the lock-commander's face. "Right," he agreed, his voice still gruff and businesslike despite the bad news. The goat-locker was a tight-knit community. Among those with long service, everyone seemed to know everyone. "Get on with it!"

"I'm trying!" the rating shouted. "Pull, Chief! I can't move him alone!"

Wordlessly I edged my way forward. "I'm the strongest man aboard," I offered. It was true enough; Jimmy's motors had been powered down a little in favor of extended battery life.

"Yes, sir!" the chief answered, stepping aside. He'd heard the stories and knew that I was telling the truth. The petty officer's leg emerged again…

…and I recognized Petty Officer Brooks. It didn't come as a surprise; I'd suspected it to be him for quite some time now. I tried to grab his belt, but it was gone; expended, no doubt, as a tourniquet. So instead I gripped the waistline of his pants just above the crotch, modesty be damned, and levered him out at an angle that no normal human could've even begun to mange.

"Thank you," the hatch-chief muttered as I stood up, cradling the huge, muscular Brooks as if he were the child and I the adult.

"No problem," I assured the petty officer. Then I looked around for a cart to place him on…

…and found none!

"What?" I demanded. "I mean…"

"Sweet Jesus!" the chief exploded, suddenly aware of the glitch in his arrangements. The grizzled veteran leapt to his feet. "Ahoy!" he bellowed down the corridor, in a voice that in another century might well have penetrated the most ferocious of typhoons. "Ah-o-o-o-y!"

But, there was no reply.

"Mouth to mouth!" Ted barked.

"Won't work on a vacuum lung!" the chief replied. "I'm going to get Greg a cart if I have to steal one!"

"You go!" Ted agreed. "I'll try anyway."

"Good!" the older man answered. Then, he was off in a flash.

So it was that I held my good friend Brooks in my arms as Ted blew air in and out of his lungs and Jimmy clenched his fists and wept in frustration. Even a vacuum-damaged lung can transmit a *little* oxygen; therefore, it's probable that Ted's efforts prolonged Brooks' life for a measurable period of time.

But not long enough. There *were* no more carts, nor enough techs to man them if there had been. When the doctor finally arrived he took a few readings, then gently shook his head and moved on to the next disaster.

Chapter Thirty-Four

We spent almost two entire days hovering motionless just outside the Nikita Point that would connect us to Earth. After a few hours of rest Jimmy and I went back to heel-and-toe watches, sitting on the catapults in the Mark I Skybolts we'd originally brought along as cargo and which were now very-much-appreciated combat gear. There were still Dracan fighters based on New Nippon, large numbers of them by any reasonable measure despite their terrible losses. They might sortie at any time, and we had to be as ready as we could be. But they never did. Probably their commanding officer was smart enough to realize that if several hundred fighters hadn't been able to blot us out of the sky, then the few dozen he had left would be more profitably employed on other missions in the future. We'd been hurt, yes. But the Dracans had practically been gutted and hung out to cure in the sun. While the Emperor might not be pleased with the miserly way that his subaltern refused to expend his subject's lives, in this case the officer in charge was serving his sovereign's interests well.

Despite the long watches I was still able to make a little time to visit sick bay. While I'd been terribly angry at first about how such a fine man as Brooks had died for no better reason than a shortage of men and gear, I had a lot of time to think things through while on sitting on the launch rail. It hadn't been anyone's fault, or at least not that I could see. *June* was a ship of war first and foremost, not a spacefaring hospital. She'd been optimized and equipped for battle above all other factors. Yes, treating her wounded was important too. But, in the very nature of things healing could only be a secondary consideration. It *had* to be that way; no one could foresee exactly how many of this or that kind of medical equipment would be needed after any given battle, and there was only so much deck space to go around. Besides, it wasn't like people hadn't given their all; the fact that the other two medical crews, the ones who'd treated Father Murton and the admiral, had come from other ships spoke volumes about the efforts that'd been made to treat every single wounded man. There hadn't been anyone anywhere near sickbay that hadn't given their best, at least not that I'd seen. Who was I going to blame? The petty officer in charge of the lock? The medical teams, whose equipment and methodology simply wasn't set up for more than one patient at a time? The engineers who'd designed *June*'s sick bay to only have so many beds?

No, it wasn't anyone's fault. No one's at all. Just one of those things that Brooks himself had taught me about so long ago, when he'd told me about how as a boy he'd tried to rescue two children out of a fire and only one had survived. It'd been pure luck back then, which had lived and which had died, just as it was pure luck this time around that Father Murton had been tossed into the cargo container atop Brooks instead of the other way around. Life was like that, I was beginning to realize. Where others tried to find meaning in life and death, warriors learned quickly that there was only random chance. How many laser-bolts had aimed at me that I'd not seen and actively dodged, but which had missed anyway? What might've happened to Jimmy if my nose-wheel hadn't failed while launching for the Drakkus raid? Or if I'd flown my original assigned mission profile, the one that ended up killing Viktor and Delana? Our lives were terribly fragile things, I was coming to understand, infinitely unlikely chains of events shaped by an equally infinite variety of random circumstances, over most of which we had no control whatsoever. It was frightening to think about, but Brooks had learned young to deal with this vision of reality and in turn it'd become the foundation of the massive, overwhelming courage that was the bedrock of his identity.

Sitting silently in my Skybolt, I resolved to try and do the same. To accept the random nature of life and strive to become half the man that Brooks had been. Somewhere far away I felt him smile and pat me on the back. After that, I was at peace.

It was harder for Jimmy than for me, of course. Though Commander Zandi, who'd taken over command of *June* for the moment, had decided not to hold an actual funeral and space-burial due to the fact that Earth was so near and so many of the men had families there, he did conduct a hurried memorial service on the flight deck. Practically everyone on board not still at action or damage-control stations showed up, including many who were really too badly wounded to be there. It should've been Jimmy's watch, but we cut a private deal and I stayed on alert a few extra hours; in return my friend was kind enough to pull up a chair and sit next to me, near the very back. Ted sat next to him, and though they only had one working human eye between them they wept a river of virtual tears. Ted had known Brooks as a boy too it turned out, though I hadn't known it. "He's the one who coached me into the Academy," Ted whispered, tears running his unruined cheek. "He's the one who got me off of my butt and taught me to *do*, not just to try." The two brothers spent most of the service hugging each other, and when Brooks' name was read off Jimmy came over and hugged my fuselage as well. It was very, very sad.

But at least when I was off duty I could go see Father Murton and Admiral Vlasilov and remind myself that not all was death and destruction. Vlasilov, predictably, was making a remarkably quick and thorough recovery. Even though little more than a day had passed since he'd been blasted away from his flagship, spent far too long breathing only the most miserable excuse for air and then been exposed to the hardest of vacuum, Vlasilov was awake, alert, and composing his report on the action. He still couldn't speak; that'd take several weeks of healing. But he didn't *need* to speak to communicate. A dour glance here and there was all it took to convey meaning to the elderly one-armed petty-officer who served as his steward; it was if they'd actually grown telepathic over the years. "A force of nature," Captain Jungmann had called Vlasilov while he was still missing, and seeing him still at least partly in action despite being hooked up to half the plumbing in sick bay did nothing but reinforce the image. He smiled when I entered his room, so wide that I feared he'd dislodge his throat-tube. Then he waved me over to him, and hugged me for such a long time that I thought maybe he'd passed out. His eyes were all red and irritated anyway, from exposure to vacuum. But the tears he shed were only for me. I'd known that he liked me, even that he liked me a lot. I'd never really appreciated, however, how deep the emotion ran.

Father Murton was in much worse shape than the admiral; blood transmits oxygen, the doctor explained, and the loss of his lower legs had nearly drained him of blood even before he'd had to do without good air for so long. "The leg wounds are very clean," the exhausted-looking physician explained. "My guess is that the original blast knocked him unconscious, then a closing automated airlock sheared his calves off. Though that doesn't explain why the severed limbs were still with him." He shrugged. "Who knows? Maybe the merchies thought they could be re-attached, and went to find them? All kinds of strange stuff happened yesterday."

I nodded; Father Murton was still deathly pale, and hadn't recovered consciousness. "Will there be brain damage?"

"The readings so far are good," the doc explained. "Not perfect, mind you. But good." He sighed. "Thomas... The fact is, your counselor isn't exactly a spring chicken anymore. While we medical-types are getting better at fighting aging, humans also grow more and more fragile over time. The padre here is going to live; I'd bet my degree on it. We'll also grow him a new pair of legs, maybe even a little better than the ones he lost. But..." He shook his head. "Thomas, the brain is a very subtle thing, as is the personality. The answer to your question depends on some very fine distinctions, such as what does and what does not constitute 'significant' brain damage. This man has undergone a huge amount of trauma; near-fatal trauma, even. A lot of brain cells have died, and the things don't exactly grow on trees as I'm sure you already know. Once they're gone they're gone, even with the best of modern techniques." He turned and looked me square in the eye. "This whole business won't do your friend any good, Thomas. You can take that to the bank. But, how severe will the damage be?" He shrugged again. "Anywhere from a significant drop in IQ and major personality damage to maybe the equivalent of five or ten years of normal aging."

I blinked and looked at the still figure lying on the gurney. He *did* look a little grayer than I remembered, I realized suddenly. And, the lines in his face were deeper, too. Father Murton was *old*, I realized suddenly; it was something I'd never really thought about before. Too old for vacuum lungs and amputations, certainly; he'd originally retired from the navy while I was still in diapers. "I see," I said slowly, feeling a new sick feeling spinning in my gut. Someday-- someday soon even, if enough damage had been done-- Father Murton might be senile. And how was I going to deal with *that*? "Thank you, Doctor."

"Sure, Thomas," the white-coated man replied, smiling blearily. He was taking drugs to stay awake; the navy permitted men in critical positions to do this under certain circumstances, but also required them to wear a large yellow tag on their shirts while dosed-up. Though the doc's lab-coat was clean and snowy-white, his tag was spattered in blood. "For you, anytime."

I spent a few minutes alone with Father Murton, even though the doctor had warned me that he couldn't possibly be aware that I was present. I'd brought his favorite rosary with me, the black one with the golden crucifix that he wore on his cassock when dressed formally. He'd prayed so long and hard on it that the beads were no longer round; rather, they were dished-out a little on the sides where his fingers habitually made contact with them. "Here you go, Father," I whispered, opening his left hand slightly and placing the beads in them.

My tutor might've been unconscious, but apparently rosaries were a more powerful stimulus than the medical profession gave them credit for. Father Murton's hand closed, then his fingers found a single bead and lovingly began fingering it as if he were praying. Then he smiled; his whole face lighting up like that of an angel. It was a beautiful, beautiful thing.

Chapter Thirty-Five

On our third day of waiting, Vlasilov called Captain Shepherd to his sick-bed. As senior able-bodied officer he'd been in charge of the task force ever since the mortally-wounded Flag-Captain Jones of *The Glorious First of June* had ceded command to him. I was visiting the admiral when Shepherd arrived; the wounded officer's batman had told me that I was welcome anytime, for as long as I liked. But when Shepherd arrived I was most politely and respectfully shown the door. So I sat with Father Murton for a few minutes in the room next door while Vlasilov met with his subordinate. Though the admiral couldn't speak, I'd read enough of his handwritten notes after various meetings to know that this was no great handicap to him; he expressed himself as easily in the written medium as the verbal.

"No, sir," I heard Shepherd say, after the social rituals were completed. My ears were excellent, and soundproofing apparently hadn't been a major concern when sickbay had been designed. There was another long pause, then Shepherd spoke again. "Yes, sir, I *have* read the intelligence estimates." This time his voice sounded a bit defensive. "There's no question whatsoever. We're easily the most powerful force within two or three Jumps of here."

Father Murton was still unconscious. He wasn't in a coma anymore; rather, he was being kept under so that the special drugs designed to salvage as many damaged brain cells as possible could do their work. My tutor wasn't even on the critical list anymore; tomorrow if there were no more pressing emergencies among the other patients he might even receive his new leg-buds. So, I didn't feel too self-conscious about my eavesdropping. In fact, it was something I could hardly avoid.

"Sir," Shepherd replied, presumably to a scribbled comment. "*June* is badly hurt; she'll have to be towed across the Nikita. Towed, sir! *Cochise* isn't in any better shape; she can make a little thrust, but her Jump equipment is pretty much slagged. And—" Suddenly Shepherd's voice was cut off, my guess was that Vlasilov had begun his scribbling again.

"Sir... We're the last effective squadron in the navy, and the Dracan heavies are still out there somewhere. What if there's more destroyers waiting at the Earth end? Or cruisers, even? There might even be carriers with superfighters, though I think we've proven we can deal with fighters of the ordinary sort. The losses, however—" His voice cut off again. "No, sir," he said after a time, his tone now strained. "I am *not* of the opinion that you can win a war without losing ships. But—"

Whatever Shepherd's counter-argument might have been, Vlasilov clearly hadn't wanted to hear it. "Aye-aye, sir!" Shepherd said next; he must have come to attention and saluted as he did so, because I could hear his heels click right through the bulkhead. Then, without a further word, he left the room. His eyes were smoldering as he stomped past the entrance of my tutor's room. As well they should've been; clearly he'd been accused of lack of aggressiveness and initiative during his time in command of the entire force. There was no more damning charge in the navy world, save perhaps for outright cowardice.

On my very first day as a warrior, Lofton Knight had explained to me that air battles were most often won by sheer bloody-minded aggressiveness. While fleet-strategy was a little less straightforward, it was clear to me that the admirals who risked ships and took losses were pretty much the same admirals who won wars. Shepherd, given the chance to show what he could do, had been found wanting in this most critical of all command-traits. Unless I missed my guess, no matter how long he remained in the navy he'd never fly a flag of his own. Fleets were far too valuable and important to allow the awarding of second chances. I couldn't say that I was surprised; indeed, I'd been wondering myself what all the lollygagging in New Nippon space was about. Each day that we spent waiting was another that Earth starved. That alone was worth accepting losses to end. Even worse, however, each day we spent drifting idly and licking our wounds was another day that the Dracans had to refuel their dreadnoughts, scratch together a squadron, and attempt to recover from what for them must have been the worst disaster imaginable. Eventually they'd be back. By the time that they arrived we had to liberate New Nippon in order to replace the Dracan ground-based fighter threat with one of our own and put together a reinforced task force strong enough to fight and decisively win. Every *hour*, much less every day, was precious beyond price. Certainly lost hours were more important than the risk of possibly losing a ship or two. Didn't Captain Shepherd understand that?

Vlaisov had once told me that if I remained in the navy long enough I'd surely become an admiral myself. Perhaps I had a little natural aptitude after all?

Sure enough, before my next alert shift was half over things began to happen. "Action Stations!" the tannoy cried out. Those few red warning beacons that'd survived the torp hits lit up as well. All of them were on one side of the ship, making it appear as if the port launching rail was about to get into a fight while the starboard was not. "Action Stations!"

"Thomas?" a female voice asked directly into my mind. "Are you there?"

It was Michelle, though why I was hearing from her of all people I couldn't at first imagine.

"Yes, ma'am?" I answered.

"Ted's busy, so he asked me to give you a call. He's conferring with the staff over on *Cochrane*. They're in charge over there now, you know."

I false-smiled to myself; Michelle was good, but she couldn't quite hide the disapproval in her voice when she mentioned *Cochrane's* staff. "Right," I agreed. "There's nothing on the pipper. So, I assume we're *finally* about to Jump?" I laid just a tiny bit of extra emphasis on "finally" so she'd know that I understood.

"Finally," she agreed, her easy smile evident in every syllable. "We've had a contingency plan in place for two days now, and we're going with it. Your job is to remain in reserve with Jimmy as a quick reaction force. We'll dispatch you as needed, on the fly."

"Right," I agreed, turning my wingtip camera to watch as Jimmy was hooked up to his 'bolt. He waved to me as he laid down on the gurney. "That makes perfect sense."

"*Roman Nose* is leading," Michelle continued; I checked my pipper, and sure enough the plucky little destroyer was moving up to the front of our formation. She'd been held in reserve during the last battle, in part to pick up Jimmy and I should it have proven necessary. Now she was the only completely undamaged fighting ship in the task force-- if you didn't count the fact that her forward main guns had been removed-- and also the only one with a full outfit of torpedoes. "The rest of the *Chiefs* will follow, except for *Cochise* of course, and then the older destroyers. The main body will hold back, since *Cochrane* can't fight effectively while towing *June*."

I virtual-frowned; if Vlasilov had been in charge, the big ships would've followed close on the destroyers' heels, while *June* temporarily waited on this side of the Nikita. He'd have done without Jimmy and I and depended on traditional firepower. After all, there couldn't be much of a Dracan force on the other side; the enemy fleet wasn't that big! Didn't Shepherd have any faith in his own intelligence officers?

"Hello, Tommy!" Jimmy greeted me from the starboard rail. "What's up?" Bard brought him up to date. Then Ted cut in, slightly breathless, to tell us the same stuff all over again. Next we had to wait while everyone formed up…

…and, right on the tick, *Nose* burst through into Terran space, the first navy ship to do so in far too many months. "Horrido!" she signaled right before Jumping, which made both Jimmy and me smile. The war-cry was spreading. Rotte would never be forgotten, it was clear.

Nose wasn't physically big enough to produce a flash-image like the one we'd gotten from *Orleans* as she'd burst through to New Nippon just a few days before. It took a discrete interval of time to do that, time generated by hull-length. But the Nikita didn't flash and pulse with energy as it had last time either, and that along with faith in Michelle was enough to make me begin to relax. Jimmy too, it seemed. "There won't be a fight," he predicted as the rest of the *Chiefs* surged through, one after the other. "There's nothing there."

"Yeah," I agreed. "I think you're right."

The only complicated thing about our battle plan had been developing a means to get information back to New Nippon space. A timetable had been worked out, similar to that used in peacetime traffic control, to prevent any ships from trying to transit the Nikita both ways at the same time. Nothing came back through during the first scheduled interval, nor the second. But, during the third, *Nose* came bursting back to bring the rest of us up to date. "No Dracans present in Earth space," she sent instantly. "Navy headquarters reports that the last enemy unit left twelve days ago." There was a pause. "The Commander-in-Chief of the United Systems Navy wishes to pass on a message to every man and woman in task force seven, including the crews of the merchantmen. 'Job well done. You have saved Earth, and in so doing have saved the future of mankind. No victory won, past or future, can ever eclipse the importance of your hard-won triumph against such terrible odds.

"Lovers of freedom everywhere salute you."

Chapter Thirty-Six

The people of Earth were indeed very grateful to us. But grateful wasn't quite the same thing as competent; *The Glorious First of June* was ordered to land in the Firth of Forth, where the navy's best surviving repair facilities awaited her. Somewhere along the line, however, a poorly-trained signalman-- almost certainly a short-service draftee-- managed to reverse a couple of digits in our landing orders. The upshot was that *June* came down near marker buoy six-one, while she was expected at buoy one-six. To make things even more interesting the berth at six-one was already occupied by the still-fitting-out heavy cruiser *Abuja*. Since unfinished ships don't carry navigation beacons, her unexpected presence-- only detected at the very last second-- proved rather a shock to *June*'s navigational staff. Commander Zandi's fill-in bridge crew of replacement officers gleaned from every ship in the task force somehow managed the impossible, however. They landed us in one piece despite the fact that none of them had ever splashed down a carrier before, much less a heavily-damaged one. We came down out in one of the marked shipping channels, where we were promptly rammed by a cursing civilian captain in charge of an improbably large string of supply barges. It was a ridiculous, stupid, and yet somehow entirely fitting end to such a long and perilous voyage. Fortunately the impact was oblique, so that no serious damage was incurred to either party. Commander Zandi invited the tug captain aboard for a drink while the VIP's who'd gathered to welcome us home hurriedly climbed aboard a fleet of 'hoppers for the short trip across the Firth. While the tug captain was aboard, at Commander Zandi's request Jimmy and I showed up on the bridge to introduce ourselves to the aggrieved contractor. It worked like a charm; suddenly all was well with his world again.

The ceremony was pretty much like every other homecoming in the long history of mankind; I'd sat through enough of them by now to realize they were essentially all the same. A bunch of kids sang "Hail the Conq'ring Hero Comes", along with similarly appropriate songs chosen from among the seven-bajillion cultures and traditions represented in the United Systems. Then there were the speeches; predictably long and boring. But still, as dull as being greeted as returning heroes was, it was terribly important to those of us who'd been through so much and faced such terrible danger. It would've been far worse *not* to be greeted. The Dracan dreadnoughts, for example, had been forced through no fault of their own to flee instead of doing battle; you can't fight much of a war without molecular batteries, after all. But, would children be singing "Conq'ring Hero" to *them* when *they* made planetfall at home after their own long mission, main guns still unfired?

Somehow, I rather doubted it.

Having task force seven make its homecoming all over the planet had confronted officialdom with something of a dilemma. Should they greet *June*, the flagship? Or, should they go meet the bulk of the fighting ships, which were scheduled to splash down at the North Atlantic spaceport? What about the merchies, who were landing in little dribs and drabs all over the place? They'd solved the problem rather neatly, I thought, by having the PM himself meet *June*, most of the civilian and navy brass the rest of the warships, and local dignitaries the merchies. Every celebration was different; in San Francisco Bay fireworks burst over the big container ships as they were towed in formation under the Golden Gate bridge, which was closed for the occasion and packed with countless thousands of riotous celebrants. In Hong Kong there were Chinese dragons and firecrackers. And in Hamburg, where half the population was still radiation-sick from the Dracan bombing of London, for one glorious twenty-four hour period beer-rationing was suspended and the drinking-places filled with the sounds of happy songs and stomping feet.

I'd planned to go back to my cabin and rest after the big blowout, but it wasn't to be. Just as things were breaking up, Vlasilov's one-armed steward sought me out. "Sir?" he asked, tugging slightly at my sleeve from behind. I'd been standing at the rail, drinking in the splendid desolation of the Firth. "Excuse me, sir."

"Yes?" I asked, turning around and smiling.

"The admiral asked me to find you, sir. He says that he needs you in his room in sick-bay. It's urgent."

It's always urgent, I thought but didn't say aloud. Unless one counted actual combat time, I hadn't been out of *June* in weeks. This had been the very first chance I'd had to just stand and take in some fresh air. But, I reminded myself as I turned to follow the Chief, no one else had had much time for rubbernecking either. Including Vlasilov, of course, who probably wouldn't see the sun for weeks to come.

I should've known that something was up from the busy hum of activity that grew more and more intense the closer I got to the ship's hospital. Because of the recent terrible overload there, in some ways normal ship's discipline had been allowed to slide. Decks normally swabbed every morning had been left to gather dust, for example, so that the responsible hands could perform more vital tasks. But now *June's* sickbay was a whirlwind of swabbing, scrubbing, scouring… It looked more like a scene from what I'd heard boot camp must be like than anything I was familiar with. The ratings just barely had time to look up at me as I passed by, and one actually dragged his mop across my left shoe. "My god, sir!" he whispered, realizing what he'd done. "I'm so sorry!"

"Never mind," I answered. "It was an accident. No big deal." Still, Vlasilov's steward made me find a little nook, where he sat me down and rapidly returned the black leather to a mirror-finish. It was just as well that I physically couldn't do this for myself, or else I'd have been forced to admit that I didn't even know *how*.

So I shouldn't have been surprised to find the Prime Minister waiting for me, sitting patiently by the head of Admiral Vlasilov's bed. Pinned to the admiral's pillow was a medal; the United Systems Parliamentary Medal of Merit, the highest decoration a man could win. I had two of them, both awarded for mere propaganda purposes, I clearly understood. But if anyone had ever truly *earned* the Medal, it was Vlasilov. Without him, we'd have been beaten before we ever began. "Sir!" I said, hitting as stiff a brace as my fake body would allow and saluting. "Congratulations!"

Vlasilov smiled a little, a rare sight indeed. Then, still unable to speak, he nodded slightly.

"Ah, Thomas!" the PM exclaimed, levering himself to his feet with the help of the arms of his chair. He was thinner now than he'd been, much thinner, even. And the once-cheery wrinkles in his face had degenerated into thick, careworn ruts. An assistant instantly reached out and placed a cane in the PM's hand; where once the device had been a near-ornament, now it was a clearly a necessity. He tottered slowly forward. "There will be an official investment ceremony later, of course. But I happened to be here, and..." With the hand furthest from Vlasilov, the one the admiral couldn't see, the PM indicated all the plumbing my Commanding Officer was still hooked up to. It was still faintly possible that he might die, and obviously the PM was taking no chances.

"Of course," I answered, smiling. "No one deserves it more."

"You and Jimmy will be well taken care of as well," the PM assured me, his eyes twinkling. "Though in your case it's becoming rather tedious to come up with new award-speeches." He smiled and extended his hand. "So, for now you'll have to accept my simple thanks on behalf of everyone who's benefited so much from your risks and sacrifices."

I took the PM's hand and shook it, but couldn't think of anything to say. When we were done, however, he held on and drew me closer. "You have a good handshake," he observed. "Especially considering that your hand makes no pretense of being real."

I smiled again; my fingers were naked stainless steel. "That was one of Father's ideas," I explained. "He put little warmers inside the fingers. My social body is much more advanced and sophisticated than, for example, Jimmy's. The original plan was for everyone to have one like this, but..."

"...but then the war came," the Chief of State agreed, nodding sadly.

"What a terrible disaster it's been for us all!" He cocked his head to one side. "I've received a letter about you," he continued. "From Alicia Wiston, my most-capable Deputy. She's formed, it seems, some intriguing ideas about your future."

I glanced around the room; suddenly everyone was staring at me, including the admiral. *So*, I thought to myself, *that's what this is all about*. "We've had conversations," I admitted. "My father agrees with her. They're becoming quite good friends."

The old man's gray eyes turned to ice. "Indeed?" he asked. :"That is… Interesting." Then, almost as quickly as it had formed the frost faded away to nothing. "We're going to be holding general elections soon, Thomas, though the exact date hasn't been set yet. As I'm sure you well remember, I dismissed Parliament. I didn't apologize for it then, and I don't now. When the bombs fell, Thomas…" He shuddered for a moment, then steadied himself. "Well… If we hadn't already been under martial law, it would've been far worse. But somehow it seems that a lot of people don't agree with me. They're calling me a dictator. A fascist, even! I had to look that one up in the dictionary."

I nodded slowly. "There are those who call the navy murderers, too, for what we did on Drakkus. Butchers."

"Ye-es," the PM replied, his eyes narrowing again as he drew out the single syllable into a long, nasal, very British sound. "Well, I for one would welcome a murderous butcher like you on my party's ticket, Thomas. We fascists are going to need the butcher-vote quite badly this time around; every shortage, every hardship is being blamed on us by the Opposition. Alicia ideas were *most* interesting, I assure you. Though I want to be certain they're practical before discussing them any further."

My own eyes narrowed; Alicia and Spence were the two hardest-core dirty-pool aficionados I'd ever known. Once they became convinced of the rightness of their cause and the unworthiness of their foes, they'd do practically *anything* to see what they considered to be the side of truth and justice come out on top. I thought back to the defense committee meeting I'd been asked to testify at, and how that one self-serving Parliamentarian from Washington State hadn't let me get a word in edgewise. What had his name been? Nagano, I suddenly recalled. Chief of the opposition. Nor had he wanted to allow the navy to build the weapons it needed to win-- he'd even tried to stop the Skybolt program and divert the money to his own district! Without the 'bolt, we'd have surely lost the war by now, and everyone would be worshipping the Emperor! But…

I stood up straight and tall. "Sir," I said, as respectfully as I could manage. "I'm a naval officer, and must perform the duties to which I am assigned. Today I'm the commander of the Top Bananas. We have only two pilots and four 'bolts, and we desperately need to work up more. There's only Jimmy and me to do most of the training, and as important as the elections are, well…"

Vlasilov reached for a scrap of paper and began scribbling. When he was done he handed the sheet to his steward, who in turn put it in my hand. "Thomas," I read aloud for the benefit of everyone present. "You're correct about the need for more Skybolts, and also about how important you are to making this happen. I cannot deny this. However, there's more to getting a full squadron of 'bolts into service than just buying airframes and training pilots. First of all Parliament must provide the funding. Despite all that has happened and the clear necessity for naval expenditure in time of war, the Opposition still wants to force the Fleet to base its strength on battleships rather than Skybolts. You know that we need both, Thomas. But you also know that we need rather more Skybolts than capital ships. Not the other way around.

"The navy cannot take an official position in Parliament, except through the Navy Minister. I can, however, inform you that I'm utterly certain the Navy Minister would be absolutely delighted if you were to stand for election. I can also tell you that nothing would please me more personally."

The note ended there, but Vlasilov had been scribbling away the whole time I was reading. The new note arrived just as I was finishing the old. "The nature of this war is about to change," the admiral continued. "Where until now one or two Skybolts have been vital components of victory, in a year we will be flying dozens. Thus, Thomas, your own personal contribution at the front lines will mean far less. We still need you, yes. No one else will command the Bananas if I've anything to say about it, and you can be assured that I most certainly *shall* have a say. However, as urgently as we need you in the Fleet we need you in the government even more.

"I know that you do not wish to do this, Thomas. But in the name of the war dead whose sacrifices might yet come to naught, I am asking you."

Chapter Thirty-Seven

Vlasilov was right; I *didn't* want to stand for Parliament. In fact, short of having to go out and kill more Dracan children, it was about the last thing in the universe that I wanted to do. But between Father, Alicia, the admiral and all the thousands of men I'd watched die, how could I in good conscience say no? The PM seemed quite pleased to hear my answer, and I have to admit that I felt a certain little thrill inside of me when I thought about actually being able to *do* something about the conduct of the war and the crafting of a lasting peace. "There won't be much to it," the PM explained. "I recognize how valuable your time is." He smiled at Vlasilov. "In fact, the navy has made its prior claim on you abundantly clear. All that will be required are a few campaign speeches, and perhaps a town hall meeting or two. Then, once you've won, you'll have to spend a few days at the new capitol in Rome. Ordinarily, of course, we'd demand far more of a young man standing for office. But in your case, I think the voters can be made to understand how thinly stretched you are. In the meantime no one is to say anything to anyone. My organization still has much groundwork to lay, and much of it is of the sort that is best taken care of quietly."

"Will running for Parliament get me out of selling war bonds?" I asked.

"Heh!" The PM shook his head and smiled. "I fear not, Thomas. *Everyone* sells war bonds, including me." He placed a sympathetic hand on my shoulder. "But this much I can promise. At least you won't have to do peddle the wretched things quite so often."

The next day, Vlasilov's staff cut me a set of what would've been dream orders for any other officer. And, I had to admit, they were pretty darned good ones even for me. I was to report to my father's estate back in New Orleans, and there act as the official navy liaison to Father's plant. I was to use my own judgment in the performance of my duties, my object being to facilitate the production and delivery of new 'bolts, and was also to work in two weeks of shore leave as time allowed. In short, I was being cut loose to do whatever I thought right regarding a critical war-production program, which was about the biggest mark of confidence any eighteen-year-old anywhere had ever received so far as I knew. I was surprised that Ted wasn't given the job until I discovered that he was being transferred to command the air group of the soon-to-be-commissioned *Tsushima Strait*, a traditional heavy carrier that was being outfitted with Polecats in lieu of Skybolts due to lack of airframes and pilots. Jimmy was going with him to take some leave, as Lofton Knight, their father, was the ship's captain. There were plenty of Polecats to go around on Earth; you could hardly walk around a navy base these days without tripping over one. No less than four factories were now up and running, cranking the things out like consumer goods. This was why Earth had never lost completely lost aerospace supremacy, though the Dracans had been able to hit targets whenever they were willing to pay the price. Now, with interstellar trade up and running again at least on a limited basis, it was proving possible to complete heavy spacecraft as well. *Tsushima* was only the first of eight or ten warships scheduled to be commissioned in the next few months. It was too bad that they'd have to settle for Polecats and, perhaps, even Gladius thruster-fighters to fill out their air-groups.

Which, of course, was why I was being sent to New Orleans in the first place.

I hadn't the slightest idea of what I was going to do regarding Father's plant; in fact, I hadn't considered for a moment that I might be sent there. It was just as well that the navy gave me something to smile about and take my mind off of my troubles as I legally separated myself from *June*.

"We'll miss you, Commander," the purser assured me as I signed my name to the papers that relinquished my claim to a cabin and dining privileges and such on my old ship. I'd just spent an hour walking up and down the hanger deck, where, seemingly, every off-duty sailor aboard had unofficially gathered to bid me farewell. It'd been very moving. "We all know what you've done, and I'm sure that I'm speaking for everyone when I tell you how proud I am to have been your shipmate."

I smiled and concentrated on trying to sign my name. Father Murton usually took care of that for me; he had my power of attorney. But his temporary replacement, Spaceman First Class Manuel Melendez, of the planet Pampas, was not so authorized. I made a sort of horrid scrawl, which the Purser was kind enough to accept. Then he turned the page and scowled. "I should've taken care of this a long time ago," he admitted. "But you've been busy, I've been busy…"

"There's been a war on," I agreed.

"Yes!" he answered. "Exactly! But, still…" He scowled again. "Sir, I know this can't be accurate. But it appears to me that you've never been paid. Not once! There's never been a payroll account set up in your name that I can find. Even worse, I can't find any record of your induction into the service. When and where were you sworn in, anyway?"

Despite myself, I grinned. If I told the truth I'd be stuck aboard *June* all day, dealing with outraged navy lawyers. "On Churilla," I explained. "The first day of the war. My paperwork's probably been lost."

"Ouch," the purser agreed, pressing his lips together in sympathy. "So, it's real then? You've actually never been paid?"

"Not that I know of," I answered. "Frankly, money has sort of been the *last* thing on my mind."

The purser smiled, then realized I wasn't joking. "Son…" he said slowly. "Do you have the faintest clue as to how much a carrier-rated pilot-commander makes, even without the combat bonus you're entitled to?"

I shook my head. "Nope."

The older man paled, then asked to be excused for a moment while he consulted his computer. "Travel expenses," I heard him murmur at one point. "My god! All of those speeches! And shipwreck allowances! Mustn't forget those. Test-pilot pay, for flying an unproven type…"

When the purser finally emerged from his office again, he was perspiring. "Commander," he said slowly. "Are you *sure* that you've never been paid?"

"I'm honestly not certain," I answered. "The checks might've gone to Father Murton."

"No," he answered. "That's against regs. Your friend Jimmy gets his in trust, but it still goes to him." He sighed and slapped a check down on the table in front of me. "I don't want to do this," he explained. "Really and truly I don't. But I'm scheduled to be rotated dirtside myself next week, and this little matter has to be off of the books before I can go." He tapped the "amount" line with his forefinger. The numbers wouldn't all fit in the little box; two digits ran off to the right. "I'll have you know, Commander, that's the biggest paycheck I've ever cut in my thirty years in deep space. By a factor of fifty." He shook his head again. "You'll have to sign a special statement for me, of course. Saying that you swore to me on your honor as an officer that you'd never been paid."

"Sure," I agreed. "Anything for a shipmate."

The purser's check was still folded up in my shirt pocket when the navy 'hopper flared out above my father's private landing field and then settled gently to the tarmac. I stole a glance at Manuel, he'd seemed rather nervous throughout the flight. It was odd, really; he'd traveled I didn't know how many thousands of parsecs since leaving home, and was the veteran of at least three space battles. Yet an ordinary 'hopper ride made him nervous as a kitten. He noticed me looking at him, and smiled shyly. I smiled back. Manuel wasn't a counselor; quite the opposite, really. He was a little frightened of my rank and fame, and couldn't have been more than a year or so older than me. Though he was rated a gunner aboard *June*, he'd been trained as a navy valet somewhere along the line. Manuel, I'd been informed, had been temporarily assigned to me as a reward. Despite his seeming shyness and fear of flying, he'd shot down two Dracan fighters at New Nippon, and scored difficult, long-range hits on a destroyer during the raid on Drakkus. Even more, he'd dashed unprotected through near-vacuum to deliver survival-bubbles to several shipmates trapped in the next turret; his voice was still a little rough from the experience, and his eyes glowed red from all the burst blood-vessels. He was going to be awarded the Fleet Star, promoted, and sent to the Training Fleet to serve as an example to the draftees just as soon as he was done taking care of me, though he didn't know it yet. I promised myself that, no matter how busy I was, I'd make time to attend his investment ceremony.

Still, I felt very much alone as I carefully made my way down the ramp to the ground, taking one slow, laborious step at a time as I always had to. Everything about the scene told me that I was home; the sun and sky were the right color, I was surrounded by greenery instead of tundra or bare rock, and, I was quite certain, the place would even have *smelled* like home if I'd been equipped with a working nose,. But it was all different somehow, and the differences had nothing to do with the subtle alterations to the plant's roofline that'd been made since I'd last walked these grounds, or the fact that most of the grassy areas had been converted to vegetable gardens. There was no one here, I realized deep down in my gut for the first time. No one that I knew and trusted and loved, to help me make my decisions and find my way.

No one at all.

Well, I corrected myself as I picked out a familiar portly figure striding towards the landing field as quickly as he could. *There was always the staff.* The somewhat-overweight figure belonged to Mr. Flowers, Father's estate manager. He was a Terran; Father preferred to employ locals whenever practical in the name of good community relations. "Thomas!" the heavyset man greeted me, white teeth flashing in his dark face. "We weren't expecting you so soon!"

"The navy gets a higher clearance," I explained. "So we don't have to wait for traffic." I accepted Mr. Flowers' extended hand and shook it. "I should've warned you."

"I'm still very sorry," he answered, not quite meeting my eyes. Clearly Mr. Flowers—I couldn't remember his first name and suspected I'd never known it—was nervous about something. "Your room is ready, of course. And—"

"Thomas!" a new voice called out; it belonged to a very tall, big-shouldered man that I didn't recognize. "Thomas!" He walked right up to me and hugged me like a long-lost child. "I'm so glad to meet you at long last! We follow your adventures every day, up in the offices!" He pulled away and extended a hand for shaking. "I'm Keith Roon, plant manager."

I didn't like to be hugged by people I didn't know. Even worse, I was in full uniform. It just wasn't *right* for a civilian to treat a serving navy officer in such a manner, whether it happened to be me or not! Especially in front of an enlisted man. I looked over at Manuel; sure enough, his cheeks were reddening. "Excuse me," I answered, accepting Roon's hand. "Have we met?"

Apparently I managed to inject a little chill into my voice, as I'd hoped. "No," Roon admitted, lowering his eyes slightly. "I was appointed by the government to try and bring the plant back into production after your father and brother left." He lifted his hands, then let them fall back to his sides. "The plant's been nationalized for the duration, you see, though I'm told you Longo's are being most handsomely compensated. The War Production Board decided it's still the best place to try and produce Skybolts even after so much tooling was carried off to Esteppe."

I nodded slightly; it was sensible enough. "And how is production proceeding?" I asked.

Roon smiled. "Very well indeed! We've hit all of our benchmarks, every last one. We've completed a dozen airframes."

My eyebrows rose. "Really?" I asked. Vlasilov's people had led me to believe that nothing was happening here.

"Really!" Roon agreed, smiling. "We're very proud."

I tilted my head to one side. "Who do you have for a test pilot? I've just hit dirt, you see, and haven't had time to read the reports."

For the first time, Roon looked a little nervous. "No one," he admitted. "The navy hasn't been able to provide a pilot yet. They're having problems with the surgery. Our doctors aren't experienced in the procedure."

That was bad news. I remembered how we'd lost a boy during brain-core surgery aboard *June*, and shuddered inwardly. Even in wartime, it was understandable that inexperienced docs would want to take it slow and easy. "How soon before you have one assigned to you?"

"I don't know," Roon admitted. His face brightened. "I can send a memo, and get you an answer by Tuesday at the latest."

I pressed my lips together again. It was inexcusable that a program-head be so out of touch that he couldn't rattle off the exact projected date of such a vital event. I'd sat through enough of first Spence's and then Vlasilov's endless planning sessions to know *that* for certain! "Well," I said slowly. "I presume you have ground-support staff?"

"Oh, yes!" the big man agreed, his head bobbing up and down eagerly. "The same team your father left behind. They're *very* well trained! We have them do demonstrations for VIP's almost every day!"

I couldn't help but wince at that; Skybolt ground-crewman were highly-skilled professionals, not circus ponies. While it might be reasonable to expect them to put on a show once in a great while, well... I could imagine what *they* thought of it all. "I see," I answered. Then I turned to Mr. Flowers. "Can you get someone to take my dunnage to my room?" I asked. "And perhaps help my friend Manuel get himself situated?"

"Of course, sir", the estate-manager replied, a knowing smile spreading slowly across his face. "And... I must say that it's wonderful to have a Longo back in charge here. Things were getting dull."

I couldn't help but grin back; I'd always liked Mr. Flowers and so had Father. "Not anymore," I promised. Then I turned back to Roon. "Let's go have a look at these twelve completed airframes," I said, smiling and putting my hand on his shoulder as if I knew him far better than I did. "Have the support team meet us there. I feel an itch to fly. And while we're on the way, perhaps you can tell me a little bit about your background in military 'hopper production, and how exactly it came to be that you were appointed to your present position..."

Chapter Thirty-Eight

Roon didn't *have* a military 'hopper production background, as near as I could tell, though as we walked across the tarmac he made a big deal of his experience producing home appliances. "Refrigerators and 'hoppers; it's all the same thing, really," he explained airily, waving his hand at the factory as if the planet's sole Skybolt production facility were the most commonplace building in the world. "All businesses operate under the same basic principles. Quality, efficiency, repeatability."

I nodded politely, even though I wanted to retch. "What happened to your refrigerator plant?" I asked. "I'd think that it's be operating full bore, with the food shortage as bad as it is."

Roon pressed his lips together. "Off-planet competition. And the damn unions! An honest man couldn't make a nickel anymore." He shook his head. "My sister tried and tried to get legislation passed to protect such a vital industry. But—"

"Your sister?" I interrupted, sensing that at last I was on the true path to understanding the situation.

The big manager smiled and seemed to puff up a little. "Sis is a Parliamentarian," he explained proudly. "Representing New Zealand; she relocated when she got married, many years ago. You've probably heard of her. Cindy Albers."

Actually, I hadn't heard of her. But, I nodded as if impressed.

"We're all so terribly proud," he explained, still smiling and holding his head high. "I used to babysit her when she was little. Imagine that!"

"Golly!" I agreed politely.

Not all of the completed 'bolts were airworthy, Roon explained as we made our slow way back to the rearmost corner of the factory grounds. We should've called for a cart, but I'd wanted time to listen and learn. The refrigerator manufacturer, naturally enough, had ordered that the fighters be stored out-of-doors, where the navy kept them in humidly-controlled hardstands as much as possible and Father went so far as to filter the air in his hangers to prevent even the slightest possibility of dust contamination. As we walked up a Longo-coveralled worker was cutting on one of the 'bolts with a torch. I winced at the use of such a crude tool, but maintained my silence. "What's this all about?" Roon demanded of the torch-wielder, crossing his arms in a domineering fashion. He was trying to impress me, I hoped; if not, then he was the worst leader of men I'd ever seen. "Who authorized you to work on this 'hopper?"

The worker jumped a little in fright, causing the flame of his torch to wiggle slightly and cut a bundle of wires he'd been trying to avoid. "Sir?" he asked, turning around and raising his heavy mask. "Didn't you… I mean…" Then he saw me. "Thomas? Is that *you*?"

By sheer luck, I recognized the man. His son David had used to go canoeing with me sometimes, and once or twice I'd slept over at his house. "Mr. Pearlman!" I replied, smiling a heartfelt smile. "How wonderful it is to see you again!?

The older man smiled so wide I thought his face would crack. "Thomas! I mean, Mr… Commander…"

I laughed out loud, and reached to shake Mr. Pearlman's hand. He had to switch his torch around and remove his heatproof gauntlet to do so; while he was awkwardly rearranging his gear I clapped him on the shoulder. "It's so good to see you!" I assured him. "And to you I'm always 'Thomas'. After I broke your son's brand-new bunk bed, how could it be otherwise?"

"Hah!" Mr. Pealrman answered, leaning his head back and directing the single syllable of laughter up towards the heavens. "I've forgiven you that long ago, son. And your father took care of the damages."

I smiled again; it was *so* wonderful to see a friendly face. We caught up on family matters; David was a pre-med student now, it seemed, and Mr. Pearlman was terribly distressed to hear that my brother Sven was ill; they'd worked closely together on a couple of prototype projects. Mr. Pearlman was a hand-fabricator, one of the best Father had ever known, he'd claimed more than once. He'd wanted to take him with us to Esteppe, but the navy hadn't had enough space. "So," I finally asked, looking him in the eye. "How are things here?"

Pearlman looked first at me, then at Roon, then back at me. "I… Uh…"

"Right," I agreed. "I understand." I clapped him on the shoulder again. "We'll do dinner, eh? Say, tomorrow night at the big house? You and the missus, and Danny too if he can make it?"

The fabricator's eyes grew wide, but before he could answer Roon spoke up again. "First," he demanded, arms still crossed. "What were you doing taking parts off of a completed airframe? Don't you know that's against policy?"

Pearlman looked at me; I smiled and shrugged. *You'll be protected,* I was trying to say. *Tell the truth.* Apparently my attempt at telepathy succeeded; he turned back to Roon and removed his hat. "Sir," he explained. "We've been taking parts off of these birds for weeks now. Didn't you know?"

The big man's face turned scarlet. "That's not allowed!"

"Well," Pearlman explained; he looked at me for reassurance, and I nodded again. "It's not as if any of these 'bolts are ever going to fly anyway. They're all defective." He looked back at me again. "That one bird we built that you flew, Thomas, it was bad enough even though we had proper equipment and your father helping us. But these?" He shrugged and pointed at the machine he'd been cannibalizing. "This was our first after we lost all of our best tools. Nothing in it lines up. I mean, sure, you can eyeball it and everything looks fine. But, the tolerances…" He shook his head and sighed. "These birds operate at accelerations and velocities that Polecats can only dream of; that's why they're so damned unforgiving to build. We're operating right on the edge of the theoretical limits. If you get even one tiny bit of weld-spatter where it doesn't belong, well…" He waved at the factory. "Maybe on Esteppe they're used to building stuff that perfectly, though frankly I doubt it. I bet your father had to go through the same long, drawn-out process there that we're going through here, trying to get past the learning curve and create specialists. So long as your father and brother were around, we made actual progress." He turned to face Roon again. "Your father didn't try to churn out large quantities of crap in a hurry and then pass it off as quality goods.

He scrapped his mistakes instead of trying to force the navy to buy them. And, even more, he involved the workers and helped them *learn* from their errors. He didn't berate or discipline them; I've rarely known such a patient man, a true pleasure to work for. He was also one of the greatest machinists I've ever known in his own right. Willy wasn't afraid to get dirty." He glared at Roon again. "We have over a thousand outstanding labor grievances, Thomas. Back in the day, a dozen was a scandal. I've run for union office myself, I'm so sick of it. I'd have quit this place outright if I hadn't been privileged to know you and your family personally. A lot of good men did exactly that. There's plenty of war-work to be had elsewhere."

I felt myself growing sick. Knowing how difficult the task would be, Father had hand-picked his workers personally, one by one. And now…

"What are you doing cutting on this airframe?" Roon demanded again. "You have no authorization!"

"This airframe isn't going anywhere," Pearlman repeated, standing his ground. "Ever. Once upon a time it might've staggered through the sky, god willing, on a good day. But we didn't build it right. Which is no surprise, since you forced us to work without a proper polymill." He shook his head and turned back to me. "You just can't build a Skybolt without a proper polymill. Period. We could've spent the time training and tuning in on subassemblies, but no…"

"You're insubordinate!" Roon cried out, waggling his finger in Pearlman's face.

"Always have been," he agreed cheerily, obviously no longer afraid. He knew me better than Roon did, and had read my intentions correctly. Or perhaps he'd finally hit his breaking point. "That's why Sven liked working with me. Or so he always said. Anyway," he continued, turning back to me. "We ran five more 'bolts before they got us a polymill." He waved his hand. "They're all junk. Numbers six, seven, and eight have skewed motormounts; they're so far off they can't be adjusted back into true. That happened because we tried to produce—again!—when we should've been dialing-in the new 'mill. By the time we built numbers nine and ten, we were starting to have worker turnover problems. People were quitting faster than they could be trained. So, nine is out of true again, the motormount problems resurfaced on ten, and somehow we screwed up the wiring on eleven so badly that I'd strongly advise you never to have yourself hooked up to it. I imagine it'd be agony. That issue might just have been fixable, but the stub-wing mating adhesive was later found to be contaminated. In my mind, that's sufficient reason to scrap her; I'd never trust her with *my* life, knowing there's reasonable doubt. So, we've never bothered troubleshooting the wiring."

I nodded. "And twelve?"

"You won't believe it," Pearlman said, shaking his head as Roon looked daggers at him. "We built that one right after the bombs fell. It's perfect, or near to it. But the carbon composites are radioactive; they came from eastern Canada, which caught the fringes of the fallout." He shook his head. "Now, there's not a ton of electronics in a 'bolt; there *can't* be, as you well know. But…"

I nodded. "Ionization," I agreed. "It could induce errors. *Would* induce errors, in fact."

"Exactly!" Pearlman agreed. He shook his head again. "And management knew all along. Did they think no one would ever notice? And it's not just the 'hopper, you know." He glared at Roon. "He exposed the workers to radiation for no good reason without even warning them. Don't expect that to be forgotten anytime soon! Man, you should have seen them hit the gate and never come back after *that!*"

"Why are you removing parts from this airframe?" Roon demanded one last time, by now desperate to reassert his authority. "Answer me!"

Pearlman shrugged and pulled a form out of his coverall pocket. "It's from the navy," he explained as Roon snatched it from his hand and began to read. "They need some parts, pronto, for a couple 'bolts that got shot up fighting the convoy through. My guess is that Thomas here knows a little something about that. Plus, they've forwarded an inventory of spares they want to stock." He smiled as his boss turned scarlet again. "I don't know the guy who signed this note, but whoever he is, he sure knows how to explain exactly what he wants. No weasel-words at all; it's refreshing, sort of. And, he doesn't seem the sort to appreciate delays. The name's Vlasilov. Do you know him, Thomas?"

I nodded and smiled. "We've met. I suggest that you make him happy. Very, very happy."

"So…" Pearlman put his mask and gloves back on, then relit his torch.

"…if you don't mind, I'll be getting back to work." He smiled at me again, the expression just barely visible through the dark glass. "And, Thomas? Would Thursday be okay for dinner? I know that Danny'll want to come; it's been a long time since you two were playmates but he never stopped thinking well of you. I doubt he can make it home from school before then, what with all the wartime travel restrictions."

"Thursday it is," I agreed, making a mental note. "Or, if you need to reschedule for Friday just leave word with Mr. Flowers." I didn't have time for socializing, not really. But via fifteen minutes of simple honesty Mr. Pearlman had just done more for me and for Longo Enterprises as a whole than I could ever pay back with a lifetime of dinners. Father had taught me well, I suddenly realized, even though I hadn't been old enough to appreciate that I was learning anything of value while bouncing up and down on and eventually breaking little Danny Pearlman's new bed. Employees were friends and social equals. Fellow human beings, not inferior serfs. Treated accordingly, they were a treasure not only in terms of generating crude financial profits, but in simple comradeship as well.

Of the two sorts of wealth, the latter was infinitely the more important. It was too bad that Roon's business-school professors hadn't spent much time on the concept of human brotherhood. If they had, he might've gotten somewhere in life on his own account instead of riding his sister's coattails. "Thank you for accepting my invitation, Mr. Pearlman. I'm genuinely honored, and look forward to a pleasant evening."

Chapter Thirty-Nine

"…too early to reach any rock-solid conclusions," I was typing laboriously into the datalink in my room. I'd last used it for a ninth-grade history paper; it was a miracle the thing still worked. "However, due to the importance of the program I feel it necessary to forward daily reports." I sighed and rolled my chair back from the desk; it was a bit too small for me these days, but at least my servos weren't going to cramp up on me. Tomorrow I'd ask Mr. Flowers to find me a bigger one. The chair was a mere side-issue; my main problem was the report itself. Here I was, just an eighteen-year-old kid, trying to make sense of what about had to be the most sophisticated 'hopper production facility this side of Esteppe. I'd already spent hours working on the document, too much of it spent cutting and pasting and rewording. No one had ever taught me how to write a formal report; I was having to make-do based on memories of the dozens and hundreds of the things I'd read in the course of my duties. It sounded easier than it was; I could only hope that Vlasilov, knowing my circumstances, would make allowances for my poor performance.

"It's clear, however, that not one of the Skybolts promised for delivery is in fact airworthy, much less combatworthy…." I went on to explain about the out-of-true airframes and such, and how I'd obtained my information through highly unofficial family connections. "I certainly trust Mr. Pearlman's word over that of Mr. Roon," I explained, without going into details about how I'd never damaged Mr. Roon's furniture. "Mr. Pearlman is a highly valued employee of long-service and immense ability; please see Father's request for his presence on Esteppe." Then, not quite sure if I was using the correct protocol, I typed in a link to Father's old correspondence, specifically the flurry of notes he'd written during the busy hours just before the evacuation. Mr. Flowers had been able to unlock the file for me, and even helped me find the part I needed. I hadn't realized it, but Flowers had apparently been a personal assistant to Father as much as his estate manager. This didn't surprise me; Father was infamous for his failure to compartmentalize the functions of his staff. With him, it was simple. He either trusted you or he didn't. If so, he asked you to help out as needed with whatever came up.

I was just explaining about the turnover problem and how the plant was losing staff faster than it could be trained when there was a knock on my door. It was Mr. Flowers, wearing a raincoat over his pajamas. Rain was pouring down outside, and I'd notices a few flashes of lightning through my window. "Hello!" I greeted him as he opened the door and stepped through. "What are you doing here so late?"

The older man smiled. "I might ask why you're still up and working yourself, young man, except I know better." He pulled a large, high-quality linen envelope out of his pocket. "This just arrived by special courier, Thomas, and I saw across the courtyard that your light was still on. I thought it might be important, so I brought it over myself."

It was a letter from Father; I blinked twice, shocked that communications with Esteppe had been reestablished so quickly. Then I looked at the postmark; it was dated before the convoy had sailed, and therefore had made the trip with me. Which was odder still, I thought as I removed the letter from its high-dollar wrapper. Why a special courier, to deliver a message that Father might have given me in person long ago?

"Dearest Son," the letter began. It was paper-clipped to a whole bundle of complicated-looking stuff. "I have chosen to send you this letter in such a way that you will not receive it until, god willing, you've arrived safely on Earth. I've done this because I'm well aware of the difficulties and dangers you face daily as a navy officer, and didn't wish to distract you from the difficult business of survival. I pray that this note finds both you and your friend Jimmy happy and whole, and victorious as well."

I pressed my lips together. Father wasn't usually one to refer much to religion or prayer, in writing or otherwise. He must truly have been afraid for us.

"At any rate, now that you are arrived safe and sound I must ask something of you. While I cannot be certain, I consider it highly likely that the United Systems government will have taken over our New Orleans production facility. I consider it equally likely that they've made a total hash of things there."

At this, I couldn't read any further. Instead, I tilted my head back and laughed my head off. Mr. Flowers looked his question at me. "It's just funny, is all," I explained. "Father suspects that the United Systems might be mismanaging his factory." Then he laughed, too. The situation could hardly have been news to him.

"Most likely," Father continued, "if there are indeed problems the navy will send you to look into them. This is due to your last name more than anything else; Vlasilov is no fool, and recognizes the power that it carries with the work force. While this would be a highly satisfactory role for you from my point of view, it does not go far enough.

"Though I cannot and do not expect you to take active control of the plant, Thomas—I recognize that your life will proceed in other directions, of which we've spoken many times and do not need to be discussed here, and also that you're genuinely not qualified as an engineer—I must ask you to do whatever you can to ensure that the integrity of the Longo name is being upheld. In the end, Thomas, all we Longos have is our good name, with our customers and employees alike. I wish to maintain its value at any cost.

"Your legal and ethical situation vis-à-vis the Skybolt program is already a tangled mess simply because you are both my son and uniquely qualified to serve in certain roles on behalf of the navy. Someday, I expect that a government attorney is going to be asking us all some very penetrating questions regarding conflicts of interest and the expenditure of government funds. But things have developed the way that they've developed, and that's that. There's been no intent of wrongdoing on the part of any of us. Therefore, I don't waste time worrying about the inevitable investigations and advise you to do the same. As you well know, my son, I've been on trial before and survived the experience; so shall you if the unhappy day should come. What's important now is defeating the Dracans as quickly, efficiently, and humanely as possible. Everything else pales in comparison.

"I don't wish to further complicate your legal situation by making you a full partner at this time, though Sven and I have agreed that nothing would please us more. However, I've included a variety of paperwork with this letter that will allow you to take any one of several actions at your discretion, from assuming full partnership if you should find it advantageous to becoming my completely-empowered agent on Earth. Peter Flowers can help you file these documents at need; I've always found his counsel to be both wise and well-considered. He's an attorney, if you didn't know, and a rather good one. He left the profession in order to spend more time with his family, a sentiment I thoroughly understand and approve of.

"I've also given considerable thought to the issue of money. Thomas, in the normal course of things, I'd have steadily increased your allowance as you grew older, watching closely to ensure that you never lost sight of the value of a credit. I'm sure that everything would've been all right; you were never greedy as a child, and in your too-few normal teen years you exhibited no tendency towards becoming a spendthrift. Your skimmer was your only expensive foible, and as I recall you earned it via good grades.

"The things I'm asking you to do on behalf of the Longo family may well cost money, Thomas. They might prove quite expensive indeed. Our other plans regarding your future may prove costly as well. Therefore, among the other paperwork I've enclosed you will find that I've set up an account in your name with the Bank of Geneva. You now have twenty million credits to call upon. I'll add here that I do *not* expect and will even be disappointed if you use this money solely for business purposes. You're a fighter pilot, Thomas, and as I so well understand you may be taken away from us on any given day, even during a routine test flight. I want you to be happy, son, and to get some rest and enjoy life when you can. At the very least, please buy yourself the finest skimmer there's ever been as a heartfelt gift from me, and don't feel obliged to stop there. If you need more cash, it can and will be arranged.

"Dean, sitting at my knee, sends his best. I'm certain Sven would do the same if he weren't slaving away as usual at the plant. Know that we love you more than life itself, and hold full confidence in your ability to represent our interests on Earth.

"Love, Father"

Chapter Forty

It was well after dawn before I finally got everything squared away. First, I had to let Mr. Flowers read Father's letter; it was essential that he understand what was expected of me if he was to be of any help. Then he insisted on calling the Bank of Geneva right then and there to make sure the transfer had gone through properly, and after that there were the legal forms to go through so that he could explain them to me… By the time he put his raincoat back on and trudged across the square to his home, the sky was turning pink in the east. And I still had to finish my report to Vlasilov!

It was all worth it, though. By the time I woke up again, not long after noon, Vlasilov's reply was already waiting for me. "Thomas," it read. "This is exactly the kind of excellent work I expected from you, and completed, I'll add, in a most timely fashion. Well done! Your predecessor as corporate liaison was, seemingly, unaware of anything except the fact that there were twelve complete-looking Skybolts sitting on the runway waiting for pilots. She also now owns a very expensive home that she cannot possibly afford on her navy pay, which makes me very sad for her. There will be a formal Board of Inquiry into all of this, just as soon as I can convene it.

"There's no need for you to report in every day, Thomas; I trust your judgment now more than ever. Don't forget that you're also supposed to be working two weeks of shore leave into this assignment; did you plan to file reports on *those* days, as well? Contact me when you feel that you've something important to say, and I promise that I won't confuse your silence with idleness when you do not.

"Vlasilov"

There was a postscript, as well.

"I can but echo and endorse the admiral's sentiments, my boy. It's no wonder the navy refuses to let you go. Expect action on these issues soonest; this memo is being placed directly atop my 'Urgent' pile and will not be removed until you report back to me that all is once again well in New Orleans."

"Matthew Pithom, PM."

Wow! I thought to myself. *That was fast! Maybe it wasn't such a terribly written report after all?*

Since it was already late in the day and there didn't seem to be much else constructive to do, I decided to get dressed and head over to the plant to shake some hands and get reacquainted with the workers. I'd always kept a pair of Longo coveralls in my closet for when I went over to the shop to do some work; just as soon as I was old enough Father had set me up with my own workbench in the tool-and-die area, where I'd spent many happy hours making things like slightly-crooked bookshelves, getting better and better every year until at the end I'd worked my way up to custom accessories for my skimmer. Though the coveralls no longer fit, they'd started out baggy enough that, with a few discrete rips and tears and much help from Manuel, I was able to wriggle my way into them.

Mr. Flowers was appalled when he saw the results. "I'll get you a new pair!" he pleaded. "I can have them here in five minutes!"

"I'm custom-sized only now," I countered. "My torso is too long for the length of my legs. And, there's other weird stuff too." I smiled and tapped my name-tag, which read 'Tommy Longo'. "Besides, new coveralls would be all clean and stiff. These are stained. I'll fit in better."

"I'll pour oil over the new ones!" Peter countered. "I'll roll them in grease!"

"That wouldn't be honest," I explained. "These stains are *real*. I *earned* them." Then I thanked Manuel, asked him to remain available, and moseyed over towards the plant.

Rather to my surprise, my workbench was still exactly where I'd left it; someone had even been keeping it dusted. No one was doing much, I noted as I strode towards it. In a cutting-edge workplace like this one machinery breakdowns and the resultant work-stoppages were to be expected; heaven knew I'd seen enough of them back on Esteppe. But here, the whole place seemed to be shut down pretty much continuously. The employees sat at chessboards and in front of holovision tanks; some were even having picnics. I had nothing against picnics, but some of these looked to be quite elaborate affairs, complete with complicated dishes that clearly implied foreknowledge that there'd be plenty of spare time to put them together. It was reasonable, I supposed, that where there was so much idle time intelligent people would find a way to fill the empty hours. It was the responsibility of any manager worthy of the name, however, to ensure that downtime was kept to the minimum.

No one noticed me at first as I walked slowly up to my tool chest and then smiled as I traced with my index finger the letters I'd clumsily engraved in it so long ago. "Property of Tommy Longo", they read in what now struck my eye as a very childish script. I grinned, then pulled out my key, stuck it in the slot, and—

"Hey!" cried an outraged voice. "Get away from there!"

"Who the hell do you think you are?" someone else demanded.

"Are you with management?" another voice chimed in. "If we've told you once, we've told you a thousand times. That bench stays right there!"

I tilted my head first to one side, then the other. "Guys…" I said slowly, turning around to face them. "It's me!"

There was a long, long silence. "Sweet Jesus!" one of the men finally called out. "It really *is* him!"

Then I got mobbed, as all the old-timers came rushing up to look at my face and shake my hand and just simply look and see for themselves that it was true. "You're a hero, Tommy!" "We're so proud of you!" "We always knew you'd make it big!"

Finally Security took notice of the situation and an officer came rolling up in a little red cart. "What's going on here?" a sergeant demanded. I didn't know him.

"It's Tommy!" Jim Peters exclaimed, slapping me on the back for about the millionth time. He'd often helped me with my little projects back in the day, as time allowed. "Todd Pearlman wasn't lying! He's back!"

The guard peered intently at me. "You don't have a badge," he observed. "How did you get onto the plant grounds?"

"It's *him*!" Jim explained. "Tommy Longo! Look at his face. For that matter, look at his hands! See how they're not real? He's a hero! The Skybolt pilot who saved the fleet! And who nuked Drakkus! He flies the birds we make here, and his dad owns the place! Don't you ever watch TV?"

"He *lives* here, you moron!" Ted Bellew observed. "In the big mansion. You may have noticed it? *That's* how he got in."

The sergeant's brow wrinkled, then went back to his cart to use his radio in private. "You stay right where you are," he cautioned me. "I'll be watching you every second."

"Right," I agreed, my tone just a shade more insubordinate than I'd intended. "You do that." Then I turned back to Jim. "How're things?"

"Just awful," he answered. Then he nodded toward the security cart. "They retired old man Mulligan, and then replaced his whole staff. Security's been outsourced."

My jaw dropped. "You're kidding!" I answered. "Father would *never*—"

But that's as far as I got. Suddenly the guard was in my face again. "Mr. Roon says you don't belong here," he explained. "So, you've gotta go. I'm to be polite and respectful, but you're not to be permitted inside the factory proper."

"What?" I cried, balling my fists in anger. "Who on Earth…"

"Mr. Roon," the guard repeated. "He gives the orders inside these walls." The uniformed man nodded to Ted. "Yes, the young man lives here, all right. And he'll be free to wander the estate. But, he has no right to be in the plant, creating a disturbance."

"I'm the official navy liaison!" I screeched, now angry beyond reason. "That ought to give me full access, even if I *wasn't* the owner's son!"

"Maybe," the guard agreed, gesturing for me to precede him so that he could follow me out the door. "If so, you and the navy will have to take it up with Mr, Roon. I just follow orders. Now are you going to make this easy on us both, or are you going to cause a fuss?"

Chapter Forty-One

I made it so easy on the guard that I'm sure he never imagined the red, bloody images that coursed through my mind, first of me tying his arms behind him in a nice, pretty bow knot, inflicting fractures as necessary along the way with my overpowered servos, and then slowly strangling the life out of him. *Kill them all!* But it *wasn't* his fault, not really. Like the man said, all he did was obey orders. So I was as insincerely polite as I knew how to be, and even wished the sergeant a good afternoon when, eventually, I was dropped off at my own doorstep with strict instructions never to enter the production facility again without obtaining permission and a badge ahead of time.

I would've raced up to my room, but my body didn't do that anymore. Instead, I was still making my slow way up the steps one by one when Mr. Flowers arrived. "My god!" he declared, reading the expression on my face. It must not have been pretty. "What happened?"

"I'm not permitted in the plant," I explained. "Without prior permission."

Peter's eyes widened. "Jesus," he muttered. "Can they do that?"

"They can try. Apparently word's gotten out that I'm not Mr. Roon's friend. What's he got to lose, at this point?"

Flowers nodded. "I'll get the paperwork."

Two hours later, I was lying on the floor of my room playing the solo version of *Rocket Sledder* and trying to think. Solo *Sledder* wasn't nearly so satisfactory as playing with Jimmy, but at least it helped me relax. I was doing quite well, really, given how little sleep I'd gotten the night before. Father often spent hours alone, listening to terrible spiritual-harmony music. For the first time, I was gaining insight as to why. The longer I played, the worse my original plan of action sounded. My gut instinct had been to hit Roon with everything I had, filing to become Father's agent and then unleashing legal hell by appealing the nationalization of the plant. No other defense plants had been nationalized, that Mr. Flowers knew of at least. Just some critical mines and large farms. And even then there'd been extensive rights of appeal; the government had *not* won all of the cases. While we were late in filing, Mr. Flowers assured me, we had an ironclad case in that our family hadn't been informed about the takeover until I'd arrived home, due to the wartime disruption in communications. We still had *months* to appeal, if we chose.

But that wouldn't have been right, I decided after a little cooling-off time and a few rounds of *Sledder*. It'd hurt the navy, would hurt the PM, and might delay Skybolt production even further. As Father had said, winning the war was priority number one.

So, I'd next put down my joystick to write a joint letter to Admiral Vlasilov and the PM, protesting my eviction from the plant both on the grounds of my status as naval liaison and as unofficial representative of my father, who still actually owned the plant even if the government was running it. I worked long and hard on the letter, cutting and pasting and rephrasing over and over and over again. But, no matter how hard I worked at it, it still felt like I was running to an adult and asking for help with a bully. "Waah! Waah! Waah!" the words screamed at me, however they were rearranged. In his letter, Father had enjoined me to uphold the dignity and respectability of the family name. Running to the authorities, I'd eventually decided, was not the correct way to do this. It'd be counterproductive at best.

My sled burst over a ridge and hit an unexpected aspen tree; it exploded, and I set my controller aside for a moment. So far, I'd been able to successfully wear so many different hats in my life because the underlying forces behind my roles had been so perfectly aligned. Being Commander of the Top Bananas hadn't conflicted with my near-filial relationship with Alicia and Spence, for example, because the Wiston's interests were identical with those of the navy. Both parties wanted to win the war, no matter what the cost, and had very similar ideas of how to best accomplish this. I'd been able to be best-friends with Jimmy as well as his CO because, again, under the circumstances we'd encountered so far there'd been no conflicts. We both wanted nothing more than to be the finest pair of Skybolt pilots we could possibly be.

But now, things were growing more complicated. What Father demanded of me in his letter wasn't necessarily what was in the best interests of the navy. He was demanding that his standards be maintained in his absence, that his way of doing things remain in force whether the navy approved or not. In this, he was demanding a degree of control. Of power, even, on the grand scale of things. His goal clearly was to create a state of affairs wherein if one wanted to buy a superfighter, one came hat-in-hand to see a Longo. I could quite likely force the issue in his favor, making use of the paperwork he'd so carefully provided. And the moment was clearly opportune; Roon's days had been numbered from the moment I'd discovered those twelve unflyable 'bolts. Even now, the comm-circuits in the PM's office were probably humming as Pithom's staff sought out alternative managers. But if I stood aside and let the PM's men choose, would the person they selected do things *Father's* way? The Longo way? Would he be loyal to *us*?

Their last pick certainly hadn't been.

I sighed and turned off my game. It was getting late and I was short on sleep. Besides, it was all so complicated! The navy had rights and needs, Father had rights and needs, our staff had rights and needs... Even Roon had rights and needs, though I rather disliked acknowledging the fact. Everywhere I looked, I could find only conflict.

So what was right and what was wrong? Roon's interests I dismissed out of hand; the sooner he packed up his desk and left the happier everyone else would be, his sister excepted. The navy's short-term interest, at least, was in getting as many Skybolts out of the plant as quickly as was humanly possible. As near as I could tell, Father's methods were the only proven means of producing battleworthy superfighters, unless one counted Dracan slave-labor techniques. The government's interests were in seeing to it that everything proceeded as smoothly as possible, and that all the mess stayed out of the courts and headlines. And the staff's interests...

I sighed as I thought about the thousand outstanding labor grievances that Mr. Pearlman had spoken of, and the huge turnover. What a miserable mess Roon had made out of their lives! They'd been *so* angry when I'd been thrown out...

Suddenly I sat up, bolt-upright. We Longos weren't accustomed to depending on either legal proceedings or governmental goodwill for our strength. We generated our own, simply by being who and what we were. Others tended to respond accordingly. Perhaps the situation would resolve itself without my having to interfere? Perhaps it already *was* resolving itself, even? And entirely in Father's favor, at that? The timing, I judged, was just about right...

I was free to wander the grounds without creating a conflict, if not the plant itself. Presumably that included the main gate, since short of taking my 'hopper everywhere I went it'd be impossible for me to come and go without using it. So, tired and sleepless as I might've been, I decided to take a little walk. My shorts and t-shirt weren't appropriate for the chilly weather, but it didn't matter enough to justify waking up Manuel, who was resting. It wasn't like I'd suffer from the chill. So, I walked the half-mile or so dressed as I was.

As I'd half-expected, there was a huge ruckus taking place; dozens of security-types were lined up shoulder-to-shoulder, faced off against a screaming mob of perhaps ten times their number. "You're Roon's dogs!" one of the protestors shouted, pointing at a guard. "Bark for me! Sit up and beg! Woof! Woof!" It was Todd Pearlman, I was shocked to see.

"Shaddap!" the guard countered, pointing some kind of weapon at one of Father's finest prototype-makers. He pulled the trigger, and suddenly the middle-aged man was thrashing about on the ground, vomiting and spouting filth from his other end. My god! The guard had hit him with a sick-gun!

That proved to be a mistake. At first, the workers went dead silent. Then an angry murmuring set in. I waited for a moment, then when the rage showed no sign of fading away I took action. "People!" I shouted, turning up my internal speaker just as loud as it would go. "Please! Don't get crazy!"

Everyone turned to face me; I sounded pretty strange with my speaker turned up. Inhuman, almost. But at least, they recognized me. "There he is!" He's back, all right!" Thank god! A Longo!"

"There *will* be justice," I promised, pointing to my friend, who was still convulsing on the ground. "For that, and for many other things. But please! No violence!"

Jim Peters stepped forward; two guards backed away to make room for him, a good sign in my book. He crossed his arms before speaking. "We trust you, Thomas!" he answered. "And your father and brother as well. But we watched these idiots throw you out; I saw it happen with my own two eyes! Who's in charge here, anyway?"

"We Longos *will* be," I promised. "Soon."

"Good," Jim answered, nodding. "That's when we'll be back to work, then. Soon. Until that time, you have our home numbers on file. We're looking forward to hearing from you. Not from anyone else.

"Only you."

Chapter Forty-Two

Crises can be very strange things. Nothing had fundamentally changed at the plant. The facility hadn't been producing working superfighters *before* the walkout, after all, so it shouldn't have been the end of the world that it continued not doing so. The walkout created no fundamentally new problems; old ones that should have been self-evident to anyone had merely come home to roost. And yet to look at the papers you'd think the world had ended.

"Skybolt Workers Walk Out; War Hero Longo Promises 'Justice'" blared one local headline. "Critical War Production Obstructed," screeched another. This one was a business publication. "No Arrests Yet Made".

I did the only thing I could do, really, which was sit and wait and calmly put together a plan of action that I thought might get the factory working again, this time properly. No, I wasn't qualified to figure out how to fix the engine-alignment problems or to put together a program to make sure the stub-wing adhesive was never contaminated again. Those issues were over my head. But I could see that the first thing necessary was a complete shutdown, probably of about ten days duration, during which the outstanding grievances could be settled and the new management could sit down with and gain the trust of at least the top union officials. Father's old quality-councils needed to be reinstated, forums where managers *had* to listen to worker gripes. The navy needed to provide a test-pilot pronto; how could anyone really *know* if the 'bolts were any good if there wasn't anyone to fly them? And so on.

When the secret meeting was eventually held, I was surprised at how many people showed up. There were four representatives from the Labor Ministry, for example, and three more from the War Production Board. The PM sent a member of his personal staff, a Mr. N'denko, and the navy sent of all people Michelle Bard. She was representing Admiral Vlasilov, who was still too sick to travel. "Congratulations, ma'am" I greeted her before the meeting, shaking her hand. She'd been promoted to captain, a well-earned reward for the ultimate success of the molecular battery-denial campaign. She'd put together the whole thing; it'd been her baby from day one.

"Thanks, Thomas," she replied, smiling prettily.

I smiled back. "I'm always glad to see you," I continued, tilting my head to one side. "But, I have to admit that I'm a little surprised to see you *here*."

Her smile faded, and her expression went sour. "Think about it, Thomas," she answered eventually. "Very hard. Eventually you'll find the answer."

My eyebrows rose, and then she quite deliberately turned away and struck up a conversation with someone else. It hurt when she did that-- hurt a lot, even. But at least left me a clue. *Think about it...*

I had plenty of time to think, once the official proceedings began. I'd offered to host the committee in the family mansion, it being located right at "ground zero" of the whole problem so to speak. That way, if anyone wanted to see what was going on or actually talk to some of the workers, it could be arranged within minutes. But instead the committee met in Baton Rouge. This made no sense whatsoever to me; while they were indeed physically a little closer to the problem than they'd been in Rome, they still weren't near enough for it to make any practical difference. We had to rely on pictures and stuff, for example, which we could just as easily have done anywhere on the planet. But this way everyone got to sample some good Cajun cooking and fill in inflated travel-expense reports, which I soon came to understand was the whole point of the exercise.

The Conference began with the crucifixion of my predecessor as naval liaison; she admitted taking bribes, apologized to her family, the navy and the people of the world, then later that night jumped off of her balcony.

The next day it was Roon's turn to testify. Father had left him an impossible situation, it seemed. The product wasn't laid out for easy production, as all decent designs should be; instead, it was burdened with impossible tolerance after impossible tolerance. The idea that said tolerances were what made the Skybolt work in the first place didn't even seem to enter his head. The most crucial tooling had been gone when he'd arrived, and there was no way to make schedule except to try and improvise. Worst of all, he'd been saddled with an overpaid, insubordinate, even actively subversive workforce. "They were spoiled," Roon explained, his eyes dripping ice when they met mine. "Spoiled rotten. They had no interest in meeting goals. Instead, *they* wanted to tell *me* how things should be done."

Then it was my turn to testify. Things got really complicated then, because I was a Member of the Board, and Board Members, apparently, just didn't do that. There was a flurry of motions and counter-motions and protests, while I sat and for the first time appreciated just how much time and money Father saved by not tolerating such nonsense in his businesses. They hadn't planned on putting me on the Board at all until the last minute, when I'd sent Mr. Flowers to see the PM's private representative with his little stack of papers. After that, they made sure that I got a nice seat right near the middle. They'd give me *anything* rather than see the legal paperwork formally filed

It should've been easy for me in the witness chair; I hadn't done anything wrong, so all I had to do was tell the truth. Roon's attorney asked some very penetrating questions about my relationship with Mr. Pearlman and why I trusted him so completely, so I explained about the bed-thing and everyone except my questioner and the man he represented had a good laugh. "I've known almost all of the lead-men since I was little," I explained. "It's just how we do things. Besides, didn't the test-data show that Mr. Pearlman was right?"

The Labor Ministry people also gave me quite a bad time; I couldn't figure out why until I realized that it was because I was a rich kid and they hated rich kids on principle. Their animosity was a lot easier to take after that, once I realized it wasn't personal. They asked me questions about overtime compensation and shift premiums and about a million other things I couldn't answer, until I finally started asking questions myself. "You're in contact with Jim Peters, aren't you?" I demanded. He was the chairman of the plant's local, though I hadn't known that back when I'd seen him first on the shop floor and then again at the gate.

"Yes, sir!" the top Labor man answered proudly. "Brother Peters and I spoke for almost an hour."

"Was he upset about overtime?" I asked.

The Labor rep pressed his lips together. "No," he finally admitted.

"Or shift premiums?"

"No," he repeated. "Though I personally find it—"

I cut him off at the pass. "What are his demands?"

"That things go back to the way they used to be," he admitted, nose wrinkling in displeasure. "That the technicians be allowed to produce quality products, not junk. That management work with them, not against them. That proper tools and training be provided. That outstanding grievances be resolved, and that the guard who sick-gunned that one worker be criminally charged." He sighed, then threw up his hands and shook his head. "They seem to think that you Longos are some kind of gods. All they really want is to work for you again."

"We're not gods," I said to the committee, meeting the eyes one by one. "Just honest businessmen." Then I pulled the plan I'd worked up out of my pocket and tossed it down on the table in front of me. "Look," I said. "We're wasting time here. Valuable time, while the Dracans build more superfighters that are going to kill who knows how many of our people. It isn't going to take an act of Parliament to get that plant going. Instead, all that's required is long hours of patient work, performed in an atmosphere of mutual trust. Building Skybolts, I'm told, isn't easy. In fact, it's one of the hardest things that anyone's ever done. No matter what anyone does here or what motions get made, there'll be further glitches and wastes of material." I looked at the Labor men. "There'll probably even be more grievances and complaints, though I think there'll be a lot less of them if you follow my blueprint." I looked around the room, then pointed at my plan again. "What do you say, people? Let's quit wasting time here, so you can get back to governing, I can get back to flying, the workers can get back to producing, and the navy can get back to winning the war. This three-ring circus is ridiculous!"

Chapter Forty-Three

Apparently things Just Weren't Done that way; there was a flurry of objections, the Chairman banged his gavel, and I was severely admonished for putting forward a plan while the fact-finding part of the process was still underway. "Only because of your youth, inexperience, and distinguished service do I let you off so lightly," the chairman intoned gravely while Mr. Flowers smiled real big at him and patted my back down low where no one could see him do it.

"You're doing fine, kid," he assured me as we broke up for a recess. "Very well indeed. Your dad'll be proud of you."

I might have been out of order, I soon understood, but that didn't seem to prevent anyone from taking an interest in the plan I'd put together. Because I moved so slowly I generally made it my practice to wait until the crowd thinned out a little before leaving a meeting room. It only took me a couple of extra minutes, yet by the time I made it out into the hallway everyone and their brother seemed to be sitting down studying a copy of my ideas. "Ten days of shutdown?" the War Production man asked me, raising his eyebrows. "Ten whole days?"

"Trust is a difficult thing to build," I explained. "Especially once it's already been broken. I think that's a conservative estimate. But, you'll note, we can also use the time for calibrating and fine-tuning the tooling with a handful of key personnel. From what Mr. Pearlman and others tell me, it's something that should've been done a long time ago. In the end, I bet you'll gain more than you lose."

"What makes you think the 'key personnel' you speak of would be willing to help?" the War Production man asked. "How do you know they just won't come in and sabotage everything to gain more leverage?"

"Because they won't," I replied. "They'd never do such a thing. Ever."

"Humph!" Roon snorted from a few feet away. He'd decided that we weren't on speaking terms, and that was just fine with me. But, apparently, that didn't mean he was above eavesdropping.

"Walking off the job is a serious matter, Thomas," the Production representative continued, peering deep into my yes. "During wartime, at least.

There are those who want to see the ringleaders arrested."

"Then they can arrest me, too," I answered, carefully not looking towards where Roon was still taking in every word. "They're absolutely right to do what they've done. Even Father would agree-- he hired men and women of intelligence and would hardly expect them to behave stupidly. You sent an idiot to supervise the work of good men, someone who so far as I can tell isn't even as qualified to run the plant as I am, simply because of who his sister is. What did you expect? And why are all of you so afraid of her, anyway?"

Suddenly there was silence up and down the hallway. "She's the Deputy Whip for the Opposition," one of the Labor Ministry men explained. "People think she's got a future."

"Ah!" I replied. "So *that* explains it! I should've pulled up her public file myself." Everyone was looking at me now, so I took advantage of the moment. "You're all terrified of the idea that someday she might be PM, and hold your careers in her hands?"

There was a long, telling silence.

"And," I added, "that's *far* more important than the men, women, and children dying at Dracan hands on the occupied worlds? More important than the soldiers and sailors I've watched killed so that you can sit around and ask inane, irrelevant questions about overtime and shift premiums at important-sounding committee-meetings?" I shook my head. "I have to say, I can't wait to get back to being a fighter pilot. They call me a murderer, and I admit that I do kill people. By the millions, at times. Yet somehow, combat missions feel *cleaner* than what I'm experiencing here."

There was another long silence, then the committee chair's hand twitched as if he were reaching for his gavel and was surprised to discover it wasn't there. But we were out of session; therefore I could say anything I pleased. "Thomas!" he barked. "Young man…"

"You're bluffing!" Roon interjected. "You'd never go to jail for shop-floor trash!"

"For my *friends*," I corrected him. "And, watch me," I replied evenly. "I've done harder things. Much harder. As you may've heard." Then I turned to the newly-minted Captain Bard. "A moment of your time? In private?" I looked around at everyone else and smiled. "It's a personal matter; nothing of significance. We're old shipmates."

She was positively glowing, apparently at what I'd just said. "Of course, Thomas. It'd be an honor."

There were little rooms situated all up and down the corridor, all of them supposedly cleared daily of bugs due to the top-secret nature of our proceedings. The captain and I selected one, then pulled the door to. She raised her eyebrows in an unspoken question.

"You're here because you know me," I said slowly. "And also because the admiral understands that I like you very much and see you as an authority-figure. Heaven knows that an intelligence officer has no other business dealing with war-production issues. He can't be here himself, so he hopes that he can influence me through you instead."

Michelle looked down at the carpet. "You're a smart kid, Thomas. I *knew* you'd figure it out."

I nodded. "You're under orders. There's no hard feelings." I sighed. "And I *do* respect you, Michelle. A lot!" Now I was looking down at the carpet, too. "Let's just lay our cards on the table and work things out, like we did aboard ship when we were planning a mission."

She looked up and smiled a little. "All right. Me first, then. The admiral loves you like a son, Thomas. You know that by now, don't you?"

I nodded. "I'm pretty fond of him as well."

"He's aware of that, too. But…" She frowned. "He also knows that you love your father, and have a debt to your family tradition. To your heritage."

I frowned. "So far as I can see, there's no conflict between what my family wants and what the navy wants."

"So far as you can see," Michelle agreed. "But put yourself in the admiral's position. He can't afford to let *anything* get in the way of the war effort. And…" She frowned. "Do you realize what you're doing here, Thomas? You're using your unique status and connections to muscle around the *government*. That's who we navy types work for, and are sworn to uphold. You're on very treacherous ground."

I snorted and gestured in the general direction of the hallway. "You don't work for the likes of *them*," I countered. "You—or we, rather—work for the people. We protect them."

Michelle's frown deepened. "Guess who *represents* the people, Thomas?" She too gestured out towards the hallway. "For better or for worse, it's always men and women like those who end up on top. We *do* work for them, like it or not. Think about it."

I shook my head and turned to look out the window; it was raining again. Everything was so green; I couldn't get over how wonderfully *alive* Earth seemed after being away for a time. No other planet could touch her; she was the most precious gem in the universe. "I've always thought of myself as working for Alicia," I admitted. "Insofar as I've ever really thought about it at all." I shook my head. "But you're right. She's *not* typical. Is she?"

"Sadly, no," Michelle explained. "And if you don't have the stomach to work with the likes of what you've seen here today, I can't imagine what you're going to do in Parliament." She smiled. "Yes, I know, Thomas. I'm waiting for the new district lines to be announced. If I can, I'm going to vote for you, regardless of what the navy makes me do in the meantime,"

I stiffened at that. "What do you mean, what the navy makes you do?"

Michelle's face went expressionless. "Consider the situation, Thomas. Up until now, you've been a perfectly good-natured and subservient little boy. But something's changed in you; we who know you well realize that it's been coming on for some time. You're becoming a man, Thomas, a man of independent means and power. And you're beginning to act like it. You're thinking for yourself, and taking you own interests into account. Or those of your family, rather; they're pretty much the same thing."

I frowned. "Ma'am," I said as respectfully as I was able. "So far as I can tell, I'm being a good officer as well as a good Longo. The interests of both groups coincide; producing Skybolts, and the more the better. It so happens that I genuinely believe that the plan I submitted is the best way to achieve that."

Michelle nodded. "And so far you'll note that I've not said a word to contradict you. I've sat silently. In rapt admiration at times, I'll admit." She shook her head. "When you're finally finished growing up, well… Wow." I nodded and started to speak, again, but Michelle continued right over my words. "But," she warned. The admiral and the navy he represents cannot help but note that you're acting very much as your father's son just now. As a result, you're being watched." She sighed, then her eyes hardened. "I've heard about the documents you've been flashing around." She picked up her purse and waved it at me. "Don't think that you're the only one carrying fully-prepared legal forms, Thomas. And signed legally-binding orders, as well. You've played straight with us so far, and we appreciate it. So I'm playing straight with you. Everyone's still friends, and everyone wants to keep it that way. But the minute it looks to me like you're putting the Longo interests ahead of those of the navy…"

I sighed and looked out into the rain again. "Michelle," I said slowly. "This isn't easy. The position that I'm in, every single day of my life. You know that, right? I hate every minute of it."

She smiled. "I believe you, Thomas. I know you too well not to. But it's only going to get harder and harder for you, as time goes on and your life grows more complex."

I nodded. "Then let's simplify things a little. Have you ever known me to lie?"

"No, not ever."

I nodded again. "All right, then. I hereby swear on my honor as an officer and the graves of the war-dead that I will never, so long as I remain a serving officer, knowingly put my family's business interests ahead of those of the people. Further, I swear that if I'm elected to office, I'll resign my seat in Parliament before I do anything to hurt the service. Nothing means half so much to me as getting this cursed war over with, and as near as I can tell supporting the navy with all that I have to give is the best way to do it."

Michelle nodded, but said nothing.

I gestured out towards the hallway. "Words may be cheap, among *that* kind," I continued. "But mine are not. You won't be needing that paperwork, Michele. Just as I won't be needing mine, at least not in dealing with you or

Admiral Vlasilov. Help me get the plant running, is all that I ask. We *must* trust one another."

"I *do* trust you, Thomas," she answered. "And Vlasilov does, as well." She looked down. "In fact, I'm a little ashamed—"

"Don't be," I interrupted, thinking about my poor bribe-taking predecessor as naval liaison, who'd taken such a long, miserable fall the previous night. She'd been trusted too, hadn't she? Perhaps she'd have been better off if the trust hadn't been quite so complete. "There's corruption everywhere, and everyone has their weaknesses. We're all human. All I ask is, just give me a chance to sit down and work things out with you before you go and get all crazy with those written orders you spoke of. To prevent misunderstandings. And I'll do the same for you. All right?"

"All right," she agreed. Then, quite unexpectedly, she wrapped her arms around me and kissed me on the nose, in a motherly sort of way. "Forgive me," she said. "But I've wanted to do that for a very long time now."

I smiled. "It's okay. But there *is* one more item of business we need to cover."

Her eyebrows rose. "What?"

"Please," I whispered, dropping to my knees as quickly as my servos would allow. "Please, in the name of all that's holy, ask the admiral to get me transferred back to flight operations just as soon as he can possibly manage it? This liaison stuff is driving me batty! I'll attend status meetings instead of ditching them like I used to. I won't complain when the deck crewman hook me up to a 'bolt over and over again for drill. I'll stand heel-and-toe alerts until the cows come home. I'll do anything! Please? Just get me back aboard *June* and away from all these political problems!"

Chapter Forty-Four

Father Murton was scheduled to be taken off his drugs and regain consciousness the next morning; in an unexpectedly humane gesture, the committee gave me a few hours off to go visit him in San Francisco. There wasn't much to our little get-together; the doctors had warned me that he'd still be very bleary-minded from the drugs, and they were correct. He didn't even seem to realize that his legs were gone. But he was very glad to see me all the same; he hugged me and wept and told me that he'd dreamed over and over again that I was killed in action. We prayed together for a minute or two, and then it was time for me to be gone.

I shouldn't have been surprised to find two strangers waiting for me at my navy 'hopper, both dressed in the expensively-casual attire that screamed "politician" to the experienced eye. "Hello, Thomas!" the female member of the pair greeted me as I turned the last corner. "I'm Parliamentarian Wan." She smiled and nodded at her companion. "This is Special Assistant to the Prime Minister Olafson. We'd like to share your flight back to the meetings at Baton Rouge, if you'd be so kind. And perhaps do a little talking as well."

It was inevitable, I supposed, that the PM's office would want to speak to me about the plant issues. And all the more so since I wasn't simply keeping my mouth shut and accepting direction. "Of course," I agreed, smiling back and bowing politely. The flight was only an hour or so long; how bad could it be? "I'm honored.

We hadn't even been cleared for takeoff yet when Wan and Olafson spun their seats around and locked them into position facing my specially-contoured one. "It's wonderful to meet you at long last," Mr. Olafson began, his smile seemingly genuine. "I've never known a hero before."

I mumbled something incomprehensible, and Wan smiled. "Don't be modest, Thomas. Your accomplishments speak for themselves. So, let them do so. Don't try to deny what is clearly true."

I didn't know what to say that, so I just smiled and kept silent.

"Well," Wan continued, after my awkward non-reply. "First, let me explain that I'm one of the PM's floor-leaders. Some would call me a key leader. A kingmaker, even. And as such I'm fully aware of your plans to stand for office with us." She shook her head and smiled. "Alicia's plan is a masterpiece. What a pity it is that she's exiled herself to a colony world for so many years. Our political landscape has been the poorer for her absence."

Since I still didn't know what Alicia's big plan was, I simply nodded as if I did. Whatever it was, it must be a doozy!

"At any rate," Parliamentarian Wan continued. "I'm here for two reasons. The first of these is to formally welcome you to the Party." She smiled and extended her hand, which I accepted and shook. Then Olafson and I did the same.

"What's the second issue?" I asked when the ritual was complete, glad to be able to say something intelligent at long last.

Wan smiled. "The committee meetings, of course. What else?"

I closed my eyes for a second and sank back into my seat. What else indeed? "All I want," I explained for perhaps the ten-thousandth time, "is to get production rolling again. There's only one known method to make Skybolts that actually fly, and that's Father's method."

"Which means," Olafson observed, "finding a qualified, humane and intelligent plant-manager."

I blinked in shock. Olafson was the first person I'd come across from the political side of the spectrum who seemed to have even the slightest clue as to the real situation. "Exactly."

He nodded. "This is doable. Who do you have in mind?"

I blinked again. "There's only two men in the universe for the job. One is my brother Sven. He's, however, so deathly ill that I fear for his life."

Olafson's eyes narrowed. "I didn't know your brother was sick," he replied. "He was who I was expecting you to name. We'd have approved." He titled his head to one side. "Who's your other choice?"

"Gunther, Father's right-hand man on Esteppe. He helped run the Stormcrow plant while Sven was still in the service, and understands everything there is to know both about the aircraft and how to maintain proper, productive relations with the employees. For some years he and Father were estranged. Fences, however, have been mended. The last time I saw them together, they were working together like family."

Wan and Olafson turned and looked at each other. "Is he the Eliteman?" she asked.

"I think so," her partner replied, scowling.

"Yes," I answered. "He's quite unrepentant about it, as well. As are many Esteppans." I paused for a long moment. "Father's an Eliteman too, you know. Due to the war emergency, both he and Gunther are actively jacking in again. So is Sven, for that matter. It's a very useful ability."

"They're jacking in?" Wan demanded, turning to Olafson again. She wasn't smiling any more. "The Elitemen are jacking in again?"

"Yes, ma'am," he answered. "Didn't you know? Alicia Wiston signed a war-emergency order so authorizing them."

"And she's a damned frankenstein herself!" Wan spat. She turned to me, eyes glittering. "Is there no one else?" she demanded. "How about you? As a figurehead, I'm sure you understand. We know and accept that you're no engineer. You could deal with employee relations, however. We'd fully empower you in that area."

I leaned back in my seat and crossed my arms. There was a little trick I'd learned a long time ago, where I could make the servos fight themselves a little and make an unusually loud whine. I did so. "I'm a frankenstein too," I pointed out. "One of the handful of frankensteins, in fact, that's winning the war for you. If you hadn't noticed."

Wan's mouth twisted up as if she'd just bitten into the sourest apple there'd ever been. "Yes. Well... Forgive me for speaking out of turn, Thomas. You're correct; it was inexcusably rude of me."

"We're all very grateful," Olafson agreed, his smile firmly back in place again. "The PM is well aware not only of the sacrifices you've made personally, but those of your family as well in working in such a risky environment. No one would've demanded this, yet your people didn't hesitate to volunteer. For that matter, we're fully aware of the contributions that Alicia's husband makes and the risks that he runs on a daily basis as well." He bowed his head. "You're quite correct when you say that between you, you're winning the war for us. It's no exaggeration."

Wan frowned again, then looked down at the carpet. "I'm sorry, Thomas," she apologized again. "That was a foul, wrong thing for me to say."

But, I thought to myself, *it's how you genuinely feel, deep down inside. Isn't it?* "I understand," I replied, bowing acknowledgement. There wasn't any gain that I could see in being small about the incident. "There's a war on, and feelings are running high."

"Indeed," Wan agreed, looking quite relieved. Then, diplomatically, she changed the subject. "I could support this Gunther person," she agreed, looking at Olafson. "Even if he *is* jacking-in for the duration, and not inclined to be apologetic about it. But... Could Thomas perhaps find time for a fund-raiser in my district? To support my next campaign?"

"Perhaps," Olafson agreed, eyeing me suggestively.

My mouth opened, then closed. This was just plain wrong, I understood suddenly. Gunther was being eased into position via political favoritism, just as surely as Roon had been. But... We *needed* Gunther, to win the war! Or Sven, if he was up to it. "I... Uh..."

"And," Olafson added, once he saw that I wasn't quite yet ready to accept the deal. "We've come to understand that the whole nationalization thing was a mistake as well. Chalk it up to wartime jitters. Once the first working 'bolt rolls off the line, we'll return full control of the plant to your family."

I sat and goggled some more, then Wan chimed in. "You gave a speech in

Shanghai last year, selling war bonds," she said. "I was in the audience. It was quite moving. You spoke about the need for unity during times of peril, unity of heart and soul as well as unity of purpose. Do you think that you could give that one again at the fundraiser?"

"I..." My head was spinning so fast that I could barely think. What was right and what was wrong? Who were the good guys and who were the bad? Suddenly, *nothing* made sense.

Until I thought about watching a private being forced to kill his own officer back on Churilla. About sitting by helplessly as the Training Fleet faced off against an incomparably superior enemy, so that the rest of us might live. About Spence's guerillas accepting near-certain death in order to get Alicia and me and a handful of others back home to where we could do our part to fight the Dracans. The war effort came first, I reminded myself, before all other things. It didn't matter what I wanted or needed, it didn't matter what Father wanted or needed, it only mattered what would win this damned war, here and now. That at least was a fixed point in a fluid universe. Cleaning up politics was a job for another day and perhaps for a different man; no one could fix everything at once. "I remember that speech well," I heard myself saying, as a little part of my soul died. It hurt *really* bad; at the rate I was going I wasn't sure how much I'd have left when the shooting finally stopped. "Sure! I'd be most pleased to deliver it again for you..."

Chapter Forty-Five

Word of Wan and Olafson's presence on my shuttle had apparently preceded us to Baton Rouge; almost the entire committee was present to greet us at the landing field. While one or two *might* have turned out to greet me, there was no way that everyone had shown up in my honor. They were there for Wan, it was clear in a matter of minutes, as each of them fawned and bowed and scraped before her. I wasn't at all surprised, therefore, when meetings were canceled for the rest of the day. Clearly, the Chinese Parliamentarian had some serious choreographing to do.

Though I was urged to stay, I told a white lie and claimed that a warning light had come on in my mannequin body and that I needed to see my ground crew. The fix was already in and everything arranged; what did they need me for anymore? The fake warning light was enough to get me home to New Orleans, where the trouble mysteriously vanished. I had a very close personal relationship with my ground crew; how could it be otherwise? The only actual doctoring required was to my troubleshooting logs.

That left me with almost an entire afternoon free and clear to do whatever I wanted. It was a little frightening, really; I hadn't had so much unscheduled time all together in one block since my leave on Esteppe. I took a few minutes to call Jimmy, who was doing fine and feeling good about how wonderful a job the surgeons had done on his father. Lofton apparently could almost pass for normal these days, his one cybernetic eye excepted. Since his and Ted's missing orbs were both on the same side, they'd agreed to maintain the family resemblance by each ordering exactly the same hardware. They both naturally had brown eyes, but chose an ungodly shade of jade green for the replacements. "It's really weird at first," Jimmy explained. "Then kind of cool after a while. I told Dad I halfway hope I lose an eye in combat someday, too. And you know what? He smacked me!"

There was a big pile of reports sitting on my desk regarding my future pilots; I paged idly through them but couldn't concentrate. There were nineteen candidates; our goal was to have a full flight of twelve 'bolts operational when next we invaded Dracan space. Nineteen was a very odd number; I couldn't help but wonder if there hadn't originally been twenty surgeries of which one had failed. In which case some poor kid had volunteered, risked everything, and lost their life without my ever meeting him or her. I pressed my lips together and resolved to visit the pilot's hospital ASAP, just as soon as I could clear a place in my schedule. They deserved nothing less from me, after all. And besides, how could we all become a tight-knit team if they perceived me as someone who didn't even care enough to come and visit while they were going through the bad times?

For that matter there were other obligations I was neglecting, as well. Delana's family had asked for a visit, as had those of several of the other lost pilots. Heaven knew they were entitled; most of them had even found the strength and good-will in the depth of their mourning to thank me for the difficult letters I'd written them describing the loss of their children. How could I not find time for such people as these? It'd originally been my intention to wait until Father Murton was up and about before taking this particular duty on. He was good with grieving people. Most priests were, I knew, but my tutor seemed to have a special gift. It was becoming clear, however, that I couldn't depend on his help with anything anytime soon. He was a shadow of his former self, and it would be for weeks if not months to come. So I wrote a memo and sent it off to my overworked personal secretary, explaining that this along with the new-pilot visit simply *had* to be worked in, no matter how difficult it might be.

Which led me to another item of unfinished personal business. Manuel was proving most satisfactory as a personal attendant. He was quiet when I needed for him to be quiet, smiled when I needed a smile, and was otherwise quite efficient. Best of all, he played a mean game of Rocket-Sledder. So I sat down and wrote him a letter asking him if he'd be willing to stay on for a bit. "I'll understand completely if you say 'no'," I explained. "A lot of people probably look at what you're doing and imagine that you're acting as my personal servant, which they consider to be demeaning. In fact, every time I see you on your knees groveling at my feet to tie my shoes for me, I feel a stab of guilt. You're a trained gunner, and quite a good one judging by everything I hear. If you were to go back to the fleet, I'd not blame you a bit. You're under no obligation whatsoever. But if you were to stay I'd be very, very grateful."

It was heartwarming, really. I'd barely hit "send", it felt like, before I got a nice note in reply. "Commander Longo," it read. "I've never had such wonderful duty as I've experienced working for you. I've met famous people, visited interesting places, and I'm learning more and more every day about cutting-edge medical stuff just from being around you. Not bad for a ranch-boy from Pampas! Best of all, sir, you don't make me *feel* like a servant. It's a *pleasure* to tie for your shoes for you. After all, I know that you cannot do it for yourself.

"I'll be glad to stay with you for as long as the navy allows me to, sir. Again, this is the best duty I've ever known."

I smiled when I read Manuel's letter, then forwarded both it and my own to Admiral Vlasilov. I was sure that he'd let me keep him; the man was already working out well, and *someone* had to take care of me. Sure, I was robbing the Training Fleet of a desperately-needed gunnery instructor. But, hey! Turnabout was fair play; they, after all, were trying to rob Aviation of a skilled valet!

There were still a few hours left before I needed to go to bed, and one more pressing issue remained on my plate. Father had instructed me to buy myself a new skimmer, and I knew him well enough to recognize that he'd meant exactly what he said. "The finest skimmer there's ever been," had been his exact words. I smiled and toyed for a moment with the idea of getting my old one out for a quick dash across Lake Pontchartraine and back. But it was nearly dark. Besides, navy security would go insane trying to guard me while I indulged in such wild antics at short notice. So instead I rang up the salesman who'd listened so patiently while I'd hemmed and hawed between various accessories and configurations as a child. I'd buy an ocean-going skimmer this time, I decided. It' be larger and less maneuverable, perhaps, but also capable in a pinch of getting me to the Bahamas almost as quickly as I could fly there by 'hopper. I'd get a blue one, I decided, with seating for four so that Jimmy and Ted and Manuel could come along, and if the dealer delivered it with the bows painted red like the ground crews kept insisting on doing with the noses of my Skybolts, I'd… I'd… I'd…

I'd do nothing, apparently. The phone rang and rang; the showroom was closed and everyone had gone home for the day.

Oh, well, I thought to myself as I slowly raised myself out of the too-small chair that I kept forgetting to ask to have replaced. *Maybe I should just go to bed early. I'll buy a skimmer the next time I have a few minutes to spare. And if I never do, then Father will just have to understand.*

Chapter Forty-Six

An afternoon off should've made the next day's endless conference meetings in Baton Rouge more tolerable, but it didn't. Even though I was by now a veteran of thousands of endless official and para-official meetings, I'd never before felt so strongly that the whole affair was nothing but a sheer waste of everyone's valuable time. Or of *my* valuable time, at least; the politicians seemed to have unlimited quantities of the stuff to fritter away on nonsense. It was rude of me, I knew, but I found myself spending more and more time playing my internal video game. Mr. Flowers would nudge me if, god forbid, something of substance should happen.

It was perhaps three in the afternoon before anything interesting took place. The chairman thumped his gavel for our normally-scheduled afternoon break. When I finally emerged into the brighter light of the hall, last as usual, Manuel was waiting for me. "Sir," he whispered. "There's someone waiting for you in your office."

My eyebrows rose; only a handful of people were even aware that we committee members had been assigned temporary work spaces for our convenience while in Baton Rouge. Mine was so ornate that I was afraid to go inside for fear of breaking something expensive. So instead I'd been using the perfectly-good plastic console in my hotel room. "Really?" I asked.

"His name is Bhata," Manuel explained. "He's from India. And, he looks really nervous."

Mr. Bhata virtually flew to his feet when I entered the room. "Mr... I mean, Your Excellency!" he greeted me, stumbling a little over the off-world honorific. "I am greatly honored!"

I extended my hand, and the Indian man pumped it energetically. His clothing was rumpled and he seemed even smaller than he really was. "I came just as soon as I heard," he explained, noting the way my eyes were wandering over his less-than-perfect wardrobe. "My luggage was lost. What a cock-up!"

I nodded and smiled as reassuringly as I knew how. "That's terrible!"

He shook his head. "It's nothing," he countered, still gripping my hand. I was beginning to wonder when he was going to let go. "Compared to the honor, I mean. I'm *so* very grateful for such a wonderful opportunity!"

I let my smile fade. "Forgive me," I replied. "But I've been tied up in rather intense meetings all day. What opportunity are you referring to?"

Just then Mr. Olafson's head appeared around the edge of my door. "Ah!" he exclaimed. "Excellent, Thomas! I see you've met Dr. Bhata."

I nodded, then gestured the Special Assistant to the PM into the room. He closed the door behind him. "We've met," I admitted, once we were in private. "But I still don't know why."

Olafson's eyes widened for an instant, then he laughed. "Dr. Bhata is an engineer, Thomas. Up until yesterday he ran by far the most successful of our four Polecat production facilities, the one in Phnom Penh. He's also the man I judged most, err… Compatible, let's say. Compatible with your family's and your work force's accustomed management style." He smiled. "I think you'll get along fine."

I looked over at Bhata, who wilted a little, and then back at Olafson. "What about Gunther?" I demanded. "Or my brother?"

"This is just temporary," the PM's man explained, his voice a near-purr. "It'll take weeks to get either of them here, you know. There's no way around it. In the meantime, someone's got to take charge." He nodded at the little engineer. "The doctor here will become the number-two man the minute a Longo man arrives," he explained. "It's already been agreed to."

I looked back at Bhata. "Yes!" he agreed. "I'm perfectly happy to accept a number-two job, what with all there will be to learn. It's a great, great honor to work with such a ground-breaking enterprise. Your father is a legend!"

I pressed my lips together, and thought for a moment. Olafson was within his rights, I decided. Someone *did* have to be in charge of the plant until Gunther or Sven arrived. The navy needed fighters, after all, and right now! More managers needed to be trained at all levels, and there was no time like the present to begin. Besides, I could hardly claim that Dr. Bhata lacked qualifications. So I reached down and took Bhata's hand again, then shook it firmly. "In that case," I said, "welcome to the family." He didn't seem to know quite what to say, so I continued right on for him. "There's no point in rushing right down to New Orleans." I gestured at the luxurious leather swivel chair behind my desk. "Make yourself at home," I urged him. "Try and find your luggage, and make any calls that need to be made. Will you need a place to stay, for yourself and your family? If so, Manuel can help you get situated in the *gasthaus*; you can stay there for as long as you need to."

Dr. Bhata's jaws worked. "I… Uh…"

"Excellent, then!" I agreed, edging past Olafson and out of my office. "You can fly to New Orleans with me, if you'd like. We'll leave just as soon as the conference is finished for the day."

"It'll be finished for longer than that," Olafson assured me, following me out the door. It wasn't difficult to keep up, as slowly as I moved. "They're going to sound the final gavel today."

My mouth opened, then closed. I'd been about to protest that we hadn't even gotten to the problem-solving phase yet, but then I'd thought about how badly I wanted things to be over with.

Olafson read my expression perfectly. "Hah!" he laughed, slapping his thigh. "Everything's in the bag, Thomas. As of twenty minutes ago the last major deal was cut. Besides, everyone's getting tired of the local eateries and nightlife. They'll officially read your proposal, then adopt it unanimously without further debate. We'd have gotten this all squared away yesterday, but there was one last sticky issue—"

Just then we rounded the corner into the little lounge-area directly outside the main conference room, and I practically walked into Roon, who'd been hurriedly moving in the opposite direction. "Excuse me!" he declared, both looking and sounding perfectly sincere.

"And me as well," I replied, bowing slightly. We'd both been equally at fault, after all.

The plant manager smiled and extended his hand. "Look," he said. "It's a good thing that we ran into each other like this, Thomas, because I want to tell you something. I'm damned grateful for what you've done, fighting for us and risking your life the way you have. You're a hero, and you've earned every one of your medals. There's no hard feelings on my end."

I accepted his hand, more out of reflex than anything else. "I… Well…"

Roon's smile widened as we shook. "You're just young, is all," he continued. "In time, you'll grow up and learn more about the world." Then he was gone, striding down the corridor on his long legs, and, of all things, whistling.

I stared after him for a long moment, then turned to Olafson. "You spoke of one last sticky problem," I speculated. "Don't tell me…"

"He walks away clean," Olafson agreed, suddenly looking worried. "Now, Thomas, don't get all—"

"He's a *moron!*" I countered, my hands balling up into fists. "Incompetent, corrupt… Heck, we *know* that at least one naval officer was bribed. Who do you think paid said bribe?"

"We'll never know," Olafson answered, shaking his head. "The key witness is dead."

My eyes narrowed. "Did she leave a note?" I demanded.

Suddenly Olafson's mouth formed a hard, thin line. "Watch that!" he cautioned me. "Watch that very closely indeed! There are limits even for you, Thomas Longo!"

By now my jaw was working with rage. "What's going to happen to him?" I demanded.

Olafson looked away. "The same thing that we've been doing with his kind for as long as there's been governments and morons with influential relatives, of course. We're promoting him. Kicking him upstairs to where he can't do any more harm." He shook his head. "We can't afford to alienate his sister any further; eventually we're going have to do business with her."

I closed my eyes, and felt vaguely ill. "Upstairs to what?" I asked. "Not that it particularly matters, I suppose. I mean, obviously the deal's already been made. But I'm curious."

The Special Assistant smiled, though he looked very tired. "We've created a new post for him. More pay, more prestige, more responsibility. In theory at least." He shook his head again. "Mr. Roon is to be named executive coordinator of all four Polecat production facilities, a position made necessary by the large volume of conventional fighters being produced. He's thrilled to death."

I titled my head to one side. "But… The navy doesn't need any more Polecats," I pointed out. "They have too many now. I just saw a report on the matter the other day."

"Exactly!" Olafson agreed, finally meeting my eyes. "The navy wants production cut, yes. But have you ever tried to convince those Parliamentarians whose districts the plants are in that there need to be cutbacks?"

I gulped.

"So you *do* see!" Olafson agreed happily. "The navy gets fewer fighters of a type they don't want anyway. Roon's sister isn't offended. No Parliamentarian is forced to accept job cutbacks among their electorate. You Longos and your people get to see the back of an idiot." He grinned like a little boy. "Everyone's happy! Is our friend Mrs. Wan a political genius, or what?"

Chapter Forty-Seven

I spent a lot of time thinking about what Mr. Olafson had said regarding Mrs. Wan's plan of action during the ride back home. A rather nasty hurricane was spinning itself up out in the Gulf; the storm wasn't a threat to hit land anywhere nearby, but despite this it was snarling up air traffic throughout the entire region. So Dr. Bhata and Manuel and I had plenty of time to sit and stare silently at one another while we waited for clearance to take off. The Special Assistant had called Mrs. Wan a political genius, and perhaps she was in the narrow sense of the word. "Everyone's happy!" he'd declared. But everyone wasn't, not really. Just the important people, who presumably were everyone that mattered in Olafson's book.

For example, Wan's solution not only left Roon's career unbesmirched by his clear incompetence, but put him in a position to do even more damage in the future. Would more naval officers succumb to bribes, then have to jump off of hotel balconies? What indignities and outrages would Roon inflict upon the Polecat workers? And worst of all, once the war was over where would he go next? Would he be placed in charge of hydroelectric dams upstream of large cities, perhaps? Or a public health-care system? Sure, in the short term booting a fool upstairs might not do a terrible amount of harm. But if he wasn't dealt with, as time passed he'd grow better-connected and ever harder to rein in. How difficult would matters become if, heaven forbid, his sister actually *did* become PM?

Then there were the taxpayers. Not only had they received a rotten return for their investment in trying to build Skybolts under Roon's leadership, an even worse situation could be expected in the future at the Polecat factories. On the surface all was well, since the navy no longer needed large numbers of new Polecats anyway. But the *right* way to scale down production was to close however many of the plants needed to be shut down, not to render all four grossly inefficient. There was a huge shortage of skilled workers at present; this was one of the war-effort's largest bottlenecks. It was stupid, criminally stupid even, to deliberately make decisions that'd result in large numbers of workers sitting around doing nothing at such a critical hour. But again, that was clearly less important to a man like Olafson than offending powerful, well-connected

Parliamentarians who happened to have Polecat-related industries located in their districts. Heaven forbid that they should ever be forced to explain to their voters that they must suffer a little temporary inconvenience in the name of ultimate victory!

I even felt sorry for the security goon who'd sick-rayed Todd Pearlman. Sure, it'd been a totally unjustified action-- I'd been an eyewitness and therefore felt qualified to judge. But once you put things in perspective the lines were a lot blurrier. The guard had made a poor decision, yes. But it was a snap-decision, made under stress and the influence of genuine fear. Roon on the other hand had not only created the larger situation that brought about the physical conflict, but had also issued the orders that made the incident inevitable. The guard was going to get the book thrown at him; my own promise that justice would be done had seen to that. He'd do hard time and carry a criminal record with him for all the rest of his days. Roon, however, was being *promoted*! Where was the justice in *that*?

I grew angrier and angrier as we sat and waited for clearance, stewing in my own juices so intently that I actually didn't notice when we finally took off for the short hop home. And then there was the matter of the dead liaison officer. Most likely, things had taken place exactly as advertised. Deeply dishonored, she'd probably committed suicide as penance for her guilt. But...

Had there been a note? If not, had one perhaps been provided? What kind of creatures walked the halls of Parliament anyway, that I felt it necessary to wonder? And how could I ever live with myself after I became one of them?

I sighed and shook my head. Some of the people I admired most were politicians. There were Spence and Alicia, for example. Both of them were old campaigners-- hard-bitten, hard-cored, hard-nosed. They'd ruin a rival's career in a minute given the chance if it'd further the causes they believed in and the ends they wished to achieve. And why not? The opposition would do the same to them if they ever got the chance; it must be eternally frustrating to those who stood against the Wistons that their enemies lived such boring, pedestrian lives. They were rich, yet took little interest in the things that money could buy. They were of the very highest strata of Churillian society; indeed, by being the sole surviving Founders they practically *defined* said highest strata. But they also lived in a bungalow when their own people were begging them to accept a mansion, and enjoyed rubbing elbows with the peasantry more than attending state functions. Spence often boasted that the trains of Churilla still rode in part on spikes he'd driven by hand. It was impossible to imagine someone like Mr. Roon, or even Mrs. Wan, taking pride in a similar accomplishment.

Did the Wistons hate politics as much as me? Suddenly I understood that they almost certainly did. Just as they hated war, another activity at which they were extraordinarily proficient.

And Father, he was getting into politics too. He was going to run for the Presidency of Esteppe, which would also automatically give him a seat in

Parliament. Yet he was different too. He'd never taken any interest in politics before; if he had, the Autarch would've been pleased to name him his deputy and right arm. I couldn't imagine *him* smiling as he explained Mrs. Wan's plan to me; indeed, the thundercloud of rage I was forced to picture on his brow rather frightened the little boy that still lived somewhere inside of me. He'd have gone along, I was reasonably sure, for the same reasons that I had. The war *had* to be won, and we had to do it with the tools and institutions available at hand, not the ones we wished for. But…

…he'd have sulked for hours afterwards. Just as I was doing.

I sighed again, and looked around the 'hopper's cabin. Since this was a navy vessel it was equipped with a pipper; I glanced at the repeater mounted on the cabin wall and shook my head. Traffic from half of Texas was being re-routed into Louisiana, and even with our military clearance we wouldn't be landing any time soon. Manuel was reading a Spanish-language book he'd brought with him from Pampas; he was used to traveling with me by now, and came prepared. But poor Dr. Bhata was simply staring at the bulkhead, looking bored. If he'd brought anything at all to entertain himself with, he'd presumably used it up during the long trip from East Asia. "Well," I said at last, trying to smile. "It shouldn't be more than another hour or two."

Bhata tried to smile back, but failed. Instead, he looked more frightened than ever.

I turned away and frowned. A pattern was developing here, and not a good one. Clearly, Dr. Bhata was terrified of me. I pressed my lips together, trying to reason out why. Was it because I was famous? Perhaps the fact that I'd nuked several cities offended his personal code of ethics? If it was *that*, I decided, I could hardly blame him. Firing those missiles had deeply offended *me*, too. But if that were the case then why would he be building Polecats for a living? They were every bit as capable of killing a city as a Skybolt; ask any Esteppan! Was it perhaps because I was a cyborg? But again, if that were the case then why was he so pleased to be getting involved with Skybolts?

Then I recalled our first meeting and everything came together. I turned again to face the small Indian. "Dr. Bhata?"

"Yes, Your Excellency?" he answered, looking frightened again.

"I'm just plain 'Thomas' to you from now on, if you don't mind." I smiled as best my plastic face was able. "I hate having a title, though I use it in public out of respect for those who gave it to me."

Dr. Bhata smiled, clearly more nervous than ever. "Of course, T-Thomas" he answered, stumbling over my unadorned name.

I let my smile fade. "I've just realized," I explained, "that you're in a rather difficult position. You've been placed in charge of a failed high-profile plant with a rebellious work force, and your predecessor has been discredited. Or at least privately he has, I should say. The public will never hear a word of it. You're also being forced to cater to the whims of a rich, snot-nosed eighteen-year-old you don't even know who, even worse, is also the most famous war-hero alive. And you've probably been forced to accept instructions, many of them mutually contradictory, from a dozen or more important politicians. Including, most emphatically, a certain Mrs. Wan who left you in absolutely no doubt regarding how seriously you're in her debt. Am I fairly close to the mark so far?"

The engineer's skin, already dark, deepened further in shade "I... Er..."

"Right," I agreed. "You can't talk about it." I pointed vaguely in the direction of Baton Rouge. "I understand. I have to deal with them too, as you saw. But, I wanted to tell you that I'm not one of them, and god willing I never will be. None of us Longos are. We tell each other the truth as best we're able and try to do what's right for everyone." I shook my head. "Put all of that political nonsense behind you, if you can. All you have to do to make me happy-- to make all of us Longos happy-- is to treat the workforce like family. In return, I promise that you'll be treated in kind. It's that simple. Report to whoever you must on the outside; I understand the position you're in. But know from the get-go that we're going to be loyal to you, and expect you to remain loyal to us in return."

Bhata's brow narrowed, then his face fell. "This situation is so complicated," he muttered. "So terribly complicated! I'm an engineer; I build things, is all!"

"And I'm just an ignorant navy 'hopper pilot," I reassured him. The best way to earn loyalty was to offer trust; Father had taught me this a million times over, though I couldn't put my finger on just when and how. "Which is why we've got to work together. As soon as we land, I'm going to go with you to the security desk and get you all signed in. They're reporting to me for now; by the time we're done, they'll be reporting to you as well. From that moment I'm giving you carte blanche. You may have heard that I've got another more-than-full-time career on my hands besides trying to run the plant; I've been ignoring it for far too long now. Don't expect me to look over your shoulder the way everyone else and their brother will be trying to do. You know how to run a fighter plant, and you have a copy of the committee's authorized plan of action. If you need me, I reckon you'll call me. My staff will be instructed to prioritize your calls just under those of my commanding officer. I'm sorry that I can't make you co-equal. But if you ever meet Admiral Vlasilov, I'm quite certain that you'll understand."

Chapter Forty-Eight

The next morning I again found myself facing an empty schedule; my secretary had been under the impression that the Conference was going to meet again, and I could hardly blame him since I'd believed the same thing myself until very late in the day. There were worse things in the world than having nothing important to do, I decided as I lay in bed for an extra twenty minutes and listened to the birds sing outside my window. Then I sighed, climbed slowly to my feet so as not to tumble my gyros, and had Manuel help me put on my Longo coveralls. They were brand new, this time; crisp and unstained. But at least there was one good thing to be said for them; they fit. While tight clothing was a lot less uncomfortable in my mannequin body than it'd been back in the days when I'd worn flesh and blood, it was still nice to be able to move freely without worrying about ripping out a seam. Sure, the garment lacked character. Well, there was one sure way to fix that!

I'd never seen the plant empty before except on weekends. It was a lonely cavern-like place when there were no people in it, haunted by the grotesque, twisted shadows of odd-shaped tooling and machinery. Usually most of the lights were off when no one was working. The tool and die area, however, where my workbench was located, was lit up like any normal workday. I frowned at the waste of power, especially given the wartime shortages. In fairness, however, I had to admit that conditions weren't exactly routine nowadays. Exactly whose job was it to turn the lights off and on when the workers had walked out? Who could be blamed for not knowing?

So I walked slowly across the work bay, looking for light switches and keeping my eyes peeled for promising bits of scrap. A long time ago, back when Jimmy had still been in his human body, he'd admired a joystick and video-console holder I'd designed for myself. I was going to make another like it, I decided, and then not only paint it Skybolt blue with genuine Skybolt paint, but also go out to the scrapped 'bolts that weren't going anywhere anyway and indulge in a little petty thievery. For the most part a 'bolt was a very utilitarian object, completely devoid of ornamentation. Every single Longo 'hopper ever manufactured, however, carried a maker's plate in the cockpit or else the nearest thing there was to one. Since Father was a both a traditionalist and a stickler for maintaining the quality image of his products, the Skybolt's plate, mounted just inside the hatch where the pilot's brain was carried, was rather something to see. Though made extremely thin to save weight, it read "Longo Industries: Skybolt Mk I" in ornate silvery raised letters on a not-quite gold backdrop. Since such plates were serial numbered, I imagined them to be rather difficult to come by. Certainly, one would look good mounted on the front of Jimmy's video-game rack. In fact, while I was out there I might just steal a second one for myself…

Though I knew the shop floor fairly well, I'd never had to shut off the lights before. I came to several switches and tried them, only to discover that they merely controlled the little spotlights above various lathes and drill presses. I was just working my way around the polymill when I discovered that I wasn't alone. There was a pair of legs sticking out from underneath.

"Hello?" I called out gently, so as not to startle whoever it was. There was nothing worse than hitting one's head on something hard, unyielding, and made of tool steel.

"Eh?" a voice answered. "Who is it?"

Finally I realized the truth. Though I should've caught on sooner from the fact that the exposed legs were wearing suit pants, not Longo coveralls. "It's Thomas, Dr. Bhata," I answered. "There's no need to--"

Before I could finish my sentence the Indian man had scrambled out from under the polymill and leapt to his feet, hitting his head along the way. "Ow," he complained, rubbing at the sore place.

I winced. "Sorry. I was just explaining that you didn't need to get up."

Bhata shook his head and lowered his hand. "It's nothing," he explained. Then his eyes seemed to fill with fire. "This machine!" he complained. "It's improperly calibrated! The horizontal index, in particular. It's not even close!"

I nodded. "So the workers tell me."

The engineer's eyes widened. "The employees knew?" he demanded.

"How could they not?" I countered. "They complained about it every single day. The 'bolts they made all ended up as scrap. There had to be a reason, didn't there? Even worse, Father hired his own setup men so that he wouldn't be dependent on the supplier's people. They *wanted* to fix it, and were fully qualified to do so. They simply weren't allowed."

Bhata's jaws worked silently once, twice, three times. Then his fists clenched. "Morons!" he exploded. "This place was run by morons!"

I nodded. "Exactly. You're just now figuring this out?"

He shook his head again. "It'll take at least two weeks to make this machine right. Maybe longer. And… I've not even looked at the rest yet."

I thought things over for a moment, then made a decision. "Would you like some help?"

"Ha!" Bhata declared, encompassing the plant with a single sweeping gesture. "Negotiations haven't even begun with the workforce! And, where else could I find specialists on short notice?"

"Oh," I said slowly, "I just might be able to rustle up a few key individuals. Strikebreakers, really. Like, say, the head of the union. He's one of the best setup men of all."

The engineer blinked. "I… You mean…."

"Exactly," I explained, reaching gently around Bhata's shoulder and steering him towards the offices. "Let's go make a few phone calls. And, while we're at it, I'll find you some coveralls. You'll fit in a lot better around here, wearing those…"

Part II

Chapter Forty-Nine

By noon, I had my little joystick holder all welded together and being readied for paint in the autosurfacer and Todd Pearlman was back in the plant, looking wary but doing what certainly appeared to me to be a quite professional job of precision-measuring a partial Skybolt airframe that he thought might be salvageable. Best of all, Jim Peters was lying alongside Dr. Bhata under the polymill. I was paying a lot more attention to them than I was to Jimmy's joystick-holder; one of the legs came out a little short, and I had to build it up some with a torch and a brazing rod. Jimmy wouldn't mind, I didn't think. Before long Dr. Bhata and Mr. Peters were passing tools back and forth as if they'd known each other for years, and were competing in inventing new names for the engineers who'd designed such a recalcitrant heap of fecal matter. By three my rack was sprayed a perfect Skybolt blue. Now it needed to be left to dry overnight. Which in turn made it the perfect time for me to go steal my nameplate.

It was wrong of me, really. Anyone even remotely associated with Skybolt production would gladly have given me all the nameplates I wanted; being who I was all I had to do was ask. Equally, I was quite certain, if I wanted those *particular* nameplates all I had to do was point at the soon-to-be-scrapped 'bolts and offer even the slightest hint that such a thing might please me. They'd be on my desk in ten minutes, gift-wrapped as likely as not. But somehow it wouldn't have been *right* for me to give a Jimmy a gift like that. The rack would mean so much more to both of us if there was an interesting tale to tell to go with it.

So I waited until no one was looking and sort of eased my way out the big back door where the completed 'bolts were rolled out. It was no great trick for me to open up the hatch of first bird that Mr. Pearlman had been cutting parts from, and then one of the dimensionally-hopeless 'bolts. I brought a crowbar with me, but didn't need it; the ID plates sort of popped off under a little pressure from my superstrong fingers. Then I tucked the plates into the front of my coveralls…

…and turned to find myself face to face with Mr. Pearlman. He was smiling. "Hi, Thomas!" he greeted me.

I'd never been so embarrassed in my life. "I… Uh…"

"Jim sent me out," he explained, still smiling. "To tell you that he thinks this Dr. Bhata guy is going to be okay." Mr. Pearlman shook his head. "Jim asked me to tell you that he's worked on polymills for thirty years now, but despite that Dr. Bhata is still teaching him things he didn't know."

I blinked. Perhaps a doctorate's degree was worth something after all. "Really?" was all I could think of to say.

Mr. Pearlman's smile faded. "The union's looked over the plan you came up to resolve this whole mess. We like it. I'm speaking for both Jim and myself when I say that."

I nodded.

"We want to go ahead and call in the lead men immediately, if you approve. And if Dr. Bhata approves, of course." He shook his head. "There's a war on. All this time-wasting is stupid."

"We need more 'bolts," I agreed. "Worse than anything else in the universe, we need 'bolts and pilots to fly them."

Mr. Pearlman looked away, then met my eyes. "I…" he began. Then he broke off and turned away again. I waited patiently; clearly my friend was trying to say something important, but wasn't quite able.

"Look," the prototype-maker finally explained, turning to face me once more. "We all feel terrible about what's happened here, every last one of us. When I think of the time we've wasted while the little boy who once played at my house flew combat against such terrible odds, I… I…" Tears were forming at the corners of Mr. Pearlman's eyes.

I shook my head. "It wasn't your fault," I declared, as firmly and as emphatically as I was able. "If anyone on Earth knows that, it's me. Not one bit of it!"

Mr. Pearlman shook his head again. "Maybe," he agreed. "And maybe not. But I've been watching you as this whole mess unrolled, Thomas. And you know what? Somehow, I think you'd have found a way to make everything work where all of us failed. It makes me ashamed."

I sighed and turned back to the unflyable 'bolts. "I've seen more failure than you can imagine over the past couple of years," I explained slowly. "I've seen men fail, I've seen equipment fail, I've seen strategies fail, command structures fail… I've even seen whole systems of government fail. That's part of what's so awful about war, I think, is that it brings out the worst in everything and everyone. It's not just the waste and the death that makes it to terrible. It humiliates and mocks us as well. You're hardly alone in your sense of guilt."

Mr. Pearlman stood silently alongside me for a moment. "You've grown, Thomas," he observed. "Straight and tall and far above most of the rest of us. For all of its shortcomings, war can do that to a young man as well. In your case, it most certainly has."

I shrugged, causing the stolen nameplates to rattle up against my metal chest. "Not that I can tell. All I really want to do with the rest of my life is sit and play video games with my friend Jimmy and try to forget."

Mr. Pearlman nodded. "A lot of combat vets are like that. It's sad." He sighed and shook his head. "In any event, Thomas, I just wanted to tell you one last thing."

"What's that?" I asked.

"That even your father couldn't have handled this situation as well as you have," he said, once again looking me directly in the eyes. "I respect him to no end, Thomas; you know that. But, what you've done here, well…" He took my hand and shook it. "The workforce will be back tomorrow morning. All of it. Jim told me to promise you that. And, he also told me to tell you that they're coming back *for you*."

Chapter Fifty

It would've been very nice if I'd been able to finish up Jimmy's shelf right away, but there were too many other demands on my time. In the late morning I spoke at a war-bond brunch on the West Coast, and then in the afternoon I met with the parents of Li Han and Liu Ming near Bangkok. Li and Liu had collided in mid-air during training; the former survived while the latter did not. But when last I'd seen Li he'd been convinced the crash was all his fault. It wasn't, of course; his training had been pushed insanely hard and fast due to the imperative necessity to stave of imminent defeat. It was a miracle we hadn't suffered more such crashes. Still, Li had blamed himself and when last I'd seen him back on Esteppe he'd been sinking steadily towards that brand of depression-induced unresponsive catatonia unique to brain-core patients like he and I. It was usually either fatal or something even worse, and there was little I could offer his parents beyond the bare fact of his survival. All in all it was a grim day. I hadn't thought there could be worse things to have to do than selling war bonds, but watching parents try to be brave and strong and then weep their eyes out anyway was so much worse that I was ashamed at myself for feeling put-out over making a silly speech.

I was rather hoping that nothing else would come up so that I could go home and try not to have nightmares about grieving mothers. However, Admiral Vlasilov sent me a message while we were racing homewards across the Pacific. "Thomas," the note read. "Something important has come up. I need to see you in person immediately, just as soon as you can get here. Nothing's wrong regarding Skybolt production; I was pleased indeed to hear that the workers returned to the factory today. You're doing excellent work and have nothing to fear. However, I urgently need to see you nonetheless."

Since the admiral was still in the navy hospital near San Diego, we hardly had to alter course at all and made excellent time. Manuel spruced my uniform up a little for me as we landed at the nearby 'hopper field, where a navy VIP van waited to speed me across town to the admiral's room. "What's this all about?" I demanded of the ensign in charge of my reception detail.

"I've no idea, sir," she replied. "Honest."

They always treated me as a VIP at the hospital, van or no. I was dropped off at the main entrance, and at least a dozen assorted muckety-mucks greeted me at the door. They took me straight back to Vlasilov's room...

...which was locked tight, and guarded by a Marine sentry. "What's going on?" I demanded.

The Marine looked frightened; his jaw worked, but no words would come out. Before he could force himself to speak a lieutenant appeared from around the corner. "Commander Longo!" he greeted me, extending his hand. "Sir, it's an honor to meet you! I'm instructed to inform you that the admiral's evening conference is running overtime. It's highly classified, sir, and you're asked to please be patient. There are chairs around the corner, if you like."

I nodded, then leaned forward slightly to look through the little window built into the door. Sure enough the room was full to the gills with admirals, and even an army general or two. I sighed; it would've been much more pleasant to still be on my way home. But since Vlasilov was one of the few people on Earth who could legitimately claim to be even busier than I was, there wasn't any sense in complaining.

"Tell you what," I instructed the Marine lieutenant. "I know another patient in this wing, a Father Murton. His room is just down the hall on the left. I'll be there when the admiral is ready for me."

"Very good, sir!" the Marine answered, snapping out a parade-ground salute. I always hated it when people did that, because my servos were so slow and my range of motion so limited that what I was forced to do in reply was more a mockery of military courtesy than anything else. But the lieutenant, like so many before him, didn't sneer. Instead he merely snapped his heels and went on about his business.

I hadn't either written or talked to Father Murton since the last time I'd visited. I'd tried to call twice, but both times I'd caught him asleep. He was asleep most of the time, the desk-nurse had explained to me when I asked. "Is that common, with this sort of thing?" I asked her.

"Sometimes," was her only comment.

Luckily, my tutor was wide awake this time when I entered the room. He was praying his rosary, his eyes closed and a serene smile spread across his features as he mumbled the timeless prayers. "Hello, Father," I greeted him, my voice low and respectful.

He opened his eyes, looking confused for a second. "Thomas?" he asked. "Thomas? Is that really you?"

I let my smile grow wider. Obviously, he'd been too sick to remember my first visit. "It's me," I reassured him, bending over him and spreading my arms for a hug. "And, I'm *so* glad to see you!"

My tutor's eyes widened and he flinched away. "No!" he screamed. "It *can't* be you, Thomas! You're dead! They say you're dead! I was just praying for your soul!"

Suddenly I was very, very frightened. More scared, in fact, that I'd ever been in combat. "I'm *not* dead," I explained, my voice as calm as I could keep it. "I'm right here! And I love you!"

"No!" Father Murton replied. "You're not real! You're a monster made of plastic and metal. Where's my little boy?" His voice rose into a scream. "Where's the *real* Thomas? What have you done with him, you murderous beast?" He threw his rosary at me, the same worn-out black-beaded one that I'd brought him in sick bay aboard *June* so long ago. "You're a city-killing demon! You murdered my innocent, loving little boy!"

Just then what seemed like every doctor and nurse in the world came running in; two of them eased Father Murton back into bed and administered some kind of shot while the majority formed a sort of phalanx and drove me from the sickroom. "It's me, Father!" I heard myself shouting over and over. "Thomas! I love you!" But it didn't do any good at all; the medical staff kept pushing me backwards and I had to either go along with the pressure or break their bones, which even at that awful moment I knew better than to do. Someone ripped open my right sleeve and brandished a hypodermic, then saw my plastic skin and realized what a silly idea *that* was. "Doctor!" the nurse with the needle cried out. "I can't... I mean..."

"It's all right," a new voice interrupted. "Put that down. Commander Longo will be just fine without it." Even hoarse to the point of near-incomprehensibility and sitting in a wheelchair, Admiral Vlasilov carried such an aura of authority about him that he was instantly obeyed.

"Yes, sir," the nurse replied, lowering the needle.

The admiral looked at me. "Thomas," he said. "I'm sorry beyond words both at what has happened and that you had to find out like this. I called you here so that I could break the news myself, knowing that you have no one else on planet. But..." He shrugged helplessly. "So much is going on. You arrived earlier than I expected, the conference ran over..."

I nodded, looking away. "Navy stuff," I agreed. "Navy stuff always comes first."

Vlasilov looked down at the ground. "Not always," he replied. "This time, perhaps I should've told my fellow admirals that there were more important things in my life. But I did not. And what is done is done." He raised his head to meet my eyes. "The doctors asked me to wait until they were certain, or else I'd have called for you two or three days back. The original brain scans were quite promising, but..." The admiral sighed. "He doesn't know me either, most of the time. I'm a war-demon."

I nodded. "Brain scans aren't a hundred-percent reliable." At least a million doctors had told me that over the years, both in regard to Father Murton's case and in dealing with several of my pilots.

"They're not," Vlasilov agreed, scowling. "Nothing in life is, as I understand better and better with each year's passing." He shook his head. "Thomas... Is there anyone I can call for you? Another priest, perhaps? Bog knows that I'm cold comfort in times of trouble."

"No," I answered. As a cyborg I couldn't quite weep anymore, but the cascade of chemicals associated with intense sadness was beginning to flow through my brain regardless. My mouth formed a rictus of pain for a moment, then by sheer force of will I muscled it back into place. "No, sir. There's no one. Not anymore. I mean…"

Then before I knew it I was on my knees, hugging the admiral so tight that it must've strained his sutures to the breaking point. "There's no one!" I bawled, sounding just like a little child. "No one at all! And there won't ever be again!"

"It's all right," Vlasilov wheezed. Between his injuries and my death-grip, it was a miracle he could get any air at all. "Cry, Thomas! Cry all that you like. Surely your counselor is a man well worth weeping over."

At long last one of the brighter navy doctors had accessed the databanks and figured out how to sedate me. I felt deft fingers tug at the back of my jacket, then swing open the little maintenance door that offered access to my moist and gooey parts. I could've fought the doctor off, could've dodged away and, strong as I was, refused to be tranquilized in the most forceful possible manner. But, I realized, I *wanted* to be put out of my misery, *wanted* to run away for a little while from a world where I had to know every single day from now on that I'd never again speak in any meaningful sense of the word to the best man I'd ever known, my mother and father both in many ways,

"No one!" I complained to Vlasilov as I began spinning down the long, dark tunnel. "No one at all!"

"You have me, son," Vlasilov whispered, right at the very end. "You still have me, poor second-best that I am. On my honor as an officer, I shall never abandon you for so long as I live.

"Rest now, and we shall begin to work this through in the morning. Together."

Chapter Fifty-One

And we did exactly that, the admiral and I. Whatever drugs they gave me were quite excellent stuff; I woke up in my hospital suite feeling fresh, relaxed, well-rested…

…and all achy-hollow inside, as if a major organ had been removed and the rest of my insides weren't accustomed to the fact yet. The pain was dull and distant, however, enough so that I was quite certain I was still under the influence of something-or-other. I could've complained, but I didn't. The admiral was right. Decisions had to be made, and in order to make them I needed to think clearly.

I was quite certain that Vlasilov had planned on breakfasting with someone else, or even more than one someone else. I even saw what I suspected might have been several disappointed invitees with lots of gold braid on their uniform being quietly ushered away as the admiral slowly consumed his scrambled eggs. For all his apparent energy and vitality he was still on a soft-food-only diet, and still spent most of his days hooked to a machine or three. He was the sole survivor, I suddenly realized, of whatever had befallen him and Brooks and Father Murton on the severed part of *June's* bridge, or at least the sole survivor in any meaningful sense of the term.

Though Father Murton's condition wasn't quite so bad, it turned out, as it had first appeared. "He has good days and bad days," his physician explained to me. "I'm sorry that you happened to come see him on a bad one."

I nodded. "The first time I saw him, he knew me. Was glad to see me, even. But he can't seem to remember it."

The doctor smiled. "That's good to hear. Perhaps he'll be glad to see you again another time." Then he shook his head. "But the fact is, mostly he's not functioning very well at all. He can still enjoy life. If you turn on his holovid, he laughs in the right places. Or at least he does when he doesn't think the actors are demons."

"Right," I agreed, sighing. I'd asked if I could try visiting again, but the doctors wouldn't permit it. My tutor was still physically quite frail, just like Admiral Vlasilov. They didn't want to run the risk of having to sedate him again so soon.

The doctor pressed his lips into a hard, thin line, then turned to look out the window. Vlasilov's room looked down on, of all things, a butterfly garden. Wheelchair-bound navy wounded could be found down there at all hours. Rather to my surprise, the admiral spent what time he could there as well. "Your friend is going to have to go into long-term care. There's no doubt of that. The only question is where."

"There's always the navy, of course," Vlasilov interjected around a mouthful of eggs. "We have places where men like him are treated with dignity and respect."

"And there is the church," the doctor pointed out. "They take care of their own, as well."

"My family would never let him suffer," I chimed in.

"Of course not," Vlasilov agreed. Then he frowned and pulled a file out from under his bedsheet. "Thomas, you may not know about this sort of thing because your own official documentation is such a mess. Your file is missing all sorts of supposedly vital paperwork." His eyes narrowed. "Is it true, by the way, that you served for almost two years before being paid for the first time?"

Even as bad as I was feeling, I couldn't help but smile. The check was still at home, folded up and sitting on the corner of my desk. I'd have to deposit it somewhere eventually, I supposed. "Guilty," I agreed.

"That story will be told and re-told for a hundred years," he predicted. "Anyway… When someone joins the navy under more ordinary circumstances than you did, Thomas, he's asked to make certain decisions about what should be done in the event of the unthinkable." He hefted the folder in his hand. "This is Father Murton's file."

I nodded slowly.

"In it," Vlasilov continued, "your friend expressed a desire to let the church take care of him. However, he was only twenty-four at the time. This was long before the Esteppan War, where he met you." The admiral sighed. "Technically, we're supposed to honor the victim's wishes. But in this case…"

"Right," I agreed, understanding.

"So," the doctor asked. "What do you think?"

I frowned. "If we ask the church to take care of him, who pays for it?"

"The navy would pay a subsidy," Vlasilov answered.

"Right, then." I nodded. It was a good thing I was still drugged up, or the answer would never have been so clear to me. "So will my family." I turned back to the doctor. "Father Murton always chose to spend his holidays among other clergy when he could," I explained. "And you've seen what comfort his rosary gives him. I can't see where it makes any sense to try and overrule his wishes, no matter how long ago he expressed them."

"Da," Vlasilov agreed, nodding at the doctor. "Let it be so, then."

"Aye-aye, sir" the physician acknowledged. Then he turned to me again, not quite meeting my eyes. "Commander," he said. "I just want you to know that I did everything... I mean, I knew from the beginning who he was and what he meant to you. I..."

I waved my hand dismissively. "I know," I answered, my face screwing itself up a little again despite the drugs. "Everyone did their best. But flesh and blood can only stand so much."

"I'm sorry, too," Vlasilov agreed. "Back when we were hit, we tried to help him. Everything was madness, all around us! We got the tourniquets on him as quickly as we possibly could, Brooks and I did. But... But..." The admiral's skin paled, and a thin sheen of sweat formed on his forehead. "But..."

My eyes closed. So even the legendary Vlasilov knew the true meaning of terror. "Admiral," I interrupted, eyes still shut. "I was there when you three were admitted into sickbay. It wasn't pretty. But I know from what I saw that you did all that you could. More than most would've managed, I'm quite certain. You don't have to tell the story if you don't want to. Not to me or anyone else. Ever. I understand completely."

The admiral's bullet-shaped head fell back onto his pillow. All the force of his personality had evaporated into nothing and he looked more than a little like Father Murton; a tired, worn-out old man who'd fought one war too many. "Thank you, Thomas" he whispered. "More than I can ever say."

Chapter Fifty-Two

It was almost dark by the time I got back home to New Orleans. I'd been scheduled for a week or more to speak at a war-bond rally in nearby Mexico City, and even though I was still doped up and all achy inside I decided to go ahead anyway. Everything went the way it always did; a lot of money was raised, and more people shook my hand and had their pictures taken with me than I could ever remember.

It was a gray and damp evening, as I rounded the end of the hedgerow that marked the edge of the house-grounds and began walking across the front yard. *No one!* A little voice was whispering in the back of my brain. *Not ever again*! Apparently the drugs were beginning to wear off, because all I wanted to do was go up to my room and cry until dawn.

Then I caught sight of two men carrying something very odd-shaped away from the house. It was big, flat, and wider at one end than the other. The thing was apparently quite heavy as well, because its bearers were clearly struggling. "Hey!" I cried out, stepping up my pace the little bit that I could. "Let me help you with that!"

The two faces turned towards me, then faced each other. "Thomas," a familiar voice said. "I don't… I mean, I'm so sorry…"

Then someone turned the big outdoor lights on, and I understood. It was Jim Peters and Todd Pearlman, carrying a 'bolt's stub-wing. On it were scrawled hundreds of signatures. "We just now heard about Father Murton," Jim explained, taking over for his stammering friend. "We're so sorry. But we honestly didn't know."

I couldn't help but smile. "It's all right," I said, reaching out and taking most of the weight. "You *couldn't* have known; in fact, I'm surprised you found out at all. I was trying to keep things as private as possible." I paused for a second. "You were taking this back to the factory?" I asked.

"Yeah," Todd said. "It just didn't seem like the right time."

"Sure it is," I countered; the *last* thing Father Murton would have wanted, I knew, was for Skybolt production to be endangered on account of him. If the workers had made a gift for me, I'd accept it both graciously and immediately. "Let's go back inside. I want a better look at this thing."

"We couldn't run anything today anyway," Jim explained as we muscled the stub-wing back up the steps. "Everything's being recalibrated and Dr. Bhata's interviewing all the foremen."

"Most of them he's firing," Todd interjected.

"So," Jim continued, "we kind of decided to—"

Before he could finish we were through the front door, and then into the reception hall beyond. There was a big cake sitting on the table with recently-extinguished candles on it. Heaven knew how many ration-points the thing had cost or where they'd come from. Arranged off to one side behind it was another, matching stub-wing, also festooned with signatures. Between them, they covered a large portion of the wall.

"We had a delegation waiting here for you," Jim explained. "They left just a few minutes back, when we, ah…"

"Right," I agreed, perfectly willing to allow my friend to dance around the issue of my recent loss.

"One of them is for you," Todd explained, "and the other is for your wingman, Jimmy Knight. We're just sorry that neither of you can enjoy the cake," Todd added.

"I'll have it sent to the shop floor," I agreed, smiling as I ran my fingers up and down the smooth metal surface. "Good luck Jimmy!" one of the well-wishers had scribbled; clearly, I was looking at my friend's gift. "Take care of Tommy for us!"

I shook my head and smiled. "Why?" I asked. "I mean…"

Jim smiled, then nodded towards where my little video-game joystick rack now stood, finished and complete, with its genuine Skybolt manufacturer's plaque mounted in just the right place. Apparently I hadn't been quite as sneaky as I imagined when stashing the plaques in the top drawer of my workbench. "Someone sort of gave us the idea that you guys might like to have something authentic to remember each other by," he explained. Then he smiled and tilted his head to one side. "You *were* making it for your friend, right?"

I laughed and shook my head. "Yes," I admitted."

"Good!" Jim declared, pulling a second identical rack out from under a table and handing it to me. Or nearly identical, rather-- when I checked there wasn't any brazing underneath to make up for a short leg. "Then perhaps you'll accept this one from us."

And that was more than I could take. Suddenly, I was crying again. "I… Guys…"

"Of course, Thomas," Todd agreed, placing his hand on my shoulder. "Too much, too fast." He looked at Jim, who nodded. "We'll go now, son. Don't worry about a thing out on the shop floor; we're going to be fine now that we're all on the same side again." He looked down at the ground. "Like I said, we just didn't know."

212

Chapter Fifty-Three

The next couple weeks passed in something of a blur. I still hurt inside, but the cold truth was that I didn't have *time* to mourn. I sold war bonds in nine cities on four continents, and that was just the beginning! I also met with Delana's and Viktor's grieving parents, attended at least a dozen vital meetings at the plant in my role as naval liaison, and then six or seven more strictly because I was Father's unofficial representative and son. Fortunately things were breaking loose at long last, production-wise; the partial airframe that Mr. Pearlman had thought might be salvageable was indeed sufficiently well-built to be used. By completing it and shamelessly robbing our scrapped airframes of every usable part, we were able to produce our first in-spec 'bolt for delivery within ten days, even before the polymill was properly lined up. I flew it three times around the airfield as the assembled staff shouted and cheered. Then I officially delivered it to the big naval air station in Florida, where dozens of would-be ground-support ratings waited to train on it.

It was a glorious day indeed; no one was prouder than Dr. Bhata, who I was beginning to hope would remain with the family business for a very long time to come. I came to trust him more and more as time went by, so that when eventually Admiral Vlasilov sent an assistant liaison to act as my aide and then promoted him to replace me entirely, I was more than satisfied that Father would be pleased at how the plant was operating. If I ever felt the need to interfere, I could wave around Father's legal papers again anytime I wanted. But with Dr Bhata in the saddle, I felt confident that it wouldn't be necessary. In fact, I almost regretted having called for Sven or Gunther to take over. What was done was done, however; one couldn't exactly recall interstellar mail.

With less to do at the factory I had more time to be a squadron commander. Vlaislov sent me a letter suggesting that I visit *Tsushima Strait* if I thought I could make time, so that I could look around and learn how things operated aboard more conventional carriers. The arrangements aboard *The Glorious First of June* during my time with her, he explained, were not at all standard operating procedure. He didn't have to ask twice; I was in Hiroshima Bay within three days, touring the ship, asking questions, and best of all getting to see all three Knights all together again in one place. Jimmy was right, I decided as his father Lofton greeted me at the ship's entry-port. You could hardly tell that he'd ever been wounded, except for his one green eye. Ted, in fact, looked by far worse of the two; he'd never found time to get his facial scars fixed, and my guess was that he wouldn't until the war was over. "My brother's pilots are terrified of him," Jimmy confided to me one night, while we were trying out his new joystick-holder. "He sort of reminds me of Colonel Rotte sometimes. Apparently he's the devil incarnate behind the joystick of a Polecat; the very first thing he did when he took over command was beat every single man in the squadron in one-on-one dogfights." He shook his head. "It's not fair, somehow. I could whip him silly with a Skybolt and we both know it. Yet, who's the better man?"

All I could do was nod and agree; ninety-eight percent or more of my own success in combat, I was fully aware, was attributable to what I flew rather than my level of skill. Things were as things were, however; the only thing one could do about it was to remember to treat Polecat pilots with the respect that they deserved. Especially the long-timers like Ted and his father, who'd been flying for so many years.

Still, Ted's Kicking Dragon squadron wasn't a group to be trifled with. Each of them had the lean, hungry look about them that was the hallmark of a good fighter pilot. Most of them were already blooded as well; the Dracans had raided the area several times during the period while Earth was cut off, and the Kicking Dragons among others had been fairly successful in driving them off. Four pilots had their first kills under their belts, and one of them had a pair. All in all, I decided, these men were far better prepared for the ordeal to come than I'd been, or even than Jimmy'd been. Or, for that matter, than my next squadron of children was likely to be.

"It won't be right away," Lofton Knight assured me from across the table; we four veterans of the disastrous Churillian campaign were dining together in his private cabin aboard ship. "But you can bet the rush will be on just as soon as you have pilots. The quicker we move the fewer countermeasures our enemies can prepare."

"There are people dying on the occupied worlds every day," Ted reminded me. "And merchies getting shot up. We need to end this war as quickly as we possibly can."

I nodded. Just that morning, I'd read in my daily written briefing, a ship had arrived from Esteppe. Among other cargo, it carried four Skybolts. With the four we'd brought with us aboard *June* and the one working 'bolt from New Orleans, we were up to nine superfighters assigned to the Bananas. That was the most we'd ever had! Plus, there were almost a dozen more flyable birds back on Esteppe. They were painted soot-black, I was told. The Butcher Birds were reforming as well. If we went into action alongside each other, it was hard to imagine how anything could stand against us. Father had predicted a rapid end to the war, and now it seemed he'd been right.

Suddenly Ted put his fork down and looked at his father. "Can we tell him, sir?" he asked.

The senior Knight scowled, then nodded reluctantly. "I suppose it can't do any harm." He turned to face me. "Your security rating is sky-high, son. But you've not been cleared for this because, in theory at least, you lack the need-to-know. I've been a squadron commander myself, though, in a fairly similar position to where you're at now. And I don't agree with the security experts. You *do* need to know."

I nodded silently.

"*Tsushima Strait* is going to war," her captain continued, "Sooner rather than later. We're going to go clear the vermin off of New Nippon so that we don't have to continually convoy all the merchies through there, and liberate the local population." He looked me directly in the eye. "We're not waiting for superfighters this time, Thomas. We're doing this job without you. That means you have a little more time than you probably think. To get ready, I mean."

Ted nodded. "I'm a squadron commander just like you are, Thomas. So, I'm only cleared for pretty much the same kind of stuff. However…" He frowned and looked at his father, who nodded again. "Well… There's never been a rule saying an officer can't make guesses."

"Right," Lofton agreed, smiling. "In fact, junior officers are encouraged to speculate, to help them develop the thought-processes that they'll someday need when serving as admirals." He reached down and pressed a button under his table, and a holomap, arranged by Nikita alignments, appeared above the remnants of our meal.

"As you can see," Ted continued, "most of settled space is a rabbit-warren of interconnecting Nikita hops. There are, however, a few choke points. New Nippon is one of these; it's the only approach to Earth. Controlling it is vital to victory."

"And, the Dracans have lost it!" Jimmy interjected.

"Right," Ted agreed, smiling at his younger brother. Then he turned back me. "Historically," he continued, "wet-navy battles almost always took place at choke-points on the high seas. If you ever look at a map of them, you'll see that even in times of relatively high-tech they almost always were fought practically within sight of land. Usually in or near some kind of strait or channel of high strategic value."

I nodded. "So," I said slowly, examining the map. "You're going to go do the final clean-up at New Nippon." I mentally ran my fingers down the various lines of approach to Drakkus. There were tons of them, if one was willing go through eleventy-six Jumps the way we had on our big raid. But there were only four reasonably direct routes.

All four of them, at one point or another, ran right smack through the Orion Nexus.

"Churilla," I whispered. "After New Nippon, we're going back to Churilla."

"There'll probably be a little more to it than that," the eldest Knight predicted. "We'll liberate some other economically important worlds first. The Dracans probably will let us, husbanding their resources for what has to be the next big fight. After all, they can read a map as well as we can."

"Ten weeks," Ted predicted. "That's what it'll take to make *June* operational again, and by coincidence that's also about how long I expect it'll take for the army to prepare an expeditionary force." He smiled. "By then the rest of the fleet will have shaken down on the small targets, like New Nippon. We'll be at peak fighting efficiency."

"Ten weeks," Jimmy repeated, whispering. He stared down at the table for a moment, then looked up at me. "Can we do it?"

"Of course!" I replied breezily, not even reminding anyone that I also had to stand for Parliament during this same crucial period of time. "No worries! It's four more weeks than I was figuring on. We'll be ready with time to spare!"

Chapter Fifty-Four

Ten whole weeks; it sounded like *plenty* of time. Until of course one considered that the only combat-qualified Skybolt pilots on the planet were Jimmy and I, and that the rest or our would-be pilots at this point were still little better than vegetables, able to make a little light flash at will but not much more. I was finally able to visit them, as I'd been promising for ages, on my way home from Japan. But it did little good that I could see. Some of my future command made their lights flash quickly for me, but were unable to respond in any more meaningful way. It was incredibly awkward, though the doctors assured me that my presence couldn't do anything but help.

My secretary usually did a pretty good job of screening my mail for me, but even so too large a pile of letters was waiting for me on my desk when I got back home. Some of it I didn't need to see; my bank statement, for example. It was probably a good idea in theory to keep a close eye on my personal finances, but that could wait until the war was over. I wrote on the still-sealed envelope that in the future this sort of thing could go directly to our accounting department. But there was some other stuff that was more worthy of my personal attention. Father had written me a letter to accompany the latest shipments of Skybolts from Esteppe. It was very awkwardly phrased, at least partly because he couldn't know for sure that I was still alive as he wrote it. His worry manifested itself in every syllable. Even worse, however, he was clearly exhausted. The letter contained several misspellings, for example, which was totally unlike him. I suspected that he hadn't had a good night's sleep in weeks. Near the end he informed me that Sven was responding to treatment, but had been barred from working until his condition improved. Then he closed by asking me to relay his best wishes to Father Murton, which made me cry all over again so that I couldn't look at the rest of my mail for a little while.

When finally I was able to continue, however, only one other item remained to be dealt with. My voter-registration card had arrived. The simple form letter congratulated me on having achieved my majority, then explained that I was eligible to vote in all local elections, those of the National Government of the United States, and perhaps most importantly in the Second North American District during the upcoming United Systems Parliamentary elections. My parliamentary district's boundaries had been readjusted, the letter further explained, due to wartime population shifts and the massive carnage inflicted on the east coast by the Dracans. Where once the second district had encompassed most of the Missouri-Mississippi Valley, now it was an odd salamander-shaped thing, running along the Gulf Coast through Texas and the Southwest, and then up the West Coast well up into Canada. I shook my head in bafflement; during eighth-grade civics, Father Murton had explained to me that Parliamentary districts, insofar as was possible, were supposed to take into account national, cultural, and natural geographical boundaries. I couldn't make any sense out of it; all the districts surrounding the Second were far more regular-shaped. Perhaps the defining factor was the coastline, I wondered? Perhaps the people of the second district shared distinct maritime interests or a seagoing culture?

Then it hit me like a bolt of lightning. This was Alicia's doing, dirty politics at its very finest! The district boundaries weren't *supposed* to make sense...

...until one took into account the fact that the Opposition leader was one Isoroku Nagano, of Seattle. Which was now, via the most strained interpretation possible of the codicils, part of the same district as New Orleans.

Where I lived and therefore where I was legally bound to run.

My jaw dropped as the beauty of it all sank in. It was... brilliant! Daring! Even the navy had cooperated by stationing me at home, removing even the slightest basis for an appeal as to my residency. And it was dirty, dirty, dirty! A wonderfully fitting riposte, in other words, to the filthy brand of politics I'd personally watched Nagano engage in during my short acquaintance with him, when he'd tried to force the navy to build more battleships instead of Skybolts despite the fact that big-gunships couldn't help win the war. Even better, I came to realize as I did a little research, Nagano himself had publicly hailed the new district boundaries as "statesmanlike" and "bipartisan". Why? That answer became clear in a few keystrokes; even a neophyte like me knew by now where to look in order to reveal a politico's motives. His last re-election had been close; too close, apparently, for comfort. This new district, historically, voted much more reliably for his party than the old one did. In fact, during redistricting negotiations he'd probably been forced to offer multiple concessions elsewhere in exchange for drawing himself a "safer" district. It was magnificent; he'd almost certainly *paid* for the privilege of being raped! He might even have suggested himself that New Orleans be added, since it always voted his way! No wonder everyone "in the know" always commented on how brilliant Alicia's plan was! What an amazing admiral she'd have made!

Isoroku Nagano was due for a terrible disappointment once he learned I was on the ballot, I reckoned. And, try as I might, I couldn't help but grin as I imagined the look on his face when he finally learned just how badly he'd been outmanuevered. *Kill them all!* A familiar voice whispered in the back of my brain. *Kill every last one of them buggers!*

Kill them I would; this time, there wasn't the slightest doubt in my mind as to the right and wrong of things. The PM and his people might be less than as pure as the driven snow, but I knew unadulterated evil when I saw it. Nagano might yet beat me, yes. He was a pro and I was just an eighteen-year-old kid. But I'd give him the run of his life, I swore to myself, in the name of all the men and women his self-serving stupidity had slaughtered on I couldn't even guess how many battlefields. With any luck at all, I might just beat him. So it was to be full military power, and all missiles armed and ready! I was in all the way aboard now, willing, eager…

..and, most importantly of all, had the taste of blood strong in my mouth.

Chapter Fifty-Five

Things happened quickly, once I got the voter card. My secretary informed me that he'd received a series of phone calls from the PM's personal assistant while I was abroad, regarding some sort of mysterious "campaign staff" that he claimed needed to be set up for me. I confirmed that yes; I'd be employing a campaign staff sometime in the very near future, though I left the poor fellow in the dark regarding whether it was for a military or political campaign. Both sorts of battles required equal levels of secrecy based on what I'd already learned, and it was still too soon to risk letting the cat out of the bag by informing anyone who didn't have the need to know. I decided to devote the whole gasthaus to the election effort excepting only those rooms required by Dr. Bhata, and met with Mr. Flowers to let him in on the secret. "I know that I can't possibly spend enough time on the campaign to do it right," I explained. "I also know that I'm young and naïve. But I trust you. Will you act as my personal representative on the staff?"

The attorney's eyes widened. "I'd give *anything* to see that bastard Nagano on the street. When they shifted us into his district, I considered putting in for a transfer to Esteppe." Then he smiled. "Of *course* I'll do it! In fact, I'll contribute to your campaign! Where should I send the check?"

I didn't know, of course, which was kind of embarrassing. But I made up for it by authorizing my attorney to transfer up to ten million credits into the campaign account from my own coffers, when and if he ever found it. Father hadn't sent me so much money with the intention of it being left to sit idle while the great issues of the day were decided. And, of course, there was no limit on the amount of money one could donate to one's own election fund.

Once I got that all set up, more and more strangers began appearing at the estate. Clearly these first arrivals were low-level functionaries who'd been made to understand that my time was far more valuable than theirs. They never once interrupted me when I was remote-conferencing with Admiral Vlasilov, for example, or complained when I was gone for two or three days at a time selling war bonds. Still, each had their demands, all of which had eventually to be met. Because their time with me was so short, it wasn't at all unusual for me to be assailed by as many as three or four at once. "Would you be willing to try a brown suit, Your Excellency?" my personal tailor asked one afternoon while measuring my left arm. Off-the-rack suits, in my case, were clearly out of the question. "Or perhaps even a maroon?"

Make them both, I'd been about to answer, *and we'll see which looks better*. But, before I could speak, a young man not much older than me interrupted from across the room. "You own a skimmer, Your Excellency. Does it have a name?"

Then, from behind me. "I'm sorry, Your Excellency. But, do you happen to know what medals the navy plans to award you for your role in the Second Battle of New Nippon? I'm trying to compile a media package, you see, and…"

"Perhaps we ought to stick with simple black," the tailor mused. "It'll make you look more dignified, as young as you are…"

"Have you formally graduated high-school?" the media lady demanded.

"What color is your skimmer? Do you have any pictures of yourself winning a big race in it?"

"…or maybe gray, Your Excellency?"

It was the purest sort of madness, yet absolutely necessary. I already understood better than most that democracy was a form of government riddled with flaws and contradictions. Yet it was only when I was forced to stand around for hours answering the most inane and irrelevant possible questions that I came to appreciate that perhaps foremost among these flaws was that a significant percentage of the electorate would indeed base their decision, consciously or subconsciously, on the color of my suit or what name I'd given my skimmer. My party and I differed with Nagano's people on virtually everything under the sun, from how the war ought to be prosecuted to tax and tariff policy. Yet what would matter to too many voters was how many medals I wore on my chest and how many races I'd won as a boy. It was no wonder that our government was such a mess; its core system of representation sprang from deeply flawed roots. "Democracy," Spence had told me once, "is the worst system of government ever developed by mankind, save for all the others." He'd sounded like he was quoting someone, though I wasn't sure. If so, whoever it was must've stood for Parliament a time or two himself.

By the time the last day of signup arrived, I was growing rather nervous. Waiting until the last minute seemed like a very bad idea to me. Anything could go wrong; the 'hopper with the legal papers could suffer a mechanical failure, there could be a fire at the Seattle Courthouse, someone might have forgotten to dot an "i" or cross a "t". "Why not file a day or two early?" I asked. "Just in case. I mean, what's Nagano going to do with two extra days?"

"You'd be amazed," Mr. Flowers assured me.

"He's right," Mrs. Hunter agreed. She was my campaign chief, and a veteran of dozens of hard-fought elections. "Trust us, Thomas. Please. We've got your best interests at heart. Giving a snake like Nagano even an extra *hour* is something best avoided."

I sighed and looked away. "I'm just nervous, I guess. Like before combat."

Mrs. Hunter smiled; she always looked vaguely like an elderly tigress when she did that. "Of course, son," she replied, her voice soft and soothing. Then she placed her hands on my shoulders and tilted her head close to mine. "But, you know what?"

"What?" I asked.

"From what I hear, son, when the fighting starts you generally do just fine." She smiled again, exposing what really should've been fangs but were not. "Be patient just a little longer, Thomas. Your papers will be filed at four-fifty-five PM local time tomorrow, barring anything short of an all-out nuclear attack. That's five minutes before the deadline. Plenty of time! The fight will truly begin at that moment. And I fully expect that you'll do us all proud."

Chapter Fifty-Six

As it happened there wasn't any nuclear attack in Seattle that day, and the paperwork declaring me a candidate for the Parliament of the United Systems went in without a hitch. This was not to say, however, that there were no fireworks; Nagano's people had been hanging around the courthouse for days, waiting to see what sort of last-minute surprise might be sprung upon them. "The longer things went, the more complacent they became," Mrs. Hunter chortled as she told me the story. "Our mole in their organization said some of them were even beginning to think we were going to allow Nagano to run unopposed. As if we'd let the snake off *that* lightly!"

I nodded and smiled, though a little nervously. The United Systems clerk, who'd apparently received my papers in a state of shocked disbelief, had spoken my name aloud. "My god!" he'd shouted. "*Thomas Longo* is running?" From there, all hell had broken loose.

"Thomas Longo?" Nagano's representative cried. "You can't! I mean, he can't... I mean, how..."

"Read it and weep," my own representative replied, handing him a 'courtesy copy' of my candidacy papers. "See ya on the hustings, asswipe." From there according to media reports, things degenerated in a hurry. My people, being more numerous, had gotten the best of it. But there was much broken furniture, and the behind-the-scenes leaders of both parties were busy for days afterwards "fixing" charges and counter-charges of assault and battery.

Clearly, it was going to be an interesting campaign.

* * * *

Nagano and his campaign staff weren't the only ones to be surprised that week, though at least from my point of view the rest of the surprises were all pleasant ones. Another freighter came through from Esteppe, the *Yooper*, bearing yet another Skybolt. This one was a Mark I*, and painted up with a red nose. Clearly it was intended for my own personal use. I was glad to see it, as the 'hopper I'd flown at the Second Battle of New Nippon was never going to be the same again regardless of how many new parts it received. Now my weary old bird could be relegated to training, where it belonged. In time, according to the navy, Jimmy would be receiving a new Mark I* as well. Just as we'd planned so long ago, the Top Bananas were going to have a single flight equipped with Mark I*'s, plus the staff flight. Which for now consisted solely of Jimmy and I, since he'd officially been named my executive officer and second-in-command and all that. My best friend was now a freshly-minted full lieutenant, and no one was prouder than his brother and father. Lofton had once given me his old lieutenant-commander insignia to wear, but his younger son got his lieutenant's bars. Someday, I resolved, when the time came, I'd pass on Lofton's lieutenant-commander's rank-badges as well. For now, Jimmy's responsibilities were training, training, and more training. It was wrong, really, that the burden had to fall on him this way. By rights, training the Bananas was *my* primary duty. But I had a campaign to run, which was every bit as important to the war effort overall. As a result I could only make occasional trips to visit Jimmy and the rest, even though Florida was practically next door. I felt bad about that, but what could I do? When the political stuff was over, I swore, I'd come back and kick the butts of every last pilot under my command in mock combat, just like Ted or Lofton Knight, or for that matter Emil Rotte would've done. If I didn't lose my edge, that was, with all the speechmaking.

And what speechmaking there was! They scheduled me to visit town after town after town, pressing flesh and meeting my would-be constituents in person. There were also three formal debates to prepare for, where I'd be expected to discuss the issues face-to-face with my good friend Isoroku Nagano. The very prospect left me shaking in my boots; having been privately tutored, I'd never taken a single class in public argument. But, the week's *other* surprise went a long way to help; traveling with my new Skybolt aboard the *Yooper* was Alicia Spencer, Deputy Prime Minister of the United Systems and perhaps the nearest thing I had left to a mother. "Alicia!" I greeted her as she quite unexpectedly appeared at the door of my home, right in the middle of a campaign staff meeting. "I can't believe… I mean…"

Then she threw her arms open and we hugged for so long that everyone began to stare. "I'm so glad to see you," she whispered in my ear, so that no one else could hear. "We've were incredibly lucky not to lose you."

I nodded, then pulled my face away from hers. "I… Uh… Father Murton…"

"I know," she whispered, squeezing me reassuringly as I was still a little boy.

The United System government, now that communications with Earth were re-established, was moving back home. "Rome's the temporary capitol," Alicia explained to me as she sat sipping a cup of Father's best tea. She liked Esteppan tea, I'd discovered while we were there together, and so I asked the cook to brew it up special for her. "Though probably in the long run it'll be moved out of Europe. People seem to think it's somewhere else's turn, after London had it so long."

I nodded and smiled. It didn't matter what Alicia was saying; she could've been reading the tax code for all I cared. Just the sound of her voice was exactly what I needed to feel better.

"Anyway…" she said at long last, carefully setting her cup in its saucer and placing both on the table, "I've come to ask a favor, Thomas. If you don't mind."

"Anything," I answered, meaning it. "Name it."

She smiled. "Well… I find myself rather at loose ends. Parliament's been in emergency suspension for months now, and won't be reseated until after the new elections. So all of my fellow Parliamentarians are out running for re-election. I, however…"

I nodded, suddenly understanding. Alicia's homeworld was under Dracan occupation. Free elections on Churilia weren't likely to take place any time soon; she'd been placed in her seat via the decree of her planetary government-in-exile, and would remain there either for the duration or until recalled. "You don't even have a house to call your own," I suddenly realized. "Stay here. We can find you a room. Or you could use my chalet in Italy if you'd rather."

The oversized rabbit-lady smiled, making her nose crinkle quite fetchingly. "Thank you, Thomas. I was hoping you wouldn't mind my sharing a roof with you." Then she turned to Mrs. Hunter, my campaign chairman. "And, since I've nothing else to do… Perhaps I might help a little with the election work? In my spare time, I mean?"

Mrs. Hunter's jaw dropped. "I…" She sputtered. "I… I'd be *honored*, Madame Deputy! If Thomas approves, that is." The older woman looked down at the carpet. "This whole thing was your idea," she acknowledged. "Frankly, I'd relish the opportunity to work with the mind that came up with such a wonderful plan." For once I didn't picture fangs in my manager's mouth. She seemed quite sincere.

"Good," Alicia replied, bowing slightly from her chair. "I recognize that I'm a Johnny-come-lately here and also that I'm not as familiar with local Terran politics as I might be. I'm *not* here to take over, Nancy. Just to advise." She turned to me. "If you approve?"

If I approve? I didn't say aloud. This was the best news I'd gotten in *weeks*! Instead of answering directly, I cocked my head to one side and squinted slightly, like Nagano so often did in the videos I'd been watching, then crossed my legs nervously, and uncrossed them again. The man was *full* of nervous tics! "I might be willing to cut a deal. What's in it for me?"

Most of the room didn't get it. But Alicia had shared plenty of conference rooms with our mutual friend. "Ha!" she replied, reaching out and slapping me on the shoulder in appreciation. "Don't worry about a thing, Thomas. So long as we all keep our senses of humor, all will be well."

Chapter Fifty-Seven

It didn't take long at all for things to heat up; the press quickly blew my contest with Nagano into a sort of mini-referendum on the conduct of the war itself. The PM's decision to suspend Parliament and declare martial law while Earth was in mortal peril had been hotly debated from the moment it was made, and probably would be for decades to come. Soon the media was perpetually parked on my doorstep—they actually worked in shifts, going to live coverage whenever my personal 'hopper came and went! It was amazing! Once I watched them break into a holo-cartoon to report that I was leaving my estate, even though I was actually still lying in bed. It wasn't until later I found out that the navy had simply decided that my 'hopper needed washing…

Not that I could use my navy ride as much as I used to. Within hours of my filing, Nagano's people were screaming bloody murder about how the military was illegally supporting my campaign. They claimed that I was abusing the system a thousand different ways, from accepting free rides to being assigned to a "gravy post" at my own home. My own staff responded by pointing to the shiny new corporate 'hopper they'd leased for me to use while campaigning, and explaining that the navy security types who accompanied me everywhere were essential for national security. "After all," Mrs. Hunter had explained to the ever-attentive cameras, "No Dracan spy could *possibly* want to kill Thomas Longo. Right? He's in no danger at all!" Then she rolled her eyes so expressively that practically everyone who watched the clip laughed out loud.

That was Nagano's biggest problem, really. Every time he attacked me, the only reaction he could evoke was laughter. Even worse, the laughter was always directed back *at him*! For years and years, Alicia explained to me while sipping tea and preparing me for the first debate, Nagano had won re-election entirely through his uncanny ability to destroy the character and reputation of his challengers. "It's much too prevalent on both sides," she explained. "We've got old wheelhorses in our own party that are just as bad as Nagano. But he's always been the uncrowned king of negative campaigning and character assassination. Now that he's running against someone like you, whom he can't hurt that way, he doesn't have the first clue as to what to do."

I nodded slowly. "If he says bad things about me, then it makes him look bad because I'm a hero. I understand that. But…"

Alicia tilted her head to one side, grinning. Clearly she knew what I was about to ask.

"But…" I continued, plowing right on ahead anyway. I couldn't help it, after all, if I wasn't intellectually enhanced like she was. "I mean… Why doesn't he talk about the issues instead, then?"

Alicia's grin widened. Clearly, she'd guessed correctly. "Because he doesn't really care about them," she explained. "His stands on the issues are designed to help him win elections, is all. None of them really matter to him one way or the other. All he cares about is who holds power and how he can then manipulate them to benefit his own interests. Again, just like too many officials on our own side." Suddenly, her grin faded. "Far, far too many, I fear. They become so enmeshed in the turning of the wheels that not only do they forget what their job really is, but they lose sight of the fact that, every now and again, they just might run across another politician who *hasn't* forgotten." She shook her head. "Nagano couldn't understand you in a thousand years, Thomas. In his mind, this election isn't about the issues—it's about *him*. So he assumes that in your mind it must be about *you*. That's why everything he does is so petty and personal. There's not a statesman's bone in the man's body; his whole life is about puffing himself up as big as possible and amassing more and more and more power without purpose or end." Alicia shook her head sadly. "It's the same pattern over and over again. The human pattern, I mean. You see it with money, in corporate life, sometimes even in academia. The purpose of power becomes power. Once that happens, all hope of rational decision-making is lost."

I nodded slowly. "And that's the real reason why you and Spencer win elections whenever you want to," I said slowly. "Because you remember that you're trying to accomplish specific goals, not just puff yourselves up bigger and bigger. Eventually, the voters notice."

She smiled again, like a teacher working with a particularly rewarding student. "In the end," she confirmed, "they always do. When you offer them a choice, that is. Which is rare enough, what with the Naganos of the universe being as common as they are." Then her smile faded again. "So… The whole planet is watching, Thomas. Comparing you and Nagano. It's our job to make sure that they like what they see. Even if things go badly for you, it'll help the others who're running on our ticket."

I nodded. It was easy to see in retrospect that Alicia had planned on the media circus. Did the talking heads even suspect, I wondered, how effortlessly they were being manipulated? Probably not, I reasoned; most of them seemed to be just as interested in puffing themselves up as the politicians and millionaires were. Not that it mattered. "I'll do my best," I promised Alicia. "Though I have to admit something."

Her eyebrows rose. "What's that?"

I sighed and looked away a time before answering. "I'm not in this for myself," I explained. "If anything, I'd like to *deflate* myself a little. We both know that I'm being honest about that, right?"

She nodded. "It's part of why so many love you so much."

"I'm in this," I continued, "because I hate this war and what it does to everyone it touches. I want to win it as soon as possible, with as little pain as possible. And then once it's over, I want to help craft a lasting peace. After all the people I've killed, it's the only way I can even begin to wash the blood from my hands." I turned and looked her in the eyes again. "We've discussed this before."

"Yes, Thomas," she agreed, nodding slightly. "We have."

I made a vague gesture with my hand. "You're brilliant," I continued. "You and Spence both. With the possible exception of Father while he's jacked-in, you're easily the most intelligent and able people I've ever known. Maybe even the most intelligent alive."

"Go on," she continued, not denying it.

"Well," I said slowly, searching for the right words. "It'd help if I knew what your plan was. For the peace settlement, I mean. So that I could know in my heart that I'm doing the right thing."

There was a long, pregnant silence, then Alicia looked away before speaking. "I can't tell you," she answered. "For a thousand good reasons, I cannot." She turned back towards me and looked deep into my eyes. "You're still a combat pilot, Thomas. There are battles yet to be fought. You could be taken prisoner."

"I could," I agreed. It was true enough, if inconvenient.

"And there are other reasons as well. Good ones, Thomas." She frowned. "Politics is very much like war, you know. It shouldn't be, but it is. In the end, you simply have to decide who you trust and who you don't." Her eyes met mine again. "Do you trust me, Thomas?"

"How could I not?" I replied. "Father does. Admiral Vlasilov does. In fact, just about *everyone* does. Or, at least, everyone I care about."

"That's not what I asked, Thomas," Alicia answered. "I don't want to know about your father, or your admiral, or even what poor Father Murton thought. I want to know if *you* trust me."

I looked away again. "You took me in on Churilla," I answered slowly. "Sure, you had a moral obligation to help me because I was a navy pilot, but you practically *adopted* me. Ever since then, you've shared everything you have with me and treated me like your own son. And besides that, well... I like the way you do things. You and Spence remind me of my own family in more ways than I can count. I've been so lucky to know you... How could I *not* trust you?"

Alicia smiled, then carefully straightened a wayward strand of my hair. "The honor has been ours," she replied. "And your trust is a greater honor still. Be patient, Thomas, and all will be revealed."

Chapter Fifty-Eight

A month prior to the election, our party was running so far behind in the polls that none of the talking heads thought we stood a chance. Wars tend to involve a lot of inconvenience and suffering for everyone involved, including the voters. And because Parliament had been sent home during the worst months, when the very hardest of decisions had been made, Nagano's party was able to blame everything on us. Were you hungry? The food rations were too low; blame the PM! Had your son been drafted? It was all the PM's fault, since he'd set the conscription rules by executive fiat. Had you lost a relative in the bombings? The PM had made poor strategic decisions; in fact, it was his fault that we were at war at all! The Opposition's arguments made me sick; Parliament had been disbanded in the first place because it hadn't been able to rise to the challenge of crafting effective weapons procurement, rationing and conscription laws. The time for partisan debate had ended when the Dracans took New Nippon; indeed, an excellent case could be made that the PM had waited several weeks too long before sending the representatives home. I shuddered to think of what condition the planet would've been in upon my return if the endless bickering had been allowed to proceed even another day. When Earth's only trade-route was pinched off, hard decisions became inevitable. Parliament had shown no signs whatsoever of being able to make them. Personally, I believed that the PM and Alicia had saved the human race from a new dark age by suspending Parliament, and a sizeable percentage of the population agreed with me.

Not enough, however. Not by half.

Blaming the PM for the war itself was an even more despicable tactic, in my book. Anyone could see that the United Systems need never have placed itself in a position where the much-smaller Dracan Empire was able to effectively mount a challenge to it. We could have outbuilt them several times over in any category of armament that one might care to name, so that they would never dare attack. Instead, the Opposition party during their own days in power had cut the navy down to nothing. Nor had they done the army any favors. They'd redirected the funds into ineffective pork-barrel programs which tended to employ large numbers of exactly the sort of constituent most likely to vote Nagano's way, while at the same time providing little or no benefit to society at large. Instead of armies of riflemen, they'd created armies of bureaucrats and tax-dependant voters, all with hands outstretched and insatiable appetites for more money and less work. Even in wartime, with their party in the minority, this privileged quasi-nobility was seemingly as untouchable as Roon. Cockroaches, I was beginning to understand, were easier to eradicate than even the smallest and least-significant of government agencies. And probably made better company, too. Yet Nagano's people wanted *more* of these costly, wasteful programs, even while the Dracans occupied more than a dozen of our worlds. Where was their sense of priorities? Had they no decency at all?

Nagano's positions were ridiculous on the face of things; everything bad that happened was our fault, the war itself being the prime example, while he and his people were responsible for all that was good in life, such as sunshine and the laughter of children. I couldn't understand how my opponent managed to keep a straight face while giving his poisoned speeches. Yet the majority of the populace apparently absorbed and believed every word. Especially when my opponent wept at the podium; he did that sometimes, if he thought the time was right. As a cyborg I could quite easily have had myself plumbed to cry on command as well. However, I refused to stoop to such tactics.

Instead, we hit him head-on with facts, facts, facts. "Nagano and his party tried to prevent my father from building superfighters!" I declared in San Antonio, thumping my fist on the podium the way I'd learned to do during a thousand war-bond speeches. My speeches drew *huge* crowds, many times the size of those who came to see Nagano. Most of them, however, were there to see Thomas Longo the war hero rather than Thomas Longo the politician. It was my job to make them interested in my politics as well. "They wouldn't even approve spare parts to keep me in the air after I destroyed the *Imperial Throne*! Where would Earth be today, without superfighters? You can't kill Dracans with slingshots!" A few seemed to listen, but most didn't care. We moved up a point or two in the polls, but it wasn't enough. Even those points faded away when Nagano pointed out with his smug smile that it was *Polecat* squadrons which had defended Earth itself against nuclear warheads, not Skybolts. "These so-called warhawks want to force our children to do their fighting for them!" he cried out in Seattle, his personal political stronghold. There were tears running down his cheeks, a sure sign to trained eyes that the man didn't believe a word he was saying. "Our beloved children, ripped away from their families far too young, then cut and mangled into living frankensteins! We don't need to sink that low! We can stand by our proven, tried conventional fighter squadrons and big-gunned capital ships."

I ground my fake teeth together so hard that my jaw-servos locked up tight. Did the man know *nothing* of strategy, about what wars were like and what it took to win one? Apparently not, because the very next words out of his mouth were a promise to seek a negotiated settlement with the Dracans as soon as possible, while they still held most of the choice strategic points and therefore had all the bargaining leverage. Was *this* how he intended to deter future aggression? By ensuring that it was *rewarded*? Was *this* how he proposed to build a lasting peace? By returning to exactly the same conditions which had brought about the current war, only with our side weaker than ever? How could he even *dream* of abandoning the brave Churillian guerillas to Dracan tyranny?

But that wasn't the worst part. At the end he took questions from reporters. I couldn't see very well, since my ground-crew was trying to unlock my jaw. But one of the newswomen asked if he didn't feel a little nervous about running against such a hero, who'd done so much for the United Systems. Nagano smiled his true smile then; not the one on his campaign posters, but rather the same icy expression he'd worn just before New Nippon fell and he was blocking the PM's every attempt to defend Earth so that he could force a vote of no-confidence and take over the government himself. "Well, Nancy," he explained, his smile widening. "I've got a lot of respect for Thomas Longo; he's certainly brave enough. That goes without question. He's earned every one of his many medals. Because he's so young, my opponent couldn't possibly have had any role in the crimes against humanity that his father was so famously tried for, so these certainly shouldn't be held against him. And yet he's no different in some ways from the many others I've run against in the past. His father is rich beyond the wildest dreams of most of us; so rich in fact that his father is paying for the entire Longo campaign out of his own pocket. Apparently my opponent sees a Parliamentary seat and the trust of its constituents as just another shiny plaything to be bought for him by his rich daddy. I mean, how many of the voters of the second district had their own skimmer when growing up? And how many had parents powerful enough to shield them from the long arm of the law when they misbehaved with such a powerful, dangerous toy?"

It was a good thing that I didn't actually need to move my jaw in order to talk; in my case, it was merely good manners. "Alicia!" I cried out, loudly enough to be overheard in the boiler-room next door. "Mrs. Hunter! Did you hear…?"

"Hush!" my campaign manager declared, rushing in. "Don't go reacting yet. Listen first."

"…over and over again, as near as we can tell," Nagano continued, shaking his head in mock solemnity. "He'd do whatever it took to win these informal races, including breaking whatever laws and endangering whoever else he had to." Nagano sighed and looked at the camera. "It must be nice to grow up rich."

"I never did that!" I exploded, thumping the arm of my chair so hard that it shattered and fell off. "Never once! Yes, I raced hard. Sometimes we even bumped into each other. But that was part of the sport! We only raced in the designated lanes, during legal hours! Father would've *killed* me…"

"Yes, yes, yes," Alicia agreed, appearing at my other side. She was staring intently at the holoscreen, not really paying attention to me. "Of course, Thomas. And I suspect you're right about your Father. He *would* have killed you." Then she turned to Mrs. Hunter. "Look there!" she declared, pointing at the left-front corner of the tank, far from Nagano's podium. "Jonah looks like he's about to have a coronary."

Mrs. Hunter blinked, then turned to face the tank herself. "You're right!" she whispered. "The man looks like his little dachshund just died."

"I swear!" I repeated. "Not ever!" But no one seemed to care.

"He's slipped up," Alicia declared. "Got carried away."

"Yes," Mrs. Hunter agreed, suddenly looking very feline. "He hasn't got a reliable source for this. And Jonah knows it."

"Who's Jonah?" I finally asked, not angry anymore since no one was listening to me anyway.

"Nagano's campaign manager," Alicia replied, still staring at the screen. "One of the finest in the business. A pity he's not more selective about who he works for." She turned back to Mrs. Hunter. "He's rattled. I'm willing to bet the farm there's good reason for it."

"Ditto," my own manager replied. Then, finally, she turned to me. "Are you *quite* certain?" she demanded. "Your father never dug you out of trouble for racing illegally? Not even once?"

"Never," I answered. "Go down to the courthouse and check."

She sighed. "That's part of the problem," she explained. "If your father actually *had* fixed things for you, there wouldn't be a paper-trail. Besides, you'd have been a juvenile. The records are sealed."

Alicia snorted in derision. "What a miserable, lousy thing for a man to do. Accusing someone of *juvenile* misbehavior! That's a new low, even for Nagano. Even though we know he's wrong, we can't prove it!"

"Thomas hasn't had time to make mistakes as an adult," Mrs. Hunter answered. "That's part of what Isoroku must find so frustrating. Anything that happened more than a few months ago, he can't touch. Or couldn't, until now. When he began making stuff up."

"Or *someone* did," Alicia countered. Her eyes narrowed again. "Thomas," she asked after a little while. "How old were you when you got your skimmer?"

"Fourteen." Then I sighed. "Father always said that sooner or later it'd get me into trouble. Until tonight, I'd proven him wrong."

Alicia didn't smile at my attempt at humor. "Fourteen," she mused. "That's only four years ago. Hardly the ancient past."

Mrs. Hunter's eyes lit up. "We can't touch the records," she observed. "But there's not a reason in the world that we can't get every single judge and juvenile officer in southern Louisiana to affirm that they never had any official dealings with Thomas."

"They're probably all still alive," Alicia agreed. "Most of them are probably still working the same jobs, in fact." She pointed towards the boiler room. "Let's hit the phones! We've got an election to win!"

Chapter Fifty-Nine

And hit the phones they did. The entire staff, myself excepted, pulled an all-nighter doing research and figuring out who was who in the local juvenile justice system. By noon the next day they not only had sworn statements from the vast majority of them that I'd never caused any trouble, but had gotten a few people who'd served as race officials during the formal matches I'd participated in to state for the record that I'd been a talented, aggressive, and remarkably clean racer.

But the big payoffs didn't come until the afternoon. I was out kissing babies in Albuquerque, so I only heard about it second hand. But apparently a local sheriff heard about all the fuss my campaign staff was kicking up among his fellow law-enforcement types and remembered something. Like any other kid with a new toy, when my skimmer first arrived I practically lived in the thing. I cruised up and down Lake Pontchartraine continually, even after dark when it was illegal to race, just because I was so excited to have it.

On one of these nights, right after dusk, I'd reported a boat with no lights to the Coast Guard and then forgotten about the whole thing. It turned out that the reason the boat had no lights was because the only adult aboard had experienced some kind of seizure, and the two children out with him were too young to know what to do. No one had ever told me that part. Alicia and Mrs. Hunter didn't waste a second; in three hours not only was the sheriff on the holovision news channels telling the story, but my people had located the boat's owner—still alive, thankfully—and his children as well. "Thank you, Thomas Longo!" the kids, still young enough to be cute, declared solemnly in unison in the resulting campaign commercial. Then the boy, whose name was Bobby, read the required legal statement at the end. "This message was paid for by the Thomas Longo for Parliament Committee." He looked very much like I had at his age, and from then on we used that footage for *all* the legal disclaimers.

The other stroke of luck was in finding out exactly who it was that'd claimed I was such an irresponsible skimmer operator. At first suspicion centered on the other kids my age, the ones I'd raced against. Mrs. Hunter thought they might be jealous at all the attention I was getting these days. But it turned out that for the most part they were my biggest supporters. A few were going to vote against me, sure. But even they sent good wishes on a personal level and reminisced with our staffers about tough races I'd won or lost against them. Then we finally found out why Nagano's campaign-manager was so nervous. One of the sheriffs we were contacting anyway in order to establish that I wasn't a law-breaker knew who the guilty party was. He'd thrown him out of a bar recently-- drunk, disorderly, and bragging about how he'd ruined me.

Who was it? None other than the security guard who'd sick-gunned Mr. Pearlman at the plant gates. He was being prosecuted to the full extent of the law, as I'd promised. And apparently he held me responsible for his problems. "I told 'em about what a louse he was, growing up!" the drunken guard had chortled to the sheriff. "They'll never elect him now!" We sent Mr. Flowers to his house with a big briefcase full of impressive-looking papers that had nothing to do with anything. When the guard opened the door and saw my attorney standing there he went white as a ghost. "I didn't mean it!" he declared. "I was drinking, not thinking right! It was all made-up!" We got a full holotaped confession, which also made a rather nice campaign commercial. For that one, we got Bobby to tape a new legal disclaimer. In addition to telling everyone who'd paid for the ad, he smiled real big and added "Liar, liar, pants on fire!" at the end.

At first, I thought all of this was just silliness. Sure, people cared if I was a man of integrity or not. But what really mattered was winning the war, right? Apparently not. Bobby's childish taunt moved us up ten points all by itself, aided by Nagano's abject refusal to either retract the charges he'd made against me or provide substantive evidence to back them. "Liar, Liar!" read the headlines on half the newspages on the planet, while Alicia and Mrs. Hunter exchanged knowing smiles. Using Bobby had been Alicia's idea; she'd explained to me that because my own face wasn't natural, I needed to sort of borrow another one that people could identify with more easily. "Bobby's perfect," she explained. "If you think about it, he says everything that's really important about you."

I blinked in confusion. "Huh?"

"He's young, fresh, and above all *different*." Alicia smiled. "He also brings in the hero factor because by now everyone knows you once saved his life."

"But..." I spluttered. "He's just a kid! And this is serious business!"

Alicia's grin widened. "Thomas... Forgive me, but I have to let you in on a little secret. You're a lot closer to Bobby's age than that of most of your constituents. They see you as a boy, too. So why not profit from it where we can?"

Despite everything Nagano did, "Liar, Liar" became the number one talking point of the campaign. Everyone on the planet seemed to be laughing about it; once my opponent grew so frustrated at a talk-show host who wouldn't drop the subject that he walked off the set in mid-interview. "Let me know when you want to talk about issues," he growled on the way out. "Instead of playground insults." That was good for another five points. According to our mole, his campaign manager was livid. He almost resigned, even.

By the night of the first debate Mrs. Hunter and I were exhausted, Alicia was having the time of her life, and we were dead-even in the polls. What was better still was that we weren't dead-even just in my district, but everywhere else as well. The whole universe was watching my race, it seemed, at least as closely as the one in their own district. A late-night holovision comedy show brought down the house by portraying the Dracan Emperor crying out "Liar, liar!" in the middle of a Privy Council meeting; the phrase was repeated so often that people actually grew mildly sick it. "Nagano's stripped his entire party of resources to beat you, Thomas," Alicia purred during our final debate-prep session. "All of his most talented people are here, instead of out helping his allies. And believe me, they won't forget it. Even if he wins he's crippled for years to come."

That was a pleasant thought to ponder as I went through the endless questions and answers, trying to get things *just* right. It was a lot harder than it should've been, because I couldn't just memorize stuff and spit it back out. No one could predict exactly what form the questions were going to take, and thus I had to be ready to improvise. I understood what my party stood for well-enough; that wasn't the problem. But *communicating* these positions in a warm, sympathetic, trustworthy manner... Well, that was another issue entirely. Mrs. Hunter was never satisfied, and Alicia was even worse.

"You've gone wooden again, Thomas!" she'd declare just about the time that I felt like I'd gotten things right. "Look in the mirror." And sure enough, I'd let my false-face grow expressionless again.

"I can't do it!" I finally exclaimed at one point. "Look, my body isn't real! I have to *concentrate* to so much as twitch an eyebrow. How can I think about that and what I have to say too?"

"I know dear," the rabbit-lady replied, instantly switching over into "warm-and-soothing" mode. "I'm different too, you may've noticed, and I have to think about facial expressions just like you do. Ear-twitches, for example, don't translate well to a human audience."

I blinked, not ever having thought of that. "Really?" I asked, raising my eyebrows.

She nodded and frowned. "Really. So I've had to develop some work-arounds. Maybe we can adapt some of them for you, too."

The result was one of the most remarkable debate-aides ever developed. Nagano and I had agreed that each of us would be allowed a small notebook to scribble in as the other spoke. We'd also agreed that it wasn't to have any text in it...

...but the rules said nothing about pictures. Alicia, gifted illustrator that she was, drew a series of captionless cartoon-sketches in my notebook, then made up a detailed story to go with each frame. Sometimes the picture wasn't even about anything that would make sense to anyone except us two; one of the frames was of Spence fishing, for example; it's hidden message was "Relax, Thomas, and enjoy yourself! Everything's going to be all right!" The notebook made everything *so* much easier; it was a miracle that no one had exploited this loophole long ago. Besides, fair was fair. My steel fingers were too clumsy to allow me to write legibly anymore, and when I'd asked for permission to use a keypad to take notes instead Nagano's people had laughed. There were to be no exceptions to the standard rules, they insisted. So what came around, went around. Some would call it cheating; Colonel Rotte would've classified the maneuver as "never giving the other bugger so much as half a chance".

This time, I was wholeheartedly on Emil's side.

Chapter Sixty

Alicia and Mrs. Hunter wanted me to rest and relax a little before the big event, but that was impossible. I was so far behind on my navy duties by then that I was ashamed to call myself an officer. So while the ladies believed me to be napping I sat down at my desk and caught up on report after report after report. Captain Knight had told me just a few weeks before that the entire nature of the war would be changing soon, and sure enough I could see signs of it already. Ships were joining the fleet at an ever-increasing rate; the first two *Warlord*-class destroyers, improvements on the magnificent *Chief*-class, were already in shakedown. *Genghis Khan* and *Attila* were faster and harder-hitting than their predecessors, being fitted with larger engines and Esteppan-pattern triple-turrets like those of *Graf Zeppelin*. The eldest of the *Chiefs* weren't more than two or three years old, and the newest were still in shakedown themselves. Yet they were already obsolescent. I gulped, and wondered when it would be my turn to follow them.

That'd be pretty soon, it seemed. Jimmy was doing his level best to get my squadron trained without me; the reports written by the regular-navy types overseeing his efforts spoke over and over again of his single-minded dedication and the "childish joy" he took in teaching others. His students were still learning basic flight skills, but some had actually been in the air. One promising young flyer, who'd decided late in the game that he couldn't stomach the idea of actually killing anyone, was slated to become the permanent test-pilot for the plant in New Orleans. It was too bad that Oskar didn't have a taste for blood, I decided after looking over his folder. He was easily the most promising pilot of the bunch. But that was just how things went sometimes; I accepted his decision and resolved not to put any pressure on him to fly combat. He was still a child, after all. Besides, he'd already risked and suffered enough in the name of defending his freedom merely by undergoing the brain-core procedure. I'd treat him as a full equal, I decided, if and when we met. Then if he happened to change his mind later, he'd be welcomed into the Bananas with open arms.

The Dracans hadn't been up to much of late, according to the latest intelligence. They were digging in like ants on Churilla, but neither hide nor hair of their fleet had been seen in weeks. Everyone figured they were hoarding their resources for a major confrontation, but Captain Bard had written an addendum to the report emphasizing that the Dracans were brave, capable, intelligent, and above all unpredictable enemies. "The sooner we retake New Nippon," she emphasized, "the more secure our position will be. From a purely strategic point of view, this operation should be undertaken as soon as possible.'

Sadly, there was a lot more to retaking New Nippon than mere strategy. The army, it seemed, would never be ready. Every time they got a formation fully trained, it was split it into two or three parts to provide cadre for new units. They didn't have enough heavy equipment, were acutely short of field guns and anti-'hopper equipment, and there weren't enough power-frames to fill the needs of even a small combat unit. In fairness, the army had been shortchanged for months in terms of both personnel and material in order to support the navy's expansion. Still, the eternal delays were frustrating to everyone involved. Judging by his margin-notes, Vlasilov was fit to be tied.

Not that the navy's own house was entirely in order-- the loss of the Training Fleet was coming home to roost, in spades. *Roman Nose* been relegated to the instructive branch, just as her captain had predicted. Incredible as it might seem, however, they were asking for *Jimmy Doolittle* as well. *Doolittle* was one of the most modern, up-to-date Fleet units! What were they *thinking*? Yet I had to admit that pickings were growing mighty thin what with losses being so heavy, and spacers had be trained *somewhere*. They wouldn't get *Doolittle*, I was certain. She was far too important as a screening ship. But how *would* they manage? Some enterprising officer was suggesting that we could mount a single working turret on however many merchies might be needed, with enough extra bracing added to the vessel for her to withstand minimal recoil forces from reduced charges. Vlasilov sounded enthusiastic about the idea. Most likely, I was willing to bet, that was exactly what would end up happening.

In the meantime, however, the navy was manning its ships with minimally-trained spacers. The results were predictable. Captain Knight's command, the heavy carrier *Tsushima Strait*, was back in the yard for repairs to her main engines. The damage was caused by a mistake on the part of a reserve engineering officer who'd been promoted beyond her capabilities. This was due, according to Lofton's report, to the extreme shortage of qualified personnel. The captain was very careful to exonerate the guilty party. "She was placed in a position that she was by no means ready for," he explained in his report. "Prior to the incident this officer repeatedly requested more training, which we were then and are still unable to provide. It's not in the best interests of the service to punish an officer who was doing her duty to the best of her ability, and who was a civilian five short months ago, for making a mistake that it was beyond her capacity to avoid. Therefore, I'm officially recommending that no formal Board of Inquiry be convened." The navy, in other words, couldn't support an invasion even if the army were ready. It might've been funny if it weren't all so serious. This was yet another reason why it was so important to maintain military strength in peacetime; once the shooting starts, it becomes many times as difficult to try and make up for lost opportunities.

I was still reading about the new ships when Alicia knocked on my door to tell me it was time to get dressed and ready. I didn't want to quit; a new light carrier was working up at Esteppe to replace the lost *Skaggerak*; she was named *Coronel* and was almost as heavily festooned with turrets as *Graf Zeppelin*. The reformed Butcher Birds, it was reasonable to expect, would soon be operating from her. But as much as I wanted to read more about my new soon-to-be operational partners, I had to re-enter the political world. Manuel helped me put on my gray suit--which after long hours of debate had been determined to be my best look-- and then we were off to Seattle, where the debate was to be held. We'd hold the first in Nagano's stronghold, it'd been agreed, the second in Salt Lake City-- where we'd been running even back when the agreement had been made, but where I how held a sizeable lead-- and the third in New Orleans, where in theory I should've held a home-town advantage. But long-term voting patterns were working against me there, and in fact I was down locally by five. It didn't matter so much where the debates were held, I supposed. The only difference I could see was in that I could expect more questions about battleships versus superfighters in Seattle, where the big guns were made. Since I was particularly eager to answer these questions, I didn't mind if I was sitting on the "Visitors" bench. We could've held all three events in Seattle for all I cared.

By now I was pretty much used to the constant presence of cameras and reporters covering my every gesture on more news channels than I could count every time I went outdoors, though it still had its comic moments. Once a large bug landed on one of my eye-lenses, and, forgetting about the cameras, I tried to shoo it off with my finger. Reporters with too much air-time to fill speculated for days on what I'd been doing and what it portended...

Nagano was already at his podium when I stepped out from behind the curtain and stood behind my own. I smiled at my opponent, but his answer was a cold, angry glare. The small audience of press-types clapped politely, however. I held my smile for them, then bowed slightly in the Esteppan manner. People loved it when I did that, my staff assured me. It made me seem a little exotic, and yet also at the same time old-fashioned and self-confident. Nagano's glare intensified, but I didn't care. Alicia and Mrs. Hunter, I'd long since decided, had Nagano's personality and motivations dead to rights. It was all about him, him, him, and I was raining on his parade. The intensity of his hatred towards me was a barometer of the effectiveness of my campaign. So, the madder he was, the better. If he grew so angry that he blew a blood vessel, better still. He might not care for me, but there wasn't a lot of love lost on my end of the equation either. Not after the things I'd seen, for which this man was in large part responsible.

Then the lights came up, the holocameras' indicators turned red, and we were on the air. Nagano was smiling his campaign smile now, and waving as everyone applauded again. I didn't bow again, because Esteppans only did that once when entering a room. Nor did I wave; my arms moved so slowly that it just looked silly. So instead I smiled again, and concentrated on finding Alicia and Mrs. Hunter out in the crowd. They were sitting in the third row, directly in front of me. Sadly, the lights were reflecting on my eye-cameras in such a way that I couldn't make them out.

I didn't have long to think about that, however. The Master of Ceremonies for the debate, who was also the head of a local civic organization, gave what I considered to be a much-too-long introductory speech outlining the history of political debate and its role in democracy in general. Then it was time for the first question. A coin-flip had been held weeks back to determine who answered first; I'd won. "Commander Longo," the reporter asked. He was a surprisingly young man, to be given such a plum assignment. But who was *I* to complain? "Your Excellency…"

I winced inwardly. The reporters had agreed not to use either my naval rank or Esteppan title during the debate. The first slipup might've been an accident, but not both. This man was no neutral, unbiased journalist. He was a plant!

"…say that such a wealthy man cannot possibly appreciate the plight of the poor. And, there's also your position on naval armaments, Commander. Seattle produces the finest naval ordnance in the galaxy, sir! Why are you so averse to purchasing it? And, finally, Your Excellency, how are you going to properly represent the people of this district while also serving actively with the Fleet?" He smiled, the expression as cold as Nagano's, and a murmur spread through the audience.

I grinned back just as coldly, then looked down at my sketch of Spence peacefully fishing in the little stream by our hideout cave back on Churilia. After that, I counted to five. When I was done, I knew my next move. One of Emil Rotte's favorite ploys in battle was to hit hard and early, so as to leave the enemy disorganized, frightened, and unable to respond effectively. Nagano clearly agreed. But Rotte had also taught me that the best way to counter this tactic was to hit back just as hard, without the slightest hesitation and without holding anything back. *Sheer bloodyminded aggression…*"Tell me, Mister… Blackguard, is it?" His name tag clearly read "Blackshard", but my version was plenty close enough. He began to correct me, but my voice was more easily amplified than his. "Are you going to ask me if I've quit beating my wife, as well?" Then I turned to the judges. "The questions asked here are supposed to be specific and about one topic only, because of my limited response time. Are you going to rule Mr. Blackguard's question out of order? Or are you people here merely for decoration?"

Suddenly the room went dead-silent; no one in living memory, Alicia had told me during prep, had ever appealed to the debate judges. This was because it tended to be seen as a sign of weakness. In this specific instance, however, I thought my actions might be perceived a little differently.

"We... Ah..." the Senior Judge spluttered. He was a very old man, and I felt rather sorry for him. Still, it couldn't be helped. "We need to confer."

"Uh..." the Master of Ceremonies replied, totally at sea. Then he looked to one of the network producers for guidance.

"Tell them we'll be right back to live coverage," he cried out, so loud that every mike in the place must have picked it up. "Once the judges have ruled."

"Right," the MC agreed, looking relieved. His eyes found the nearest camera. "We'll be right back, folks, just as soon as the judges rule." All the red lights went out and we were off the air. Suddenly the previously-silent studio was full of shouting, arguing spectators, someone was banging a gavel, and the network producer was shouting obscenities at whoever was at the other end of his little boom-mike. I smiled again, this time the fierce grin of combat that I could never actually wear while in the cockpit, and turned to face my opponent. "Nice try," I offered, nodding my appreciation.

But Isoroku didn't say anything back. He simply stared and scowled. Then he did the last thing I expected. Instead of replying, he simply looked down at his notebook and began scribbling.

At first I didn't understand. Then, slowly, it came to me. The man was terrified! Possibly for the first time in his entire political career! I could smell the stink of fear a mile away; I'd been taught the art by one of the very best, in fact. Suddenly Nagano reeked of it. *Thank you, Colonel Rotte*, I whispered to my one-time mentor. *You may've made me a coarser, uglier man than I might otherwise have been. But you also taught me how to come out on top when it really matters.*

Chapter Sixty-One

It soon became clear that nothing was going to happen anytime soon; ten minutes after we went off the air people were still running around in circles yelling at each other. Without asking anyone for permission I retired to my little prep-room, where Alicia and Mrs. Hunter joined me within a minute or two. Mrs. Hunter was nervous about what I'd done, but Alicia was practically trembling with excitement. "That's my Thomas!" she said as she burst in. "That's the Tommy I know and love! I *knew* we could count on you!"

About thirty minutes after the camera shut down, the Senior Judge showed up as well. "Mr. Longo," he began, once we let him in. "We agree that the question you were asked went well beyond the established rules of the debate. However…"

My eyebrows rose, and Alicia's ears twitched. "However?"

"However," he repeated, "Well… Things aren't as simple as they may seem. Mr. Blackshard represents the largest newspage in Washington state, you see, and—"

"I see," I responded, not waiting for Alicia or Mrs. Hunter. "Well, then. Thank you for your time." I stood up and fumbled at unbuttoning my suit coat. "It's been nice to meet you." Then I rose up on my tiptoes and looked over the old man's head. "Manuel? Can you come help me get out of this getup? We're going home."

The old man's skin went white. "But… You've made a commitment, sir! You owe the voters a chance to see where you stand on the issues!"

I shrugged. "Whatever." Then I looked at Alicia.

"Thomas agreed to come here and participate in this debate based on the premise that fair questions would be asked, in an unbiased and open forum," she explained for me. "You yourself just acknowledged that the very first question he was asked didn't meet this standard. Therefore, his commitment stands null and void."

As if on cue, Mrs. Hunter switched on the holotank. "…unbelievable development in the Longo-Nagano race," the commentator was eagerly saying. She switched the channel.

"…accusations of biased questions…"

"…handled himself brilliantly in my opinion, John…"

"…shockwaves still reverberating around the world's newsrooms…"

The Senior Judge went pale again. "Let's lay all the cards out on the table," Alicia declared. "If you refuse to enforce the rules and Thomas goes home right now, he's flat-out won this debate. Your organization comes away looking like Nagano's choirboys, and Thomas is a hero for standing up to you. You understand that, right?"

"I… Uh… Mrs. Wiston…"

"That's 'Madame Deputy' to you," she barked.

He paled further. "Madame Deputy--"

"And you don't want that," she continued, speaking right over him. "Because you *are* Nagano's choirboys, as you've just proven. So either enforce the rules or we walk," she declared. "You've got fifteen minutes."

Chapter Sixty-Two

In the end the debate *was* resumed, though it took a little longer than the demanded fifteen minutes. Mr. Blackguard's credentials were revoked and he was escorted from the premises. For the rest of the night, I made it a point to crane my neck a little so that I could catch a glimpse of each reporter's notes as they asked their questions. Interestingly enough, Blackguard's question had been neatly typed out well ahead of time. All of the rest of the reporters worked from hand-scrawled notes clearly thrown together in just a few minutes. The inference was obvious.

Despite this evidence of evil intentions, from that point forward I had no reason to complain about bias. The questions might've been hand-written, but they were fair. Even the tough ones. "Lining my own pockets?" I asked in reference to a question about whether or not I was personally profiting from the Skybolt program. Alicia had encouraged me, insofar as it was possible, to begin my answers to every question with the syllable "lie", and to emphasize it slightly. This was a not-so-subtle reminder of our "liar, liar" campaign. Nagano understood perfectly well what I was doing; he gritted his teeth every single time.

"Most of my family's wealth, which I acknowledge is considerable, is derived from mineral extraction. We're making far more from our mines than from Longo Industries. In fact, we lost money by the truckload for over a decade on our 'hopper manufacturing operations. Father built the New Orleans facility strictly out of his own pocket, foreseeing the likelihood of war. Overall, counting the bad years, we're still operating at a large net loss." I shrugged. "Not that we can't afford it, mind you. My family is hardly asking for charity. And who knows? We might yet come out ahead financially. If so, know ahead of time that we probably won't apologize for it. But to claim that we're lining our pockets on war-production contracts is ridiculous! We would've been far ahead to stay home on Esteppe, mind our own business, and quietly profit from the upswing in rare-earth-mineral prices caused by the war." I smiled. "I'd be a rich playboy instead of under military discipline. My brother wouldn't be ill from radiation poisoning, either. Maybe we Longos aren't so bright after all!"

Another question was even harder to field. This one was about the suspension of Parliament. Nagano answered first. "Uniformed men came and frog-marched me off of the floor of the House of the People!" he declared. "I wanted to weep for humanity's terrible loss. Right before my eyes, freedom died! The will of the people was suborned by a bunch of right-wing militarists!" He pointed at me. "Like that one, right there! He wasn't part of the government at the time-- I acknowledge that. But he's backing the criminals who turned our government into a dictatorship, backing them with everything he has! And profiting from it, to boot!"

"Life can be ironic," I countered when it was my turn. It was vital to answer both competently and completely; this issue was the ideological crux of the election. Most of the time, when people come under attack they tend to rally around the party currently in power. That hadn't happened this time, and the PM's suspension of Parliament was, most analysts believed, the reason why. "Mr. Nagano is correct when he says that I wasn't part of the government at the time Parliament was suspended. Yet I *was* in London during much of the period in question, attempting to testify about the effectiveness of the Skybolt in combat." I shook my head and looked Nagano in the eye. "Perhaps my opponent has forgotten how he blocked me from saying so much as a single word about the weapon that has done more than any other to keep Earth and the United Systems free. He also spurned the PM's offer to work out a compromise, almost *any* compromise, rather than topple the government at a time when large-scale attack and perhaps even invasion and conquest were imminent." I shook my head in disgust. "I was *there*. I saw it happen, though no one planned it that way. This man wanted to be PM so badly that he and his party undermined the war effort. They were so effective in their machinations that the government wouldn't even approve spare parts for the single Skybolt we possessed at the time." Genuinely angry now, I pointed at Nagano. "Just in delaying the Skybolt program alone, this man has killed I don't know how many good and decent human beings. Some of them were my fellow pilots, boys and girls willing to give everything for their freedom and yours. My squadronmates were forced to go into battle half-trained because this man and his party delayed things so effectively. They wanted to win a majority. Nothing else mattered to them. Most of my friends *died*!"

Nagano's mouth opened, but I cut him off at the pass. It was my turn to speak, not his. "I was also, by the purest of chance, present on the Floor when Mr. Nagano was arrested and removed—*not* frog-marched!—from the building." I looked down at the floor and shook my head. "It was one of the saddest things I ever saw. My opponent is right; democracy was terribly damaged that day and an awful precedent was set." I shook my head again. "I wasn't on Earth during the bombings. My duties took me elsewhere. But of course I've seen the horrific images and read the mind-boggling statistics. There are billions of dead. Billions! I was raised on Earth myself, don't forget. I can see how much has changed. That everyone's a lot thinner, for example." I paused and looked around the room, trying to meet every eye. "How much worse would it have been if our government had remained totally paralyzed? Parliamentarian Nagano's minority coalition, under his personal leadership, failed to agree to build effective weapons during one of the most terrible wars ever fought. I was there and saw it with my own eyes or else I *still* wouldn't believe it. How are we to know what might've happened had Parliament, as deeply divided as it was, still been in session when the hell-bombs landed? Rationing, for example, had been under discussion for weeks. But the minority blocked it every time it came to a vote. Why? Merely to bring more pressure to bear for their no-confidence push. How many more might've died, had we not immediately nationalized all foodstuffs? There wasn't a day to spare! And would it have been the rich who starved? Or perhaps more likely the poor whom my opponent claims so persistently to speak for?"

The Skybolt versus battleship issue, apparently so dear to the hearts of Seattle residents, wasn't brought up again until the debate was almost over. Nagano gave his usual spiel about the unshakeable strength of the battleships and how they remained the true measure of the relative strengths of governments. "The Dracans didn't conquer so many worlds using superfighters," he pointed out. "They relied and still rely on large fleets of solid, hard-hitting heavy-gun capital ships. They're the backbone of the Dracan navy, as well they should be." He looked down at his lectern. "My opponent likes to point out that my party allowed the Dracan fleet to expand in relation to ours in the years immediately prior to the war. He feels that this was a primary factor in their decision to attack us. In this, I will acknowledge, perhaps he is right. Though, I hasten to point out, their peacetime tonnage never exceeded our own."

But their ships were all newer, I didn't say aloud. *Twice as effective, ton for ton, as ours.* Nor would I; my reply time was limited, and trying to explain why modern ships had such an edge in combat would take far longer than I had. Better to concentrate on simpler issues.

"…when we sit down at the negotiating table with the Dracans and outlaw superfighters as the inhumane abominations they are," he continued, voice calm and rational-sounding, "We'll insist on a comprehensive naval treaty as part of the peace settlement." He turned to face me. "We made a mistake, Mr. Longo. We admit it, and we can learn from it. From this point forward, we'll permit no imbalances in naval strength to develop between us and the Dracans. The first thing we'll do after the peace settlement is to lay down a dozen of the most powerful battleships ever built, matches in every way for the Dracan's rightly-famous *Imperial Throne* class. We'll expand our shipyards and ordnance works here in Seattle, and never let the Dracans get ahead again." He turned to face the cameras. "You can take that to the bank."

Then it was my turn to speak. But somehow I couldn't. Nagano's proposed policy was wrongheaded on so many levels that I couldn't imagine where to begin. "I… I …" For the first time the entire night, I found myself stuttering. Nagano's eyes widened slightly, as he scented blood at long last…

…and then I looked down at the picture-book Alicia had made for me. Some of the drawings were rather good. I frowned, then tore one of them out. "Like it or not," I began, "what is, is. Reality speaks with an implacable voice-- you can dance around facts for a time, but eventually even the most skilled politician must face them." I smiled at the Opposition leader. "So let me try to put this in the simplest possible terms for you." Then I held the torn page up in front of me. "Can everyone see this?" It was a drawing of me in my Skybolt during the Battle of the Orion Nexus, in the act of killing the *Imperial Throne*. Alicia had included it to remind me that I should present myself as a bonafide, impeccably-credentialed military expert whenever I had the chance. I watched as a camera zoomed in on the notepad, then continued. "That's me," I explained. "Destroying the biggest battlewagon ever built. In a Skybolt."

The crowd was staring at me in rapt silence; even the moderators seemed spellbound. So I tore another page out. "This is me again," I explained, "killing another *Imperial Throne*-class battleship on Drakkus. I caught this one while she was trying to up-ship. It happened on the same raid where we nuked the Drakkan capital. About five hundred conventional fighters tried to stop us, but we got through anyway. There were eight of us. Two survived." I shook my head. "Let's see. How many Dracan conventional fighters did it take to nuke Earth? Three hundred or so, if memory serves. Plus more on the diversionary raids." Then I found a picture of the Stormcrow plant back on Esteppe; Alicia had included that one to remind me to acknowledge the wartime sacrifices of the civilian population. "See how small this factory is?" I asked. "It's probably the leading superfighter production facility in the universe just now. How easy would it be to keep a superfighter program secret? The Dracans have superfighters now too. I know because I've fought them. While we dithered and argued, they made steady progress. Thanks in large part to my opponent we've already thrown away much of our early lead, and many more innocent people are going to die because of it." I shook my head, lips curled in disgust. "Of *course* the Dracans will sign a treaty outlawing superfighters! Look at their record; they'll sign *any* treaty! Getting them to *honor* it is, however, another matter entirely. How many treaties did they break, I wonder, when they invaded Churilla, enslaved the population and tortured the POW's?"

By then I was so angry I could hardly speak any more. So I decided not to. Instead I carefully stacked the sketches one on top of the other, with the one of me shooting down the *Imperial Throne* on top. Then, breaking protocol, I walked the two steps over to Nagano's lectern and dropped them on top of his own notes. "Which part of this do you not understand?" I asked my opponent. His eyes were hard and cold, like those of a cornered rat. "Tell me, and maybe I can explain better."

"Mr. Longo!" the Senior Judge declared, banging his gavel. "You're out of order. Please, return to your podium!"

I nodded; he was right, of course. I'd gone too far, probably much too far. I turned to take my proper place again…

…and suddenly my security detail was surging forward. "Turn off those cameras!" the marine captain in charge ordered. "Now!"

"What is this?" Nagano demanded. "Another stunt? More theatrics?"

"Sir," the captain declared, grasping my right arm and pulling me towards the rear of the studio. "You're to come with me. Priority Alpha."

It was happening too fast; my mind was refusing to shift gears. "What…"

"Priority Alpha, sir!" he repeated, shaking my arm urgently. "Come *on*! We've got to *go*!"

"Yes," I muttered, looking at the still-live cameras. "Of course."

"I don't believe this!" Nagano spluttered. "What…"

But I had no more time for Nagano. As the captain tugged me through the rear exit, my brain finally shifted out of neutral, and I remembered what Code Alpha stood for.

Attack imminent!

Chapter Sixty-Three

There was mass-confusion at first; all sorts of formal protocol arrangements had been made regarding who was to leave the debate first and when, so that my privately-hired limo was parked behind Nagano's, and the navy's security van was waiting behind that. The moment the captain carried me through the outside door—he'd been selected to head my security detachment in part because he was so large and strong that he could carry me many times faster than I could walk—he was already screaming for the van to come pick us up. "Move, move, move!" he ordered into his com-unit, not even breathing hard from his exertions.

"I don't have room, sir!" the driver replied. "These idiots parked in my designated clear-lane."

"*Make* room!" the captain bellowed.

The big van surged forward. Though the vehicle looked ordinary enough from the outside, it was as well-armored as a light tank and very nearly as powerful. My limo didn't stand a chance against it. The long black vehicle folded and bent and skidded forward until it was in turn driven into Nagano's ride, which then was likewise ruined.

"Get in, sir!" the captain ordered, shoving me forward as the door swung open.

"Right," I agreed, moving as quickly as I was able. This clearly wasn't quickly enough; I was only halfway in when I felt the captain's huge shoulder thrust me forward, so that I landed on my face.

"Sorry," he apologized, climbing in after me and lifting me into a seat.

"That's quite all right," I answered; at least I could speak as quickly as normal people. Not that the captain was listening. The instant I was in my seat he pivoted to his left to shut the van's door.

But a brown-furred arm barred his way. "I'm coming with you!" Alicia declared. It was an order, not a request.

"Yes, ma'am," the captain replied, pulling her aboard almost as roughly as he'd handled me. Either he was one of the quickest-thinking human beings I'd ever met, or else he'd planned everything out ahead of time so that he'd know what to do if the Deputy Prime Minister demanded to accompany me. He even waited while Alicia's own lead bodyguard came pounding up and scrambled aboard behind her. Next Mrs. Hunter tried to get in, but the marine slammed the door in her face. "Sorry!" he explained after the door closed, when she couldn't possibly hear him anymore. "Official traffic only."

Somehow, the driver knew when the door closed. He didn't wait for orders this time; even before the captain was seated our vehicle was surging forward again, driving the remains of the ruined limos before it. There were sparks and scraping noises and once something that might've been a small explosion, and I hoped the chauffeurs had been smart enough to bail out. Then we were out in the street. Our driver threw the van into reverse, freeing us from the wreckage. "Where's the cops?" his voice demanded over the intercom. "Sir! There's supposed to be cops."

"Damn!" the captain answered. He hesitated a split second, then gave his order. "Run without them, Ernie. Flat out. I'm responsible."

"Yes, sir!" Ernie replied. Then he hit his accelerator…

…and the world turned into a long, dark tunnel. The engine roared, the tires spun and shrieked, and we were shoved deep into our seats. "Don't worry," the captain assured us. "Ernie's the best there is. He didn't merely graduate from high-performance bodyguard-driving school. He used to be an instructor there."

That made me feel a little better, at least until we finally found our police escort. They were coming down the street in the opposite direction, running almost as fast as Ernie was and using both lanes. There was another prolonged bout of tire-squeals and van-lurching, then somehow we were all going the same direction in a sort of vee-formation, with our vehicle protected on all sides.

"What's the threat?" Alicia finally asked, once things had settled down a little. It was my job to ask that question, and I felt a little guilty that I hadn't. Mostly that was because most of my mind was still on the debate. Passages from the closing statement I'd now never make were still echoing through my head. … *must choose between a quick, cheap peace and a costly but lasting one… the sacrifices of our war-dead must not have been in vain… we cannot stop fighting with no victory won, or our children will have to fight and win this same battle again in our stead…*

"It's a Dracan raid," the marine officer explained. "The enemy's popped through Nikita number two at New Nippon, with a huge vector on. A bigger vector, I'm informed, than anything our ships can Jump with."

I nodded; the Dracans had been ahead of us in that particular technology since the first day of the war. Apparently they were getting even better as time passed. "Go on."

"They broke through with a bunch of fast-moving stuff. One light carrier, four light cruisers, a bunch of destroyers. They're aimed directly for the jump to Earth, and then to come out of our Nikita heading almost straight for us. Everything's lined up perfectly for them. According to the report from *Sitting*

Bull, who jumped to warn us as soon as the Dracans popped through, they'll be here in two and a half hours or so."

"What about the squadron at New Nippon?" Alicia demanded.

"According to *Sitting Bull*, the Dracans have too much vector to intercept. We've been caught flat-footed; no one considered that they might be able to move so fast. Our ships will only get off a few salvos, and maybe some torpedoes." He looked at me. "If we had superfighters stationed there we'd have been able to intercept the bastards, no problem. Damn Isoroku Nagano!"

I pressed my lips together but said nothing. Nagano remained a problem, yes. For the moment, however, he belonged on the back burner. "This doesn't make any sense," I observed eventually. "Sure, the Dracans can blast from Nikita to Nikita at a nexus, particularly one where the points are bunched so close together. But, once they get here, they're trapped. There's only one exit from this system, and they'll burst through heading directly away from it. It'll take them forever to turn around, even if they slingshot a planet. We'll be able to intercept with so much force that they won't have a prayer. They're toast."

Alicia nodded. "It's a suicide mission." Then she paled. "Thomas…"

For once I was thinking just as fast as she was, genetic modifications or no. "It's a nuclear raid," I whispered. "They're going to drop as many hydrogen bombs as they can, to make their losses worthwhile. With luck, they might even knock Earth out of the war."

Alicia nodded. "And with just a light carrier…"

"It's superfighters," I agreed. "It *has* to be! Every single one in their inventory, most likely. Nothing else makes sense." I turned back to the marine captain. "Hurry," I urged him. "In the name of everything holy, move this crate just as fast as you possibly can!"

Chapter Sixty-Four

The captain took me at my word. He spoke a single command to Ernie, then we eased through the police escort and left them in our wake. Whatever the Seattle Police Department was driving these days, it wasn't any match for a navy VIP van. Hopefully they were closing the highway ahead of us; we hadn't seen another car since almost colliding with the escort. If they weren't, Ernie would simply have to improvise.

"We can't possibly make it in time," I finally observed aloud. My navy 'hopper was parked right alongside my rented machine, out at the airport. Even at VIP van speeds, we were a good half-hour away from takeoff. Then there was the trip across North America, the confusion of loading and unloading, the time it would take to mount me in my 'bolt... "We have to do something different." I turned to the captain. "Tell my 'hopper to meet us at the next interchange," I ordered. "Just make sure there's no hospitals or anything like that in the landing-area first. We'll make the transfer there."

The marine gulped, and so did Alicia. Landing a 'hopper anywhere but in a designated, properly-shielded area was a major felony, and for good reason. The drive-motor would blow out everything electronic for several miles around. There'd be millions in damage, people would have to leave their homes... Individuals requiring special medical care might even die. Yet clearly it had to be done. Apparently Alicia agreed, because when the captain looked to her for confirmation she simply nodded.

Whoever was piloting my standby shuttle that day was surely on his mark, because my bird was waiting for us in the median not ten miles further down the road, still settling down on her landing-legs as we came screeching to a stop. By then our vehicle, equipped with full military shielding, was the only thing moving for miles in any direction. It was also, save for the shuttle itself, the only thing showing any lights. Ernie had to thread us through several hundred yards worth of stalled vehicles, shoving some of them out of our way with the van's dented but still quite functional battering-ram of a nose. I glanced over at Alicia, who was looking very glum indeed. If this were another false alarm, like the one we'd experienced on Esteppe...

But it wasn't. My obviously-capable pilot had the pipper hot and running

253

for me, so that I was able to study it as he up-shipped from our improvised landing-field and began the race towards the Skybolt base in Florida. As he did so our pip changed from steady navy blue to blinking, indicating an emergency military priority flight. Oddly enough another pip just a couple of hundred miles south of us was blinking the same way, and was headed in the same direction. My blood froze. "Jimmy?" I asked, looking up at the ensign whose job it was to brief me.

"Yes, sir, she responded. Her hair was a bit awry and her lipstick smeared, but her voice was steady. "He was visiting his brother in Los Angeles."

I pressed my lips together, but said nothing. We were stretched 'way too thin, Jimmy and I both, for us to be able to maintain anything resembling continuous availability in case of attack. Besides, we weren't supposed to *need* to maintain a round-the-clock watch, what with so much of the navy being between us and the Dracans. *What is done, is done,* I told myself. There wasn't any point in wasting time on second-guesses. There'd be plenty of opportunities for that later.

The rest of the pipper display held few surprises. Intelligence had drawn in a dashed red line indicating the anticipated Dracan line of attack, including the longest vector-arrow I'd ever seen. Wow! I stared and stared at the thing, then shook my head in wonder. Certainly *our* navy couldn't hit a Nikita moving like that! Even though the screen was filled with blue dots, it was clear at the first glance that only a few of our ships were in any kind of position to intervene. *Cochrane* had been on a gunnery exercise, shooting up targets on the Moon. She might get in a few long range salvoes. *Genghis Khan* and *Attila,* shepherded by *Graf Zeppelin,* had also been out on the firing range. All three of these vessels were thrusting for all they were worth and, being faster than the much larger *Cochrane,* looked likely to make the intercept. *Khan* and *Attila* were both green ships. Their training was incomplete. But being the latest and greatest more than likely they were manned with the pick of the navy, especially regarding the officers. *Jimmy Doolittle* had just up-shipped from the Firth, along with half a dozen *Chiefs* and one lone prewar-pattern heavy cruiser, the *Cairo.* Plus, of course, there were absolute swarms of Polecats ready to rise from everywhere on the planet. That was the one good thing about Polecats; it was a lot easier to scramble them in a hurry that it was a Skybolt. On impulse, I reached over and turned the comm unit to the Kicking Dragon squadron's channel.

"…going to be very fast," Ted Knight was explaining to his flyers. "Faster than anything you've ever seen. Even the simulations don't do it justice. If we're extraordinarily lucky, we *might* get a chance to shoot at one of them. If so, don't try to conserve ammunition. Fill the air as full of fire as you possibly can. Burn your guns right out; we don't care about barrel life, just this once. You'll never get more than the one chance, so make the best of it."

I smiled, remembering. Ted had flown practice missions twice against me over Esteppe, and once against Rotte. It must have been terribly frustrating for him, perhaps even humiliating. We'd both killed his Polecat time after time, seemingly without effort. Rotte, who'd killed well over a hundred Polecats for real, hadn't been particularly polite about it either. But Ted stayed in the air with us anyway, learning what he could from his repeated drubbings. Though the senior Knight had shot down two Stormcrows back in the day, both of them while taking off, Ted's father wasn't able to fly anymore. That left Ted as the navy's leading expert on the forlorn, miserable, and perhaps even hopeless art of defending against superfighters with conventional weaponry. "Hello, Ted," I greeted my old friend on the special channel we shared as fellow squadron commanders. "This is Thomas."

"Thomas!" he answered, his voice full of relief. "Are you going to make the show? We need you, kiddo! And how!"

"It's going to be a near-run thing," I answered, glancing at the clock. "I was at the debate. And you were with Jimmy."

"Yeah," he answered, sighing. "If I hadn't flown my 'cat to LA, I'd have missed this one myself. How do you want to handle things?"

"Jimmy and I might not even make it at all," I admitted, looking at the clock again, and that long, long Dracan vector arrow. "If we do, we're the fast-movers. How about your brother and I clean up the leakers?"

"Leakers!" he snorted. "We'll be lucky to take down one or two without you. Aren't *you* the confident one?"

"They can't be as good as Rotte," I reminded my friend. "Not as good as me, even. They've rushed things along so they could pull this off before we retake New Nippon and shut the door entirely. So the pilots have to be green as grass. Sucker them, and they'll fall for it."

"Maybe," Ted answered, his voice a little flat.

Rotte had been too hard on Ted, I suddenly understood. The old warrior had taken me under his wing because I was a bonafide Esteppan war-hero and a brain-core, just like him. As gruff and as coarse as Emil had been to me, by his standards he'd treated me like royalty. But he'd seen Ted as an old enemy. Being Rotte, he'd therefore reflexively done his best to crush him. With, apparently, considerable success. "Look," I said. "First, there won't be all that many of them. There *can't* be; we're limited to a dozen 'bolts per light carrier, and we've been doing this longer than they have. Second, they've got to get past *Doolittle* and *Zeppelin* and the rest. Vlasilov told me once that they were designed partly with superfighters in mind, to try and stay a step ahead. You've seen what happens when Jimmy and I try to attack *Zeppelin*. You think the Dracans will have it any easier?"

"Right," Ted agreed, suddenly realizing what I was doing. "I get it, Tommy. Sorry."

"No problem," I assured him. "You've got a tough row to hoe, compared to Jimmy and me. We understand."

Ted's mike clicked twice, then he changed the subject. "All right, then. You and I are the senior squadron commanders. I'll go ahead and contact Air Defense Central and let them know what we think. My guess is, they'll approve."

"Like they have any choice," I observed. "Jimmy and I won't get there in time to do much *but* chase leakers. This fight is pretty much in the hands of you regular-navy guys. It's up to the Polecats and cruisers." I paused, then realized that there really wasn't anything else to say. "Good luck, Ted," I finished up, a little inelegantly. I might legally be an adult, but I still felt pretty awkward sometimes. "Kill them all!"

"Kill them all," he agreed grimly. "Horrido!"

Chapter Sixty-Five

A Skybolt wasn't just a machine; it was a living organism. Father's doctorate degree was in alloplasty, not aeronautical engineering, and it was every bit as correct to think of a 'bolt as a sort of artificial organ as a warplane. Because there were living components, and because the pilot's brain was a living thing as well, there were some things about mating up to a 'bolt that no one ever could quite explain. For example, I always adapted quicker than Jimmy did, though there was no good reason why this should be so, and back when Viktor had been alive he'd usually been up and functional in half the time it took me. It was just one of those things. Therefore Jimmy and I were ready for takeoff within seconds of each other despite the fact that his 'hopper had beaten mine to Florida by a clear five minutes. Both of us were studying our pippers intently as we rolled out onto the tarmac. The battle was already well underway.

"*Sitting Bull* is toast," my wingman observed. He'd toured the vessel not too long ago, as a morale-boosting event for her crew, so that he was able to put names and faces to the steadily fading icon. "She's been hit twice."

I clicked my mike twice by way of acknowledgement; two hits was about all it took, for a destroyer at least. *Bull* had relayed the news of the attack back to Earth, then waited just on our side of the Nikita with torpedo tubes hot and ready. It was too bad there hadn't been any other United Systems vessels in position to back her up. *Sitting Bull* had died alone, though she'd sold her life dearly. Where once there had been four Dracan light cruisers with the attack force, now there were only two. One of these had never come through the Nikita, and presumably had been accounted for by the New Nippon squadron. The other, however, belonged to *Bull*.

Sadly, the carrier remained undamaged.

"They're still running right down the groove," Jimmy observed, probably to change the subject as much as anything. "Our cruisers have split up."

I clicked my mike twice again. *Zeppelin* and the two *Warlords* had started out almost astride the big red arrow that indicated the Dracan's likeliest course. But they were thrusting off to one side now, while *Doolittle* and the *Chiefs*, older ships all, were moving into position to cover the other side. In essence

Zeppelin and her escorts were covering the western hemisphere, while *Doolittle*'s entourage covered the east. That left the poles open, but who wanted to nuke an ice-field? I virtual-frowned. *Doolittle* had a heavy cruiser with her, though she wouldn't be of much use against superfighters. And, she had five *Chiefs* as escorts, while *Zeppelin* was alone, save for her two *Warlords*. *Doolittle's* force looked to be by far the more formidable of the two, on the pipper at least. But I'd flown against both *Zeppelin* and *Doolittle* in exercises. While *Jimmy Doolittle* was a very fine gunnery ship indeed, more than a match for most of the rest of the fleet, *Zeppelin* and the *Warlord*s were equipped with the deadliest weapons in space. Or, more correctly, the deadliest weapons in space against superfighters. The three-ship formation would be *much* more difficult to get past, I decided, than the *Doolittle* group. Looks were deceiving, in this case. And, though the *Warlord*s were still green, they *had* just been at the gunnery range...

Would the Dracans understand this? Probably not, I decided. They had no equivalent of *Zeppelin* to exercise against, and few if any of their pilots who'd come into range of her had lived to tell the tale. The attack force would try to run past the smaller group for sure, I decided. "It's a sucker trap," I explained to Jimmy. "Probably something Vlasilov or his staff came up with. They'll face the three ships instead of the seven. I'd bet money on it."

"Ooh!" Jimmy crooned appreciatively. He'd tried to attack *Zeppelin* too, after all. "I *like* it!"

"Me too," I admitted, hating every second of delay as we taxied, taxied, taxied along. I wanted to take off so badly that I could feel it in every rivet. A 'bolt's antigravs were many times more powerful than those of any other 'hopper, however, and the airbase wasn't quite as well-shielded as it might have been. I'd been strictly ordered to roll as far as I possibly could from the main complex before launching. "Use your judgment, Commander," the admiral in charge had instructed me in person while I was being hooked up. "The army has air-defense missiles here. Don't ruin them unless you absolutely have to."

So far, the army's precious missiles were safe enough; I couldn't understand why the Dracans were putting off launching. The longer they delayed, the more time we had to react and move things into position. In fact, it was starting to look as if I'd blacked out part of Seattle for no good reason at all. That wasn't going to look at all good on Election Day; I could just picture Nagano waggling his finger at me at the next debate...

I looked at the pipper again and sighed. Were the Dracans *ever* going to launch? What were they waiting for, anyway? An engraved invitation? Did they think we were going to be *surprised* to see superfighters, for heaven's sake?

Then, suddenly, *Cochrane* appeared all by herself from around the back of the Moon. Her mains guns spoke...

...and the Dracans couldn't hold back any longer, for fear their sole carrier might be wiped out by a lucky, long-range hit. The pipper beeped as more red icons appeared. "One, two, three…" Jimmy counted. They were superfighters, sure enough.

"…nine, ten, eleven…" I continued.

"…fourteen, fifteen…" Jimmy's voice was suddenly very tight. "Tommy…"

"It can't be!" I declared, probably echoing the sentiments of half the navy. "It just can't be!"

"Eighteen!" Jimmy declared, once the new bogies quit appearing. "Thomas, there's eighteen of them!"

I checked my navigation systems; we were now almost far enough from the army's installations to safely up-ship. It would have to do. "Launch!" I ordered. "I don't care how many there are! We'll kill them all!"

Chapter Sixty-Six

It's an axiom in aerospace combat that as relative vectors increase, combat simplifies. This was one of the first things I'd learned while training to demonstrate Skybots for Father, a fact so elementary and obvious that it's quite easy to overlook. In other words, the faster the fleets and fighters move, the less time there is for maneuver and fancy tactics. We'd made that work in our favor while raiding Drakkus; due to our high vector, over half the Dracan ships in nearby space hadn't been able to move into position to fight at all, the ultimate in battle-simplification. More importantly, for the same reason we'd had to engage only a relatively small portion of the Dracan homeworld's fighter defenses, Rotte's magnificent stand against multiple squadrons after he'd been cornered notwithstanding. Now the tables were turned, however. A Dracan raid with even more vector behind it was coming in. Most of our ships weren't in position to intercept, and the attacking superfighters would be able to run right past most of our own defensive 'hoppers. A few squadrons—not many!—would be able to get in front of the Dracans and make a single head-on pass. After that, they'd never be able to get into firing position again.

And, sadly, that described the situation for Jimmy and me as well. As fast as our 'bolts were, there was no way in the time available that we could head out towards the enemy, then turn around and thrust the opposite direction and make a tail-chase of it. We weren't any better off than the Polecats, in that we'd be limited to a single head-on pass ourselves. Our only advantage over the more traditional birds was that, because of our speed, we were a lot more likely to be able to get in front of the Dracans than any individual Polecat squadron. That, and we could afford to wait and try and engage the Dracans deep inside the atmosphere. They had to shed some vector by then, or else they'd burn up.

Neither Jimmy nor I had ever had a chance to train with Fighter Control Central, and thankfully someone there was intelligent enough to issue Jimmy and I "free chase" orders. Therefore I was in charge of our deployment, not someone who'd never even seen a Skybolt up close and in person. I examined the pipper carefully; sure enough, our enemies were setting up to try and run past *Zeppelin*, though they were thrusting to swing as wide of her as possible. That swing, in turn, was moving them towards an attack on the Americas; I countered by flying out into the Gulf of Mexico, where I could run up to full power without breaking things like delicate army missile batteries.

"They're going to shave *Zeppelin* mighty close," Jimmy observed. "Why aren't they swinging wider? They've got power to spare."

That was a good question, I decided. Then, it came to me. "What if they don't?" I asked.

"Huh?" my wingman replied.

"I mean... Look, Jimmy. See their track on the pipper? What have they actually done so far that a regular fighter couldn't?"

"Nothing," he agreed, beginning to understand. "And... There's *no way* they can have eighteen superfigters. *We* don't have that many, and we're months ahead in production."

"Right!" I agreed. "We use decoys on our raids all the time! The Dracans are kind of doing the same thing, except with actual fighters. That's why they launched so late, too! So we wouldn't figure it out for as long as possible!"

"Jeez!" Jimmy complained. "I feel so dumb!"

So did I, actually. Or at least I did until I switched over to the squadron-commander's channel, where the announcement was just now being made. "...not all superfighters. Repeat, our latest intelligent estimates indicate...."

I switched back to Jimmy's link, feeling a little better. "Fighter Control agrees," I replied. "They're not all superfighters." And, sure enough, a few seconds later our pippers updated to reflect the new picture. Instead of all being superbirds, the little cloud of Dracan pips were now simply "bogies".

"So," Jimmy speculated. "How many of them *are* supers? I mean, some of them *have* to be. Otherwise this whole thing makes no sense."

I clicked my mike twice, and thought about what I knew of light carriers. *The Glorious First of June* had originally been designed for twenty-four conventional fighters. But Skybolts took up more room, not so much on the hanger deck but in terms of support staff and machine-shop requirements. Vlasilov was planning on re-equipping *June* with a dozen Skybolts, a single flight. Dracan light carriers were roughly the same size as ours. And, their superfighters, being first-generation birds, would if anything require even more space. Certainly, Stormcrows were harder to keep aboard a carrier than 'bolts. So, if there were eighteen pips...

"Not more than six," I predicted. "And probably only four or five. That's all they've got deck space for. It fits our estimates of their production-rate, too." I virtual scowled. "I feel so stupid! We should have figured this out sooner."

"Don't be so hard on yourself!" Jimmy countered. "You're doing fine in my book!" He laughed, for the first time his usual, cheerful self. Being outnumbered two or three to one was a *lot* easier to swallow than nine! "The brass didn't figure it out, either. And they didn't have a fighter and wingman to manage."

That was true enough, I decided. Or at least it made me feel a little better

Graf Zeppelin and her escorts were thrusting for all they were worth, forcing the Dracans to swing wider and wider. You could tell that our ships were running as hard as they could from the fact that *Zeppelin's* formation was falling apart; ships moving at full speed have no reserve for station-keeping. Still, they were roughly in line ahead, *Khan* leading, and in good position to do some damage. The Dracans couldn't evade forever; if they fiddled around long enough *Doolittle* and the *Chiefs* would be able to join the party as well. I did some rapid mental math. The geometry of the situation dictated that the longer the Dracans dithered, the further west their bombing runs would have to be. Europe was now totally out of the question. So I altered course to the west as well.

Just as we came onto our new heading, the Dracans made their move. Instead of trying to pass as far away from *Zeppelin's* squadron as possible they suddenly turned and thrusted almost directly towards the three ships, clearly aiming to blow past them before they could properly aim. I virtual-frowned and shook my head. This was going to be ugly, so ugly that I didn't want to have to watch. The fighting was taking place a long way from Earth, in conventional-fighter terms. There couldn't be a lot of "bite" for the Dracan antigravs to work with. The superfighters would be all right, with their huge motors. But the regular fighter pilots would be experiencing mushy, vague controls and grossly-reduced power. They were little better than targets…

…and the superfighters had to hold station on them, or else they'd reveal their true identity and draw all the fire!

I virtual-shook my head again as *Zeppelin*, *Attila*, and *Khan* seemed to explode, and remembered what it'd been like to fly right down the muzzles of so many rapid-fire guns. Who did the Dracans have planning their missions, anyway? Certainly decoys were wonderful things to have along on a raid. Not so wonderful, however, that they were worth sacrificing a superfighter's greatest assets, its speed and power. Yes, we'd succeeded through using decoys. But our fake 'bolts had been equipped with superfighter-class motors, so that we'd only had to slow down a little. How could the Dracan admirals be so stupid?

Was it perhaps because they were growing desperate?

"They'll come out hot and fast," I predicted to Jimmy. "The surviving supers, that is. The rest are toast. They'll never make it."

Jimmy clicked his mike twice…

…and, sure enough, out of the maelstrom emerged three red pips, coming fast and hard.

"That's it, then!" Jimmy crowed. He was far happier than I was. "Just the three! Hooray!"

"Hooray," I echoed. Yes, it was good that there were only three enemies left. Yes, I was glad that the number of cities that might be nuked had been greatly reduced, and even that my own odds of personal survival had just increased dramatically. But still, as I swung us still further west to effect the intercept. I couldn't help but think about the three terrified brain-cored kids mounted in the enemy 'hoppers.

Kids who should have been smiling and happy and playing at home with their brothers and sisters, but who instead had just passed through a terrible ordeal of fire, and who also had to know that no matter what else happened, death was coming for them much, much too soon.

Chapter Sixty-Seven

By now my wingman and I were approaching the coast of Texas, running at half throttle and trying to guess where the Dracans were headed next. "San Francisco," I suggested. "Or Los Angeles. They're the most important cities left in North America."

"Mexico City," Jimmy countered. "Or maybe even Sao Paulo. To spread out the damage. They haven't hit South America yet."

I virtual frowned, but said nothing. It was all just a guessing game, really. The Dracans might well be carrying enough warheads to hit a dozen cities or more. Who could know for sure, until—

Then it finally happened. "They're breaking up!" Jimmy cried out. Sure enough, the three Dracans were splitting off on separate headings. "One to Central America," he judged. "One to the Pacific Northwest. And one..."

"....right here, almost," I finished Jimmy's sentence for him. We'd discussed breaking up into one-'hopper raids for the Drakkus mission, but had decided that the odds were better with two-plane elements. Obviously, our enemies didn't concur. "We can't get them all," I observed. "Not in time."

"There's three squadrons of Polecats over Venezuela," Jimmy answered. "Plus, there's the army's missile battery at the Panama Canal. If we've got to leave one uncovered, that's the best."

I blinked to myself; Jimmy was growing. Six months ago he'd never have made such a suggestion. Probably it was due to all the responsibilities he was taking on training the new pilots. He was also, as it happened, correct. "Agreed," I replied. "Which one of the others do you want?"

There was only the slightest of hesitations. "Give me the Texas raid," he answered. "The other one's going to be a tougher job. And, Tommy... Well, you're still a lot better pilot than I am."

"Not for long," I answered, meaning every word. "You're coming along fast, old friend." Then there wasn't any more time for chatter. "Good luck, Jimmy! I'm outta here!"

With that, I went to full military power and was gone. Jimmy was right; this was going to be a tough interception, and the sooner I began the better my odds.

Northern California, I decided after zooming my pipper's scale down a little. The rest of the battle was now irrelevant to me, or at least for the moment it was. I'd intercept the Dracan over Northern California unless he dropped his bombs and turned away first, which was unlikely given his current course and speed. Or, unless the Polecats got him. There were two squadrons rushing in, the Adams and Eves over the Sea of Cortez, and the Kicking Dragons somewhere near Los Angeles.

"Top Banana One, Top Banana One," my radio called out. "This is Adam One."

"Roger, Adam," I replied. Adam One was the commander of the Adam and Eve squadron.

"We're not going to make it," the commander answered, sounding as if his heart were about to break. "Have you any advice?"

I examined my pipper again. "Head west," I decided. "If he bombs San Francisco, he's likely to head out to sea, where there's no missile batteries."

"Roger," Adam One replied.

Then it was Ted's turn. "We got lucky, kiddo," he exclaimed. "We're coming in with everything we have. I expect to get a shot."

"Great!" I answered. "We're currently on a collision course. I'll swing a little north and leave you a clear sky."

"Exactly what I was going to suggest," Ted replied. "My boys are liable to shoot at anything moving at superfighter velocities. We don't need any accidents."

"Right," I agreed, shuddering inwardly. That was one I hadn't thought of! "You take the first whack at him and I'll clean up if he leaks through. Just like we agreed."

Then the radio clicked twice and Ted was gone.

There was only a minute or so left now, and then things were going to happen very quickly. I took a moment to expand my pipper and check on Jimmy; he was doing fine, coordinating with the Dixie squadron just as I was working with his brother and the Kicking Dragons. He was maybe fifteen seconds from making his firing pass, and I was sorely tempted to wait and watch. But I didn't have the time to spare. Even though it was one of the hardest things I'd ever done, I tore my eyes away from Jimmy's battle and focused on my own.

The Dracan should almost be in visual range by now, so I cross-connected my nose-camera to the pipper and let it try to pick up the raider. It did, and for the first time I was able to actually see my enemy. He was much like the other superfighters I'd fought in general form and shape. But there was a new hump behind the center of the fuselage. Were the Dracans still monkeying with their basic superfighter design? Apparently so, and if that was the case it was good news indeed. I knew from being around Father and the plant so much that nothing slowed down production so much as continual design changes. Except for Mr. Roon, of course. He was a special exception.

Maybe we could appoint him to a job on Drakkus?

"I'm lining up!" an Eastern-accented voice cried out. Most of the Kicking Dragons were Korean, Chinese, and Japanese.

"Me too!" cried another.

"Shoot!" ordered Ted. The sky lit up with lines of little red laser-bolts. They danced all around the Dracan, who almost immediately began firing back. There was a flash among the Dragons, then another smaller one on the Dracan's left stub-wing.

"We hit her!" a new voice called out.

"I'm hit too!" someone else responded. "Mayday! Mayday! May—" Then there was another larger flash, and silence.

Just that quickly, it was my turn. I cranked my camera magnification all the way up, something I rarely had the luxury of doing in combat. The Dracan was carrying four weapons and, though the image was less than ideal at such high magnification, it looked to me like the left stub-wing was indeed damaged. It was blurry, as if it were vibrating badly. I flipped back to the pipper; sure enough, he was slowing down! That was one of the bad things about fighting inside the atmosphere; damage that didn't matter in space often caused big problems when you tried to drag it through the soup.

"He's hurt," I confirmed. "You hit him for sure." Polecats didn't have such good cameras, so the Dragons probably didn't know. Then there wasn't any time left; I called up my gunsight, lined myself up...

...and winced as the Dracan opened fire at me. I *hated* head-on firing passes-- over and over again Rotte had taught me that they were to be avoided except under the most extreme circumstances. "It's pure luck who wins, head on," he'd growled. "If you depend on luck long enough, eventually you'll lose."

But it *wasn't* pure luck, I reminded myself as I selected both cannons on my Mark I* and let fly with all I had. I was equipped with two guns now to my enemy's one. Bigger ones, too. It was still a crapshoot, in a sense. Now, however, the dice were loaded in my favor. Our laser-bolts crossed in mid-sky...

...and then I saw two bright flashes as the Dracan zoomed by. Two hits! And I'd not been damaged at all! Instantly I hauled myself around in a pursuit curve, even though it was probably futile. Three hits was a lot of damage for *any* 'hopper to absorb, even a nearly-solid-metal superfghter. If I was very lucky...

Sure enough, the Dracan was losing speed quickly now. His port wing was still blurry, fluttering not in the manner of a butterfly's wing reacting to a gentle summer breeze, but rather in the insanely-rapid metal-ripping fashion one might expect of deformed metal exposed to an unremitting hypersonic vortex. The whole fighter was blurry now, it was shaking so violently, though the pilot seemed determined to see things through to the bitter end.

"Bail out!" I urged him on the universal frequency. "Dracan pilot over the west coast, bail out! You've done all that you can do!"

But he hadn't. Even as I continued to swing around and complete the now-simple intercept from behind, the superfighter's left stub-wing fell away…

…and from the right burst two missiles.

Chapter Sixty-Eight

The radio immediately went nuts, though I no longer had time to pay any attention to it. "Vampire, vampire, vampire!" Ted cried out, using the traditional navy code-word for a missile launch. "Two tracks, visual bearing north by northwest"

"Full nuclear alert!" Fighter Control called out. "All batteries are released. I say again, all batteries are released!"

"...for the City of Imperial Learning!" the Dracan pilot cried out on the common frequency. "Payback in full!"

By then I'd swung almost all the way back around to the north. The crippled Dracan superfighter was little more than a flying scrapheap; I killed it even as her pilot cursed me by name. I didn't like having to finish him off that way, but for all I knew he might be carrying an internal warhead. Or he might even try and crash into a city. Dead, however, he could certainly do no more harm.

That left the missiles. I mentally advanced my throttles all the way forward to emergency overboost, and left them there. Missiles were fast, yes. Since they carried no gee-sensitive pilots, they'd long been equipped with more powerful motors than Polecats. But Skybolts were faster still. At least by a little. That was why I'd always preferred gravity bombs to missiles, back in my demonstration-flight days. Bombs were harder to shoot down.

"Clear the area, Top Banana One!" the fighter director ordered. "Immediately!" I knew what he wanted me to do and why-- he intended to let the army fire their interceptor missiles, which carried fusion warheads of their own. They'd do terrible damage and irradiate large areas of the countryside, though it wouldn't be nearly so bad as what the Dracan missiles would do if allowed to detonate. Our enemies tended to employ the filthiest sorts of warheads, the kind that poisoned large areas for centuries at a time. But even the defensive bursts would be bad enough. Even worse, likely as not the enemy bomb would still get through.

"Negative, Fighter Control," I replied. "I can make the intercept. Tell the army to go ahead and shoot, if they like. I'm staying right here." Then, I turned off his channel.

One of the missiles wasn't moving quite so fast as the other, and was aimed further to the west. It was thrusting only in fits and starts; most likely it'd been damaged by all the shaking. I came to it first as I completed my long half-circle; the thing was tiny and I only had time for one pass. I thought about Rotte and the impossibly tiny groups he'd routinely turned in at the gunnery range; how I wished that *he* were here, instead of a mere pretender like me! But he was dead and I was the man in the hot seat. I concentrated on my gun sight like I never had before…

…and blotted the missile out of the sky with, I suspected, my very first round. It flashed and went up in a small ball of fire, much like a conventional fighter. Then I was past the thing, and chasing after its sibling.

This was a tail-chase pure and simple, and my edge in speed wasn't nearly as great as I'd have liked. It was still dark here in… Oregon, I suddenly realized. I was in Oregon, and the missile was targeted for Seattle! How ironic! I was headed right back to where I'd started. Perhaps I could drop in at Nagano's place for coffee and a little pleasant conversation afterwards?

By now my engine temperature indicators were well into the red, and my nose and the leading edges of my wings were glowing as well. I'd never flown a 'bolt so fast through an atmosphere, and I was pretty sure that no one else had either. I was already well in excess of Father's specified design limits for both engines and airframe, but I tried not to worry. He over-engineered *everything*; it was almost an obsession with him. "There's nothing to worry about," I reassured myself aloud, using the 'bolt's external speaker. "Everything's under—"

Then a large glob of something that glowed flew back and smeared itself over my nose camera. I was melting! For just an instant I considered reducing power…

…and then the radio spoke again. "Call it off, Thomas!" It was Ted. "You can't do this. I used to plan your missions. I know as much about what a 'bolt can do as anyone.'

No you don't, I didn't reply as more glowing goop flowed back onto my fuselage. I was watching from my wingtip camera now, which was turned inwards. It was kind of pretty, really. I looked like a cartoon image of a meteor in flight. Most likely I was lighting up the sky for hundreds of miles around! *No one except Jimmy and I really understand what a Skybolt can do.*

And, I'm quite certain, it can do this.

Then I switched back to my gunsight. It was kind of awkward, since I usually aimed with my nose camera. But I could crosslink and use a wingtip unit as a backup. It just took a little Kentucky windage, was all. The range , however, was still very slightly too long.

"Thomas!" Ted roared. "Get out of there!"

Suddenly a huge flashbulb went off above and slightly behind me; an anti-missile, I supposed. I barely felt the blast, and the same was probably true for the Dracan missile. We were flying very low now, deep in the atmosphere, and moving much more quickly than the shockwaves from the anti-missiles could propagate. Sure enough, the enemy weapon was configured for a filthy, fallout-inducing ground-burst. Which was all the more reason why I couldn't break off the chase.

Now we were down almost to treetop level, and I had to laugh as a darkened patch of city loomed up ahead, the place where my navy shuttle had caused a blackout only what? Three hours before? Finally the missile came within extreme range. I fired a burst and missed clean because of the weird angle of my gunsight. I corrected, fired another burst, and missed again. The shots went on to strike the ground beyond the missile; not only was I failing in my mission, I was strafing a friendly city! Could I do *nothing* right? Another big glob of molten stuff peeled off of my nose; this time, something more solid underneath was exposed. It glowed a dull red, whatever it was, rapidly shifting to yellow. I'd been getting warning lights for ages now; suddenly, a dozen or more of them lit up all at once, some of them blinking to indicate increased urgency.

I lined up to fire again…

…and nothing happened. My guns! I checked the board; my guns were out! They'd melted! Downtown Seattle loomed ahead; if the bomb had been equipped with common sense it would've detonated itself long since so as to deny me the slightest chance of defeating its purpose. It was merely a stupid piece of metal, however, where I was alive and able to make decisions. Improvise. My brother had told me about that once, when I'd just been a demonstrator pilot. "Show them that you can think," he'd urged me. "That makes you far more dangerous."

"Thomas!" Ted called out one last time, reading my mind. "For the love of god, don't do it!"

But I did. If the Dracan bomb blew me up, then that wouldn't be so bad. It'd be fitting, even, after I myself had blown so many others to kingdom come. And best of all I'd never have to nuke anyone else, not ever again. The missile was only a yard or two in front of me now; I could practically reach out and touch it.

So I did. The closing speed didn't seem much, but all of the 'bolt's rather impressive mass was behind the blow. My blunted, glowing, softened nose rammed hard into the rear of the missile, just a little off-center. This in turn forced the weapon to slew slightly sideways…

…which at our current airspeed instantly induced a catastrophic amount of drag. The missile slammed home into the side of my fuselage, there was a bright flash…

…and then everything went black, black, black.

Chapter Sixty-Nine

"…all the ablative material," Sven observed from his wheelchair on the other side of my sickroom. "Every last bit of it!"

I nodded absently and smiled. It was good to be with Sven again after so long. He wasn't much for sentimentality, but that wasn't the same as saying he didn't care. "Every last bit of it!" he repeated, waving his pipe for emphasis. "You *abused* that airframe, Thomas! You *deserved* to crash!"

I smiled again. Father and Sven were two peas in a pod; having grown up around them I'd long since learned how to interpret what they really meant. "You abused that airframe!" really meant "Good god, my beloved brother! Please, be more careful! You could've been *killed*!"

"I did crash, eventually," I pointed out. "Or the 'bolt did, rather. I punched out." It was good to lay on the nice, soft snowy sheets and not have much of anything to do. When the salvage-charge-- a small non-nuclear warhead included in all nuclear missiles to discourage tampering—went up, the explosion shattered my fighter and gave me a terrible concussion. The doctors had kept me in a drug-induced coma for almost twelve weeks in order to allow the brain-repairing medications to work in peace. Fortunately, my outcome had been better than Father Murton's. But then, I was a lot younger.

It was also good to be with family again. Sven was so much older than me that he was more of an uncle than a brother, but that didn't mean that we still didn't love each other an awful lot. Rather to my surprise, Father had transferred him to the New Orleans facility instead of Gunther. "It's the only way to keep him out of the Stormcrow plant," Father had explained to me. "We've done a lot of cleanup, but there's still too many rads in the air. Sven is especially sensitive and he just can't accept the fact. Besides, it'll help to have another blood-relative around that the workers and staff will trust and listen to. Gunther's in seventh heaven; we're best friends again, and he's working sixty-hour weeks. His wife is pregnant at almost fifty, and he wants me to stand as the child's godfather. Isn't life wonderful?"

Unexpected miracles indeed! The reason Gunther was so happy was because he was now working out of Father's old office, overseeing all Esteppan Skybolt operations. It was his dream come true, the ultimate dream-job for any Esteppan aviation engineer worthy of the name. He'd resigned himself to building boring, mundane cargo-'hoppers for the rest of his life, and now he was at the pinnacle of his dreams.

Of course the reason that Gunther had risen so high was that Father was now the President of Esteppe; he'd run for office and won in a walk. The best part of that, in my book, was that he'd traveled on the same liner with Sven to vote his seat in Parliament in person, at least for a time. My home-planet had never really abandoned its militaristic heritage; the godlike treatment accorded Colonel Rotte and the way the Stormcrow workers' lips had curled in disgust as they described their peacetime jobs spoke volumes about their true feelings. Esteppe had been defeated but never broken, and now Father was seen as the key figure in bringing warrior-pride back to his home-planet. Sure, there were still a few who muttered "traitor" in dark places and behind closed doors. Now that Esteppe was once again playing a key role in a great military campaign, however, all was forgiven. Besides, everyone knew that a few more hydrogen bombs might've sterilized the planet. And though few spoke of it, there was a growing understanding that, after a certain point had been passed, their glorious stand against the United Systems wasn't anything to be proud of after all.

"We can add more ablatives," Sven observed. "But, Thomas, it's all extra mass! And, the greater the mass, the poorer the maneuverability! Especially when it's so far from the center of gravity!"

I'd just opened my mouth to explain that I thought the current ablative-package had done its job just fine when there was a knock on my door. "Come in," I said instead.

It was Mrs. Hunter, my former campaign manager and now my Parliamentary secretary. I'd won my election too, it seemed. By an even bigger margin than Father, after so many voters had watched me blazing across the sky over their heads chasing a warhead. Best of all I'd won while lying helpless in a coma, not having been forced to kiss even one more baby. It was most pleasant part of the entire campaign. "Hello, Thomas," she greeted me. Then she nodded at my brother, whom she didn't know very well. "Your Excellency."

He smiled back, looking only slightly pained. Hardly anyone remembered that Sven had, long ago and in another war, won an Esteppan noble title in his own right. But trust a savvy political operative like Mrs. Hunter to be in the know.

"Sven prefers to go by his own name, just as I do," I explained to the woman who carried ninety-eight percent of my political workload. "Both in public and in private, in his case."

"Of course," she answered, curtseying to my brother in apology. "I'm sorry, Dr. Longo." Then she turned back to me. "The doctors tell me you'll be ready to leave the hospital tomorrow?"

I nodded. "It's one of the advantages of being a cyborg," I explained. "No muscles to atrophy. I've felt fine ever since they woke me up. But, they wanted to observe me a little bit longer."

"Excellent," Mrs. Hunter agreed, looking down at the big stack of folders nestled in the crook of her right elbow. "Parliament's already in session, you know."

I nodded; their first official act had been to send me a huge get-well wreath. The thing had been so big that it couldn't be kept in the hospital. So Mrs. Hunter had it sent to the crater where my Skybolt had ended up; it was a pretty impressive hole, people told me, though I hadn't been able to go see it myself. Nor would I ever, probably. Folks from all over the world were sending get-well floral displays there, and supposedly a veritable mountain of the flowers had piled up. There was even talk of not ever filling the thing up, of preserving it as a memorial to the bomb that didn't fall. I was grateful that people cared, sure. But showing up in person would be far, far too embarrassing.

"You have to attend at least one session," she continued. "To be formally sworn in, though of course you're already voting in absentia. To receive your medal, as well. And to give your freshman address."

I nodded again, though I didn't really feel like it. They'd voted me a third Parliamentary Order of Merit, something that no one else had ever received. I didn't like that; not at all! The first one had been awarded to me strictly because the people needed a hero during the darkest of times; I could accept that, but never be comfortable with it. The second was for pushing a couple mental buttons and nuking thousands of university kids on Drakkus. That too had been a job that needed doing. But it was hardly something to be proud of or decorated for; the only part of that whole monstrosity of a mission I felt at all good about was helping Jimmy get out alive. And to receive yet *another* of the highest awards Parliament could give, just for ramming a warhead after being too incompetent to perform a proper intercept and shoot the launching fighter down when I'd had the chance? It was ridiculous! I'd seen *real* heroes in action, on Churilla and in the Training Fleet when they'd made their death-ride. *That* was the real McCoy! But when I protested and then refused the decoration, Admiral Vlasilov came by and yelled at me and made me promise to accept it with good grace.

"I didn't write up that citation just to have some ungrateful child make an idiot of me!" he'd roared. It was the first time he'd ever treated me like that. But he convinced me that it was for the good of the navy and would help win the war. So, I eventually said I'd wear the thing. Though I wasn't sure if he really *could* order me to, as he'd threatened.

"When can Parliament work me in?" I asked Mrs. Hunter. "I mean, I know they must be pretty busy."

My manager's mouth dropped open for just a split-second, then snapped shut again. "Trust me," she answered eventually. "They'll work with you on scheduling. I'm *quite* certain of that." Then she looked down at her folders again, and her brows knitted. "I think you ought to do all of this at once," she said eventually. "It'll have more impact that way."

"It'd save a trip to Rome," I agreed. "At least one. The less time I spend traveling, the better. I don't even know anyone back in the squadron I'm supposed to be in command of, except Jimmy of course." I looked over at Sven. He seemed amused about something, though I couldn't figure out what. "I've got so much work to do aboard *June* that it isn't even funny."

"And there'll be a state dinner," Mrs. Hunter continued remorselessly. "You can't get out of that. There'll be a formal reception beforehand, so this is effectively an all-day affair. You'll sit at the PM's right hand. After all, you delivered him a majority when no one else in the universe could've. Then there's the inaugural ball. And your formal presentation to the Esteppan delegation; everyone recognizes your special connections there, so that won't be a problem."

"Argh!" I cried out, letting my head flop back onto my pillow. "And this is the easy, light-duty version of being a Parliamentarian? Someone call my doc! Give me more drugs! I wanna go back into the coma!"

Chapter Seventy

I was pretty well caged in, Parliament-wise. Mrs. Hunter was correct in that I had to attend my own swearing-in and receive my medal. And, I supposed, I also had to give a freshman address. They were an old tradition among Parliamentarians; every new member, in his or her first few months, gave a speech on the issues dearest to their hearts. The speeches, invariably delivered by green, untried politicians, tended to be long, rambling, and incredibly boring. No one ever paid any attention to them, except maybe for a few supporters back in the home district. But the tradition ran deep, and I supposed I had to honor it. This was something I couldn't delegate to Mrs. Hunter. Even though I was certain she'd do a better job.

They discharged me from the hospital early the next morning, and I was startled to find Father waiting for me in my navy shuttle. "Thomas!" he greeted me, arms spread wide. We hugged for a long time, even though he'd been to visit me in the hospital twice since I'd woken up and I didn't know how many times before. "My son! I'm so proud of you!"

When we were done embracing, Father smiled and sat down, so that we could begin strapping in. "If you don't mind," he suggested, "I think that we should go straight to Italy. We can use your chalet there; it's only an hour or so from Rome. Unless there's something you need in New Orleans? Or someone you want to see?"

"Not really," I admitted, after meeting Manuel's eye and getting the thumbs-up from him. "Besides, the Alps are pretty this time of year, and I've been cooped up in a little room for days. Maybe we can eat dinner out on the balcony?"

"Of course!" Father agreed, his wide smile standing in stark contrast to his black Eliteman's robe and shaved head. One got the impression somehow, looking at an Eliteman, that they weren't supposed to smile or laugh. Yet, there wasn't any rule against it, or at least there wasn't that I knew of. "On the balcony it is!" He looked over at Manuel. "Would you be kind enough to send the request ahead, my friend, once we've taken off?"

"But of course," my valet agreed, bowing slightly in his seat.

Father and I spent the rest of the trip catching up on this and that; he told me funny stories about his run for office, and I shared the one or two interesting things that had happened to me on my own campaign trail. "By the way," he pointed out while we were over the mid-Atlantic. "I'm very, very pleased with how you handled the issues at our New Orleans plant. You struck just the right note with all the right people." He clapped me on the shoulder. "And Dr. Bhata is a true gem. He's every bit as fine a man and engineer as Gunther. You were right to trust him, too." He smiled. "We're going to try and keep Dr. Bhata in the family. I have my staff putting together a permanent job offer for him. On a par with Gunther's."

I smiled back. Father had already let me know that he was happy with my business dealings in his name, but this was high praise indeed. And it was good to know that I'd done right with Bhata as well. Since I probably wasn't going to be any kind of decent engineer myself, judging by how poor I was at calculus, it was a relief that at least we'd found someone else who could do the work I should've been doing myself. "I got lucky," I answered after a time. "Just like in so many other things."

"Hmph!" Father snorted. But he didn't say anything more.

When we finally landed in Italy, the first thing I noticed was that someone had plowed all the snow off of the entire 'hopper field, not just the little corner my navy launch needed. And, they'd also plowed all the sidewalks and driveways running all over the property. There wasn't anything *wrong* with doing this, of course, but it was unnecessary and perhaps even expensive. I shifted uneasily in my seat. I'd owned this estate for almost two years now, and somehow I'd never gotten around to giving anyone instructions of how I wanted it taken care of. For that matter, who was paying the staff? Had Father or Mr. Flowers arranged it behind my back, or was that part of the gift? If the latter, did I have the *right* to give instructions? I'd never really wanted an estate in the first place, not even one in such a beautiful place as this. It came with too many responsibilities. But the people of Italy had given it to me, and that was that. What kind of an ingrate would I be if I asked them to take it back? Besides, I had to admit that it *was* kind of convenient, what with Parliament being held in Rome and all.

Maybe I could find out from Mr. Flowers who was in charge? If I asked really nice, he might even fly over for me and take a discreet look to make sure that everything was being run on the up-and-up…

I was still worrying about who was paying for snow removal as I slowly clomp-clomp-clomped my way into the entry hall and around the corner to the big open space that did multiple duty as holovision room, informal dining room, and entertaining area. The holovision was already on, I noticed, and rotated to display its images up on the ceiling. I pressed my lips together in irritation. Sure, I wanted my staff to make themselves at home. This, however, was stretching things a bit too far, even for my tastes.

Then it hit me. I couldn't quite see the holovision images; my angle was wrong, and there was a low archway blocking the view. The sound, however, was instantly recognizable. It was someone playing *Rocket Sledder*! And that someone could only be…

"Jimmy!" I cried out in delight, actually tripping and falling on my face, I was in such a rush. Even worse, I tumbled my gyros. I hadn't seen him in forever, it felt like. He'd called me almost every day in the hospital, but his duties had prevented him from visiting in person. "Jimmy! Bring up a two-player screen! I'll be right there, just as soon as the world quits spinning!"

Chapter Seventy-One

We played three entire games before really speaking to each other, one of them very nearly a record performance. Jimmy was getting better almost weekly, it seemed, despite the fact that he had almost as little time to practice as I did. My friend was growing up fast.

"..chased him most of the way across the Gulf," he was explaining as we crashed and burned together, ending the third game. Get two veteran fighter pilots together, and it's only a matter of time until the conversation turns professional. "He got past the Polecats, but in doing so he scrubbed off a lot of speed. I killed him over the water, before he could launch."

I nodded and hit the reset button. I'd read the reports, of course. But that wasn't the same thing as discussing things face to face. "I shouldn't have let mine launch," I said as the game flashed through its start-up graphics. "It was a huge mistake. I missed when I had the chance."

"You didn't miss, Tommy!" Jimmy corrected me. "You hit him twice, both of them solid. I've seen the tapes! Plus the Polecats nailed him, too." He sighed. "You're just too hard on yourself, is all. The odds were, he should have gone down. That he didn't was plain bad luck." He pointed at the holodisplay "Like when our sleds hit trees on the other side of blind jumps. You just can't help it."

I frowned and set down my controller. "He got past me and fired," I repeated.

"And you got both the missiles!" Jimmy replied. "Tommy… Your intercept was a lot harder than mine. No one else on the planet seems to have a problem with how you handled yourself. Why should you?"

I shook my head and sighed, then turned off the video game. Clearly play-time was over. "I don't know," I answered eventually. "I really, truly don't know. But I feel like I should've done *something* differently. So many people almost died…"

Jimmy looked out the window, then back at me. "It's like this, whether you accept it or not," he said. "You're a hero. The reason you're a hero is because you keep doing the right things, time after time after time."

"I just happened to be at the right *place* at the right time when the shooting started," I pointed out, a little sulkily. "That's most of it."

"Maybe it is," Jimmy answered. "Who am I to argue that? Would *I* be where *I* am today if my father hadn't been a famous fighter pilot? Or if we hadn't already started to make friends the night before the war began?" He shrugged. "The important thing, in my book, is what you've made of your opportunities. When I look back at everything you've accomplished since we first met, the first thing I want to do is turn green with envy. I honestly don't see how you could've done much better. It's almost like you've got some kind of inner compass built into you, one that tells you what your next move ought to be. Even more, you've never done anyone dirty along the way, or at least not that I know of. That's the really amazing part, to me. Your head ought to be the size of the Singapore Tower. But it's not. Instead, you're sitting here about to receive your third Order of Merit-- all of them well-earned, I might add-- and take your elected seat in Parliament. Yet here you are, bitching and moaning about how you're not as good a combat flyer as you might be." Jimmy shook his head and sighed again. "Tommy, if I didn't know you so well I'd question your sanity."

I tried to speak, but a new voice intervened. It belonged to Alicia Wiston, though I hadn't noticed her enter the room. Perhaps she'd dropped in to discuss politics with Father? "If you want to find fault, Thomas," she said, "consider that there were only two Skybolts available to intercept three Dracan attackers. Both you and Jimmy were, eventually and with help, successful in shooting down your targets. No bombs fell, where there were Skybolts available for defense. But in Latin America…"

I pressed my lips together and turned away. Latin America was another thing I tried not to think about; whenever I did, I started feeling vaguely ill. It'd been my decision and no one else's to leave the people there uncovered. Mexico City, Sao Paolo, and Buenos Aires were all gone. The Panama Canal would've been gone as well, save that the army shot down the incoming missile. The Dracan ripped right through the Polecats without them even getting a shot off; the pipper-movie looked almost like a replay of any of several instances during the Esteppan war when Rotte's Butcher Birds had gone over to the offensive. *Jimmy Doolittle*'s task force had finally cornered him and blotted him out of the sky when he'd tried to rejoin his carrier. If they hadn't, who knew how many *more* cities might be gone?

"If you want to look for someone to blame for something," Alicia continued remorselessly, "look at those who made certain that there wasn't even one more working Skybolt ready to defend us when we needed it." She shook her head. "You and for that matter your father and I did everything-- *everything!*—in our power to defend those cities. If it'd been left up to us, we'd not have lost so many crucial weeks and months. Our consciences, Thomas, as well as yours, should be clear. Don't blame yourself for only scoring two hits—usually enough to be lethal!-- on a difficult target during a head-on pass, when according to your own reports success under these conditions is more a matter of luck than anything else anyway. Instead, concentrate on wondering why on earth you didn't have more fighters under your command to help you!"

"That's what the voters did!" Jimmy agreed, nodding emphatically. "Everyone says so. Even the talking heads!"

I closed my eyes and sighed. Then a new voice chimed in. "Da, Thomas," Admiral Vlasilov agreed, stepping around Alicia and into my living room. "I perhaps understand your feelings better than most, having ordered so many ships and even more men to their deaths. I spend hour after hour in my cabin, watching the tapes and seeing them die over and over again. I can see where I made mistakes, where my decisions killed men who need not have been lost." He closed his eyes. "Sometimes I see their faces and voices as well. Yet overall my profession judges me a success. I believe that history will judge me a success as well." He shrugged. "I hate the fact that I'm merely human. But, what can I do?"

Despite the fact that I was wearing shorts and a t-shirt instead of a uniform, I scrambled as quickly as I could to my feet; the admiral's presence always had that effect on me. A whole crowd had formed without my noticing; in addition to Alicia and the admiral, Captain Bard was there, and both Knights, and... My god, the Prime Minister!

"Surprise!" Father declared, stepping out in front of all the rest. "Welcome to your swearing-in party, Thomas! And to your medal-winning party, as well. There'll be a formal dinner later in the week, of course, with all sorts of dignitaries and media-types present. But this is the *real* dinner, the one we hope you will truly remember and enjoy. It'll be highly informal, in deference to your preferences. You'll note that even the PM is wearing sweats." The leader of the government smiled and waved. "So there's no need for you to go get all dressed up; there's plenty of time for that over the next few days. And, we've moved dinner out to the balcony. At your request."

"I..." I stammered, not quite able to make my speaker work. "I..."

"Surprise," the admiral repeated; someone had already put a drink in his hand, it seemed. He raised it high. "Congratulations, Thomas. It couldn't happen to a better man."

Chapter Seventy-Two

The informal dinner proved to be everything that more formal affairs were not and could never be. Even though Jimmy and I didn't eat, we watched in glee as the highest-ranking dignitaries in the United Systems sat around in casual clothing on my balcony with the Italian Alps in the background, eating barbequed chicken, corn on the cob, and cucumber salad. Even Alicia seemed happy with the menu choices for once; she tore into the corn as if she'd been starving for months. "The chicken tastes a little funny," Sven explained to me at one point. He knew how much I missed the taste of food. "Probably because the cooks are Italian."

"But funny in a good way!" interjected the PM, who was sitting on Sven's left. We were making no pretense of precedence whatsoever, sitting in a higgledy-piggeldy mess that had nothing to do with rank and everything to do with who enjoyed who's company. Everyone seemed to be having a wonderful time; even Mrs. Hunter, who was normally a stickler for rank and social protocol. "Pass the salt, Madame Deputy?"

"I'll trade it for more corn, Prime Minister. Until then, I'm holding it hostage."

The PM looked at me and rolled his eyes. "How I pity the Wiston's political rivals back on Churilla. They have to deal with *two* of them!"

"I pity the Dracans," I countered, "Even though they're currently dealing with just the one."

"How true, Thomas," the PM agreed, exchanging the corn that had been sitting at his elbow for the requested salt. "How very, very true."

When dinner finally wound down, the PM tapped on the table and called for everyone's attention. "As some of you know," he began, "early last week the armed forces of the United Systems liberated New Nippon."

I blinked. No one had whispered a word to me, and there hadn't been anything in the news, either. The censorship must've been total.

"…just arrived, fresh from the battlefront. Would you care to tell us the tale, Captain Knight? I'm not asking for a formal report, of course. Just dinner conversation."

The elder Knight smiled; he and Ted were the only ones present in uniform, and now I knew why. *Tsushima Strait* must have just hit dirt a few hours ago. "The operation was a total success," he explained. "Admiral M'bele's plan worked perfectly. If you're familiar with it, then you know exactly how the battle went. We had a few problems with the assault landing, but they were directly attributable to poor training. We'll do better next time."

"What about losses?" the PM demanded.

"Almost none, for the navy," Lofton replied. "Just a few landing-craft officers. As for the army... Sir, I'd rather they made their own report. I don't believe it was any worse than expected, but there *were* casualties."

Meanwhile, there was a little interplay going on between Jimmy and Ted. Jimmy met his elder brother's eyes and raised his brows inquiringly, then Ted held up three fingers. He'd made three kills! Jimmy grinned, and I gave my friend a big 'thumbs-up' as well. Unless I was mistaken, Ted was now the leading Polecat ace in the fleet.

"...civilian losses," the PM was continuing, looking rather grimly down at a toothpick. "Compared to what the Dracans were doing to them on an almost daily basis, I mean."

"An effective Resistance was just developing," Lofton agreed. He looked away from the table. "Sir, the navy's report will contain references to numerous mass graves. Most of the educated classes were killed off."

Alicia scowled. "Just like back home."

"Atrocity after atrocity," the PM agreed. "It seems to be the Imperial way." Then he turned back to Lofton. "You're certain that we're not going to be dislodged?"

"Absolutely," Captain Knight reassured the Chief of State. "The Dracans were poorly supplied and had used up most of their 'hoppers trying to stop our initial convoy. Many of the dead were starving."

"Starving," the PM repeated. Clearly, the fact that his enemies had been suffering offered him a considerable degree of satisfaction. "That is good news indeed." Then he changed the subject. "What about the prisoners? Are we getting anything of value form them? Or have you heard?"

Lofton frowned, and put down his half-eaten chicken-thigh. "Sir... he said slowly. "They didn't surrender. Almost none of them did. There's only a small habitable zone on New Nippon; I presume you're familiar with conditions there?"

The PM nodded, and so did everyone else. Most colony worlds were bare rock, except in small areas centered on towns and cities. New Nippon was no exception. Despite being the eldest of all colonies, the planet was mostly still empty. This was because crafting a functional biosphere out of such unpromising stuff as was to be found there was an enormous challenge. It might take millennia. "Well, sir," Lofton continued, "The colonists signaled us while we were still in orbit. They gave us the locations of all the Dracan strongpoints. We hit them hard from the air, then landed before the dust settled. Our enemies fell back in disorder." His face became hard. "The New Nipponese slaughtered every survivor they could get their hands on, and those they didn't get rallied at a ridgeline just outside the habitable zone and dug in deep." The captain looked down at the table. "It would've taken weeks to dislodge them, sir, and we'd have lost thousands of good men. If we left them there they could bombard New Tokyo at will. So we nuked them. Neutron-bombed them, just like they did to us back at the Kammhuber Pass on Churilla. It was the cheapest, most effective way." His eyes rose and met those of his Commander-in-Chief. "If we took as many five prisoners out of fifty thousand or more Dracans, I'd be amazed. The rest are dying of radiation-sickness as we speak."

Chapter Seventy-Three

Suddenly I was glad that I hadn't eaten; if I'd still had an actual stomach, I was quite certain, I'd not have been able to hold down dinner. Of all the awful, terrible things I'd seen and been through, walking through the Kammhuber Pass after it had been neutron-bombed was easily the worst. The people there had died slowly and horribly, knowing all the while that they were beyond all hope. Some had killed themselves immediately. More had clung to life just as hard as they possibly could, while their bowels turned to bloody water and their vitality drained away and the horror of it all ate slowly at their sanity…

"Thomas?" Alicia asked, looking at me worriedly. "Are you all right?"

"Yes," I answered, forcing a reassuring smile and looking around at the pleasant little dinner group that was ultimately responsible for unleashing one of the greatest horrors ever to curse mankind. Admiral Vlasilov was munching unconcernedly on yet another chicken leg, I noted. Had he ever watched a man die of radiation poisoning, I wondered? Would it matter if he had?

Alicia's eyes narrowed. She knew well the horrors I'd seen, better than anyone else at the table. I'd described them to her in tearful fits and starts while she sat and sketched them for her little comic book of my adventures that everyone in the galaxy seemed to have read. "It had to be done, Thomas," she explained gently. "You know that."

I nodded, but said nothing. It was true enough; if Captain Knight had laid out the situation honestly, of which I had no doubt, then there simply hadn't been any other decision to make. Unless one wanted to sit and write thousands of letters to grieving parents, like the ones I'd written for far too many dead Top Bananas and never, ever wanted to write another of. The Dracans could've surrendered. They hadn't, however. They'd been the first to employ such a wretched weapon. What came around, went around; that was the cardinal rule of warfare. To ignore this was to first fight with one hand tied behind one's back and then to lose. But still…

Captain Bard had told me once that there came a time in warfare when you felt as if you were kicking your helpless enemy in the genitals over and over just as hard as you could with a steel-toed boot. And you kept kicking, even while your enemy moaned and writhed and coughed up blood all over you.

284

That was what victory felt like, she explained, in the real world. That was how you could tell you were winning, when the hope in your enemy's eyes faded and he was left to helplessly scream out his life and die right before your eyes. And if you didn't keep right on kicking while he was down, the next thing you knew he'd be back on his feet kicking *you*...

War was miserable, I decided for about the thousandth time. It was the worst and most awful thing there could ever be. Except bowing to the Emperor, of course; that was a given. I'd never sought this fight, I reminded myself; I'd still been a child when it began. But I was up to my neck in it now. I thought back to all the good men and women I'd seen die, and suddenly I was angrier than I'd ever been before in all my life, even angrier than when I was fighting Dracans. This was *wrong*! It had to be *stopped*! People had tried before me, I knew. They'd given their best, and failed utterly. But that was no excuse for not trying.

"It had to be," I agreed, after a too-long silence. "I know it's true. But that doesn't make it right."

"No," the PM agreed. "It doesn't. We lose sight of that, sometimes." He sighed, but said no more.

"We're trapped," Captain Knight observed. "In the most miserable position possible. As a species, I mean." He looked at me. "We're smart enough to do almost anything we put our minds to. Make weapons, terraform worlds, jump across interstellar space. Yet we can't quite figure out how not to slaughter each other. And more often than not in ways that we'd never willingly subject some poor dumb brute of an animal to."

I looked over at Ted, whose eyes had suddenly gone dark. The truth was written all over his face; he was the commander of the Kicking Dragon squadron and it was therefore axiomatic that he'd not asked his men to do anything he wasn't willing to do himself. It was Ted who'd dropped the terrible bomb, I knew, just as certainly as if I'd watched him do it. "I know how it feels," I said slowly, looking my friend in the eyes.

"Yes," he agreed, as everyone else at the table slowly figured out what I already knew. "You do."

"There's only one way for people like us to ever become clean inside again," I continued. "No victory won will ever do it, unless the victory is made to mean something." I turned to the PM. "We've all done terrible things, those of us sitting at this table. Every single one of us. Things that would never be excusable outside of the context of war, and maybe not even within it." I hesitated, unsure of what I was trying to say. "We've got to build a better universe out of all of this horror. Things have to change, in the most fundamental way possible. We can't ever fight another war as awful as this one, and everything we've destroyed along the way will be for nothing unless some kind of real, meaningful progress is made. We've got to make humanity a better species. One that won't do this to itself anymore."

There was a long, long silence. Then the PM smiled, and gestured towards Father and Alicia, who by chance were sitting together. "Exactly, my son," Father replied, reaching up with one hand and pointing at the socket in the back of his skull.

"Exactly," Alicia agreed, wriggling her ears a little more exaggeratedly than usual.

"Yeah," Jimmy agreed, putting his elbows on the table and doing it in such a way that the electric motors made far more noise than usual. "I'm on-board too."

"They don't want it," the PM cautioned me. "I didn't want it, for that matter, until I came to have so much personal contact with so many of you. And, of course, the voters hate the idea. Only the Emperor is less popular, and that's not by much. Every poll agrees on this. If we try to push things now, my government will fall in twenty minutes flat. In fact, if my party rank-and-file even *dreamed* we were having this little chat, I'd be out of office so quick my head would spin." He smiled. "But there will come a time, Thomas, when we'll be free to act. We'll have to move quickly, and decisively. And when that time comes…"

"…we'll win. One way or another."

Chapter Seventy-Four

"We'll win," the PM had assured me. Yet as I scrambled about like a madman for the next few days preparing for my mercifully brief stint as a serving, active Parliamentarian, I couldn't help but ask myself over and over again exactly how he was going to pull it off. He was right about the poll numbers; I verified it just as soon as dinner wound down and everyone went home. The Dracan Emperor excepted, gengineering and "frankensteining" were about the least-popular political causes out there. There were only seven Parliamentarians on record as being in favor of fully legalizing these activities, of which Father, the Wistons and I made up the majority. The rest were from Esteppe as well. Yet oddly enough the Wistons and I, obvious and unhidden violators of the supposed sanctity of the human form, held the highest United-Systems-wide approval ratings of any politicians, period. Mine was so high that when I saw it I gulped and got off the page as quickly as I could. It was hard to understand how people could so strongly disapprove of 'borging and gengineering and yet like the results so much. Somehow, they must not be thinking things all the way through.

Maybe the PM somehow meant to help them do so, and *that* was how he intended to secure everyone's future? Almost certainly not; I'd already experienced plenty enough politics to know there wasn't much hope of ever getting voters to actually *think*. You had to appeal to their emotions and better natures, not their brains. If you expected to win them over, that was.

When my big moment finally came, everything was choreographed to a "t" for me. All I had to do was remember where to stand, when to smile, and give a few carefully scripted speeches. As promised I accepted my medal in good grace, along with another endless series of gifts from the grateful citizenry. This time they included the keys to the cities of Seattle and San Francisco (where the first missile was probably heading), a chalet actually *inside* Yosemite, and lifetime access to the High Roller Penthouse in any of several casinos in Lake Tahoe and Las Vegas, which would likely have been in the fallout patterns. I was deathly afraid the whole time I was up at the podium that someone was going to promote me to captain, which would've been even more ridiculous given my age and skill-level than being a commander was. I'd made both

Admiral Vlasilov and the PM promise me they wouldn't do it; reluctantly, they'd agreed. In exchange, however, without telling me ahead of time they made me an honorary Colonel of Marines, a position the PM explained had been resurrected just for me. It carried a significant lifetime pension I didn't need, entitled me to wear a marine uniform I hadn't earned, and, damn it, made me nominally equal to a navy captain in rank. Though it wasn't nice of them to blind-side me like that, I smiled and accepted the honor right along with all the rest. They chose Jimmy to present it to me, probably because they knew I'd bite the head off of anyone else. "Keep quiet, Tommy," he whispered in my ear as he shook my hand at the podium. "It's not our fault that you won't accept what you deserve."

Immediately after this little ceremony I took my Parliamentary oath of office, swearing to respect, honor, and uphold the Constitution of the United Systems. I wasn't alone as I did this; there were almost two thousand Parliamentarians all told, and between illnesses, the dislocations caused by the war and other factors quite a few us had missed the original mass swearing-in ceremony. Eleven of us stood and took the oath together including, to my shock, one Isoroku Nagano. He hadn't been elected to anything but was a bonafide Parliamentarian nonetheless, having wangled an interim appointment from the Provisional Government of New Nippon. He had strong family ties there, it seemed. I extended my hand to my former rival as he and the rest stepped up to join me, but the bastard cut me cold. Later I found out, he'd done it with foreknowledge and malice; though there were dozens of cameras covering the ceremony, not one picked up the insult. He'd worked things out ahead of time and made sure he was standing in just exactly the right place to get away with it.

Not that Nagano was a terrible threat, for the moment at least. The election had turned into a shellacking, and my party had a rock-solid majority. While I was helpless in my coma Nagano had tried to blame me for the loss of the three Latin American cities, claiming that I'd allocated my targets based on "the politics of prejudice" instead of sound military strategy. His position had gained a little traction in heavily Latino districts, enough so to unseat one long-time friend of the PM who previously had been in no trouble. But Alicia, filling in for me on the campaign trail, had over and over again pointed out that it was Nagano himself who'd ensured that there was a Skybolt shortage to begin with. "Even one more," she'd cried out passionately from dozens of rostrums. "Even one more, and we might have saved who knows how many lives? And why is it we didn't have that one? If it weren't for Nagano and his cronies, there'd have been *dozens*!" Her arguments had carried the day, and what had been the narrowest of races turned into a rout.

I was exhausted by the time the formal State dinner was over; at least ten thousand times I stood and smiled and held the hand of a perfect stranger while a photographer dutifully clicked away, gritting my teeth all the while about the fact that I should've been spending quality time with the new pilots of the Top Banana squadron that I was at least theoretically in command of. Still, it was amusing to contrast the behavior of the PM and Father and Alicia at this event to how they'd comported themselves over barbequed chicken back in my villa. There they'd laughed and smiled, or at least they had until the subject of the war came up. But this time, every word and gesture was deeply considered before delivery. I wasn't a skilled enough politician to ad-lib in such a manner at a venue where the play was for keeps and I knew it. So I just smiled a lot and limited myself to inane talk about my skimmer-racing days and how much Jimmy and I liked to play *Rocket-Sledder*. All the time Mrs. Hunter sat at my elbow and monitored every word I said. "You did just fine," she assured me when it was finally over. Then she gave my arm a little squeeze. "Come now. We've just got to get you over to the special Esteppan reception, and then we'll call it a night."

So I groaned, then did it all over again for the Esteppan dignitaries. They weren't much different from the more run-of-the-mill United Systems types except for the fact that they all called me "Your Excellency" and bowed to me repeatedly. I had to put my medals back on for this affair, of course, so I clanked and clinked even more than usual as I made my slow, clumsy way around the room, posing with everyone. There was at least one nice thing about the Esteppan reception, though. Instead of discussing skimmer-racing and video-games again, I was able to make small-talk about what it'd been like to fly with Colonel Rotte and the other Butcher Birds. They saw Rotte as a great hero and wanted to know everything I could remember about him. Before the night was out I'd promised to sit down after the war with the planet's official historian and record it all for posterity. I liked that a lot better than being made a Colonel of Marines; Rotte *deserved* to remembered, warts and all. All the Butcher Birds did, for that matter. They'd stood off the United Systems' best, while outnumbered almost a hundred to one. That *deserved* commemoration. Certainly *I'd* never done anything so noteworthy.

Before the night was out, I was made a Butcher Bird myself. Emil had all but adopted me already, but now it was official. Father handed me a certificate inducting me into the Esteppan Reserve arm of the United Systems military and naming me commander of the Birds. This wasn't quite as farfetched as it seemed; in point of fact, it was long-established tradition that the commander of the Top Bananas was the senior squadron commander in the entire navy. That was why I was a full commander instead of a lieutenant-commander like all the other squadron leaders. Since the Birds were almost certainly going to be operational before the Bananas, Esteppe being set up so much better to support a superfighter unit, I really *would* effectively be in command of them for a time. I'd also always be in distant charge of them in combat as well, whenever both units were flying together. Perhaps it was for the best that the relationship was formalized; otherwise all sorts of annoying problems rooted in planetary pride might've arisen. "They're coming to Earth for final training," Father explained, smiling. "In part specifically so you can work with them."

I smiled and looked around the banquet room; suddenly all the Esteppans were absolutely bursting with pride. It was *their* weapon that was winning the war, and now it was *their* squadron that'd be operational first. It was overwhelming, really, to see how much this meant to the people of a recently-defeated planet. "As a proud son of Esteppe," I said carefully, "this is a great honor indeed. I'm no Emil Rotte; there'll never be another ace as great as he. His shoes are far too large for me to fill. But I'll do my best."

"There may never be another Emil Rotte," the Minister of Defense replied, eyes shining. "But there'll never be another Thomas Longo, either. Three cheers! Hip-hip, hooray!"

"Hooray!" everyone echoed, so loud in the little room that I had to turn down my microphones a bit. "Hooray! Hooray!"

I looked down at the floor and smiled back, trying not to think about the miserable, starving Dracans on New Nippon who at this very moment were dying in droves of radiation poisoning. Either that, or crawling miserably into the hole that'd become their grave and detonating one last grenade.

Chapter Seventy-Five

My freshman address was scheduled for the next afternoon so that I could finish up my business, formally sign my vote-pairing agreement with a gentleman from the opposition who wanted to go serve in the army, and get back to being a fighter pilot again before I forgot how to fly. I was so eager to be done with the thing that I could hardly stand it. Ever since the big dinner at my Italian villa, Alicia and Father had let me think of little else.

"It's just a formality," I protested once, in the middle of a rehearsal. "No one ever listens to these things, anyway."

"They'll listen to *yours*," Father countered grimly, as Alicia nodded her agreement. "Count on it, son. You have to get this one right."

I sighed and shook my head, but went back to work. Learning formation flying while Rotte poured sarcastic comments directly into my mind had been hard, I'd thought at the time. And I'd also thought that it was hard to stand heel-and-toe watches back on Esteppe. But *nothing* was harder than writing and delivering a truly important speech, I soon came to understand. *Nothing!* Especially since I wasn't using a speechwriter.

"Thomas," Father corrected me gently when I asked him what he wanted me to say. "This is *your* freshman speech. Mine was delivered over a month ago, while you were still asleep in the hospital." He closed his eyes in pain. "I know you haven't had time to watch the recording, but someday you might want to. It was largely about you."

Nor had Alicia been much help. "We worked to get you elected, that's true enough," she replied when I explained that I felt I was being left high and dry. "But we don't *own* you, Thomas. Nor would it be right for us to *try* to own you. You'll have to do this part yourself." Then she smiled. "Though you've really nothing to fear. You're quite the public speaker when you really try. Your inner honesty rings like a bell, loud and clear."

So in the few hours I could scrounge here and there I had to write my own speech. That wasn't to say that I didn't have help; once I'd produced a rough draft first Mrs. Hunter and then everyone else went over it with a fine-toothed comb for me, asking me if I really meant that *all* navy personnel were heroes (of course I didn't; that was just a dumb mistake in phrasing) and if I *really* wanted to distance myself from the PM's position regarding wartime excise taxes (I hadn't even realized I was doing so.) But for the most part, they didn't alter a thing. "Are you *sure*?" I asked Mrs. Hunter. "I mean, will it be all right?"

"You're a Parliamentarian now, Thomas," she'd replied, looking into my eyes. "'This is a very special speech for you. It isn't supposed to be about party unity or log-rolling or pork for the folks back home. This is your once-in-a-lifetime opportunity to talk about what's nearest and dearest to your heart without fear of Party censure. Sure, your colleagues might be a little upset if you took a strong position against them on something important to the platform; you're a party member after all, and expected to show your support on key issues. But otherwise you're being offered a free pass, an opportunity to show the world that you can be a statesman. You'll never have another such opportunity. Certainly, you'll never get to do it again with a clean slate and carrying no political baggage." She shook her head slightly. "We groomed you for office, Thomas. I'll even admit we spoon-fed you a pre-prepared list of positions to take. That's not so bad; lots of first time politicians start out like that. But this…" She shook her head. "This is *yours*, Thomas. It'd be criminal of me to try and take it away."

So I tore up my speech and started all over again, this time pouring my heart out. Father was still making suggestions as a Parliamentary page almost as old as I was knocked on my office door. "Sir," she said, gulping in excitement, "It's time."

"Gut," Father grunted, handing me back my speech. It was covered with little notes in his neat, meticulous handwriting; I'd have perhaps ten minutes in the anteroom to study the proposed revisions. Then he turned to me and adjusted my tie. "Your speech is excellent," he assured me. "Far better than your first effort, though at the time I thought even it was plenty good enough."

"Thank you," I mumbled, as Father struggled a bit with the knot. It wasn't easy for a man to work on another's tie, Manuel had told me once, until he'd grown accustomed to doing so. "Go," he said finally, slapping me on the shoulder. "Make me proud, as you always do."

Chapter Seventy-Six

"Ladies and Gentlemen of Parliament," I began, as I stood alone behind the Speaker's podium and faced the most powerful individuals in the galaxy. The words were as traditional as the freshman speech itself; the first paragraph, at least, I hadn't had to sweat bullets over. "Allow me to introduce myself. My name is Thomas Longo, and I come to you by the grace of and with the support of the people of the Second North American Parliamentary District." It was traditional at this point for a freshman to extol the virtues of his or her region-- the opportunities it offered for tourism, for example, or its business-friendly atmosphere. Sometimes new Parliamentarians even congratulated successful sports teams. But I'd decided that none of that sort of thing was appropriate in wartime. There were few tourists these days due to all the travel restrictions, and business was booming everywhere so long as one was willing to trade in weaponry. Besides, if there was one thing I'd learned from selling so many war bonds it was that short, direct speeches struck home hardest.

"I am by a few days the most youthful person ever elected to this august body. Certainly, it's true that I'm very young." Carefully I paused to smile. "As a young man, I share many of the traits commonly attributed to youth throughout history. I laugh easily, for example. I think that's one of the very best things about being young. I also enjoy things that go fast, such as racing skimmers. I spend too much time, perhaps, playing video games. And I'll admit something here that I never revealed on the campaign trail-- I absolutely hate doing homework."

A wave of laughter rolled across the Assembly Room, admittedly emanating mostly from my own Party's side of the aisle. "It's true," I acknowledged, "that we young people are in some ways shallow. By the very nature of things we haven't yet had time to gain the kind of experience that brings great events into perspective. It is also true that we can be impetuous and emotional. We're still somewhat subject to the great storms of adolescence, and our brains are still undergoing their final stages of development. Yet despite all of this, our forefathers saw fit to allow persons as youthful as myself to stand for Parliament, to serve in the highest offices of the land. During the campaign, as I flew from town to town between speeches, I often asked myself how and why this could be. Eventually, I came up with an answer.

"For all of our shortcomings," I continued, letting my smile fade away, "we young people have unique virtues as well. Physically our strength and endurance is unmatchable—this is why we send our young to war. Our minds tend to be far more open and flexible than those of older people; we haven't yet lived long enough for our beliefs and prejudices to ossify into something immutable and unchangeable. We're able to bend where many of our elders would break."

I looked around the chamber, meeting as many eyes as I could. "Most of all, however, we young people haven't yet forgotten how to dream. We're natural idealists, as yet free of the cynicism and naked drive-to-power that seem to be the most important factors in so many politicians' lives. Sure, we want to win. But even more, we still want what's *right*. Just like, I think, the average guy on the street wants what's right."

The Assembly Room was dead-silent, now. A distinct chill was filling the air; I plowed on regardless. "It's been my lot to go more places and see more things in my short life than most people experience in all their decades. I've witnessed a planet's fall to hostile invaders, seen several cities vaporized, and been in close proximity to more deaths than I ever want to know. I've done my share of the killing, too; my hands are no cleaner in some regards than those of the meanest Dracan. But perhaps in part because I'm young, I can solemnly assure you that I've hated every minute of this war with all the passion my soul can muster. There are those who claim that there's glory to be found in battle, that war can be an exciting, positive experience. I would very much like to take such a person by the hand and lead them across the battlefields I've known, where countless people young and old have given their best and then died both anonymously and miserably, unknown heroes all. No oath sworn to some abstract political entity motivated these heroes to give their all; it had to come from inside, had to be part of them from the moment they were born. And, no battle fought has ever taken place without consuming the lives of far too many of these remarkable men and women.

"This is not to say that I'm against the current war; far from it! I'm one of only a tiny handful of individuals present here today who've experienced the horrors of Dracan occupation firsthand. The Emperor calls himself a liberator, but if the behavior of his minions on Churilla genuinely reflect his definition of human freedom and dignity, then I'd rather be dead than 'liberated'. It's a sad fact, perhaps the saddest fact in the entire spectrum of the human experience, that from time to time we're compelled to fight wars in order to remain free. We're forced to impose our own concepts of right and decency on those who would not only choose to live another way, but would instead force *their* way of life upon us against *our* will. Indeed, human history to date seems largely to be a catalog of such wars, one after another after another, cold names and dates in black and white. To most people, these names and dates are all that these wars shall ever be, and perhaps that's for the best. But when I read of them, after seeing what I've seen and having been the places that I've been, a different picture emerges. What I picture are rotting corpses by the million, the dead, decaying bodies of uncounted men and women who were mostly still young and healthy, who laughed easily, and were still chock-full of hopes and dreams when their lives were stolen away from them."

I looked around the room again; it was still as silent as the grave. "We can do better than this," I assured the men and women of Parliament, and beyond them whatever tiny percentage of the human race might be curious enough to turn off their sitcoms for a few minutes and tune me in. "We *must* do better, this time around. Every year our weapons grow sharper and our arms longer; as serious as the damage to Earth and Drakkus is to date, it could've been and still may yet be far worse. Next time, who knows? Perhaps the worst shall come to pass and entire planets will be rendered uninhabitable. Are we so rich in terraformable worlds that we can afford to throw a dozen or so away every few decades? Are human lives so cheap that a few billion of them lost now and again in some petty squabble or another are of no real import?"

I grasped the sides of the podium and leaned forward, no longer needing my notes. "A friend of mine recently observed that the human race is trapped. We're smart enough to figure out how to do almost anything we might wish to, except for one crucial missing item. That one vital omission is how we might live peacefully together, in harmony. We've been working at it for millennia now, admittedly harder at some times than at others. During these same millennia we've progressed technologically all the way from ram-equipped biremes to fusion-weapon-capable superfighters. Yet judging by recent events, we've made no discernable progress at all on the art of getting along with each other."

I looked around the room again, still gripping the podium. "It's time for that to change, my fellow Parliamentarians," I said, challenging each and every one of them with my eyes. "It's time for us to take a real look at ourselves and confront whatever it is in our makeup that's both so intractable and so bloodthirsty that we've never been able to overcome it in any meaningful way. It's time for us to take charge of our most essential selves and destinies and make whatever improvements are necessary to ensure our future survival. Yes, we must pursue this current war to complete victory; the fight was not of our making, and anything less than total triumph leaves a warmongering tyrant seated on a throne he doesn't deserve. Drakkus and all the other Imperial worlds must be freed. Yet we must also fight for something more this time. We must as victors ensure that the youth of tomorrow, the youth of *all* our tomorrows, are never forced to die as heroes again. No victory won will be meaningful if all that's accomplished is a little resting time before the *next* war, and no victory won can be called complete if it doesn't lead to a fundamental change in human nature itself. If all of our efforts, if the deaths of so many heroes leads only to yet another war, another dark stain on the pages of history in an endless series of dark stains, then we shall have failed by any reasonable measure and the ultimate result must inevitably someday be the darkness of the grave for us all."

I met the eyes of my audience one last time. "There are those who call me a hero. Whenever someone does so to my face I try explain to them that I've seen real heroes in action, and that I don't halfway measure up. There's no one who respects our heroes more than I do-- I even respect the Dracan heroes, who from their own point of view are merely defending their own twisted version of truth and justice. But when will enough be enough? How many thousands of millions of our own young and how many of our biggest cities are we going to kill off before we grow serious about making real changes in ourselves and how we think about things? What exactly would it take for us to improve ourselves, anyway? Can't we at least consider the possibility that, just maybe, with today's technology and resources we really could transform ourselves into a better and more decent species? If we were for once to seriously make the attempt, I mean. "

Then I looked down at my notes and began stacking them, signaling my audience that I was nearly finished. "Maybe I dream too much," I explained, shrugging slightly. "Maybe I really *am* too young and too idealistic to deserve a place in this body. Maybe I'm immature and should stick to my studies for a few more years. In another world, under other circumstances, that's almost certainly what would've happened. I'd have grown up a very ordinary young man indeed; certainly not an eighteen-year-old Parliamentarian and already a veteran of many battles. But we live in *this* world, not the one we might wish to live in. And in *this* world my childhood has ended under very unlikely circumstances indeed, circumstances so peculiar that I ended up standing behind this particular podium on this particular day, instead of in some anonymous classroom flirting with a pretty girl and not paying proper attention to my professor." I picked up my speech and made the Esteppan bow that, I'd been told, my constituents so loved. "In *this* world, it happened that I'm here addressing you today as an elected member of this government, not safely locked away with all the other young dreamers. And so you in turn are forced, for these few moments at least, to listen to a young man's idealistic ravings instead of bickering over whose district the next new munitions factory will be located in." I smiled my coldest smile, the one that Colonel Rotte had taught me. "Be very careful, my fellow Parliamentarians. Idealism can be contagious. For that matter, so can wanting to do the right thing. Make sure you wash your hands as you leave the Assembly Room today! If you don't, you just might become infected. And then, if such a thing were to happen to enough of you, oh my!

"Who knows what disasters might befall the art of government as we know it today?"

Chapter Seventy-Seven

I was already changing into my navy uniform when another page came knocking. Fortunately Mrs. Hunter was in the outer office to deal with him. "Thomas," she called though my door. "Don't get undressed yet. The PM's asked you to come see him in his office."

I sighed and closed my eyes; Manuel had just begun helping me take my trousers off. He looked up at me inquiringly, and I shrugged. "I don't have time," I explained, raising my voice so that I could be heard through the expensive, heavy door. "I'm supposed to report aboard *June* by six. You know that."

There was a long pause. "Thomas," my chief political aide eventually replied. "Who's the commander-in-chief of the navy?"

"The PM," I replied, sighing. All I wanted was out of Rome, really. More than I'd ever wanted anything in my life. It was a nice enough town, I supposed. But these days it was full of politicians. Therefore I hated the place.

"Then it makes sense," Mrs. Hunter continued sweetly, "that the PM should have first call on your time." There was another long pause. "I'll ring up the Navy Department and find someone there to talk to. Or, better yet, I'll have one of the PM's aides do it. All right?"

I gulped. In some ways, as an MP I outranked most of my superior officers. Before the election, Captain Bard had taken me aside to explain how much said superior officers were going to resent that. "It's hard on them, Thomas," she explained. "You've always been a very special case; I doubt you've any idea how much the navy's been forced to go out of its way in order to accommodate you and the other superfighter pilots. You've been granted access and input far in excess of your rank, because you're the only expert we've got. But once you're a Parliamentarian, too…" She shook her head. "Choose your fights carefully. You'll need to stand your ground on some things, I'm sure. In everything else, however, you'll have to be a model subordinate officer if you're going to win and hold the respect of others. Many will be insanely jealous."

"I… Uh…" I replied intelligently as Manuel waited for me to make up my mind. Being late reporting aboard my ship wasn't the best possible way to get off on the right foot with a new CO, now was it? Especially one that more likely than not was wary of me to begin with. But there really wasn't any choice that I could see. "All right then," I capitulated. "Have our office staff call *June* direct, and explain to the captain's secretary why I'll be late. For heaven's sake, don't use the PM's people. No matter what, don't go *there*."

"Aye, aye, sir," Mrs. Hunter replied; we were close enough friends by now that I understood her mock-naval response to be an attempt at humor.

Then I looked down at Manuel. "Dress whites," I directed. "Just like we planned. If he's my ultimate commanding officer, then by golly a uniform ought to be plenty good enough for him."

The PM's eyebrows rose slightly when I stepped through his door dressed in dazzling white, but he said nothing about it. Nor did the gaggle of other politicians already present in the room. I only recognized two of them, the Secretaries of the Army and Navy. Plus Alicia; I didn't see her at first, because she was kind of short, and standing in the back. "I'm sorry it took me so long to get here, sir," I apologized to my host as he rose to shake my hand. "You caught me changing clothes."

"Of course," the head of my party replied. His smile widened. "That was *some* speech, Thomas. Congratulations!"

"Hear, hear!" echoed an elderly man I didn't know. He was wearing the most expensive-looking suit I'd ever seen, and holding a gold-handled cane.

"Everyone's talking about it," the Secretary of the Army added. "Everyone!"

I shrugged. "It's just how I feel about things, is all. No big deal."

"Heh!" the PM replied. He reached down and pressed a button underneath his desk, and the far end of his office wall turned into a big holovision tank.

"…most heartfelt and sincere speech I've ever seen, John," a female newscaster was saying. Then the PM hit the button again and again.

"…truly remarkable beginning…"

"…worthy of our greatest hero…"

…threw down the gauntlet today during his freshman speech to a crowded Assembly Chamber today…"

"You see, Thomas," the PM continued as he killed the screen. "I wasn't exaggerating. Everyone really *is* taking about it."

I blinked, rather caught off guard. Why hadn't Mrs. Hunter warned me? Though, she *had* looked at me kind of funny as I'd left my office… "Well," I said slowly. "It's the only speech I'll ever give here. So, I guess I'm glad that people liked it."

The Navy Minister coughed, and looked at the PM.

"Ye-es," the PM answered, stretching out the word as was his habit when under stress. "There are those in the Party who think you could serve best by staying right here, son. And supporting the war from the Floor."

"You've fought so much already," the Navy Minister added. "No one would think the less of you. There isn't another man alive who's taken such risks."

"It's not right that you should face combat again," the army's political representative added. He wasn't a member of my Party, I knew. But I suspected it was only a matter of time. Already he was one of the PM's closest and most trusted confidantes. He looked over at his navy counterpart. "If he were mine, I'd simply not allow it. This man is a treasure. He's our future. We can't afford to lose him."

My mouth dropped open. "B-b-but," I stuttered. "I mean—"

"You see what I'm up against, Thomas," my supreme commander interrupted, not quite meeting my eyes. "In all honesty, I can't say that they're entirely wrong."

My jaw worked but no words would come out. I looked at Alicia, who so far had said nothing. Her face might've been made of stone, even. Clearly she wanted me to work this out on my own. Finally I came up with the proper reply. "There's a terrible shortage of pilots," I explained. "You know that! Especially combat-experienced ones. I have a whole squadron to train with just Jimmy to help me. Plus I need to work with the Butcher Birds. I can't do all that and hang around Rome too!"

"We'd like to appoint you to the War Cabinet," the elderly man said, after a short silence. "I'll admit up front that you'd be filling a relatively junior post, one without much actual power. Your elevation would largely be for morale-building reasons, and in all honesty for political purposes as well. But…" He leaned forward. "'Not much' power is *not* the same thing as 'no' power. I've heard tales about how you handled the issues at your father's factory, young man, and I at least am not fool enough to believe that you'd accept a purely figurehead job. Nor am I fool enough to offer you one; you need to be nurtured, son, to be given jobs of steadily increasing importance until you're capable of doing anything." His eyebrows rose. "I mean, I assume you're not such a young idiot as to think you can begin with a senior job?"

My mouth opened and closed again. "I… I…" Then I looked away and forced my recalcitrant body back under control. "I don't want any job at all, sir. Except to fly with my squadron."

"That speaks well for you, son," the navy man answered, looking deep into my eyes. "It speaks very well for you indeed. No one's ever called you a coward. But I'd like you to consider something. You said a lot of brave and powerful things at that podium today, things that I believe have needed to be said for a very long time. It's one thing to talk big, son. It's another entirely, however, to make good on such strong words." His eyes narrowed. "You're brave son. Of that there's no doubt. But, are you brave enough to stay here and fight for what you believe in? Brave enough to climb down into the sewer and exterminate rats?"

I didn't know what to say at first, until I caught Alicia's eye again. She was still sitting as silent as the sphinx; my guess was she'd promised the PM that she'd not interfere in my decision. "Look," I said finally. "I don't *want* to be a politician. It's not how I plan to spend my life. Nothing personal, but I *hate* this stuff."

"How can you possibly hate it when you're so bloody *good* at it?" the old man asked, gripping his cane and shifting it so that he could rest his chin on the handle. "Don't ask me to check my common sense at the door, son. No one succeeds in a field they truly hate."

"I *do* hate politics," I assured him." Just like I hate war." I pointed at my medals. "But so far I seem to be doing fairly well at *that,* too." There was a snort of laughter in the back of the room, but I ignored it and turned back to the PM. "Seriously, sir... I'm greatly honored by your offer. But I cannot and will not accept it. No one can replace me aboard *June*." I looked at Alicia next, meeting her eyes as well. "I mean... Imagine what it'd be like if I *did* stay here and joined the Cabinet, and then a bunch of kids got killed in battle. It'd be my fault! And yours too, for not putting them under the most skilled leader available, and not giving them the best training possible. We might even lose a battle that we don't need to!"

There was a long, long silence. Then the PM sighed and looked at Alicia. "You told me so," he admitted.

The rabbit-woman smiled. "I did. Sir."

"Indeed," he agreed, as the old man with the cane scowled and looked away. "But..." My commander-in-chief turned back to me. "Thomas, I'll grant that we can't take you away from your squadrons just yet. I grant it reluctantly, mind you. Your arguments, however, are unassailable." He sighed. "Still... My good friends here are correct when they say that you've become an irreplaceable resource on this end of things as well." He shook his head. "I've never before witnessed the beginnings of such a promising career, son. Never! Nor, I daresay, have many others. Not once in a thousand years do events conspire to such a degree." He stood up, walked around from behind his desk, and placed his hand on my shoulder. "Someday this office shall be yours, son. I feel it in my heart and soul. Not only shall it be yours, but itll remain so for many, many years. Good years, for all of mankind."

"Hear, hear," the man in the back said again.

"You're the future, Thomas," the PM repeated. "You're *our* future. And because you're our future, I'm giving you an order that you're going to hate. It's a direct order, neither to be questioned nor disobeyed. Do you understand me?"

To that, there could be only one reply. "Yes, sir."

"Good," he continued. "Commander Thomas Anthony Longo, you are to fly no more combat missions and to take no more risks with your personal safety than are absolutely necessary to the training and development of your command. Only in the most dire of emergencies are you to face the enemy again." He smiled gently, trying to take the sting out of it. "You've done enough. Let someone else win a medal for once."

But I was having none of it. "Aye-aye, sir!" I responded formally, making the mockery of a salute that was the best my mannequin-body could manage. And then, seething with rage under my calm-seeming exterior, I marched out of the room without waiting to be dismissed.

Chapter Seventy-Eight

Direct orders from the Prime Minister were not things to be taken lightly, I discovered almost immediately. Captain Han greeted me in person when I reported aboard ship, even later than expected due to unforeseen traffic delays. She was warm and enthusiastic and as near as I could tell quite willing to give me my head and let me run my department pretty much as I saw fit. I couldn't ask for anything more from a captain. Except, of course, for the fact that the Prime Minister had already personally called her and informed her that I was no longer to be risked under almost any conceivable circumstances.

At first it didn't really make much difference in my day-to-day life. Since it'd been much too long since I'd flown, I spent a full day wringing out a brand new Mark I*. This one was painted soot-black and destined to be assigned to the Butcher Birds, but at least temporarily it was mine. Predictably, therefore, it was adorned with an Order of Blood red nose and more kill-emblems and mushroom-clouds than I liked to think about. Though I had to admit that the newest additions were pretty cool; a pair of X'ed-out mushroom clouds representing the two missile-kills I'd made over the West Coast. These at least I could feel unreservedly good about. Since Jimmy was still leading the Top Bananas through their primary flight training, I felt that I should work with the Esteppan squadron first. It was just as well that I had so much time with the new bird; Father and the rest had made subtle improvements in the interfaces. Either that, or this particular Mark I* was just an especially good match for my nerve-endings. I liked it very much, I decided, and for once pulled a few strings on my own behalf to make it mine permanently. The 'hopper felt more like a part of me than anything else I'd ever worn, including my trusty old mannequin-body. It was *me*, which should've been frightening but somehow was not.

Coronel arrived in-system the very next day, and by evening was floating in the Firth of Forth not far from *June*. I flew low over her, more out of curiosity than anything. The two vessels weren't quite sisters, though the family resemblance was clear. *June* was a bit smaller, and equipped with the older-style twin guns instead of the Esteppan vessel's triple mounts. Apparently *Coronel*'s crew was on the bounce; even though they couldn't have had much notice that I was coming the deck was packed with sailors when I made my pass, all of them waving and cheering. When I rocked my wings in acknowledgement and came around a second time, they cheered and waved harder than ever. It was kind of embarrassing, really. But, it was also good for morale. Or at least I hoped so.

That evening I met Major Sean Ferguson, the sixteen-year-old leader of the Butcher Birds. There weren't all that many people of Irish descent on Esteppe, but somehow they kept rising to positions of prominence all out of proportion to their numbers. The Ferguson family was almost as eminent as my own in Esteppan society, specializing in banking. As we sat down to what for any normal naval officers wouldve been a discussion over drinks, I pointed out that it was a little odd that we'd never met.

"But we have!" Sean responded. "I climbed the Stahlberg with you. That was when I decided to become a fighter pilot, no matter what. Some of the other guys climbed with you, too. None of us will ever forget."

The rest of our conversation would've been familiar to any combat pilot from any period of history; we talked training, training, training. "I think we've done pretty well," Sean explained, crossing his mannequin-legs in a clear display of confidence. "We had Hans and Wolfgang to help us, after all. That put us way ahead of the Bananas, though of course that's not their fault."

I noted the slightly condescending tone in his voice. "You think you're ready for combat? *Completely* ready for combat?"

Sean should've picked up on the warning in my tone, but he didn't. "Yes," he answered, nodding. "I think so."

"Hmm," I answered. In point of fact, the new Butcher Birds *had* enjoyed an advantage in having Hans and Wolfgang around to help train them. But Hans and Wolfgang weren't Colonel Rotte, not by half. In fact, the two surviving old-school Birds had less than a dozen kills between them. While Rotte had respected their courage, they'd been left behind to guard the ships at Drakkus for good reason. In any fighter force a handful of truly superior hunters of men rack up the vast majority of the kills. The rest, though they give their best, are mere also-rans. The difference only becomes clear once the actual fighting begins; there's no certain way to tell ahead of time who the successful ones will be. "Well," I replied slowly, looking deep into Sean's eyes. Was he a killer or an also-ran? "We'll have to put that to the test, I suppose."

Sean's eyes glittered. "I can't wait."

Easy meat, Rotte's voice whispered inside my head. *He's an overconfident fool. Immature, to boot.* "Tomorrow?" I asked, rising to my feet. "At dawn, over the Atlantic Exercise Area?"

"You and me?" he asked.

"That'll do nicely," I agreed. "For a beginning."

Sean's eyebrows rose. "For a beginning?"

"Keep the rest of the squadron on standby," I explained. "Before the day's done, I expect that I'll be working with you all."

Chapter Seventy-Nine

My meeting with Major Ferguson broke up earlier than planned. This was just as well, because the interview left me deeply unsettled on many levels. Just as soon as I'd seen my fellow fighter pilot to the exit-port I turned around and headed back to my cabin. There was a lot of work to be done, much of it stuff I should've taken care of long ago instead of frittering away my days making bad speeches in Parliament. Like, studying the Butcher Birds' personnel files.

Sure enough, the closer I looked the more fully my worst suspicions were borne out. Major Ferguson wasn't the only blue-blood in the squadron, not by half! The pilot roster read almost like an abbreviated version of Esteppe's equivalent of *Who's Who* magazine; in fact, when I laid them out side-by-side the degree of correlation was terrifying. Every single Butcher Bird was well-connected, well-financed, and well-known in society. Worst of all, their military ranks seemed to very closely reflect their social standing.

It was no coincidence, I was quite certain. Opportunities for military glory attract Esteppans as surely as moths are drawn to candles. Strings had obviously been pulled, and quite forcefully at that. This was to be expected, at least to some degree; I'd been around politics enough now to understand that much. Besides, I could hardly complain, having pulled a string or two for Jimmy myself during his selection process. But…

…I examined the Butcher Birds' files again, and shook my head in despair. Yes, I'd selected Jimmy for pilothood against the advice of the majority of the counselors; I'd admit that to anyone and my best friend was fully aware of the fact. My interference, however, had come relatively late in the selection process. By then he'd honestly beaten out thousands of other would-be fighter pilots, maybe even tens of thousands, by scoring at the top of the pack on a regimen of tests that I doubted I could ever have passed myself. I'd picked him from among the best of the best, in other words. Not from the population at random. So far I felt that the results clearly justified my decision. But the new Birds, however, hadn't even tested out particularly well. While as a group they were academically ahead of their peers, it wasn't by all that much. No more than could be explained, certainly, by the fact that most of them had enjoyed, like me, the advantage of personal tutors. They were also a shade more mature and stable than the general population, but again not remarkably so and certainly no more than could be explained by their inborn advantages in life.

I sighed and paged listlessly through the files. Technically my own family was entitled to use the preface "Von" before our surname. We didn't do so, however, because we felt that it sounded ridiculous; 'Longo', after all, was of Italian derivation. Yet there was no shortage of "Von"'s in the Butcher Bird's roster; eight of them, in fact, out of a dozen. Plus, an actual Serene Highness. What was I going to do with *him*, I wondered? How did one bow when one was a Skybolt? For all its other shortcomings, Earth had done a much better job than Esteppe at pilot selection. Delana's parents, for example, had been middle-class. And, as everyone who'd ever flown with her knew, she'd easily been the best of us all. Somehow, I doubted that I'd find her like among the Birds. Or, for that matter another Colonel Rotte; his father, I suddenly recalled, had been a minor government functionary. Apparently even the Autarch had been less class-conscious than modern-day Esteppans.

I shook my head in frustration, then dashed off a letter to Father explaining the situation. He hadn't been President when things had gone wrong, and with any luck he wouldn't allow it to happen again. In the meantime, though…

I sighed again, then turned off the monitor and called Manuel to help me dress for bed. In the meantime I'd just have to do the best I could with what I had, even if it meant that a lot of people might die who really shouldn't have. Just like I'd been doing for what seemed like forever, now.

Ever since this verdammt war had started.

Chapter Eighty

By eleven o'clock the next morning I knew that my work was cut out for me. Not only had I shot down Major Ferguson nine times in virtual combat, four times one-on-one and the other five while he was leading all or part of his squadron, I'd also watched him throw one hissy fit after another at the "incompetence" of his own men. It was one of the most unprofessional displays I'd ever seen, more suited to a spoiled-brat child than a combat leader. But of course Sean *was* a child, and apparently a spoiled brat to boot. This was something that was easy to forget when one was talking to a Skybolt or an immaculately-uniformed mannequin-body instead of the boy Sean truly was. I gritted my teeth and seethed, but said nothing. Changes would have to be made, yes. But they could at least wait until I'd talked to a few counselors.

Overall the Birds performed wretchedly. They were hesitant and defensive in simulated combat, which was the surest way to incur losses that I knew of. Most of their training seemed to be centered around the formation of defensive circles where they would supposedly be safe from attack. This tactic was apparently the brainchild of Hans and Wolfgang, the last-survivors of the original Birds. Colonel Rotte would've laughed the whole idea out of existence, and my guess was that once upon a time he probably had done exactly that. Circling endlessly about in enemy skies accomplished nothing whatsoever that I could see. It didn't destroy targets, it didn't kill enemy fighters, and it didn't achieve objectives. Instead it merely offered the enemy time to react. This was the antithesis of the unremitting bloodyminded aggressiveness that won battles and by extension won wars as well. But now, with no Rotte to overrule them Hans and Wolfgang were free to preach the gospel of air superiority as *they* saw it, unedited and unmodified.

The results were disastrous. When I assigned the Birds to defend a fixed point on the surface of the sea they simply formed their tail-chasing circle directly above it, with each 'bolt covering the one immediately ahead. In theory, the formation was unassailable. In practice, however, the results were pathetic. At first I amused myself by slashing in at high speed, wiping out the target before the Birds could react, and then escaping unhurt. Then when that grew boring I made things a little harder for myself by seeing how many Birds I could splash and still make a clean attack and getaway. By then, the Birds were terrified of me, and as soon as the first soot-black 'bolt was "killed", the rest scattered in chaos and confusion.

"Your pilots have good technical flying skills," I explained to Sean as we flew side-by-side back to *Coronel*. I'd dismissed the rest of the squadron for the afternoon, so as to give them a chance to think over what they'd seen. Meanwhile I was trying to dwell upon the positive with their leader. "Their formation work was excellent, for example. No one did anything overtly dangerous."

"So, we didn't make any really basic mistakes," Sean muttered. He sounded angry more than anything else. "We just our asses shot off over and over again by a single enemy, was all."

I virtual-scowled to myself. All day long I'd listened to Sean berate his men and never accept a smidgen of blame himself. Even when I'd beaten him one-on-one, he'd never congratulated me or asked me how I'd won so that he could learn from the experience. I was just about to point out that it wasn't his fault that his squadron's core battle-doctrine was flawed, that in the greater scope of things this was one of the smaller of the many wartime screw-ups I'd borne witness to, when he finally went over the top.

"It isn't fair!" Sean exclaimed. "You've got a better 'hopper, because your father builds the things! That's why you beat us! You cheated!"

That was the final straw. It was my job to develop fighter pilots, not babysit spoiled brats. Men and women were dying every single day in droves, and there just wasn't enough time to wait for Sean to grow up. What had to be done would be neither pretty nor enjoyable, but utterly necessary nonetheless. "Major!' I snapped.

"Yes, sir!" he answered.

"Return to base," I continued, my voice remaining harsh and distant. "Report to your counselor as soon as you're dismounted, and then accompany him to my cabin aboard *The Glorious First of June*. See me there."

There was a long, long silence. "You're going to remove me from command, aren't you?" he asked.

No, I didn't answer aloud. *I'm going to kick you out of the program entirely*. "Report as ordered," I said instead.

"You evil cheating bastard," Sean answered. "You're afraid I'll steal some of the glory, aren't you?"

"There isn't any such thing as glory in combat, Sean," I answered. "And those who seek it there are fools. Though I expect that's not something you're able to grasp quite yet." Then I sighed aloud. "Report to my cabin just as soon as you're dismounted. We'll discuss matters further at that time."

Chapter Eighty-One

Sean wasn't just immature; he was potentially dangerous, as well. I remained in the air until he was firmly planted on *Cornel*'s weather deck, for fear that in his childish anger he might attempt something truly stupid. I'm still not sure precisely what I'd have done if, say, he'd attempted to ram either his own ship or *June*, but the fact that I feared such irrational behavior from him at all spoke volumes about his unfitness for Skybolts. When he and his counselor finally arrived in my cabin—after an unforgivably long delay, though that hardly mattered any longer—Sean was a lot quieter, almost subdued. He wouldn't meet my eyes at all.

"Sir," Dr. Weiss greeted me at my desk, coming to attention and saluting for both himself and his charge. The doctor was Sean's counselor and had been his tutor for many years. Though he had no navy background, as near as I could tell he was doing his level best to emulate Father Murton. His file was full of positive remarks from those who'd seen him in action. Predictably, the elderly man looked terrible. He had to know what was about to happen. My guess, in fact, was that he'd been expecting it all along.

I made things as easy as I could on both of them. Though I did so more for the benefit of Dr. Weiss than Sean, who somehow I couldn't force myself to like. "You're out of the program," I said, simply and firmly. "It's not your fault, really. Sean should never have been selected to come this far. Not one in five thousand teenagers has what it takes to face the enemy in a Skybolt." I met Weiss's eyes. "Sean has neither the maturity nor the willingness to learn that are required of a navy pilot."

Sean's tutor bowed his head, and I read agreement in his face. "Yes, sir."

"I'm going to do my best," I continued, "to ensure that all records of this incident remain sealed in perpetuity. Sean is still sixteen, after all, and he's shown incredible bravery just in undergoing the brain-coring procedure and expressing a willingness to serve in such a dangerous role at such a young age." I turned to face the major. "If you want to serve, Sean, it still may be possible for you to work as a test pilot. Though you're probably going to have a much harder time convincing the navy here on Earth to trust you than you did on Esteppe, where your father's name counts for so much. Test-piloting is a vital, sometimes even dangerous job that *someone* has to perform. And who knows? Spend a little time doing that and perhaps the navy will reconsider you as a combat pilot. I certainly have no doubt regarding your technical abilities; it's your general level of maturity that I take issue with. As a rule, that's a problem that the mere passage of time cures."

A mannequin body couldn't weep, of course. But the human brain behind it could, and I knew how to read the signs. "Sir..." Sean whispered. "I'll do anything. Bust me back to lieutenant; I don't care. Just let me fly combat. I... I got mad today and went too far. I admit it! It's just... I wanted to beat you *so* badly."

I shook my head. Someday every single member of the Birds squadron was going to go out on a mission with four nuclear torpedoes tucked beneath their stub-wings. Could Sean be trusted with nukes? Something deep inside of me said no. Or at least, not yet. So I gently shook my head. "No, Sean. Not for the time being, at least." Then I faced Dr. Weiss, who seemed to be examining me very closely indeed. "Take care of him," I urged. "He's not a bad kid, I'm sure. Just not one of the very special ones we need. Dismissed."

Weiss nodded, then clicked his heels together in the Esteppan way. "Aye-aye, sir," he acknowledged. Then they both about-faced to leave; even Sean, in his android body, did a pretty good job at it, far more smartly than either Jimmy or I could manage. Perhaps martial movements came naturally to Esteppans? Then, with his back turned to me, Dr. Weiss spoke again. "All the time," he said, "While we were training they told us 'Father Murton this' and 'Father Murton that'. They even showed us films of him in action, taking care of you and helping you along." He shook his head. "What a great man he must once have been. It's been a privilege to meet you as well, Your Excellency." Then and only then, the pair marched out.

Yes. I definitely felt sorry for Doctor Weiss.

Chapter Eighty-Two

It was amazing, really, how much of a stir one little personnel move could cause; a few weeks after I cashiered Sean, once enough time had passed for the news to travel all the way to Esteppe and back, a huge pile of papers appeared on my overworked secretary's desk, most of them covered with fancy Esteppan official seals. "Sir?" he asked me during one of our hurried daily meetings. "What should I do with these? At first I thought they were from your father. But…"

I looked through them and shook my head. Sean's father, a Baron with his own family seal, had apparently been devastated by the news. He'd written me maybe a dozen letters, none of which I had time to read. Not only that, but he also filed an official appeal of my decision. This was especially impressive since, in order to do so, he'd first had to create an appeals process. Apparently the Baron Ferguson knew how to make things happen quickly when he chose to. I sighed and instructed my assistant to package them all up as neatly as he could and forward them to Admiral Vlasilov, with an apology from me on top. "Explain that I don't have the time or knowledge to deal with this sort of thing on my own. The admiral will understand. Though," I predicted, "I bet *his* people won't know what to do with them either."

Father was clearly a little vexed with me over the matter, though his letter carefully didn't say so. He trusted my judgment entirely, it explained, and understood that I had to do what I had to do as a serving navy man. He was proud, he said, that I'd made a difficult decision. And he'd back me up all the way. Still, the next five pages were an explanation of just how badly the cashiering of Major Ferguson had damaged his political situation; apparently the Baron was spitting nickels at what he saw as a personal betrayal after supporting Father unreservedly in the elections and was now doing everything he could to undermine the Longo administration. Which, it seemed, was plenty. "Please, Thomas," the letter should've concluded, but didn't. "I know you have a tough job to do. But can you perhaps avoid pissing off any more of my best friends along the way?"

Luckily that didn't prove necessary. With the passing of the major a fresh breeze seemed to blow through the Butcher Birds. They didn't suddenly become any more competent as fighter pilots. But they *did* begin to ask questions about why it was that I kept kicking their butts in the air, and intelligent ones at that. They were scared stiff of me, yes. And in a way perhaps that was a good thing. It was an even better thing, however, that they respected me and maybe even wanted to be like me. It made me feel as if I were an old man, like maybe even thirty or so. The main thing, however, was that they began to *learn*.

When I first showed up during off-duty hours in *Coronel*'s gunroom, everyone made a big stir and fuss. Even though this was supposed to be no-military-discipline-zone for Skybolt pilots, people scrambled to their feet and saluted. Even the counselors, who should've known better than to violate the rules of their own sanctuary, hit some of the most ridiculous-looking braces I'd ever seen. One of them even did so with a steaming-hot pepperoni pizza in his hands.

"Hey, people!" I told everyone, shaking my head and gesturing everyone to sit back down. "I'm just one of the kids here, come over to play. That's okay, isn't it?"

Actually I was now over eighteen, and when someone finally got around to writing official regulations covering this sort of thing, which probably wouldn't happen until at least a decade after the Dracans were finally beaten, the administrative officers would undoubtedly determine that as a legal adult I should no longer have romping-rights in the gunroom. It was probably inevitable-- certainly it was going to be a terrible mistake when it happened. Because, as always, the best, most meaningful training sessions I ever delivered came from behind a video-game joystick.

"Aww!" I complained while playing the officially sanctioned *Skybolts and Polecats* training game, designed especially for us young pilots. The thing had cost the navy millions of credits, all of them wasted in my book. What an awful, boring waste of time! "This thing sucks! Let's play *Invasion: Esteppe!*"

"Yay!" His Serene Highness cried out, falling over backwards onto the floor in glee and tumbling his gyros along the way; *Esteppe* was clearly one of his favorites too. Soon as many as four of us at a time were forming up in simplified Polecats, trying to shoot down Stormcrows. "You see," I began. "The most important thing is to be on the offensive, every second of the game. Never, *ever* give your enemy time to think..."

Between the video games in the evening and flying all day every day with one young Butcher Bird after another, soon I was putting in sixteen-hour days again. It should've been worse than being in Parliament, but somehow it wasn't. I *liked* working with the Birds, I discovered, every bit as much as I'd once enjoyed training the Top Bananas. Slowly but surely I labored to bring out the best in each of my pilots. His Serene Highness Prince Ludwig proved to be a gifted marksman, once he no longer had Sean blaming him for all the squadron's failings. The Duchess of Markheim was very nearly as good at evading enemy fire as Delana had been; she was a dancer, too, and I filed a brief with the navy encouraging them to give preference to skilled dancers of both genders during the pilot-screening process. Plain old untitled Ernst Haeckel was an outstanding dogfighter; he was the first of the Birds to shoot me down, and I did my best not to let the gleeful cheers of his fellow Esteppans make me feel bad when it happened. (Of course, it helped that I'd swung my evasive turn out a little wide on purpose, a fact that I planned on never sharing with anyone so long as I lived.)

In the end the eleven surviving Birds could be said to have become a fairly decent fighter squadron, after a few weeks of intensive effort. Where once they'd been cocky, now they were quietly confident. Where once they'd been hesitant, now they were sure and swift. Where once they'd been defensive-minded, now they were ready to rip the throat out of the first Dracan they saw. There was only one problem. For all their progress, nothing resembling a squadron commander had emerged from among the new pilots. Sure, I had a couple of good flight leaders; rather to my surprise the Prince turned out to be one of them. Still, there wasn't a single boy or girl among them who was even halfway ready for the top job. The Butcher Birds at this point in their development were wholly dependent upon me as their squadron commander in almost every sense of the word. I was their tactician, their support system, their operational brain. Without me, they were still little better than babes in the woods. And I'd been prohibited from flying combat.

Chapter Eighty-Three

"They're ready," I replied to Admiral Vlasilov's question in the peace and quiet of his cabin. He'd summoned me there after a long day of training during which Ernst had shot me down again, this time without any help, and the Prince's flight had over and over again driven me away from the target he'd been assigned to defend. "Not for high intensity operations, I mean. But they're ready to be blooded."

"Da," the admiral agreed. He was sitting alongside me, admiring the endless rows of mooring lights which represented the anchored Fleet from his stern cabin window. This was his way, I'd come to understand, of indicating that he wanted to talk stuff over in detail and find out what I *really* thought about things. On more formal occasions he remained behind his desk. "If everything works out as planned, there should be an opportunity to offer them some easy kills before they come up against serious opposition." He poured some more tea from his bubbling samovar, then sipped at it in silence for a few moments. Vlasilov was grayer than he'd once been, in both hair and skin tone. His wrinkles were deeper as well. Though he still seemed to be filled with a sort of crackling energy, the effect wasn't nearly so intense as it'd once been. He'd never fully recovered from his injuries yet here he was working himself to death again, commanding the navy's most powerful striking force and, therefore, bearing the fleet's largest burden. For the first time, I appreciated what a truly great man he was.

"And the Bananas?" he asked, after properly savoring his tea.

I looked away. "They're better than the Birds," I admitted. "Better selected, better trained, better almost everything." I sighed. "Admiral, I gave it my best. Honestly I did. But-"

"Bah!" Vlasilov interrupted, holding up his hand to cut me off. "I've read the reports, Thomas. You've done fine work, better than I hoped for. It's not your fault that the Esteppans sent you nothing but noblemen. Equally it's not your fault that we've stretched you too thin. You can only accomplish so much."

"They're not that bad," I replied, feeling vaguely obliged to defend the men under my command. Or, at least sort of under my command. "One thing I think we've learned from this mess is that we may be making the selection process too strict. The Birds will make a fine squadron, in time. Probably just as fine as the Bananas. It'll take them a little longer, is all. In fact, if they hadn't been mistrained to start with, then who knows? They might have come along just as quickly as the A-team."

"Heh!" Vlasilov replied, his expression as inscrutable as always. "I don't think that it'll matter much how we select our future pilots. Or not to me, at least. These two squadrons, they're all that we'll have time to field before the war is over. Let the young people worry about what comes after. For me and for my purposes, there is only the present."

I nodded. While I'd been flying in circles over the North Atlantic, the army and navy had been busily liberating planets in areas that the Dracans weren't willing to risk their fleet to hold. There hadn't been any big ship-to-ship actions, but nine worlds were no longer under the Dracan yoke. "All that's left is Churilla and then Drakkus herself," I answered. "The Dracan fleet will contest one or the other in an all-or-nothing battle. Which battlefield they choose is up to them. Not us."

The admiral's eyebrows rose. "My staff spent most of the morning trying to convince the Prime Minister that the Dracans will make their stand at one of those places. He seems to fear that they'll hit one of our invasion fleets instead."

I shook my head. "That wouldn't make any sense. By now we're far more powerful than the Dracans in terms of landing forces. Losing a few troopships would be a terrible tragedy, yes. But we're still not that far ahead of them in fleet strength. If they gut our navy, they can still win the war. Or at least sue for terms instead of surrendering unconditionally. The only places they can hope to win a battle are at Churilla, where they can use their high-speed Jumping tech to best advantage among all those Nikitas, or else at Drakkus herself, where their supply lines are shortest and ours are at their longest and most vulnerable. I mean, what are they going to do? Attack Earth again, where all the advantages are on *our* side? Or oppose the invasion of a non-critical planet, where they have everything to lose and nothing to gain? I think not."

Slowly, Vlasilov smiled. "You're growing up fast, Thomas."

I shrugged. "Maybe. Maybe not. If so I wish it were faster. Because I have a problem that I simply can't solve on my own."

Instantly the admiral's smile vanished. "Is there anything I can do?"

"Perhaps," I answered slowly. "I guess you know that I've been barred from flying combat."

"I do," he acknowledged, not commenting further.

"Well…" I continued. "You know, I just told you that the Birds are ready for combat. But really, they're only ready if I'm flying with them."

Vlasilov's eyes slowly closed. He was a navy man, so I didn't have to explain further. "I see."

"Jimmy's pretty much taken over as squadron commander of the Bananas,"

I continued. "I hardly know any of them, even. And he's done a great job, too! I mean, I just told you that they're better than the Birds. But if you take Jimmy out of the equation…" I sighed. "They're rookies, sir. All of them, in both squadrons. If you were to send the Bananas into combat without Jimmy, they'd be toast. Just like the Birds would be without me. I've become their commander. They *need* me."

The old man sipped at his tea again, then stood up and strode wearily to his desk. He kept a sweater there for when he grew cold. Which was far too often these days. It was an incongruous powder blue. "Go on," he encouraged me as he slipped it on.

I nodded; at least he was listening. "There isn't anyone to substitute for me, sir. No one at all, any more than there's anyone to substitute for Jimmy. I don't need to lecture you about how leadership works, sir; you've taught me more about the subject than anyone else. But I *do* have to point out that a commander is worse than useless unless he can and will lead his men into combat, facing the same risks that they themselves are taking."

"Da," Vlasilov agreed, settling down alongside me once more. "This is certainly so."

"It's a fundamental principle of command," I continued, warming to the subject. "Perhaps even *the* fundamental principle. And there really isn't anyone else available. I *have* to fly combat, sir. Or else half of your superfighter force will be practically useless during the biggest battle of the war."

Vlasiloz sipped at his tea again, then scowled as if suddenly the flavor had gone bad. "Bah!" he complained, setting his navy mug down. "You're quite convincing, Thomas," he agreed. "I cannot dispute even one of your arguments."

"Plus it's a matter of honor," I continued. "I'm in the navy too. So long as I wear this uniform, I should have to share the risks. Just like you do, sir."

Vlasilov nodded. "All of this is true." Then he stood up and held out his hand to help me up out of my chair; somehow, without my noticing it, our discussion had ended. "Thomas, I'm deeply flattered to hear you say that I've helped you learn how to lead, for indeed you are a promising young leader. Still, it's clear that you have much to learn. So if I am to serve as your teacher, let me suggest a lesson. Tomorrow morning, instead of attending the morning briefing I want you to look up the term 'chain of command' on your console. As you study it you'll come to understand that the chain of command is every bit as vital to discipline, order, and combat effectiveness as personal leadership is." He smiled. "It's one of the things we swear an oath to obey. And, you'll also find that the Prime Minister far outranks mere admirals like myself."

I closed my eyes and sighed. "Do you really expect me to stand by and watch my friends get themselves killed? That'd practically be murder!"

Vlasilov didn't answer. Instead he smiled again and opened his door to allow me to leave. "You're a good officer, Thomas," he said. "And a good man, as well. I'm quite certain that you'll conduct yourself in an honorable fashion under all conceivable circumstances. Thank you for visiting, son; it was good of you to come. But it's time for an old man to rest."

Chapter Eighty-Four

I already had plans to fly with the Bananas during Vlasilov's morning briefing, as he probably well knew; Lieutenant-Commander Barnes was my new alter-ego on administrative matters and she covered routine meetings for me. All I had to do was glance over her carefully-transcribed highlights. Still, I took the admiral's advice and looked up "chain-of-command" just as he'd suggested before going to bed that night.

The navy's official page on the subject was a little frightening. It was filled with stern warnings about the overriding need to obey orders and the severe penalties awaiting those who failed to do so. I could certainly understand why all of this was necessary. When I gave, say, His Serene Highness an order, I didn't have time to explain why I was giving it or to offer him a briefing on the situation overall. Combat created a fluid, rapidly-changing environment, one in which there simply wasn't time for questions or even hesitation. "Aye-aye, sir!" could be the only proper reply to an order, or else the navy would soon be totally unable to function. Even if the order in question meant that the recipient would die while others lived.

Yet there were exceptions to the rule, and quite fascinating ones at that. First, no serving navy man or woman was required to obey an illegal order. Examples of illegal orders included those requiring the subordinate to perform forbidden or immoral acts. I squirmed a little in my seat while reading this part, because some of the things that were specifically mentioned as illegal were pretty much standard procedure on Churilla, such as executing prisoners. The War Cabinet hadn't repudiated the actions of Spence's guerillas, or at least they hadn't the last time I'd checked. In fact, the latest word I'd gotten on the subject was a speech the PM had made in Parliament recently praising my friend and his band of desperadoes in the most immoderate language possible. Apparently the information I was looking at was a bit outdated. Spence was clearly doing the right thing given what he was up against, no matter what the regulations said.

There were other exceptions listed as well, most of them involving decision-making by higher-level commanders. A commander on the spot, for example, was under certain circumstances considered justified in disobeying the orders of a physically distant superior if he or she was so far away that they were clearly out of touch with the reality of a given situation. I remembered the captain who'd sent Admiral Lutjens looking for Davy Jones back on Churilla and smiled. Sometimes physical distance wasn't the only reason why a superior might give unrealistic orders. Even back then, I'd known that Captain Yan had done the right thing. It was good to know that the navy at least in theory agreed.

Disobedience was also justified if the superior officer in question was either insane or a traitor, though the database urged extreme caution in both of these circumstances and admonished any would-be mutineer to seek out the advice and counsel of as many of his or her fellows as possible before acting. It was very rare, the page explained, for things ever to get this far. There were alternative mechanisms available for dealing with this kind of situation under almost any conceivable circumstance. These other mechanisms were to be employed whenever possible.

Then at the very end the navy added one last "catch-all" paragraph. "Ultimately," it read, "the best guide as to whether an order should be obeyed or not lies in one's own heart and brain. The service does not expect blind obedience when such obedience would undermine either the mission of the fleet or the safety of its members. 'Any damn fool can obey orders!' a great saltwater admiral once raged, commenting on a great opportunity for an important victory thrown away due to the blind, unreasoning obedience of a fellow admiral. In that particular instance, hundreds of thousands if not millions of men, women and children eventually died due to one man's inflexible interpretation of the chain of command. The United Systems Navy specifically requires of both officers and enlisted men that, when time allows, common sense be applied to the interpretation of orders and initiative be displayed in pursuing said orders' higher purposes. While the violation of orders can indeed result in a court martial and even a conviction, it is stated here for the record that disobeying an order for the purpose of attempting to accomplish a higher goal shall be recognized as a legitimate defense. The navy accepts that it cannot demand both blind obedience and personal initiative of a subordinate at one and the same time."

I sighed and turned off my console. I was too tired to think any more about the legal basis of orders; there'd be plenty of time for that tomorrow. It was long past time for bed, and I was planning to get up early so that I could visit with Jimmy for a few minutes before flying. Except for in the air, we hadn't seen each other in weeks. I didn't need to work with the Bananas, really; they were about as good as they were going to get in the absence of actual combat experience. But apparently spending time with me helped their confidence quite a bit. Jimmy had been using me as an ogre, it seemed. "Thomas would never tolerate that!" he'd declare when a maneuver went badly. So my good opinion mattered. Besides, technically I was still their commander, even if I didn't even know half of their names without prompting. I *owed* them at least a few dogfights, and probably a few social visits to the gunroom, as well.

I sighed again and rested my head down on the console for a moment. Vlasilov was right; I *was* spread too thin. I'd finally hit the point where I wasn't doing a good job at *anything* anymore. Instead, I was spending my time running from crisis to crisis, never quite spending long enough anywhere to make things truly right and becoming more and more of a fifth wheel. It was a good thing the war was almost over—I wasn't sure how much more I could take. If I were wearing a human body, I wondered, would I appear as gray and haggard as the admiral? Would I have lines on my still-young face and need to wear a sweater when it was perfectly warm in the ship?

I let my mind wander aimlessly for a bit, wondering what it must be like to have nothing more important to worry about than college classes and feeling a vague sense of guilt about letting my remedial calculus lessons slide. Then the images and feelings grew blurrier and mingled together in a sort of swirling mélange until I was addressing an angry Parliament in my Skybolt-body, explaining thorough the fuselage-speakers how I was going to use my own initiative and disobey their orders to do more math homework until I could get the Butcher Bird's work stoppage settled. Then things turned darker and I was strangling the life out of a Dracan in the bottom of a closet. But the Dracan wouldn't die and wouldn't die and wouldn't die, even though her eyes bulged and blood ran from her ears and radiation-sickness shrunk her head until it was just a great bleeding skull. Then finally Ensign Eaglish went limp and I drifted helplessly away, watching his forlorn little light blink-blink-blink until it too was absorbed by the infinite blackness.

Chapter Eighty-Five

It wasn't any wonder that I woke up in a foul mood after not getting enough sleep for the bazillionth night in a row. Even worse, what little I got was spoiled by the way I'd sort of wandered in and out of consciousness, draped over my console instead of lying properly in bed. At first I took it out on Manuel, who countered by being extra-polite and smiling even more than usual as he attended to my most basic needs. Then I reminded myself how unjust I was being to a good and decent man, apologized, and did my best to get on with my day.

It wasn't easy, though. Every time any little thing went wrong I felt myself trying to revert to growling and snapping. "You should suck it in tighter!" I admonished a Top Banana who was having trouble keeping up with me while serving as my wingman. "My god! What do you think this is? A verdammt cheerleading squad? People *die* over this kind of nonsense!" Then I realized that I was turning into Colonel Rotte and had to apologize again. Yes, I had to admit to myself, everyone in the Bananas *did* want to be like me and imitate my exploits, though God himself might well wonder why anyone would wish on themselves what I'd been through. But deep down they feared me as well; Jimmy was right about that. I was a mass-slaughterer of men and they were still innocent children. Given this fact, how could things be otherwise? It was an uncrossable wall that separated us aces from everyone else; the longer I lived, the better I understood the colonel.

Still, I didn't have to *become* him. Or at least I hoped that I didn't. Certainly I could fight the process, and one way I did so was by canceling a morale-building meeting with the support teams aboard *Coronel* to spend the afternoon video-gaming with the Bananas. Despite being quartered just down the hall from them somehow I'd never found the time. Besides, there'd be plenty of opportunities for me to meet with *Coronel*'s men on the way out to Churilla. We played some *Invasion: Esteppe*, but mostly everyone else sat around and watched as Jimmy and I set a new all-time record at *Rocket-Sledder*. As worn-out and headachy as I was, somehow I was able to put all of my inhibitions aside and go on a total tear, a once-in-a-lifetime combination of reckless abandon, lucky choices, good breaks and perfect coordination with my teammate. "I don't usually play this well," I muttered to the Bananas when it was finally over. "Ask Jimmy."

But they didn't believe me. Instead one of them solemnly printed out the victory screen, and had Jimmy and I sign it. "This is going on the gunroom wall," she declared.

"Yeah!" an ensign agreed. His eyes were glowing with admiration, as if I'd just shot down a whole squadron of superfighters. "I've never seen anything like it! Not even close!"

Which made it all the harder for me to know, as he did not, that when his Big Day came and he faced down death for the first time I'd not be there for him. It hurt so bad that I had to look away from those shining, eager eyes.

As much as I wanted to stay and play some more there was someplace else I had to be that evening, an appointment far more difficult to cancel than a ground-crew appearance. Alicia had requested that I come to Rome for a visit, and since I'd agreed more than a week ahead of time it wasn't something I could easily back out of. We sat down to dinner as usual and caught up on personal stuff while she ate and I watched.

"…another letter from Spence," she explained between mouthfuls. "He sends you his best, and said that he hopes to see you soon. He knows it's almost time." She shook her head. "I sometimes wish he wouldn't write; communications are so terribly risky. But then I'd hate that too."

I nodded dutifully; Alicia was deeply worried about her mate of more than a century. She missed him more than anyone else besides me knew, I suspected, which probably made it all the harder for her. There was a sort of joyous glow missing in her, one that sometimes flashed momentarily to the surface when she was with me. It was something very special, that glow; it reflected a love and devotion that was as extraordinary in its way as the Wistons' intellectual and leadership abilities. I brought it out in her sometimes, I supposed, because I reminded her of home. The emotion, however, was so special and even so inhumanly powerful that unless you knew to look for it you'd never note its absence. Everyone else on Earth probably imagined that Alicia was thriving as Madame Deputy, that she was living the finest hours of her life. I, however, knew better. She too desperately needed for the war to end.

"Things are worse than ever back on Churilla," she continued. "There's no food; the markets are empty. The only factories running are the ones producing molecular batteries for the Dracans, and the situation is so desperate that Spence is allowing them to keep on operating. If he doesn't, there won't be any food at all."

I nodded again; what was there to say, really?

"We were already overpopulated," she continued. "There were never enough resources to go around. Now Spence thinks as many as a quarter of us might be dead. Though he can't be sure, of course; the last thing the Dracans want is an accurate count." She shook her head. "The Emperor must hang.

There's no other way."

"We can't do anything else," I agreed. "Like Father Murton told me once, history demands that crimes of this magnitude be punished. Or else they'll be repeated."

Alicia pursed her lips. "We've committed crimes too, of course. You can't wage war effectively without doing so. Not a winning war, at least. But at least we can honestly claim that we weren't the aggressors. We didn't fire the first shot."

I nodded again. There'd been longstanding disputes with the Dracans, sure enough. We might not even have been in the right on all of them. But we hadn't tried to settle things by occupying Dracan worlds and slaughtering their intellectuals, either.

Alicia sighed again and put down her fork. "The Emperor must hang, yes. That's a given. He and all his upper aristocracy. But... What else are we going to demand of the Dracans, Thomas? When we have them on their knees, I mean?"

I looked away. "No more extreme militarism," I pointed out.

"No more extreme militarism," Alicia agreed, nodding. "Until, of course, domestic order breaks down on their planets. That happens when you lose a major war, you know. Once you remove the established leadership, chaos erupts; it's happened over and over again in history. Then we'll either have to occupy them ourselves or else tolerate a new Dracan Army. One built, I'll add, out of officers and men left over from this same Imperial outfit we're so eager to rid ourselves of. The militarists, in other words. Returned to positions of power."

"We have to occupy, then," I said. "We can't let the Imperial Army reform!"

Alicia shrugged. "And if we do that," she replied, "then every little thing that goes wrong will, in the minds of the Dracans, be the United System's fault. No bread? Blame the United Systems, not the Emperor for moving the farmers into war production a year back so that no crops were planted. No job? You'd have one, if the United Systems would spend more money on rebuilding. Your son died in a wreck? It's the United Systems fault for not providing proper traffic control. Got a rash? Why isn't the United Systems sending more dermatitis cream? And so on; once our troops hit the ground they'll become everyone's whipping-boy." She sighed. "It's hard, accepting foreign uniforms on your own soil. If we're not careful, soon it'll be Churilla all over again but this time with us as the Dracans. It's happened before."

I frowned. "So, what do you think we ought to do?"

"Be magnanimous in victory, demand no reparations or unreasonable territorial concessions... In short, be good neighbors. Live and let live." She sighed. "But I'm in the minority, I fear. Most of Parliament wants to bleed Drakkus for every drop they can get."

I nodded, having somehow found the time to follow the debates. At least in a shallow sort of way. "It's Nagano again."

She nodded. "He's drawing his moral authority from the fact that he's now representing New Nippon, a world raped by the Dracans." She looked away. "If we held a vote on this today, moderates like me would lose. Worst of all, Nagano knows it."

"Of course, every last one of my fellow Parliamentarians has sisters and cousins and nieces and nephews who'd be just *perfect* for jobs with the Occupation Authority," I grumbled. "High officials, every one of them." My headache, which I'd shaken while playing video games, was coming back.

"Of course," she agreed, looking terribly sad. Then she met my eyes. "Some want to annex the Dracan Empire outright. And then everyone else everywhere, peacefully if possible. If there's only one government, they reason, there can be no more wars."

"And soon there will be no freedom," I countered. Esteppe had been forcibly annexed and still didn't like it. In this one thing if no other I felt that their gripe was absolutely legitimate. "The whole universe under one Parliament? There'd be no place left to run if things went badly. No planet where people who wanted to live differently, under different laws, could flee to. That'd be the biggest tragedy of all!"

"I agree," the Deputy Prime Minister stated, sounding very formal. "And so does Spence. There's nothing more dangerous than giving *any* group of politicians a total monopoly on power." She shuddered. "Especially the ones I'm working with every single day."

There was a long, long silence. "The Fleet's about to ship out," I observed. "Everyone knows it. We're almost ready."

Alicia nodded. "Yes."

"You want me to stay behind," I continued. "You want me to accept a minor cabinet post, like that old guy offered me, and help you work all this out. You *need* me, in fact. That's why you asked me here tonight. That and to say good-bye, of course. But you haven't been able to work up the courage to ask me outright."

Alicia smiled. "I'd have gotten there. Eventually."

I smiled back. "Eventually. And I'd have given you this same answer." I looked down at the tablecloth, then met Alicia's big, pale-blue eyes. "I can't do it."

She pressed her lips together. "Why not, Thomas?" she asked, her voice calm and reasonable. "What's so terrible about working to do the right thing, in the place where you can do the most good?" She tilted her head to one side. "Surely by now you realize that Parliament really *is* the place where you can do the most good. For all of Mankind."

I kept my eyes lowered. "There's more to it than that," I tried to explain. "I mean… what kind of man would I be if I left these children I've been training to face combat on their own? While I spend the rest of the war sitting in a comfortable, safe office arguing all day? You're right, you know. I *can* do more good there, I think. In the short term, at least. But…" I shifted uncomfortably in my seat. "For how long? If I were to abandon my men like that, what would it do to *me*? To my soul, I mean? How long would I be a force for *good*, in other words, if I were to try and build on such a flawed moral foundation?" I shook my head. "It's bad enough that I behave like Colonel Rotte sometimes, as you well know. How long would it be until I turned into Nagano, too?"

Alicia's eyes narrowed. "I'll admit it," she said after a long moment. "I never thought of that." Then she turned away. "Thomas… Is it really necessary that you accompany the Fleet? I mean, there'll be more pilots to train right here on Earth soon. Isn't that an honorable enough occupation for you?"

"They'll never see combat," I predicted. "The war will be over. So there'll plenty of time for me to work with them later." I shook my head and thought about the glowing-eyed ensign who'd so admired my video-gaming skills earlier that afternoon and realized that I didn't even know his name. "These two current squadrons are the kids who're going to bleed," I explained. "They're the ones who're going to have nightmares for the rest of their lives and blood on their hands that won't ever quite wash off. Don't you think we owe them something? More specifically, don't you think that *I* owe them something? Even more, perhaps, than I owe the government or the people of the Second North American District?"

Alicia's left ear wriggled nervously, then her whiskers bristled; she wasn't used to losing arguments, I could tell. But at least she succumbed gracefully. "All right, Thomas," she agreed. "Go with the fleet, and do what you have to do. But, please…" It was her turn to look away. "Come back to us?"

Then we were on our feet and hugging one another as if we truly were mother and child, weeping like babies. "Do what must be done," she whispered in my ear. "Listen to your heart. But remember that you have obligations here as well."

"I'll remember," I promised. "And, I swear to you, I'll always do my best to do what I see as the right thing regardless of anything else. I'm real big on that, and getting bigger every day."

Chapter Eighty-Six

By now I was an old hand at Fleet departures. I sat and smiled through the PM's "good hunting" speech, then cheered mightily at Alicia's far more bloodthirsty follow-up. The PM's speech might have gone down better with the general populace, the budding politician inside of me noted. But hers was right on target with the audience at hand. Then we up-shipped, this time with dozens of warships and six brand-spanking-new planetary assault ships. Once again I missed the spectacle; by tradition the flagship took off first and I was aboard her. But, I consoled myself, someday I'd be able to watch a fleet depart from another perspective entirely.

The trip out to Churilla was also much like any other outward journey; for a time we stumbled about and tripped over each other and made terrible messes of our drills. Vlasilov scowled and threw up his hands in despair, the petty officers screamed until they were red in the face, and over time things grew better.

Oddly, the outward-bound trip was a lot shorter than I was used to; these days United Systems fleets sailed where they pleased while Dracan vessels were the ones forced to take circuitous evasive routings. I had only a handful of days available to me when there was a mass near enough by to work with the squadrons, so when I exercised them I often spent twenty hours or more in my 'bolt. The rest of the time I spent teaching tactics and, now that there were fewer distractions, bonding better with my pilots. I also religiously attended the special strategy classes that I'd been able to persuade Captain Bard to reinstate. She was the task force's chief strategist now, and busier than ever. It was natural that at first she wanted to delegate the responsibility to someone else. But then I explained to her that of all the things and people that'd helped me along, her classes had mattered the most. "Well," she replied, blushing a deep red and looking down at the floor. "In that case, how can I say no?"

At first she repeated some of her earlier sessions on how victory in war was akin to pitilessly kicking someone to death and about how U-boats and other technology had blurred war's old standards of chivalry and morality. Instead of paying attention to Michelle I watched my fellow pilots faces as the true horror of what they were about to do began to sink in. They could deal with it, I decided, or at least most of them could. The rest, well... The ones who actually wept, I carefully and with Jimmy's blessing assigned to the reserve flights.

Finally, just before arriving in our theater of operations we began covering new material. I leaned forward eagerly. War might be ugly. It might even be the most awful thing there'd ever been. But I was a professional, and I'd never been able to find anyone else anywhere who seemed to understand its ultimate essence as well as Captain Bard did.

"War isn't logical in the conventional sense of the word," she began after the usual pleasantries. "As I've explained to you before. It's not logical to destroy so much wealth and so many lives, it's not logical to employ violence in order to achieve one's ends and means, it's not logical to risk the very survival of humanity itself over what by comparison are relatively trivial issues. And yet once war begins we inevitably do these very things. This is because once the fighting starts a whole new logic takes over, one in which material possessions mean nothing and lives little more. Even worse, any party in war who chooses to ignore this special logic of conflict does so at their mortal peril. One of the best ways I know of to lose a war is to try and apply peace-logic when the enemy is using war-logic."

The captain remained silent for a long moment, ensuring that her words sank in before continuing. "Making the mental leap from peace-logic to war-logic is a very difficult step," our teacher continued. "And that's probably a good thing, because if war were any easier we'd certainly have killed ourselves off many centuries ago. It's perhaps easiest for professional warriors to make the switch, because at least in a theoretical sense we think in terms of war-logic all of the time." She smiled. "I've spent more years thinking about how best to destroy the Dracan Empire than I care to admit, employing every dirty trick in the book along the way. And so have most of the other career-officers you'll meet. We've lived our whole adult lives, in other words, familiarizing ourselves with and preparing ourselves for war-logic.

"And yet even we have difficulties in adapting. It takes to time to grasp, in the emotional rather than the intellectual sense, that killing other men has suddenly become not only an acceptable action but one necessary to survival. It takes time for one to come to appreciate that your enemy really *will* kill you for no better reason than the uniform you're wearing, unless you kill him first because of the one *he's* wearing." She sighed. "Again and again in the history books, you'll find that military units of all kinds which have actually seen combat tend to be far more effective than those who have not yet been exposed to the logic of war. They've made the mental changeover, where those who haven't yet been 'blooded' have not. This is why so-called 'veteran' units have always been so prized by generals and admirals; they're truly ready to fight where 'green' units, no matter how well-trained, have yet to accept the war-logic mindset."

She looked around the room, meeting everyone's eyes. "Now, if you think things all the way through, you'll soon come to realize that if getting *into* the warmaking mindset is difficult, then leaving it and going back to peace-logic might prove difficult as well. And such is indeed the case." She smiled slightly. "Has anyone here ever heard of a place called 'Masada'?"

A Butcher Bird raised his hands. "Of course!" he answered. "They were great heroes!"

Bard smiled gently. "Some consider them so," she agreed. "Tell us about them."

"They were Jewish rebels," he explained. "The Romans were trying to suppress them, and our religion. But they were in an unassailable fortress, and held out for... well, years I guess."

"And what happened to them?" our teacher asked.

The young man blinked. "They all died," he answered. "Every one of them. But, they took an awful lot of Romans with them!"

"That they did," Bard agreed. "But, in the end, what did they *accomplish*?"

The boy looked confused. "Well... They became a legend! Immortal!"

"Hmm," the captain replied, now looking confused as well. "But... They raised no more children?"

"No," the boy answered.

"They wrote no more books, to perpetuate their ideas?"

"No."

"They didn't extend their culture any further, or perhaps even convert the Romans?"

"No. Of course not!"

Bard shook her head, still looking confused. "Then... How were they such great heroes?"

There was a long silence, until pretty soon we were all looking confused. Then the captain smiled, and congratulated the boy for knowing his history. "It stands to reason," she repeated, "that, once having made the difficult transition into the logic of war, people might also have trouble transitioning back into the logic of peace."

There was another long, long silence.

"Masada is the archetype of a pattern we see repeated again and again throughout history," she continued. "During the American Civil War, for example, the South fought on long after all hope of victory had passed. So did Germany and especially Japan during the Second World War; Germany, in fact, actually went on the offensive late in the war, chasing hopeless dreams of past victories." She sighed. "Typically, the more militaristic a society is to begin with the harder it is for them to put aside the logic of war and switch back to the logic of peace."

"And," I replied, slowly grasping the relevance of the topic. "The Dracans are a militaristic culture."

"Exactly," she answered. "Very militaristic indeed."

"They've already lost," a Top Banana added. "But they can't accept it."

"Or won't," A Bird added. "Esteppe did that, too."

Bard smiled again; clearly she'd failed to mention Esteppe's long agony on purpose. "And what did it take to finally persuade Esteppe to give up?" she asked.

Suddenly there was a long, cold silence in the room. "The navy nuked us," a Bird finally replied. "Over and over again. Until the Autarch was betrayed by Thomas's father and overthrown." The boy looked at me, then turned away.

"Thomas's father employed the logic of peace," Bard explained. "He was able to switch his mindset back to it when those around him could not. Then he had the courage to do what had to be done. I assure you that had he not 'betrayed' his people, none of you Birds would be here today. You see, I was busy helping write the plan for the final sterilization of Esteppe when the Autarchy finally collapsed. It was one of my first active-duty assignments."

There was another long, long silence. That was *not* in the history books, though not one of us doubted that our instructor was being anything but honest with us.

Captain Bard looked down at the carpet. "I've told you this," she continued, "to try and help you understand why it is that we expect the Dracans to fight harder than ever, insofar as their reduced means of making war allow. And to prepare you for what may come next." She looked at me.

"Unless there's a Willy Longo to be found among the Dracan aristocracy. Which is probably too much to hope for."

Chapter Eighty-Seven

Captain Bard, of course, always knew where we were going and what we were going to do there before we pilots did; after all, she was the one in charge of strategic planning. Plus, the admiral had promised me a chance to "blood" my rookie pilots prior to the big assault at Churilla. So I wasn't at all surprised when a sort of electric thrill began spreading through *The Glorious First of June*, the special sort of thrill that only happened when by ones and twos various department heads and sailors began figuring out that action was imminent. In my case I knew that we'd be fighting soon the minute that the ground crews were instructed to cease all training teardowns. Many of our repairmen were still more than a little green, and their petty officers had been working their men's fingers off to make up the shortfall. Oftentimes half our 'birds had been rendered unserviceable at any given moment in order to allow our mechanics to learn. Now they were to be rested and as many 'bolts as possible held in flyable condition at all times. Which added up to a slightly-overcrowded thirteen aboard *June*, since she was still accommodating my soot-black Mark I* as an extra, and a mere eleven aboard *Coronel*, since we'd never found the Birds a new squadron commander. I'd suggested that the imbalance be addressed by having me move my quarters, but Vlasilov would have nothing of it. "We need you here for mission planning, Thomas," he'd replied. I had to admit that he had a point. There wasn't anyone else more experienced at putting together attacks based on superfighters than me.

Soon Captain Bard summoned me to her private working spaces and I began earning my keep. "It's New Connaught," she declared as soon as the hatch swung shut behind me. "We're invading."

I looked down at the big simulated pipper displaying the system and what we estimated the Dracan defenses might be like, then shook my head. "Why?" I asked. "There's only one Nikita, like Earth. So there's no geographic advantage to be won. The population is tiny. The planet has no mineral resources to speak of either. So what do we gain for our trouble?"

Bard frowned. "Ask the PM," she answered. "Or else put on your own political hat and figure it out for yourself."

That was the only clue I needed. "It's Dracan territory," I replied slowly.

"Annexed by them at knifepoint long before the war. The PM wants to show that we're taking the war to the enemy's homeland. Even though this part of their homeland is pretty useless, it's the only place we can get to just now."

"Probably," Michelle agreed, smiling now that I'd worked it out for myself. "In any event, this objective was assigned to us by the government. It's not for us to reason why."

I nodded. "It gives me a good chance to blood my pilots, so I suppose I'm all in favor of it, too."

"Probably everyone is," Michelle agreed. "Except for the poor bastards who're going to die on and around New Connaught for no good war-winning reason." She sighed and shook her head. "At least we'll be able to blood the army types, too."

It didn't take long for Michelle to lay out her tentative plan of attack. "We'll hold the heavies at the Nikita," she explained. "Just in case the Dracans go insane and decide to come out and fight a losing battle for no good reason. Massing at the Nikita is pretty much standard procedure for a one-link system. But…" She frowned and shook her head. "New Connaught's Nikita is pretty far out, Thomas. Your fighters' antigrav's won't have much in the way of mass to work with. Do you think we ought to take the carriers further in?"

I scowled. There were dangers either way. If we moved the launch-vessels in close our superfighters would be effective right from the get-go. The carriers, however, would perforce be poorly escorted since the bulk of the heavies would remain at the Nikita. Which in turn meant that if the Dracans had a surprise in store for us, our mother-ships would be highly vulnerable. On the other hand, if we kept *June* and *Coronel* out near the Nikita where the rest of the task force could support them, the Dracans would have literally hours of notice whenever we raided. Even worse, merely navigating so far from a mass wasn't any fun at all. If any of us pilots made even the slightest miscalculation, we'd find ourselves drifting away helplessly, beyond all hope of rescue. "I see why you're consulting me," I said at long last, after studying the situation intently.

Michelle nodded. "It's not an easy decision." Then her mouth formed a hard, grim line. "The admiral will make the final determination, of course. It's his job. But I bet he'll do whatever you suggest. Your pilots are a key factor."

I scowled again, then rubbed at my chin. There were no whiskers there, of course; plastic skin didn't tend to grow much in the way of hair. But on my real body, well… who knew? We Longos tended to mature late, physically at least. Still, however, it was about that time. I lifted my eyes to meet Bard's. "Bring them in close, is what I recommend," I said finally. "Defensive-minded thinking rarely wins a war. Instead, you have to take chances and hit, hit, hit just as hard and as often as you can." I smiled. "You're one of the people that taught me that."

Captain Bard smiled back, and hit a button on her pipper. Everything disappeared, then reformed with the fleet disposed exactly as I'd suggested, planned out down to the tiniest detail. Clearly, my decision had been anticipated. "And you've learned well," she replied, reaching out and patting me on the shoulder. "Very well indeed."

"Thank you," I answered, smile fading. The most difficult decision might've been made, but the hard work was just beginning. "Now, let's figure out exactly how we're going to structure our strikes…"

Chapter Eighty-Eight

"…going to be continually striking with one squadron while we hold back the other as combat air patrol," I explained hesitantly, the pointer feeling unfamiliar in my hand. In the past Ted Knight had handled such crucial briefings before the high-rankers for me. But Ted had his own squadron now, and I was on my own. It was more challenging than addressing Parliament; my fellow officers raised much more intelligent objections than lawmakers did. "The Bananas will go in first, then when they've expended their bombs the Butcher Birds will take their turn. We'll keep right on taking turns like that. It's not an ideal setup in terms of maintaining continual air support, but at least this way we're guaranteed to have fighters protecting the carriers at all times. That's got to be our primary goal. Neither unit will be cleared to hit ground targets until the other is ready to defend the task force against a counterattack. We lack the skills for anything more complex."

"Da," Vlasilov agreed, nodding soberly. He'd approved the basic plan two full days ago, but managed to look interested anyway.

"My objections still stand, admiral," our resident army general complained. His name was Dayton. "This setup leaves us little or no flexibility to call in targets as required on a minute-by-minute basis. It's not the kind of close air support we've been trained to work with."

I sighed silently to myself. General Dayton was the largest pain in the ass I'd ever worked with outside of the political arena. He was among the most senior officers in the army, but so far hadn't been entrusted with a combat command. The reasons for this were rapidly becoming crystal-clear to everyone except him. "This is self-evident," Vlasilov replied, his voice dripping calm reason. "As Thomas himself just pointed out, his plan maximizes fleet protection at the cost of effective, rapid support for your men. There has to be some kind of tradeoff, after all; our resources are not unlimited. There *will* be air support. It will merely be intermittent, is all."

"We should wait," Dayton countered, making a fist and lightly pounding it on the table so as to emphasize his point. "Until we have more superfighters. Or at least some Polecats to dedicate entirely to ground support."

"Bah!" the admiral replied, his brows narrowing. "If we had more superfighters, we'd use them to defend our carriers even more thoroughly. And, don't forget, the Polecats are training for Churilla as we speak." He shook his head. "New Connaught should be a walkover for you, General. We estimate that you outnumber the Dracan garrison by as much as ten to one. Why are you so concerned with air support?"

Dayton flushed and began to stutter. "It's our doc... I mean, the troops have trained with continual air support. I... We..." Suddenly, I was very glad that Dayton hadn't been assigned the far tougher job of invading Churilla. Instead he'd remain behind on New Connaught as military governor. Which, I was certain, was no coincidence at all.

"Of course," Vlasilov replied smoothly. "Your objections are noted. We'll work through this one step at a time. Once we're dead certain that the Dracans can't mount any sort of significant counterattack, you'll have both squadrons assigned to nothing but ground support."

"Yes. Well... I mean, I..."

"Good," Vlasilov continued. "I'm glad you agree."

Most of the rest of the meeting was like that, as practically every department-head in the task force found fault with my deployments. Maintenance complained that I was demanding too much up-time of the birds; in their opinion, we should be thinking ahead to Churilla. Intelligence complained that there were no birds allocated to photorecon work. Even one of Michelle's underlings spoke up and complained that the carriers really should remain with the heavies out near the Nikita; in her department, low-rankers who sincerely disagreed were encouraged to speak out. However, I believed in my plan and defended it against all comers. I spoke over and over again of my pilots' lack of experience and need for a controlled, structured first-combat experience. "It's so easy to forget they're children," I pointed out. "They're fragile, and need to be eased into the hard reality of war."

"You weren't," Bard's underling pointed out.

"And you have no idea how badly I wish I had been," I replied just as sincerely as I was able.

"We all do, Thomas," Vlasilov replied, his joints popping as he rose slowly from his chair. "You have no idea how badly most of us wish things were easier for you." Clearly, in his mind, the meeting was over. For a long moment General Dayton remained seated, then he frowned and rose as well. Vlasilov noted this, then turned his head so the general couldn't see and winked at me. I smiled back, and for a moment we grinned at each other like a couple of youthful conspirators. Then the admiral's smile faded, and his face became gray and strained again. "There is one more matter that remains to be resolved, Commander Longo," he continued, growing more formal. "A personal issue. Would you care to accompany me to my cabin and discuss it with me?"

I felt my grin fading as well; there was not the slightest doubt in my mind as to what the "personal issue" was. In my last, formal version of the air strike plan, I'd called for the employment of all twenty-four superfighters. And all twenty-four pilots as well. Including myself. "Aye-aye, sir!" I replied. Though I tried, I wasn't quite able to completely prevent my anger and resentment at being ordered out of combat from revealing itself in my voice.

Much to my surprise, Vlasilov didn't grow angry in return. Instead he grinned again. "We'll make it as quick and as painless as possible," he promised me.

My frown intensified for a moment, then I made a hard decision. "Sir," I said slowly. "If I'm to have a fair hearing, I expect this to take some time."

Suddenly the rustling and bustling sounds of several dozen officers leaving a major meetings ceased, and the room went dead silent. No one present except for Vlasilov, *June's* captain, and myself knew what the big disagreement was all about. But, if they expected an explosion from the admiral, they were sorely disappointed. "Da," he agreed, smile still in place. "For you and for this particular issue, I have all afternoon. I may not be able to offer justice, Thomas. This is not within my power. At least, however, I can offer sympathy in nearly unlimited quantities."

Chapter Eighty-Nine

If Admiral Vlasilov had been a politician, my line of argument probably would have succeeded. In a politician's world, everything is fuzzy and gray and amorphous. Hard and fast rules have little meaning for those empowered to write new ones; they're temporary inconveniences, nothing more. Black and white are unheard-of; lawmakers live in a land of invariant gray. Not so admirals, unfortunately. Even though he agreed with me time and time again as I laid out my case, the answer always came back the same. "You have your orders, commander, just as do I. They come from the highest of levels; clearly you cannot appeal."

"But…" I'd complain, and begin all over again. The Birds were dependant on me, both psychologically and in terms of tactical skill. I was the best pilot in the fleet, even better than Jimmy, and skill *mattered*. In point of fact, I was probably more effective than the other eleven Butcher Birds put together. I hated bragging on myself, but it was *true* and Vlasilov knew it.

"You have your orders, commander," he repeated pleasantly for about the fifth time, and I felt my fists balling up in fury.

"People are going to be killed if I don't fly!" I protested. "We might lose ships or even a battle! Not here maybe, but at Churilla. This was a stupid decision, and you *know* it!"

Up until that moment, Vlasilov had met my every sally with infinite patience and a slight smile. Now his smile faded. "That is not for me to judge, Thomas. And you well know it!"

"I'm sorry," I apologized, instantly repentant. "It's just…"

Suddenly the admiral was all sympathy again. "Stupid orders happen, Thomas. They've happened again and again all through history. You read about some of them when you looked up that data page on the chain of command, didn't you?"

I nodded, all empty inside now that my rage was spent. Like a little kid after a tantrum, I supposed.

"It's happened again and again," he repeated. "The most famous example took place at the Battle of Copenhagen. Admiral Nelson, the greatest naval officer who ever lived, had fought a terrible battle against the anchored Danish

Fleet and was just on the verge of winning when he was ordered to withdraw by his superior. Who, as it happened, was aboard a ship so far away from the fighting that he couldn't possibly have understood what was going on."

"Really?" I asked.

"Da," Vlasilov replied. "Nelson was blind in one eye, due to an old wound. When his signal officer informed him that the squadron was being recalled, the admiral simply held a telescope up to his blind eye and said 'I don't see a thing.' That's where the expression 'turning a blind eye' comes from, in fact."

I suddenly felt a slight sense of hope. "And he won the battle?"

"Of course," the big Russian replied, levering himself to his feet. "On his own responsibility, mind you. He didn't argue with his admiral. He simply *acted*, knowing and accepting the consequences that might've come with being wrong."

"He didn't argue with his superior officer and try to get him to accept the responsibility," I answered, beginning to understand.

"Exactly!" Vlasilov agreed. "After all, Nelson was already the toast of England after what he'd already accomplished at the Nile. Who was going to court-martial *him*? Putting the King himself in the docks would've caused less of an uproar." Vlasilov stepped around the desk and wrapped his arm around my shoulder in a very fatherly way. "Of course not every naval officer is a famous hero, effectively immune to censure. Nelson had special advantages that way. Which he never abused, I'll add. Only that one time did he flagrantly disobey." The admiral turned me around and looked deep into my eyes. "I can't think of another naval officer in all of history who was similarly immune from prosecution, who really had nothing to fear even from a 'guilty' verdict, I mean. Can you?"

"Not one," I lied through my teeth, suddenly feeling much better than I had in days and days. "Not a single verdammt one."

Chapter Ninety

Most of the crewmen of Vlasilov's task force seven spent the last week before arrival at New Connaught on drills, drills. They went on right up until the very last day, when everyone was allowed to rest. We pilots spent this same period talking and gaming as Jimmy and I continued to hammer home the need for relentless aggressiveness at all times. "Kill them all!" we urged, "before they kill you!" Then on our last day before combat the gunroom of *The Glorious First of June* played host to the Butcher Birds, and amid much laughter and raucousness Jimmy and I took on all comers at *Invasion: Esteppe!* We kicked their butts, too, which sobered them considerably. As we'd intended from the get-go, of course. It was a shame that Jimmy wasn't my wingman anymore; working together as an experienced team we probably in truth were the most lethal weapons-system in the galaxy.

Our ground crews mounted us up about two hours before we hit New Connaught's single Nikita, so that we didn't have to wait too long in our 'bolts. We were loaded out with four anti-ship torps apiece, so as to cover the remote possibility that the Dracan Fleet might be awaiting us on the other side of the Point. Captain Han tried to order me not to even mate up with my fighter, but I countered by pointing out that the PM had said that if there ever *was* an emergency, I'd be allowed to fly combat again. Given that it took so long for me to get ready, the only way I could be possibly prepared for such an emergency was to be all hooked up in advance. She didn't like it at all, and we had our first argument ever. In the end, however, I was responsible directly to Vlasilov, not her. She could've ordered her deck people not to cooperate, I suppose; if she had, then I'd have been helpless. Instead she gave in and I was made ready for flight without any further argument.

I'd very carefully never informed the Birds that I wasn't allowed to fight any more, and the air was electric with chatter between the pilots before takeoff. Jimmy and I had made the decision to permit such personal conversations on an unrestricted basis right up until the launch sequence began; we were dealing with kids, after all, not disciplined adults. They needed to vent their excitement, and as near as we could tell there wasn't any harm to be found in abusing the comm net prior to combat. Besides, Jimmy and I had often chattered the same way. If anyone had tried to stop us, we'd have resented it.

"I'm going to splash me a destroyer!" Jenny de Meers declared.

"There won't be any Dracan fleet units at New Connaught," the Prince countered. I was monitoring the Birds' channel, of course, while Jimmy listened in on the Bananas. "The admiral won't need us until we assault the planet itself."

"If there *are* fleet units waiting for us," I interjected, "remember our plans. No one is to try and take out a warship alone. We're going to be a long way out from any good masses, and we'll have to coordinate everything very carefully. Stay with your wingmen and let us leaders do our jobs."

"Aye-aye, sir," the price replied. Was there a slight mocking tone in his voice? I couldn't blame him if there was, I supposed; after all, I'd been hammering home the same points over and over again for weeks now; I probably *did* sound a bit like a nervous old woman. But… After all our training did he *still* think it was just a game? I opened my mike to chastise him, then clicked it off without speaking a word. As near as I could figure, the Price's remaining childhood could be measured in minutes. There was no point in me spoiling it for him, not at this late date.

"Don't worry, Thomas," a new voice interjected, a soft one bordering on the delicate. It belonged to Isaiah Pearlmutter, who'd answered Captain Bard's question about Masada not so long ago. "We're kidding around now, sure. But we're ready. And we've you to thank for it. We were so stupid before!"

"Ja!" another Bird agreed. "Real rookies! It's a great honor to fight alongside you, Thomas. Your Excellency I mean, just this once. A greater honor than I ever hoped to know. You've taught us so much!"

Just then, the deck officer of the *Coronel* chimed in. "Jump in two minutes," he reported.

"Jump in two minutes," *June*'s deck officer agreed.

"Roger," I acknowledged for my men. Then I switched back to the squadron-circuit. "And I'm very proud of each and every one of you. "You're going to do a fine job. Kill them all!"

"Kill them all!" they chorused back, so full of enthusiasm that it chilled my blood.

"Horrido!" the Prince added.

"Horrido!" I agreed, as on my pipper the task force began rearranging itself into the long, single-line formation required to transit a Nikita Point. This was it, I knew, the moment of truth for uncounted thousands of us. The same basic scene was being played out thousands of times over among the ships of the task force, I knew, as we few veterans did our best to steady the rookies and brace them for what was to come. "Horr-i-do!"

Chapter Ninety-One

Attila and *Genghis Khan* led us through, followed by the heavies and *Chief*-class destroyers> Then came us carriers, followed by the helpless troop transports. In two or three minutes at most our task force was dominating local space; nothing could exist anywhere near us, unless Vlasilov suffered it to live. I scanned my pipper over and over again, waiting for it to update. But, no matter how long I waited, no red pips appeared.

"It looks like Fleet Intelligence was right," I said at last. "There's no enemy ships here."

"No fighters rising from the planet, either," the prince pointed out. He was an element leader, and thus permitted and even encouraged to discuss the battle when time permitted. I'd wanted him for my personal wingman because his marksmanship was so good. Plus he was learning to be quite aggressive, and I had high hopes for him. But because I wasn't permitted to go into combat, I'd chosen to include all the weakest pilots in my own four-'hopper element. It was yet another example of how political interference subtly weakened military strength; the *right* way to organize a fighter squadron was to put all the best pilots together and let them show the rest the way to excellence.

"They wouldn't be coming up this early, unless they were supers," I countered, a bit testily. "And even supers would be better off waiting." The Prince should've figured this out for himself; it was obvious enough.

"But…" Jenn asked. "Sir, why aren't we getting any pips on New Connaught itself? It's been long enough, by now."

I virtual-frowned to myself; Jenn was one of my least-promising pilots, but at least she was asking the right questions. "I don't know," I answered. "Let me see what I can find out." Then I switched to my command-bridge link.

"…unconditionally," a Dracan-accented voice was saying. "Absolutely, sir. Without question."

"There are no military units present at all?" Vlasiov's voice demanded. "How can this be?"

"They pulled out," the Dracan-voice replied. "Two months back. Apparently they realized that you were coming and decided to fight again another day."

"Who did you say that you are again?" General Dayton demanded. He didn't sound happy.

"President Psilovowski," the Dracan repeated. "Leader of the Provisional Free Government." He paused, sounding very tired. "Believe me, we're very glad to see you. Almost as glad as we were to see the back of the last Dracan off the planet."

"Da," Vlasilov answered, sounding thoughtful. Meanwhile I began to feel a deep sense of relief; perhaps there'd be no combat today after all. "Well… In that case, prepare to be occupied, Mr. President. Offer no resistance and there'll be no violence."

"You have my word," Psilovowski replied, sounding relieved. "Would you like for us to deliver hostages? My sons among them?"

There was a long, long pause. "No, Mr., President," the admiral answered. "That won't be necessary. We, you see, are not Dracans." There was another long pause. "Don't resist us in any way; that's enough for now. We'll let the politicians sort out the rest."

Both the Birds and the Bananas were terribly disappointed when I spread the word that the operation had changed in nature from an invasion to an occupation, which underlined just how little they still understood about war despite all the efforts that'd been made to educate them. We watched our pippers as the troopships performed their carefully-choreographed dance, just as if there actually were active resistance to be stamped out. As the transports discharged their landing craft, Vlasilov called. "Thomas!" he greeted me. "Isn't it wonderful?"

"Ja," I replied, meaning it as only a veteran could. "Though I bet General Dayton is fit to be tied. This was his one-and-only chance at the history books."

"He's being professional about it," the admiral replied. "But that's not why I called." He began using his "official" voice again. "Thomas, so far everything's going perfectly. There's been only one report of resistance, just outside of New Dublin. And frankly I'm suspicious of that one."

"How so, sir?" I asked.

"Green troops often panic, Thomas, and see things that aren't there." He sighed. "Still, I must do something. Could I persuade you to have your Skybolts overfly the area for a time, low enough so that the residents will know that you're there? Low enough even to crack a few windows, perhaps?"

"Aye-aye, sir!" I replied promptly. "Would one element of each squadron do?"

"Perfect!" Vlasilov replied. "See to it immediately."

It was the work of only a moment to order four 'hoppers from each squadron to launch for New Dublin. "We want cracked windows," I explained, "but no flattened buildings. Weapons are not to be energized without specific orders."

"Aye-aye, sir," Jimmy replied. He was in command of the Bananas' first element, and I'd deliberately included him to keep an eye on things.

"Aye-aye, sir!" the prince replied as well; he'd be in charge of the four Butcher Birds.

The eight fighters launched without difficulty and began what would've been an excruciatingly boring mission had it not been for the fun involved in knowing that they were doing minor damage in the city below. "This is great!" Isaiah cried out.

"I never thought I'd draw combat pay just for violating traffic rules," Jimmy agreed. Even with the window-cracking factored in, eventually flying in circles was bound to grow dull. This must have been especially true for teenagers who'd so recently been all keyed up anticipating their first life-and-death combat.

"Watch your formation, number four!" I chastised a Bird at one point. "You're opening up from your wingman."

Click-click, came the wordless acknowledgement. I scowled; a double-click might be okay between wingmen, but it wasn't the proper response to a censure from the squadron commander. I almost chewed out the unfortunate number four, then bit off the words. It was the stress, I decided, and the disappointment. Not deliberate insubordination. "All right," I began. "We're going to do a relief here. First we'll launch—"

But I never finished my order. Out of nowhere a red inverted "v" appeared on my pipper, aimed directly at the Bird's slowly orbiting formation. It was a missile! Then a second, and a third!

"Break left!" I cried out, the words more reflex than anything else. "Nownownow!"

Instantly, the Bananas complied. Sadly, however, they were not the ones in the most danger. "What?" the Prince demanded. "I mean…"

"Nownownow!" I repeated, watching the tracks come racing in. Where had *they* come from? I mentally hit the button that flashed my pipper-image to the bridge, then gave another order. "Guns hot, people. Jimmy, stand by to take out that launcher!"

"Roger," my best friend agreed as his element swung clear of danger.

"Mein Gott!' the prince cried, for the first time picking up on what he should've seen long milliseconds ago. "Break left!" he repeated, physically leading his pilots into the maneuver at last. "Break—"

But it was too late by then. All three missiles slammed home, two of them into the prince's 'bolt and the third into that of the luckless Number Four. Neither bailed out. According to the telemetry, death was instantaneous.

"*June!*" Jimmy demanded his voice tight and angry. His element was on the attack now, roaring low and fast in the general direction from which the missiles had come and to hell with the collateral damage to New Dublin. "Gimme some intel! I need that target on my pipper!"

"Wait one," the bridge replied, the officer's voice also tight and angry. "It appears that we have a friendly-fire incident here. That's why you have no target."

"Friendly fire!" I exploded. "What blithering idiot—"

"Thomas!" Vlasilov interrupted me. "Stand by!"

"I can tell which blue launcher it was, now that I know it was one of ours" Jimmy interjected. "Just give the word and I'll blow it to hell."

"You know better than that," I countered.

"Yeah," he replied, pulling his element up so that he wasn't cracking masonry anymore. "I guess."

"You do," I reassured him, even though I was at least as sick at heart as he was. Then I spoke to the bridge. "Have we got our trigger-happy army friends under control yet?" I demanded.

"Da," Vlasilov replied, now sounding as angry as I was. "They've acknowledged the mistaken launch." There was a long, long silence. "Recall your men," he ordered at last. "That's the only certain way to prevent more such mistakes. And know that General Dayton is absolutely mortified. He wishes me to inform you and your men that there will be a full inquiry and court martial."

"There'll be funerals, too," I countered. "Two of them. Inform the general of *that*, if you'd be so kind." Then I sighed and switched back to my more usual channel. "Return to base," I ordered, my voice softening. "All units, return to base. When you get here, report to your counselors immediately. We'll need sworn testimony from all of you, eventually. But that can wait."

Chapter Ninety-Two

To General Dayton's credit, he attended the funeral services for our two dead children. So, by his order, did the commanding officer of each and every field missile battery in his invasion force. Not only that, but he ordered the entire crew of the battery that'd actually fired on our 'bolts to attend as well, a half-dozen of them attired in bright-orange prison jumpsuits. Three of the jumpsuited men committed suicide that night, thus more than doubling the death-toll of the whole wretched incident. Maybe their deaths should've made me feel better, but they didn't. Underneath the jumpsuits they were scared young men not that much older than me, who'd made a terrible mistake under equally terrible stress. It wasn't something that they should've died over. Or, at least I didn't think so.

But the dead remain dead, no matter what anyone thinks of the rights and wrongs of their passing; that too is something that every veteran learns early on. I transferred my quarters over to *Coronel* just as soon as I reasonably could, this time not asking for Vlasilov's approval. It was just as well that I did. For hours after the deaths of their friends and squadron-mates, the Birds sat around the gunroom and silently stared off into space. Their counselors didn't know what to do, but I did. Colonel Rotte had told me once about how the Birds traditionally dealt with losses. "You can't simply pretend it never happened," he'd explained on the way home from a long, drawn-out mock dogfight we'd fought to a draw. "Pilots are human too. On the other hand you can't let it affect operations either. So I created a tradition."

Therefore, after a little time had passed I gathered the other Birds around me and explained to them what needed to be done-- what the Birds had *always* done. First we went to the prince's cabin, and then that of Marie von Blum. We divided their property into three piles. The first, which contained anything of either significant monetary or sentimental value, we carefully bagged up for the parents. The second, consisting of video games and other inexpensive but useful items, we divided among ourselves. And the third, which consisted of items best forgotten (like the mildly pornographic magazine I found under the prince's bunk), we simply trashed. Like so many of Rotte's suggestions it worked like a charm, offering the survivors far more closure than even the most

343

elaborate funeral ever could. The intimate little ritual brought us closer than ever to our departed friends and to each other as well, while at the same time allowing us each in our own way to say farewell. How had Rotte known that someday I'd be passing all this stuff on to a new generation of Birds? And how awful it was that he wasn't here to do it himself!

There was a myth prevalent throughout the United Systems that we Esteppans were born fighters. Natural soldiers, in other words, a warrior-society without peer. This myth was born in Esteppan society's love of uniforms and medals and grew into maturity during the planet's prolonged defense, when she actually did in fact hold off the United Systems and all her dozens of worlds all by herself for month after month. But the myths were nonsense, I'd always thought. Certainly I was no natural warrior, any more than my father or Sven was. When I thought of a typical Esteppan I pictured the Stormcrow workers; happy, big-bellied middle-aged craftsmen who liked to drink beer and sing together after finishing up a hard day's work, then go home to their loving, equally plump wives. A more unmilitary image was hard to imagine.

Yet I had to admit to myself a few days after the deaths of the prince and Marie that perhaps there might be something to the myth after all. On the theory that it was best to climb back onto a horse immediately after being thrown, I asked the admiral to close us off a piece of space for exercises. And so it was that the very day after the funeral I watched in amazement as the surviving Birds flawlessly executed maneuver after maneuver with a precision I hadn't seen since watching the original Birds perform together under the direction of the colonel himself. It was amazing, it was shocking, it was almost jaw-dropping how big the improvement was. All of the nervousness, all of the hesitation, all of the game-playing were gone as if they'd never been. Where once I had commanded a squadron of children, suddenly I was now in charge of young men and women. "Commanders always cherish blooded units," Captain Bard had told her little class. But this went beyond far beyond that. Was there after all something deeply rooted in the Esteppan psyche that, once activated, turned us all into exceptionally efficient killers? Or would the Bananas after losing some of their own react in the same deadly-cold vein? I could only shake my head and wonder.

That, and enjoy every minute of cleaning the clocks of the Top Bananas in a simulated furball not a week later. We not only killed nine of them to three of us, but destroyed *June* as well! With us only having ten 'hoppers to their twelve! I could almost feel old Emil patting me on the shoulder…

There was one exception to the sudden improvement in the Birds' performance. One of my pilots, who happened to occupy a particularly critical position, went into a bad slump. His gunnery scores dropped, he grew snarly and short-tempered, and while he didn't do particularly badly in the big Birds-Bananas melee, he didn't exactly live up to expectations either. I suspected some sort of personal problem, but couldn't quite figure out what it might be. In most cases I'd have spoken to his counselor, but this time that wasn't an option. So I decided to look up *Coronel*'s chaplain and get his advice.

"…not bonding properly with my squadron," I explained, my voice tense and hesitant. "I mean… Jimmy is my best friend, right? And I was really close to Delana, too." I shifted uncomfortably in my seat. "But… Somehow there's a wall between the Birds and me. I can command them, but no matter how hard I try I just can't *connect*."

"I see," Father Kordel replied softly.

I shifted in my seat again. "They're going to die, some of them. Two of them already have. I should've been more upset than I was. They deserve so much more from me than what I've been able to give. Emotionally, I mean. Like… I wasn't even quartered with them until last week. I tried to move over here before then, but not hard enough. If I'd really pushed the matter, I'm sure I could've made it happen. I knew that staying aboard *June* was bad leadership, but I let it be." I looked away. "I don't deserve these kids, Father. I don't deserve *anything*!"

The priest looked away. "That's a lie," he said simply. "And you know it."

I sighed. "Well… Maybe I *have* done some good things, though not nearly so many as other people seem to think. Certainly, though, I shouldn't be in charge of a squadron. I mean, look at how much better Jimmy is at the job!"

"I agree, frankly," Father Kordel replied, still looking away. "You *shouldn't* be in charge of a fighter squadron." He shook his head and turned towards me at long last. "You shouldn't even be a combat pilot, Thomas. Not at eighteen. Nor should you be a Parliamentarian, wrestling with intractable issues and slimy professionals. For that matter, you shouldn't even be mediating labor disputes—yes, yes," he replied, smiling as I looked up in surprise. "I've heard about that one, too." Then his expression sobered. "Thomas… You've been through more than any healthy teenager should ever be asked to endure. Now you're paying the price. One of the documented side-effects of excessive long-term stress is difficulty in achieving emotional contact with others. It's bad enough with ordinary veterans. But with you…" He looked directly into my eyes. "You've lost Delana, you've lost other squadronmates, you've lost Father Murton… In a sense you've even lost your father and brother. It's not like you ever see them anymore."

"And they've changed so much," I added. "Grown."

"Plus," the priest continued, "there's the corrosive effect of the war itself. All the fighting and bloodshed you've seen. The men you've killed." He met my eyes again. "The bombs you've dropped."

My shoulders sagged, as if I were carrying the heaviest burden the world had ever known. "Yeah. Those."

Father Kordel shook his head again. "You're a wonder, in a way. An absolute wonder! How you remain sane at all is more than I can possibly imagine." His eyes narrowed. "You realize, don't you, that most young men carrying your load with so little support from others would be in a psych ward by now?"

There didn't seem to be much to say to that, so I didn't try.

"Combat veterans," he explained, "often complain of an inability to feel emotions after undergoing the trauma of battle. The more intense the negative experiences, the higher and thicker the wall these veterans tend to erect around themselves. It's a defensive measure, really. Meant to prevent the pain of further loss." He sighed. "A person can lose only so many friends and loved ones before they begin to fear the pain so much that they shut off their feelings. It's a hardening, of sorts. Though one that's only surface-deep, I fear. True strength comes through relationships."

I felt my eyes narrow.

"It's what you're experiencing, I think. You've built a wall between yourself and the Birds, a defensive wall. It's common enough." Kordel was far colder and more academic than Father Murton had been; I wondered if perhaps he'd experienced a few losses himself? "Certainly it's nothing to be ashamed of. Some even consider it a healthy adjustment, inasmuch as anything related to war can be referred to as 'healthy'. The best way to deal with it is to talk about it, to understand it, and to learn to be brave again." He steepled his fingers. "Would you like a new counselor, Thomas? If you do, it can be arranged."

I thought about it a moment. "No," I said finally. "I'm a squadron leader and a Parliamentarian. I can't go back to being a boy with a guardian, not ever. No matter how badly I'd like to."

"None of us can," the priest replied, "As much as we'd like to as well." He sighed. "If you want my official diagnosis, here it is. You're ridiculously overstressed at far too young an age. Overworked as well. You've been through absolute hell, and it's one of God's not-so-minor miracles that you're still functioning as well as you are. You ask far more of yourself than anyone else ever would, and see only your own shortcomings in the mirror every morning where everyone else sees towering strength." He sighed. "It can't go on forever, Thomas. Flesh and blood can only take so much. Eventually something's got to give. But…" He looked away. "I have to admit that I can't see where there's much to be done about any of this. I'm a man, not just a man of God. As a member of the human race I can only look upon you and what you're doing with a sense of wonder and gratitude." He stood up and bowed. "And, Your Excellency, I can only hope that you'll be strong enough, long enough. For even I can see that you can't stop now."

Chapter Ninety-Three

You can't stop now. Father Kordel's words rang through my head over and over again over the next couple weeks as the army regrouped and re-embarked and resupplied and re-everything else a fighting force had to do before leaving the scene of one invasion and moving on to another. It wasn't a swift process. Which was probably just as well, since that gave us navy types more time to collect reinforcements and perform more drills.

We picked up another Warlord-class destroyer, the *Arminus*, plus the Polecat-equipped *Tsushima Straits* for ground-support. Having *Tsushima* with us was especially good for Jimmy, since his father and brother were aboard. On the day the new carrier arrived I sent Jimmy written orders requiring him to take three day's leave, then was happily surprised to receive near-duplicate orders myself from Admiral Vlasilov. It was a rather suspicious coincidence, this happening so soon after I had talked to Father Kordel, but not so suspicious that I could say for sure that there was a connection. Vlasilov might very well have come with the idea all on his own, so I decided not to hold it against the chaplain. Besides, the priest's words made *so* much sense! He was right; I *was* building a kind of wall around myself and whenever I tried to break it down I discovered that it was made of sheer raving terror. Eventually I'd have to do something about it, but now wasn't the right time. Not with the biggest and probably last major campaign of the war in the offing.

Predictably Jimmy and I mostly spent our three days together, a lot of the time with Lofton and Ted. I could be myself around the Knight family in ways that I couldn't anywhere else, even in my own home. All of us were highly-decorated war heroes, and even more importantly all of us understood how little that truly meant in the greater scheme of things. Father Kordel was right that I'd built myself a defensive wall, but around the Knights I could let it down a little. Sure, we might all be dead in a few days. But somehow it didn't seem to matter so much with the Knights around.

Both Lofton and Ted were brimming with confidence about the Churillian operation. "We have twenty-two superfighters!" Lofton exulted. "Twenty-two! And look at what you two have accomplished in the past all by yourselves."

"The Dracans will commit everything they have, this time," I countered,

"Including their supers. I can feel it in my bones."

"All the better to splash them," Ted replied, sipping at a glass of wine. "Kill them all!"

I smiled despite myself. More and more Polecat pilots were repeating Rotte's favorite saying these days. I wasn't certain that he'd have appreciated the irony.

"We *do* have overwhelming force, Tommy," Jimmy pointed out. "They can put up a fight, yes. But they can't win."

"And we four couldn't escape from Churilla either," I pointed out. "That was impossible too."

There was a long silence. "In a sense you're right," Lofton said eventually. "In the same kind of sense, to an extent it's even healthy to think that way." He put down his dessert fork and looked me deep in the eye. "But… Are you all right, Thomas? I mean, *really* all right?"

I looked down into my empty plate for a moment before answering. *You can't stop now*, Kordel's voice repeated in my head. *You can't stop now.* "All right enough to fight," I answered finally. "Though… Sir, I'm glad it's coming to an end. I have to admit that I'm getting a little tired."

Lofton smiled, then reached over and tousled my hair. "You're a good kid," he said. "The best. And one of the finest fighter pilots I've ever known."

I smiled back, glad again that I couldn't blush anymore. "You taught me to think offensively, sir. To understand that sheer bloodyminded aggression is what wins wars. And you're still the only pilot who ever shot me down in mock combat with a regular fighter."

It was Lofton's turn to blush, though with so much plastiskin sewn into his face he didn't do that very well anymore either. "I got lucky," he acknowledged. Then his smile faded. "And I'll admit something to you, Thomas. I'm getting tired too. It's been one long damn war."

"To peace," Ted said, raising his half-empty glass in a toast.

"To victory!" Lofton corrected him, raising his own.

"To the navy," Jimmy suggested, "Which gives us both."

"To our children," I suggested, my slow-moving arms clumsily raising my own glass. "That they may never make war again."

"Amen," the other three answered; I hadn't realized it was a prayer. Then Ted and his father drained their glasses to the dregs, while Jimmy and I sat and realized, with a sudden thrill, that perhaps it might not be so long before we could taste wine again ourselves.

Chapter Ninety-Four

In many ways, developing an air-plan to support the Churillian operation was much easier than the New Connaught operation had been. We had *Tsushima* and her Polecats with us now; it was a simple thing to delegate her 'hoppers to full-time ground-support and hold back the superfighters from *Coronel* and *The Glorious First of June* for operations against the Dracan Fleet when and if it showed up. But as always, there was more to it than that. We'd be landing so many troops and supplies, for example, that the transports would be vulnerable for days. All of that time, we'd be subject to counterattack. No pilot could remain mounted in a 'bolt forever. Yet because the Orion Nexus was so complex, at any moment we might find ourselves suddenly involved in a huge naval battle. So suddenly, even, that we wouldn't have enough time to man up our 'hoppers before our enemies were upon us. It was an intractable problem, one that grew worse the more you thought about it. I found myself looking back fondly upon the Drakkus raid, where the mission parameters had been far simpler.

Laying out an attack was always easier than planning a defense; this was part of why the aggressor tended to have such an overwhelming advantage. Everyone knew it; this was part of why "sheer bloody-minded aggressiveness" was such a powerful factor in victory. And we *were* on the offensive, I reminded myself, overall. In taking Churilla back we'd go a long way towards ending the war in our favor. But on a tactical level my squadrons would in essence be on the defensive, like it or not. So I had serious problems to solve.

In the end I sat down with Michelle and worked out a plan wherein the Bananas and the Birds traded off twelve-hour alerts, during which we pilots would simply sit in our torpedo-loaded 'bolts and wait for the Dracans to show. This would require heel-and-toe watchkeeping for no one knew exactly how long, and that wouldn't be easy. Jimmy and I had survived several weeks of such duty back on Esteppe, however, and being a fighter pilot wasn't supposed to be all fun and glory. What my best wingman and I had once accomplished, our new pilots could manage as well. In addition I wrote in a six-hour "all hands" alert to cover the period immediately after we invaded Churillian space, just in case our enemies were there waiting for us. They wouldn't be, we were all sure; it'd suit their purposes far better to come pouring in through one of Nikitas when they were good and ready rather than fighting us at our own highest point of readiness. Just in case, however, we superfighters would all be available. Besides, the Kicking Dragons aboard *Tsushima* might need help winning local air superiority.

When the big day finally came, everything went exactly as foreseen. Or almost exactly, I should say; no one ever dreamed, for example, that Spence's guerillas would contact us within seconds after our lead ship transited Nikita Number Four to inform us that the Dracans had demolished and booby-trapped the port facilities at Churilla City, that the occupying army had been reinforced to the tune of an entire additional division, and that exactly forty-seven enemy Dracan 'hoppers were believed to be in flyable condition. This last was particularly good news because we'd been led to expect at least a hundred. It wasn't until much later that we learned our original estimates had been very nearly correct until only a few hours previously. The guerillas, at terrible cost, had sabotaged the rest. Even more unexpected was the final portion of the guerilla's message.

"Welcome, brave liberators!" Spence's ever-optimistic voice boomed out across the bridge. "Welcome to Free Churilla! Above all, welcome back Thomas! We've saved some Dracans for you!"

Chapter Ninety-Five

At first it appeared that the only Dracans Spence had saved for me were army-types. We saw no Dracan naval vessels at all except for a single destroyer, hovering by one of the exits. It hung around just long enough to satisfy itself that we were indeed the main invasion force, then vanished. Clearly it was carrying the news of our arrival. Therefore for the first day there wasn't much for the navy to do, save covering the landings. We didn't even do much of that. Since we hoped to encourage the enemy to expend his fighters as quickly and as fruitlessly as possible, we sent only Polecats to cover the landings. Our enemies would hopefully come up to engage the 'cats, whereupon we'd launch the instantly-ready Birds and Bananas and commence ripping them to shreds. The Dracans didn't rise to the bait, however, so we sat on our launch rails and waited, waited, waited while huge battles raged down on the planet below.

The dirtside casualties were high, but the outcome was never in doubt. By H-hour plus three we'd secured two large landing-zones, one at each end of the Kammhuber Pass. "They're going to fight for Churilla City, it looks like," Captain Bard opined on the bridge circuit. "See how they've concentrated their missile batteries there? Along with at the Kammhuber, of course."

I virtual-nodded-- if anyone in the task force knew how vital the Kammhuber was to Churilla's defense, it was me. "I can understand trying to hold the Pass," I answered. "But why are the Dracans fighting for Churilla City? We surrendered it without opposition the first time around. It doesn't have any strategic value."

"To inflict casualties," Michelle explained. "To make the war more horrible, and create more ugly images in the press. The Dracans perceive us as weak and unable to stomach house-to-house fighting among civilians. The bloodier they can make this battle, they reason, the more likely we are to seek a negotiated peace. The reinforcement division went there, so clearly the Dracans believe it's an important strategy." She frowned. "We can't use heavy weapons in the built-up areas for fear of slaughtering the civilians. It'll be a bloodbath. All small arms."

"What about airstrikes?" I asked.

"Artillery is more accurate than any bomb," Vlasilov interjected. "And the army won't even be able to use that."

"I was thinking of strafing," I answered. "It's not as effective as bombs, but still useful."

"Maybe eventually," the admiral answered, sounding very tired. "But for now I can't afford to risk the losses. Remember those missiles!"

I virtual-nodded again, then checked the time. We Birds had been on alert for almost half a day; it was time for us to rest. I hadn't pulled a twelve-hour alert since I couldn't remember when, and I was more tired than I ever remembered being back on Esteppe. "Well," I said finally. "We'll know more tomorrow. In the meantime, I'm about to pull the Birds offline."

"Yes," the admiral acknowledged. "Of course. Get some rest, Thomas. I have a feeling we're going to need you tomorrow. Or the day after, at the very latest."

I virtual-nodded again; until the transports were completely unloaded we were terribly vulnerable. We couldn't maneuver worth a darn with the cargo-carriers tying us down. It was as if we had one foot stuck in a bucket. Even worse the Dracans understood this as well as we did, they themselves being past-masters at the art of spaceborne invasion.

They could be counted on to plan accordingly.

Chapter Ninety-Six

We Birds were almost through our second twelve-hour alert when things finally started breaking loose; there was only an hour left in our shift and the Bananas were already beginning the process of mating up to their birds. I was busy monitoring the ground battle, paying only passing attention to the endless chatter between my squadron-mates. So long as the tones of their voices remained upbeat and happy, I didn't interfere.

"...down to thirty-eight birds, according to the Resistance," our intelligence officer was reporting. "They claim to have sabotaged nine more. Though how they've managed it I'll never know."

Through sheer hatred, I didn't answer aloud. Having been there I understood that it was hatred which made the guerillas so dangerous, nothing more and nothing less. Hatred made them willing to take fantastic risks and sacrifice themselves in immoderate numbers in order to achieve their goals. People didn't like talking about hatred, but it was one heck of a motivator. In fact, it was difficult to imagine waging an effective war without it. "They're holding back," I observed. "To support their fleet when it arrives."

"Almost certainly," Vlasilov agreed. He paused for a moment, and I could almost see him sipping his tea. "How is the unloading going?" he demanded.

"Very well, sir," Jennifer Tyrose answered. She was Vlasilov's army liaison. "All the transports are down now, and we've got the floating cranes deployed and working. Give us another thirty-six hours and the landing force will be supplied for a month."

"Da," the admiral replied laconically.

"The sooner the better," Captain Bard added.

I virtual-nodded as well, even though no one could see me do it. So long as the transports were floating helplessly on the sea below, we superfighters had *two* targets to defend, not just one. If the Dracans wiped out the transports, our army would be forced onto the defensive in order to conserve munitions and power; if it remained unsupplied too long, it'd be forced to surrender. But if the Dracans hit our carrier fleet, superfighter operations would soon come to a screeching halt. All our repair and support facilities were aboard *Coronel* and *June*. In the absence of superfighters our fleet was no match for that of

Drakkus. Destroying either target could hand the Dracans a huge advantage.

"Tommy?" a new voice chimed in. It was Jimmy, mating up to his 'bolt. As squadron commanders he and I were the first in and the last out, so that no one else was on alert status longer than us.

"Heya, Jimmy!" I replied on our private channel. We hardly ever got to talk any more. "What's new?"

"Not much," he answered, sounding tired and grumpy. "Any news on the tactical front?"

"The Resistance has been busy," I answered. "There's only thirty-eight fighters left, or so our friends down below tell us. I'm inclined to take it as gospel myself."

"Me too," my best friend replied. He'd seen Spence's men in action just like I had. "And the army?"

"Unloading fast," I answered. "Though not fast enough."

"There is no 'fast enough'," Jimmy pointed out. He yawned again. "It'll be this watch," he predicted. "While we Bananas are on duty."

I virtual-nodded. "I'm surprised it hasn't happened already. In fact—"

Just then a red spot appeared on my pipper. It was a Dracan destroyer, popping through at Nikita Number One. "Alert!" the bridge talker declared. "Alert!"

"Perfect!" Jimmy declared. "Right at shift change! How lucky can we get?"

I smiled to myself. Back when we'd started the heel-and-toe watches, I'd offset the schedule six hours in order to have both squadrons up and ready during the initial attack. Presumably the enemy had figured out by now that we stood twelve-hour watches. Michelle and I had actually rather hoped that the Dracans might not allow for the offset. By their clock, based on the observations of the lone destroyer we'd seen, they'd probably estimated that right now we were as far from a shift-change as it was possible to get. I virtual-smiled to myself, then let the non-expression fade. Yes, the captain and I might've foxed them. Or else it might be pure luck. Either way, we still had one heck of a fight ahead of us.

It took mere seconds for the destroyer to grow a vector-arrow, and it was a huge one. Then another destroyer popped through, and another. By now *Almirante Cochrane* was blasting away; she'd been stationed centrally, where her big guns could cover all the entrances except for Numbers Two and Six. Accompanied only by a small escort, she was herself vulnerable to any determined Dracan attack. *Cochrane* was expendable, however, where the carriers and transports were not.

I watched as the big rounds roared across space, narrowly missing the lead destroyer. The second salvo, already fired before the first missed, straddled but did not score a hit. Desperately the Dracan began thrusting at ninety degrees to his current course, attempting to throw off the aim for what was shaping up to be a third-time charm. But one of the big laser-bolts struck home regardless, and the warship went up in a sheet of flame.

By then the sky was lousy with red pips; Dracan destroyers were pouring in at Number One, Number Two, and Number Five, all of them at insanely high vectors. Then more powerful units began to flash into existence, all at Number Four. I watched as one, two, three heavy cruisers popped through. The third was one of the extra-heavy cruisers specifically designed to defend the space around Drakkus itself, with lots of speed and torpedoes but not much in the way of range. I virtual-shook my head; if they were deploying *those* in this attack, well… The next thing I expected to see appear on my pipper was a kitchen sink.

The situation was developing exactly as Michele had predicted it would. The Dracans were hitting us from everywhere all at once in the hope that our command and control would break down. It was the kind of assault that there wasn't any way to plan for, save through endless drill and strict discipline. "Where are the heavies?" an unknown voice on the bridge demanded. "I don't see anything heavier than the cruisers yet. Or any carriers, either!"

"They're trying to get us to commit our defenses first," Michelle replied, her voice very calm in contrast to that of the unknown man who'd spoken before her.

"Da," Vlasilov agreed. "Signal *Cochrane*'s group to close on the main body. Everyone else is to adopt formation 'B'."

"Aye, aye, sir" the chief signalman replied.

"I've got three 'bolts ready," Jimmy interrupted on our private channel. "What are we waiting for?"

"The heavies," I explained. Then I switched to the Bird's channel, and explained the same thing. "We've gone to formation 'B', which is defensive in nature. Until we know where the main threat axis is, there's no point in launching. We'd be just as likely as not to head off in wrong direction."

"Ja," Isaiah agreed softly. He'd ended up my wingman after we'd been forced to reshuffle due to the friendly-fire losses. He was only an average pilot, but had a level head and knew how to obey orders. Besides, I had a gut feeling that he was exceptionally brave. In some ways he reminded me of Rotte's favorite wingman, Gustav. Bravery and unquestioning obedience would be enough, I hoped; it'd be my job to provide everything else. We were now operating in two elements of four and an element of two. Isaiah and I made up the element of two.

So far there really wasn't much of a battle. The surviving Dracan destroyers from Number Two linked up with the cruisers from Number Four, but their vectors weren't quite right to close immediately with our ships. Instead they'd have to thrust for a very long time, perhaps even several hours, before their relatively small guns and torpedoes could be effective. Meanwhile *Cochrane* was blasting broadside after broadside at them, though not so luckily as before. She winged a heavy cruiser, and vaporized another destroyer. But that was all.

"Where are they?" the unknown voice demanded again.

"It'll be Number One," Michelle predicted suddenly. "Look at the angles. When we planned our deployment, we came up with two possible concentration loci. The cruisers came through aimed directly for the one we didn't use. They aren't stupid. How much do you want to bet that the main group will be headed right for the one we *did* choose?"

"Da," Vlasilov agreed. "I concur." There was a short pause while he considered the implications if Bard were correct. "Five points to starboard," he declared at last. "Bows down ten degrees. Signal *Cochrane* to conform independently."

I studied my pipper. Every rivet of my Skybolt body yearned to launch, but it was still too soon. "Steady, Thomas," the admiral chided me, even though I hadn't spoken aloud.

"Aye-aye, sir," I replied. Was the man a mind-reader on top of all his other talents?

Then, as if all the Dracan vessels' helms were controlled by a single hand, the cruiser-destroyer group came about ninety degrees and began thrusting for all they were worth, the special high-speed defense-cruisers slowly pulling away from the rest. "What?" someone asked. "That doesn't make any—"

Even as he spoke, however, suddenly a torrent of new red pips began to appear, not from the expected Nikita Number One, but from Number Four. And, they were headed directly for Churilla and the army's transports!

"Damn," Bard mumbled, taken aback at being proven wrong for once.

"It makes no difference," Vlasilov comforted her as the pips began to take on identities. There they were, at long last-- the cream of the Dracan Navy with the older battleships *Serene Mountain*, *Crown Prince*, and *Aurora* leading the line. Then the pipper flickered again, and there was the superdreadnought *Imperial Scepter*, apparently finished well ahead of schedule, followed by the *Imperial Seal*. They were merely escorts, however, along to safeguard the main Dracan threat safe from counter-attack. Even the most powerful warships ever built couldn't hit the transports themselves, not while they were dirtside and protected under miles of atmosphere.

But carrier-borne Dracan fighters most certainly could. I waited expectantly…

…and sure enough, there they came, right on the heels of *Imperial Seal*. No less than five carriers, three of them heavies and two lights. Chock-full of conventional fighters, I was certain, plus whatever few supers the Dracans had been able to rush into action. *These* were our proper targets; I clicked over to Jimmy's channel. "Do you see what I see?" I asked.

"You betchum," he replied. "How do you want to do it?"

"How many of you guys are ready?" I countered.

"Five," he answered. "Give us twenty minutes and we'll all be on-line."

I paused for less than a second. "We can't wait," I decided. "The Birds go in first. We'll do what damage we can and you guys clean up after."

"Roger," Jimmy replied, sounding slightly disappointed.

"It *has* to be this way," I explained, trying to make my friend feel better. "You're the Bananas only experienced combat leader. So I have to send you all together as one unit. And you *know* we can't wait any longer to get started."

"Yeah," he agreed, still sounding less than enthusiastic.

"Cheer up!" I countered. "We'll probably have to settle for battlewagons. That'll leave you the carriers." I virtual smiled. "Good luck, Jimmy!"

"And to you, Thomas!" he answered, sounding a little better. "Horrido!"

"Horrido!" I agreed. Then I switched back over to the bridge channel.

"...should launch immediately," Michelle was saying.

"We're ready," I answered before anyone else could speak. "Or we Birds are, at least. Give the Bananas twenty minutes."

"Da, Thomas," Vlasilov replied. "Your targets are the enemy heavy vessels, especially the carriers. Do you understand your orders and the situation as a whole?"

"Ja," I replied, my own accent coming out a little under the pressure.

"Excellent," the admiral replied. Then he made it official. "Launch all second squadron fighters! Good hunting! Kill them all!"

Part III

Chapter Ninety-Seven

"Kill them all!" Vlasilov had just ordered me; the words echoed over and over again in my mind as I sat poised last in line on the starboard launch rail. I'd had to spot myself there because, in theory at least, I wasn't supposed to launch at all. And he'd wished me "good hunting" as well. Did that constitute official permission for me to enter combat? Was it a simple oversight on his part, a mis-speech in a moment of terrible stress? Or was it just possibly a deliberate attempt to allow me to "miscommunicate" my way into combat? Most likely the latter, I decided; Vlasilov was far too experienced a combat leader to make that kind of silly mistake. Though, of course, no inquiry could ever prove that the whole thing wasn't just a terrible misunderstanding, with no single individual bearing all of the blame. Not that it really mattered; I was going to fly this mission come hell or the entire Dracan Fleet. Since both were currently to be found in nearby space, I felt confident that I was doing the right thing.

By that point the only thing left that could've stopped me would've been if the catapult crew simply refused to launch my 'bolt. That didn't happen, however. Like the well-trained machine they'd become, the ratings pumped us Butcher Birds into space like rounds from a well-served cannon; boom, boom, boom! All ten of us launched in under ninety seconds, a new record. "Thank you, *Coronel*," I said as I roared down the rail. "Outstanding work."

Click-click went the deck officer's mike, an abbreviated acknowledgment. "Good hunting!" he added.

The situation hadn't changed much during the distraction of the launch. The Dracan heavies had formed a line-ahead to translate the Nikita, just as we had to do. Now they were contracting into a cylinder-shaped formation, with *Scepter* and *Seal* out front to take the bulk of the punishment. Not that this slowed them down any-- in half an hour they'd be well within normal-fighter launch range of the transports. The supers could launch any time they wanted to; Churilla was plenty close enough to provide an anchor-mass. I wondered what they were waiting for.

By then the Birds were done forming up, so I swung my nose towards the enemy concentration. "Our targets are the heavies," I repeated, just to make sure that everyone understood. "The carriers are the most urgent threat, but we need to take out the battlewagons too. It's long range, but eventually they'll either shoot up *Coronel* and *June* or else drive them out of the system. Either way, that'd be very bad news for the United Systems."

"Ja," my first element leader replied.

"We may not be able to make it all the way in," I answered, watching my pipper as *Cochrane* swung down under the rest of the task force so that her line of fire wouldn't be fouled by the lighter ships. She was our only dreadnought-- modern and well-founded as she was, I wasn't giving her very good odds of surviving the next two or three hours. "There's not enough of us, and you can bet that at some point there's going to be one hell of a dogfight. The main thing is to hit a target. I don't want any weapons left unfired. A cripple is nearly as valuable as a kill; don't waste all four warheads on any ship unless it's an *Imperial Throne*-class battleship." I paused for effect. "Those things tend to survive a lot of punishment."

"You oughta know," Jimmy's voice whispered directly into my brain; I hadn't known he was listening in.

I ignored him. "Accept an easy target if one presents itself," I encouraged my pilots. "The Bananas will be right behind us. Just kill heavies, and you'll be doing your job."

"The Bananas are lousy shots," one of my pilots griped.

"Ja!" another agreed. "And they listen to lame music too."

"So we'll have to make it easy for them," a third agreed. "The babies."

I sighed to myself; at least morale was high. "Whatever," I agreed. By now we were racing towards the enemy at a huge vector; I'd long since gone to full military power. "I'm very proud of you," I said after a long pause, while I searched for words and failed to find them. "And Colonel Rotte would be proud of you too. Horrido!"

"Horrido!" they all agreed at once, jamming the channels hopelessly.

"All right," I continued as the Throne-class battlewagons opened fire. Their huge rounds seemed to be headed straight for us at first, then arced harmlessly below as they sought out *Cochrane*. Their curving was an optical illusion, but the display was still rather pretty in a spitting-cobra sort of way. When we'd reorganized the Birds, I'd assigned my weakest fliers to the first element. They'd get the slowest, least maneuverable targets I could offer them. "Number Ones, you're for the old ships. They're slow, but they have thick armor and big guns. Take 'em out!"

The flight leader was willing, if inept. "We'll kill them all!" she declared. "Every verdammt one!"

"Second flight," I continued, "I know the odds are against you, but I want you to try and pick off a carrier or two. If you can't make it that far, attack a target of opportunity. I trust your judgment." And I did, too. Or at least I did since they'd done so well against the Bananas in our most recent mock battle. They'd been the real stars, all the more so since I'd personally not lived up to expectations.

"We'll kill 'em deader than hell," the young flight leader declared. His mother ran a highly-successful infant's toy business, and I wondered for an instant how she'd react if she overheard her once-cherubic fourteen-year-old speaking in such a manner. "Dead Dracans all over the sky!"

"All over the sky," I agreed, though having already seen that particular sight a few times I had no desire to repeat the experience. "Isaiah and I will take on the *Thrones*," I added, more for the sake of completeness than anything else. I believed that it was always wise to keep everyone as well informed as possible.

But..." my first flight-leader objected.

"Sir!" the second repeated. "You can't! I mean..."

"Sure we can!" I countered, carefully saying 'we' so as to include Isaiah. "There's only two of them! If I allocated a whole flight Butcher Birds to just two targets, the colonel would rise up out of his grave and strangle me!"

"He'd do it, too!" Jimmy added. Strictly speaking this was a breach of about fifty communications protocols and several basic command principals. But at that particular moment I wasn't about to complain. "You have no idea!" Then he switched to the private channel. "Tommy!" he protested. "Wait for me! Please? That's too much, even for you!"

"I can't," I answered, again privately. Then I switched back to my squadron channel. "All right. You have your assignments. From here on in it's all about flight discipline and stick and rudder skills." I paused. "You're going to kick ass. I know it!"

"Let's hear it for Tomas Longo! Three cheers!" my first-element commander cried out. "Hip-hip, hooray!"

"Hooray!" everyone echoed, and I felt terribly embarrassed.

"Thank you, Thomas," Isaiah added, on our private line. "For trusting me."

Would he still be thanking me, I wondered, when the Dracan fire was all over him like stink on shit and the superfighters had him boxed in and death was staring him in the face? "I trust you with my life, Isaiah," I answered. "As you're trusting me with yours. We're partners; there's no need for thanking either way." I looked down at my pipper; the sky was a totally confused mess of red- and blue-dominated swirls. This battle would be fought on a ship-to-ship and 'hopper-to-'hopper basis. There'd be little room for grand strategy or command and control, by me or anyone else. In the army, this sort of thing was called a "corporal's battle". Soon I'd be just another element-leader, another corporal unable to affect much of anything beyond the actions of my wingman and myself.

I hadn't spent nearly enough time with the Birds. I'd not even bunked with them until far too late in the game, and even though I'd made a sincere effort I hadn't been able to bond with them emotionally. All I'd been able to offer them was a little retraining work and then to lead them into battle personally. At this point, all I could do was hope that the Butcher Birds wouldn't need anything more.

No matter how much they deserved it.

Chapter Ninety-Eight

The *Thrones* fired again and again, our ships making no reply. *Cochrane* was conserving her power supplies, it seemed, after firing so freely at the light forces earlier. Having watched *Coronel* launch her birds, the Dracans were instead concentrating on *June* and *Tsushima*, each superdreadnought targeting one vessel. A salvo passed uncomfortably close to *Tsushima*, who was in the middle of recovering an airstrike-- for a terrible second I thought we'd lost her. But the huge laser-bolts somehow passed safely though they must've scorched her hull in the passing. As if this were a signal *Almirante Cochrane* opened fire once more; if it'd been up to me she'd never have stopped in the first place. Meanwhile the Dracan cruiser-and-destroyer force was closing in from the far side, in a sort of three-dimensional pincer movement. *Jimmy Doolittle* and *Louis Bleriot* were moving to counter them, accompanied by half a dozen *Chiefs*. They'd be hopelessly outclassed but might well buy enough time to allow us fighters to rearm and make a second strike.

If, of course, there were any superfighters left to rearm. Or, for that matter, any carriers for the survivors to land on.

Soon the space between the two forces was full of fire; the older Dracan battlewagons had finally came into range, and then the lighter guns of their heavy cruisers. It was a very uneven battle at this point, with only *Cochrane* and eventually the brand-new heavy cruiser *Toronto* able to reply. Not surprisingly, the Dracans drew first blood, one of their older vessels scoring a lucky first-salvo hit on *Cochrane*. But the heavy vessel simply shrugged off the blow as if it hadn't happened and continued to pump out fire in reply. She was targeting *Imperial Seal*, and on her fourth salvo scored a hit of her own. *Seal* flared brightly but continued shooting and showed no sign of falling out of formation. Her fire did, however, become notably less accurate.

"Good for *Cochrane*!" Isaiah transmitted; by now we Birds were well separated, each element spreading out towards their various targets. My wingman and I were braking now, so as not to run past the *Thrones* too quickly. Since they were leading the enemy line, Isaiah and I would be the first to attack. When the time was right, I swung us around so that we were charging in on their port flank.

"Yeah," I agreed, trying to sound cheerful. The Dracans hadn't launched their superfighters yet, and I couldn't figure out why. Perhaps they'd given up on them? Not likely!

"Where are their verdammt supers?" Isaiah huffed. I checked another box in his favor; he was asking the right questions at the right time. Perhaps I should've made him an element leader after all?

"I can't figure it out," I admitted. "If they wait much longer, we'll be too close to intercept."

"Ja," my wingman agreed, sounding glum.

Then there wasn't any more time for conversation, as our Skybolts tore through an invisible line and the Dracan ships began firing their light and in some cases even their medium and heavy weapons at us. It was every 'bolt for himself now, and I had no time for anything but the barest glance at Isaiah's position as I twisted and writhed and dodged through the fire.

"Mein Gott!" Isaiah whispered, probably unaware his mike was live.

"It gets worse," I answered, "the closer we get. This isn't anything." I climbed hard, then swung left and down to avoid a particularly heavy burst. A glance showed me that Isaiah was still with me. The maneuver broke us out into a bit of clear space; I took the opportunity to glance at my pipper. The first element was almost ready to begin their attack run, while the second still had a long way to go. "It's all right," I reassured the other Birds. "Everything's—"

Just then, a single light round slammed into Isaiah's left stub-wing. It wasn't too bad; there wasn't anything vital located under the skin at that particular point, and the round struck at such a shallow angle that most of its energy was wasted. But it still made a bright flash, and presumably lit up angry red lights in Isaiah's head as well. "Scheiss!" he cried, suddenly swinging away from the enemy.

I conformed to his turn so that we'd stay together. "It's all right," I repeated, examining his airframe carefully with a wingtip camera. "You're not hurt at all. It's just a scratch."

"Ja," Isaiah replied, falling back so that I was the leader again. "I'm sorry."

"No worries," I answered, arcing back onto something resembling an intercept heading; by the time we were done dodging and weaving who knew what angle we'd strike from? "Now you know what it's like. You're ready for it."

"Ja," he repeated, sounding calmer. "Thank you, Thomas. It won't happen again."

I double-clicked my mike, then returned to the squadron channel. "…follow me in," my first element leader was ordering. "Ernst, you take the *Crown Prince*…" Since everything seemed to be going so well I switched back over to my pipper, spinning almost casually past another stream of laser-bolts; the enemy gunners were finding the range again. Even as the pipper-image formed in my mind, it blinked …

…and then reformed, showing a cloud of fighters emerging from all five Dracan carriers.

"Enemy fighters!" the controller aboard *June* cried out in warning. "Massive enemy fighter launch!"

Another stream of laser-bolts rose from a nearby destroyer, then a second. The Dracans seemed to have mounted a lot more light guns on their ships since last I'd fought them. I decided that this one was shooting far too well; something needed to be done. I swung hard right, then rolled over on my back and dived on the enemy vessel, straight down towards his weather-deck. Just then yet another stream of fire emerged, forcing me to swing left and spoil my aim.

Not Isaiah's, however; without orders, he squeezed off a single torpedo. The range was too long, especially since my wingman's skills were a bit below average. But he got lucky. "Horrido!" he cried out as the elderly, practically-unarmored Dracan vessel went up in a huge explosion. "Horrido! Horrido!"

"Splash one," I agreed, already swinging right again to set my next run. The pipper was screaming for my attention, and I needed most urgently to look and see where the Dracan fighters were headed and how many of them, if any, were supers. But I simply didn't have any attention to spare. We were well into the Dracan escort-shell now, and under more fire than I could ever remember. It was almost like a simulated attack on *Zeppelin*.

Just then a light cruiser came looming up out of the darkness; either it was maneuvering wildly or else I was more disorientated than I'd known, to be taken by surprise at its sudden appearance. I swung hard left and passed so closely underneath her that I could've counted the plates in her bottom. She began to spin, so as to present her guns. I dove away, then looped around to face her. A quick glance showed that Isaiah was still right with me. "Splash it!" I ordered; the fewer torps he carried the more maneuverable his fighter would become and the easier time he'd have dodging.

He didn't acknowledge; there wasn't time. Instead he simply fired. The enemy vessel, already spinning, also began thrusting hard right. Isiah's torp missed, but it wasn't wasted. The unplanned series of maneuvers left the cruiser headed directly for the old battleship *Aurora*, an unhandy, pigheaded juggernaut of a warship if I'd ever seen one. Eventually, I predicted, they'd collide. Either that or such chaos would be unleashed that the Dracans would begin fouling each other's lines of fire and making it impossible for the group of ships to function as a unit.

"Scheiss!" Isaiah cursed. I wanted to console him, but there wasn't time. Already we were up against our next challenge, two more old destroyers swinging to cut us off. My virtual-mouth dropped slightly open; one of the silly fools looked as if he was trying to ram me! It took a mere thought to swing me past; as I did so I sent two streams of cannon-fire into her bridge as payment for her audacity. A Skybolt's guns weren't anything like powerful enough to lethally damage a warship; it'd be difficult even to destroy a merchie with them. But they could inflict casualties, and with a little luck I might just have killed a captain.

As we flashed by the destroyers, their hulls masked us for a second or two from the rest of the Dracan vessels. This finally gave me chance to check the pipper. Sure enough, the enemy carriers were disgorging a cloud of fighters. Dozens of them! Most would be ordinary 'hoppers, almost useless so far out from Churilla but growing steadily more effective as time went by. Among them however, had to be a handful of supers, a half-dozen or so according to our best estimates. But which ones?

Then the Dracans answered the question for me; eight birds suddenly spilt of from the rest and began racing for Churilla, their speed and power testifying to their identity. I virtual-scowled; now I understood the Dracan's delay. I could either intercept them or I could attack the *Thrones*. Not both.

"We'll take 'em out!" Jimmy assured me. "Launch in two minutes!"

I double-clicked my mike, then frowned again. Jimmy would get a crack at them, sure enough. But the geometry wasn't favorable for him. He'd only be able to make a single, head-on pass. The enemy would be moving so fast by then that, even if the Bananas tried to turn around and chase them, they'd never make it until long after the transports had been attacked. All the while, the Dracan heavies would be firing away at our own outgunned ships.

Another stream of fire roared by, joined by a second and a third, all from slightly different angles. I spun and twisted, my mind mostly still on the intercept problem. We Butcher Birds were going to hurt the Dracans, I estimated. But we weren't going to defeat them all by ourselves. Even as I studied the pipper, *Cochrane* flared from a serious hit. Everything depended on us superfighters; we were our fleet's primary strength. *Everything!* And here we were, all of us out of position! "Flag bridge!" I demanded, making a sudden decision.

"Here, Thomas," Michele replied.

"Stand in towards Churilla," I suggested. "You'll force the Dracan supers to swing wide. Maybe I'll be able to catch them from behind."

There was a pause that would've seemed a lot shorter if I hadn't spent the whole time avoiding a sudden barrage of medium-caliber laser-bolts; apparently we were now within range of the dreadnought's secondary turrets. Having no other targets close enough to distract them, they were occupying themselves blazing away at my wingman and I.

"You're faster than a Dracan superfighter," Michele replied. "But are you that much faster?"

It was a fair question; too bad I didn't know the answer. Nor did anyone else. "Do it," I urged.

"We'd have to stand in closer to the battlewagons," she continued, obviously thinking hard. "They'll get more hits."

Michelle might've had the luxury of thinking things through, but just then I didn't. A new burst of fire came in from the right; Isaiah dodged by veering sharply towards me. I wasn't angry with him, as he'd clearly had no choice. But his maneuver forced me directly into the place where I was expecting a medium-sized round to pass; only by spinning on my axis was I able to keep it from striking home square in the middle of my stub-wing.

"Oops," Isaiah apologized. I clicked twice, then spiraled hard to the left to avoid more rounds.

Then the vista I'd been waiting for opened up before me, obscured only by the distracting flickering of dozens of muzzle-flashes. There they were, two *Imperial Throne* class battlewagons, just beginning to sheer away. We were still too far out, really. But the targets were very large. "Fire," I ordered Isaiah; his last two torps leapt forward just as I was forced to swing hard left again. He'd chosen the nearer vessel as his target; it was *Imperial Seal*, rendered instantly recognizable by the large scar on her superstructure left by *Cochrane*'s earlier hit. There was no time to wait around and see if my wingman scored; suddenly the intensity of the incoming fire doubled or perhaps even tripled as the Dracans first grasped how deeply we'd penetrated their formation, then reacted to the fact. I spiraled hard left, applying vectored thrust along the way just to make things more complicated. It was a tough maneuver to expect someone as green as Isaiah to emulate, but I had little choice with the incoming fire as thick and heavy as it was. Still, he did a credible job…

…right up until the moment the first round of a long stream of fire caught his 'bolt dead-center and exploded it in a blinding flash.

It's rare to experience a shock wave in space, but apparently I was close enough to my wingman's 'bolt to pick up one. Or else maybe I caught some debris. Either way, I was suddenly pitched hard to the outside of the sharp turn I was making, so hard that for a split second everything went black.

Suddenly there was a second flash, larger but much further away than the first. It was a torpedo, striking home somewhere nearby. "Horrido!" a voice cried into mind, though I was still too stupefied to understand. "Splash one *Imperial Throne*!"

Disembodied brains tend to recover more quickly from physical shock than do normal ones, but it's still not instantaneous. I thought that I was myself again, or at least mostly myself. But the part of my brain that was thinking I was fine was apparently just as messed up as the rest of me. I dodged a stray heavy round, then searched the sky. Behind me and to the right, the *Imperial Seal* was indeed staggering out of the line of battle with much of her upperworks either missing or glowing red hot. She wasn't dead, though-- not by a long shot! Her after guns were still blazing away, and she seemed to be at least mostly under control. She was crippled, though, and that was good enough. I wasn't quite sure why it was good enough, but that was what I'd told the Birds just a few minutes ago, wasn't it? And if I'd said so, it must be true. I was their commander, after all! Or at least I thought I was, probably. My head hurt when I tried to think about it. There were a bunch of yellow lights glowing somewhere around the edges of my consciousness, and even a single red one. They were trying to tell me something, but it didn't seem terribly important.

It didn't matter, I decided. *Imperial Scepter* was now leading the enemy line, and that *did* matter, though again I wasn't entirely sure why. Near her-- that was where I was supposed to be! Laser-bolts were flying all around me, so thick that I felt I could reach out and grab a handful. My 'bolt weaved and dodged, much like a punch-drunk boxer wobbling across the sky. I stood my 'hopper first on one wingtip, then the other as I cut and ducked and vectored my thrust, working my way ever closer to the enemy flagship. I was alone now, which left me far freer to maneuver than if Isaiah had still been with me. He could never have kept up. Even Jimmy couldn't have. Which gave me an idea. I'd ring him up! "Jimmy!" I cried out into my radio, virtual-grinning. "You'll never guess where I'm calling from!"

"...second flight will conform," Jimmy was ordering. Then I heard a click as he switched back our private channel. "Tommy?" he demanded.

Suddenly my head swam again and things cleared up a little. My god! What was I doing chatting with Jimmy in the middle of a battle? He had important things to do besides talk to me. "Sorry," I murmured. "I got knocked a little goofy for a minute there."

"Tommy!" Jimmy repeated, his voice now full of anguish. There was a short pause, as he consulted his pipper. "For the love of god, do you realize where you're at?"

"Sure," I answered. "I'm about a hundred feet under the keel of an Imperial Throne-class battleship, holding formation. Everyone's shooting at me." I paused for a moment. "That's bad. Isn't it? That they're shooting at me, I mean."

"You're still goofy!" he cried. "Break right! Break right! Nownownow!"

That finally broke the spell. Instantly I swung out of my self-imposed slot in the Dracan formation and pulled away from the dreadnought. In the short run that made things worse, as her guns were unmasked and they began blazing away at point-blank range. But I was too close to hit, as fast as I was; the Dracan muzzles couldn't swing quickly enough to follow me. I raced away for a moment, then looped back...

...and released all four torps. The range was so short that not only were they sure hits, but all of them would strike home at practically the same place. Then I looped a second time and raced away for all that I was worth. Presently there was a huge flash behind me, the biggest I'd ever seen in all of my battles to date.

But I barely noticed. By then, all of my attention was focused on the eight Dracan superfighters running hell-for-leather towards Churilla.

Chapter Ninety-Nine

"Horrido!" the radio cried out again and again. "Horrido! Splash one *Imperial Throne*!" Even Ted Knight chimed in; he'd just landed back aboard *Tsushima Strait* in his Polecat, and was rearming to intercept the wave of incoming conventional fighters. His voice was easy to pick out among the rest. "Good job, kiddo!"

But I didn't reply to any of the congratulatory messages. My head was beginning to hurt in a very serious way, and I was growing rather nauseous as well. This was quite a trick, seeing as how I hadn't had a gastro-intestinal tract in years.

"Tommy?" Jimmy asked, but I didn't speak to him, either. Not because I didn't want to, not at all! But somehow I couldn't; two clicks of my mike was all that I could manage.

By now the red and yellow lights in my mind were becoming painful. They wouldn't go away until I paid attention to them, so I forced myself to do so. The yellows were nothing important; I'd lost my backup antigrav cooling system, which wouldn't matter in the slightest unless something happened to the primary. Most of the problems, however, were related to my bio-systems. I was suffering from a concussion, the rest of the yellow warnings informed me. But the red one, that was more severe. I still wasn't sure if I'd been hit by a fragment of Isaiah's 'bolt, or if I'd experienced a shockwave. Either way, an important connector had torn loose.

I was bleeding.

It wasn't painful, in any normal sense of the word. All I felt was a sort of tingling that encouraged me to check the red light regularly. Nor was I losing vital fluid at too terrible a rate; I could survive for about an hour, so long as things didn't get any worse. But I'd lose consciousness long before then. Exactly when that would occur, my flight systems weren't sophisticated enough to tell me.

I turned back to the pipper. This took a little longer than usual, as my mind was having trouble focusing. That was okay, however, because the volume of fire from the Dracan fleet had fallen to practically nothing. *Imperial Seal* was still popping away with her aft mounts, though not very accurately, and so were the destroyers and several cruisers. But *Aurora* had a very familiar-looking light cruiser sticking out of her side about a hundred feet forward of her engine outlets and *Crown Prince* was swinging out of line, wracked by internal explosions. Only *Serene Mountain*, alone among the enemy dreadnoughts, seemed fully-functional and battleworthy. She, however, had swung away to the disengaged side of the Dracan formation, presumably to avoid superfighter attack, and her guns were currently masked. This last dreadnought might still be full of fight, but for the next few minutes at least she'd not be shooting at much of anything. Plus, against all expectations, my second flight had driven their attack home as well. Two Dracan carriers, a heavy and a light plus several of their escorts, were colored in dead-ship pink. The net result was that for the first time, the two sides were at something resembling equality in terms of traditional firepower. *Cochrane* was still blazing away with three of her four main turrets, *Toronto* was unscratched, and even *Zeppelin* and the Warlords were nearly close enough to open fire. Vlasilov had chosen to shorten the range, as I'd requested.

I didn't need to consult the pipper to locate the Dracan supers, or for that matter their conventional fighters. My nose camera was locked on them, and I'd long since gone to full military power in pursuit. "First flight," I called out, looking for support. "Report in."

"This is three," Ingrid replied. "I have four with me, but he's heavily damaged. I think his radio's out. One and two are gone."

I pressed my virtual lips together before answering. The first flight had attacked the older battewagons. This mission had required them to fly a little further away from Churilla than mine. While they could certainly intercept the conventional fighters, I didn't think they had a chance of catching the supers. It wasn't worth even trying, I decided. There had to be survivors, to build a new squadron around. "Go home," I ordered Ingrid. "Escort Pieter. Your element did very well. I'm proud of you both."

Ingrid didn't reply immediately. When she did, there was a quaver in her voice. "Thank you, your excellency."

I clicked my mike twice, then switched frequencies. "Second flight," I called out. "Report in."

There was no answer.

"Second flight," I repeated.

Again, there was only silence.

Staring at the pipper too hard made my head hurt, and rapidly-moving superfighters weren't the easiest things in the world to make out anyway. Still, I studied the screen intently. No matter how hard I tried, I couldn't find anything left of the second flight.

A deep-rooted wave of anger rose in me; I bared virtual teeth, then turned on my external speakers and screamed my rage into the eternal vacuum. Yes, we Birds had hit the Dracans and hit them hard. Harder even than our most optimistic estimates. We'd left the Bananas a mop-up job, nothing more. But, the *price*!

I screamed into the vacuum again, this time until things started to go black around the edges and I felt myself start to sort of fade out. A few seconds passed, during which I maintained course and speed through pure instinct. Then a familiar voice brought me back to reality.

"…your telemetry, Thomas. Are you all right?"

It was Vlasilov, finding time to worry about me in the middle of directing the greatest battle he'd ever fight. "I'm fine," I lied, lining up my nose camera on the nearest Dracan conventional fighter, the one on the far left of their formation. They were headed towards Churilla too, though not nearly as quickly as the Dracan supers. I wouldn't have much time to shoot, but I didn't plan on wasting any of it.

"Your telemetry doesn't agree," he replied. "You're hurt, Thomas. Come home immediately."

I swung a little to the left as the Dracans grew and grew and grew in my gunsight. "I don't see a thing," I murmured, lining things up just so.

"You don't…" Vlasilov's voice sort of trailed off. "Thomas! This is not the time or place for… You didn't understand me, son!"

"I'm out of my head," I replied steadily. "Knocked silly. Delusional, even."

"Thomas!" Vlasilov exploded. "Get back here!"

"Just now," I answered, "Colonel Rotte outranks you. And believe you me, Admiral, he has business here. All of Esteppe has business here. We're collecting on a debt, you see." Then, I disabled my entire communications module.

"Thank you, son," the colonel said in my mind. Perhaps I really was delusional, but I'd felt his presence very strongly ever since I'd seen just how well his Birds had done and learned what a terrible price they'd paid for it. "We kill them all this time, ja? No verdammt survivors. Not a one!"

"Ja," I replied, steadying down and trying to concentrate on my gunsight. There'd be no pity this time, none at all. "Just don't joggle my elbow, all right?"

Chapter One Hundred

The Dracans were spread out in a wide line-abreast, broken up into subunits of fours and then the fours into pairs. It was a good formation to adopt when facing a head-on assault, which these Dracans were about to do. The Bananas were closing in fast. It was, however, a lousy setup for defending against attack from the side and rear.

"Steady," Rotte whispered in my ear, as I swung wider and wider to the left. "This will require exquisite shooting, Thomas, as well as very precise timing. Your timing has always been satisfactory and then some. But your shooting…"

"Yeah, yeah, yeah," I whispered back as I glanced up at the onrushing Bananas. This was going to be close. Rotte had never been happy with my scores on the gunnery range; his own had bordered on the superhuman. Only once had I ever shot a group as tiny as the ones he routinely turned in.

"If you can do it once," Rotte whispered, "you can do it anytime. You just have to want it badly enough. Don't be a weakling!"

I pressed my virtual lips together and nodded; he was right, of course. That was what winning wars was all about; being willing to work just that little bit harder and take risks just that tiny bit more insane than the ones your enemy was willing to accept. That, and being just a smidgen crueler and more ruthless. The rule even applied to wartime factory workers, apparently.

"One, two, three! Snap shot after snap shot. They're all ducks lined up in a row for you, Thomas! Stupid buggers, every one. Kill them all!"

"Kill them all!" I muttered back, springing into action. I'd long since moved into range of my first target, who'd nervously been sliding further and further out of his slot in the formation. He had to have known that he was about to die, and was growing more and more terrified with the passage of every second. At the first sign of fire on my nose he broke discipline entirely and tried to soar away. But it was too late. My laser-bolts struck home and he was dead in an instant.

I reactivated my communications module, and switched to the common frequency. "Horrido!" I sang out in triumph. "Horrido! I kill every one of you beggars! Every verdammt one!" Then I snapped my nose to the right like a machine and fired another ridiculously short burst. Every bolt struck home, and another Dracan died. "Horrido!"

Just then the Bananas came roaring up. In theory we should've coordinated our attacks. But Jimmy and I knew each other well; he did exactly as I would've asked and struck the far side of the enemy line. Four of them died, killed by the combined fire of the Banana's twelve 'bolts, while only a single Dracan bolt struck home on one of the third flight's birds. The Skybolt flared, but did not explode. Presently, it swung around and headed back for *June*.

Not that I had any time to worry about the rest of the fight. Rotte was living through me, aiming and firing with a precision I could never have achieved on my own. It was me doing the killing, part of me knew, me doing the flying and the aiming and the slaughtering. I'd just gotten that much better and grown that much stronger since last time, was all. But something in my mind had snapped as well, so that it was also very much Rotte who was, once again, slicing through the enemy like a hot knife through butter.

"Not bad at all," I congratulated him when it was done. We'd shot down eighteen fighters. It would've been impossible for anyone but Rotte.

"You're far too easily satisfied," he countered. "And not nearly aggressive enough. We've only just begun! Watch closely!" Suddenly we spun around on a dime and began a second run.

"We don't have time!" I objected. "The supers—"

But Emil didn't even let me finish my sentence. "You verdammt beggars!" he screamed on the general frequency, firing our twin cannon out into empty space. "You butchers of children! I'll show you what dead means! By god I will!"

And that was enough. The Dracan formation, already cut to bloody shreds, suddenly ceased to exist as individual fighters raced off in a thousand different directions seeking simple survival. "Ja!" Rotte cried out, firing the cannon again. "Run, you beggars! Run like cowards when you come up against a real man!"

My virtual-jaw dropped; it was brilliant. Attacking as ones and twos the Dracans could never hope to do any damage. And with any luck at all the Bananas were about to kill their carriers. The Dracans didn't have a hope of reforming the survivors for a coordinated strike, not during this war at least. No, Emil hadn't quite "killed them all". But he *had* rendered them impotent, which was effectively the same thing.

"A good many actually will die," he pointed out with a huge virtual grin. "Look at how hard they're running. How much do you want to bet that half of them forget their navigation and run too far away from Churilla for their motors to bite? Then they'll just drift away and die slow. Those ought to count as maneuver-kills, by god!"

"They should," I agreed.

"Tommy!" Jimmy cried out again; I'd left my radio on the general frequency, where he'd found me. "Go back to *June*! Please? There's red stuff coming out of the side of your 'hopper! I think it's blood!"

I frowned and turned the communicator off again. I liked Jimmy; in fact, he was the best friend I could ever hope for. But for now, I had other priorities. "He's a good kid," Rotte observed. "But you're worth two of him in combat. Maybe even three! What a superb killing machine you've become!"

I didn't answer; it didn't seem right somehow. Instead I concentrated on chasing down the Dracan superfighters. The only reason I had a prayer of catching them was that they were being forced to swing extra-wide to avoid the fire of the fleet, while I could cut straight across their curve. I still wasn't sure I'd make it. The Bananas had apparently accounted for two of them during their head-on encounter, which had taken place while I'd been otherwise distracted. It was six to one now. Good odds, I reckoned, with Rotte on my side.

"We'll catch them, all right," Rotte assured me. "At re-entry time, if not before. We just won't slow down so much as they do."

I nodded. "Ja. I've played meteor before, where they probably haven't. I know how much this old bird will take. And my brother's improved the design some since then."

"That's my boy!" Rotte answered gleefully. "Everyone dies, in the end. But not everyone covers themselves in glory along the way! I'm so proud!"

"This is all very easy for you," I pointed out. "You're already dead."

"And you're not?" Rotte retorted. "Look at your instruments."

I'd been trying not to look for some time now; concentrating instead on the steadily-enlarging image of the lead Dracan superfighter. But now, at Rotte's urging, I did so. It was kind of hard to read the text, what with the black spot that was developing in the center of my field of vision. As near as I could tell, about a third of my blood supply was gone. "I've got plenty left," I assured the colonel. "It'll last long enough."

"Ja," he agreed. "Besides, being dead isn't so bad. No one asks you to sell war bonds or run for offices you don't want anymore, once you're dead."

I didn't quite pass through the task force on my intercept course, but my track was close enough for me to be able to take a good naked-eye look-see. *Cochrane* had lost another turret, but for the first time I thought she might actually survive the battle. *Toronto* had taken a heavy hit and slewed out of line. It wasn't clear if she'd make it or not. But now the range was so short that the multiple light guns of our smaller ships were in play, hosing down the enemy with seemingly limitless streams of not-so-tiny laser-bolts. *Zeppelin* and *Arminus* were moving out to one flank, while *Genghis Khan* and *Attila* swung out to the other. Clearly, a coordinated torpedo attack was in the offing. In the distance, *Doolittle* and *Bleriot* along with their brave *Chiefs* were fighting a desperate battle of their own. But this was a sideshow. Whoever won the main engagement would come to the support of their cruiser force and the intervention would prove decisive

Meanwhile, I was closing on the supers faster than I'd dared hope. "Either they're holding back," I observed, "or else they're not nearly so fast as we thought." This was the first time we could be sure that we'd seen them running flat-out in a vacuum.

"Your father is a genius," Rotte replied. "They've copied his engine design, but haven't mastered it. The Dracans should never have started this war—by what process they deluded themselves into believing they might win is beyond me."

I shook my virtual head. "It was their stupid politicians, I bet. They lost touch with reality. Just like ours keep trying to do."

"Ja," Rotte agreed. "We warriors, we do the killing and the dying. But not the warmongering."

For just a tiny second I pitied the Dracan children I was about to kill. After all, they were pawns too. Then I walled the emotion off utterly. There wasn't time for that, not now. The lead Dracan element began to brake for atmospheric entry, then so did the second and third.

I, however, did not.

The enemy 'hoppers were swelling fast, now. Or at least I thought they were; there seemed to be something wrong with my camera. The images were growing very dim. I was close, now, very close.

"Close enough," Rotte declared, and I fired at absolute maximum range. The rounds struck home, and a Dracan super flared and died.

"Good shooting!" the colonel exclaimed, and I smiled blearily. It was growing difficult to concentrate now. The Dracans continued to slow themselves down, and I shot down a second, then a third. Red lights began to flash, as my navigational systems began, rather belatedly, to figure out that I no longer could slow down enough to avoid burning up.

"The beggars are helpless!" Rotte chortled. "They can brake and be shot down or they can burn. You've trapped them, Thomas!"

"No," I answered soberly. "I could never burn children to death, Colonel Rotte. *You've* trapped them."

"Whatever," he replied, shrugging. "You, me, we, they, it doesn't verdammt matter in the end. Everyone dies. Just as you are about to die."

I mentally shrugged back. "They won't get to the transports. That's what matters." Then I slowed down just a tiny bit; it was no longer necessary that I close the distance. All that was required was that I remain exactly where I was relative to my enemies. Nothing more.

As I watched the remaining three Dracans ceased braking and therefore remained out of range. In mere seconds they hit thicker air and began to glow. Then my own 'hopper began to glow as well.

"Turn off your pain circuits, Thomas," Rotte advised. "They're of no further use, under the circumstances."

"Ja," I agreed, doing as my mentor had suggested. But I couldn't turn off the cameras, as much as I wanted to. Slowly the Dracan supers grew hotter and hotter. It was a lot worse than my missile intercept had ever been; I'd started out inside the atmosphere on that one, and hadn't been moving at anything resembling interplanetary velocities. Would they burn all the way up, I wondered? Or would they eventually turn and fight? If they did come after me, the advantages would all be on my side. I'd kill two, maybe even all three while they came around, my position was so perfect. Then the last one would, unless I somehow screwed up, be easy meat as well, what with me starting out behind him. And what were the odds of me screwing up, now that Rotte had joined me? Slim, nil, and none. I'd already won.

Assuming I didn't run out of blood first, that was.

In the end the Dracans chose to burn, probably hoping to get off at least a long shot at the invasion fleet before meeting their maker. We were only a hundred miles or so from the landing ships when we crossed into daylight, screaming over the barren sea of rocks that made up so much of Churrilla's tiny land mass. The Dracans must've been in agony by then; one of them had tumbled and split into ten thousand fiery fragments, and I'd watched an attack-missile burn off of a second. I tried not to imagine them as infants writhing and screaming in a furnace. After all, what kind of victory could possibly be worth that? My own fighter wasn't in much better shape; I'd lost my main camera long since, and the nose was melting and dribbling back along my fuselage. "It's not so bad to burn," the colonel assured me. "You get used to it."

"I hope so," I answered. "I expect we'll both be burning for rather a long time, once all of this is over."

"Ha!" Rotte replied. "Well met, Thomas! It's been good to know you."

"And you," I replied. I couldn't punch out until the Dracans were dead; for all I knew, once I was off of their tail, perhaps they might manage some kind of attack after all. Better not to take the chance. Besides, I was almost bled-out anyway. "Horrido!"

"Horrido!" Rotte answered, as everything faded to gray. I was almost blind now...

...but not so blind that I missed the flashes as the last surviving superfighters broke up in front of me. So, my Skybolt had proven tougher than the Dracan design after all!

"Punch out, you idiot-child!" the colonel roared, as I sat and gaped. "Raus! Raus! Raus!"

Under that kind of tongue-lashing, I of course 'raus-ed' instead of thinking. "Boom!" my ejection charges went...

...and almost instantly I blacked out again.

The last thing I saw was my 'bolt transforming itself into a meteor shower.

Chapter One-Hundred One

Someone was screaming, I realized blearily. Rather, he was doing something worse than screaming. There was probably a word for it, but I wouldn't have known what it was even if my head hadn't been splitting and my non-stomach roiling and my gyros tumbling over and over again, unable to reset themselves. Whoever was making all the racket must have been in total agony. Every exhalation was a top-of-their lungs incoherent screech, and every inhalation a sort of sobbing gurgle. It went on and on and on for what seemed like hours, as I floated back and forth across the borderline that divides consciousness from troubled sleep. There were other screamers, too, but none so loud and persistent as this one. Whatever else was wrong with him, his lungs were as healthy as could be. I was just finding a sort of reassuring regularity in his cries when, quite suddenly, the sound was cut off in mid-gurgle.

That woke me up a little, at least enough to check my systems readout. Everything was green or yellow, all except for the gyro module. That was blinking red, which meant that a manual reset was required. To do that I'd have to lift my head until it was vertical. "No," I muttered to myself. "Not that!" Even such a trivial effort seemed as impossible as leaping over the Moon. I was getting better, the lights assured me. But for the moment, all I wanted was to sleep.

I must've moved slightly, because someone in the room with me realized I was awake. I heard them leap to their feet. "Sir!" a Dracan-accented voice cried out. "The prisoner is conscious!"

That was enough to bring me the rest of the way around, pronto! Despite the fact that every servo in my survival-body felt as if it were full of sand, I sat up in bed and opened my eyes. It didn't help much, because everything was still spinning. Yet clearly I was in some kind of hospital room.

And sitting on the chair next to the bed was a Dracan enlisted-man's garrison-cap.

"No!" I whispered to myself, trying to leap to my feet. I had to get away! But I wasn't going anywhere, it soon became obvious. There was a sort of collar welded around my neck and anchored deep into the stone wall. I yanked at it, just as hard as I could. But it didn't budge at all.

Then a Dracan dressed in a bloodstained lab-coat stepped into the room.

He examined me carefully, while taking great care not to approach too closely. "Are you in pain?" he demanded eventually.

I debated whether to answer him or not. Then I heard one of the more distant screamers start up again and realized this man, enemy or no, had other business to attend to. "No," I answered. "Though I need to do a manual reset on my gyros. To do that, I have to sit straight up. And I'm not sure that I can, without help."

The doctor nodded, then snapped his fingers twice. An orderly with no hat instantly appeared and stood at attention. "Assist the prisoner!" the doctor barked.

Instantly the orderly was at my side, so eager to help that he practically lifted me off of my bunk. "Whoa!" I protested as the world spun even faster. "A little forward... There!" My internal light went from blinking red to blinking yellow. "I'll need thirty seconds like this," I explained.

The doctor nodded soberly, crossing his arms. As everything clunk-clunked back into place, I took the opportunity to look myself over a little. I was pretty much intact, but one of my tripod legs was badly bent; I'd be walking with a limp until I could get it fixed. My father had added a pair of short arms equipped with gripper-fingers to the survival-body since the last time I'd worn one. They emerged from just under my neck. The left one was mangled to the point of uselessness.

"You came down in our front lines," the doctor explained. "The troops had been under heavy air-attack; they beat you with clubs and rifle-butts. Fortunately, a general was nearby. Even more fortunately, your engineers chose to use standard fittings in your construction." His brows narrowed. "One of our front-line medics discovered that our transfusion bags would mate up with your inputs. Once you were evacuated, I repaired your broken blood-line."

"Thank you," I replied, unable to nod until the gyros were done.

"Don't," he answered. "I also disabled your suicide option. My family lived in the City of Imperial Learning." Just then my stabilization system finally recovered. It must've been obvious that I no longer needed help remaining upright, for the doctor snapped his fingers twice and orderly stepped back and stood at attention again. "Good," he said, looking me over. Then he turned to leave. "You have much to answer for, Commander Longo. Don't thank me for saving your life. I've done you no favors at all."

Chapter One-Hundred Two

They left me to stew for a good little while; how long, I'm not quite certain. Long enough ,however, for a new screamer to take up residence not far away. "Jeez!" I finally said to the orderly, who'd been left to keep an eye on me. "Why don't you get these people some painkiller?"

"We've been out of most medicines for hours," he replied. "Causalities are far higher than anticipated." Then he frowned and turned away. "Please. I've been ordered not to speak to you. Don't ask me any more questions."

I sort of false-shrugged and sighed. "Whatever." Then I began to examine my room in detail. There wasn't much to it; it'd been cut out native rock, the same kind of rock, seemingly, as Spence's old guerilla tunnel. I wasn't anything resembling a geologist, but I knew that the stuff was hard and difficult to bore through. The furnishings looked old-fashioned and poorly-made, but were brand-new; it was if a fifty-year-old factory back home was still putting out the same tired, unimproved products. The sheets were of a very coarse weave and the medical instruments had crude, unfinished corners. Some of the switches sat off-center in their recesses. In fact, in the whole room the only item which seemed to be of quality manufacture was the orderly's uniform; clearly, no expense had been spared there.

Boredom was just beginning to seriously set in when, suddenly, there was a large explosion and the lights dimmed. Then there was another and another and another, until dust rained down from the ceiling. It was a barrage of some kind; probably artillery, given the regularity of the blasts. It was quite frightening at first, especially since my head still hurt. But the orderly didn't react at all. So neither did I. He seemed rather disappointed at that.

Eventually the barrage lifted and the screaming resumed its place unchallenged as the background music of the hour. I was trying to figure out how many distinct voices I could make out among the chorus when, quite suddenly, a large, bulky figure appeared at my door. Instantly the orderly snapped to his feet and saluted.

"At ease," the big man replied. His hair was done up in the intricate braid work that marked a member of the highest levels of Dracan nobility. "Leave us. I want to be alone with the prisoner."

"At once, Governor!" the orderly replied, smiling a big false smile and practically tripping over his own head as he bowed and scraped his way out into the corridor.

Governor? I asked myself. I'd seen the Dracan Military Governor of Churilla on the news many times while in hiding with the guerillas; this was not the same man. He studied me in silence for a moment, then closed the door that separated my room from the rest of the hospital. Next, he turned and looked me over some more. It went on and on, until he finally broke the silence. "It is customary," he said eventually, "to bow in the presence of royalty."

My eyebrows rose. "It is also customary," I replied, "to bow in the presence of a member of the Esteppan Order of Blood. So how about we call it even and settle for exchanging cold stares?"

Despite himself, the governor's lips curved slightly. "You're as irreverent as I was warned you'd be," he answered me. "Perhaps it's a symptom of your youth." Then he out and out smiled, and sat down in my visitor's chair "So be it, then. We may consider courtesies to have been exchanged. Have you been treated well, Commander?"

My eyes narrowed. "Since regaining consciousness, yes."

"Yes," the governor replied, nodding. "I've been informed of the unfortunate circumstances surrounding your capture." He looked down at my mangled arm and bent leg." Most regrettable." He smiled again. "I am Prince Pierre Montblanc, at your service. Thirty-third son of the Emperor."

I simply nodded. The Emperor had dozens of sons. It sort of went hand-in-hand with the harem-thing. He never seemed to run out of jobs for the younger ones.

"And of course," the Prince continued, "you are Thomas Anthony Longo, Parliamentarian and highly-decorated war hero." He smiled slightly. "The slayer of many, many of my people. Or, will you attempt to deny it?"

"Thomas Anthony Longo," I replied. I hadn't actually attended any classes about what I should do if taken prisoner; there was never any time. But even I knew this one. "Commander, United Systems Navy." I paused, embarrassed. "I don't know if I actually have a serial number or not. Probably I do; I think it was printed on my paycheck. But I never memorized it."

"Ha!" the Prince laughed, actually slapping his knee. "We have much in common, you and I. In theory I'm a field marshal in the Dracan Army. Certainly I receive the pay of one, among other compensations. But I don't know my serial number, either." He eased back into his chair. "I, however, have had a far less active military career than you have."

There didn't seem anything to say to that. The Prince was studying me again, but I didn't know what he was searching for. Eventually he broke the silence. "You fought well today."

"All of us Butcher Birds did," I answered. "I wasn't around long enough to watch the Bananas."

"Yes," he answered. "Your whole squadron did in fact distinguish itself. But you, personally..." He shook his head in what appeared to be genuine admiration. "I'm in a way sorry that you've been captured. Despite myself, I find your accomplishments quite remarkable. Heroism knows no boundaries. You don't deserve trial and execution."

I didn't even blink, having figured that part out long ago. "Thomas Anthony Longo," I repeated. "Com—"

"Stop!" the Prince ordered, holding up his hand to silence me. "We won't follow that tiresome road." He tilted his head to one side. "Is it true that you recently turned down a cabinet post in order to return to combat?"

I could see no harm in admitting this, so I nodded.

"You're close to the PM and actually intimate with Madame Deputy." He rubbed his chin. "And as you so correctly reminded me earlier, you're of noble blood."

"Look," I said. "There's not much you can do to torture me. Certainly there's nothing you can put together in the time you have left, before you're forced to surrender."

"Ha!" the big man countered. "My father has issued an Imperial Decree that Churilla is to be defended to the last man and the last round. That's why I'm here, to ensure that His august and lawful wishes are properly carried out." Montblanc's eyes narrowed. "There will be no surrender. Your army may wipe us out, but we'll leave behind a desert. A radioactive one. Without a single live civilian in it."

I smiled a little, despite the ugly images. When I'd made my departure we'd been well ahead in the space battle. Now I knew for certain that Vlasilov must have won. Otherwise Prince Montblanc wouldn't be speaking of last stands. Nothing would be entering or leaving the Orion Nexus without the admiral's permission for a very long time to come. There would be neither reinforcements nor evacuations for the Dracans. Ultimate victory for the United Systems was a certainty.

"Don't mock me!" the Prince growled, seeing my smile and knowing exactly what I was thinking. "Someday, Thomas Longo, you may know defeat as well."

"I've already known defeat," I replied. "In the Kammhuber Pass, under a neutron bomb." I shook my head. "It wasn't pleasant."

The Prince paled momentarily, then turned to face the rough-cut rock of the wall. "Yes," he replied listlessly. "I suppose you have."

There was another, long awkward silence. "I met your father once," the Dracan eventually said, apropos of nothing. "Just after he was cleared of crimes against humanity. It happened quite by chance; at an engineering conference in London." He smiled again. "My own father wanted to make an engineer of me, a superintendent of industrial production. But I found that I could never quite master calculus."

I blinked, but said nothing.

"At any rate," he continued, "I was still but a student, and your father was one of the speakers. There was almost no one there, Esteppans still being social pariahs at the time. But we Dracans, we've always been social pariahs too, and therefore less choosy than most. I attended, then afterwards granted him a brief audience." He shook his head. "Your father was so quiet and unassuming that it was difficult to believe he was so brilliant. We should've offered him a job and a title of the first rank. I suggested it, in fact, but the higher-ups never acted." He sighed. "So much might've gone so differently!"

"He wouldn't have accepted," I consoled him. "He's hated authoritarian regimes, ever since the Autarch."

"Authoritarian?" the Prince demanded, looking scandalized. "But I'm the protector of the Churillian people, against the exploiting capitalists and intelligentsia." Then his expression altered subtly, so that I'd understand that he was well aware of the truth. "You're probably right. We were doomed long before the opening salvo was fired."

There was another long awkward silence. I was almost convinced that the interview was about to end and that I was about to be taken to my "trial" when the Prince reached deep into one of his uniform pockets and pulled out a little box, Then he placed it on the bed beside me. "Your father," he continued, after switching the thing on, "was a traitor."

I opened my mouth to protest, then quite suddenly closed it. Suddenly, many things about this interview were beginning to make sense. "He ended a useless war," I countered. "A hopelessly lost war, in which people were dying for no sane reason."

"Like I said," the Prince answered, looking away again. "A traitor." Then he turned back to me. "He was made certain promises by the United Systems. And these promises were kept."

"They were," I agreed.

Montblanc's eyes narrowed. "Are *you* prepared to make promises, Parliamentarian Longo?"

I gulped, then looked at the box on the table. "That," the Prince explained, "is a jammer. To prevent any records from being made of this conversation. Save for the one that the box itself is making, of course. I'm no fool."

"I… Uh…" I temporized.

"I realize," the Prince continued, his eyes boring into mine, "that you're only a boy, by some measures of the word. On the other hand, you're also a nobleman whose influence extends to the highest levels of your government." He tapped his breast pocket, which was full of datachips. "I have much to offer you, your excellency. Codes, troop dispositions, convoy schedules, the location of vital supply dumps…" He frowned. "Our generals aren't fools; you realize this. Your army will shed much blood retaking the Kammhuber. We've been digging in for months. And when the fight is over the rail network will no longer be worth much. Many more will starve, despite your best efforts to feed them. Taking Drakkus itself will be far worse."

My mouth formed a thin, hard line. This man, almost certainly a war criminal many times over, was trying to sell out his nation in order to save his own hide!

"There's more!" he added, misinterpreting my expression. "I have deep, strong connections back on Drakkus. I can persuade others to defect, as well! Many others! I have information of great military value regarding our dispositions there, as well."

Despite myself, my lips became thinner still. Was this what it'd been like for Father, I wondered? He *had* been guilty of some of the lesser charges; certainly enough of them to hang. But, he'd never been prosecuted on those, due to his essential cooperation in ending the Stormcrow menace.

Was this why, even after all these years, he sometimes had trouble looking Gunther in the eye?

Then I sighed and it was my turn to stare at the wall. Only a few hours ago I'd burned several Dracan children to death in the name of victory. I'd done far worse on the day I'd nuked Drakkus proper. I thought about the doctor who'd just treated me; I'd killed his family and countless others. I'd even strangled a woman to death with my bare hands, here on this very world! What could be worse than this damn war going on and on and on? Setting a single murderer free, justice unfulfilled, didn't even begin to compare! Alicia would agree, I knew; she was essentially pragmatic under all the bloodthirstiness. So was the PM. They'd back me to the hilt. Even Spence would approve, I knew, though he wouldn't like it any more than I did. Anything, to end this verdammt war!

And Father? Prince Montblanc had made his position on matters of this nature clear enough. Damn him.

I let the silence drag on and on, just to make the Prince sweat a little. It was best that he be reminded that not all the leverage was on his side. Then I turned to him and met his eyes. "What exactly do you have in mind, your highness?"

Chapter One-Hundred Three

Two hours later I found myself seated in the largest, most opulent military vehicle I'd ever seen in my life. It was an amazing thing, really; a cross between an all-terrain vehicle, hovercraft, and VIP limo. The thing must've cost a fortune, but Prince Montblanc didn't seem to think there was anything unusual about it. "Load the prisoner in the back," he directed, and the squad of infantry that was guarding me obeyed. They needed the help of a cargo-handling power-frame; because my survival-body was such an odd shape, standard restraints were useless. So they'd welded the lead from my collar to about half a ton of scrap iron instead. It was very effective.

I paid close attention to every detail, though so far everything was going as planned. It'd taken the Prince and I almost half an hour to work out a detailed arrangement, the essence of which was that he'd take care of breaking me out of prison and I would then take charge of getting us to a safe place. The Prince was carrying a microtorch that'd make short work of my leash. I couldn't wait until it was cut; the lead was too short, and it was impossible to find a proper way to sit. The setup was most awkward, even though my joints didn't cramp anymore.

Then three of the soldiers climbed in back with me, a sergeant sat down in the vehicle's back seat and the driver held Montblanc's door for him. With regal calm he took his place, then the chauffer dashed around to his own seat. Finally, we set out on our way. I was very nervous; the Prince had refused to tell me how he intended to cover his end of the bargain. "I have a plan," was all that he'd say. "All the necessary resources are in place." Which was fair enough, I supposed; I still didn't have a clue as to how to get us safely into the hands of the guerillas. I knew a few old passwords and hand-signals from my time with Spence, but surely they were obsolete by now; indeed, anyone using them would probably be assumed to be a Dracan operative. Still, contacting the insurgents seemed a safer course than trying to cross an active battlefield. The United Systems forces were still limited to two small perimeters near the sea, with intense fighting taking place all around them. Anything that moved was likely to become a target for the guns of both sides.

Montblanc's driver seemed to be fully aware that his vehicle was unique and highly conspicuous; we'd boarded it close up against the steep wall of the quarry that the Dracans had expanded into a field hospital; my guess was that this was intended to make overhead photography difficult. Then the driver chose a route that took us down narrow valleys and, eventually, down the high-rise-lined streets of Churilla City. It was very dark, probably the middle of the night. Michelle had been right, I realized as we purred effortlessly down the streets while those few Dracans and terrorized civilians up and about so late lined the curbs to bow their respects to the VIP vehicle. Churilla City was absolutely full of troops. Liberating it was going to be a bloodbath!

Unless, of course, the Prince's data proved useful.

The streets grew steadily narrower, and the buildings older and more decrepit. Churilla had never been a rich planet, and during her early days the colony had nearly failed more than once. Back then the colonists had thrown together buildings any way they could; décor and durability being luxuries for the affluent. The result was the nearest thing to a slum I'd ever seen on a colony world. The last time I'd visited this neighborhood Spence had made me a Founder of Churilla, and I'd been awarded my first Order of Merit. The ceremony had taken place in a tunnel left over from the very earliest days of the settlement. Its entrance had been under a restaurant, I remembered.

And, I remembered, the restaurant staff had been members of the Resistance!

Suddenly the truck made a hard right, down a dark and narrow alleyway. There were plenty of these about, most fouled with trash and worse. The three guards in back with me looked surprised; up until then, we'd been squarely on-route to the Presidential Palace, or whatever the Dracans had renamed it. But they said nothing.

"Out!" their sergeant was suddenly bellowing, as he threw open the back of our vehicle. "Out! Out! Out!" The soldiers didn't hesitate; in an instant I was alone.

Then the Prince was standing alongside the truck. "Form a perimeter!" he ordered. "All eyes out! There are guerillas everywhere!" Without hesitation, the men obeyed. Then the Prince turned to the sergeant. "Give me your weapon!' he demanded.

In any other army, the NCO might've hesitated at obeying such a strange command, coming as it did at the end of such a string of strange and inexplicable activities. Or, perhaps not; none of the orders, after all, had been in any way illegal or more than passingly suspicious. The Prince snatched the sergeant's rifle out of his hand, then checked to make certain it was fully charged. "Men!" he cried. "There's a traitor among us! He's secretly sending out signals intended to allow the enemy to home in fighters and rescue their hero!"

"No!" the sergeant declared, falling to his knees; it was obvious whom the Prince was referring to. "No! Your highness—"

Blam! went the blast-rifle, and that was the end of that. "Eyes outward!"

the prince ordered my three guards. "Cover the end of the alley! They could be coming at any second!"

The privates all lined up, rifles raised and ready, then the Prince stepped up behind them. *Blam! Blam! Blam!*, and it was over.

Next the Prince turned on his driver, who was apparently unarmed. "No!" he whispered, licking his lips. "Your Highness! I'm no traitor! I've served you for many years! Since you were a boy! Who will braid your Royal hair in the morning? Who will serve your soup, warmed just so? Who will—"

Blam! the Prince answered, rejecting the appeal. For just a moment he looked down on the ruined body of what had apparently been his personal bodyservant as well as his driver, then he turned to me. Though I examined his face as carefully as I could, I couldn't detect a trace of emotion. "No one must know," he explained as he opened the truck's tailgate and handed me the minitorch. "No one. Not even faithful old Ross."

I accepted the tool, then turned away, disgusted. Part of the deal had been that no one, including me, would ever disclose the Prince's treason; he didn't want to have to deal with the shame of it. The official story, instead, was to be that I'd overpowered my captors and taken him prisoner. But I hadn't… I mean, who'd have thought…

"Hurry!" the Prince urged, pulling a pair of plain coveralls out of his briefcase and pulling them on over his gaudy uniform. "We haven't got much time!"

That was true enough; I gripped the torch in my one good manipulator and set to work. In seconds I was free. "Here," he urged me, removing another item from his briefcase. It was a handgun. "Take this! If we run into any Imperial troops, I'll pretend to be your hostage."

If we ran into any Imperial troops, I decided as I accepted the firearm, and there wasn't any way to deceive them, then I'd kill the Prince if it was the last thing I did. After what I'd just witnessed, I wouldn't hesitate a second. I'd never actually enjoyed killing anyone before; it'd be a new experience for me. "All right," I agreed, waving the muzzle at my "hostage". "We'll go down the alley a little further, then make a right."

"As you wish," the Prince replied. As near as I could tell he'd given me a perfectly functional weapon. He was an intelligent and resourceful man, despite his ethically-challenged nature, and seemed to understand that, having come this far, his best chance of survival lay in full and complete cooperation. Without a word, he turned and walked off in the direction indicated.

Now, it was all up to me.

Chapter One-Hundred Four

We weren't doing half badly I reassured myself as we reached the end of the filthy little throughway and, as planned, made a right turn. Of course we weren't moving very quickly; the Prince had already had to stop and wait for me twice due to my bent leg. And I still had no idea of where we were; the right turn had been chosen at random. But, I decided, overall things were going pretty well. The Prince had chosen a good spot for his executions, I had to hand him that. The entire area seemed to be abandoned. "We'll go a block down that way," I indicated, casually waving the gun again. "Then we'll start looking for a—"

Suddenly, out of nowhere the muzzle of a blast-rifle appeared at my throat. "Silence!" a voice demanded.

I felt myself relax slightly; the voice had a Churillian accent.

"Drop the gun!" it continued.

I let the thing clatter to the pavement. Then the rifle-muzzle pulled back slightly. "This way!" the voice urged, as suddenly a half a dozen more shapes materialized out of nowhere. "Now!"

The Prince obeyed instantly, and I moved as quickly as I could as well. Which wasn't nearly fast enough, apparently; at a gesture, the dark figures snatched me up and began running with me. "I'm a shot-down United Systems pilot," I whispered into the ear of one of the men. "And the man with me is my prisoner. He's not to be harmed!"

"Silence!" he ordered again. This time, I complied.

We rounded the corner at a fair clip, the Prince breathing hard from his unaccustomed exertions. Then the group's leader tapped out a staccato little beat on a trash dumpster, using the butt of his pistol. The dumpster rolled away…

…exposing a trapdoor underneath!

"In!" he demanded. "Now!" Once again the Prince didn't hesitate. But, damaged as I was, I simply couldn't climb down the ladder no matter how hard I tried. Sirens were sounding in the distance now; apparently, the Dracans were just now noticing that their governor had been misplaced. "Are you fragile?" the leader demanded as I tried and failed to pick my way down through the tiny manhole.

"No," I answered, wincing at I knew must come next. Without orders, two of the men grabbed me, turned me upside down, and tossed me headfirst through the opening.

"Ow!" I protested when I hit bottom; it happened a lot sooner than expected, so that I didn't have time to brace myself.

"Crawl!" a new voice urged. "For your life!"

I did so, almost immediately hitting my head again on the low ceiling. The tunnel couldn't have been more than a couple feet high. "The prisoner," I whispered again. "He isn't to be harmed, no matter what! We need him alive and unhurt!"

"Yes," the leader answered from behind me. "We know. Now, crawl!"

Our journey seemed to go on forever. The tunnel had apparently been dug by hand; it was pitch-black inside, of course, but I could feel the walls bulging in irregularly here and there as I squeezed my way down it. I couldn't be sure, but judging by the sounds the last man in line was knocking out the supports as he passed. Sometimes there were caving-in noises. Anyone who tried to follow us was in for a long, dangerous journey. Eventually a dim source of light began to reveal itself far in front of me; it flickered and wavered as the multiple writhing bodies between me and it blocked its glow. But as time went by it grew stronger.

"Here's our first stop," the leader said, as he eased himself out of a sort of hatchway. When my head emerged, I could see that the tunnel's outlet was located near the floor of what appeared to be some kind of factory. Certainly the place was noisy enough to be a factory; in the distance I could hear all manner of heavy machinery running. The guerilla, for by now I could be certain that this was what he was, reached down and helped me to my feet. "You didn't need to introduce yourself, Founder Longo," he observed, smiling for the first time. "Ever since you were shot down, your navy friends have been flooding the airwaves with your picture and notice of a huge reward."

I nodded and smiled back; why hadn't I figured that out for myself? The concussion, perhaps? Then I reached out with my one functional manipulator. "Pleased to meet you… what was your name again?"

"Louis," the man replied, grinning again and accepting my "hand". He bowed. "I'm deeply honored."

"I'm deeply grateful," I countered. Then I repeated the process with the rest of the group.

"We've met before," Louis observed when I was finished. "Do you by chance remember me?"

I examined his face closely. Like the rest he was filthy, worn-out looking, and gaunt to the point of starvation. The Dracans were starving all of Churilla, quite deliberately. The merest survival-ration of food was allocated only to those who worked in the Dracan war-industries; if they had no extra, in theory there'd be nothing to share with the insurgents. "No," I answered. "I'm sorry. But I've met so many people…"

"Oh!" Louis replied, blushing a little. "I think that perhaps you might recall me. If I were to remind you properly, that is." Then he pulled out a gold coin, and held it up so that I could see it. I blinked; it was a perfectly ordinary twenty-credit piece…

…just like the one that, on the very last day of peace, I'd thrown off a bridge for a young Churillan to dive after! My eyes widened. "Why… I…"

"Ha!" Louis replied. "You do remember!" He held up the coin in triumph. "Did I not tell you, over and over again, that Founder Longo himself had tossed this into the river for me? That I really did meet him? That is why I shall never spend this coin! Never!"

Some of the other guerillas looked at their leader in wonder, while others turned away, unable to meet Louis's eyes. It was easy enough to tell who the skeptics had been.

Then Louis turned to the Prince. "Who is this creature?" he demanded, his voice suddenly far less friendly.

My eyes narrowed. "You don't know?" I answered.

"He was riding in a VIP vehicle," Louis answered. "That means he's a high-ranker, all right." Then his face softened and he faced me again. "Did you really kill all of those Dracans in the car with you, Founder? All by yourself?"

I didn't like it, but I'd made a promise in the name of the greater good. "Yes," I lied. Then I turned to the Prince, and my eyes narrowed. "You're not half so famous as I imagined you'd be."

"I only just arrived on-planet," he countered. "With the last wave of reinforcements. I haven't had time yet to make any public appearances." Then he turned to the Churillans. "I am the head of the Ministry of Education. Duke Andre Lamont, at your service."

Lies, lies, lies, I thought. Nothing but lies, and all of them unfolding right in front of men whom I knew to be the true heroes of this terrible war. It made me feel dirty inside. But what I could do except keep the charade right on going? If this man wasn't a Prince, the navy would find out soon enough. Though the one thing he surely could *not* have been was the Minister of Education; a man in a purely administrative position wouldn't have access to such an important prisoner as myself. For my money at least, he was the genuine article and telling the truth about his recent arrival. "We have to get him out of here," I replied, changing the subject. "To someplace where a pickup can be arranged."

"And you, as well," the guerilla replied. He waved his arms. "This is a molecular-battery factory. It operates three shifts, seven days a week, providing the Dracans with power-sources." He smiled. "But not-so-good power-sources, I fear. Churillian industry was never renowned for its quality-control. And since the invasion?" He shrugged. "What a scandal!"

I smiled, understanding. "Which means, I suppose, that large quantities of stuff comes in and out all of the time?"

He nodded. "Exactly." Then he looked up at the dirty old clock on the wall. "The morning pull will be in three hours. I think we can have you two ready by then."

Chapter One-Hundred Five

As a little boy, I'd been very fond of Halloween. I'd gone out trick-or-treating dressed as various superheroes, a ghost, and even several different cartoon characters. But never in my wildest imagination had I ever imagined that someday I might masquerade as a molecular battery.

It was logical enough, I supposed; just an extension of the same principle by which Spence and Father Murton and I had once traveled these same rails inside shipping crates. Since that time, however, the Dracans had grown far more careful about rail freight. Crates were opened and sometimes even hurled off cliffs at random, in order to discourage their use as makeshift passenger compartments. Molecular batteries, however, were extremely valuable to the Dracan war effort. On top of that they were heavy and required powered equipment to move. Even with such equipment, unloading a whole railcar full of the things for inspection was quite a job. So the Dracans didn't do it very often.

"…and," Louis was explaining, wearing a big grin, "you'll even show a full charge if tested. So don't panic if they pull you for a search."

I nodded, impressed. Though their enemies had grown more careful, the guerillas had in turn become more sophisticated. The Resistance was going to seal each of into our own fake unit, the oversized kind that was big enough to power a small community for as much as a year. And, also, the kind that the Dracans needed most to power their fortifications. There was little danger they'd interfere with *this* shipment.

"You're only going to have half the interior to yourselves," he continued. "The other half is real, which is where the charge comes from. You'll breathe through the standard cooling vents."

I nodded again. It made sense. Then I looked at the Prince, who was paling rapidly. "You got a problem?" I demanded.

"I…" he stuttered. "I mean…"

"Are you claustrophobic?" Louis demanded. "If so, speak up and we'll drug you."

"No," the Dracan replied, eyeing his proposed hiding-place carefully.

"Then what's wrong?" the guerilla demanded.

"Nothing," the Prince replied. Then he climbed over the edge of the casing and down into the fake battery. "I'm ready."

Louis made an imperious hand-gesture to one the factory-men, who drove his material-handler forward and, with great skill, set the heavy lid delicately in place. Next two more workers stepped forward, sealing the Prince in. "Well," the young man declared, grinning to me. "His beacon won't work anymore now! He's enclosed in lead."

I blinked. "Beacon?"

"Of course!" Louis replied, laughing in merriment. "You're wearing one too, if you didn't know." My mouth opened, but Louis continued right on. "It's not your fault; we know that. It may not be your prisoner's fault that he's wearing one, either. They're tiny things, easy to plant and difficult to detect without proper tools." He held up a hand-scanner.

"I… But…"

"Ha!" Louis replied, bending double and slapping his thigh. "We deal with this sort of thing all of the time; if we couldn't, how do you suppose we survived so long?" He pointed to a green light on his scanner. "That's a jammer. These days every guerilla on the planet carries one with him, all of the time. The Dracans lost contact the moment I came within twenty feet of you." His grin widened. "Eventually they'll follow the collapsed tunnel, of course. But that'll take time. By then we'll be long gone from here. In fact, if we did the job properly Churilla might just be free again before they figure it out. There were false leads built in, as well."

I smiled too, but only for a moment. Tracers? I'd been away from the Resistance for too long it seemed, fighting a less devious sort of war. "Are you sure?" I finally asked. "Unless I miss my guess, we've got total air superiority by now. If we really needed to, the task force could punch right through and evacuate not only the prince and I from this very spot, but you and your men too."

"I'm sure, Louis replied, still smiling. Then his expression faded, too. "Founder?"

"Yes?" I answered.

Louis looked away. "This Prince you've captured…"

I sighed. "There's something fake about him. Isn't there?"

My new friend nodded. "I didn't want to say anything… I mean, you're a great man, while I'm but a poor—"

"You *are* a great man," I interrupted. "And your fight has been much harder and more dangerous than my own. Don't ever underestimate what you and your fellow Churillians have achieved here, Louis. It's a far greater accomplishment, won at a far greater cost, than anything I've ever done."

Louis blushed so red I feared he might suffer a stroke. "Founder! I mean…"

I smiled and patted him on the shoulder. "Never mind. We don't have time.

Now, what about the Prince?"

The guerilla frowned again. "I've fought many Dracans. And, I've even taken a few prisoners. They resist like wildcats, even long after all hope is gone. All of them. Without exception."

I nodded slowly. "This one is slime, Louis. Utterly without honor and self-respect." I looked away. "I'd like to tell you more. But I can't. There's security issues involved. I'm sure you know all about that sort of thing."

"His hair is braided properly," Louis continued, speculating. "That's an art-form in and of itself. I believe him when he says he's a nobleman. But…"

"But?" I asked.

"That hair… It's *too* elaborate for a Duke. And…" He frowned again. "Founder, I swear to you that I've seen that face somewhere before. I can't quite remember where, but the minute I laid eyes on him chills began running up and down my spine." He looked me in the eyes. "And I can equally assure you that no Dracan Minister of Education would have that effect on me." He smiled. "No matter how badly they've polluted everything else they've touched, the Dracan schools actually aren't half bad!"

Chapter One-Hundred Six

I had a lot of time to think during the three-hour train ride to wherever I was going. Any Dracan inspections, I was told, would take almost certainly happen before I ever really got moving. None took place, so I was left to lie in the dark in peace. It was the first time in many weeks, I reflected, that I'd had time to just think about stuff. Which was just as well, because my recent experiences were certainly worthy of mulling over. First there was the battle, and all the deaths. The Butcher Birds had suffered horribly, I knew. But how about the Bananas? Was Jimmy still alive? If not, I decided, it was better that I didn't yet know.

And, I asked myself, why was it that I worried about Jimmy instead of those Birds who I knew for fact were shot down? Certainly, there would've been some successful ejections among them. But still… What was happening to me? Why could I not make myself care as much about those wonderful, brave children who'd trusted me so? I'd lost a wingman, for crying out loud, and yet here I was mooning over whether or not Jimmy might be dead!

Who was I becoming? Would I ever be able to make new friends again? Were the scars too thick? How deep did the damage go?

Then there was the Prince to worry about. On the one hand, I could understand how a man might betray his country and even his family under the exigencies the local Dracans were facing. With the space battle won there could be no escape for any of them, save through surrender. Surrender would probably be quite difficult for a Dracan nobleman, much less a prince, to live with after the war. We were going to hang the Emperor; that was a given. But it was equally certain that we'd not hang all of his dozens of children. That'd be an atrocity, since most likely only a handful were guilty of war crimes. The rest of them would go on much as they had before, as wealthy aristocrats. Even if we confiscated their property, which was in and of itself unlikely, they'd soon be back on top. There were few things harder to kill off than a claim to nobility. Take His Serene Highness, for example, who'd died in the friendly fire incident off New Connaught. His family's claim to princedom dated back over seven hundred years, almost six hundred of them having passed after the nation he was supposed to be prince of had ceased to exist. Yet after all that time people still bowed and scraped. His family was one of the most important on Esteppe, both socially and financially. My captive Prince could ill-afford to put himself in a bad odor with his brothers and sisters, given that they'd remain influential for generations to come. I sighed and shook my head in the darkness. What was it about humans anyway, I wondered, that made us adore royalty so? Was there something written in the human genome that made us want to accept family dynasties as the natural way of things?

Not that such a system produced particularly good results, I reminded myself. Parliament, for all its corruption and waste, was a much better way to run things. Even Nagano, the lowest, most disgusting Parliamentarian I knew, was ethically head and shoulders above the Prince. I shuddered a little, remembering the Dracan cold-bloodedly shooting his own valet. Despite all I'd seen and done in this war, I'd never taken in such a revolting, disgusting sight. The faithful Ross's last wail of despair as his patron pulled the trigger would live in my nightmares forever; there could be no doubt of that. All the more so since a little voice in the back of my mind kept telling me that I should've seen it coming, and that therefore at least partially the horrid crime was my fault.

I sighed and shook my head again, thinking back over everything I knew of the Prince. At first I'd been surprised at how much he and I were alike, right down to our having failed as would-be engineers due to our inability to master higher maths. We were both born to wealth and privilege, both younger sons of men of great power, scions of long-standing dynasties that dated back to the original days of the colonization of the universe. We were both at least moderately bright as well, I allowed. Yet, how very differently we'd come out! I was, rightly or wrongly, seen as a hero. People really did like me, I admitted to myself, though I knew they wouldn't if they knew me better. But the Prince...

He was everything that I hated. Arrogant, ruthless, self-centered. A murderer and traitor. All the things that I'd rather die than become.

Maybe that was why I couldn't understand what was going on? Because I wasn't accustomed to thinking in such a sick, twisted manner? Curling my lips in disgust, I tried to picture myself executing Father Murton as he moaned in betrayed misery. At first I wanted to retch, but then a couple things came clear. This wasn't the Prince's first murder, I realized. Not by a long shot. The man who could pull the trigger under such circumstances must've hardened himself first over a long period of time, by killing again and again and again.

And who on Churilla, a little voice asked in the back of my mind, has killed so many times? Not second-hand, through others; that wouldn't have been enough. Who'd killed people up close and personal often enough that it became easy and natural? And who would also have access to one Thomas Longo, once he was taken prisoner? Then I laid my head back on the battered old pillow that Louis had tossed in with me at the last minute. The Prince didn't have one, and suddenly I hoped that he'd never have another so long as he lived. For I knew now who he had to be, why the guerillas hadn't recognized him, and why he'd been so eager to risk everything in exchange for my word of honor that he wouldn't be prosecuted.

I'd captured myself a Prince all right; Louis was correct about the hair-braiding thing; Ross himself had wailed about caring for his master's "royal" hair as he'd died. And, said Prince probably *was* carrying vital military data in his breast pocket, and had all the social contacts that he was so eager to claim. But he was no governor, any more than I was a lemon meringue pie. If he'd been the governor he could never have pulled off the whole defection thing. There'd have been too many guards.

No, I realized, wanting to vomit. My Prince was the head of the secret police, the man who'd been in charge of interrogating, torturing and killing god only knew how many guerillas and innocent suspects. He'd kept his face secret so that he wouldn't be an assassination target. Of all the Dracans anywhere, second only to the Emperor himself, he was probably the one most deserving of the noose.

And there he was, riding safely and securely just a few feet away from me, probably planning his post-war life and congratulating himself on seizing such a brilliant opportunity to survive when death had seemed so certain.

Chapter One-Hundred Seven

I wasn't alarmed when the train's brakes suddenly slammed on and, almost before we'd come to a stop, the door flew open. I'd ridden Rail Guerilla before, and knew how such things were done. Soon there were muffled voices, followed by the sound of powered cargo-handling equipment. I felt myself being lifted and carried, then everything went silent for a few moments as, presumably, the operation was repeated for the Prince. Next there was a dull thud alongside me as he was set down, and the roar of the locomotive as the train went off on its way once more.

"We'll be cutting you out in a few minutes, Founder," a friendly-sounding voice reassured me. "We've got to get you to a safer place."

"Let me out first!" I shouted back, hoping I'd be heard. "Don't open up the other battery until I've had time to speak with someone in authority!"

There was a long, pregnant pause. "Right," the voice agreed at last. "Can do." Then the cargo-handler seized me again, and lifted me onto another platform. I waited a few seconds for the Prince to be laid alongside me again, but this time apparently we were riding separately. Instead of another reassuring "thud", I heard a motor start up, this one much smaller than the locomotive's, and we were on our way once more.

It'd been so long since I'd been able to smell anything that I hardly missed it anymore, but at least I could still sense temperature. The air coming into my vents back where I'd been trans-shipped had been much cooler than what I'd been receiving while in the boxcar. I'd have bet my bottom dollar that if I'd been able to detect its scent, the stuff would have been dank and moist and smelled of tunnel. Now, however, the air was warming up again. This time, even though I couldn't smell there was something different about it. The oxygen content seemed lower; my respiration-fans were running at a higher power than they usually did. Somehow, I felt that I must be full of dust. Was I in a mine?

Apparently so, because when the little train finally stopped and the workers cut me out of my prison, they were wearing facemasks with headlights mounted on them. So were the half-dozen heavily-armed guards, who stepped forward and made absolutely certain that I was who and what I was supposed to be. Only after this treatment was completed were the main lights turned on.

"Tench-hut!" the leader of the armed men bawled out as his men snapped to attention in my honor. They were a ragged, unsynchronized, threadbare and even filthy lot compared to the hundreds, even thousands of smartly-uniformed soldiers, sailors, and marines whose salutes I'd previously received. But never was my heart so warmed.

"At ease," I answered, still wriggling out of my prison. It was a long, complicated task, what with the damage to my leg. "Thank you. Please, you don't have to do that for me."

The group's sergeant relaxed ever so slightly. "It's our honor, sir."

Then one of the workers who'd cut me out turned to face me. "This way, Founder, if you'd be so kind. There's someone quite anxious to see you."

I smiled, despite myself. It'd be Spencer, I knew in my heart, though he should've been far too busy to make time for me. But first there was unfinished business. I peered off into the darkness, looking for the Prince's battery.

"He's in another chamber, sir" the sergeant reassured me. "Under strict guard. Nothing further will be done without orders."

"Thank you," I answered, nodding and smiling again. "It shouldn't be too long."

Then I was being led down an endless shaft, angling downwards. "It's almost half a mile down this adit, sir," my guide explained. "This is an old zinc mine. We brought it back into service just for the Dracans. They can never get enough metals, and this operation is the only one on the planet they never, ever have production trouble with."

"And, you were so eager to please your customers that you even dug a few extra side-tunnels along the way," I observed. "Tunnels that you didn't bother telling them about."

"Indeed!" the young man agreed, beaming. "Why should we trouble the Dracans with a bunch of extra paperwork, when they're so busy with everything else?" His grin widened. "There's a war on, after all."

"So I hear," I answered, smiling back.

The adit we were descending seemed to lead directly away from the ore body; the further we lowered ourselves beneath the surface, the cleaner the floors and walls became. Eventually we came to a metal door. "Saint Matthew," my guide declared, his voice clear and distinct. "Guiding the Virgin Mary."

With an audible click the massive panel unlocked itself and swung open. There was another identical one just beyond. "It's an airlock," I was told. "For safety reasons." We let the first door close behind us, then the second opened…

…and there was Spencer, standing there wearing his usual ratty clothes and leaning on his beat-up old walking stick! "Welcome, Thomas!" he declared, throwing his arms wide open and letting the cane fall clattering to the ground. "Welc—"

But, I didn't even let him finish the word. It should've been physically impossible for me to race across a room in a damaged survival-body. Somehow

I did it anyway. "Oof!" Spence said as I crashed into his welcoming arms and, rather pathetically, tried to hug him back with my one working stubby little gripper. "Oh my!" he declared over and over, as I rubbed my cheek up against him as a child might a stuffed animal, just barely able to keep myself from weeping. "Oh, my!"

"I never thought I'd see you alive again!" I sobbed at one point. And, "I never thought I'd live to make it back here! I've missed you so much!"

"And I've missed you," Spence answered, seeing that I was done for the moment and edging away a little so that we could converse more normally. He smiled. "I hear that you've flown high since we last met. Even higher than either Alicia or I expected."

I looked away. "It sort of just happened," I explained. "I don't want to talk about it right now, if you don't mind."

He smiled. "Believe me, I both understand and empathize completely." He looked over my head and nodded, and then a group of others entered the room. "I hope you don't mind, Thomas," he explained. "We've been in private for the last few minutes, but…"

"Right," I agreed, though I didn't like it. It seemed like there was no end to duty. This was probably, I was beginning to understand, because there wasn't. Short of the grave.

About a half-dozen men and women filed in. I knew one of them; he'd been Spence's military advisor from Earth back before I'd escaped. "Hello, Thomas!" he greeted me, his broad Michigan accent still as powerful as ever. It was amazing to me that he'd survived so long with it. I smiled and nodded back, then turned to Spence.

"Now," he said. "You and I have much catching-up to do, Thomas. Much indeed! But it'll have to wait; we've arranged for the navy to pick you up just under three hours from now, along with some of the rest of us." His eyes narrowed. "But first… Tell me about this so-called Prince you've captured. And perhaps you'll also be so kind as to explain why it is that I must not see his face until you've spoken to me."

Chapter One-Hundred Eight

Spence might have been pleased to see me, but he didn't remain happy for very long. I made him send everyone back out of the room, so that he and I were alone again. From the very beginning it'd been clear that I'd have to tell either him or another high-ranking guerilla the whole story, and eventually Admiral Vlasilov and the Prime Minister as well. My bargain with the Prince covered these three individuals, and no others. Word might well spread; I was under no illusions that the PM, for example, would be in a position to keep the truth entirely to himself. But when the leaks happened they wouldn't be my fault. I'd given my word, and that was that.

"I see," Spence commented a few sentences into my explanation. As I went along his brow furrowed, his eyes hardened, and a sort of red glow seemed to emerge from the top of his head. Even worse, he made no further comments at all.

"…and that's about it," I said in conclusion. "It wasn't until I was on the train that I figured out who he probably was." I wasn't looking at my rabbit-friend anymore by then; he was so angry that I didn't want to have to see it. It made me feel almost like a little boy again. "I'm sorry," I added lamely.

"Humph!" Spence commented, his first utterance in far too long a time. Then there was long, pregnant silence. "This man. Is he unusually large and muscular? And swarthy to boot?"

I nodded, not wanting to speak.

"Damn!" Spence cursed. "It's probably him, then; that's about all the description we have. All these long months, I've dreamed…" Then, he bit the words off. "Thomas," he said slowly. "Forgive me. I'm very angry, yes. But not at you. Let me make that completely clear. So far as I can tell you've done nothing wrong here at all. You were absolutely correct to make this deal. And yes, I'll stand behind it. As I suspect will everyone else. All the reasons you gave are perfectly valid, and I'd have backed you even if all you'd accomplished was saving your own skin; your life is worth a thousand of his, any day of the week."

I let out a virtual-breath I hadn't realized I was holding.

Spence smiled, though it was clear he didn't want to. "Besides, it's still just barely possible that this so-called Prince isn't who we think he is." He glanced at the clock on the wall. "We have just enough time to find out."

Things moved quickly after that. The Prince's battery was moved to a secure room, and the same detail that had supervised my own removal began cutting him out. Meanwhile Spence and I watched through a one-way window. My friend had given his men the strictest orders imaginable without quite telling them what to expect, and you could see that they were even tenser and more alert than they'd been while freeing me. When they were about halfway done I heard a noise behind me; it was a medical orderly, pushing a wheelchair. "Sir?" the man asked.

"Just a moment," Spence replied, his eyes growing hard again. "We won't keep her any longer than we absolutely must. I promise."

Her? I asked myself. In the dim light at first there hadn't appeared to be anyone in the chair at all, just a big pillow. In fact, I'd figured that the rig was for the Prince to ride in if they drugged him or something. But sure enough there was a face peering out of the lump. Or rather the remains of one. The mouth was a lipless gash, the nose repeatedly twisted and broken, and the skin burned and sliced so many times that it consisted merely of ridge after ridge of scar tissue. The woman's very skull was misshapen; it looked to me like someone had done something to her inner ears. Her eyes had been removed too, gouged out judging by the look of things. Her vision had been restored, however. In each mutilated socket a single camera-lens was mounted. She gazed at me for a moment, then turned away in shame.

Turning her head was about the only thing she could do for herself; all four limbs had been amputated. High. That was why I'd mistaken her for a pillow.

I was just about to ask Spence why in the name of god he'd dragged this poor wreck of a woman away from her hospital bed when, quite suddenly, the Prince's lid swung open. "Sit up!" the leader of the rifleman demanded, waving his muzzle threateningly. "Now!"

Looking more than a little bedraggled and carefully keeping his hands in full view at all times, the Prince complied.

"Now," Spence instructed the orderly. Without a word, he rolled his quadriplegic charge through the door, bringing her face-to-face with the Prince.

"Yeaaa!" she screamed almost instantly upon entering the room, her lipless mouth clearly unable to form words correctly. "Yeaaa! Yeeaaa!"

The Prince squinted back. "Juanita Marin," he replied. "I never figured to see you again." He smiled. "And here I thought I'd cauterized those optic nerves properly."

"Yeaaa!" Juanita replied, a stream of drool running down her chin. Though her cry hadn't changed much, it'd somehow transformed itself into the most vile curse I'd ever heard. "Yeaaa!"

I looked over at Spence. He was standing ramrod straight, his powerful, gengineered hands clenched into fists. "I'm sorry," I repeated, though the words

400

seemed pitifully inadequate.

"Don't be," he answered, the fists relaxing slightly. "We've already been through that." Then he flipped a switch on the intercom. "Get her out of there," he ordered. "Thank her, on my behalf." Spence waited until the Prince's victim was gone before speaking again. "Welcome, Prince Nogandeaux," he said finally. "You chose an excellent bondsman."

The Price smiled, the expression not expressing the slightest sense of relief. "His unexpected arrival was a stroke of the greatest good fortune, Founder Wiston," he replied, clearly recognizing the distinctive voice of his chief enemy. "One must take advantage of lucky breaks if one is to flourish in a challenging environment. This opportunity literally fell right out of the sky."

Spence's hands were fists again, though his voice remained warm and resonant. "Your bargain will be honored," he continued. "Assuming, of course, that you have the promised military data?"

The Prince smiled, then with an overly-elegant gesture intended to reassure the men holding the guns that were still pointed at him, he patted his shirt-pocket. "Here!" he said smugly. "The locations of major troop concentrations, supply dumps, anti-aircraft batteries... Practically everything an enemy could ever want, covering both the Churillian defenses and to a lesser extent those of Drakkus as well."

"Damn!" Wiston swore again, though he cut his microphone off before speaking so that no one but me could hear him. "Take it from him, Jesus," he directed one of the gunmen, after re-activating the circuit. "Then bring it all to Sherry's office." He turned to me again. "The navy will get the originals," he assured me. "But we'll make a copy for ourselves first." His face went hard again. "Too bad I can't make a copy of *him*," he continued, stabbing an angry finger in the general direction of the Prince. "Dozens of copies! Then I could amuse myself for the rest of my life hanging the bastard over and over and over again."

Chapter One-Hundred Nine

After all that came before, my rescue was sort of a letdown. The army had known all along that they had to make contact somehow with the highest-ranking members of the Resistance so that they could coordinate their strategy and activities. Besides, Spence was head of the Provisional Government as well. It was his job to try and bring something resembling justice and order out of the vortex of fire that was, for the second time in too few years, about to run amok across his homeland. There was no question that he and his staff could perform these duties far more effectively aboard the specially-converted liner *Lawrence Highridge* than in a few cramped tunnels hidden underneath a working zinc mine. There'd been plans to evacuate him from the very beginning; over time, these schemes had grown and grown in scope until they constituted a full-scale assault landing. "The railroad is a key line of supply," Spence explained to me as we hurried down deeper under the ground. "So, since they've got to land to get my people out anyway, the army is going to set up a permanent bridgehead right across the tracks. With any luck the Dracans'll be forced to withdraw fifty miles."

"Their position will have been turned," I agreed, pretending more knowledge than I actually had.

"Exactly!" Spence agreed, gasping a little as he limped along. Due to my injured leg I was riding on a hospital bed. In the old days, Spence would've been able to keep up easily; I'd personally watched him hike the legs off of hardened guerillas more than once. But somewhere along the line he'd damaged his right ankle and was now limping almost as badly as I was. What other battle-scars did he carry, I wondered, hidden away under his thick fur and cheery manner? He'd seen action, clearly enough. Judging by the godlike reverence that the guerillas displayed around him, he must've acquitted himself well. "You've learned a lot about war since we last met, Thomas."

I laughed, a bit too loudly. "More than I wanted to." I admitted. "Far more. So, how are we going to link up?"

"The simplest plans are usually the best. Our army friends know we're down here; they're going to take the surface above us in—" he glanced at his watch—"about seven minutes, now. We've been watching for weeks and know where every last Dracan foxhole is. Therefore, so does the army. The fight should be over almost before it begins. When things quiet down my men will pop up their heads up and hope that your army isn't so trigger-happy that they forget they have friends on this world as well as enemies."

I nodded, then frowned. It didn't seem particularly heroic to sit and wait hundreds of feet underground while someone else did my fighting for me. But, I had to admit, just now I wasn't much use at that sort of thing. At the moment I couldn't fire a blast-rifle if my life depended on it.

The preliminary bombardment, when it began, was enough to stir up dust even down in the most protected part of the mine. Spence's advisor from Michigan had assured him that we'd not even notice the explosions, but that didn't prove to be the case. Though the rock beneath our feet didn't kick and heave it did sort of vibrate, and there was a continuous dull rumble. Spence had evacuated the entire complex down into the safest areas, all except a handful detailed to collapse both entrances to an old, shallow shaft that it was anticipated our enemies would seek shelter in. About halfway through the bombardment a guerilla came running up and whispered something in Spence's ear, and he smiled his fiercest smile. "Success!" he explained to the rest of us. "Almost two hundred of them are trapped in there without air or power. An entire battalion! God himself couldn't dig 'em out in time; there'll be a huge gap in the defenses. One of our finest operations ever!" There was no cheering but soon everyone was grinning, all except for the Prince. He was lying in a drugged stupor on a bed just like mine. I wasn't smiling either. Mental images of terrified, soon-to-be-dead Dracans scrabbling about hopelessly in the darkness didn't make me smile anymore, I feared. All I wanted was for all the pain to stop.

Soon the ground stopped shaking and we knew that directly above our heads the landings were taking place. "The hour is at hand," Spence declared in his rich, resonant voice.

"Hip, hip! Hooray!" someone cried out, and everyone began to cheer.

It was indeed a great moment, I supposed, if you'd had to live with a Dracan army of occupation for more than two long, hungry, brutal years.

"Hip, hip! Hooray!" Next they cheered me, and then Spence, and finally he led them in the biggest cheer of all for themselves and what they'd accomplished against such terrible odds and in face of such horrid danger. I joined in that one, at last giving in to the power of the moment, wholeheartedly and without reservation. Churilla, outwardly a poor, poverty-stricken world that should never have been colonized in the first place, had proven itself rich in those things that really mattered; courage and valor. In these things Churilla was wealthier than any ten other worlds, so far as I could see. These men and women *deserved* to be cheered.

"Hooray!" I cried out as loud as I could, forgetting in all the excitement that my survival body was equipped with a megaphone to help me contact potential rescuers. "Hooray!"

Everyone turned and stared at me, then we all laughed and hugged each other until we cried. For the first and only time during the entire war I felt like I was right where I belonged, standing as one with other war-scarred people who could understand how and why I hurt so much inside. Michelle was right about victory, I decided; it *did* feel a lot like remorselessly kicking a helpless man to death as he begged for mercy. But she was wrong as well, I now understood. Victory also felt like a great weight being lifted off of one's heart, like emerging out into the sun again after being trapped in a dark airless hole for so long that beauty and love were merely fantastic rumors. Sure, there was still fighting to be done-- plenty of it, if we had to invade Drakkus proper. These people's war, however, was almost over and by virtue of my earlier time among them I was enough part of the team to share their simple joy at surviving. Corks popped, carefully hoarded wines flowed, and random couples danced lively Churillian jigs. All the while Spence stood and grinned like a sainted grandfather watching his descendants caper on Christmas morn.

The party grew wilder and wilder as the Prince snored and Spence beamed and more champagne flowed. Until eventually, as it had to, the end finally arrived in the form of a marine officer in full combat gear making his way determinedly down the tunnel. I nudged Spence in the ribs, then pointed him out. "Right," he agreed, sobering instantly. "Thank you." Then he waved his hand above his head. "Yo! Over here!"

Almost as if a signal had been given the riotous noise dropped away to nothing and a path appeared through the mob. "Much obliged," the officer muttered as he edged his way in our direction. "Excuse me!" Then he was facing us. "Commander Thomas Longo?" he inquired officially, though he had to know who I was. "Provisional President Spencer Wiston?" We nodded, and despite the fact that he was under arms and therefore not obliged, he saluted us as if we were standing on a parade-ground. "I'm Major Luong, sirs. Of the First Marines. Your ride is waiting upstairs."

Chapter One-Hundred Ten

A few hours later I was lying in sickbay aboard *The Glorious First of June*, bored out of my skull. During my short, eventful naval career, I'd so far managed to pretty much steer a course around the meaningless red tape that did so much to make naval officers' lives miserable. Mostly this was due to the fact that the higher-ups understood that it wasn't in their own best interests for me to waste my limited time on petty nonsense. But this time, I was caught cold. According to regulations, anyone who'd been a POW must immediately undergo a full, detailed medical workup upon repatriation. It didn't matter that I didn't have a normal body anymore, or that I'd only been held captive for a few hours. Everything had to be done by the book under these circumstances, and that was that. Even Admiral Vlasilov refused to rescue me. "It'll only take two days, Thomas," he explained, sitting in my visitor's chair. "You can catch up on your paperwork."

I tuned away. The only paperwork of substance that needed dealing with was already done. Jimmy and I had already written our letters to the parents of the dead. There were fewer than expected, due to the fact that Father had improved the Skybolt's ejection gear. We'd lost a lot of 'bolts, yes. But only five pilots. Even my wingman Isaiah had made it, despite the fact that he'd ejected in the heart of the enemy fleet. Though he'd had a narrow escape, being on his last five minutes of air when the pickup was finally made. My fellow Bird had already dropped by to visit, grinning like a fool. "No matter what happens to me from now on," he declared, "I've been your wingman in real, honest combat. No one can ever take that away from me."

"And you were a good wingman," I assured him. "A brave one. Thank you, Isaiah. I'm just glad that you're alive."

Even better, in lieu of a written report the admiral had already accepted a recording of my verbal statement to him covering both my combat activities and subsequent events on Churilla. This recording had, of course, been immediately placed in a lead diplomatic box, triple-locked, stamped "Top Secret" so many times that we'd nearly run out of red ink, then forwarded by fast courier back to Earth. The data the Prince had delivered, apparently, was everything he'd claimed it to be. Our army was already acting on it, and dozens of cursing Dracan generals must even now be bemoaning the run of "bad luck" that was suddenly ruining their every enterprise. Vlaslov had added a cover letter, one that he'd read aloud to me, endorsing my actions up and down the line.

Or at least he'd endorsed my actions after bailing out…

"Now, Thomas," he said, straightening up in his chair. "I'm glad that you're feeling so well. However, we have one last important matter to deal with." He reached down into his briefcase and pulled out a folder with my name on it. "You've violated a standing order. Need I remind you which one?"

I turned away and faced the wall. "You know why I did it," I answered. "You even agree with me, I think. Your orders just before launch were suspiciously vague."

Vlasilov nodded. "I do agree with you, at a certain level," he replied, "Furthermore, in violating this order you saved the lives of dozens if not hundreds of fellow servicemen and made a probable victory both certain and overwhelming." His eyes narrowed. "You also performed so well in combat that my staff is still abuzz over how many enemy units you either directly or indirectly destroyed-- even now your final tally is still being calculated. Your performance bordered upon the superhuman; one of my staff said it was as if Colonel Rotte himself were alive again, minus the oversized ego. I personally consider it likely that your recent sortie will, for a very long time to come, stand as the single most perfect mission ever flown by a navy pilot." He shook his head. "I was in command, yes. Yet I think this battle will always be remembered as your victory. And I must say that I find this assessment fair."

I blinked. "But… But…"

"Ah," Vlasilov agreed, nodding. "There is indeed a 'but'." His eyes narrowed. "You knew that you were not to fight again."

"I did," I agreed. "But…"

Vlasilov held up his hand. "It is our function as officers," he continued, "to obey orders. Though sometimes we are allowed to be creative about it." The ghost of a grin lightened his features. "It is my duty to maintain discipline among my officers. And I shall perform this duty, no matter how unpleasant it may be."

For the first time, I began to understand. "Sir?"

"Let me make things perfectly clear, son. You've been officially charged with disobedience to a legally given order. You may if you choose demand a formal trial by your peers. In which case you will be given every opportunity to present what I'm quite certain will be an excellent defense, one in which you'll be forced to demonstrate beyond the shadow of a doubt that the Prime Minister interfered in naval affairs far beyond his level of expertise and issued orders that significantly reduced the effectiveness of our fleet in wartime. All sorts of nastiness is liable to ensue." His smile widened. "Or, Thomas, you can accept non-judicial punishment. In which case I, as your commanding officer, will alone and without recourse determine the depth of your guilt and dictate punishment accordingly. I might add that once you've agreed to this there can be no further appeal. Nor can there ever be another trial; are you familiar with the concept of 'double-jeopardy'?"

I nodded, still a little confused. "Uh-huh. I think so, at least."

"Good," the admiral continued. "Now, Thomas. Which is it to be? A messy, public trial? Or will you trust me to deliver a fair and reasonable verdict?"

I didn't have the slightest doubt. "I'll trust you, sir. Every day of the week."

Vlasilov bowed slightly, which I was fairly certain wasn't standard disciplinary procedure. "Thank you, Thomas. I'm truly honored." Then he pulled out a sheaf of papers and began signing them. "I'm finding you guilty, Thomas," he explained.

I nodded, having already figured that part out.

"But," he continued, "I'm also finding that there were indeed numerous mitigating circumstances. So many in fact that as the local officer in command I'm hereby suspending the order against your flying combat, at least temporarily, based on the fact that the fleet is seriously depleted of qualified pilots and that your level of performance with this weapon, due to your long experience and high level of natural aptitude, truly is unique. I only wish that this clear, unmistakable evidence had manifested itself earlier, so that this terrible misunderstanding need not have taken place to begin with. I also find merit in your assertion that my orders might just possibly have been a bit unclear. I don't claim to be perfect, Thomas, and the bridge of a flagship during a fleet engagement is a noisy, confusing place where subtle communication errors are far too common. Even we admirals often misunderstand each other under such pressure. Therefore…" He paused while scribbling some more. "…I'm nominating you for another Parliamentary Order of Merit, which I feel it safe to assume will in fact be awarded without delay. I'm also promoting you to captain whether you like it or not." His face hardened, and he paused in his writing for a moment to look me in the eye. "I'm not tolerating any more nonsense on that score, Thomas. There will be new rank-insignia waiting for you in your cabin when the doctors are finished with you. They were once my own. You will wear them until others become available. At which point if you choose to continue to wear mine I shall be deeply honored."

I gulped and nodded again. "Aye-aye, sir."

"Finally, we come to the matter of punishment." Vlasilov scowled, and tapped his chin with his stylus. "What do you think would be fitting, Thomas?"

I looked down at the floor, my head still spinning. "I don't… I mean…"

"Of course you don't," the admiral continued. "I don't either. So…" the tapped his chin again. "How about two month's pay and thirty days confined to *June*? With so few fighters left we're moving all Skybolt operations over here anyway and sending *Coronel* home."

I gulped. "But..."

"Flying time excepted, of course." He began scribbling again. "And visits to other ships within the task force. And time on Churilla as well; it's reasonable to assume that you may have official business there too." The scribbling went on and on. "We'll also factor in the time aboard you've already served..." He looked up and smiled. "Why, Thomas! It looks like you've already paid your penalty in full! You're free to go! Now, was that so bad?"

Chapter One-Hundred Eleven

It didn't take too long after leaving sickbay for me to begin to wish that I was back there again. Yes, all my paperwork was now caught up. But there were still a million things to do in trying to slap together a functional superfighter squadron out of the wreckage the Dracans had left us. "Nothing except a battle lost can be half as melancholy as a battle won," Jimmy declared to me as we walked side-by-side down the gunroom corridor."

"Heh!" I snorted, understanding his meaning as only a veteran could.

"The Duke of Wellington said that," he explained as we turned a corner; moving as slowly as we did, at least we had plenty of time to talk when going places together.

"Never heard of him," I answered. Jimmy had gotten a list of books from Captain Bard and was perhaps spending too much of his time reading them. I wished he'd spend more time video-gaming and less studying, to keep sharp. There'd be plenty of time for book-learning when the war was over. Still, it was kind of nice to see that he was settling down on a career as a military officer. He'd always wanted to be one, and now they'd have to let him into the Academy for sure. He also had been promoted too for his own part in the recent battle and as likely as not would outrank half his professors. I only wished that I could make up my own mind about what I wanted to do with my life. Every time the subject came up my head began to hurt. Every door in the universe was waiting to fly open for me; I could do practically anything I wanted to do. Be whoever and whatever I wanted to be.

But … Who and what *did* I want to be? The more choices one had, perhaps, the more difficult finding the answer became.

"Wellington had this really cool infantry tactic," Jimmy explained, his eyes lighting up as he warmed to his subject. "He'd use the brow of a hill—"

"Thomas!" Michelle interrupted, just as my friend and I were about to make the last turn into the ready-room. "I was just looking for you!" She smiled. "How are you feeling, Captain? After your recent adventures, I mean?"

I smiled back; Captain Bard had been too busy to make it to my sickroom in person, but had sent a very nice note. "Just fine, I guess. What's up?"

"There's going to be a staff briefing in ten minutes," she explained. "The admiral will be there. He asked me to see if you could make it."

I nodded. Whenever Michelle was extra-busy, excitement soon followed. "Of course. What's up?"

"I can't say, here and now," she answered, looking at Jimmy. "But if you two were to figure out on your own what our next strategic objective has to be and when we'd be best off getting started on it, well... I'd hardly be to blame for that, now would I?"

My best friend and I looked at each other. "There's no place left..." I began.

"...except Drakkus itself!" he exclaimed. Then his face fell. "But, we're not even close to being ready to invade; the ground-fighting's still only just beginning here."

"We're going on blockade," I whispered, looking deep into Michelle's eyes to see if I was right. Sure enough, they twinkled. "Drakkus has multiple Nikitas. The only effective way to cut the planet off is to maintain a fleet right in their front yard. We don't need the army for that."

Captain Bard smiled. "You're both *such* good students!" she answered, not quite confirming our speculations. Then she turned back to me. "We all know you're just off the sick-list, Thomas. But you might want to take what little time you have to study the latest readiness figures. Whatever our next operation might be..." She smiled and winked. "...your people will have a big part in it."

I smiled back, then sighed. What I really wanted to do was to sit around with my pilots for a little while and try to relax. But clearly it wasn't in the cards. "I'll be there."

Chapter One-Hundred Twelve

Planning out an invasion of Dracan space was a lot easier this time around. During our first visit we'd merely been a hit-and-run raiding force, outgunned by the defenders. Our survival had been totally dependent upon our high vector; in any kind of sustained fight we'd have surely been ground to dust and sooner rather than later. But what a difference a year made! The entire strategic situation was transformed. The cream of the Dracan fleet had been reduced to a complex series of navigational hazards drifting in Churillian space. Our enemies had managed to extricate almost nothing from their Orion Nexus disaster; one obsolescent and heavily-damaged battlewagon, one equally-devastated special-purpose planetary defense cruiser and a handful of destroyers. Add to that a few scattered squadrons and convoy escorts scattered here and there throughout Dracan space and that was all the Dracan Navy there was left.

That and a few superfighters, perhaps.

"Our best intelligence estimates are that the Dracans plowed everything they had into the Nexus battle," Michelle explained in her situation assessment. "As well they should've. It was their last, best chance to win." She waved her pointer, and a hologram appeared above the conference table. "This *Confucius*-class cruiser, for example, was still incomplete, minus her after turrets. Her gunnery was also absolutely wretched throughout the fight. It's a fairly safe bet that she was never shaken down properly." Michelle shook her head. "They've already scraped the bottom of the barrel. Most likely there'll be no supers. It's only been a few days, after all. If they'd had any more close to completion, they'd have delayed their Orion counterattack for them."

Vlasilov turned to me. "As you already know, sir," I explained, "currently we can launch only five Skybolts. At one time it was thought that we might be able to fly seven in a few days. Unfortunately, the current estimate is six. We found more damage in one of the wounded birds."

"Da," Vlasilov agreed bleakly. "Will that be enough? We won't be attempting to attack any ground targets, Thomas; that can wait until the Polecats are finished here on Churilla. If we place *Cochrane* properly her guns can cover two of the three Nikitas. The third, the one down in the atmosphere, will have to be watched by your Skybolts."

"A lot depends on how good our intelligence is," I replied. "Michelle believes that the Dracans have nothing left; if that's the case then even one or two should be enough. If she's wrong, well…" I shrugged.

The admiral nodded. "Of course."

"We could watch that last bolthole from the other end," Bard added. "But that'd divide our fleet, which is always dangerous. Or we could wait. That's always an option and in this case perhaps the safer one. We're growing stronger all the time. But the longer we wait the longer the war drags on. And—"

Vlasilov waved his hand in irritation. "Yes, yes, yes," he replied. "We understand that, captain."

"And there's another factor, as well," she continued, ignoring her superior's uncharacteristic display of bad temper. "According to the latest information from home, the Emperor himself is still on Drakkus. Our friends in the neutral embassies claim that everyone near the throne is in a state of panic, that no one can make a decision and that the government is paralyzed. If he should decide to move his inner circle out into the hinterlands…"

"Da," Vlasilov agreed, looking even sourer than he had a moment ago. "He could hide out for months. Or maybe even find asylum." Then he looked at me. "'It seems to be a law of nature, inflexible and inexorable, that those who will not risk cannot win.' A great American naval officer said that, Thomas. Later he became a noteworthy and successful Russian admiral, of all things."

"Really?" I asked, blinking. It seemed to be my day for quotations.

"Really," Vlasilov confirmed. Then he turned back to Captain Bard and scowled. "Any further word on *Cochrane*'s repairs?"

"No, sir," she replied. "The last we heard, her main battery won't be on-line for three more days."

"Bah!" the admiral complained. Then he turned to me again. "In three days you can have your composite squadron up and running? In a combat-worthy state, I mean? We can provide a training area and a ship or two to serve as targets."

"I can," I promised.

"Good," he answered, smiling for the first time. Then he looked up and down the table, meeting everyone's eyes. "He who will not risk cannot win," he repeated. "In time of war, offering an enemy enough time to collect their wits after a good stiff blow is almost always a mistake." His eyes turned hard and cold. "The task force will translate to Drakkus seventy-two hours from now and take up blockade stations, to be described in your written orders. We'll leave a few light units behind in support of the invasion fleet; under the circumstances they should suffice." He scowled. "The sooner we begin to strangle this beast, the sooner it'll die. And if we move quickly enough, who knows? They won't be expecting us so promptly, I don't think. We might get lucky and catch them with their trousers down."

Chapter One-Hundred Ten

I expected more trouble integrating the two Skybolt squadrons into one unit than we actually experienced. They'd done their basic flight training on two separate worlds, after all, and the pilots themselves arose from two very different societies.

The navy generally preferred to man ships and 'hopper squadrons with crews that all shared the same cultural heritage; this was intended to reduce internal frictions and promote teamwork. Only academy-trained officers tended to move from ship to ship, and with new vessels coming into commission so rapidly even that rule was often being broken. These days, the navy was so short on skilled help that they were taking whoever they could get and herding them practically nonstop onto the nearest ship. *Graf Zeppelin* was entirely officered by Esteppans, for example, most of whom had served in the short-lived navy of the Autarch. So was *Coronel*, for that matter. Because of this, both functioned a bit differently than the rest of the fleet. I was worried about mixing Esteppans and Earthers, noblemen and commoners, all together in one basket. But I needn't have wasted the emotional effort. By then they were veteran fighter pilots far more than they were either Esteppans or Earthers, and therefore shared so much in common that once-important differences paled by comparison. Even though they hadn't fought side-by-side in the same formation before, we'd wargamed the two squadrons against each other enough that they'd learned to respect each other. Besides, both had racked up fine combat records and Jimmy and I had drilled them so hard and so long in our own techniques that the differences in initial training had pretty much faded away to nothing. There were a few key differences in radio protocol that needed to be worked out, but wherever possible we followed what I came to call the "Horrido" rule. The Top Bananas' official victory cry was "Splash one", while the Birds cried out "Horrido!" Instead of forcing one side or the other to change long-hallowed patterns of behavior we simply agreed to use both interchangeably, as I already did. There were dozens of cases where this rule was applied, from pre-flight inspection procedures to prioritizing radio traffic. Both systems made sense; with so few of us left, we could be informal and still make things work. Someday the navy would get around to writing official manuals and ruin all the friendly cooperation forevermore. For now, however, we kids could play together however we liked.

And play we did, with a discipline and ferocity I'd never seen before. Everyone had lost close friends now, and everyone understood what war and death were all about. Everyone had scored kills as well, or at least all of those I planned to allot 'bolts to at Drakkus had. There were more pilots than aircraft now, due to the successful ejections. So Jimmy and I were free to pick and choose. Isaiah was very proud to be selected to command the third element; he was the only other Bird besides me to make the cut. There were others who were deserving, yes; we'd have ended up with four Birds and two Bananas, if Jimmy and I had been allowed to have our way. But one of the Birds had suffered a severe concussion during bailout, and unlike me was making a slow recovery. Another was having recurrent nightmares; though she begged to return to combat I sided with the counselors and held her in reserve. We weren't expecting serious opposition, so why should I take a chance on damaging Ingrid further? Ho from the Bananas was very nearly as good, and his blood ran as cold as ice water.

Our 'hoppers were mostly Banana veterans as well, as we Birds had taken the lion's share of the losses. The battle-scarred jumble of soot-black and sky-blue fighters looked hideous in the hanger; the deck officer scowled every time he bustled past. Since Jimmy and I had decided it'd be best if we became wingmen again we both had to fly the same type, either a Mark 1 or a Mark 1*. Everyone, in fact, needed matched pairs. So in order to make things come out the best possible way I had to assign both Isaiah and myself blue ex-Banana 'bolts, and a former Banana into a soot-black fighter. No one complained, which I took as a good sign. Kids grew up fast in combat, it seemed. At any rate Jimmy and I both ended up in 1*'s, which was a good thing as the more heavily-armed fighter was a bit harder to handle. We both liked the newer model better, but it wasn't for novices.

Predictably, not two hours after I'd informed the techs who was assigned to which bird, they'd already painted the nose of mine bright red and festooned it with kill-symbols. I still thought the result was both ugly and in the worst possible taste, but said nothing. Traditions were important, I was coming to understand. The flight-deck hands worked hard at a thankless task, and if a little artwork made them happy, well… Once in flight I hardly noticed.

It didn't even take us the three full days to work up; I was well satisfied by the end of the first though I didn't tell anyone but Jimmy. We were already scheduled for torpedo practice on the second day, which in my opinion at least was far less challenging than fighter versus fighter combat, or else I might've ordered a rest-day instead. Usually Vlasilov assigned *Zeppelin* and *Cochrane* or a couple of the other more modern ships to serve as our target, both to offer us a better workout and to give the target's gun-crews a little practice as well. This time, however, he did something different. While he did choose one modern vessel—*Arminus*, still practically brand-spanking-new out of the yards, and yet to experience even a mock superfighter attack—he also sent us the converted passenger liner *Lawrence Highridge* to shoot at.

I couldn't figure it out at first; maybe, I reasoned to myself as I "killed" her over and over again with the most minimal of effort, it was because all the other vessels in the task force were busy. Or maybe it was to give *Arminus* a little experience in shepherding such a helpless charge; perhaps she'd soon be detached on convoy duty or something. Nothing I could come up with really made sense, however, until I recalled how upset all of us superfighter pilots had been at the idea of shooting up helpless merchant vessels back before the big Drakkus raid, during the campaign to deprive the Dracans of molecular batteries. If it hadn't been for the colonel and his original Birds, we youngsters might well have turned back. And what would our job be on blockade duty? Blowing unarmed, helpless cargo-carriers out of the sky, of course. That was one thing I admired about Vlasilov. Yes, he made mistakes; waging war was a complex thing and no commander escaped without making an error or two. But he always learned from the experience and never, ever repeated one. This time around his young pilots would be better prepared for what was expected of them. Which pretty much amounted to murder, of course, though the textbooks gave it prettier names, like "supply interdiction" and "mercantile warfare".

So I wasn't too terribly surprised when, after being dismounted from my 'bolt, I found that Captain Bard had been detailed to give all of us pilots a special lecture about the vital necessity and strategic imperatives that lay behind the destruction of helpless merchantmen and their crews. I frowned when I found the card ordering me to attend lying on my desk; I'd already had the class, thankyouverymuch, and had long since shed most of my inhibitions against killing Dracans, pretty much whenever and wherever I came across them. But I lucked out. Tucked under the order was an envelope addressed, oddly enough, to "Parliamentarian Longo". No one I knew of aboard *June* or for that matter any of the other ships of the task force would address me in such a manner; I was "Captain Longo" to practically everyone except for a handful who hadn't got the word yet and were still addressing reports to "Commander Longo" instead. My pilots would have simply typed "Thomas" on the envelope, except for a few of the stiffer Esteppans who might still prefer "Your Excellency" when being formal.

There wasn't any good way to solve the mystery, I decided eventually, without opening the envelope. So I did. Instantly the answer became apparent. There was no mistaking Spence's fluid, anachronistic longhand; it was much like that of his wife. "My dear Thomas," the note began. "I know that you've been terribly busy of late winning the war, and heaven knows that I'd not willingly stand for an instant in your way. However, I must ask. Have you been keeping abreast of the political situation at home?"

I frowned a little. Every three days or so, whenever the courier ran, I received a special data pack coded to my personal key. It was a summary of all the official actions of Parliament since the last update. My own personal Parliamentary staff was allowed to attach anything they thought I might want or need to see, from personal notes to letters from my constituents. The outline alone often ran a hundred pages or more, and recently I'd taken to scanning the thing for notes from Alicia and then filing the rest away unread in the special secure databank the navy supplied elected officials with. The last three remained unread period, though I'd planned to skim them later that night. I didn't feel at all guilty about the way I was neglecting Parliament; I'd warned everyone involved that there weren't nearly enough hours in the day to both fight a war and do even a passingly-miserable job of representing a district full of voters. Everyone had nodded and smiled and assured me that it'd be okay, that everyone including the voters would understand. Now, however, apparently something had gone wrong.

"A certain degree of war-weariness tends to develop during any prolonged conflict," Spence's note continued. "However, what's developing back home seems to be something quite extraordinary. A peace-at-any price movement has sprung up, seemingly out of nowhere. Their position is that we've effectively won the war and surely the Dracans will listen to reason now, if only we'd sit down and talk with them instead of pounding their heads. Even more, there are powerful accusations of war-profiteering and Parliamentary corruption being bandied about, many of which seem to bear a certain aura of truth about them. Almost all of them are aimed at either members of our own party or those who've joined our coalition.

"I've been badly out of touch myself, Thomas, and as you can imagine am quite busy too. These developments, however, are of such a serious nature as to demand both immediate attention and immediate action. They are quite obviously the forerunners to a confidence vote designed to bring down the government and force new elections. While I've been expecting such a ploy once the fighting is over, I find it most remarkable that even the most militant of Opposition politicians would attempt such a divisive maneuver while there's still shooting taking place. But there it is. Alicia wrote me a long letter—she sends you her best, by the way—explaining a bit of the history behind all of this. Yet the more I read, the more I realize that I need to speak in person with someone who has firsthand knowledge. In particular, Alicia informs me, I must hear directly from you about a certain Parliamentarian Isoroku Nagano. Beyond that, she won't say a word about him.

"So, Thomas, I'm terribly sorry to interrupt. But I feel that I must ask if you can possibly find an hour or two in your busy schedule to come visit an old friend and talk politics? I'll rework my appointment-book entirely around yours; the rumors are flying about an upcoming close blockade of Drakkus, and if there's anything to them I'm quite certain your hands are full indeed. But what's the point of winning the war if we can't build a meaningful peace? What has been the point of all this death and destruction, if the human race cannot learn and grow from it? I'm a student of history, Thomas; no victory won has ever led to a lasting peace once it's been milked for short-term political gain. You and I want something larger, Thomas; so does the PM and many of his best friends. We have a unique opportunity before us—one that I believe may never come mankind's way again. A chance to enlarge humanity, to grow like we've never grown before. If we lose control of Parliament now, Thomas, we lose everything. So if at any time you can accommodate me, I'd be most indebted. I'd not ask, except that I know we share a common cause.

"Your Admiring Co-conspirator in Superhumanity, Spencer Wiston"

Chapter One-Hundred Eleven

"…think he felt like he deserved to win," I explained haltingly to Spence the next day. "It had, after all, been his district for a very long time. The man who held it before him was sort of his mentor. It was the root of all his power as minority leader, too. He sort of became a laughingstock when I won. They made all kinds of terrible jokes about him losing on holovision."

"I see," Spence answered, looking out his porthole. The navy had done very well by Spence, setting him up in a huge luxury suite that served as both his presidential office and living-quarters. His new working area was many times the size of the little desk-nooks that he and Alicia had maintained back in their little bungalow, and I rather suspected that my friend would've requested something far smaller and less ostentatious given the opportunity. Thank heavens I was serving aboard a warship where space was so crucial, or else they might've tried to set me up the same way! "And you think he bears a grudge?"

"Oh, yes!" I agreed. As unpleasant as talking politics was, it still beat sitting through the mercantile warfare workshop that my fellow pilots were currently suffering through. I felt especially sorry for Jimmy, who needed it as little as I did. He, however, hadn't been able to offer pressing political duties as an excuse. "Nagano cut me cold, the one time we met in person afterwards, even though I offered him my hand." I sighed. "It wasn't pretty,"

"I imagine not," my fellow Parliamentarian replied, still looking outside the ship. I craned my neck a little, and realized that he was gazing down on Churilla, where the land-battle was still raging. The Dracans had used a nuke earlier in the day, and we'd replied in kind. This didn't bode well for the upcoming Battle of Churilla City, which promised to be destructive enough even without the intervention of mushroom clouds. Finally he turned to face me. "And now that he's back in office, he's probably more ruthless than ever and throwing every lever he can to get that minority leadership job back." He titled his head to one side. "I'm curious, Thomas. You were never interested in politics before you ran for office, were you?"

I shook my head. "Not at all."

"I didn't think so," Spence continued, smiling slightly. "You didn't seem the type back when I knew you before. And if anything you seem even less so now."

"I'm not," I agreed, looking down at my feet. "I didn't want to run for anything. But Alicia and the rest... They convinced me that I sort of had to. Even the navy pushed me a little, though they really shouldn't have."

"And thank god you rose so successfully to the challenge," Spence replied, smiling. Then his face grew serious once more. "What do you see as the real differences between the parties? On a core level, I mean? Outside of how they wish to prosecute the war?"

"Not much," I admitted. "The Opposition wants the government to spend more on certain things, while my side wants the same money spent on other stuff. Most of the other Parliamentarians seem more interested in propping themselves up than anything else, maintaining power so that they can keep their cousins and uncles and other supporters in key positions." I sighed. "They care more about where war industries are going and who'll be running them, for example, that what they're actually making or if it'll help us win. There's a few who really care, like I think that you do, and Alicia does, and even the PM and the Minister of the Army. He's from the Opposition, by the way, and I think you'd like him." I shook my head. "But I despise most of the rest. To be quite honest with you, they disgust me. Almost as much as the Emperor does. All they want are the benefits of power without any of the responsibilities."

Spence smiled slightly, and looked at me for what felt like a very long time. "You have excellent instincts, Thomas. I hate them too, you see. For pretty much the same reasons that you do. I despise them with all of my heart and soul. So does my wife-- even more than I do, I suspect. That's why she's able to rend and tear them so heartlessly."

I nodded. "She's a demon, politically. The news commentators claim she 'rips her opponents' hearts out'."

"So," Spence said after another long pause, "You hate them, and I hate them. Why do you suppose that is?"

I smiled back, refusing to be baited. "I'm only eighteen going on nineteen, and haven't had much time to think about things of that nature lately. But I bet you've got it all figured out."

My lapine friend smiled back, flashing his incisors. "Well met, Thomas! Well met, indeed! You are, I predict, going to be a regular hellion in university. And I salute you for it. A certain group of staid self-important old professors deserve exactly what they're going to get from you." Then his expression sobered. "Though I think that's the nub of it right there."

My eyebrows rose.

"Excessive ego," Spence elaborated. "It's the most deadly of all sins because it leads directly to the acquisition and abuse of power." He waved his hand, the gesture taking in his opulent office. "Some people like this sort of thing," he explained.

"I know," I replied. "I don't understand it at all. I mean... It's nice to have a bit of property, maybe, and even cool toys like skimmers. But..."

"But there's a limit," Spence agreed. "At least for you, there is. I could reduce your wealth to one percent of what it is today and you'd be perfectly content with what was left."

I nodded. "So long as I have a comfortable place to live and a few nice things, what more could a person want? You understand; you're the same way."

Spence smiled again. "Thank you for saying so, Thomas. And, I like to think that it's true. The happiest times I've ever known, I spent hammering spikes into ties and puttering around with the family greenhouse and compost heap while Alicia played piano in the distance." His smile grew. "Wealth doesn't mean much on a freshly-opened world, Thomas. People come to respect one another-- or not-- based on how hard they work and the content of their character. There isn't much room for putting on airs."

I nodded back. "Esteppe was only founded a few years before Churilla," I agreed. "When I was little, Father told me the stories about our hungry-time, and how my great-grandfather earned the trust of his fellows. He eventually was put in charge of the food supplies."

"I'm not surprised," Spence answered, nodding slowly. "The planetary founding families, or at least the ones who did well and earned the respect of their fellow colonists, are still pretty much in charge on the outer worlds."

"Including you," I pointed out.

"Including me," he agreed, soberly. "And the Longos. And the Dracan Imperial family as well."

I winced. "Don't remind me."

He shrugged. "Truth is truth. There's an ointment surrounding every fly, you see, and a rule to every exception. In their case they didn't earn respect. They took it at gunpoint, and were far enough out into the lawless lands that no one stopped them. From there, things just sort of took their course."

I nodded. "People don't like wealthy, powerful families; I learned that on the campaign trail. But for all our faults we're better than the Dracans."

"Almost everyone is better than the Dracan Imperial family," Spence agreed, smiling again. "It's not much of a distinction. Your Prince is actually very true to the spirit of his dynasty's founders. The apple, in his case, didn't fall very far from the tree."

"I hate power," I said eventually. "Because that's what it all comes down to, ultimately. Naked, raw power."

"Heh!" my friend agreed, leaning back in his chair. "You always were a quick student, at everything but the higher maths, at least." His face sobered. "You aren't still letting that bother you, are you? It's no shame for a man to lack talent in something. I can't, for example, play a proper game of chess to save my life."

My eyebrows rose again. "Really?"

"Honest injun," he assured me. "I'm lousy at poker, too. And discovering that weakness, I assure you, was far more expensive than learning about my shortcomings at the chessboard. Alicia is still angry about a certain little incident, all these years later. I couldn't accept, you see, that when I was good at so many things I might be deficient in something that looked easy. My own ego did the rest of the damage. I was young once too." He titled his head to one side, making his ears flop a little. "The key to succeeding in life is to learn one's strengths and play to them while also charting out and avoiding one's weaknesses. So far, though I'll agree it's largely been a matter of luck, you seem to be doing pretty well at that."

"Pure luck," I agreed, glad to finally find someone that understood.

"Well…" Spence corrected himself, shifting uncomfortably in his chair. "Not quite *pure* luck. The strengths you're playing to, in addition to quick reflexes and a quicker mind, are mostly strengths that you've had to develop in yourself. That you had to earn, in other words. You're brave, Thomas—remarkably so, in a world where bravery is far more commonplace than most people realize. You're also honest, so honest that habitual liars instinctively despise and fear you. Your heart is true, in other words, just as your great-grandfather's apparently was back when he was put in charge of guarding the colony's food during the famine." He shook his head. "I've never been able to figure out why it is that some people come out well and others fail so miserably. I've seen the noblest behavior imaginable from the sons and daughters of scum, and I've also seen children so badly disappoint their eminently worthy parents that the thought of it still sickens me. It therefore can't merely be a matter of pure genetics or a proper upbringing, though I'm convinced that both are factors." His face hardened. "Even more, I've never been able to figure out why it is that liars and people with otherwise weak egos—for it takes a weak ego to unduly cherish power and wealth—tend to be so successful in politics. It doesn't even matter what form the government takes; in a monarchy, flatterers and schemers become privy counselors. In a despotism, they become commissars or party officials. In a democracy, they become senators and Parliamentarians." He shook his head. "It's almost as if the human race were willfully blind to the true nature of those who continually end up leading them. Or else are too stupid and lazy to do anything about it."

"But you're not blind," I pointed out. "Nor stupid or lazy."

"Look who's talking!" Spence retorted. "I first ran for office because someone wanted to nationalize all of Churilla's leading businesses. My railroad was among them, and I had no intention whatsoever of surrendering what I'd fairly earned without one hell of a fight; if I'd lost, I just might've led an armed insurrection rather than peacefully submit to that kind of legalized theft. But even more, I couldn't stand the idea of seeing my pride and joy misrun by appointed bigwigs who didn't know the difference between a sleeper and a pullman, but who were related to all the right people." He shook his head. "In every government I've ever been a part of, there are a few decent and honorable men among the rotten apples, though only a sprinkling of them. You can usually pick them out by the fact that they live simply and don't put on airs. They're not natural politicians, like the others. If you ask them, you'll usually find out that they first ran for office because they were madder than hell about something. Just like I was madder than hell about losing my railroad for no good reason."

I nodded slowly. "And I was mad about the way the war was being misrun."

Spence nodded and smiled. "Exactly."

I squirmed in my seat. "Sir," I said, in my best "respectful" voice. "This is all very interesting; very interesting indeed! But… What does it have to do with me, and why was it so urgent that we have this talk right now, before I go out on blockade duty?"

Spence looked out his porthole. "I know that you want a just peace, Thomas."

"More than anything," I answered.

"As do I." Rather suddenly, he stood up and walked across the richly-carpeted floor to where his big revolver dangled in its shoulder-holster from a peg, the same rig he'd been wearing the day I met him and which, presumably, he'd rarely taken off during the long, brutal Dracan occupation. He reached up and touched the worn leather of the holster, and sighed. There were, I noted, many fewer cartridges in the loops than there'd once been.

"Our current methods of government stink, Thomas. All of them. Because they're outgrowths of a fundamentally flawed human nature. Imperfection breeds imperfection, and war is only one of many unpleasant results. We won't end war until we fundamentally alter what it means to be human."

I nodded. "We've had this conversation before."

He nodded back. "So we have. There's been much water under the bridge since then, however. Alicia told me that you're fully committed. But you're young, Thomas. I had to be sure."

"My father has a plug in the back of his head," I replied. "So does my brother. My home planet fought nigh unto the death for the right. And I'm a cyborg."

"You're a cyborg, yes" he corrected me gently. "But not just any cyborg. You're a very angry one, deep down inside."

I nodded. "Madder than blazes," I admitted. "There's no excuse for the wretched things I've seen, and for the even worse things that I've been forced to do. None! Not if we can do better."

Spence nodded, then drew his revolver and hefted it in his hand. His nose wrinkled in distaste, then he slid it back into place. "I pray," he said, "That I will never again have to draw a weapon in anger so long as I live."

"And I wish that I didn't have to kill any more Dracans," I replied, "Though I rather suspect that I shall."

"Me too," Spence agreed, frowning. "Though how many is open to question. Let's hope that it will be only a relative few." He sighed, then sat down behind his desk again. "What we want to accomplish, really, is to change the gengineering laws. Legalize jacking in and frankensteining." He looked at me fiercely. "They *work*, Thomas. We're living examples. There's no other proposed cure out there that holds any promise. For the good of everyone who will ever live, we must arrange it so that these practices are legalized."

"It'll be an uphill fight," I predicted. "People sort of listen to me, if you know what I mean. But once I start talking about Father or brain-coring…"

Spence frowned. "Of course. I would expect as much." Then he shook his head and pointed at what I assumed was Alicia's letter, the one that'd warned him of the Opposition's maneuverings in Parliament. "In this kind of environment, it'll be even more difficult." He sighed. "Between you and I, for my money Nagano will pull it off. It's much easier to destroy something than to build it, and that includes a governing coalition. The people of Earth, where most of the voters are, have suffered hunger and nuclear bombings under their current leader. Their PM wants to fight on while the Opposition promises peace, new jobs, more food, and better pay. It doesn't matter that they can't deliver, or that if they end the war too early their children will simply have to fight it again and again and again until they finally get it right. They're saying what the voters want to hear. And those politicians who value winning above all else, whose only principles are rooted in puffing themselves up larger and larger to cover up how small they really are inside, will defect for fear of losing all they hold dear." Spence frowned. "The government, I predict, will fall. Soon."

My mouth fell open. "Spence, I--"

"Oh, we'll fight it every inch of the way. I've been wrong before, Thomas; many times! But I'd be lying to you if I claimed that I thought that this was going to be a winning battle. And I respect you too much to lie to you."

"Th-Th-Then…" I stuttered. "Th-th-then, all of this is for nothing! We're just blind, ignorant animals, killing and mutilating each other for no good reason, suffering and dying so that…"

Spence waited a long time for me, but I was unable to finish the sentence. "Now, son," he chastised me, rising from his desk and walking around me so that he could place his hands on my shoulders from behind. "All is not lost."

I looked up at him, feeling about twelve years old. I must have looked it, too, because he smiled in a very parental way. "As I just said, we might still win the big fight in Parliament. And if not in Parliament, there are always other, more direct ways to get things done. But…" His face grew very, very serious. "In any event, we need for the war to end as quickly as possible. Before the rot sets in back home. You understand that, right?"

I nodded.

"And," he continued remorselessly, "You're in a position to help make that happen. Aren't you?"

I nodded again. "Sir," I said. "I'd do that anyway. For everyone's sake."

"Good boy," he answered, releasing my shoulders. "That is why I called you here today, before leaving to go on blockade. To make sure that you understand where things stand and how important a quick, total victory is. That, and one other thing."

"What's that?" I asked, still looking up at him like a little kid.

"I also want to ask you a favor."

My eyebrows rose.

"Keep believing," he said. "No matter what happens, win or lose. Keep believing, no matter what. Even if one day Nagano ends up becoming PM."

"Do you have another plan in mind, if he does?" I asked.

"Of course," Spence replied, grinning again. "It's the damnedest thing. For I don't know how many millions of years now, the human race has continually spread and grown and prospered and bettered itself more or less continuously, no matter what the obstacles. Isoroku Nagano might flatter himself to the contrary, but somehow I don't think that he's the man to end that kind of long-term historical trend." His grin grew into a full-fledged smile. "Nor is he the man to stop Alicia, your father, and me all working together. And you too, of course. In many ways, you're the most formidable of us all."

Chapter One-Hundred Twelve

Moving from ship to ship within the task force wasn't the easiest thing imaginable; one had first to be approved for an intership shuttle and pilot, which typically had to be reserved days ahead of time. I'd line-jumped in order to be able to attend my urgent meeting with Spence. Used my rank, prestige and elected office, in other words, to interject myself ahead of someone else who also had important business and who now was forced to work around me. Was this unknown man or woman cursing me at this very moment, I wondered as I floated effortlessly home from the liner that was serving as Spence's provisional capital? Were they raging against the privileged kid who knew all of the important people, got all the big medals, and who they had to salute first even though he was far too young to have actually earned that kind of respect? Was I just as bad, in other words, as all the strutting peacocks on the floor of Parliament that I so despised, but so far detached from everyone else's reality that I couldn't see it anymore? Sarah Fowler would've thought so, though I'd personally seen to it that she'd never speak her mind again. She'd hated wealth and privilege at the gut level, and would gladly have confiscated everything that Spence and I had in the name of fighting poverty. That was wrong too, I thought. Especially since, no doubt, she'd have put her supporters and relatives in charge of dividing up the spoils…

I shifted in my seat a little, not wanting to think about Sarah Fowler and how she'd sold out to the Dracans and the way she'd squirmed and quivered and struggled as I'd throttled the life out of her. *June* was at almost the other end of the task force from *Lawrence Highridge*, and the trip consumed almost an hour at a pod's stately pace. That was much too long to spend dwelling on a killing. I did plenty enough dwelling when I should've been sleeping at night; that, and drifting across the wasteland that lay between wakefulness and dreamland, imagining that I was condemned to personally strangle each and every Dracan I'd ever killed and feel them die under my own hands. No, I spent plenty enough time remembering Sara Fowler; there was no need to give her anything extra.

So to distract myself I picked up one of the endless stream of reports it was my duty to read, and which at best I barely managed to keep up with. This one was on the two new fighter squadrons currently taking shape, again one each from Earth and Esteppe. Pilot selection, it seemed, was still underway. They wanted my input. It was difficult at first to put Sarah's dead, staring eyes aside and focus on dictating my comments for the people back home to ponder. I was continually learning more and more about what made a good fighter pilot candidate, and because the subject genuinely interested me I was a little startled when without warning my pod jarred into its mating-ring.

By the time I had my paperwork all neatly stowed away the pressure had equalized and the pod's pilot, a senior boatswain at least twice my age and probably specially detailed to make absolutely certain nothing bad happened to me, stood rigidly at the salute as I exited his vessel. "Thank you, bos'n," I muttered as I left. "It was a very smooth ride."

"It was my privilege and honor, sir!" he replied, still stiff and formal. Was the older man being honest, I wondered? He might've said the same thing to any one of dozens of Parliamentarians I knew whom I considered to be a total waste of space. For that matter he'd probably say the same thing to Isoroku Nagano himself, were he to come a-visiting. How could I know what another person really thought of me, in his heart?

Then I pressed my lips into a thin, hard line and realized that I was thinking nonsense. That was what friends were for, or at least good ones. Friends and family both. They served as guideposts; in selecting those who I admired, I suddenly understood, I'd also been deciding who I wanted to become myself. And who could ask for better role-models than the oddball collection of remarkable individuals I'd somehow surrounded myself with? Were I ever to grow too big for my britches, Father could be trusted to pin my ears back properly in a minute. To him I'd always be a son, not a bigwig war hero. Or Jimmy would grow sulky and distant and not want to spend time with me anymore. For that matter, Spence and Alicia were fine, fine people; if I became something repulsive and ugly, would the truth not be reflected in their eyes? Alicia had already corrected me once after I'd made a fool of myself aboard the tanker *Nelson Rockefeller* back on Esteppe. I loved her all the more for it; the experience, I now understood, had been as unpleasant for her as for me. But she'd done it anyway, because she cared. As I someday would correct someone I cared about. And Admiral Vlasilov... I shuddered inwardly at what he'd say and do if I let my ego grow all big and puffy. He was the antithesis of puffiness, the epitome of self-discipline, the embodiment of honor. If I strayed too far he'd be there for me too, cold and hard and loving.

And of course there was Father Murton. Yes, he was in many ways gone. But he'd live inside of me for as long as I chose to listen to him. Which, I took a moment to pray, would be for however long I might last myself. He deserved nothing less. Then there was Brooks, too...

I was plenty self-absorbed as I strode down *June*'s passages, mind a thousand miles away. It wasn't until she actually touched my sleeve that I noticed the ensign who'd apparently been trying to get me to notice her for quite some time.

"Huh?" I asked, still half-befuddled.

"You're wanted in the conference room, sir," she explained, relieved that she at least hadn't had to actually hit me over the head in order to get my attention. "Immediately. Something terrible has happened."

Suddenly I forgot all about strangled parliamentarians and the lampposts that guided my life. "What?" I demanded.

Her eyes widened, and she suddenly appeared almost as young as I was. "It's the admiral, sir. He's had a stroke."

Chapter One-Hundred Thirteen

Sickbay was directly on the route between the pod docks and the conference room; I might be needed urgently, but I also couldn't see where sticking my head in for two seconds would do any harm. I suddenly felt lost, and only finding out more about Vlasilov's condition could make me feel better.

As it happened I couldn't have timed things better. I came in just as the doctor stepped out of the main treatment room, so that I actually caught a glimpse of the admiral himself. He looked very pale and drawn, though his eyes were open. "It's our fault," the medical man said, glancing up and seeing that I was there. "He's been on a severe drug regimen ever since he was wounded and breathed so much vacuum, back when the bridge was blown off." The doctor frowned. "Things got a little out of balance, and we didn't notice."

"So it wasn't a stroke after all?" I asked.

"No," the doctor explained. "Though I can certainly understand the confusion; at first we thought it was, too. He grew confused on the bridge and started issuing irrational orders." The doctor's eyes narrowed. "He wanted you to come and save him and a petty officer and a clergyman, sir. Would you know anything about that?"

I gulped. "That's who he was trapped with," I explained. "One of them didn't make it, and the other was brain-damaged. I'd guess he's not really over the experience, though with him being who he is no one else would ever know. It's not the sort of thing he'd ever talk about."

The doctor frowned. "I see." Then he turned to face the treatment room. "The admiral will make a complete recovery, don't you worry about that. It'll only be a week or so, once we get the balance right again. Though…" His frown intensified.

"What?" I demanded. Having lost Father Murton to brain damage, I wasn't in any mood to be trifled with.

"He'll probably never hold an active command again," the doctor explained. "This sort of thing… Once it happens, the higher-ups begin to ask questions and have doubts. If the admiral were still an up-and-comer, they might take the risk. After all, this incident was the direct result of a war-wound, most honorably suffered. But… Vlasilov was borderline for a fleet command health-wise even before this, sir. He's never fully recovered his strength and probably never will. They were hanging onto him to finish the war because everyone knows he's the best we have. But now… The Admiralty doesn't like it when key officers collapse in the middle of an operation, sir. They don't like it at all. No one will criticize the man; in fact, most likely he'll be promoted into greater responsibilities. But…"

I nodded. "Thank you."

The doctor nodded. "I thought you ought to know, since you're clearly so important to him.

I blinked; then nodded and thanked the doctor again before leaving for the conference room.

Chapter One-Hundred Fourteen

Pretty much everyone aboard *The Glorious First of June* was aware that we pilots couldn't move very quickly under our own power. Therefore it'd become customary to start meetings without us and let us catch up later on anything important we might've missed. "Attention on deck!" a staff-lieutenant roared out as the door slid open in front of me.

"At ease," I answered just as quickly as I could, before anyone really came to their feet. They were coming to attention because of the traditions surrounding my Parliamentary Medals of Merit. I didn't like it, but it was one of the few formalities surrounding me that Vlasilov had refused to allow me to suspend for the duration of the war.

"What's this nonsense?" the man at the head of the table demanded. It was Captain Shepherd of the *Almirante Cochrane*, the task force's senior captain. He was in charge now that Vlasilov was out of sorts. The gray-haired man met my eyes. "I mean, come on! You have the right, but—"

"The admiral insisted," Michelle explained, looking daggers at Shepherd. Suddenly I remembered that they didn't like each other; the two had totally opposing views on how a war ought to be run. Up until now Vlasilov had mostly let the offensive-minded Captain Bard have her head. Also, the last time that Shepherd had been in charge the admiral had rebuked him for being grossly overcautious. Suddenly, I didn't like the look of things at all.

"I see," Shepherd replied, nodding slightly by way of apology. Then his face grew stern again. "What took you so damned long, anyhow? Your pod docked forty minutes ago."

I could've explained about slow-turning servo motors and long corridors. Instead I walked stiffly and ponderously to my usual chair, moving even less expeditiously than usual. Damn it, I was a captain too! Shepherd's substantive equal in rank, not some snot-nosed ensign! If he wanted to chew me out, at least he ought to have the courtesy to do so in private!

"Sickbay was directly on my route, sir," I answered evenly. "And I knew that everyone here would want an update. I obtained some information there which is almost certainly pertinent to this meeting. It wasn't a stroke; the admiral is suffering from a medication imbalance. It's a lot less serious, but his doctor informed me that he won't be himself for a week or so."

Shepherd's frown intensified. "When you're told to report immediately to one of my meetings, mister, you will doubletime in the future. Do you hear me?"

"Mister" was the proper terminology for addressing ensigns, not captains. I looked over my shoulder theatrically. "Was that comment addressed to me?" I demanded, finally beginning to lose my temper.

"You know that it was!" Shepherd replied. Then, he backed off a little. "Please, be more considerate of the rest of us, Captain Longo. It's bad enough that we had to wait for your political consultations to end. Do you do that sort of thing often, by the way? Make use of your political privileges, I mean?"

That was quite enough. "Only when my duties demand it," I replied, my voice as cold and cutting as I knew how to make it. "Whenever my elected office requires me to display initiative and daring, that is." There was a sudden sharp intake of breath at the table; everyone present was well-aware that the last time Shepherd had been in command, these were the very qualities Vlasilov had found lacking in him. After the big Dracan defeat at New Nippon he'd held the relief convoy up for days based on groundless fears of a second Dracan task force waiting in ambush. Who knew how many starving civilians had died, waiting those extra days for food?

"Why, you young…" Shepherd was turning a very nice shade of purple and that was plenty gratifying in its own right, but even better his spluttering gave me a moment to think. What was all of this really about, anyway? It'd come from nowhere, lightning from a clear blue sky! I'd sat down at dinner tables with Shepherd four or five times at various functions, and had even met his wife once. All of that, I realized suddenly, had taken place before he'd been rebuked by the admiral, before he'd messed up so badly that he'd probably never have a chance to fly a flag of his own. And now here I was sitting directly across the table from him and his broken career, wearing the same captain's bars at age eighteen that it'd taken him his whole life to earn and the ribbons for three Parliamentary Medals of Merit for good measure, with a fourth on the way. My god! The man was so jealous he could barely contain himself!

Others could see it too, apparently. "George," Michelle began. "For Christ's—"

"Quiet!" Shepherd ordered, his eyes not wavering for an instant from mine. Then, very slowly, he relaxed a little. "We're getting off on the wrong foot here," he observed.

More so than you'll ever realize, I didn't say aloud. The fact that I worked so hard not to develop an overstuffed ego didn't mean I was automatically willing to play doormat. "Yes, sir," I replied instead.

"We've got to work together," he continued. "Closely."

I nodded, but didn't smile. "Yes, sir."

"Admiral Vlasilov would want us, too," he continued.

Finally he'd scored a telling hit. "He would," I agreed. Then I extended my hand across the table.

Shepherd accepted and shook it. "All right, Thomas," he said, smiling slightly. Then he turned to Michelle. "What's our status?"

"We're almost ten hours from initiating the close blockade," she replied, distaste sill evident in her expression. "All final orders have been cut and delivered."

"I don't like it," Shepherd replied. "Never did, really. *Cochrane* still isn't at anything like a hundred percent." He looked at me again. "And your squadrons are at less than half strength."

"There's also no Dracan Navy left," I countered. "All my pilots will be required to do, I'm told, is cover one Nikita against at most light opposition. We can easily manage that with what we've got."

He frowned again. "I don't believe," he continued, "that the admiral would've supported this plan had he been fully aware of how badly off *Cochrane* still is. Perhaps his mental condition has been slowly deteriorating for some time, so that he failed to comprehend my report as thoroughly as he normally would've? Our main guns were knocked totally out of calibration!"

"It'll take you an extra two or three salvoes to find your target," Michelle replied evenly. "More likely two, on a merchantman. Which, along with a destroyer or two, is the most we expect to fight."

Shepherd turned back to me. His forehead was glistening. "Your fighters aren't just reduced in numbers," he pointed out. "You've had to form a composite squadron, as well. Your people aren't used to working with each other."

"The lead element will be Jimmy Knight and myself," I countered. "We've fought many battles together. Successful ones."

"You two can't be on duty all the time," he replied. "There could be a massive superfighter counterattack. I could lose half the fleet!"

"Jimmy and I aren't the only qualified pilots," I answered, trying to remain calm. There were excellent reasons to believe that we wouldn't be seeing anymore Dracan supers anytime soon; if our enemy had them, they'd have used them a few days back in the main battle. "Everyone has combat experience under their belts now. Some have earned medals for their bravery. Two are now aces."

"It's also very late in the game to cancel such a big operation," Michelle reminded Shepherd. "We've got supply vessels dancing complicated jigs as many as three Jumps back, and even the yards back home are adjusting the refit schedules based on their understanding that we're going to be at Drakkus for some time to come."

Shepherd's face paled visibly. "You've already sent word back to the Admiralty?" he demanded. "That was fast!"

"We have," Michelle confirmed. "My staff is highly efficient."

"I see," *Cochrane*'s captain replied, perspiring more heavily now. Shepherd might be a good officer in most regards; he almost had to be, in order to have been entrusted with such a responsible posting. And I knew for fact that he was a solid, reliable ship-handler and all-around spacer. I'd attacked his ship in drills more times than I could recall, and never once had I found the slightest thing lacking in either his preparations or maneuvers. But, as was becoming more evident with each passing minute, he was totally unfit for higher command. He always had been, probably, and now Vlasilov's rebuke had broken him beyond repair. "Never take counsel of your fears," it said in one of Jimmy's books. He'd pointed the passage out to me just that afternoon; it was a quote from one of history's more colorful and successful generals. Now I understood why this was such good advice for a man who had to make top-level decisions. Too much doubt could break a man—had broken this one, in fact

Suddenly an inspiration hit me. "I'll put it writing, sir."

"Put what in writing?" he demanded.

"That no Dracan superfighter will get through to the task force," I answered, smiling as innocently as I could. "It'll be my responsibility if they do."

Michelle's eyebrows rose, as well they should. The suggestion was ludicrous; I couldn't promise such a thing, nor could Shepherd abdicate his responsibility so easily if the worst came to pass. But our new commander was eager to grasp at straws, it seemed. "You'd sign such a document?" he demanded. "In front of witnesses?"

"Sure!" I agreed, trying to sound as boyishly innocent as my youngest pilot. "Bring it on!"

Amazingly enough, Captain Shepherd did exactly that. He drafted the letter himself right out in front of everyone, editing each phrase a dozen times over so as to ensure that every ounce of responsibility landed on my shoulders instead of his own. He even made me accept responsibility for any losses caused by the battleships and cruisers the Dracans no longer had, then went back and modified the phrase to make sure it also covered secret weapons no one had heard anything about yet as well. The longer the drafting went on, the more difficult it became for the other officers present to conceal their disgust. Finally Shepherd collected his document and left, clutching it to his beast as if it were some kind of security blanket. "We translate in just over nine hours," was his final statement. "Dismissed.

"I've never watched a man lose his mind before," a lieutenant-commander of signaling commented once he was gone. "And I hope to god I never have to see it again."

"I'd rather have Vlasilov utterly mad than Shepherd sane," another officer added. "And with Shepherd gone round the bend himself…"

"That'll be quite enough of that," Michelle barked, though it was clear that she agreed with every word. Then she looked at me. "Thomas has the right idea, as usual. Captain Shepherd is our commander and we have to do whatever we can to support him. The mission comes first; let's keep our eyes firmly on defeating the Dracans." She smiled at me. "Good work, kid. I'd never have thought of that one."

Chapter One-Hundred Fifteen

Nine hours later, precisely as planned, I was sitting in my Skybolt body on the port launch rail, eyeing Jimmy as his own 'bolt was chivvied the last few inches into place. "You all right?" I asked him over our private channel.

"Right as rain!" he agreed, cheery as always. Then his tone grew more serious. "I'm glad we're back together, here at the end of it all."

I clicked my mike twice, which between us meant more than words. Jimmy's 'bolt had developed a last-minute life-support glitch, and for a little while it had appeared that I might have to pair up with Isaiah again. But the sweating, cursing techs had put things right, and now we were properly lined up for launch. We'd elected to break up into three flights of two and keep four of us on watch at all times. It'd be a brutal schedule to maintain; quietly, I'd already put out the word that any pilots sleeping on standby were neither to be awakened nor disciplined. But with the Dracan homeworld so close at hand, it seemed the only prudent course. Plus all of us were on special standby for the translation, so that all six operational fighters stood ready for liftoff in case something unexpected awaited us on the other side of the Nikita.

Not that we were going anywhere anytime soon; at the very last minute—and perhaps even a few seconds beyond—Captain Shepherd had altered our plan. Instead of bursting into Dracan space in a long, heavy, undefeatable mass assault, he was sending *Attila* ahead to reconnoiter and report back. It was a bad decision on multiple levels. First, *Attila* was a brand-new Warlord-class destroyer and therefore very valuable; if there were a trap on the other side, then we could find out just as easily by sending a far more expendable ship. Second, if there *was* a trap, which we had no reason whatsoever to suspect, *Attila* would be forced to fight her way clear of it alone and unsupported. And third, suppose *Atilla* didn't come back? What then? Would we send her sister *Genghis Khan* through alone next to see what had befallen her? And, when she didn't return, would we then send *Arminus*? My head hurt from trying to follow the twisted logic that lay behind Shepherd's decision; try though I might, I couldn't come up with one single reason why he'd done what he did. The only benefit I could see for anyone except the Dracans was that perhaps it might lower his own personal anxiety level a notch or two.

My head hurt for other reasons as well. I'd had to ask for a medic to come and induce sleep for me after the big meeting. I almost never did that, partly because I didn't think the rest I got that way was as good and partly because, since becoming a squadron commander, I'd learned that an inability to sleep was considered a major red flag by the counselors. While I was no longer subject to their down-checks, I knew that somewhere a flight surgeon was keeping tabs on me just as thoroughly as Father Murton ever had. So I usually did without rather than ask for help. But this time… I sighed. Whenever I'd been right on the verge of snoring, I'd either imagined over and over again how awful it must've been on the bridge when Vlasilov became confused, or else grew angry all over again at Captain Shepherd. Mostly, it was Shepherd that kept me awake. I simply couldn't understand how a man could be in the navy for so long and rise so high, yet break down like that when the pressure hit a certain point. He was a lot older than I was, and certainly far better trained and educated. So how could he be so indecisive? Was it maybe because he understood the consequences of his actions better than me? I didn't think so, not since I'd been there to see Churilla fall. No one could live through that and not learn something about high stakes. At any rate, it was foolish to let him bother me so much. He was only going to be in charge for a week at most. By then Vlasilov would be recertified fit for duty. It'd take far more than a mere public breakdown to damp *his* fires; while his days in command might be numbered, he'd run things with a firm hand indeed during the time he had left. Then the Admiralty would either send out a replacement, or…

…or, just maybe, the war might be over. And that was indeed a happy thought indeed, wasn't it?

Michelle agreed with me, up and down the line. "We can carry Shepherd for a week," her private note to me had read; it was stamped "Most Urgent", so I'd taken the time to read it before reporting to my 'bolt. "And we must do exactly that. It's our duty." She'd already contacted the brass back home, she explained, using private channels. Blockade duty was simple enough; there'd be no snap decisions to be made. Or at least there shouldn't be. "Just do your job, Thomas," she urged me. "It's plenty big enough. Leave the rest to us professionals." And Captain Bard was right, I knew. I had more than enough on my plate, for an eighteen year-old.

Still, my head throbbed

"There she goes!" Jimmy observed as *Attila*'s pip hit the Nikita and vanished. That was yet another thing that was wrong with Shepherd's modification to the plan; because she had to turn right around and come back the way she'd came, *Attilla* couldn't carry much vector as she Jumped. If there were indeed a trap, she'd trigger it while moving dead slow. Then we'd all have to wait while she reversed yet again to rejoin us. That wasn't any way to run a railroad!

We waited and waited. In the past I'd made it my policy to monitor the bridge channel under circumstances like these, so as to remain completely and totally up to date at all times. But here and now, what was the point? Until *Attila* came back no one would know anything anyway. And the idea of listening to Captain Shepherd further emasculate our battle plan made my head hurt even more. If someone wanted me, they knew where to find me. In the meantime I sat and played my internal video game in blessed silence.

"Thirty seconds," Jimmy observed.

I clicked twice, then saved my game and brought up my pipper. If all was well, *Attila* should reappear… Now!

Nothing emerged from the Nikita.

I sat and waited. Ten seconds, twenty, thirty. Nothing. Then I turned on my bridge monitor.

"..clearly there *is* something dangerous on the other side!" Captain Shepherd was declaring, his voice ringing with self-righteous triumph. "We're going to have to stand down, then reinforce for a full-fledged, properly-planned ass—"

Just then, in mid-word, the Nikita flared and *Attila* popped back through, braking heavily. "Sorry!" she signaled almost immediately. "We had to splash an escort-destroyer. Pitiful little thing, really—she only carried two torps. We'd have been back sooner, but we had to maneuver to avoid them."

There was a long, cold silence. "Where's the main Dracan fleet?" Shepherd demanded. "Where's the enemy? Make a full report, damn it!"

"There isn't any! That little destroyer was the heaviest unit in the sky. But we have to hurry! There's a liner preparing for takeoff from their main spaceport! A big one!"

Chapter One-Hundred Sixteen

At a certain point, apparently even a Captain Shepherd could be forced to take immediate action. The rest of the task force was all nice and lined up and drifting steadily towards the Nikita, *Cochrane* leading the way due to her thick armor. Captain Shepherd had returned to the surroundings of her comfortable, familiar bridge, though he really should've remained aboard *June* and in close proximity to Bard's flag staff. For long, wasted seconds I waited as my commanding officer tried to find a reason not to proceed. Then, finally, he gave the necessary order.

"Follow me!" he declared, as his battleship's tremendous motors fired, full power ahead. Behind her were the two remaining Warlords, then *Doolittle* and *Zeppelin*, and finally us. As we closed in on the transition point, I rang up the flag bridge. "I'll want to launch the first flight immediately," I told Michelle. "Unless there's good reason why not."

"Right," she agreed, "My sentiments exactly." She paused. "Thomas, that liner…"

I clicked my mike twice. We both knew who was probably aboard her; it didn't take a genius to figure it out. Back when Churilla had fallen, Father Murton and I had been lucky enough to hold tickets for a stateroom on the *Argus*, the last liner out. While we'd ended up not accepting the ride, a mob of people had surrounded us at one point, waving huge sums of cash and otherwise abasing themselves in an attempt to catch the last lifeboat leaving the war zone. Humans were pretty much the same everywhere they were encountered, and I was willing to bet that Drakkus was no exception. Aboard that liner, I was quite certain, could be found the richest, most influential and powerful of all Dracans, blindly stampeding like cattle away from danger. It'd probably taken them days to make up their mind; according to our intelligence their decision-making system had broken down. But now, everyone that could wangle a seat was running for all they were worth. Every square of inch of that liner was almost certainly crammed with self-important humanity.

And, I was willing to bet, said self-important humanity included the Emperor and his Imperial Household among their number.

"Come on!" I silently urged *June's* captain. This was unfair of me; we couldn't Jump until it was our turn, after all. I had no reason to be so angry about the fact that we weren't at Drakkus yet. Except, of course, for the fact that Shepherd had already wasted a vital hour with his silly *Attila* foray, an hour which might make all the difference in the world in whether or not the Emperor made his escape, and whether the war went on for who knew how many extra months. "Gahrrr!" I complained aloud to Jimmy. "Vlasilov set everything up so that we might maybe catch the Dracans with their pants down by arriving sooner than expected. We would've gotten lucky too, but Mr. Prissybritches threw it all away!"

"Lucky how?" my friend demanded.

I blinked to myself; perhaps it wasn't so obvious. "That liner," I explained. "It's probably the elite of the planet, trying to escape. Including the Emperor."

There was a long, cold silence. "Geez!" he said finally. "And they've got Nikita Number One down inside their atmosphere!"

I checked my pipper; while Drakkus rotated on its axis, the Nikita remained motionless relative to the planet's core. "At least it's almost halfway around the globe for them. We may have a chance." I virtual-scowled. "Unless we spent the next twenty years stuck in traffic!"

Chapter One-Hundred Seventeen

Either *June*'s captain must have figured it out too, or else Bard leaned on her. In any event, she did what she could for Jimmy and I by thrusting a little extra-hard and treading so closely on *Zeppelin*'s heels that our collision-warning siren went off. Then, even before the queasiness of translation died away, Jimmy and I received twenty-five gee kicks in our posteriors and we were flying side by side into combat, just like the old days.

"She's up-shipped," my friend observed.

"Yeah," I agreed, scowling and swinging us onto an intercept course. "That's odd. They're not on a direct track for Number One."

"They're still swinging around," he explained. "I bet they were going for Number Three originally. But now that we've shown up, well… Any port in case of storm!"

I clicked twice, then switched to Michelle's channel. "Don't—" I began.

"Who authorized your launch?" Shepherd interrupted me, clearly in a state of rage. "Answer me, Captain!"

There was more than one Captain on the circuit, fortunately. Otherwise, I might've embarrassed myself by using some of the more colorful words and phrases Petty Officer Brooks had taught me. "Thomas is authorized to launch on his own initiative," Michelle explained patiently. "Ever since he was promoted to captain. It's his right as an air group commander of superfighters. You probably haven't had time to familiarize yourself with the new standing procedures, sir."

"I… Uh…" Shepherd continued, wasting my time when I should've been ordering the launch of my second element for backup. "Cover the task force, Captain Longo," he ordered. "We're at our most vulnerable while transitioning."

"Yes, sir!" I replied, not altering my course a single degree; I was racing directly away from the main body, barreling down towards Drakkus on a full-throttle attack run. I paused fifteen seconds, all the while gaining vector, then explained. "I'm going to cover the task force by going to investigate that large bogey, sir. It may've been misidentified, and therefore could conceivably be dangerous."

"You mean the liner?" Shepherd demanded. "She's no threat. And, I'm receiving new intelligence…" Suddenly my pipper blinked as I was updated as well. "She's a hospital ship, Captain Longo. Red Cross-marked, and therefore entitled to safe, undisturbed passage."

I virtual-scowled. "Sir," I replied, "the Dracans began this war with a sneak attack utilizing smuggled fusion weapons and killing millions of civilians. They've committed atrocity after atrocity ever since, almost nonstop. I've witnessed some of them personally." I let my voice grow soft and conspiratorial. "Surely you don't suppose that they'd stoop to abusing hospital-ship privileges?"

There was another long silence, as Jimmy and I all the while covered more miles. At least, I congratulated myself, Shepherd's indecisiveness could be made to work both ways. "We're going to make the intercept, I think," Jimmy whispered in my ear. He knew that I was too busy to work it out for myself; it was part of what made him such a superb wingman. "Unless that fat slug of a liner can move faster than it is already. Which I doubt." There was a short pause. "Or maybe she'll splash down somewhere."

"This planet's practically all dry land," I replied. "They had to dredge out an artificial lake to create their spaceport. There's probably isn't any other body of water big enough to handle her. It'd take forever to turn something that big and awkward all the way around. She's better off to run for the Nikita."

"Then she's ours," my best friend observed. "Unless we're ordered to let her pass. Or we get shot down."

I clicked my mike twice again; Drakkus might be fresh out of all of the other implements of war, but she still had plenty of air-defense missiles and batteries in service. I was picking up intermittent warnings every few seconds as the weapons-operators tried the range. It was still too long, though. For now.

"I…" Shepherd stuttered. "I mean…"

"The Emperor is very likely on board," Michelle explained for Shepherd's benefit. "Would you have him escape? How long might the war drag on then? How many more deaths would there be? How many more resources squandered, planets ruined?"

Then, a new voice interrupted, speaking on the common frequency in a sharp Dracan accent. "Sheer off, United Systems skyhoppers," it warned. "You're attacking a registered hospital ship, entitled by treaty to free passage."

"Uh…" Shepherd commented.

"It's full of infants and young children," the Dracan voice continued, "attempting to flee the war zone. You're savages, yes. But will you sink this low?"

There were only seconds left; on the planet's surface a missile battery fired. And, I remembered with a gulp, there had indeed been a last-minute attempt made to evacuate as many children as possible from Churilla, though in far less elegant vessels. "Jimmy!" I said on our private channel. "What do we do? You just had the class on attacking merchantmen!"

"We're supposed to stop and inspect her, if you want to get all technical," he answered. "But, we can't do that! We're Skybolts! And there isn't time for anyone else to get to her!"

It was worth a try anyway, I decided. "Dracan liner!" I declared on the common channel. "Heave to and cease all maneuvering. You will remain in your current position until you receive a new course to follow, whereupon you will be boarded and inspected. If you're what you claim to be, you'll be allowed to proceed unharmed."

"Captain Longo!" Shepherd screamed. "That is far in excess of your authority!"

"Yes," I answered back. "It certainly is. Now quiet down, won't you? I'm busy fighting the war."

For a long time, there was nothing but silence over the channel at my outrageous comment. Then Captain Shepherd finally found his tongue. "It's all your responsibility, then! I wash my hands of it! Expect to face a court-martial!"

"Right," I agreed absently; by then court-martials were the last thing I was worried about. A few years in the brig were nothing, compared to ending the war early. I'd suffer them gladly.

"Uh…" the Dracan finally stuttered; now it was his turn not to know what to do next. Down on the planet below, a second missile battery fired, then a third. We didn't have long before the warheads arrived. Meanwhile the liner didn't waver an inch from her declared course. "We don't have to submit to your dictates!" he declared eventually. "*Emperor's Mercy* is a properly-flagged Dracan naval vessel, duly registered as a hospital ship. You have no right to search her."

"She'll submit to search or I'll blow her out of the sky!" I roared. The missiles were closing in now, and Nikita Number One was looming close. "It's your decision!"

"The ship is crammed with infants!" the Dracan shrieked, "Little ones, napping in their cribs and suckling at their mother's breasts! Will you tarnish the name of your navy forever? Of fighting men everywhere?"

"Will you sacrifice them in the name of enforcing a verdammt legal principle?" I roared back "Heave to, or I swear on my honor as an officer that I'll kill every living thing aboard your precious liner, babies or no. Do it now!"

"You have no right!" the Dracan shrieked, his voice growing hysterical. "You're an animal! A barbarian! Unworthy of your uniform."

"And about to be two missiles lighter, too!" I declared. "You have five seconds. Four. Three…"

"No! You must not do this! It's *wrong*!"

"One… Zero!" I declared.

"A missile apiece?" Jimmy offered. "Just in case?"

"If that's the way you want it," I replied.

"Most definitely," he answered. "Emperor or the brig either one, together all the way. I've never been prouder to be your friend."

"Thank you," I answered. "Or I yours. Take careful aim. We have time enough for that."

"No!" Shepherd ordered. "You can't do this! We have to sit down and work things out and-"

"No!" the Dracan echoed; it was a wail of despair. "Nooooo!"

"On target," Jimmy reported.

"Me too," I answered. "Now!"

And as one our torpedoes raced off of their rails, soared through the sky, and detonated deep in the vitals of the alleged hospital ship *Emperor's Mercy*.

Chapter One-Hundred Eighteen

I'd never seen a large ship moving at cruising speed through an atmosphere shot down before; the result was… staggering. In a vacuum dying ships tended to remain all in one piece; even when they exploded bits and pieces like turrets flew off but the main hull tended to remain intact. Not in a high-speed airflow, however. The initial torpedo hits were just the beginning. *Emperor's Mercy*, if that was really her name, peeled herself like an egg and then turned herself inside-out as she careened across the sky out of control, no longer under power and screaming her death agonies. Her innards trailed behind her like so much confetti. Some of the bits and pieces were corpses, I was quite certain; or at least soon-to-be corpses. It seemed to me that almost all of them were of right sizes and shapes to be adults, though I couldn't be certain. Jimmy and I hung around and watched the liner die for as long as we reasonably could, not because it gave us pleasure but because I needed to know the truth, if I possibly could. But soon the missiles arrived, and we had to go to high-boost to avoid them. Even then I got a little sloppy from trying to watch the liner die when I should've been dodging, and one detonated far too close for comfort. I took a small fragment and yellow lights appeared in my mind.

"You all right, Tommy?" Jimmy demanded.

"Yeah," I agreed, a little sheepishly. How the others were going to ride me when I got back, after taking such a dumb hit! "It's a little damage in the interface, is all." The interface module was where my survival capsule hooked up to the 'bolt; it was what translated my thoughts into actions. "Nothing serious, but… Damnit! I want to go down and look at the wreckage! Once it's all fallen, I mean. To see if they're babies or not!"

"If there were any babies on that liner," Jimmy reassured me, "You can bet your life that their hair was all done up in ornate braids." He paused for a minute. "Tommy, if it really had been a ship full of children they'd have stopped for inspection. It's not worth you taking a chance in a damaged 'bolt just to go look. And you know it."

"Maybe they wanted to create an incident," I answered glumly. "To make us look bad."

"If so," Jimmy countered, "then all they did as make themselves look like idiots. Yes, hospital ships are allowed free passage. But they're subject to inspection, all right. It's just that hardly anyone thinks to ask anymore because it's been so long since anyone's been in a situation to safely board one. Everything you did was legal."

"I sure hope so," I grumbled, watching the debris rain down on the desert below. Most of it was landing near one of the big scars left over from my last little visit; we'd used very dirty bombs in retaliation for the fact that the Dracans had used the same kind on Earth. So the whole area was probably uninhabitable. Which in turn meant that meant there couldn't be any functional missile batteries nearby…

"Tommy!" Jimmy interrupted my thoughts; he'd been my wingman a for very long time. "Don't be an idiot, all right? It doesn't suit you."

I looked at my yellow lights again and sighed; one of them indicated that the connecting ring, the physical link between me and my 'bolt, was cracked. If there were enemy superfighters in the sky, or if the ghost fleet that Captain Shepherd was so terrified of were to suddenly appear out of nowhere, it might be considered brave to fly into action with a cracked mating ring. But under the current circumstances, well… Jimmy was right. It was just stupid. "All right," I agreed. "Let's go face the music."

Chapter One-Hundred Nineteen

And what music there was! Captain Shepherd screamed and ranted and raged and threatened me all the way back home to *The Glorious First of June*. "You hit a big one, mister!" he kept repeating over and over again. I didn't understand what he was talking about until Jimmy interrupted on our private channel and informed me that the phrase was academy-slang for "You really screwed up bad". A couple of times Captain Bard tried to interrupt, but Shepherd shouted her down. "Don't try to defend him, Michelle! He'll be in irons within the hour! And so will his wingman!"

"Who'll be flying air cover?" someone asked; I didn't recognize the voice. "How will we enforce the blockade? Can the rookies do it all on their own?" But Shepherd made no answer.

Things grew even worse after Jimmy and I landed. I expected to be dismounted and arrested; it wouldn't be pleasant, but at least I was ready for it. It seemed, however, that *everything* was destined to go wrong that day. "You're wedged in real good, sir!" my crew chief explained. "We're going to have to cut that broken mating ring. You're going to be out of touch while we're working. The cords would be in the way."

"Right," I agreed. It'd been a long time indeed since I'd been left without any sensory input for more than a few moments. None of us pilots enjoyed the experience. "Get to work, then. I know that you'll be as quick as you can."

"No quicker than you want us to be, sir," the burly man replied, leaning close to my audio input and whispering. Behind him a squad of marines had formed up. They were there for Jimmy and I, no question about it. "We know what happened, both last night at the meeting and today on the mission. If you'd rather us take our sweet time..."

I virtual-smiled despite myself. "Just do your job the way you'd normally do it," I answered. "But thanks for the thought."

"You're very welcome," he answered. "It'll be a good two hours, maybe longer. Are you ready?"

"Ready," I agreed.

"All right, then," he said, reaching for something. "Here we go... Now!"

Suddenly I was formless, bodiless, blind, deaf, and mute. When I'd first woken up after my brain-core surgery it'd been much the same. Back then the experience had been a nightmare. It'd gone on and on and on, not for two hours but several days while I tried to learn how to blink a simple light on and off. I'd been much younger then, and frightened as well. If I hadn't been pumped full of don't-worries, I might've lost my mind. This time was pretty bad, too, in its own hideous way. Being out of contact was bad enough, but I still didn't know the truth about so many things! Had we killed the Emperor? A ship full of infant-refugees? Or maybe something else entirely? And, what would the brig be like? Would they let me have my mannequin-body, at least? Would Jimmy and I share a cell? I sure hoped so; that wouldn't be so bad.

For what felt like an eternity but probably wasn't more than a few minutes I replayed the last couple of days over and over again in my mind. It'd all happened so fast! According to the doctor, Admiral Vlasilov's medication imbalance was probably the medical staff's fault. So a single overworked medico had misread a prescription or whatever, and boom! Here was the whole task force in a state of disarray, and me about to be clapped in irons by the sorriest excuse for a second-in-command I'd ever imagined. Had Vlasilov had even the faintest idea of how unfit Shepherd would prove as a pinch-hitter? Surely he had his suspicions. But in that case why hadn't he replaced the man? Did Captain Shepherd maybe have a relative in Parliament, like a certain idiot named Roon I'd once known? Or was the navy actually *that* short on skilled line officers? Presumably it'd all come out at the court-martial; Father would see that both Jimmy and I received not just competent counsel but the best there was. I snarled to myself; if there was one thing I'd learned how to do, it was stand my ground and fight. And by god Shepherd would know that he'd been in a dustup!

The images whirled around and around and around in my mind; soon I was no longer certain if I was awake or dreaming. Not that it particularly mattered. I could've fired up my video game, I supposed, and used it to maintain a little structure in my consciousness. Somehow, however, the idea of doing so made my headache worse; *that*, of all things, was still somehow leaking through. The emptiness went on and on and on-- for days, I could've sworn, endless hour after endless hour without break or interruption.

Until, finally, someone shone a light in my eyes. Mannequin-body reflexes weren't so different from human-normal ones. I blinked, then raised my right hand to ward off the glare. "Thomas?" an unexpected voice asked. "How are you?"

It was Michelle. "Fine," I answered, sitting up. "But..." I wasn't on the hanger deck anymore. Nor, apparently, was I in the brig. Instead I was coming to in sickbay. And... "Where are the marines?"

Another shape surged forward. The light was still too bright for me, so I didn't recognize him until he spoke. His rich, strong Esteppan accent identified him as Captain Jungmann, of *Graf Zeppelin*. What was he doing aboard *June*?

"Don't worry about the verdammt marines, your excellency. That's all been taken care of."

I blinked again, still trying to clear my vision. The room was incredibly crowded; it seemed that half the fleet's officers were gathered around my bedside. In addition to Jungmann and Bard, there were the captains of *June* and *Doolittle* and *Sitting Bull*... Even the first officer of *Cochrane* was present, hunched awkwardly over the foot of my bunk so that his head wouldn't bump into the big medical readout. "I don't..." I began. "I mean..."

"You've been out of touch a little longer than planned," Michelle explained; apparently she was the group's designated spokesperson. "Almost an entire day."

I cocked my head to one side. "It felt like an awfully long time," I answered. "Was the mating-ring *that* messed up?"

"Not really," she answered. Then she looked down and sighed. "Thomas, let me just be up front and tell you straight. There's been a mutiny."

"A mutiny?" I repeated, my jaw dropping open.

"Of the blackest sort," Jungmann agreed. "It was totally illegal. In criminal violation of every regulation in the book. Vile, nasty, brutish."

"Captain Shepherd is being held against his will in sickbay back aboard *Cochrane*," the battleship's first officer explained. "He's madder than hell. I'm afraid he may have a heart attack or something."

I looked around the room again; now I could see a little better. Everyone was smiling, which made no sense at all. "What... I mean..."

Captain Bard grinned at Jungmann, who grinned back. "We mutineers have taken over the task force--"

"We're a scurvy lot, aren't we?" Jungmann interjected.

"...and have placed Captain Shepherd under arrest."

"Legally, we have little standing," *Cochrane*'s executive officer explained. "But morally... Sir... After what he did to you, and the position he placed you in..."

"He's a miserable weakling!" Jungmann declared.

"And incompetent to boot!" *Doolittle*'s commander added.

"We couldn't just stand by and watch," Bard explained. "Not after the example that you set. When you stood up to him, with everything on the line."

"You were kept out of touch so that you can't possibly be charged," Jungmann added. "Not with mutiny, at least. We let them brig Jimmy for the same reason." His face darkened. "If the United Systems government were even to *try* and charge you, your excellency, well... Maybe Esteppe might just *win* this time around, by god!"

"And maybe half the navy might side with her," *Sitting Bull*'s CO added. "Including," he explained, gesturing around the room, "all of us."

I gulped. "You mean... You guys..."

"We did," Bard replied, straightening her back and standing tall. "And we don't regret it."

"Not a one of us!" an officer in the back said.

"We did exactly the right thing!" another added. "You showed us how to be bold."

I laid my head back on my pillow and closed my eyes. "Oh. My. God."

Jungmann smiled, then pulled out a scrap of black leather and put it over his left eye. "Ahrrr!" he declared. "I'd hoist me the Jolly Roger, but the Dracans might die of confusion. Ahhr!"

"What about the Dracans?" I asked after a very long time. "I mean, the liner…"

"You did indeed kill the Emperor," Michelle explained, eyes shining. "You and Jimmy together. And most of his relatives and high advisors with him. There were children aboard, yes. But they were the Emperor's children, and there were only a few. It was his fault for exposing them to such danger. Or so I see it. He could've hove-to and surrendered."

I opened my eyes. "And the war?" I asked, almost too frightened to ask.

"It's over, we think." Michele replied. "There's still plenty of fighting going on down on the planet, but it's all between rival Dracan groups. Gangs, really. There's no government left, just a bunch of armed mobs squaring off against each other and fighting over the best looting-places. We expect that the other Dracan worlds will probably be reduced to the same state within weeks if not days. Every few minutes a mayor or general or some high mucketymuck of one stripe or another calls and tries to surrender. We accept, but…" she shrugged. "We have no troops, so we can't protect them from each other."

"We could fly airstrikes," I suggested. "Set up liaisons and try to restore order that way."

"Is that what you'd like us to do?" Michele asked quietly.

My jaw dropped again, as I searched the sea of faces around my bed. All of them, I realized were seeking something from me. Though exactly what, I still wasn't quite certain. "If it's practical, it might be a good start," I answered. "Do we have enough marines aboard the task force to hold and secure a small bridgehead? Working with one or more of the muckety-mucks, I mean. If so, we might be able to begin to enforce order." I scowled. "There's innocent people suffering and dying down there for no good reason. Surely we can find a way to help?"

"I'll make a contact list, your excellency," Jungmann declared, clicking his heels in an Esteppan salute. "We'll see who's willing to cooperate down below and what resources they control."

"I'll work with him," *Cochrane*'s exec suggested. "After all, there's not much chance we'll be needing the big guns anymore. Nor for a very long time to come, god willing."

Then everyone was volunteering for this and that, all working together again in one, coordinated group. Soon I was alone with Michelle. "I…" I tried to say, "I mean…"

She smiled. "Hush, you!" she whispered, as if I were but a small child. "It's all over, for the moment at least. Your part is done. Why don't you lay here for a while and take a nap?"

"B-b-but…"

Her smile widened, and she laid her head over on her left shoulder. "I'm a strategist by profession, Thomas. I never attended the academy. But when I became an officer I had to learn about leadership. There were classes."

I nodded wordlessly.

"There's a thousand different styles of leadership, we were taught. Authoritative, collaborative, positional, personal… In the end, all are equally valid and work equally well. So long, that is, as when the Big Day comes the would-be leader passes the leadership test."

"What's that?" I asked, now very confused.

"The leadership test is… When things really go to shit, who do the followers turn to?" Her smile widened. "I've never seen anyone score a higher grade. In fact, I'm not sure it's even possible. Unless you want to become royalty, that is."

I grimaced. "No thank you."

"I thought you might feel that way," she replied. "Though you might just pull it off. It's been done before, after all." Then her smile faded. "Thomas, when the admiral is up and about again he'll take over and sort out this mess. I can't even begin to imagine how, but that's why he gets to fly a flag and I don't. Until then… Well, I don't think it'd be a good idea for you to fly any more missions. We need you here, safe aboard the flagship."

I nodded. "This time, I think you're right."

"Good," she agreed. Then, she turned to leave. "Get some rest Thomas. You've won one war today and deserve a break. But I suspect an even more dangerous one is brewing back home."

Chapter One-Hundred Twenty

I spent practically every minute of the next few days sitting at my desk. It was a nice desk I had to admit, if a bit battered. Certainly it was nicer than I'd have chosen for myself; when I became a full commander someone automatically upgraded my perfectly-serviceable steel unit to real walnut. No one consulted me about the matter; if they had I'd have stuck with my old friend. This was doubly true since the new desk was larger and I'd chosen to remain in my undersized quarters in the gunroom so as to be closer to my pilots. By now I'd spent months tripping over the thing, and every time I'd transferred from *June* to *Coronel* and back sweating ratings had been forced to muscle it down too-tight corridors, each journey adding a new set of scratches. In other words, what was supposed to have been a status symbol was mostly for me an albatross. Though now that I was practically living at the thing, I was beginning to appreciate how useful a little extra paper-stacking space could be. Despite this, I didn't think I'd ever come to prefer wood over stamped metal.

I was just reviewing a situation-report on the occupation when a knock came at my door; creating a working occupation government out of next to nothing was proving almost as challenging as fighting the war had been. We captains had decided at one of our daily "leadership meetings", where all the decisions were made, to send back to Churilla for the army division that was being held in reserve there. Originally it'd been earmarked for the bloody Battle of Churilla City. That meat-grinder of a battle, however, now would never be fought, which in turn left the troops free for occupation duties elsewhere. Did we mere captains have the legal right to order an army general around? Of course not. But I signed the orders anyway, and word had already come back that the unit was en-route. They were expected momentarily. "Is that General Bliss?" I asked Manuel, who was proving himself a pretty fair administrative assistant as well as valet.

"No, your excellency," Captain Jungmann replied, stepping into my little room. "It's me. The admiral's ready to return to duty. He's called for all of us to meet in the conference room. I'm sure word is on its way to you, but I happened to be passing down the corridor, and…" He shrugged.

I nodded and gulped. "Right," I agreed. I'd requested a daily update from sick bay on the admiral's condition. He'd recovered exactly as predicted, from raving madman to one of history's greatest leaders of men. They'd had to use additional drugs to flush the other ones out of his system. These new formulations had left him weakened and subject to sudden uncontrollable fits of trembling. He'd been advised to use a wheelchair when moving any significant distance, and to lean on a cane for extra stability whenever he stood. But he was back to being himself, of that the medicos were quite certain. His body might be frailer than ever, but his mind was perfectly fine. For that matter it'd probably been okay for the last two days, though the doctors hadn't been prepared to take the risk of allowing him to resume command.

The conference room wasn't any further away than it'd always been, but this time it felt like it took three times as long to get there. The idea of going to the brig hadn't fazed me one little bit, so long as it was Shepherd who sent me there. In fact, by the time that push came to shove I was ready to wear punishment from him as a badge of honor. But Vlasilov was a very different story. A verbal rebuke from the admiral would carry more sting than a long prison sentence from the likes of Shepherd. Captain Jungmann seemed to feel the same way. He wasn't wearing his eye patch anymore or talking like a pirate. "This'll be ugly, by god!" he muttered as we stood aside and allowed an engineering party moving something large and heavy to pass by from the other direction.

"Not pretty at all," I agreed. "But I wouldn't change a thing."

"Nor I." Then the working-party was past and we traveled the few remaining feet to our destination.

Vlasilov kept us waiting, though I couldn't be sure if this was deliberate or not. A wheelchair didn't move much faster than my servos did, and the admiral wasn't used to being delayed by such a handicap. When he did finally arrive he was accompanied only by his one-armed valet, who was carrying the biggest pile of reports I'd ever seen. "Attention on deck!" the junior officer present cried, and all of us stood at attention.

This one time, Vlasilov kept us standing. Instead of giving the order to be seated he steered his chair carefully first down one side of the long, crowded conference table, then the other. Along the way he met the eyes of each officer, and held them for a long, cold moment. Whether by chance or by design he came to me last of all. "Captain Longo!" he demanded.

"Yes, sir!" I replied, back ramrod-straight and eyes front and center.

"Are you a mutineer?" he asked.

"Yes, sir!" I repeated, without hesitation.

"Have you been issuing orders to units not under your legal command?"

"Yes, sir!"

"Did you initiate an occupation of Drakkus not only without proper authorization, but without even consulting the government?"

"Yes, sir!" I repeated again. This time, however, someone else chimed in.

"Sir!" Michelle barked. "There was chaos. He saved thousands of civilian lives. Someone had to take the responsibility."

"And he didn't do it alone, no matter what he says," Jungmann added. "We kept an eye on him, and backed him all the way. Sir!"

"Silence!" Vlasilov bellowed, so loudly that his face paled afterwards, and he was forced to gasp for breath.

"Sir?" I asked, my tone less formal. "Do you need help? I mean…"

Vlasilov held up his right hand, palm-out; it was trembling, a little. Then, he shook his head. "No," he continued in a conversational tone. "I'm fine, Thomas. Though thank you for asking." Then his eyes and tone hardened again, and he rolled his chair around behind me. "Do you believe you've grown bigger than the navy, Captain Longo?" he demanded. "Smarter and better and more important than the government that gave you your command? Have all those medals eaten your brain?"

"No, sir!" I belted out. "I just did what I thought was right, sir!"

For what felt like an eternity, Vlasilov sat there, his hard, frigid eyes boring holes in my back. Then he finally nodded. "You're dismissed, Captain Longo," he said. "Return to your duties. I'll be calling upon you presently." There was a long pause. "The rest of you," he continued as I began making my slow, laborious way out the door, "have *much* explaining to do."

Chapter One-Hundred Twenty-One

I don't claim to know what the all-time record for conference-room marathons is, but this particular one lasted just over fourteen hours. No record was kept, and once it was finished no one ever spoke of it again. It became a non-event in the best navy tradition, something that simply never happened—sort of the same way that it came to pass that no mutiny had ever taken place anywhere except in Captain Shepherd's fevered imagination. In reality he'd broken down on the bridge much as Vlasilov had a few days earlier. It was most unfortunate that *Cochrane*'s bridge-recording gear had been damaged in the battle, and that the equivalent gear aboard the flagship was also down for maintenance during those crucial hours. Shepherd's memories of the surrounding circumstances were very different than everyone else's and a recording might've gone a long way towards clearing things up. But, hey! Sometimes that was just how things went. The navy never claimed to be perfect. Just war-winners, was all. And apparently that was good enough for both Vlasilov and then the Admiralty, when they in turn investigated the incident many weeks later.

When the admiral finally came to see me after the long, draining meeting, his skin seemed to be made of parchment and he could barely hold his head up. Before leaving Earth this last time I'd spent far too much money on a pound of good Russian tea of the kind that he loved so much. When he arrived at my cabin, a boiling pot of the stuff and a mug awaited him.

"You certainly have cheek," he declared, nodding at the boiling kettle as he maneuvered his wheelchair into my living-space. Manuel had helped me clear an area for him, or he wouldn't have had room at all.

"I'm smarter than the navy," I countered, shrugging. "My big medals have eaten my brain."

For just a second, I thought I'd pushed things too far. Then instead of exploding Vlasilov laughed out loud. It seemed to do him good. "Thomas…" he finally said, shaking his head and reaching for his tea. "I never know what to expect next from you."

I let my smile fade. "I'm glad you're well," I offered at last. "When I heard you'd had a stroke, I… Well…"

"Bah!" the admiral replied, waving his hand airily. "I'm far too wicked to suffer a stroke. When I go, it'll be something much less pleasant that finishes me." He smiled slightly. "This is excellent tea."

I nodded. "I ordered it direct from St. Petersburg. The shopkeeper told me it's the best there is. It was to be a gift when the war ended." I shrugged. "Well, it's ended."

"It certainly has," he agreed. "And thank you." His smile widened. "Thomas… What the others did…. The mutiny, I mean."

I nodded my understanding.

"It was wrong," he continued. "It was also inevitable, mind you. But it was still wrong. They're the best and brightest officers in the fleet. They should've found another way."

"They would've," I answered. "Except for the fact that things moved so quickly. That, and…" I hesitated.

Vlasilov gestured with his teacup. "Go on."

"Sir… " I said slowly, "they did it for me. I wouldn't have wanted them to, and they knew it. That was why they kept me in isolation. But…" I looked away. "

"You're correct, Thomas," he answered. Then, still trembling slightly, he poured himself a second cup and stirred in sugar. "That's why I'm here; to make sure that you realize this. And to tell you that I found your personal behavior, in contrast to that of your fellow captains, to be unquestionably correct and honorable. Your record cannot be made to reflect this, because of course there will be no record of anything. But I wanted to tell you personally that this is how I see things." He paused. "By rights, Captain Shepherd should've *ordered* you to shoot down that liner. You're only eighteen, for god's sake! He *owed* that to you, on the off-chance that you might've been wrong."

I pressed my lips together, but said nothing.

Vlasilov sighed. "Anyway, Thomas… I too have been waiting for the war to end, though I fear I have no gift for you. Or at least not anything that can be wrapped or placed in a box." His eyes narrowed again. "Long ago, back when I first accepted this command, I made a deal with my superiors. We were losing, you see, and many of the flag-officers were reluctant to accept field-commands that appeared to promise only death and defeat."

I blinked. "Then," I said slowly, "these same flag-officers have no business wearing a uniform."

The admiral chuckled. "That sort of officer, like the poor, will I fear be always with us. It seems to be a law of nature." His face sobered. "Anyway, Thomas… As a reward for accepting this command, I was offered my choice of assignments for my next berth. And I've decided."

My eyebrows rose. "Indeed?"

"Originally I intended to ask to be placed in charge of postwar superfighter development. While that remains a very attractive posting indeed, I've found something else that I think I'll like better. Something even more rewarding."

"What's that?"

"I think," Vlasilov declared, after taking a moment to savor another sip of tea, "that I shall ask to be put in charge of training and personnel development. This isn't considered to be a plum job; in fact, it's something of a dead-end. The posting even lies beneath my rank. Yet my career is winding down anyway, and I find that there are more important things in life than collecting more stars on my shoulders."

"You'll collect them anyway," I predicted. "No one else could do what you've done, sir. It won't be forgotten."

"Heh! You'll be surprised at how quickly we fade away, we old men. The only ones who'll remember and honor us are that handful that follow in our footsteps." He smiled again. "And that, strangely, is enough. In any event, this is neither here nor there."

I nodded, still not understanding.

"As chief of training, Thomas, my office will be located on the grounds of the Academy. While I won't be the superintendent—that job is *far* below my pay-grade—I'll be looking over his or her shoulder, so to speak. By tradition I'll also be allowed to teach a class or two if it strikes my fancy. And it shall, I think." He set down his mug and looked into my eyes. "I'm making these plans because I've found working with you and helping you along so rewarding, Thomas. Thank you, for helping me to learn something new about myself that I'd never have suspected without your presence in my life."

I blinked. "I—"

Vlasilov cut me off with a hand-wave. "You have a great life ahead of you, Thomas. And I'm not such a great fool as to imagine that it won't involve Parliament. With such dizzying heights available to you, the navy can't offer much in comparison. And yet…" His eyes twinkled.

"Sir," I said, "I don't know if I could become a midshipman, after—"

"Oh, no!" he cut me off again. "You're a man now, Thomas, not a boy! Putting you through the Academy could only ruin you! That's not what I have in mind at all!"

I tilted my head to one side. "Sir?"

"As head of training," he explained, "I'll also be in charge of the War College, for the army and navy alike. While academically you're not ready for such a challenge—a lot of the courses are considered the equivalent of post-doc classes in mainstream universities— I can set you up there with a whole staff of personal tutors at your beck and call and the freedom to learn whatever you'd like for pretty much as long as you'd like. The best of everything." He leaned forward. "You're a great officer, Thomas, and both the navy and the human race would, I'm certain, find the investment well worth our while. If you choose to stay in the service, you'll be a serving admiral for perhaps as long as sixty years. Longer than anyone else has ever managed, certainly. By the time you're done the navy will have been entirely made over in your image. And, Thomas, I can't imagine a better thing to have happen to this tired old service."

I blinked. An admiral for sixty years? But, I was eighteen now, and,,,

Vlasilov read my face and grinned again. "No, Thomas. I haven't promoted you again. But it's inevitable. The politicians will see to it, if no one else. More likely your enemies than your friends, because it'll make them appear to be good sports at no real cost to themselves." His grin widened. "Even after you've left active service, they can still promote you. It happens all the time."

My mouth dropped open. "I…"

"Ha!" Vlasilov laughed. Then he drained his mug and set it down on my battered desk. "I know that you have many other avenues open to you, Thomas. So it's unlikely you'll stay with us. Honor, however, compels me to at least try and come up with a fitting reward after what you've suffered and accomplished." He shook his head. "It's still pitifully inadequate."

I looked away. "I'll consider it," I promised. "But… There *is* one thing I'd ask."

"Yes?" Vlasilov asked, raising his bushy eyebrows.

"Jimmy," I said softly. "Take care of him. He wants a navy career more than anything. And the other surviving pilots too, of course."

"Hah!" Vlasliov laughed again. "I would've done that anyway, Thomas; do you think I'm some kind of ingrate?" He shook his head, still smiling and looking ten years younger than when he'd entered the room. "The entire service will take them under our collective wing. Don't you worry for a minute about that." His eyes narrowed. "But you're the main prize-- I've known that from the very beginning. And while I might be denied you, I'll not have it said anywhere or by anyone that I didn't give it my best try."

Chapter One-Hundred Twenty-Two

It took almost a month for the navy to send out a new flag officer to replace Vlasilov. During that time things went on much as they had before. The occupation troops were landed exactly how and when our conference of captains had worked out, and the foreign-office types back home didn't even raise an eyebrow at the arrangements we'd make with the local Dracan officials. The rioting died away slowly, first at rifle-point and then later because food shipments began to arrive. Everyone's economy was in a terrible mess from the war, but the Dracans were far worse off than we'd ever been. Food had never been quite as scarce as it'd grown on Churilla or even Earth at the height of the crisis, but industry had virtually come to a standstill and there were plenty of loose Dracan belts as well. Which was just as well, I decided. Better that everyone should have suffered, so as to reduce the chance that some damned fool might want to pick another fight anytime soon.

What was left of the Dracan Navy came in and surrendered as well, in little dibs and drabs as word percolated through the Empire that the fighting was finally over. Some of the Emperor's surviving warships splashed meekly down in their assigned berths, guns trained fore-and-aft as directed. The crews of these vessels then placidly filed off to the POW camps for processing. They weren't detained for any great period of time, just long enough for the record-keepers to settle up their final pay and for a discreet search to be run against a list of known war-criminals. Generally these ships were in first-class fighting condition when they landed, with brass freshly polished and main armaments still carefully sighted-in. A few, however, insisted on making hard landings and warping their hulls, then opening the seacocks so that the once-proud ships sank straight to the bottom. These vessels had been captained and officered by fanatics, and therefore their ordinary crewmen had to be considered suspect as well. Once they were fished out of the slimy, moderately-radioactive swamp that constituted Drakkus's sole spaceport for the time being, the men of these vessels were taken away to sturdier, more permanent camps for much longer stays. It was the darnedest thing. Practically every Dracan Navy war-criminal we were looking for was to be found on one or another of the scuttled ships.

There was little or nothing for me do during these final weeks except sit in meetings, look important, and nod blankly. It was just like the old days, back in Spence's cave during the formation of the Churillian resistance. We never flew any actual attack missions in order to discourage the rioters; rather, we found that the masses were terrified at the very sight or sound of a Skybolt. This wasn't an unreasonable fear, by any means. Skybolts had after all reduced the population of Drakkus by almost a quarter. Even more than that, however, the Dracans had apparently used images of our superfighters as propaganda bogeymen, the terrible evil which it was necessary for all Dracans to sacrifice and pull together in order to defeat. While it wasn't actually true that we Skybolt pilots decorated our cabins with the scorched skulls of children, as their holovision programs claimed, apparently the confused survivors took it as gospel. I wondered if they thought we all talked like Colonel Rotte as well? In the end it all worked mostly to our advantage. Whenever we wanted to disperse a mob, we just sent a lone 'bolt to fly circles over it and maybe fire a few cannon-rounds into the empty air. It worked like a charm, and no one actually got hurt. Nor did it demand much of my squadron; we dropped down to having only one pilot on alert at a time. What luxury! People actually had time to study!

I had a lot of time on my hands too, though I didn't use it for class work. There was too big a pile of Parliamentary reports waiting for me, and more arriving all the time. Spence was now adding a summary of his observations to each package; while I was grateful to him and had even specifically asked him to send me his thoughts, I hadn't realized how long-winded he could be. It was what one ought to expect from a renowned author, I supposed. Besides, though I didn't want to admit it to myself I rather suspected that a careful analysis would show that every word and sentence was indeed both important and relevant. The real problem, in other words, wasn't that Spence was wasting my time. Rather, the root of my difficulties was that being a proper Parliamentarian involved many more hours of effort than I really wanted to put into it.

I sighed and squirmed in my seat as I read one of Alicia's long letters, lovingly and meticulously annotated and illuminated by Spence's marginalia. There'd been a great outburst of joy back on Earth at the victory announcement; people had danced in the streets for an entire day and a night and then another day after that. The Opposition were caught off guard at first; they hadn't expected victory to come either so quickly or completely. They'd even been forced to interrupt their continual smear campaign for a few days, while unconvincingly indulging in an orgy of "me, too!"-ism, claiming equal credit for the tremendous accomplishment. But now it was back to business as usual. Every day a new scandal was erupting, all of them on our side of the aisle, while the voters were being assured by our political enemies that, once the war-reparations payments arrived, their tax-burden would be eased, their sufferings would be, their children would be happy and smile all the time, and lemon-drop sunflowers would grow along the sidewalks for all the good Opposition voters to pick and feast upon whenever they liked.

"The pity of it," Alicia explained in her private note, "is that the voters are falling for it. While I've not seen as much of Drakkus as you have, Thomas, the picture we're building up back here isn't very promising. The factories are old and decrepit, the economy is shattered due to the bombings, the merchant fleet is practically gone, and the population-- while historically hard-working and law-abiding when not reduced to desperation—isn't particularly skilled. Where are these enormous reparations going to come from? What are the Dracans going to pay with? We're going to have to bail *them* out, in the name of simple humanity."

Spence highlighted this portion for me, then added his own note. "They'll demand that our government extract a mountain of gold," he predicted, "then blame us when no windfall arrives. It'll all be our fault, to the common man. If they pull this off our party won't return to power for twenty years; maybe longer."

There was more. Nagano had won back his minority-leadership post, though by what combination of extortion, arm-twisting, and casual reference to ancient closet-skeletons I couldn't even begin to imagine. Every day he was looking smugger and more self-assured as he led the counter-attack during open-floor sessions. "I don't know him as well as the long-timers," Alicia observed. "But it looks to me as if he thinks he can bring us down if only he can find right the issue to base his confidence vote on. What that issue will be, I fear I cannot predict."

The rest of the stuff was even more depressing; the continuing scandal-attack was as nauseating, disgusting, and sick-making a list of personal peccadilloes and improprieties as I'd ever seen in my life. "Most of these charges won't stick," Alicia explained. "Half are pure fabrication, and the rest contain varying degrees of fantasy-elements as well. But there's just enough of a kernel of truth in some of them, and just enough people in responsible positions willing to misrepresent facts and make the lies seem true, that the cumulative effect is devastating. Thomas, for once in my life I truly do not know what to do. Yes, we too are capable of digging up dirt. But what a dilemma! There's not nearly enough of the stuff lying about for us to seriously damage Nagano's people unless we lie and slander and twist the facts the same way that our enemies are. And if we do that, then we'll be just as bad as they are and won't deserve to hold office any more than they do! Besides which, we might unleash such a wave of disgust and distrust of government and politicians in general that the people's belief in democracy itself is damaged. Eventually most of our Parliamentarians will be cleared of these charges, though some will probably be falsely convicted, and a few truly guilty parties with exceptional legal staffs will go free. But at the end of the day, Joe Voter will only be aware of the fact that every night on the news, over and over again, he's heard nothing but a long series of allegations of corruption and fraud on our side of the aisle.

People tend to assume that only the guilty are accused of crimes, Thomas, even though that's not at all the case. 'Innocent until proven guilty' is fine in theory, but only in theory. Certainly it's never applied to politicians seeking re-election. We have a choice between accepting this unearned label as criminals and worse, or else fighting back in such a manner as to endanger the fabric of society itself."

"This is part of why politics is such a rotten business, Thomas," Spence added in the margin. "I'm not at all surprised that this is happening, and am a little surprised that my wife is so upset. She should've seen it coming as well. Personally, I can't wait to be clear of politics again. And, I'm sure, neither can Alicia."

"Me too," I said aloud, sighing and laying the report aside. I didn't have any answers either.

Then the new admiral finally arrived. We held a formal change-of-command ceremony down on the hanger deck, and officers from every ship in the task force came over to pay their respects. Admiral N'werke was much taller than Vlasilov, and ten years younger. He was quite a handsome man, and had been highly decorated for his administrative work assembling a scratch force for the final defense of Earth during the Dracan blockade. Somehow, however, despite the fact that he said all the right things. ("You are most honorably relieved, sir!" he'd declared, saluting Vlasilov with the utmost respect at the end of the ceremony. "Most honorably indeed!) he was a very different sort of creature. One that I didn't like nearly so well.

"Peacetime leadership isn't the same as wartime leadership," Michelle explained to me when I asked her about it. "Admiral Vlasilov was a truly great wartime leader. He didn't shine nearly so bright when there was no actual war to be fought, however." I still wasn't sure what she meant by that, but when N'werke sent for me to come see him in his new (and Vlasilov's old) quarters, his smile seemed forced and his manner artificial.

"Is there anything at all I can do for you, Captain?" he asked, once the pleasantries were dispensed with. "Anything you need that you're not getting? Are you being granted enough time for your Parliamentary duties?" The interview was more than half over before I finally figured out what the real problem was; the man was terrified of me! What did he think I was going to do; induce the other captains to mutiny against him? Make negative speeches about him and the navy in Parliament if he didn't kiss my butt properly? It was just as well that he carried orders relieving me from my current duties in order to make one last war-bond tour—there were still plenty of bills to be paid. My orders also specified that I was to be assigned no other fixed duties in deference to my responsibilities as a Parliamentarian. They also carried confirmation of my fourth Parliamentary Medal of Merit; I was to be decorated by the PM in person.

"So," the admiral explained, smiling just a little too wide. "We've got to transport you back to Earth, with bond-selling stops along the way. Is there any particular ship you'd like to have for the trip home? *Cochrane*, perhaps? She's easily our most comfortable."

I gulped; it's not every day that a man is offered the use of a dreadnought as a personal taxi. "Well… " I said eventually. "My first stop is on Esteppe. There's a navy yard there. Are any of our ships due for refit?"

M'werke pressed his lips together, then rang up his flag-captain. It was too much, I supposed, to expect a brand-new admiral to be intimately familiar with the ships under his command so soon after taking over. Still, I suspected that Vlasilov would already have known. "*Graf Zeppelin*!" he replied eventually, hanging up. Then he smiled again. "She's due and past due for a refit, and a long shore leave for her crew as well. Esteppe is even her home port. We couldn't spare her up until now, with her gunnery being so exceptional." His eyebrows rose. "Would *Zeppelin* be adequate, Captain Longo?"

"Quite," I agreed, nodding slightly, "I think she'd do just fine."

Chapter One-Hundred Twenty-Three

All ships of war are crowded, and have been since the very beginning of things. In ancient times there were dozens of rowers and archers to accommodate. In later years, because armor plate was so heavy it became vital to design ships to be as small and compact as possible. This was difficult, but somehow naval architects still managed to keep their products livable. Or more correctly, they were livable when brand-new. As the vessel aged, however, technology would invariably progress and as a result there was a continual need to mount more and more gear. This tendency towards incremental growth was still every bit as operative today as it'd been in the days of iron steamships. Many small guns as opposed to fewer large ones, for example, not only took up more space in their own right but also required more men to crew them. So did new sensor-suites, improved safety and survival gear, and engineering enhancements in the ships' motors.

More crewmen in turn required more officers to command them, and more facilities to feed them, launder their uniforms, treat their wounds, and so forth. Every once in a great while an innovation came along that actually reduced the need for manpower, but this was a relatively rare event. Overall the game was a losing one, and the parties that did the losing in question were those who had to spend their entire careers sleeping in too tiny a bunk in too small a bunkroom aboard too crowded a ship. It was even worse aboard a vessel like *Zeppelin*, which had been hastily designed to meet a war-emergency situation. Her hull was based closely on that of the preceding *Doolittle* class, but those ships had been equipped with a third less guns. Somehow the necessary extra men had been crammed in, but then more and more essential war-equipment had been added as well. Despite the fact that in military terms *Zeppelin* had unquestionably been one of the great success-stories of the war, she was also so far the only vessel of her class ever built, and almost certainly would remain so. If the entire navy had been forced to live under such appalling conditions, re-enlistment would've dropped to something approaching zero.

Then Admiral Vlasilov, Spencer Wiston and I all showed up one day for passage on her run back to Esteppe, each of us a VIP rightfully entitled to a cabin of our own. "We don't have much to offer," Captain Jungmann explained as we reported aboard. As head of a planetary government, Spence was the highest in precedence. He was awarded Jungmann's cabin; in turn, *Zeppelin*'s commander would share that of his first officer. Vlasilov was offered the chief engineer's quarters.

"Bah!" he declared, "We should never have been assigned passage aboard this ship to begin with. What idiot ever suggested such a thing?" I remained very quiet, while Spence eyed me suspiciously. But Vlasilov was merely asking a rhetorical question. "If you don't mind, Captain," he continued almost without a pause, "I'll go hitch a ride aboard *Arminus* instead. This is no reflection on you or your men, I assure you. Yours is easily the finest cruiser in the fleet; my reports have so stated many times, as you well know. But…" He patted the arm of his wheelchair. "I 'm confined to this ironmongery for another few days, and simply must have more room to maneuver."

Jungmann clicked his heels and smiled. The Warlord-class destroyer was accompanying us in order to make permanent repairs to her patched-over battle-damage. She was Esteppan-built too, which I hadn't realized because her name sounded so Latin. "*Arminus* it is, sir; I'll arrange a shuttle immediately." Then he turned to me. "In that event, Thomas, you shall have the chief's quarters."

I felt pretty bad about kicking the chief engineer out of his home; he was a gray-headed old man and I was only eighteen. On the other hand Manuel was a necessity for me, not a luxury, and he'd be sharing my already-tiny room. The chief didn't seem too upset about it, particularly after I gave him an autographed model Skybolt for his grandson and invited him to bring the boy to visit me at the Old Home Place sometime. It was the least I could do, under the circumstances.

It was sort of strange to be aboard a navy vessel and have no specific job to do; I'd been in the same position twice before, of course. But on those occasions I'd been hurt and distraught and had spent practically all of my time in sick bay. On this trip, however, I seriously began to wonder if my real name and title weren't "Excuse me, sir!" Whenever I wandered about the ship, which I truly wished to see and learn more about, I was continually in someone's way. The Esteppan crew was wonderful; they loved me as one of their own and I found myself responding in kind. They referred to themselves as "the toughest verdammt crew in the navy", with some justice given their perpetual state of overcrowding. But proud words didn't make it any easier on them when my slow-moving servomototors and the vessel's long, narrow passages combined to make a man late to his station during a drill. Once early in the voyage I followed an ordinary seaman whose way I'd blocked and explained to the petty officer myself what'd happened. That seemed to make things worse instead of better, however, so I didn't do it again. Instead I spent a lot of time either in my own cabin, or Spence's.

My friend seemed to enjoy the company; he too suddenly had too much time on his hands. At first he hadn't wanted to leave Churilla while there was still such chaos down on the surface, but then his staff had persuaded him that they had matters under control and that it'd best for the planet if he showed his face in Parliament and appealed personally for rebuilding funds. "Not that either of those things were really what tipped the scales," he explained to me one day while sitting on the other side of a chessboard. Sure enough, he was a terrible player. "The truth is that I was mooning so badly over Alicia that I couldn't get anything done anyway. So they sent me to Earth to get me out of their hair."

I smiled, then moved a knight. I wasn't much good at chess either. But Spence didn't play video games, so there weren't many other choices. "Sometimes you have to do what's right for yourself," I reassured my friend. "Not always what's right for everyone else."

"Indeed," Spence agreed, frowning comically. I'd just forked his rooks. "If you don't at least minimally take care of yourself and your own needs, soon you won't be able to help anyone else." He looked up at me. "Are you looking forward to going home, Thomas?"

I shrugged. "I'm not quite sure where home is anymore."

"That's reasonable enough," Spence agreed, taking the offending knight with his queen; I'd missed that one. "A quarter of your life, perhaps more, has passed since you last had a stable place to call your own." He shook his head. "We're all quite sorry it happened that way."

I smiled wistfully. "I can't even imagine what a so-called normal childhood might've been like. Maybe like the leave-time I spent with Jimmy, but all of the time?" My bishop was lined up with Spence's queen now, I noticed. It wasn't on purpose—I just hadn't noticed before. Instead of taking his best piece I simply began resetting the board for a new game. We didn't really care who won or lost. Which was just as well, I supposed.

Spence smiled a little, thinking I'd conceded. "Probably quite a bit like that," he agreed. "Though of course I wouldn't know either. I was very much alone as a young man."

"Really?" I asked. "I somehow assumed you grew up with Alicia."

"Oh, no!" he countered. "She was from Manitoba, and I from Kansas." He pursed his lips, sending his whiskers pointing off in all directions. "We shipped out to Churilla together, of course. But…" He shook his head. "We were both still children, you see. I was twelve and she was ten. Gengineering had just been outlawed, but everyone kept assuming that someday we'd marry each other anyway."

I nodded; it certainly seemed obvious enough in retrospect.

"But…" He smiled again. "I was a fairly bright child, as you might imagine. And so was Alicia. We were both been mocked for being bunnies, and neither of us enjoyed the experience." His eyes narrowed. "Being different when you're young can leave scars. Rather deep ones, in fact. For many years Alicia Redder was the very last person on Churilla that I ever wished to marry.

Or on any other world, for that matter. And, she pretty much felt the same way about me."

"Really?" I asked, my eyebrows rising.

"Oh, yes!" Wiston continued smiling fondly as he remembered. "We were civil to each other, more out of mutual sympathy than anything else. But whenever anyone else tried to pair us up, it was full-scale adolescent rebellion time!" He shook his head again. "I never planned to marry at all, since the new law denied me children."

"But…" I said eventually. "I mean, how…"

"Heh!" the big rabbit continued. "Don't ever underestimate the power of the human drive to pair-bond, Thomas. In a very real way she and I were destined for each other. Made for each other, even. I mean that literally, Thomas, though very few others know it. According to our parents, who set the whole thing up, our children were supposed to be something very special indeed. Alicia and I were designed specifically to be the ideal parents for these children, not to be the final successes in our own rights." His eyes misted over for a moment, pondering what might've been. "Though we've done at least fairly well for ourselves, I think. Anyway, by the time we were forty both of us were mature enough to realize that we were just being silly and stubborn. The wedding was the social event of the decade, and we've been radiantly happy together ever since."

I smiled. "I wish I'd been there."

Spence smiled back. "It's the privilege of age, son. I just hope that I'll be able to attend *your* wedding." His eyes narrowed. "When are you getting your real body back?"

"Once this last bond-drive is over," I answered. Then I turned away. "They've been delaying maturity on it as much as they can, so the nerve-endings won't close up and make it so they can't put me back. I'll look like I'm younger than I really am. About sixteen. Maybe even fifteen."

"Heh!" Spence replied, though there was no venom in his laugh. "Fifteen, and four Parliamentary medals! Won't that look strange!"

I frowned. "They didn't tell me about that," I explained. "The shrinks decided I shouldn't worry about looking dorky. For my own good, they said. It might affect my combat performance." I frowned. "I wonder what else they never told me?"

"They were wrong to hold that back," Spence replied, "Very wrong. I'm rather surprised, really. They must not know you at all."

"It's a blanket policy," I explained, "One that applies to everyone. I suppose I'll get used to it, eventually." I shrugged. "In a few years it won't even matter. Maybe they can speed up the maturation process some to make up for it." I looked down at the little hatch in my arm where the length was adjusted. "All this time they've been readjusting this mannequin-body to match my growth back home. It didn't amount to much. I just thought I was going to be short, was all. Mom wasn't very tall, and people say that I take after her. But…"

"You're going to be as tall as your father and brother," Spence predicted, "At least as tall as them."

"Probably," I agreed. "Now I know that I'm just behind schedule, is all. At least that's one good thing."

"Here's another," Spence predicted. "Nobody expects you to look like a kid, Thomas. Everyone knows you're only eighteen, or at least in their head they know. But in their hearts, with that mannequin-body to help fool them, you're at least thirty. So I bet you won't be recognized very often in public. Or at least not like you otherwise would be."

"Everyone treats me like I'm thirty," I agreed. "Or even older. Sometimes I even treat myself like I'm thirty."

"Yes, you do," Spence agreed. "And I'm guilty as well." He looked me in the eyes. "Have you made your big decisions yet? The kind that all eighteen-year-olds have to make, I mean? About what you're going to do with your life."

I frowned. "Everyone wants me to stay in Parliament," I answered. "Or else in the navy."

"That's not what I asked," Spence observed. "Not even close."

"I know," I answered. Then I sighed. "I'm obliged to stay in Parliament, I think. At least until we get the final peace treaty negotiated and settle the frankensteining thing. It's what's right for the human race, I think. And a matter of personal honor as well. Maybe even unfinished family business."

Spence nodded. "I agree and can but applaud. After that?"

"I don't know," I admitted. "I keep trying, but all I can come up with are blanks." I looked the rabbit in the eye. "I don't know what I want to do with my life, Spence! It's a terribly important decision,-- I understand that fully! And one that needs to be made soon as well. But every time I try to make a plan…" I let my sentence die, unfinished.

"That's because you don't know who you are, son," Spence explained. "Hardly anyone does at eighteen; I certainly didn't. It's one of the great ironies of the human condition, I've always believed, that we're forced by our biology to make our most important, life-impacting decisions at the very time in our lives when we're least equipped to make them-- while still young and inexperienced." He cocked his head to one side. "Though, Thomas, I must say that you of all eighteen-year-olds can hardly claim inexperience."

"Heh!" I replied, smiling back.

"If I were you," he continued, lowering his eyes back down the chessboard, "I'd not make any plans at all until I knew who I was inside. Being rich, you have the luxury of waiting. Take a year off, or even two."

"Two whole years?" I whispered back. "With nothing at all to do?" I thought about how I was getting in the way in *Zeppelin*'s corridors all of the time, and shuddered.

"Not necessarily nothing," Spence pointed out. "You could do all sorts of things. If you gave me two empty years, I'd write a book or three. Alicia might compose an operetta, or paint." He smiled. "Or, I might go fishing, and she might loaf around the house. Two years can pass a lot quicker than you might imagine!"

"Heh!" I agreed, trying to picture Alicia loafing. It was impossible, though the idea of Spence spending two whole years doing nothing but fishing… That one, at least, I could see happening.

"You've been living a life entirely dictated by outside events," Spence explained, his voice taking a more serious tone. "You've been making decisions, yes. Important ones, even. But they've been decisions pressed upon you from the outside." He reached out and placed a hand on my shoulder. "Don't be too hard on yourself; a billion veterans from a million wars have come home after the fighting was over and found out that they didn't even recognize the place anymore. You're hardly the first who doesn't know what to do next."

"I guess that's true," I admitted.

"It is!" he assured me. "It's in all the history books. Especially the ones I wrote!" He smiled again. "Don't push yourself too hard just yet. We have this one last hurdle that both of us agree you're committed to see through to the end. After that, who knows? By then maybe everyone else in the universe will be dead, so you won't have to make a decision after all. We can at least hope, eh?"

"Heh!" I laughed.

He smiled back. "Never take life too seriously, Thomas. It takes all the fun right out of it."

Chapter One-Hundred Twenty-Four

People referred to Drakkus and Esteppe as being on opposite ends of the United Systems. It was one of the great oddities of galactic geography that in fact they were only five light-years apart—veritable neighbors, even. But in terms of Jump-geography the story was very different. It took us six weeks to get to Esteppe from Drakkus, and even worse our route didn't take us close enough to Earth at any point along the way to make it worthwhile for Spence to take a more direct routing. "Alicia will meet me at Esteppe," he explained to me one afternoon, smiling. "That's all I need to know. Besides, I've never been offworld much. I hear your mountains are beautiful."

Our mountains *were* beautiful, of course. Especially so at the Old Home Place, where I assured my friend that he and his wife were welcome to second-honeymoon in peace and quiet for as long as they liked. Still, I didn't like the idea of Alicia and Spence and I all being away from Parliament at once, even if it was supposed to be out of session. Doubly so since Father was away also; while halfway home I'd received an exultant letter from him. It went into great detail regarding the extent to which the red carpet was to be laid out for me and Spence, who after all was a major-league war hero in his own right and therefore automatically dear to the hearts of Esteppans. There were going to be parades, dinners, dedications… I sighed and shook my head, looking up and down the long list of events our presence would be required at. Perhaps Spence and Alicia weren't going to get a chance to second-honeymoon after all, my promise notwithstanding.

I also spent more time studying my Parliamentary packages from Alicia. The latest ones sounded quite bleak, as if she'd resigned herself to defeat at the hands of Nagano. "I will *not* lower myself to that level," she declared near the end of her most recent letter, the last one I'd receive before seeing her again in person on Esteppe. I frowned at the words, feeling distinctly uneasy inside. She and her husband were both gengineered beings. Weaknesses at the chessboard notwithstanding, "genius" wasn't too strong a word to describe their intellects. Furthermore, both of them were veterans of a century of legislative bickering, infighting and even civil war. If they couldn't stop Nagano from blocking our peace-plans and pointing a new way to the future, then who could? For that matter… If Spence and Alicia couldn't find a way to win then didn't that sort of kill our whole theory that, since the self-government problem wasn't soluble by humans, we'd create superhumans to solve it for us?

I sure hoped Father had some ideas. If he didn't, then… Maybe I'd spend the rest of my life throwing parties and racing my skimmer after all. Because one thing was for sure; no matter what happened, I wasn't lifting a finger to help Nagano reshape the universe into his vision of how it ought to be, no matter how many votes he won. Not *ever*!

One night while I was lying awake with the lights out something important occurred to me. Here I was, a Parliamentarian about to take on the fight of my (hopefully very short) political life in support of gengineering and brain-jacking, yet I knew very little about either procedure. I believed in them both, of course; Spence and Alicia spoke volumes to me about the lost possibilities of frankensteining, while Father's achievements stood on their own merit as well. In a sense I knew all I really needed to know just by being familiar with these remarkable individuals and what they were capable of. And yet…

My brows furrowed. In all of my life, I couldn't remember even once hearing anyone speaking on holovision about frankensteining. Which was truly odd, given that there were still a few Spence's and Alicia's left scattered here and there about the galaxy. You'd think that such odd and distinctive and-- so far as I knew-- accomplished individuals would sort of stand out, wouldn't you? Yet, they didn't. For all the media noticed them, they might as well have never existed. Anthros were mentioned in a few history books and there were pictures here and there, all of them of individuals long dead. Even when they actually got press, like when Alicia performed, there was never any mention made of their non-human status. Nor any photos.

Wasn't that a little bit odd?

Manuel was out playing poker; since gambling was illegal aboard ship I pretended to believe his cover-story. Which in turn meant that I had the cabin to myself. So, wearily and grateful that I didn't have to get up early the next morning and report to either the flight deck or the conference room, I typed my user-ID into my computer and requested an article on frankensteining.

All that came up was the kind of thing I'd seen as a child.

Next I searched Spence and Alicia by name. Spence's books were listed, as were Alicia's better-known compositions and paintings. Alicia's article had been updated to reflect her wartime position as Madame Deputy, while according the data I had Spence was "possibly an important leader" in the anti-Dracan Resistance. No mention whatsoever was made of their bunnyhood; while one solitary hologram of them standing together outside their bungalow was included, outside of that one purely visual reference they might as well have been entirely normal people.

Father's entries were in much the same vein. He was pictured weeping in the dock at his war-crimes trial, as was to be expected, and there was no mention of him becoming President of Esteppe—again, this was probably because his file hadn't been updated lately. The article spoke of him merely as the designer of the Stormcrow/Skybolt series of superfighters, and made no mention whatsoever of his far more important role in pioneering the art of brain-jacking.

Next, I searched "gengineering" and got a tiny three-line article explaining that this was an abhorrent and unethical technology long-since discarded by civilized men. "Brain-jacking" got me a blank screen…

…and, soon after, a knock at my door. It was frustrating, really, having a visitor just then. I was busily searching the ship's library for any and all references to brain/computer interfaces, and finding nothing except a few highly-technical references to prosthetic eyes, ears, and limbs. Even when I typed in my Parliamentary password, which was about as high as clearances came, I couldn't find anything about my father's truly important work. Just because his partner was the Autarch, I grumbled to myself, didn't mean that credit shouldn't be given where it was due. So I was a little miffed when the knock came and interrupted my research. I slowly tramped over and hit the "open" button…

…and there stood Captain Jungmann, in full uniform. "Thomas," he greeted me, his face sober. "How are you tonight?"

"Kind of busy," I answered, wondering why Jungmann was fully dressed so late in the evening. "And you?"

"Sleeping well, your excellency," he replied, now smiling ruefully. "Until, that is, my watch officer woke me up to let me know that someone was accessing… Shall we say, certain areas of the ship's library?"

I blinked. "I… How…"

Jungmann shook his head. "Please, Thomas," he explained. "We have an alarm set up because brain-jacking is such a sensitive subject to we Esteppans. There are still a few radicals about, you see, and some are violent." He sighed. "Usually we quietly file the data away. If a pattern emerges certain gentle inquiries are made. So far, that's only rarely been necessary. Usually it's just some sincere young crewman with a little time off who's trying to understand his planet's past a little better." His eyes narrowed. "Up until now, at least."

You have no right! I almost objected. But aboard a navy ship a captain did indeed have the right. An obligation, even, as part of his duty to safeguard his command. "So," he said eventually. "You can read whatever you like; certainly I'm not going to try and prevent you. But…" His eyes narrowed again. "You're a young Esteppan too, Thomas, just like my youngest crewmen. So… Perhaps you might be trying to come to grips with your planet's history as well? In which case, I'm here for you." He cocked his head to one side. "Would you like to talk about the war and the Autarch, Thomas? And your father's place beside him?" He smiled. "In your case, this is hardly a job that I can delegate to a chaplain."

I smiled back, then remembered what Jungmann had said to me back in *The Glorious First of June*'s sickbay, while wearing an eye patch and playing at being a pirate. It was right after he'd been one of the ringleaders of the mutiny against Captain Shepherd, the one that never happened. "If the United Systems government were even to try and charge you for what you've done, your excellency," he'd said to me. "Well… Maybe Esteppe might win this time around, by god!"

At the time, I'd thought that he was joking. Now, however, I wasn't quite so sure.

Chapter One-Hundred Twenty-Five

It was hard to know who felt more awkward and out-of-place as we sat and had our little talk; Captain Jungmann or me. "I have nothing to hide" were his opening words. Yet like most Esteppans of a certain age, his body language argued strongly that he did. He experienced great difficulty meeting my eyes, for example, and his voice was often a dull, flat monotone. This was not at all like him.

Apparently, last time around Jungmann had experienced a very short war. "I wasn't there for it all," he explained. "Most importantly, I wasn't around for the bad part at the end." He'd been first officer aboard a destroyer, one of three that made up the Autarch's entire navy. "That's what people don't understand today, Thomas," he explained. "They try to label us as the aggressor, yet we built no offensive weapons. If we'd wanted create an empire, before the shooting started we could easily have built several dreadnoughts and maybe even a carrier or two for your father's Stormcrows. Had we done so, we'd have won. But in the beginning at least, the Autarch wasn't warlike. He was simply trying to find a better way of living, of making people's lives deeper and more fulfilling through brain-jacking."

I frowned. "Then why was there a war at all, if the Autarch wasn't an aggressor?" I asked.

Jungmann sighed and looked down at the floor. "Sinister black robes and shaven skulls, I suppose, even though both were common on Esteppe for many decades before the war. Titles like 'Eliteman' and 'Autarch'. But, most of all…" He scowled, and for once met my eyes. "The United Systems was scared, son. Terrified, even, that we just might pull it off."

I shook my head. "But… Why could they possibly be so frightened of? Didn't the Autarch and Father promise to license the tech?"

"They did," Jungmann agreed. "The Autarch eventually went mad, Thomas. Spectacularly so. We all know it, so that's how he's remembered. But it was the war that caused the madness, not the other way around. Up until then, he was, well…" *Zeppelin*'s captain frowned. "Frankly he was much like your father, Thomas. I knew him at university. He wasn't one of my professors, but because he was so eminent I made it a point to meet him." He smiled. "And your father taught my basic biochemistry class, though I don't think we ever so much as spoke. I'd be amazed if he remembered me."

My eyebrows rose. It was a small universe indeed. "Then… How did the friction begin?"

"Trade issues," Jungmann explained. "Once people began jacking in, even the limited number of jackers that we could originally support, Esteppe's whole economy blossomed." He smiled. "Your family's mines used to be worked by men, Thomas. Now the ores are extracted by tiny robots. Did you know that technology was invented by an Esteppan, using brain-jacking?"

I shook my head. "Really?"

"Really," he assured me. "Because jacking was used to develop them, your family probably still collects a small royalty on the things." He smiled. "There were dozens of such inventions, one after another. A tidal wave of cash came flooding in, and suddenly we were incredibly wealthy."

"Someone told me once that it was wealth that caused the war."

Junman's brow furrowed. "I can see where some might think so," he allowed after a moment's consideration. "But, I was there. So far as I can tell, all the makings of a disaster were already in place long before the gold began flowing our way." He shook his head. "The real root of the war, you see, was power."

My eyes narrowed. "Esteppe was becoming too influential. A rival, in other words."

"Ja," Jungmann agreed, nodding slowly. "We were the first of the colony worlds to come close to being able to look Old Earth in the eye. To tell her to go to hell, in other words, and make it stick. We were crushed for our impertinence." He met my eyes again. "Drakkus was the second such world."

I looked away, suddenly appalled deep in my soul. "I… But…"

"Heh!" Jungmann chuckled. "Don't worry, Thomas. The two wars were completely different affairs, at least in my book. I volunteered to fight Drakkus, don't forget. And that after fighting *against* Earth—for, you see, the United Systems is really just Old Earth under another name—the first time around. The Dracan Empire was a wretched business, Thomas, a blemish on all mankind. We're far better off as a species with it gone." He frowned. "But… I fear that I cannot in my heart say the same thing about the Autarchy."

"It was flawed." I said after a long moment's consideration. "The Autarchy, I mean. Deeply and irrevocably flawed. As proven by the fact that one man's unchecked madness did so much damage."

Jungmann bowed slightly in agreement. "Of course it was flawed," he agreed. "Even the Autarch himself thought so. 'This is just a temporary arrangement,' he explained before he was elected—and he *was* elected, don't forget!—'until we learn more about how our new knowledge and tools can be employed to help us govern ourselves. It 'll be my goal to upset as few applecarts in the meantime as possible'." He smiled. "And, you know what? He was as good as his word until my destroyer squadron was attacked without warning at the Great Bear Nexus. My ship was shot out from under my feet before we could even get to battle-stations. I was sound asleep in my bunk." He scowled. "We were not the aggressors, Thomas. No matter what anyone says. The ships we were convoying carried new tech that Earth felt shouldn't be allowed to spread. It would've cost them far too much money."

We sat side by side in silence for a very long time. "So," I said at last. "You see the Esteppan war as Earth snubbing out a potential rival."

"I do, your excellency," he agreed. "Now they tax us and control us and keep us firmly under their thumb, so that we can never endanger their supremacy again. Sure, we get to vote. But with such a tiny population, are we properly represented? I think not. Besides, we never wanted to join their silly confederation in the first place; we turned down every offer they made until finally we were forced to accept the one punctuated with mushroom clouds." He shrugged. "Just look at our relative contributions to the Dracan war, Thomas. Who really won it, Earth or Esteppe? The answer is both, really. But through my prejudiced eyes at least, war-ravaged Esteppe contributed substantially more towards victory with less than a tenth the population." He smiled and patted the nearest bulkhead. "This ship is just one example. The gun mounts that helped us along so much were derived from experimental concepts dating back to the days when I was in the Autarch's navy. They're brain-jack tech, in other words. But don't tell anyone." He rolled his eyes." If you do, the verdammt fools are liable to order their most valuable ship scrapped on sight."

I snorted and turned away; the reaction was only too likely. Then I met his eyes. "We threatened their power," I said at last. "That's your interpretation?"

"Yes, your excellency" he agreed, rising slowly to his feet. "And thus their way of life. A lot of others agree with me, though I can't say for certain just how many. It's not the kind of question one asks in a public opinion poll."

I nodded. It fit, was the worst thing. All too well. "And you'd like to see Esteppe leave the United Systems?" I demanded.

For a long time, Captain Jungmann stared at the floor. "I wear the uniform of the United Systems," he acknowledged. "And I've sworn an oath. I served proudly against the Dracans; they were the enemies of decency everywhere."

I nodded again. "But you wish to be free of Earth's oversight?"

"We should choose our own path," he answered. "Are we not entitled? Who are the people of Earth, to deny us the right?"

"Perhaps we're entitled," I replied, non-committally. "Or perhaps not. What makes you think that Esteppe can govern itself any better than Earth can? The record so far leaves a bit to be desired."

Jungmann smiled. "We'd work it out," he assured me. "After all, we're smarter than they are." His grin widened as he stepped towards my door. "Or at least we're smarter than they are when we're jacked in. That's an indisputable fact."

Chapter One-Hunred Twenty-Six

I didn't sleep very well after my interview with the captain. By then, I suppose I should've grown accustomed to having my world turned upside down on a regular basis. But like the childish fool that I was, I kept reaching out and trying to find little islands of stability in my life. Why couldn't everyone agree on what wars were about and what constituted a just peace? It would've made my life *so* much simpler!

By mutual agreement, Spence and I didn't set up the chessboard the next day. Instead we played gin rummy. I'd never played card games before, but apparently they were still popular when my friend was young. He and Alicia played all the time, he claimed. I had no reason to doubt him; the way he stomped me over and over again bespoke decades of skill. "Gin," he said eventually, laying down his cards.

I bit off a curse, then tossed my hand in. There was no point in adding up my score; I'd lost the game by a huge margin. "It's a good thing you're not a Dracan admiral," I observed.

"Heh!" he chuckled, shuffling for a new hand. Then he slowly put the cards down. "Is something bothering you, Thomas?" he asked. "You don't seem nearly so chipper as usual."

"I'm not," I admitted. Then, without naming Captain Jungmann specifically, I outlined the conversation I'd had with "an Esteppan officer". "He might've been beaten," I explained. "But his attitudes haven't changed at all. He's only going along with the United Systems way of doing things because he's been forced to."

Spence nodded. "I see."

I sighed. "I guess I just don't understand. I mean, we fight wars to settle disagreements when we can't resolve them in any other way. Right?"

"Right," the anthro-rabbit agreed, eyes narrowing attentively. "It's the only ethical justification for warfare. It's only legitimate function."

"But…" I protested. "The issue's still not settled! Not even after all of those deaths and the passage of so many years! Ca—I mean this Esteppan officer, he still believes in the Autarch as much as he ever did. You can tell, just from talking to him. He'd go back to brain-jacking in a minute, given the chance. And bring an Autarch back, too!"

476

Spence smiled. "And how are we so different?"

"We're campaigning for change through a legitimate Parliamentary system," I explained. "We want to change the law through elected representation, not fight a war!"

"The Autarch didn't want to fight a war either," Spence pointed out. "Or so my own researches convince me. All he wanted, and for that matter all that Esteppe wanted, was to be left alone and be allowed the right to trade freely with others." He tilted his head to one side. "Captain Jungmann is absolutely correct on that score."

I blinked, then decided that attempting to hide things from geniuses was futile. "But... Jacking was illegal on Earth. It was illegal almost everywhere, in fact. If Esteppe did it anyway when no one else was allowed, how could others compete?"

Spence smiled slowly. "No one else can compete with frankensteins like Alicia and I, either. Or with cyborgs such as yourself, in aerospace battles at least."

I blinked. "That's true, I suppose."

"Absolutely," Spence affirmed, setting the deck of cards down. "Trust me on that. It's why we were outlawed to start with." Then he lowered his ears and smiled. "I told you once before that Alicia and I didn't support the Esteppan war. Don't you remember?"

"Vaguely," I admitted. "But it's been an awful long time ago."

"And you've done a lot of growing up since then, as well," he agreed. Then the smile faded. "Part of growing up, Thomas, is coming to understand that just because people fail to agree about something doesn't mean that everyone can't still be right."

"Huh?" I asked, confused.

Spence sighed and focused his eyes on something very distant. "When in the course of human events..." he began to quote. Then he shook his head and started over. "Well-intentioned people have been disagreeing since time immemorial, Thomas. We just finished fighting a very black-and-white sort of war, a conflict in which it should be obvious who was in the right and who wasn't."

I nodded.

"But," Spence continued, "Even this one wasn't all so black and white as it seemed on the surface, perhaps." He smiled. "Would the Emperor have been elected to retain his office just before the war, if an election had been held?"

I pressed my lips together and thought. "Almost certainly," I decided. "The Dracan people were completely brainwashed."

"So we say," Spence replied. "But... if you'd asked them on the day before the first bomb fell if *we* were the ones who were brainwashed... Well, how do you think they might've answered?"

"But..." I stuttered. "I mean..."

"What defines absolute good, Thomas?" Spence continued remorselessly. "And what constitutes total evil?"

"I'm Catholic," I replied eventually.

"You are," he agreed, nodding. "I, however, am not."

There was a long, awkward silence. "But if…" I said eventually. "I mean, Spence…"

"There's no 'if' to it, that I can see," my friend answered, leaning back in his seat and crossing his arms. "I can absolutely guarantee that you and I disagree on more than a few fundamental principles regarding the nature of good and evil. About what's right and what's wrong, in other words. Given this fact, isn't conflict between our viewpoints inevitable? And, if so, does this make one of us 'evil'? Which then in turn begs the question… Which one? And how can we tell?"

I sat and stared at the top of table for what felt like an hour. "But… You and I… We can always work things out!"

"So far," my friend agreed. "And even when the day comes that we can't, I'm sure both of us will go a long way to avoid antagonizing the other because we want to stay friends. Still…" He scowled again. "I broke a thousand Church laws during the war, Thomas. In fact, I not only encouraged my followers to behave like animals, but did so myself. You saw it."

"I broke a few rules too," I admitted uneasily.

Spence smiled. "Even Father Murton understood." Then his face grew hard again. "But, seriously now. Are we United-Systems-types pure lily-white? And, by extension, were the Dracans absolute midnight-black?"

"I—" No matter how hard I tried, the words simply would not come.

"Then there's the whole self-determination thing," Spence continued, beginning to shuffle his cards again. "How much authority is it right and proper for a majority to exercise over a dissenting minority, even in a representative democracy? What happens when two schools of thought develop over a truly crucial issue, one too fundamental for a society to find a way to compromise on? Is the majority entitled to suppress the minority view, call it 'evil' and 'wrong' and try to indoctrinate said minority's children in the 'correct' way of thinking? Alternatively, at what point is the minority entitled to begin to think of themselves as a separate people, entitled to self-government so that they can live their lives by their own standards of right and wrong?" Spence sighed. "When in the course of human events…" he repeated, then shook his head. "History isn't appalling because it's so full of blood, treachery and abuse of power, Thomas. It's appalling because nothing truly important ever gets resolved. The bloodshed just goes on and on and out, without rhyme or reason. None of the really vital questions are ever settled; most of the time no one even thinks to ask them out loud." He sighed. "All that gets firmly resolved is who's going to bow to whom."

I looked down at the table again. "Then, we've got to change things," I replied.

"How do we go about it, then?" Spence asked. "Let's be totally, completely frank here, Thomas. If we do manage to pass a law allowing frankensteining and brain-jacking, then, well… Face it. We're going to do so against majority opinion. We'll have betrayed the spirit of democracy, if not the letter of the rules. The only conceivable way to finagle it through is to attach it to a budget bill or something. The majority is and will remain against us."

"That's wrong, too," I observed.

"It is, in a penny-ante sort of way," Spence agreed. "But remember, we've just agreed there aren't any pure blacks or whites."

Finally, I couldn't take it anymore. "They're *stupid*, Spence!" I declared, slamming my fist down on the arm of my chair as best as my motors could manage. "Idiots, all of them! Anyone can see that it's time for us to grow! That it's a sin that we've already had the tools at hand for so long and refused to use them. They're idiots, and they decide which way to vote for idiotic reasons, like how a candidate's suit fits or who produces the funniest commercials!"

"They're idiots, all right," Spence agreed, smiling. "And you're sounding more like the Autarch every single minute, my young friend. Even the accent is right; his wasn't very pronounced either." I opened my mouth to protest, but Spence smiled extra-big and held up his hands to cut me off. "Now, now, Thomas! I'm sorry; perhaps I struck too sensitive a nerve."

I closed my mouth, and thought for a moment before speaking. "Your apology is accepted," I agreed.

"Heh!" Spence answered; clearly in his own mind he hadn't backed down an inch. And, I had to admit, he'd boxed me in very neatly indeed. I either believed in pure representative democracy or I didn't. "Are a thousand uneducated yokels wiser than one learned man?" he asked, after a moment had passed.

"No," I replied. "Of course not."

"So why do we settle important issues by counting noses?" my friend asked, still smiling gently. "Think hard, Thomas. This one's for bonus points."

"Because…" I said slowly, picturing all the interacting power-cliques in Parliament. "Because… In our society, a thousand yokels are *stronger* than one wise man."

Spence smiled so wide that the expression barely fit on his face, then drummed his feet in joy. "Yes!" he declared excitedly. "Yes! Yes! Yes! I knew that you'd get it!"

I found myself smiling back, despite the awfulness of the truth I'd just grasped. "The thousand men are stronger," I continued, "because they can rebel, or get together and go on strike, or whatever. Democracy is merely a recognition of this power. It doesn't matter in the least if they're right or wrong. Besides, when one man runs things alone, more often than not he turns out to be a yokel too."

"Like the idiot Emperor who just attacked us and started a war he couldn't possibly win," Spence agreed, still smiling. "Oh, Thomas! I'm so proud of you! So, in that case…"

From the tone of Spence's voice, I could tell that he wanted me to expand upon the new principle I'd just discovered. "All political power is rooted in other forms of strength," I continued. "In interplanetary affairs as well as domestic. The power can be economic, technological, or even just sheer numbers. But always, political leadership is rooted in some kind of raw power."

"Even when it appears on the surface to be otherwise," Spence agreed. He seemed almost to sparkle, he was so pleased with me. I could see now that he truly *had* been gengineered specifically to be an ideal father; looking back I wondered how I'd missed figuring that out for myself a long time ago. He was as genuinely happy for me as he could ever have been for himself. "Might really does make right," I said slowly to myself. "By definition, since the winners get to define the morality of the entire group."

"Exactly!" Spence agreed. "If my guerilla movement had failed, I'd be the antichrist. But I didn't lose. So I'm a hero instead."

"Yeah," I agreed, understanding slowly dawning. "If the Emperor had won, I'd be a notorious war-criminal." I looked up the grinning rabbit.

"Both of us would've become dark, sinister figures of legend, whose names would be evoked only to frighten small children." he assured me. "Like that of the Autarch.

"Yeah," I repeated softly. "Though in his case he really did go nuts." My smile faded. "He destroyed my brother's mind, you know. Trying to persuade Father to talk."

Spence's happiness instantly evaporated. "I'm sorry, Thomas," he answered. "I truly didn't know that. Though I was of course aware that such things happened, and far too often at that." He looked away. "History isn't a laboratory, you see. There can be no controlled experiments, and our reagents are far from pure. You can never be certain ahead of time what kind of havoc the impurities will wreak." Then he turned back to me. "Everything is eternally gray. Though we can help make it either lighter or darker gray through our own actions; we must never forget that."

"Lighter or darker, as we choose to define right and wrong," I pointed out. Then I sighed. "Spence," I said slowly. "As a species we're still operating under the law of the jungle. That's the essence of what you've taught me here today."

He nodded. "Exactly. At base level it's the only form of social order that humanity's ever known, though I prefer to imagine that it's been leavened with human love and kindness from time to time." He smiled again. "Your average uneducated yokel is a good and decent person, Thomas, by their own lights at least. That's another constant of human history, found wherever and whenever there have been people. But, when there's conflict…" He shrugged. "Power matters. It's a lot easier to pin down who has the power to enforce his or her will than to work out who's right and wrong in some indefinable cosmic sense. A lot less futile, as well."

"And war is the ultimate means by which human power is tested." I'd been so confused when I woke up that morning, but now everything seemed crystal-clear. I owed it all to Spence, of course. Was that what it really meant to be a genius, I wondered? Tracing subtle patterns in the fabric of reality, until with a binding flash everything suddenly fell into place? I frowned. "Esteppe will rebel again." I predicted. "Over exactly the same issues as before. It's inevitable."

"Eventually," Spence agreed, beaming. "Nothing's certain in this universe, mind you. But I tend to agree."

"Over a differing vision of right and wrong," I continued. "And over what constitutes the proper rights of a dissenting minority culture. If they go about it properly this time and plan ahead, Esteppe will win. Earth's imperial power will be shattered forever, when that happens."

"It will," Spence agreed. "The consequences are incalculable."

"They'll fight it with everything they've got," I continued, wincing as I grasped the true awfulness of it all. "It'll be a *terrible* war! Worse than the one before, by far. Worse even than the Dracan war! The Nagano's of Parliament won't roll over and give up their power. Not without doing as much damage as they possibly can first."

"And," Spence added softly, "Just maybe you and I aren't the only ones that've figured all of this out?"

"Father!" I whispered. "He ran for President; I never really understood why!"

"And Nagano," Spence replied. "Why do you think he hates you so?"

My jaw dropped. All the wheels in my brain were spinning at top speed now. But perhaps for the first time in my life they were all spinning in the same direction. "We can't fight another war," I declared. "We just can't." No victory won could ever be worth the cost of the titanic, futuristic struggle I was already putting together in my mind. None!

"Then we must prevent it," Spence answered, picking up the long-neglected deck of cards. For just a moment his eyes hardened, as they had the night I'd watched him systematically mutilate a Dracan corpse. Then he began to deal a new hand. "Just don't forget the most important thing of all," he added, almost as an afterthought. "If prevention fails, our second-best outcome is victory. Sometimes you have to be old-fashioned about things."

Chapter One-Hundred Twenty-Seven

It was just as well that we were nearly to Esteppe by the time Spence and I had our little talk about the ethics of power and the power of ethics. For a solid week afterwards I had a recurring nightmare in which Spence and Alicia and the PM and I were trying to conduct an orchestra. The instrument-players were sitting in Parliament Hall, the old one in London that didn't exist anymore, and the musicians were all wild, bloodthirsty animals of the most dangerous and disgusting sort. There were lions and giant cobras and half-leeches and, worst of all, a Nagano-thing that looked just like my fellow Parliamentarian except for the fact that his mouth was round and jawless and lined with row upon row of serrated, triangular teeth. Instead of batons we were equipped with whips, the sort that cut deep and excised chunks of flesh when properly handled. "Play, damn you!" the PM would cry out, and a sick chorus of screams and screeches and broken melodies would sort of lurch along to a misbegotten beat, while we whip-wielders encouraged the stragglers. It'd go on and on, getting worse by the second until finally Nagano would lead a successful rebellion and drive us from the podium. Then the beasts would tie us into their still bloody chairs, Nagano would mount the rostrum, and declare "Now you shall play!" Fortunately, I always woke up then; while I never quite figured out what would happen next, something deep down in my soul assured me that it was very, very bad.

We broke into Esteppan space five days ahead of schedule, mostly because partway home *Arminus* succeeded in fixing some engine-room damage that should only have been reparable in a shipyard. We made better time after that, and no one was gladder than me. By then all I wanted was to get my fundraising tour over with, visit my family, and then finish things out. Though this bond-selling series was to be far less demanding than previous tours-- I was to fly over the crowds as a Skybolt in most cases rather than address them directly—I was still quite eager to have it over and done with.

Part of it, I supposed, was that I wanted my body back. Now that the prospect was finally at hand, I wanted it more than ever. Even more of it, however, was the politics. Ever since Spence had explained the true situation to me I'd felt like I was walking on eggshells, terrified of every little cracking sound. Part of me had transformed back into a frightened adolescent eager to entrust the adults around me with all the difficult decisions; the same part of me, I suspected, that was having bad dreams. But another, newer part refused to yield an inch. It constantly whispered nastiness in my ear, such as "Aren't you as smart as the rest of them? Look at the mess *they've* made of things! You could hardly do worse!" And, of course, "If you give up, all the decisions will be made by Nagano." I listened very carefully indeed to these voices, not so much for the content of their words but rather the tones in which they were spoken. Was there a trace of Colonel Rotte in them? I couldn't detect any, no matter how hard I tried. But then, Rotte was cunning. He knew how to keep a low profile when it suited his purpose. So long as I lived, I'd have to maintain a careful watch. Rotte could be useful, as Alicia had pointed out so long ago. In his way he even deserved to be honored. He also desperately needed to be kept locked firmly away from all that was good and decent in the world during those times when wholesale massacre was not on the day's to-do list…

Esteppe went nuts when we popped through into their local space. It was a bit awkward, as dozens of celebrations and greetings had been planned. Our being so early spoiled some of them, such as the scheduled attempt by New Rotterdam to greet us by using their city lights to form a replica of the Parliamentary Order of Merit that could be recognized from orbit. Admiral Vlasilov had one of those too, so the tribute was meant for him as well. The published plan, someone explained to me later, specified both a fixed date and "the night of *Zeppelin*'s arrival in orbit", which turned out to be different days entirely. In the ensuing confusion parts of the city experienced an unplanned blackout, while in others husbands and wives called each other frantically to organize impromptu light-switchings. We ended up hitting dirt before the whole thing could be worked out, though the admiral and I sent a joint thank-you note anyway.

There were a thousand little debacles like that one, all because some genius had repaired the unfixable *Arminus*. Another problem was that there was no mooring available in the navy yard big enough to accommodate *Zeppelin*; a nearly-complete dreadnought, the *Wilhelm von Tegetthoff*, occupied our intended slot and wasn't scheduled to be moved for two more days. So we were redirected to splash down at a minor merchie port near the equator. It was warmer there, sure enough. But it was also a quarter of the way around the planet from any major population center and practically at the antipodes of the capital. Usually when a large spacecraft hits the water the red-hot hull makes a distinctive sound that combines elements of sizzling and splashing. In our case, however, all of this was drowned out by the shattering of a million plans to properly welcome us home.

No one minded much that I could see. Or, at least, none of us aboard *Zeppelin* did. I stood blinking in the bright sunshine, feeling the friendly yellow rays pour through me as I watched the deck crew make us fast to the big mooring-buoy. There was a nice breeze blowing as well, one that according to

Manuel smelled of plowed earth and fresh flowers and a world still mostly unspoiled. I looked up reflexively, as I had a thousand times before during my last visit to Esteppe…

..and realized in my heart for the first time that it was over. No Dracan raids were coming in, and I didn't have to worry about having to steer a Skybolt into the teeth of the enemy. Nor would I ever have to do so again.

I smiled. My heart finally understood. The war was over.

"It's great, isn't it sir?" Manuel asked, reading my mind. He was getting better and better at that as time went by; if he was interested I'd already decided that I had a lifetime job to offer him. Even after I left the navy I'd probably still have to wear my uniform sometimes on ceremonial occasions. And who else in the universe besides Manuel knew how to arrange all those damned medals properly?

I nodded and sighed. There was a large birdlike object orbiting a nearby cargo ship, I noted presently. It was a seacrow, closest surviving relative to the long-gone stormcrow. "Look!" I urged, pointing. "You don't see one of those every day!"

Manuel whistled a single low note. "Wow!" he whispered. "Seacrows are nearly extinct!" Then he turned to me. "Aren't they supposed to be bad luck, sir?"

"It's a silly superstition," I replied. "Just like the old one that killing a stormcrow made a man more virile. All that lies like those accomplish is to make people more willing to destroy something rare and precious." I scowled. "The locals are working very hard so that we don't lose the seacrows, at least."

"Good," Manuel replied, after a very long time.

We could've stood like that forever, watching the seacrow wheel across the sky and allowing the warm land breeze to blow the stink of space out of our uniforms. But nothing that good could last forever. "Captain Longo!" a voice cried out from the foot of the companionway that led up to the weather deck. "Captain Longo! Where are you?"

"Up here!" Manuel replied for me as I inwardly winced. Was there no end to military interruptions in my life?

But this one wasn't entirely military. "Sir!" the young ensign declared. He saluted smartly, then handed me an envelope. The young officer was huffing and puffing. "I was told to get this to you as quickly as possible, sir!"

"Thank you," I answered. Then, as the ensign retreated I handed the thing to Manuel, who opened it for me without comment. It was marked "secret", but Manuel was cleared and it would've taken me three times as long to open the blamed thing myself. Inside was a standard navy message form, with another "secret' seal on it. "Urgent!" it declared in large red type. "Flash Traffic! Eyes Captain Thomas Longo *Graf Zeppelin* only! Vlasilov."

It was from Admiral Vlasilov? Why of all people would *he* be sending me an urgent official message? Manuel and I exchanged glances, then I apologetically turned my back to him, tore the seal, and began reading.

"Thomas," the admiral had sent. "This will be in the media in a matter of minutes. But, I thought you should know immediately. A skyhopper full of VIP's exploded on takeoff here just a few seconds ago. They stopped to welcome us home first because we were on the way, then planned to travel on to greet *Zeppelin*. Their 'hopper blew up while departing, not five seconds into the flight. It looked like a bomb to me, but I don't claim to be an expert in such matters. Don't panic, Thomas, because I'm certain there were survivors. In fact, I personally saw at least a dozen people swimming in the water. Some fell free, while others ejected successfully in capsules. They're being picked up as I dictate this note.

"Thomas, the PM was aboard. Along with Madame Deputy, your father and your elder brother. There's little that anyone can do at this point except pray."

Chapter One-Hundred Twenty-Eight

"*Whoop!*" *Zeppelin*'s siren rang out suddenly. "*WhoopWhoop! Whoop!*"

"Up-ship!" Manuel translated for me; I'd never had time to learn all the standard navy signals. "Emergency up-ship!" He looked very confused.

"It's not an attack," I reassured him. "Or at least we're not going into battle. Come on, we've got to get below!"

Captain Jungmann was right to rank his crew as among the very best in the entire navy. While his battle-stations times and the like tended to be a bit slower than those of other ships, this was due to overcrowding rather than lack of drill or professionalism. Vlasilov had always understood this and made allowances. "When it really matters," I'd heard him say more than once. "I can count on *Zeppelin*." And so it proved this time. It'd clearly been impossible from the get-go for me or for that matter anyone else caught on deck when the siren went off to make it all the way to our assigned acceleration-couches. Even worse, because we'd just hit dirt and in theory at least were once again at peace, every idle hand on board had been out sunning him or herself. There were emergency couches for such occasions, but you could only keep a crew drilled and sharp at so many different things. Most captains let things like emergency-acceleration-couch training slide. I was sure that *Zeppelin*'s captain had done the same. Yet despite the worst-case and completely unexpected nature of the scenario, *Zeppelin* was back in the deep-black within ten minutes of the first siren warning. Perhaps these sailors really were the "toughest verdammt crew in the navy"?

By the time we hit orbit, I'd begun to at least tentatively put two and two together. Jungmann had upped-ship on his own authority, I suspected, in order to keep Spence and (I had to admit it) especially me as safe as possible until the situation down on the planet's surface was firmly under control. Certainly there was no safer place for us to be in the entire Esteppan system at the moment than aboard a fully-alerted and spaceborne *Zeppelin*. I explained everything as well as I could to Manuel as we lay side-by-side on our inflatable couches; one of the advantages of being equipped with a speaker instead of a throat was that I could still communicate clearly at nine gees.

"You go commandeer a holomonitor, sir," Manuel suggested as soon as the thrust eased off some. "I'll take care of stowing our lift-off gear, then find you."

"Thank you," I replied, rising to my feet just a little sooner than was really safe.

The nearest holoset turned out to be located in a bunkroom; three dozen or more ratings, crammed in like sardines, had been watching it during takeoff. "Sir!" they cried out as I stepped in. "Sir! Your father… The PM…"

I waved my hand in acknowledgement. "Ja," I agreed. "Thank you. I know."

For a frustrating moment the crewmen continued to drown out the commentators, then I could finally hear. "…appears to me to have been deliberate, Dieter."

"Ja, Magda," Dieter agreed; he was the reporter at the scene, standing on what was clearly a navy pier. In the background a thin thread of black smoke rose into the otherwise pristine blue sky. "Everyone else here seems to think so, as well. This was definitely a high-order explosion, something you just don't get from molecular batteries as a rule."

"Ja," Magda agreed. Then she switched to what I'd been waiting to see. "For those of you just joining us, a short time ago a skyhopper carrying Prime Minister Matthew Pithom, Madame Deputy Prime Minister Alicia Wiston, and our own President William Longo among other dignitaries exploded on takeoff and crashed…"

The video rolling in the background was both short and ugly. A large, plushed-out VIP 'hopper carrying, curiously enough, Longo Industries markings, was rising from the weather-deck of a Warlord-class destroyer, presumably *Arminus*. The warship was festooned with flags, and her decks carpeted with saluting sailors and marines. Exactly as Vlasilov had described, about five seconds into the flight there was a loud explosion. The 'hopper was just clear of *Arminus* by then, so that practically all the debris went cascading into the ocean. Sure enough, a significant number of what looked to be survivors fell as well. Almost instantly the men on *Arminus*'s deck sprang into action, throwing lifesaving gear over the side and doing whatever else they could to help. I squinted at the too-small image; a man with a cane seemed to be directing them. Was that Vlasilov himself? More likely than not, I decided.

The commentary had continued right along uninterrupted, but I'd sort of tuned it out for a moment. Now it percolated back into my consciousness. "…not common practice for the PM and Deputy to travel together, Dieter?"

"Ja, Magda," the reporter on the spot replied. "But there was some kind of confusion this morning. As you might've noticed, the 'hopper that crashed was not actually an official government vessel. Instead, President Longo offered his corporate 'hopper, and the suggestion was accepted. All the official vessels were grounded."

"All of them?" Magda asked, here eyebrows rising.

"All of them," Dieter confirmed. "Some were down for maintenance, in anticipation that Thomas Longo and the other navy men would be arriving later in the week. However…" He scowled.

"Yes, Dieter?" Magda prompted.

"I hesitate to report this," he explained. "But, while I was shooting some routine footage in the capitol very early this morning, I noticed squad after squad of security police patrolling the Presidential 'hopper pad." His scowl intensified. "They informed me that it was just a drill. However…"

"Ja," Magda agreed, her face suddenly dark and angry. "This perhaps explains many things."

Chapter One-Hundred Twenty-Nine

Manuel and the marines found me at almost exactly the same time; just as my valet came sidling up alongside me a squad of battle-armed troops appeared at the bunkroom door.

"You are requested to come with us, sir," the lieutenant in charge explained, "For your own protection."

"Ja," I agreed absently; it was odd how just the simple fact of being around so many other Esteppans encouraged my accent. During the long trip out I'd even caught Manuel "Ja"-ing from time to time. "Of course. Where to?"

"The conference room, just above the bridge." The young officer looked relieved; apparently he'd expected to have to pry me away from the holoscreen. "The captain is setting up a communications center for you there. And… Sir, I'm so sorry."

Zeppelin's meeting facilities were less than half the size of those aboard *June* or even *Coronel*; this was because, overcrowded as she already was, she hadn't been fitted out as a flagship. No one in their right mind, after all, would try and cram an admiral and his staff into such an already overpacked vessel Still, there was plenty of room for Spence and Captain Jungmann and myself, along with the five engineering officers who were busily removing complicated-looking diagrams from the bulkheads. The disaster had apparently interrupted a planning session for *Zeppelin*'s upcoming refit.

"Thomas!" Spence greeted me as I entered the room. He looked stricken, more so than I'd ever seen him before. "They just… I mean…" Finally, he pointed mutely at the big holoscreen, now tuned directly to a satellite feed. They were hoisting someone strapped into a wheelchair up onto the deck. He wasn't moving. The image wasn't large enough, really. But I still knew. "Dean!" I hissed.

"He was on board," Jungmann confirmed, clearly making an effort to keep his voice under control. "The navy sent me a guest list. I was supposed to arrange things so that you and your brother had a little private time together, Thomas. It was intended to be a nice surprise for you both."

My jaw dropped open. I'd been readying myself for almost anything. But somehow it'd never occurred to me that poor, brain-damaged Dean… "No!" I cried out, as I watched them lay my brother on a gurney. Water poured out of his nostrils, and even worse the medical techs didn't seem to be in a hurry. "No!"

"This is an uncensored feed," Jungaman explained. "Live from *Arminus*. I thought… Perhaps I was wrong."

Then Spence and I were standing in the middle of the room, holding each other tight. "Leave it on," Spence directed, as I took a moment to weep. "We can take it. Thank you for finding it for us."

Then the door opened again and the ship's chaplain appeared, with a medic at his side. The medic would be carrying a hypodermic and just then that was the last thing I wanted. So I forced myself to stop crying and turned to face the screen again. By then more bodies were being swung aboard. I didn't recognize any of them, though that didn't mean anything. The cameraman was working from a bad angle so as not to get in the way, and some of the victims were severely mutilated. "How many were there, anyway?" I demanded at last.

"A hundred passengers and four crew," Jungmann answered. "A full load."

"None of them alive so far," Spence muttered, his voice dead and hopeless. "Not a single one."

"These victims are all from the water, sir," Manuel observed. "Some of the passengers got out in escape capsules; we saw film of it on the news." He paused, looking uncertain. "I've been on a lot of these trips. The VIP's are always nearest the capsules."

Spence nodded soberly, then his eyes narrowed. "That's true," he agreed. Then he turned to Jungmann. "Where are the capsules? I don't see any here."

Zeppelin's captain already had a phone to his ear. "They're coming aboard further aft," he finally explained. "So are the survivors from the water." Then he stood up and threw open the conference room door. "Stephanie!" he roared. "This is the morgue feed! Get me survivors!"

"Yes, sir!" a distant feminine voice replied. There was a long pause…

…and then a new image appeared, this one of a sailor opening up a capsule. He threw the lever, the hatch swung clear…

…and there was Alicia, wearing the scorched ruins of one of her overly-frilly dresses and wide-eyed in shock. "I…" she said, as a dozen helping hands reached down to help her to her feet. "I…"

"It's all right, ma'am," a medic replied, his tone respectful. He looked her up and down. "Are you in pain? Is anything broken?"

"I…" she repeated, at a loss for words for the first time since I'd known her. Then, her face screwed up. "Spence!" she bawled. "Oh, Spence! Where are you?"

"Alicia!" her husband answered, physically reaching out towards the tank. "I—" Then, he shook his head violently and turned to Jungmann. "Captain? May I send a signal?"

"Emergency flash priority," Jungmann agreed, smiling. "The bridge is yours, sir."

Then Spence was gone. I couldn't blame him for forgetting about me, given the circumstances. But I still felt very much alone until Jungmann stepped up behind me and placed his hand on my shoulder. On the holoscreen they opened another capsule. This one contained a crewman, a steward judging by his uniform. He was dead; messily so. It looked to me as if the capsule's ejection charge had fired, but then he'd hit some debris and been killed by the shock . Pure bad luck, in other words. "My other brother," I asked eventually. "Sven. Was he aboard too?"

"Yes, Thomas," the captain answered. "I'm afraid so."

"They've found another survivor in the water," someone said from the other end of the conference room; the resourceful engineering officers had set up a second holoset there. "In good shape, too. A Mrs. Frances."

"Dean's nurse," I whispered. "I'm glad for her. She's a very good woman." Jungmann gently squeezed again, but said nothing.

Then they found Sven and the army minister, floating almost side-by-side. Neither had made the capsules, but by some miracle they'd both survived their fall. Sven was hacking and coughing up blood, and there was a deep gash in his shaven head. Meanwhile the army minister was doubled-over vomiting. Two medics came racing up to steady the army man, but he shook his head violently and pointed to Sven. "Take care of him," he insisted. "Both of his legs are broken; he saved my life, the damned fool!"

Next they found the rest of the flight crew, all alive. "It was a verdammt bomb!" the pilot exploded as soon as his cocoon swung open. He was bleeding and had a mouthful of broken teeth but was still full of fight regardless. "In the galley stores, by god! I'd bet my life on it!"

An hour passed, then a second. They hadn't found Father's body yet, but with each passing minute it became clearer and clearer that corpses were all that anyone expected to recover so late in the game. He and the PM both were still missing, for that matter. Somehow I couldn't make myself care so much about Mr. Pithom just then, even though I really did like him. Spence was back in the room, standing tirelessly alongside me. It was growing dark at the scene of the crash; all that we could see anymore was the shattered, half-submerged hull of the 'hopper bobbing morosely in the little wavelets. According to the media, it'd come to rest on a mudbar. There were a dozen or so welders clambering about atop the wreck, torches twinkling in the twilight. "Thomas," Spence said, finally. "I…"

"No," I countered, the single syllable a flat imperative. "I will *not* lose my father and brother on the same day. Not like this. I just won't."

There was another long pause. "Son," Captain Jungmann said. "I understand—"

But he never finished the sentence. Suddenly one of the welders began waving excitedly. Then she stood up and began dancing on the sunken hull. "Over here!" she shouted, voice thin and distant. "I need a stretcher party, nownownow!"

Everyone in the conference room leaned forward slightly, as if the inch or two thereby gained might reveal new details. There hadn't been any victims found in a very long time, so there was no shortage of stretcher-parties. One surged forward and without a second's hesitation disappeared down into the shattered 'hopper. "That water is very cold," Jungmann observed.

"I doubt anyone could have survived in it for so long," Spence agreed. They were trying to prepare me, I knew, trying to soften the blow.

It was well-intentioned, but I still wasn't having any. "Father's a very difficult man to kill," I countered. "The Autarch didn't execute him, the tribunal didn't hang him, the radiation in the factory didn't even make him sick, and by god no coward of an assassin is going to get him now! It just can't happen this way. Not to him!"

There wasn't much Spence or Jungmann either one could say to that, so instead they just stood by me as more minutes passed. Finally, a stretcher appeared… covered in a sheet.

"Thomas," Jungmann said again, very gently.

"I…" I stuttered, my faith finally failing "I…"

…and just then a second litter emerged. This time there was no shroud, and a dozen eager medics surged forward to help. "Alive, by god!" Spence observed.

The cameraman, whoever he or she was, zoomed in as best they could. The resulting image still wasn't very satisfactory, as the camera mount was unstable so that everything was vibrating all over the place. But it was enough. "His head is bald!" I pointed out.

"And that's an Eliteman's robe, sure enough," Jungmann agreed, shaking his head in wonder. "The verdammt thing's probably why he's still alive; they're lined with thick fur. It should work in the water, too. Or at least I think so."

"It should," Spence agreed. He turned to me. "Thomas, I…"

"I know," I said, nodding. Then I nodded to Captain Jungmann, too. "And thank you as well. Now, when do you think that it'll be safe for us to hit dirt again? I suspect that both of us Parliamentarians are about to be very busy for a long time to come."

Chapter One-Hundred Thirty

The very first thing that Spence and I did when we were at long last allowed down to the planet's surface was visit the survivors. Not only were the people close to us all in the same hospital, they were all being treated in the same ward. This made a lot of sense; the security precautions had to be experienced to be believed and for once no one complained. It would've been prohibitively expensive to post so many guards at more than one location. Personally, I thought the that whole thing was a little over the top, especially *Zeppelin*'s refit being delayed so that she could continue to provide a safe refuge for the government in the event of further violence. "The toughest verdammt crew in the navy" had suffered much for a very long time in winning the war, and was already long overdue for leave. Instead of being allowed to take it, however, they were required to spin endlessly through the sky literally within sight of their homes and loved ones, yet not allowed the slightest break in their duties. *Arminus* would've served just as well as an emergency refuge, I thought; even though she was smaller. But no one asked my opinion.

Neither Sven nor Father could possibly have known I was present when I stopped by their rooms; both were in comas. Sven's was intentionally induced, to promote healing. Father's, however, was something else entirely. He and the PM had apparently been trapped together in a flooded compartment, sharing an air bubble. The PM eventually died of hypothermia and lack of oxygen, but Father, as I already knew, was made of sterner stuff. "It's not like Father Murton," were the first words out of Doctor Nuemann's mouth when he met me in the corridor outside of Father's room. Doctor Nuemann was our family doctor; he'd delivered me, in fact.

I pressed my lips together. "Exactly how?" I demanded.

Everything was different, it rapidly became evident. I nearly drowned in the flood of medical jargon. Mostly, as near as I could make out it was a matter of the ambient temperature and the fact that Father hadn't lost any significant amount of blood, as my tutor had. "The cold probably saved him, Thomas," he explained. "I'm just a general practitioner, of course. Not a specialist in such things. But the experts are consulting with me closely, and keeping me very much in the loop." He blinked nervously. "I'm your family doctor, Thomas. I've always leveled with you Longos even when the news was bad. Haven't I?"

I nodded; during my childhood a potential treatment for Dean had emerged. It'd been the most unpleasant task of Doctor Neumann to explain to Father, a superbly-qualified medical professional in his own right, why my brother was a poor candidate for the new methodology. I was young enough that I'd spent the time outside in the hallway playing with a toy tractor, but even back then I'd known the sound of angry shouting when I heard it. Afterwards, however, Father had respected Doctor Neumann more than ever. "You have," I acknowledged, bowing slightly. "We remain most grateful for your candor."

The doctor beamed for a moment, then returned my bow. "I'm proud to be associated with your family," he answered, "Every last one of you." Then he got back to business. "Thomas... Forgive me, but you're not yet so well-educated as your father in medical matters."

I nodded, acknowledging this.

Neumann smiled slightly. "Then please simply take my word for it. Your father should make a complete recovery, and that includes his wonderful mind." His smile widened. "I won't ask you not to worry, because I know that after your previous experiences you must. But have faith. All shall be well. It's only a matter of time."

I nodded again, accepting the prognosis. "Good." Then something else occurred to me. "How long will he be out?"

"At least a week," Neumann answered. "As will your brother. Sven will certainly be brought around then, though it'll take far longer for his body to mend." The doctor scowled. "Those are compound fractures in his thighs, Thomas. Plus he's suffered extensive damage to his internal organs. He's been fitted with an artificial spleen."

"Right," I agreed, already knowing these things.

"Your father's coma, however, may go on considerably longer. He went into it naturally, and while we could artificially induce consciousness we've learned that this usually isn't a good idea unless there's no alternative." He tugged at his chin. "I'd give him ten days. Maybe even a fortnight. But it's just a guess. Both of them will be out of circulation for several months. Drugged into a near stupor."

"I see," I answered. Then I looked past Dr. Neumann; just a little way down the corridor Spence was emerging from Alicia's room...

...with Alicia on his arm! She was fully dressed and looked as healthy as could be!

Doctor Neuman's eyebrows rose, then he turned to see what I was looking at. "Ach!" he replied, nodding knowingly. "What a remarkable couple!" He turned back to me. "You're quite lucky, you know."

"Oh, yes!" I assured him, smiling and bowing my good-bye as I headed off to greet my friends. I hadn't had time to visit Alicia yet, just as Spence still hadn't seen Father and Sven.

"Thomas!" Alicia declared, her face lighting up in pleasure. She spread her arms. "Come here!"

We hugged until I began to grow embarrassed at making such a spectacle of myself. Then I pulled away and smiled. "I was so worried about you," I babbled, still full of pleasure at seeing at least one of the survivors up and mobile and functioning. "You have no idea!"

"Hah!" she countered, making a dismissive gesture with her hand. "Now you know what it's been like for me to sit at home while you go play fighter ace!"

My smile widened; it'd been far, far too long since I'd seen Alicia. And she'd… She'd almost….

"I understand that your father and eldest brother will make full recoveries," she continued. Then her smile faded. "I'm very sorry about Dean."

Suddenly I didn't feel so happy inside anymore. "He was so full of love," I whispered.

"So I've heard," Alicia answered, taking a moment to groom a stray lock of my hair back into place.

"It was almost as if he were born for the sole purpose of suffering for the sins of others," Spence observed. "Though of course my wife and I never knew him."

I nodded. "You'd have liked Dean," I agreed. "Everyone did." Then I sighed and changed the subject. "There'll be a state funeral, I suppose."

Alicia nodded. "In a few days. When I feel up to officiating."

My eyebrows rose. "You're going to officiate?"

She nodded. "I must. It's my duty." Her eyes narrowed, then she shook her head. "Thomas… I know you've been through a lot. But…"

I still didn't get it, I fear. "Yes?"

"With the PM dead," Spence explained, "Alicia is in charge of the government."

"All of it, this time," she explained.

I blinked. "Wow!" I answered eventually.

"Which also means," she continued, "that I'm in charge of getting the investigation underway." She suddenly looked old. "First things first, Thomas. Your Captain Jungmann, of *Graf Zeppelin*. Would you describe him as loyal? There are certain reports circulating about him, you see."

"I… Uh…" I stuttered at the unexpected question. "He's loyal to me. And certainly to Father as well. In any event he's a man of honor. His word is good. I'd stake my life on that."

Alicia's eyes narrowed to slits. "Well… That answer says quite a lot about the true state of affairs in the universe these days, doesn't it?" There was a long silence, while she and Spence locked eyes, just like back in the cave. "I'm going to put the navy in charge of security, then," she decided finally. "Him specifically, reporting to Vlasilov. The admiral, in turn, will head the investigation committee." She sighed. "There's been some kind of breach in the Esteppan security forces; until we work out the who's and what's and where's of it all, I think I trust your Jungmann more than I do any of them. Even if he is a revolutionary at heart."

"Aren't we all?" Spence observed.

Alicia smiled her cold, political smile. "We'll have to return directly to Earth, of course; the death of a PM dictates a new election. But we don't have to leave until I'm feeling up to it, which will happen when *I* decide that I'm feeling better, and not a moment sooner." Then she turned on me again. "We're going to get to the bottom of all this, Thomas. We're not leaving until we've learned everything we can learn about who set that bomb and why. It wouldn't be safe."

Chapter One-Hundred Thirty-One

That very afternoon Admiral Vlasilov and I found ourselves sitting across from each other at a desk in the port captain's office. Spence was expected at any moment. We hadn't even begun forming the committee yet, but already its eventual conclusions were becoming obvious.

"Whoever organized this assassination attempt," Vlasilov observed as we passed the latest reports back and forth to each other, "was a trained professional."

"Ja," I agreed, scowling as I pored over the most recent data in from the field. It'd been a bomb, sure enough; the whole galley area tested positive for Dracan explosive residue. We'd even been able to pin down the approximate date of manufacture; approximately six months before the war. "I doubt we'll ever catch them."

"Da," the admiral agreed, sighing and sipping his tea. Vlasilov had always treated me differently than his other officers. There'd never been much formality between he and I. Originally this was because I was so young and untrained, and in that context our oddball relationship had made perfect sense. But now things had progressed even further. Ever since the PM had died, the admiral had begun treating me almost as an equal. Sometimes he even deferred to me in certain matters. I was having a hard time figuring out why that was; if I'd been able to think of a polite way to ask outright, I would've. He still stood head and shoulders above me in every conceivable way; education, experience, and rank. Perhaps it was because with Father and Sven out of the picture he saw me as at least the temporary head of the Longo clan and therefore was showing his respect accordingly? We were after all rather important people, I'd come to realize. That was my working hypothesis, for the moment at least. "This wasn't the work of amateurs, Thomas. Nor was it the result of a last-minute improvised plan."

I scowled. Dracan explosives didn't necessarily mean Dracan assassins, though they obviously offered a strong clue. "My guess is that they've been ready to kill Father for a long time now. But, once the chance to bag bigger game came along…"

Vlasilov nodded. "I suspect they originally planned to kill your father and yourself. But they settled for Esteppe's President and the bulk of the United Systems cabinet instead."

I looked away and frowned. I could see why the Dracans might want to kill me. I'd killed plenty of them, after all. But who else might want me dead? No one that I could see.

The plot had required two distinct and separate groups to work together in a closely coordinated manner. First, the Esteppan government's entire VIP 'hopper pool had to be put out of action. Operational security was apparently too tight at the main hanger to allow anyone to sneak a bomb on board. It was, however, sufficiently lax to allow a small group of mechanics to sabotage a few key items in such a way as to ground the entire fleet. Once the dirty work was done, someone then killed most of the mechanics as well. This had been accomplished in a most indiscriminate fashion; many died in a beer-hall explosion near the hanger, for example. The explosives used there were Dracan as well; from the same manufacturing batch, even. Over half of the facility's mechanics were murdered the afternoon of the crash, even though it seemed certain that at most a handful could've been involved in the conspiracy. Someone was covering their tracks and doing their best to muddy the waters in every way possible.

The bomb-planters themselves had done very nearly as well. The Longo 'hopper drafted into service was older than the government models and therefore didn't have automated galley-servicing gear. The ship's food and drink, therefore, had to be carried aboard by hand. This was where the most serious security lapse had occurred, an oversight apparently brought about by the continual chaos of schedule- and ship-changes. The saboteurs simply abducted and killed two of the normal servicing crew and substituted men of their own. They'd even clocked in for their shift; we had good film of them doing so. Which did us no good whatsoever; their faces didn't appear in any files available to us on Esteppe. Not that the bombers were particularly hard to find; they too died within minutes of leaving the airfield, even before their bomb exploded. Or at least we were pretty sure they'd died; the two bodies found in the burning commissary truck matched up pretty well with our pictures.

"It was a long-standing plan," I agreed after a long time. "Impeccably executed."

"Professional work," Vlasilov replied, lowering his paperwork and looking deep into my eyes.

"Ja," I agreed, sighing again. At first I'd been eager to pin the whole thing on Esteppan separatists who hated Father and the United Systems. But they weren't capable of such a sophisticated coup. Or, at least, no one in the United Systems intelligence services thought so. I didn't at all like what options that left on the table.

Just then Spence entered the room; he wasn't formally part of the committee but no one was fool enough to try and deny him access. "Admiral," he greeted Vlasilov, nodding politely. Then he turned to me. "Thomas! How are you, son? Anything new to report?"

"I'm tired," I replied, leaning back in my chair and sighing. "And no, not really. There's more autopsy data, but not much else."

"Thomas is correct," Vlasilov added. He sighed and closed the folder he was reading. "Our conclusions are pre-ordained. From here it's all a matter of police work." He shrugged. "Young Thomas and I are wasting our time, if you ask me. There was a bomb. It caused the crash. This is indisputable. Ferreting out the plotters is hardly a suitable task for naval officers."

Spence nodded. "I cannot but agree with you gentlemen, to be perfectly honest. You're not heading the committee because its task lies within your fields of expertise, but rather because of the fact that your integrity is unimpeachable. When the time comes for us to say publicly that the crash was the result of a bomb, people are going to need to hear it from individuals they trust and believe in. It's an important role, though a dull one."

My eyebrows rose. Spence was carrying an "Eyes Only" folder with warnings in purple script. Purple was the highest-ranking color of all, usually seen only on reports meant for the PM. My own top-secret dispatches were all in the much-lower-priority red.

The big rabbit smiled and lifted the envelope. "Yes, Thomas. Sometimes it's nice to be the acting PM's husband." Then his face sobered as he laid the impressive-looking folder on the table. "I've brought this for you both to look at; Alicia's approved. I'll not insult you two after all you've been through by lecturing you on how vital it is that this information remains confidential." He smiled again.

There was only one copy. I looked at the admiral, who shrugged. "Go ahead, Thomas," he urged me. "You first. I'll make some more tea while you're reading."

The folder was sealed with some sort of special tape. It didn't rip easily, and when I finally put some real effort into the project I practically ripped the report in half. It was frustrating sometimes, being so clumsy. At least I'd not damaged things so badly that the report was illegible; that would've been embarrassing indeed!

Spence's document was a report from a United Systems listening post operating here on Esteppe, one that monitored the narrow-bandwidth hyperwave frequencies that could, in a limited sort of way, broadcast through a Nikita. Once Father had begun brain-jacking again in order to facilitate fighter production, certain parties in the intelligence community began recruiting the other surviving Elitemen for other programs. One of these new recruits was a mathematician with an interstellar reputation; he'd been assigned the job of code-breaking. Even jacked, his had been a daunting task; the Dracans were assiduous code-breakers in their own right, and took numerous countermeasures. During the last days of the war, however, the Esteppan had finally figured out how to read the enemy's mail. By then the accomplishment should've been largely academic in nature; we'd already won the big fight at the Orion Nexus, and the Dracans practically had no fighting ships left. The United Systems spooks were actually in the act of dismantling the listening post when out of nowhere a new message in Dracan code suddenly came in. "Regulus," it read after decoding. "Immediate."

Three days later the PM's ship was bombed. With Dracan explosives.

"But…" I protested when I was finished. "It takes a *huge* ground installation to broadcast on hyperwave. There aren't any ships large enough."

"That's true," Spence agreed.

"And we've occupied all the Dracan worlds," I continued.

"Yep," Spence agreed again, nodding.

"But… It's impossible, then! No one could've sent it!"

"Oh, I don't know about that," the big rabbit replied, looking grim. He sighed and looked down at the floor. "There's more to that report, Thomas. Something that Alicia and I felt should never be entrusted to paper at all."

My eyebrows rose, and the admiral looked up from his reading.

"In addition to breaking codes," Spence explained, "these experts can also trace signals. It's all quite esoteric and top-secret; probably no one else in the galaxy even suspects that we might have this capability. Otherwise they might've done more to cover their tracks." He sighed and shook his head. "The order to kill the PM, it seems, originated on Earth."

Chapter One-Hundred Thirty-Two

The admiral and I spent another couple of days going through the formalities of forming our committee of inquiry, then we took time off to bury the dead. Or bury most of them, at least; while our service memorialized everyone, only native Esteppans were to be buried in the mass grave near the crash site. The rest of the bodies would be returned the their respective homeworlds for internment,

Alicia's speech was brief but poignant. I wept a little in my non-teary way twice, once when the PM was eulogized ("He was a man of calm courage, deep loyalty, and strong convictions," Alicia said, tearing up a bit herself) and when she spoke of Dean as well. ("Sadly, I never met this remarkable young man, whose innocence was twice violated by the forces of evil.") The funeral was held in Esteppe City's largest church, but there still wasn't half enough room for everyone. The planet didn't have enough population density to justify building really large meeting halls of any stripe. All of us chief mourners sat together up in the front pews; the woman on my left was the wife of the steward who'd died so messily in the escape capsule. The rest of the space was taken up by all the assorted dignitaries who felt obliged to attend, from Admiral Vlasilov to the chief of the 'hopper pilots union.

I hadn't been to many funerals except the military ones held on board ship for fellow fighter pilots. Therefore I could hardly claim to be an expert on what typically went on. Yet somehow I couldn't help but feel that there was something very wrong with this one. Instead of sadness the church was filled with a sense of barely-suppressed rage. "Bloody-handed cowards," was how one rabbi referred to the still-at-large assassins. "We pray that these diabolical villains shall meet the end that they deserve," a minister echoed. Yes, there was weeping and sadness at the ceremony. But there were also clenched fists and an unspoken but deep undercurrent of rage. If Father had actually died, I began to appreciate about halfway through, or for that matter if I'd been aboard, well… This crowd, at least—and I had no reason to believe that the rest of Esteppe felt any differently—would've been ready to go to war against anyone they felt might be accountable, no matter the cost of the fighting or the odds against victory. Even with Father still alive they were in a nasty temper indeed.

"Amen!" the congregation-- made up of Esteppe's most responsible leadership-- eagerly replied to a particularly bloodthirsty petition to heaven. I leaned my head against the back of my pew and closed my eyes. It was happening again, I realized sickly. War might not be imminent, but it was becoming inevitable sometime in the near future. The conflicts and rivalries between the cultures of Earth and Esteppe ran deep; they'd already led to massive bloodshed once. Was there any reason to assume that they'd prove any more resolvable now? If so, I surely couldn't see how. A second Esteppan war would dwarf the Dracan conflict. Esteppe, rearmed and having learned from previous mistakes, would be a far tougher nut to crack today than it'd been a generation ago. Certainly Father was a far more cunning and able leader than the Emperor had been. Nor was there any question of whose side Churilla, which dominated the crucial Orion Nexus, would take. There'd be no way to hold Esteppe prisoner in her own star system this time around! Even today, right this minute, Esteppe could field a powerful task force centered on *Coronel*, *Graf Zeppelin*, and soon the nearly-complete dreadnought *Wilhelm von Tegetthoff*. *Tegethoff* had a new Esteppan-designed fire-control system, probably developed as the result of brain-jacking if the past as any guide. Even though her guns were significantly smaller in caliber than those of *Cochrane* or an *Imperial Throne*, she was equally well-armored and her technological sophistication would probably make her a match for either. *Arminus* had been produced locally as well. Where one escort had been built, so could others; small ships were quick and easy to produce compared to carriers and battlewagons. Captain Jungmann would make a fine admiral, perhaps even a match for Vlasilov. And with the latest and greatest superfighters at my disposal, I could...

Good lord! What was I thinking? Had I gone mad with the rest of the mourners?

"...a tooth for a tooth, an eye for an eye, a life for a life," one of Esteppe's most conservative clergymen was declaring, shaking his fist in anger. No one responded directly, but a rumble of approval filled the church. Esteppe had voted overwhelmingly for Father's and my party, and always had. His big hurdle at election time had been to win the primary; the general election was never in doubt. For that matter, practically all of the colony-worlds supported my party. It was Earth's huge inward-looking population that consistently supported Nagano and his centralized-government positions, the ones that ensured Earth held all the strings and always would. That was part of why it'd been so crucial that I win a seat on the homeworld; my victory ran against the established tide.

I squirmed in my seat. The more I thought about the state of the United Systems, the more frightened I became for the future. Once upon a time I'd wanted to end war forever, to change and improve human nature and the human level of intelligence so that we could work out our problems in a peaceful manner. I'd gone so far as to nuke entire cities with this goal as my only justification. Yet here I sat, calmly contemplating another even more terrible war. I might even find myself obliged to drop a thermonuclear weapon on Seattle, the very same place that I'd nearly died defending from the Dracans and which had gratefully voted me in as their Parliamentarian.

Did anything related to humans and to humanity make any sense?

"…as it always has been, so shall it always be," intoned the fundamentalist. He wasn't shaking his fist anymore and his voice had calmed itself to a sort of fatalistic dirge. "World without end, amen."

"Amen," everyone else in the church repeated. But not I. Instead, I balled my fists in silent rage until I stripped a gear in my left hand. We needed *change*, not throw-up-your-hands-in-despair stasis!

Finally, as the service finally ended and a mortician closed Dean's coffin-- which I'd soon be escorting to its grave-- I calmed myself a little and tried to think rationally. My brother had loved everyone in his slobbering, happy, brain-damaged way. That was the part of human nature I wanted to honor and uphold, not the self-aggrandizement of the Emperor or the cold calculation of a Nagano. My responsibilities were to the Deans of the universe, not the hotheaded fundamentalists. But, what was I going to do if the angry Esteppan masses ever found out that the order to kill their legally-elected leaders had originated on Earth? Nagano, the more-than-likely future PM, almost had to be the guilty party. After all, who else had anything to gain? Could anything possibly incense Esteppe any further than such a revelation? Perhaps the likelihood that Nagano had issued his death-order through a murderous war criminal like Prince Nogandeaux? After all, who else on Earth was likely to have knowledge of the codes that controlled the obviously still-very-much-alive Dracan intelligence network? Alicia and Spence and I had been over this a thousand times in the privacy of her apartment. We had no proof, but everything fit together so well that it was a near-certainty. Knowing both parties personally, I had no difficulty at all imagining Nagano and the Prince getting along just famously, laughing and smiling together over the finest of meals…

War just might be an inevitable outgrowth of human nature after all, if the Prince and Nagano were good examples of what it meant to be human! No matter how awful and futile combat was, perhaps we humans were getting exactly what we deserved for being such grasping creatures. Perhaps I'd been a young, idealistic fool to imagine that war as an institution might be done away with. But by God I'd not let this war happen, not without doing everything I knew to stop it! By all the charred corpses I'd left in my wake, I swore, and by all the injustice and suffering that my brother Dean had known, I'd not let the likes of Isoroku Nagano and Prince Nogandeaux manipulate the United System into another war.

Not this time!

Chapter One-Hundred Thirty-Three

The next few weeks were pretty rough, though not everything was totally miserable. In addition to my excruciatingly-boring work in regards to the commission, I had other dignitaries to meet with and more pleasant duties to perform. I found time, for example, to return to the Stormcrow plant and thank everyone there for the extraordinary contributions they'd made towards victory in the Dracan war. No less than seventeen of these men and women died of radiation poisoning, all of them quite horribly, and most of the rest were sickened to one degree or another. No one really knew how badly the survivors' life-expectancy had been impacted; in fact, there were three universities lined up to study their future health.

The Esteppan government struck a special medal for the survivors and it was my privilege to attend the investiture. Father and the navy had already seen to it that the workers became wealthy; now, with unique medals to wear, they suddenly found themselves near the top of the Esteppan social heap. Most didn't seem to think they deserved the honor, but it was obvious to anyone with any sense that they did. The Stormcrow facility, for all its radiation-related technical problems, had produced seventy percent of all Skybolts used in the war. They'd suffered almost none of the quality-control problems that so plagued the New Orleans facility. More outstandingly still, the Mark I* had been developed and produced there exclusively.

As much as I liked and respected the staff back on Earth, facts were facts. The Stromcrow workers weren't supermen. But *something* had allowed them to markedly outperform their Louisiana counterparts in every measurable category and under far less favorable circumstances. "It was better management," Gunther assured me when I asked, and perhaps he was right. The Esteppans were a little more experienced, as well. Still, I felt that there was something else involved that I couldn't quite put my finger on. For example, as much as I respected the New Orleans staff I somehow couldn't picture them voluntarily, even cheerfully, working in a potentially lethal environment the way the Esteppans had. Perhaps it was something inherent in Esteppan culture?

Something, rather akin, perhaps, to whatever it was that'd motivated so many Churrilians to give up their lives and sacrifice their wealth in order to drive out the Dracans?

I genuinely enjoyed the award-ceremony, but then things got even better. I'd been hearing rumors of a Mark II Skybolt for some time now, but as a combat pilot I'd been too much of a security risk to be let in on the details. Now that peace had broken out I was not only brought up to speed but allowed to take several flights in the new 'hopper. It was one of the most wonderful experiences of my life! Someone somewhere had taken careful note of every little complaint and suggestion and done their level best to make improvements. The "II", as it was affectionately known, was faster, easier to service, stronger and in all respects a better bird than the older Mark I's. All II's also carried the twin-cannon of the Mark I* that I'd so come to love, while at the same time being more maneuverable than the single-gunned version. I felt invincible while flying the II, and this probably wasn't entirely an illusion. I'd learned early in my studies that even tiny inequalities in fighter performance translated into large imbalances in kill ratios in time of war. In no other field of combat was up-to-the-minute technology so important. The only factor more critical to victory was pilot skill and experience, which was why a handful of aces always made such a huge percentage of the total number of kills. "*Coronel* is coming out of the yards in three weeks, fresh from refit," Gunther explained with pride after I'd been dismounted from the new model. "We'll have six II's ready for her!" I was impressed; with six Mark II's ranged on her flight deck alongside six older Skybolts, she'd easily be the deadliest thing in the sky.

I also made an appearance at Esteppe's new Butcher Bird Academy, a military school set up especially to select and train 'hopper pilots. It was a grueling, harsh place, one whose rigors I probably wouldn't have survived as a boy. At least it was open to everyone, so that in the future our pilots wouldn't all be noblemen. There'd always be more volunteers than squadron-slots and, I supposed, the weeding-out had to be accomplished somehow. Better that it be done through excessively-high standards than social ranking. The first hurry-up class, which had missed the war anyway despite all the haste, would graduate in time to ship out on *Coronel*. The surgical facilities were named after the boy who'd died during his brain-coring aboard *The Glorious First of June*, back what seemed like forever ago. Even better, the attached counselor training wing was named after Father Murton. There was a large sculpture-park off to one side of the central quadrangle devoted to the original Butcher Birds, complete with a life-sized bust of Colonel Rotte and a replica of his Stormcrow. The other three sides had been left empty, though the academy's director had been very persistent in his efforts to get me to pose just-so for holographs while standing in one of the empty slots. I didn't want to be memorialized as a killer of men! But how could I say no?

I was also able to squeeze in a day or two of actual, real, genuine honest-to-goodness time off back at the Old Home Place. As the senior functional Longo at the moment I had the run of the house, and more servants at my beck and call than I was really comfortable with. Still, it was nice to be able to count on having the main reception room at my disposal when the Vice-President of Esteppe came to pay a call. I didn't know much about how to receive such an eminent guest, but fortunately the staff did.

The visit didn't go at all as I'd imagined it would; Vice-President Schnee insisted on bowing to me regardless of the fact that he outranked me by any measure, and the image of him doing so was instantly flashed all over the planet. Even more embarrassing, however, was our dinner conversation. Schnee spent the whole meal asking my opinion on this and that and the other thing, half of his questions relating to domestic Esteppan matters about which I knew little or nothing. When I protested that I didn't know enough to comment on a proposed government takeover of a large tract of unproductive but privately-owned land to create a planetary hunting reserve, Schnee simply smiled. "You're your father's son," he explained. "And much, much more. What you think *matters* to the rest of us. It's all right that you're uninformed for the moment. We understand that you've only just returned from a long war and an even longer exile. So you're forgiven. But you must *study*! Earth may borrow you from time to time, but your roots are here. This is your home, and we'll be needing you eventually. In the meantime I'd be honored if you called from time to time and consulted with me. Especially until your father recovers."

Then, much too soon, Admiral Vlasilov called me back to the real world of grinding hard work. His Committee of Inquiry began meeting every morning, examining in excruciating detail what'd happened aboard the doomed Longo Industries hopper that'd killed the PM. It was necessary, I suppose. But my *heavens* was it tedious! Evidence was formally admitted, experts summoned, and the condition of every weld documented. As Vlasilov had predicted, the outcome was a foregone conclusion. Still, the admiral and I had to sit stoically through the whole affair and pretend to be paying close attention, he sipping tea and I doodling endlessly on a legal pad kept carefully screened from the cameras. It was our names and credibility that mattered, not our minds. How the admiral survived the experience without an internal video-game to play, I'll never know.

In the afternoons I met with Alicia and Spence. Madame Deputy's strategy for the election was to play for time, to delay, delay, delay in the hope that some new factor or scandal would emerge that might improve our odds of victory. It was a bankrupt plan from the very beginning, as she herself well knew. Yet the simple truth was that our side was pretty much out of cards to play. So she spent most of her days in the hospital, running the government from a sickbed she no longer really needed and leaving it only for short periods to deal with the most unavoidable of official functions.

"…thought we'd get more out of the bump," Spence was complaining late one afternoon. The "bump" was a slang-term the Wistons had coined for the little uptick in popularity our party picked up out of sympathy when the PM died. Apparently there was a significant block of voters who supported whichever party they felt sorrier for at any given moment. "But it's fading fast."

"That's because of the negative coverage on my hospitalization," she answered. "It seems that the media suspects I'm dragging things out for political purposes. Imagine that!" The rabbit-woman rolled her eyes.

Spence smiled, but only for a moment. Then he paced back and forth some more. "We've ruled out redistricting," he pointed out. "Perhaps we should reconsider?"

"We can't," his wife replied. "Earth's already been redistricted by emergency decree, and the other worlds aren't even close to due."

Spence pressed his lips together and kicked at an imaginary rock. "I keep forgetting," he admitted.

"You were rather busy elsewhere at the time," Alicia answered, smiling. "Being brave."

"Heh!" the former guerilla leader replied. "It's ironic, really. You and I wouldn't have any trouble being re-elected. Yet, because everything's still so messed up from the war back home, we won't even be running. Churilla's not ready to hold elections yet."

"It's just as well," Alicia answered, her smile fading. "Frankly, Spence, I don't have any desire at all to serve in an Opposition role. I thought that Churillian politics were filthy. And they are! But compared to *this*…" She frowned and shook her head. "I'm not going to sit in that chamber and acknowledge a murderer as my leader. He even tried to kill me, don't forget! I'm just not, Spence. Or at least not for a moment longer than I absolutely have to." She looked away. "After the elections I'll be resigning. Sorry, dear. But you'll have to find someone else to kiss Nagano's hindquarters."

I frowned and pressed my own lips together; the longer these sessions went on, the more depressing they became. Alicia was getting daily reports from her staff back home; polling data, demographics, clippings from key journalists… Things were looking just awful. I'd hold my seat, but Nagano's people would nearly sweep the rest of Earth. With a few oddball pickups here and there off-planet, that was all he needed. The campaigning hadn't even begun yet, but the conclusion was already evident. Almost to a man, Earth's voters had decided that our party was corrupt, violent, not in tune with their needs and interests, and worst of all had simply been in office too long. Yes, we'd won the war. The voters were duly grateful; we of the coalition that'd brought about victory would be well-thought-of in the history books, and people would willingly raise glasses to us at social functions for the rest of our lives. But for now they were tired of us and wanted to try something new.

"I want to resign as well," Spence replied. "I'd really like to, in fact. But…" He frowned and met Alicia's eyes. "Churilla needs us. You know that. We're the only ones who can unify her during reconstruction." He scowled. "The fact is, I've been away too long already."

"You have a sick wife," Alicia pointed out. "Churillians understand and respect family obligations. Still…" The corners of her mouth turned downwards. "I don't enjoy politics any more than you do, Spence. I agree that one of us has to suffer, at least for a little longer. But why should both of us have to? Next time Churilla gets invaded *I'll* serve as President during the recovery. But this time, you're stuck."

"Heh!" Spence replied.

Then I interrupted. "What makes Churillians so special," I asked slowly. "That you're willing to suffer for them but not for anyone else?"

There was a long, long silence. "Now, Thomas…" Spence began.

But I continued right on over him. "A Nagano victory is a tragedy for all of the outer worlds. Right?" I demanded. The rabbits nodded mutely, and Spence opened his mouth again. Again, I didn't give him a chance to continue. "Why are we just sitting here accepting this?" I continued. "Why aren't we fighting?"

"Because of these," Alicia replied gently, picking up a stack of polling reports and holding them out for me to look at again. "Thomas, we're beaten. Sometimes it's best to accept a shellacking rather than struggle. In the long run you lose less that way."

"B-b-but…" I spluttered. "B-b-but… This is Nagano we're talking about here! A…a murderer, we have every reason to believe! He's actively collaborating with the most evil human being I've ever met. And we're supposed to accept this man as our *leader*? When our own worlds and I don't even know how many others despise him almost as much as we do?"

"Thomas…" Spence said, his voice soft now. "Son…" Then he looked down at the floor and shook his head. "We can't win this election. We just can't."

"We're flushing everything down the toilet!" I complained, throwing up my hands to the accompaniment of a dozen overloaded servos. "Everything we believe in! Nagano will ruin it all! He'll suspend brain-jacking, no one will be gengineered… I bet he even lets the Prince be in charge of Drakkus again, though firmly under his thumb. At least for now." My eyes widened. "In fact…"

Spence smiled his nastiest smile. "You're just now figuring that out, Thomas? If your old buddy isn't the Crown Prince yet, I'd not care to underwrite life insurance policies on any remaining older brothers."

"They'll be forced into the United Systems," Alicia predicted. "Just like Esteppe was after she was defeated. In this case, however, I bet the Prince will be able to guarantee votes for Nagano's party. A whole empire's worth, in fact."

"They're quite docile, the Dracans are," Spence added. "Easily led. Especially if your Prince is allowed enough autonomy to maintain a secret police force behind the scenes."

"Which he certainly will," Alicia continued. "So that he'll continue to be able to kill Nagano's rivals for him." She closed her eyes and sighed. "It's the end of all decency."

"The logical and ultimate result of democracy run amok," Spence agreed. "First, there's name-calling and bickering. No one can get anything done. This begets genuine hatred. Next come the false prosecutions and other abuses of power to ruin the careers of rivals. All justified, of course, on the grounds that the Opposition is causing such problems that there's no other way to move ahead. Eventually, officials are stamped out in a more permanent fashion." He shook his head. "Oh, my poor government!"

"Don't waste your sympathy on *them*," Alicia hissed. "Instead, feel sorry for the poor, ignorant voters who expect decency and justice from their leaders. How extraordinarily silly of them!"

There was another long, hard silence. Eventually I broke it "So. You're just giving up?"

"We're *beaten*, Thomas," Alicia replied. "At least at the polls."

"One of the advantages of an unnaturally long life," Spence amplified, "is that you learn there will always be another day."

I felt my fists ball up. "But… There won't be, this time. Once Nagano has the Dracan vote to add to Earth's, how will he ever lose his majority?"

The answer was a long, stony silence.

"Remember how we said that the only long-term hope for humanity is growth?" I asked. "Through gengineering and brain-jacking? How will we legalize either with Nagano and his successors in office?"

Once again, I was answered only with silence.

I turned to face Spence. "When," I said slowly, "in the course of human events…"

"Thomas!" the big rabbit declared. "Don't even *say* it! What are you *thinking*, son?"

"Nothing that you haven't thought about before me," I countered, my fists still two hard balls of anger. "Nothing that Father hasn't thought about, either. And you damned well know it!"

Strangely, Alicia was calmer than her husband. She was the deadly one, I'd heard it said on Churillia. The one who'd cut out your soul and eat it for breakfast. "We can't win," was her far more pragmatic reply. "I admit it; I've been considering it too. For months, even. But we simply cannot win."

"Really?" I countered. My eyes narrowed. "What makes you so certain? Are you a naval officer, all of a sudden?"

"Thomas!" Spence answered. "Son, I *am* a successful guerilla leader and therefore a strategist of some practical experience. And—"

I cut him off cold, never turning away from Alicia. "It's the navy that really matters," I explained. "It's just the way things are. He who controls the Nikitas and the space immediately around the planets controls all. You know that from your time running things." I turned to Spence. "Hear me out. That's all I'm asking."

There was another long, hard silence. Alicia ostentatiously checked her security monitors before speaking again. "I won't support a civil war. That's flat off the table. We've just finished slaughtering far too many innocents."

"It'd be a risk," I acknowledged. "But a manageable one, I think. And he who will not risk cannot win. All of us here understand this basic truth."

There was another long silence. Finally Madame Deputy spoke again. "What do you have in mind?" she asked.

I closed my eyes and thought long and hard before committing myself. When in the course of human events… "Give me until tomorrow. And have Captain Jungmann meet us here. We'll need him from the getgo."

Chapter One-Hundred Thirty-Four

We needed the captain's help, all right. And that of dozens of others as well.

Next after Jungmann was the vice-president, who bowed to me again and agreed to everything I suggested. He seemed a bit relieved, in fact.

"Your father is still very ill," he reassured me. "But I'm certain that he would've seized this opportunity as well."

Schnee and Jungmann were old friends as it turned out; my, what a small universe we revolutionaries lived in! Things began to happen almost immediately. *Wilhelm Von Tegetthoff* suddenly moved back into the number-one priority slot for attention in Esteppe's overstressed shipyards. For a time she'd been downgraded in order to expedite the replacement of merchant shipping losses from the war, but no more! Though her trials were cut short, we had her spaceworthy in six weeks. *Zeppelin*'s major refit was cancelled, though a short furlough for quick repairs and leaves was substituted. *Arminus*'s priority rose in the repair yards, as well.

After seven weeks of endless testimony, the Committee of Inquiry reached its inevitable verdict; the crash was the result of an assassination attempt by persons unknown and still at large. Vlasilov expected to leave Esteppe once this work was done, but instead he found himself assigned to investigate and report on the Butcher Bird Academy, with an eye towards determining whether or not the facility should be emulated on Earth. Alicia engineered this among many other things for us in her role as acting PM. The admiral was perhaps the sharpest man I'd ever met, and I suspected that if he wasn't kept busy he'd figure out what was coming next. I knew him to be highly sympathetic towards brainjacking, after such long and intimate contact with the Skybolt program. Nor had I ever detected in him anything but respect and admiration for the Wistons. Still, the admiral was not a man to take his oath lightly. He'd dedicated his entire life to the United Systems and its Parliamentary system, and I felt that it was in everyone's best interests if he were kept in the dark regarding the true state of things. If he wanted to join with us later, well... I was well-connected enough to ensure that he'd be welcomed with open arms. In the meantime he was assigned a nice piece of busywork, while Jungmann and his cohorts respectfully but efficiently monitored the admiral's every communication back to Fleet headquarters.

Even as things were he made us rather nervous with his pointed comments regarding the idiocy of delaying *Zeppelin*'s refit yet again and his musings on why exactly it might be that the Esteppan branch of the Navy Office was still appointing an all-Esteppan suite of officers to an important vessel like *Tegettoff* when the war was over and Academy graduates once more available. In fact, I'm pretty sure he had it all figured out right at the end. At our last meeting over lunch in his office, he asked me numerous leading questions, in effect all but pleading with me to level with him. "You're perhaps the greatest man I've ever known," was the only answer I could offer. "I've trusted you with my life many times, and it'd be my pleasure to do so again should we ever fight another war together."

"Together," he replied, his eyes narrowing.

"I know how you value honor," I shot back. "But honor can at times become a very complex thing." I looked away, not quite able to meet his eyes. "Trust me, sir?"

"I…" Vlasilov began. Then he tried again. "You…" But somehow he couldn't find the right words.

"Sometime in the rather near future you may well find that honor has become a very complex thing in your own heart as well, sir. If so, you know where to find me. And if not, well…" I saluted, just as snappily as I could manage. "Pleasant voyages! It's been an honor."

"Thomas!" Vlasilov croaked. "Please! At least let me…" But his voice faded away, and suddenly he looked very old. "I understand," he said eventually. "Or at least I believe that I do." He scowled. "And maybe I *do* have some thinking to do."

"Take as long as you'd like," I answered, lowering my hand from my forehead. "And know that I love you like a second father either way."

Eventually the day came when things could be put off no longer, and the secretly-declared Esteppan navy up-shipped for Earth with Admiral Jungmann in command. Spence had long since departed for home, where he and his most trusted intimates were busily learning everything they could about the new navy base and other key installations that were already being rebuilt there to replace the one the Dracans had ruined. Churilla was the fleet's single most important facility off of Earth, dominating as it did the Orion Nexus. What the navy hadn't figured out yet, and what we hoped wouldn't need to be demonstrated too forcefully, was that the facilities there were completely untenable in the face of determined local opposition. Even the Dracans with all of their brutality hadn't been able to operate on Churilla with any kind of efficiency once Spence set his mind to preventing them. Alicia had followed her husband home, again claiming ill-health from the crash. While she hadn't yet resigned, her formal letter was sitting atop my desk aboard *Coronel*, waiting for me to deliver it.

Hand-deliver it, in fact. To Nagano. In person.

I was rather looking forward to it.

Chapter One-Hundred Thirty-Five

By then I was almost comfortable in the job of a squadron commander and captain of superfighters. I knew *Coronel* like the back of my hand from my previous service aboard her, and was already friendly and comfortable with my pilots, many of whom had I'd flown with at the Second Battle of the Orion Nexus. (Alicia had ordered all the surviving Butcher Birds back home to Esteppe for leave, claiming political necessity and telling the not-so-white lie that it'd be the Top Banana's turn next.) Still, it took me a couple of days to get used to seeing everyone in black uniforms. We'd broken those out immediately after transiting the first Nikita, once it was certain that word of what was happening couldn't possibly get out. Jungmann and I had worried that we'd have trouble, especially among the younger ratings who like me couldn't remember an independent Esteppe. But our fears proved groundless. The men roared and cheered as I gave my speech on the intership circuit, swearing to them on my honor as a Brother of the Order of Blood that I had reason to believe that Isoroku Nagano had killed their Prime Minister, martyred my brother and tried to kill my beloved father as well.

There were disturbances, yes. But these consisted not of protests, but rather of angry mobs waving their fists and shouting in the various ships' corridors. "Freedom!" the men chanted when I was finished. "Freedom! Freedom! All hail Thomas Longo!" Eventually the old uniforms were expelled out the nearest airlocks, a handful of loyalists were brigged under the most humane conditions possible, and our little fleet continued on its way through the cold, dark interstellar night.

I worried a lot about the fact that the ratings were "hailing" me, though under the circumstances I supposed it was better than many of the alternatives. It was even worse when all the officers of the fleet, led by Jungmann, swore an oath of personal loyalty to me. "I'm a democrat," I explained to them once they were done bowing and scraping. "Not a monarchist, and certainly not an Autarch. There will be free elections once the crisis is past. I swear it."

"We believe you," Jungmann replied for them all, bowing again. "Because we know your character, your excellency. You walk among us as an equal, just as you always have. If we didn't honor your word, we wouldn't follow." It was the nicest thing that anyone had ever said to me, the nicest thing that anyone *could* say to me. Yet the words left me feeling hollow and frightened inside. Not so long ago, Captain Bard had observed that I just might be able to make a king of myself if I tried. What I had in mind was a little different, yes. But not enough different for me to be able to sleep easily at night. Instead I laid awake and asked myself tough questions. What was power, anyway? Who legitimately had the right to it, and why? What was its true purpose? Then after not finding any easy answers I'd call the medics and have myself drugged into unconsciousness. At one time I'd feared doing this because the doctors might downcheck me from combat operations. Now they wouldn't dare.

Which frightened me even more, of course.

Because I had so many veterans in the squadron, more than I'd ever had before, our unit came together quite painlessly this time around. I drilled with them sometimes, familiarizing myself with my new red-nosed Mark II and keeping my reflexes sharp. But I didn't fly so much as I once had. I was blessed with good solid flight-leaders now, and the only way they could grow was for me to stand aside and leave them in charge from time to time. So instead of spending so many hours in the cockpit, I made use of the opportunity to catch up on personal affairs. Some of these had been long neglected. I wrote letters to Captain Bard and many of the other officers and politicians I'd come to know while growing into a man, thanking them for what they'd done for me and trying to explain why I was doing what to them must appear to be such a terrible thing. I had the most trouble with the ones addressed to Lofton Knight and his son Ted; I'd fought alongside both of them, after all, and they'd done as much as anyone to help me become who and what I was.

My letter to Jimmy would've been the hardest one of all. But somehow I never did quite manage to write it.

We hit Earth's Nikita like a midnight express train, dark and fast and closed-up tight for battle. *Tegetthoff* led the way, followed by *Zeppelin*, *Arminus*, and finally *Coronel*. We weren't at war, but it was an obvious assault-Jump. After all word might've leaked out, and who knew what reception might be waiting for us?

Everything was peaceful in Earthspace, however, and as we stood down from battle-stations I sincerely hoped that things would remain that way. "We were drilling," Admiral Jungmann explained airily to Earth Traffic Control as all of us pilots except the ready-flight dismounted from our aircraft. He'd kept his old uniform, as had the bridge-crews of all our ships. "The war may be over, but I'm flooded with green hands. It's a shambles, I tell you!"

I virtual-smiled to myself as I sat and waited to be disconnected from my Mark II. In point of fact our battle-station times were better than ever, even on poor abused and overcrowded *Zeppelin*.

"Next time, obtain clearance!" the admiral in charge muttered. "Your reputation precedes you, Captain. I'll have no unauthorized emergency up-ships taking place in *my* jurisdiction!"

"Captain" Jungmann smiled back tightly but didn't respond. Twice in his career, *Zeppelin*'s captain had lifted his vessel without orders. Each time he'd been fully justified, and once he'd proven himself the only commanding officer in the entire fleet both able and willing to take the initiative. Vlasilov had praised him publicly, a rare distinction indeed. One of Alicia's last little contributions to our mission had been to delay the return of task force seven from Dracan space. While Vlaslov had been removed from command, during the war he'd concentrated the best and brightest officers in the fleet there. Then Alicia transferred the remaining promising flag officers to positions in the Dracan Occupation Forces. It was a beautiful thing; Nagano had actually helped her along since she'd allowed him, in tacit recognition of his upcoming victory, to name their replacements. Practically all of them were "political" admirals, like the late and unlamented Admiral Lutjens of Churillian-surrender fame. And most of the rest were the same crowd who'd screamed so loudly against the idea of "wasting" money on Skybolts. We had little to fear from the likes of them.

"I *will* have order," the admiral repeated. "At all costs." Then he signed off without even welcoming us "home". This was a deliberate insult, but somehow Jungmann didn't seem to mind. Instead, he carefully followed proper procedure in filing for permission to extend his "drill" by deploying *Tegetthoff* and *Zeppelin* across the approaches to Earth's Nikita while *Coronel*, now escorted solely by *Arminus*, continued her "simulated" assault-curve towards the home of mankind.

We hadn't been in-system for more than a couple of hours before I got the message I'd been waiting for. It was a very polite note from Nagano's Chief of Staff, inviting me to dine with the Opposition leader in Rome. A reply was already written and I had it sent immediately. My mannequin-body was malfunctioning, it explained, and required emergency servicing in New Orleans. Would the honorable Mr. Nagano care to meet with me there, at Father's estate? Of course, the reply came back; even Nagano couldn't afford to be seen as unsympathetic towards a returning hero's war-related maladies. But it'd be forty-eight hours before he could clear his schedule for such a journey.

"That'll be wonderful," I replied, trying not to smile as I laboriously typed away with my slow, awkward fingers. "Forty-eight hours from now is just about perfect. You have no idea how much I'm looking forward to sitting down with your boss and speaking face-to-face with him about some important matters of great interest to us both."

Chapter One-Hundred Thirty-Six

It was probably a good thing that I'd been drugging myself to sleep instead of lying awake. I'd need all of my wits about me for the next couple of days, and would have very little opportunity to rest. I sent to New Orleans for a corporate shuttle just as soon as we were within range and *Coronel* had shed enough vector to allow a rendezvous. Eventually we were goig to end up in a highly-elliptical circumpolar orbit, but for now we were still pretty hard to catch. Not that anyone was in a position to threaten us-- there wasn't another completed, functional warship anywhere within Earth-space at the moment except for the training-fleet vessels, and among them only much-battered *Roman Nose* represented a genuine danger. While in the past the navy had employed retired warships as trainers, the Dracans had created rather a serious shortage of those. Now, except for *Nose*, the navy was using converted merchant hulls equipped with low-powered turrets, ships that were absolutely useless in combat and which bore courage-inspiring names like TV-37. *Nose* was still operating with only half her armament, however, and even better was currently laid up in the yards for something or another. If everything went well, she'd never have time to up-ship. I certainly hoped that this would be the case, as I wasn't certain I could find it in my heart to put a torpedo into her after all she'd done for me.

Longo Industries maintained a small fleet of shuttles on Earth; I'd specified the largest of these for my trip home. This was very much out of character for me; in fact, I'd only ever been on the ship twice before, both times accompanying Father on a sales mission. While she was on the way out the navy offered to send me an even bigger official 'hopper complete with an honor guard if I needed more space, but I politely turned them down. The last thing we wanted was for the navy to see all those black uniforms! There was room enough on the Longo vessel for forty marines plus Manuel and I and a few other odds and ends, which was all that I thought would be required. Neither of the pilots batted an eye at the armed troops; both were native Esteppans and long-service employees, recently transferred to Earth.

They also happened to be close friends of Admiral Jungmann.

Timing is everything, when you're running a revolution. We landed near midnight on Saturday, when the Skybolt plant and surrounding grounds were deserted. There were a few guards that required silencing, but I'd already made certain that the truly crucial security positions were filled with loyal long-service Esteppans. They cooperated marvelously. Eagerly, even, once they saw the black uniforms and had finished cheering themselves hoarse. The marines, all of them thoroughly briefed, went right to work. By the time Nagano arrived Earth didn't have a functional superfighter factory anymore. Nor anything even remotely resembling one. We'd destroyed all but one of the incomplete birds as well--all without the outside world knowing a thing. The Dracans might've been very good indeed at cloak-and-dagger work; it was their forte, even. But, that didn't mean we Esteppans were totally inept.

The marines carefully didn't do any externally-visible damage. So when Nagano's official 'hopper landed alongside my own, he still didn't have a clue as to what was going on. Father's household staff, all screened for loyalty, greeted the Opposition leader at the landing pad with all the necessary bows and flourishes, pacifying the visiting Parliamentarian with the explanation that I was still partially immobilized by the difficulties with my mannequin-body and therefore unable to greet him personally on the tarmac. The truth was that, though I was perfectly willing to accept the risk, Nagano had an armed guard of his own. The Wistons had made me promise that I wouldn't give them even a fleeting opportunity to take a shot at me should our cover suddenly break. At this point I was too valuable to lose. Reluctantly I'd agreed, and thus was sitting in a power-chair I didn't really need.

That the chair had once belonged to Dean didn't improve my mood at all.

"Thomas!" Nagano greeted me as he strode alone into the special VIP reception hall that Mr. Roon had ordered built out near the landing pad during his tenure. "What a marvelous place this is! No wonder you prefer to meet me here instead of in Rome! You have far better facilities than I do!" It was an awful place, in my opinion, overdone in teak paneling and black leather with ostentatious real-gold highlights. The overall effect was a sort of sick parody of the dark and blocky Esteppan style of the rest of the buildings. Roon had chosen the location because it overlooked the plant's exit, where new Skybolts were rolled out and tested. The hideous thing had cost a mint, diverted scarce resources during a time of planetary shortages, and as near as we Longos could tell served no useful purpose whatsoever except to impress important idiots. That Nagano actually liked it was just icing on the cake. However, it had one key point in its favor for today's meeting. Because the new Skybolts required engine run-ups upon completion, the entire structure was highly shielded. Not a single radio-wave could enter or exit. Just to be on the safe side one of *Coronel*'s flight-deck crews, dressed for the moment in Longo coveralls, had started up the motors of the plant's last flyable Skybolt. This made it even more impossible for signals from ordinary gear to get in and out.

I looked out through the thick, shielded glass to where some of Nagano's bodyguards stood huddled in a circle. One of them, shouting to make himself heard over the screaming fighter engine, was waving a useless walky-talky. I smiled and nodded at my guest. "Oh, this is nothing," I answered easily. "Someday you'll have to come see the Old Home Place."

Nagano smiled, sat down, and we began exchanging pleasantries. The first thing my guest did was to apologize for being so rude to me on the floor of Parliament . "I wasn't myself, Thomas, I assure you. I can't imagine what I was thinking." Then he inquired about my health.

"It's just a bad servo," I lied smoothly. "But it's a major one, and I've already used up all the in-stock replacements. It happens pretty often, you see. I'm still using an early design."

The Opposition leader made smoothly sympathetic noises until dinner arrived. As usual I had empty plates placed before me even though I couldn't eat, and Nagano (who'd obviously been well-briefed) ignored the fact that I never so much as picked up my fork. Slowly, inevitably, the conversation turned towards business. "So," Nagano said, picking delicately at a fine Esteppan fruit-filled dessert that I'd not enjoyed in far too long. "We have an election coming up."

"So we do," I agreed, nodding slightly.

Isoroku put down his fork, wiped his lips, and then laid his napkin down over the remains of his feast. "I must say," he said slowly, "that I find Madame Deputy's behavior inexplicable. She hasn't campaigned for her party at all."

"She's still quite rattled from the explosion," I explained. "I fear it may be the rabbit-thing. Innate fears and all of that."

Nagano's face lit up for an instant, then went blank again. "Gengineering," he observed, "was outlawed for a reason. I know that you're very close to the Wistons, Thomas. Given your tragic experiences on Churillia, how could it be otherwise? I'll also grant that they're brilliant in a limited sort of way. But... Surely you can see that they're not quite human? In their souls, I mean. Where it really matters."

"Perhaps," I agreed, not quite lying. Nagano was right. They *weren't* human. Which was the whole point of the thing.

There was a long silence, during which our plates were removed and tea was served. I'd chosen the same kind that Vlasilov liked, and Nagano's eyes went wide at his first taste of it. "My heavens!" he declared. "This is wonderful! I've never had anything quite like it!"

"It's Russian," I explained. "Not oriental."

"It's magnificent, is what it is!" Isoroku sipped again, and a look of bliss filled his face. "You're full of surprises, young man. You always have been, and in a way I'm glad to see that you still are. There are those who believe you're something very special. I begin to understand why."

I smiled again. "I'm fuller of surprises than you ever dreamed."

"Heh!" Nagano answered, slumping back in his chair and crossing his legs. "I'm not the antichrist, you know. I recognize that you hate me, and I even understand why. You're young and idealistic." He frowned slightly. "You're also going to be re-elected."

I nodded wordlessly.

"Re-elected in my old district, and by a rather large margin at that." Nagano scowled and shook his head. "You've won that fight, Thomas. I must admit it and let the past go. I've lost, and you've won. Fair and square."

"Thank you," I replied, nodding and wondering what it'd cost Nagano to utter those words. Plenty, I hoped.

"You're welcome," Nagano replied, smiling again. "There! Was that so bad? Here we are, treating each other like civilized men. Who'd have thought it?"

I smiled slightly. "Certainly not I."

Nagano took another sip of tea, then leaned forward again. "Thomas…" he said slowly, turning and looking out the big picture window at the Skybolt, which was still straining against the test stand. "Yours is a very important family in this universe. Admit it, son! You know that it's true."

I nodded silently.

"And so is mine. We go back hundreds of years; once upon a time my ancestors and yours were allied in a great war. Have you read much about history, Thomas?"

"A little," I admitted.

Nagano smiled. "Of course, you've had so little time… Anyway, our people have worked together before." His smile faded. "You can't advance your ideas unless you wield genuine power. Which I'm prepared to offer you. I can make you a better deal than anything your current party can. With me on your side, your district becomes the safest in the world; I of all people ought to know! You'll *never* leave office-- I won't even ask you to cross the aisle, or at least not yet. It's traditional, after all, for a PM to place an Opposition member in at least one key Cabinet seat. And it's a *good* tradition." He cocked his head. "I know you've been offered a post in the past. Which one, may I ask?"

I decided there was nothing to lose by speaking the truth. "My choice of several lower-tier positions. So that I could learn from the experience.

"Hah!" Nagano replied, looking up at the ceiling for the moment. "A mere pittance, for a man of your stature!" He lowered his eyes again to meet my own. "Navy Minister, Thomas. Nothing less. Commander of all that you so love. That's what I'm offering you." He folded his arms. "I'm a generous man, am I not?"

I smiled; everything was going exactly as Spence had predicted it would. Except that he thought I might actually be offered the position of Deputy, if I pushed a little. Once I accepted a cabinet position under him, after all, Esteppe would never again accept me as her leader. It would poison my position there utterly—I'd be perceived, quietly and respectfully, as something of a sellout. An ordinary man with feet of clay, in other words, instead of an unbesmirched hero. So why not wiggle the knife a little, I decided. My marines still needed a few more minutes to get everything ready. "I don't know," I answered, looking down into my lap and adjusting my tie slightly. "If I take things slowly, well… Father's job will come open someday. It's only planetary, I know. But there's a certain cachet to running one's own house. As I'm quite certain you understand."

Nagano smiled again, though this time there was a hint of ice behind it. I could almost see the wheels spinning. *Does the young fool understand how powerful he truly is?* the Opposition leader was asking himself. Then he spoke again. "Well, there's another option. You could serve as my deputy, Thomas, though for that you'd have to change parties. That's not so bad, given that you're young. People understand that it takes a little time for a politician to find himself and his true beliefs." Nagano smiled again. "You'd be my successor, eventually."

I'd be dead in a year or less, I didn't answer aloud. Instead I sighed and reached under the little lap-apron that was covering my legs. It'd been Dean's too; I was wearing it upside-down, exposing what should have been the dull blue backing. The side facing inward was decorated with little printed bunnies. Dean had loved bunnies. And, I had to admit, I was rather fond of them myself. "I don't think so," I replied. "I have a better plan for my future, you see. This letter," I continued, pulling out an envelope, "is from Alicia Wiston. It contains her resignation. I can vouch personally for its authenticity."

Nagano reached out and accepted it, then tore it open and read. His brows narrowed. "I don't understand—"

But I'd heard enough from Isoroku Nagano for one night. "This second envelope," I continued smoothly, producing a second letter, "contains my own resignation, complete with an explanation for my actions addressed to the people of my district. It'll be made public."

"What?" Nagano asked, spluttering slightly. "I…"

"This," I continued, pulling out a third envelope, "is an official letter from the President Pro-Tem of Churilla, Spencer Wiston. It constitutes official notice that Churilla is severing all ties with the United Systems, effective immediately. Your navy has ninety days from this moment to pull out all of its forces. If they fail to comply, said failure will be considered to constitute an act of war." I paused a moment for effect. "Given Alicia's resignation, you're top dog now. So, this letter is in fact properly addressed to you."

"I …" Nagano spluttered again. He didn't even open Spence's envelope, accepting its contents on faith. "You're bluffing," he declared. "And even if you're not, you'll never get away with it."

I raised my eyebrows slightly. "Really?" Then I hit a button under the table and a pipper-screen appeared in front of the big window. "Do you know how to read one of these?" I asked politely.

"I… No," Nagano finally admitted. "I never figured out the vector-arrows."

I nodded gravely. "Well, this is a specially-modified screen," I explained. "It displays the forces of the Esteppan Navy in blue, and those of the United Systems Navy in red. Not much is moving just now, so the arrows don't really matter."

Nagano gaped. "Es…Es…"

"Yep," I answered, calmly reaching under my wheelchair for a pointer placed there for this very purpose. "There's an Esteppan Navy again. I'm a captain in it, actually. The pay is excellent; they at least send me a check every month. Unlike some others I might name." I smiled. "And that large blue blob is an Esteppan dreadnought, Isoroku. Do you see any red ones hovering about just now?"

"I… No."

"Very good!" I explained. "Nor much in the way of other United Systems ships, either. See, you understand better than you think!" I waved the pointer. "And over here is *Coronel*. My ship, with a dozen superfighters aboard. How many supers does Earth have ready, I wonder? Right at this particular moment, I mean."

"Enough to blow you traitors out of the sky!" Isoroku raged. He was red in the face and his fists were balled.

"I don't think so." I waved my right hand in a certain way, and suddenly the plant's hanger doors swung open. All of the interior lights were on, revealing the kind of destruction that only a group of determined marines instructed on exactly how to do the worst damage possible can make of things. They'd even lit a couple of small fires for appearances sake, at my special request. "They had hours to do their work," I explained with pride. "We got all the completed birds, too, except that one making all the racket out there. Maybe I'll fly it home; it still belongs to Father. You haven't paid for it yet; I checked. And even more importantly, we not only got your primary stash of spare parts, but we've also destroyed the tooling you need to make more of them. The blueprints as well, actually. And all the spec-sheets."

"This…" Nagano growled. "This… Guards!"

I made another hand-gesture, and the Opposition leader's head of security was carried in. We'd had to cuff him hand and foot and even put a muzzle on him, as he was a very dangerous man indeed. Not nearly so dangerous, however, as a squad of marines. "You rang?" I replied in his stead.

"War!" Nagano finally screamed. "This is war! You want war, and you shall have it!"

"Well," I said slowly. "Perhaps you're being a little hasty, Isoroku." I pulled out another envelope and tossed it on the table. "This is Esteppe's declaration of independence. I'm sort of fond of how it begins; I chose the opening phrase myself."

Nagano made no motion to open it and admire Thomas Jefferson's timeless prose, so I continued. "I'm also informing you—unofficially, of course, as I hold no Esteppan office—that my homeworld and Churilla have signed a treaty of mutual defense. Directed squarely against you, actually." I smiled again. "We'll be inviting plenty of other worlds to join it soon enough, but I think the two of us working together are more than a match for anything you can put in the sky anytime soon. If you choose to make war, you'll have to fight for the Orion Nexus again. With just the superfighters you have on hand, mind you. And very few spares. Down near the planets, where the engines of my advanced Mark II fighter, of which you have none, will bite nice and strong." I smiled Rotte's smile. "I've fought two battles there already, and did fairly well both times. It's almost like I have a home-field advantage. Are you quite certain that you want to challenge me there?"

By now the Opposition leader, or acting PM rather, since Alicia's resignation was official, was white with rage. "You'll pay for this!" he swore. "So help me, you'll pay!"

"On my brother's grave," I replied, meeting his hard, cold eyes and not giving an inch, "I hope and pray that you'll make the attempt to collect. If you do, so help me God I'll kill you all. Now, next week, next year, or next decade. It doesn't matter when. I don't like your kind, Isoroku. In fact, you make me sick. Declare war on me and mine, and I'll kill your friends and destroy the sources of your wealth and burn you with hellfire until Earth screams for surrender. And, I might add, as likely as not until a certain former Prime Minister Isoroku Nagano finds himself hanging from a lamppost somewhere with a mob poking sharp sticks into his corpse and a bug-eyed expression of surprise still pasted all over his face. *That'd* be a victory truly worth winning, Isoroku. Ja it would!"

At that, Nagano blinked. "What do you propose?" he finally asked.

And I knew that I'd finally won a proper victory. A bloodless one, at long, long last.

Epilogue

"Dad says that war can make or break a man," young Dean said as he and I raced across the foggy Morning Sea. We had the whole ocean to ourselves; mine was the only skimmer out on the water so early, and as likely as not would be the only one to leave harbor all day long. Dawn was a newly-opened planet, jointly sponsored by Churilla and Esteppe, and the population could still be counted in the hundreds. We were on our way out to check the fish-traps, my primary job these days. There were robots monitoring the facilities too, of course. But every now and again it was wise to look things over with a human eye. Robots had no common sense. Even worse, they didn't relish a good skimmer ride. "He says that war is a filthy, wretched thing, and that it breaks most people." He turned to face me, blinking his big blue eyes. "But when it makes a man instead, the results can be spectacular."

I shrugged, making my servos whine. Dean was an adorable little thing, with all-white fur that required constant grooming. Even the gold-plated socket mounted at the base of his skull looked somehow like it belonged there. All children are by nature full of promise. Dean, however, shone so brightly that sometimes he made me want to shield my eyes. "Maybe," I answered. "It's pretty awful. The worst thing that can ever happen. Listen to your father; he knows what he's talking about."

"From the hottest furnaces emerge the finest steel," Dean explained, probably quoting someone famous. He was fiercely, sometimes even frighteningly, intelligent.

I shrugged again, then eased off the throttle and maintained a firm hand on the helm as our hull settled down into full contact with the water. The skimmer bucked and bounced, then settled in for a nice slow glide up to the net proper. I shut down the motor as we drifted alongside, then unfastened my seatbelt and walked over to the rail. It was a beautiful morning, one of an endless series of beautiful mornings on what I thought must be the most perfect planet ever colonized. Said beauty was a mere bonus; Dawn was chosen for settlement entirely due to its strategic location. It was two hops from Esteppe and three from Churillia and the precious Orion Nexus. Eventually, when local development had progressed far enough, we two firm allies would build a major combined military base here. Suddenly, Dean was standing close alongside me. "The net looks clear to me, Uncle Thomas," he observed.

"Me too," I agreed, smiling down at my sort-of-nephew. "But let's take a moment to relax and enjoy the scenery anyway. All right?"

Dean nodded, though he clearly wasn't happy. Standing and watching the seacrows circle—they were thriving here better than on Esteppe itself-- wasn't nearly as much fun for a ten-year-old as zipping across the water at breakneck speed. There was no doubt about it. My nephew was every bit as much a little boy as he was a supergenius.

"I was reading about you the other day," Dean continued, since just standing and quietly watching the sky was obviously much too boring a way for a young man to spend his summer vacation. "The Earth people call you an ungrateful traitor. Or some of them, anyway. Power-mad, even."

I nodded. "That they do."

"But you're not power-mad," Dean continued. "Anyone can see it. You live in a tiny little house, and do menial work just like all the other colonists." He smiled. "Though, you do have a very nice job."

I smiled back, saying nothing.

"Even that makes sense, though. Because you're a naval officer too, and can only work part-time. Sometimes you have to do other things." His eyes widened. "Are you going to fly with Uncle Jimmy today?"

"Perhaps," I replied, watching the seacrows wheel about in their endless search for shoals of fish. "If you'd like for me to."

"Please!" Dean begged, bouncing up and down on his toes in the most irresistible manner. The Mark IV had a live holocamera monitoring system built in, and my nephew absolutely loved watching from my point of view as Jimmy and I mixed it up over the sea. The Knights had turned up one day at the Old Home Place, destitute and desperate. Nagano had pegged them as friends of mine, cashiered them out of the fleet and persecuted them off of the planet. His loss, so far as I was concerned, was our gain. These days Admiral Knight commanded task force two, Captain Knight was CO of the new battlecruiser *Franz von Hipper*, and Jimmy was my next-door neighbor. He still wore his mannequin-body, just like me. And as we always would now, unless some kind of unlikely biotechnical breakthrough happened. There was always a price to be paid for military supremacy, and he and I were among the ones paying it. After all the years of practice and drills and so much actual combat, nothing in the sky could touch us. Sometimes interplanetary tensions built up. Whenever that happened Jimmy and I would sigh, put on our uniforms, board a carrier, and let it be known that we were in the area. So far the result had always been peace. Someday we'd be too old to fly, though no one knew how long a disembodied brain might live. But with any luck by the time that happened there'd be a generation or two of Deans scampering about the universe, perceiving that which we earlier, more primitive marks of humanity were too stupid to take notice of and finding solutions to the problems that'd plagued mankind for much, much too long.

I looked down at Dean and thought about all I'd given up. His dazzling promise was well worth every sacrifice, at least as I saw things. Jimmy, I knew, agreed.

"You're not a king," Dean continued, pursing his lips in thought and making his whiskers stick out all every which-way, just like his father's sometimes did. "Becoming one, in fact, could only diminish you. Though I think your role in society bears a certain resemblance to that of Gustavus Adolphus."

I smiled again. Jimmy had hooked me on military history; I'd read many, many times of Gustavus. "You'd compare me to the Lion of the North?" I asked. "Sweden's greatest warrior-king?"

"Sweden's greatest king, period," he corrected me. "Maybe the world's."

"But he died on the battlefield."

There was a long silence as Dean thought things through. "Mrs. Bard—she's my history tutor, you see." He smiled real big. "You ought to come meet her sometime, by the way. She thinks the world of you. I'm sure she'd be very grateful for the opportunity."

I nodded solemnly.

"Anyway… She thinks that's part of what made him so great. Gustavus lived a relatively austere and honest yet also triumphant life, then died right in the middle of his last great victory, before the glory of it all could go to his head. So he's remembered at his prime. As almost a perfect man, in other words, the stuff of legends. As important as his life was, what he became for Sweden after his death was his greatest achievement." He turned and looked at me. "It's much the same for you. But harder, I imagine. To be a living legend as opposed to a dead one, I mean. You have to live up to the image every single day. That's who and what you really are, I think. Mankind's greatest legend, ever. You're what binds everything together, the single figure that everyone holds in awe. Even Earthers feel the pull, though their government won't admit it. Someday I believe you'll unify even them. After all, nearly half the United Systems Navy took your side and deserted, once word got out about what you'd done and why. You hold no formal office, yet you're easily the most powerful man alive. Presidents and Parliamentarians and diplomats line up three deep for a few minutes of your time. All of them understand that a quiet promise from you is a worth a thousand screeching rants from Prime-Minister-For-Life Nagano." He shook his head. "Our confederation is a loose one. Without your personal influence it would've shattered a dozen times over by now over petty little squabbles. It's *you* that keeps the peace these days, sitting here on this backwards little colony world, and it's not just because you're such a fine combat pilot. You do it by *not* being a king, by *not* flaunting your wealth, by *not* putting on airs and surrounding yourself with entourages and go-betweens and all the other trappings of power." He shook his head. "I think you've tapped into something basic in human nature, Uncle Thomas. Something that we'd lost and was having a very hard time living without. But I'm not quite old enough to understand exactly what it is yet."

I chuckled. "Dean, for your own sake I hope that you never are old enough. Because then you just might feel a sense of duty as well."

The young rabbit looked away; like his father, he didn't enjoy being teased. So I tried to make it up to him. "Look," I said. "We've got five more stations to check. If we run flat-out, we can finish in two hours."

"Hooray!" Dean replied. He liked running flat-out, all of the time. Someday I'd buy him a skimmer of his own. Once he'd earned it, of course.

"While we're doing our checks, I'll see if Jimmy is up for a tussle. And Grandpa Vlasilov is scheduled to hit dirt this afternoon. He'll be at my place for dinner. Classes have let out at the academy, you see."

"Yay!" Dean cried out again, dancing about the deck. "He tells the *best* stories!"

"So he does," I agreed. "And tomorrow Father and Sven are coming to visit as well. Father wants to check your brain-jack interfacing; he thinks you're ready for a bandwidth-upgrade."

"That'd be *great*!" Dean agreed. He literally wriggled with joy at the prospect. "That's why I enjoy spending my summers with you so much, Uncle Thomas. Every day is always better than the last."

I smiled back, then reached out and gently stroked the soft fur of Dean's head. "Every day is always a gift," I replied. "And every sunrise a new ray of hope.

"Just like you."

The End